THE
GOD
SCROLLS

A Tale of Aliens, Egyptian Priests, and the New World Order

MICHAEL J. RHODES

Ancient Elders Press
HUMBLE, TEXAS

THE GOD SCROLLS

Published by:

Ancient Elders Press
P.O. Box 2555
Humble, TX 77347
www.AncientEldersPress.com

ISBN: 978 - 0 - 9825970 - 8 - 8 Paperback
978 - 0 - 9825970 - 4 - 0 eBook
LCCN: 2017960647

Edited by Balsiger Editing Services
Cover design by Michael J. Rhodes

Orders can be obtained at www.AncientEldersPress.com

To my loving wife, Wendy

Best Wishes,

Michael

CONTENTS

CONTENTS

CONTENTS

INTRODUCTION

This story was inspired by real life events. My personal interaction with the secret government, Illuminati, aliens, MKUltra, the eugenic bloodlines, dimensional beings, mind control implants, voice to skull technology, electronic stalking, parallel dimensions, and dark magic is true.

The dark side exists, and they have an agenda!

The scrolls are from my version of the Creator.

GENERAL DISCLAIMER

All names, characters, businesses, restaurants, non-government groups, schools, colleges, universities, headlines, notes, memos, telegrams, dissertations, inventions, scrolls, parchments, doodles, automatic writing, dreams, out-of-body experiences, visions, actions, and incidents in this book are fictitious. Any resemblance to actual persons, living or dead, is purely coincidental.

No animals or typewriters were harmed in the making of this story.

Reverse engineering of this book is strictly prohibited.

MEDICAL DISCLAIMER

This book is not intended as a replacement for medical advice, doctor's care, or medical attention of any kind. Anyone seeking medical assistance should put this book down now and see his or her physician before the doctor can decline your insurance and raise his rates.

SPIRITUAL/RELIGIOUS DISCLAIMER

In addition, this book is not intended to deter anyone from any spiritual or religious pursuit. If you need assistance, please consult or pray with your local God, priest, rabbi, monk, spiritual guide, shaman, celestial being, alien, fairy, dragon, or obtain your own fortune cookie for advice.

CHAPTER ONE

HERE A SCROLL,
THERE A SCROLL

Present Day...Cairo, Egypt

"Here I am, lost again. I turned left, then right, and then left down that dusty street. No, wait a minute. Stop and think," I told myself. "It was a left, another left, then a right. That's how I got here.

"These streets are all starting look the same. I passed that merchant earlier, too. No, it only looks like the same merchant. Great, now I am arguing with myself. It's no wonder I'm lost."

So there I was, a misplaced tourist stranded somewhere well outside the boundaries of Khan el-Khalili in Cairo, Egypt—one of the oldest marketplaces in the world. Not a terrible place, but not a place I wanted to be lost in, especially since I had no bearings to get me back home.

You see, I'd decided to forgo the camel t-shirts, perfume shops, and cartouche makers—the touristy parts of the Khan—and venture to where the locals go. That's how I ended up lost. I kept walking farther and farther away from the tour group as I got caught up in the allure of a new adventure.

I had walked for about thirty minutes and turned down any side street that piqued my curiosity. I'd thought I was keeping good directions to return back to the group, but my mental map had gotten lost after about the seventh or eighth turn. With a nervous tone, I sighed out loud, "I'm in trouble!"

I tried diligently to find my way back, but after walking in a circle for twenty-five minutes, I manned up and admitted to myself that I was lost. I pretty much had no other choice at this point but to stop in a shop or three and ask for directions. Unfortunately for me, though, since I was so far from the tourist area, none of the shop owners I'd met could speak English. And when I came out of the third shop, I completely lost all sense of direction. I couldn't even remember if I'd come in from the right or the left.

I've done that in the shopping mall before, too, but this was completely different. There wasn't a mall map to help me find my car back at the orange parking lot. One wrong turn could write me into tomorrow's headline:

Tourist Makes Wrong Turn and Kidnapped by Extremist Group
Beheading at Ten
News at Eleven

A little bit of panic started to rise in my belly. They say the gut will tell you how you really feel—you know, follow your gut instinct and all—so I decided to stop what I was doing, sit down on the sandy curb, and take a few long, slow breaths. I let my mind relax and go into a pseudo-trance state to help calm me down. I meditated regularly for the health benefits, so this was nothing new to me.

During this little episode, an unfamiliar voice chimed in my head. It was very comforting and stated clearly, "Relax. You will be just fine."

"Whoa! Who was that?" I thought to myself. I started to wonder what had just happened, which, fortunately for me, took my mind off of being lost at the moment. I looked around to see if anyone from my tour group had shown up to guide me back to safety, but no one was there.

I pondered again, "Whose voice was that? I didn't think that thought on my own. I was meditating and it just popped into my head." And something else unexpectedly happened: a calm, relaxing feeling rushed over my entire body. I felt great, re-energized, and ready to find my way back. It was like I'd gotten a super-loaded shot of B-12, mixed with a powerful sedative to calm the nerves.

Without thinking, I abruptly stood up and wiped the dust off my hands and pants. This created my own mini dust storm. After the dust settled from my dilemma of being lost and my minor hallucination, I gathered my belongings and looked up into the blue sky to get my bearings. Once I spotted the afternoon sun, I started walking toward the north.

After clearing my head and hiking about fifty paces, I had this strange feeling like I was supposed to go left at the next corner. It was as if someone or something was guiding me in that direction. Since I was already lost, I didn't fight the urge and headed down that way. I cleared my thoughts again and took another twenty steps or so. That's when the voice returned, "Go into this shop."

"What's going on here?! Now I'm hearing voices in my head when I let my mind go blank. Who is this?" Of course, no one answered, but the same message repeated a second time, "Go into this shop." Then the voice faded away. So I thought, "What do I have to lose?" My adventurous side started to flicker again. "And who knows? Maybe the owner can get me back to the Khan."

I turned to the shop and opened the metal-framed glass door. The string of bells that hung from the inside handle jingled and ruined my ninja stealth mode entrance.

"Come in! Come in!" welcomed the shop owner. He flailed his right arm then his left arm wide open to entice me to look around his store. He looked like a female model working at a car show, even though his elderly body lacked the curves of a sexy twenty-year-old.

"All honest pricing here! When you get home with all your goods, you won't be able to say *Eeeee-gypt me.*" He laughed and laughed and put his hands on the glass countertop, which covered a case full of jewelry.

"E-gypt me…he jipped me. That's pretty clever," I chuckled out loud.

"We almost never get tourists this far out from the Khan. But while you are here, you might as well take a look around. I have plenty of jewelry and statues that you can take home as gifts."

"What gave me away?" But I already knew, as if my Caucasian looks, sandy-blonde hair, and the camera hanging around my neck didn't scream out *tourist.*

Without missing a beat, he laughed, "It was your lack of robes and fez, of course." Then he leaned forward on the display case with all his weight on his palms. "Tell me, what are you looking for?"

Now, if you've ever been to the shops in and around the Khan, you

3

already know that many of the store owners will strike up a conversation with you to make a sale. If you tell them what you want, they'll haggle with you on price until there is a happy medium, so you can pretty much kiss your money goodbye. If they don't have what you are looking for, they'll sell you the closest item to it as if you'd been searching for it all your life. And if that doesn't work, then they'll take you fifteen blocks away to their brother's shop to ensure that they separate you from your Egyptian pounds.

"Well, I'm looking for two things at the moment. I'm lost and need directions back to the Khan—"

Before I could say another word, he blurted out, "Oh, I can get you to el-Khalili real easy. It's no more than a camel's spit away. What else are you looking for? Did you see this fine diamond-banded Swiss watch?"

I glanced at the watch he was holding, then looked around his tiny shop. It was a typical Egyptian one-room storefront that was no bigger than a couple hundred square feet. Like most jewelry shops around the Khan, there were a number of glass cases filled with gold and silver rings, watches, bracelets, necklaces made of precious stones, and a few jangly ankle bracelets. There were also a few white wooden shelves filled with Egyptian-style statues and trinkets, and a single storeroom in the back. I didn't think he had what I wanted, but there was no harm in asking.

"I'm not really looking for watches, but I was in search of something usually not found in the tourist shops. That's how I ended up here—aside from being lost. Maybe you can tell me where I can find some scrolls of papyrus with hieroglyphs painted on them. My daughter loves puzzles and anything that needs deciphering. She asked me if I could find some while I was on my trip." To stop him from trying to sell me the typical touristy pictures on papyrus, I added, "I'm looking for real text on real scrolls, not the souvenir stuff."

The shop owner paused for a moment with a strange look on his face. Then in a mysterious way, he said, "It just so happens that I have some papyrus in the back room. Wait right here," and he bounded off behind a long, blue curtain which acted as a door.

I yelled to him, "It's not like I am going anywhere! I'm lost, remember?!"

I heard him speaking in his native tongue to what must have been a relative or a shop helper. All I could make out was *Yalla! Yalla!* After a few heated words shouted back and forth, my ears picked up the sound of boxes being thrown around. About ten seconds later, and with a forcefully painted grin, he re-entered the main shop holding a medium-sized package in his hand. Before he could get all the way through the doorway, though, the blue curtain flailed in the air from his forceful entrance and partially covered his face and shoulders.

I could tell that he was disturbed by this comical event. The curtain on his head took away from his respectable, business-like demeanor. With a frantic motion, he wrestled with the curtain a little bit until it untangled from his upper body. After regaining his composure, he stepped closer with the box stretched out in front of him.

"Look at all the papyrus I have for you. This is a prize catch, no?" he grinned with an assured look of a sale. "Your daughter will love these. What's her name?"

"Hara"—a smile came to my face as I thought about her—"and my name is Michael, Michael Whyse. What's yours?"

"I am the provider," he quickly replied, "which fits me well, since that is what my name means. You seek, I provide. Now where did I put that cloth?" His bottom half stood motionless, but from his waist up he turned frantically from right to left and back again to look for the cloth.

"A quiz! My daughter would like this. But since she isn't here, do I get the pleasure of knowing your name?"

"Mudads," he answered eloquently, as if to honor his name, "my name is Mudads." He was still looking around for the cloth. "Ah, there it is," he exclaimed.

Before setting down the box, Mudads opened up a large piece of black felt and placed it on the glass counter. He pulled at the twine knot, lifted the lid, and tipped the box in my direction as if to tease me with a small glimpse. After giving me a wink, he promptly set the box beside the cloth to prepare for his presentation.

I could tell that he'd done this before, but maybe not with papyrus, more so with the jewelry that he sells. He pulled out a pair of white cotton gloves and slipped them on his long, bony fingers. Next, he pulled out an elongated pair of wooden tweezers with felt tips on the ends.

"Ah, I get it," I mused to myself. "This is how someone would show a prized stamp to a stamp collector. Boy, he's really going all out for this presentation. And who am I to stop him amidst the show? Besides, I still don't know how to get back to my tour group."

"This is some presentation," I remarked out loud.

"I am glad that you are impressed. These are very old scraps of papyrus, and I don't want to tear or smudge any of them." He gestured with a furious *come here* motion, which was accentuated by the white gloves. "Come! Come! Take a look."

I stepped up to the counter ready to declare, *These aren't what I was looking for, but thanks anyway.* I was preparing myself for the coming haggle of price. I'd played foreign tourist many times before, and I knew the set-up was in motion. I didn't say it, though, as if something inside me kept me from blurting it out.

One by one, Mudads used the tweezers to pull out more papyrus scraps. I watched as he laid them out somewhat scattered on the cloth. He would look at a piece, ponder for a moment, and then decisively put it down in a special spot. At first, I thought it was part of the show, as they seemed to be randomly placed on the cloth. But as I looked further, a pattern was emerging, almost as if he was intentionally putting together a specific shape. I kept quiet as he removed the remaining pieces from the box.

"What do you think? This is the find of a lifetime." His anticipation for an agreeable response was evident.

"This is a remarkable set of papyrus scraps. I especially like the royal blue, purple, and gold colorings. But there are no hieroglyphs, only Egyptian-looking geometric symbols." I was a little bit interested, but I didn't want to let him know. "It's not really what I was looking for. My daughter likes to translate languages, you know, solve puzzles."

Mudads countered with a new sales pitch, "Ah, but this *is* a puzzle. It is a puzzle that has not been solved by anyone here. Nobody knows what it means or says except for the person who made them. My father gave them to me years ago and showed me this pattern. I am sure I have it correct." Then he asked politely, "So, what do you think this is worth?"

"How could I tell you what it's worth," I chuckled, "especially if it's an unsolvable puzzle, right? Besides, I really am looking for papyrus with hieroglyphs. And if you look carefully at the symbol you've created, there are missing pieces, which means it's an incomplete puzzle." I said that assuredly, but I really didn't know if I was correct or not.

"Yes, I can see how you might come to this conclusion, but I can tell you that this is a puzzle worth solving. I can feel it. And I am not the one to solve this puzzle, as I am a mere provider for those who seek. I am a simple merchant who likes to serve. You have a path to follow, and only you can walk the steps to enlightenment."

In my mind, I thought, "What the heck is this guy selling me now? *I have a path?* He's probably used that line more than once to make a sale. I'd better politely get out of here before he pulls out the deed to the Nile."

As if not to miss his cue, he expressed lyrically, "I can tell that you might be in *denial,* for one who has a path often doesn't know it until he takes the first step."

"Denial," I snickered. "Is that another Egyptian joke: De-Nile?" I laughed and laughed.

His tone changed to a more serious nature. "I want you to take a closer look at these symbols. Do any of them mean anything to you? Do you recognize any of these pictures?"

"Well, I can tell you that the shape you've made forms an incomplete circle and the lines look like a Coptic cross."

"What did you just say?" He gave me an uneasy glance with his head tilted slightly.

Not feeling so sure of my answer—since he'd questioned me—I reiterated, "The shape...it looks like an incomplete sphere with two lines that resemble a Tau or Coptic cross."

The expression on Mudads' face became even more serious. As I went back to admiring the two shapes, he turned his body away from me and uttered to himself, "He must be the *one.* He knows the symbol for eternal life, but he does not remember yet."

He spun around abruptly. "Let me tell you something..." He looked directly into my eyes. "I had a vision not long ago, a dream that someone would come into my shop and ask for papyrus. In that dream, I also saw a great battle between two Egyptian dragons. One dragon was white with light emanating from its entire body. The light expanded until it formed a blazing golden-white sphere. Inside, the dragon remained calm and centered, as if nothing could do it any harm.

"The black dragon, however, looked more like an ominous mist, and it was surrounding the white dragon. I could feel evil and darkness as it blew fire upon the white dragon's sphere. I sensed death. Then I woke up in a cold sweat."

He paused for a moment, and then asked, "Do you know what I am talking about?" He was hoping for some confirmation from me, as if I'd had the same dream.

7

His stare was a little unnerving, but nothing to make me run out of his store. I thought, "He's being awfully intrusive for a simple shop owner. I wonder where all of this is going."

I broke our gaze for a moment, then I explained, "I haven't got the foggiest idea. I'm a philosophy teacher at a university back home, and I don't put much stock into dreams and visions. You could very well have eaten some bad falafel or bad dates."

Feeling a little frustrated, Mudads empathized, "I understand, Michael, but we take dreams very seriously here. My brother had a similar dream, and he also saw a white dragon, but his dragon was holding a papyrus scroll with a scarab on it. This is very unusual, don't you think? You are here looking for hieroglyphs on papyrus, and both he and I happen to have some."

"Is it that strange that a shop near the Khan has papyrus in stock?" It was a little harsher response than I'd intended, but I was caught off guard. To make up for my actions, I added in a softer tone, "It's true that some shops will stock the touristy papyrus, but I've never been to one that had scrolls with writing on them."

I took a step back. "If you don't mind, I'd like to take a picture of everything you've laid out. It looks very...hmmm...intriguing." I felt a little uneasy at this point, and I also knew that I had trapped myself into a sale by showing more interest.

Looking a little rattled himself, Mudads encouraged, "Please do. Should I wrap this up for you?" He paused for a moment, almost as if he was searching for something to say that would keep me in his shop. "I think you should consider buying these for your daughter. If nothing else, it will make a good story for your philosophy students and a great puzzle for her."

My camera made the usual motorized clicking sound as I snapped a number of pictures from multiple angles. I took five photos in total. "I'd like to buy them, but there are missing pieces and no instructions." I was just trying to get out of buying them all.

He gestured with a finger in the air, as if to raise my curiosity. "I have a solution for you...a compromise, if you will."

In my mind I knew this was coming. I also hated that it worked. "Alright, what's the compromise?"

"My brother's shop is on the way to the Khan."

I mocked in my head, "Here we go, off to the brother's shop."

"We will stop in for a coffee and smoke the hookah. Then we'll get you to where you need to go." Mudads started picking up the papyrus pieces and placing them carefully back in the box. He hummed an unusual melody to pass the time. It was very Mediterranean sounding, more like a stanza from a prayer than a song. It was odd, but alluring at the same time.

After he sealed the box and rewrapped the twine, he turned and disappeared behind the blue curtain. I thought that I might have dissuaded him from continuing to push for a sale, but a minute later he re-entered the main shop with the same box under his left arm. "There goes that idea out the window," I snickered under my breath.

"My helpers are done with their lunch and will watch the store. Come, let's go meet my brother." He walked around the counter and placed his right hand on my shoulder to guide me out the door.

I was putting a lot of faith in him at that point. In all rights, he was a stranger and could have taken me anywhere that he pleased. But I had done this once before with my wife, Constance, while we were at the Street of the Tentmakers, otherwise known as Sharia el Khayamiya in old Cairo. A shop owner had taken us to his uncle's home to see his handmade pillow cases. After looking at the amazing craftsmanship—and not finding what she liked—the gentleman brought us safely back to Khayamiya.

When my focus returned after my quick flashback, I looked at my trusty Las Vegas odds sheet and decided to go with Mudads. I wouldn't recommend this to any other tourist, but he seemed very trustworthy. It felt like he was a long-lost friend, and I still needed to get back within two hours before our tour bus left the Khan, so I went.

He walked very briskly in front of me as if he had a purpose beyond getting me to his brother's store. While he walked, he hummed that tune again. It was strange, as if I knew what he was humming. "I swear I've heard this before," I whispered.

Very softly, I hummed along. When I did this, I got a jolt of energy that ran through my entire body. I shook as if I had a chill, but it wasn't cold outside, not one bit. It was Egypt and in the upper nineties.

"That's odd. I know this song. What is it?"

"You know this song?" Mudads was cautious. "How do you know this song? It is very old and not known by many."

"I don't know. I heard you hum it in the shop, and then while walking. I just know the tune. But it's not really a song, is it?"

"We should not talk about this here in the open. Wait until we get to my brother's store."

"That was strange," I thought. "What's with all the secrecy over a little tune?" Mudads continued humming, and I joined in. We looked like our own holiday parade, with him in front and me trying to keep up on the uneven stone streets. When he heard me humming along again, he abruptly stopped singing. I finished the tune and kept quiet after that.

We traveled for another ten minutes or so, passing rows of shops and people dressed in a variety of different outfits. I could tell there was a mixture of religions by what the women wore. Some were covered in black robes, and their faces were hidden with the traditional niqab or burka, while other women's outer robes and scarves were as colorful and vibrant as the rainbow. The men, however, were mostly in white robes, jeans, or pants suits, with a few donning some grays, browns, and blacks. About an eighth of the men wore the traditional skullcaps, turbans, or the occasional kufiya (a draped headscarf and band). There was no doubt that I was not in Kansas anymore.

I decided to break the silence and inquired, "What's your brother's name?"

"Hanif. His name is Hanif. His store is just up the next street, around the bend, and next to a spice shop. He sells some of the best perfumes and incense in all of Cairo. If we are lucky, he'll have all of the other boxes of papyrus." He turned back to look at me with a smile as we crossed the street. After rounding the corner, we stopped directly in front of his building.

Interestingly, Hanif's store front looked a lot like his brother's, but with a small twist. It had a similar glass door with the long string of bells and a sign over the door with something printed in Arabic that I couldn't read. But this shop had a colorful mural painted on the huge glass window next to the door. The flowers and walking path in the mural looked a lot like one of the shapes on the papyrus that I'd seen in Mudads' shop. Being a store that specializes in scents, most wouldn't think twice about the mural of flowers. But since I'd seen the papyrus, it caught my attention right away. Before entering, I donned my tourist cap once again and stopped to take a few pictures. How was I to know of the importance of this mural later on?

CHAPTER TWO

HANIF'S SHOP OF WONDERS

As soon as I walked through the door, my eyes were treated to a mystical blur of colors. The east and west walls of Hanif's shop were filled with perfume bottles and gold-plated oil burners. They were handmade by craftsmen who worked in the back half of the store. Each bottle was unique and colored with pinks, reds, greens, purples, and blues. They looked dazzling as the late afternoon sun hit the mirrors behind the display cases and also shone on the ceiling. The multi-faceted glass, accented by the mirrors facing each other, reflected the light and gave the illusion that I was in a cave filled with gold, crystals, and diamonds. And the smell was intoxicating. Heaven was the only word that could describe my nasal experience.

On half of the north wall, at the back left of the store, were small, medium, and very large bottles of assorted oils. At least thirty boxes of incense, ranging in all different shapes and sizes, lined the other shelves. The other half of the wall displayed a half dozen pictures painted on papyrus that hung above a red velvet couch with two matching chairs on either side. A hookah sat on the floor in front of the couch, along with a small table.

The two sections of the store were split in the middle by a very large doorway. It was rounded at the top and open so the customers could see the glassmakers hand blowing perfume bottles and oil burners in the adjoining room. It looked almost like a cave entrance, but much nicer, as his shop was very well kept. A split stairway went up to the apartment above, and the lower staircase led to a large storeroom beneath the store.

As soon as the door swung shut behind me and the bells stopped ringing, Mudads set the box down on the closest countertop and called out to his brother, "Hanif! Hanif, come quick! I have someone here that I want you to meet!"

Hanif arrived within seconds from the other room. There was no doubt that he was Mudads' brother. They could have easily been twins, but I could see a little more youth in Hanif's face and eyes. His body was a little more slender, too, but not by much.

"Come in! Come in!" welcomed Hanif, with his arms spread out wide and motioning around the shelves of his store.

"Where have I seen that before?" I mused to myself.

I looked at Mudads and chuckled out loud, "Yup, he's your brother alright."

"What brings you to my shop in the middle of the day, Brother? It's not like you to come before you have closed up and finished dinner." Hanif stretched his arms out in front of him to give Mudads a brotherly hug. They both greeted each other in Arabic, "Allah ma'ak." (God be with you.)

After their short exchange, Hanif glanced at me, then back to his brother. "And who is the honored guest that you have brought into my store?"

"This is Tumaini from another land." He gave Hanif a wink that only a brother would recognize. "His name is Michael, and he is a welcome guest in our home."

Hanif walked over toward his displays and gestured for me to come closer. He gleamed with pride. "Is he looking for the best smells in all of Egypt? I promise you will not find any donkey sweat in these bottles. Only the finest of incense and perfumes are allowed on my shelves, that I can assure you.

"What are you looking for? Is there a special someone you would like to give a gift of alluring smells or sexy scents to? Maybe you like to meditate and need some myrrh, frankincense, or our special family blend, *Incense from the Temple Gods*? By the look in your eyes, you must see something that I can show you."

"I'm impressed." I lifted my nose in the air and breathed in. "With all the scents filling my head right now, I could easily close my eyes and take a trip into fantasy land. They're very calming"—I searched for the rest of my description—"and pleasantly overpowering at the same time."

"Why, thank you," Hanif smiled. "You obviously know good quality scents when you smell them."

He turned to his brother. "Who is this charming fellow, Mudads?"

"Hanif, come here. I need to tell you something." Mudads looked toward the small box on the counter, then back toward Hanif with a concerned look on his face. He paused for a moment and waited for his brother to speak.

"I knew Tumaini would come," Hanif whispered excitedly to his brother. "My dream foretold this."

"You were always the believer. Mother and Father named you well."

Hanif turned away from his brother and looked straight at me. "What is it that you seek, my friend?"

"Well, two things to be exact. One is the way back to the Khan—"

Without missing a beat, Hanif boasted, "Oh, I can get you to el-Khalili real easy. It's no more than a camel's spit away."

I laughed so hard that I just about spewed the sip of water I'd taken. There was no doubt that they came from the same mother.

"What was the other thing that you seek?" he prodded, as if it were a secret quiz question. "Do you see it in my store?"

"My daughter, Hara, would like some hieroglyphs to decipher. Do you have any papyrus scrolls hidden in your shop anywhere?"

Hanif grinned before politely excusing himself, "Wait right here, please." Then he walked through the arched doorway where he disappeared for a few minutes.

While he was gone, Mudads suggested that I should smell my way around the shop and tell Hanif what I liked best when he returns. "Even if you don't buy anything today," he told me, "my brother likes to know which scents attract people the most. It helps him to prioritize his stock."

Since I meditated frequently, I was able to recognize the usual oils and incense. The one that really caught my attention was his special blend. I picked up the thick incense rod and held it under my nose until Hanif returned.

———•◦•———

When Hanif appeared through the doorway, he had five hat-sized boxes with him. Each of them was wrapped with twine in the same manner as Mudads' box.

My head was swooning a bit from the incense. "Hanif, I really like this special blend of yours. I swear it could take you to the afterlife. It's like... it's almost like a shortcut to heaven. Or is it a way to open a dimensional portal?" I joked. "What's in it?"

"It is a secret recipe that is only known to a few. I carry it in cones, thin rods, and thick sticks. How much would you like to take home with you?"

Laughingly, I answered, "How much do you have in stock? Do you ship overseas? This is amazing. You could travel to the outer realms of the mind with this stuff."

I leaned in a bit. "Is it legal? I mean, I won't get busted for taking this through Customs, will I?" He smiled, and I leaned back and gestured with my hands. "I'm kidding, you know. Please take what I said as a compliment."

"I did," he replied happily. "A compliment is the best reward for an artist, and making this blend is a true art form. And yes, we do ship overseas. You should make sure to take one of my business cards as well. It has all of my contact information for when you run out."

While I picked up a few cartons of his special blend, Hanif lined up all five boxes on one of his display counters and opened the attached lids. The boxes were made of thick, woven straw, and the insides were lined with red cloth on the lid, sides, and bottom. And most importantly, each box was filled with scraps of papyrus that were kept in sealed plastic bags.

Just like his brother had done at his shop, Hanif put on a pair of white gloves and picked out a number of pieces from each bag. He made sure to set each piece down in front of the box that it came from. He also pulled out a scroll from the last box and carefully unrolled it. Then he used two empty perfume bottles to hold down the ends of the scroll to keep them from curling back up. He placed a white handkerchief under each bottle so it wouldn't damage the paper. Once his display was ready, he asked me to inspect the contents on the counter.

It was like hitting the jackpot. Each piece of papyrus seemed to be as old as the pyramids themselves—all but the fourth box. The pieces in front of the fourth box looked like they had been made within the last few years. The paint was different, not as worn, and much more vibrant and defined than the other pieces. The hieroglyphs were very common symbols, and they could easily be deciphered with an Egyptian hieroglyph alphabet decoder ring.

"Hanif," I called to him, as to honor his expertise, "the fourth box doesn't look like the rest. Why is that? And I can't recognize any of the symbols on the other pieces of papyrus." I pointed to the pieces in front of the third box. "Is there a primer or a code to unscramble the messages? A lot of them look like the papyrus that Mudads showed me."

Again, Hanif and Mudads looked at each other. In Arabic, Hanif indicated to his brother, "He knows that something is unusual about the other four boxes. Shouldn't we tell him?"

(Still in Arabic.) "Not yet," replied Mudads. "Let us see how this plays out."

Hanif smiled in my direction, but I could tell that something wasn't quite right. It seemed strange that they didn't speak English around me all of the time. It was as if they were hiding something, but it also felt like they were hoping I would figure out what was going on.

"You are very perceptive, my good friend," complimented Hanif. "The fourth box contains about two dozen scrolls that I rescued from the trash. A friend of mine owns a well-known papyrus shop near the Cairo museum and was going to throw them away. They don't use banana leaves there to make their papyrus, I can assure you. He only uses authentic papyrus." He flipped over one of the pieces from the fourth box to let me examine it. Then he continued, "His students apprentice for quite some time before they get to become artisans for his store. These were copies of copies based upon old Egyptian poems. They are good replicas, but they did not meet his standards for sale, so he planned to burn them. As you can see, most of them are torn into large pieces. I took the lot from him and intended to make a mosaic for my shop, but I never got around to it."

He looked at me with his original friendly form. "These would make a great gift for your daughter, don't you think? She could piece them together and decipher the poem. I'll even throw in an oil burner for her with some scented almond oil. What is that common American phrase? Oh yes, *burning the midnight oil*. She will be busy for many moons with this present."

"This is great. And thanks for the extra gift. It's just what I was looking for. But what about the rest? Would you part with these as easily? I have to admit that I am drawn to the contents of the other four boxes."

"What draws you to them?" asked Mudads with an unusually inquisitive tone.

I stepped to the left and leaned over the counter to get a better look. "I don't know. I'm drawn to them somehow, just like I was drawn to the pieces you showed me back at your shop. I can't really explain it, but I feel like I have seen them somewhere before. Maybe I saw them in a book or another store. Who knows?" I shrugged.

I turned toward Hanif and asked with a higher pitched voice, "If I decide to take them, is there a primer I can use to translate them? Do you know what they mean?"

Mudads stepped forward to his brother's side. "As I said in my shop, this is your path to take. We know not how the puzzle will bless the seeker, but the seeker will know when the task is completed."

"I have a feeling that you will be much rewarded and find fulfillment from this venture," added Hanif. "Come, let us sit on the couch. Do you partake in the hookah?"

Not wanting to leave the subject so quickly, and to get a better look, I walked over to the fifth box and glanced inside. There were a number of scrolls in the box, at least eight or nine from what I could tell.

Nervously, Hanif asked, "What are you doing?"

"Well, if you want me to take the goods, don't you think I should be able to inspect the goods, too? Don't worry. I'll take great care in handling them."

Mudads put a hand on his brother's shoulder to relax him. "Let him see the scrolls, Hanif. He should know what he is getting if he is to take them on his life's journey."

I thought to myself, "There he goes with this life's journey crap again. He doesn't need to lay it on so thick; I'm already interested. I just like how unique they look and want to see if I can recognize the symbols."

To show both brothers that I meant to take good care of the parchments, I picked up one of the extra handkerchiefs from the counter and covered my entire hand with it. Then I picked out all of the scrolls and laid them on the table in a row.

One scroll in particular caught my attention. It was wrapped in silk ribbon and sealed with a wax stamp. The stamp had a tiny scarab jewel embedded in it and appeared to be made of pure gold. When I picked it up, the sun moved into perfect position to reflect in all of the mirrors and beveled perfume bottles. My entire body was covered in white patches of light, just like a disco ball would do, but with a thousand more tiny mirrors. It was so brilliant that I could barely see.

Hanif yelled to his brother in Arabic while shaking his shoulders, "Mudads! Mudads! Do you see? He is the white dragon from my dream. He holds the Scroll of Neter—the God Scroll. Tumaini has returned. He has returned, Mudads. He has returned!"

(Still in Arabic.) Mudads exclaimed, "Yes, I see! He is the one! He is Tumaini, and he has come to finish what he started many lifetimes ago. Fortune has shined on us to see our brother return. But we must not tell him everything just yet. He must choose the path on his own, for that is how it was written."

I wasn't really paying attention to Mudads' or Hanif's expressions because I caught a glimpse of myself in one of the mirrors. My body was all lit up from the reflections. I laughed, "I look like I belong on a disco floor."

Keeping with the spirit of the moment, I spun around in a circle and looked at all of the colors on my clothes. When I stopped, I saw both brothers staring at me, and I became very self-conscious. "What? I was just having a seventies flashback. Is there something wrong?"

Feeling like a school boy who'd just gotten caught picking up the teacher's answer sheet, I set the scroll carefully back in the box and stepped away from the counter slowly and in a comical fashion. As if scripted, both brothers did the familiar head-tilt that dogs do when the dog doesn't understand what you are saying. I stopped backing up, and we all laughed together at the situation.

Hanif motioned. "Come, sit down on the couch with me while Mudads puts all of the papyrus back in the boxes. I will have my wife prepare us some coffee."

I still had questions about the symbols and the scrolls, but I figured I could ask them while we were relaxing. It's the first chance I'd had to sit down in a few hours, so my feet and back were looking forward to a little break.

<hr />

I watched Mudads handle each piece of papyrus as if he were holding a newborn baby. Then he wrapped the boxes and moved his beside the other five. Meanwhile, Hanif came back into the room humming a different tune than the one Mudads had sung earlier. I had no idea what came over me, but I instinctively hummed the last part of the tune with him as if I had written it myself.

Hanif was so caught off guard by the event that he tripped on the edge of the rug and dropped the tray that carried three tiny ceramic coffee cups. He rushed toward me, completely ignoring the broken china on the floor. "How do you know this song?" He was very emotional, almost angry that I knew the tune without being told I could sing it.

I stammered, "I...I...I don't know. I just knew it. Just like I knew the tune that Mudads hummed."

"Mudads, does he know the other tune, too?"

He looked back at me and pleaded, "Please sing it one more time."

Pursing my lips and taking a deep breath through my nose, I hummed Hanif's melody from beginning to end. "See, I just knew it. It's like I was born with both songs inside of me." There was no doubt in either of their minds now that I knew the tunes instinctively.

I was a little nervous again. It was as if I'd used a secret handshake from a college fraternity. I pondered, "How could such a short song cause such a stir?" Neither of them spoke yet, so I asked, "Is there anything wrong?"

Mudads answered, "It is perfectly fine that you know them, Michael. Not many do, and it is a tradition that we pass down within our family tree. It tells us that you are one of our brothers."

Just then, Hanif's wife, Rehema, burst into the scene. "Hanif, what is going on here?! I heard a crash coming from downstairs. What did you do to our coffee cups?" She bent down and started to pick up the larger pieces. "Just look at this mess! Is everyone alright?" She said all of this very fast and without taking a breath.

"Relax, Rehema," Hanif replied calmly. "Don't you see that we have a guest with us?"

Turning around to the couch, she expressed concernedly, "Oh my, I am so sorry." She looked at me and bowed her head. "I didn't see you there. Please excuse me." She wiped her hands off on her apron and came to give me a kind handshake. "I apologize for my abruptness. Are you hurt?"

Bending forward to shake her hand, I smiled, "I'm fine, and you have a most beautiful shop. I'm Michael."

"The pleasure is all mine. And my name is Rehema. Would you like some coffee? Wait here," she stated very motherly-like. "I will be right back with a fresh brew and some gullash." She quickly darted away from the main room.

A moment later, an employee came in with a rag and a dust pan. He cleaned up while Mudads and Hanif invited me to sit back down. Both of them repositioned the bookend seats so we could talk easier. Hanif then told the gentleman who was cleaning to take over the store while he and Mudads got more acquainted with me. The gentleman took the coffee-soaked towel and pieces to the back room and briskly walked to the front of the store to man the register.

After a moment of silence, I looked both brothers in the eyes. "I have to ask you a serious question. These scrolls aren't lost artifacts or government property, are they? I mean, I'm not going to get busted for stealing ancient antiquities, am I?" They both were temporarily speechless, and I continued, "I've heard of this type of thing being done before. Some innocent tourist gets arrested at the airport because he unknowingly bought something the Egyptian government says it owns." Before they could answer, I gestured with my hands. "I have to tell you, I'm not looking forward to spending the rest of my life in an Egyptian prison. Where did the other scrolls come from? And with all respect, please don't respond with that *I have a path* stuff again. I'd like your honest answer."

Mudads sighed a little dejectedly, "I would have hoped by now that you would have trusted us."

"It's not that I don't trust you. I...I do," I stammered a little. "It's...it's that I don't trust my own judgment all of the time. OK, maybe I'm a little scared. I just want to be sure. Put yourself in my shoes. Doesn't it seem strange that I got lost, came into your stores, and you had exactly what I was looking for? What are the odds? It's a little...well...actually, I don't know how to describe it. You both are so friendly and accommodating. It seems too good to be true." Before they could reply, I continued, "And then there are the two little tunes that I knew. You told me not to talk about one of them while we were in the street. What's going on here?"

Hanif urged his older brother, "We must tell him, Mudads. He deserves to know the truth."

Mudads took a long breath and waited for a moment. He rubbed his hands on his pants as if he were a little nervous. Deep in his heart, he was hoping I would believe what he was going to say without having to divulge too much. "Michael, I can assure you that you are the rightful owner of these scrolls and the rightful owner of the contents in the box I brought along. When you leave here with all of these boxes, you will have made an honest transaction. They belong to you, and they are yours for as long as you want them. Does this give you any peace of mind?"

"Yes, but what about the song that you wouldn't talk about in the street? What's up with that? And why did Hanif drop the coffee cups when I sang the other tune? How many customers go through this much just to buy a gift for their daughter? Can you see why this has me a little on edge?"

"Perhaps I can explain," expressed Hanif.

"I wish you would," I implored.

"You see, Michael, we take dreams and visions very seriously in Egypt."

I interrupted, "I know, Mudads said the same thing."

"Well, let me continue, please. Do you believe in reincarnation? Do you believe in past lives?"

"As I told your brother, I really don't put too much stock into visions, dreams, or reincarnation. I'm a philosophy teacher back home, and I question everything. My last name even starts with the word *why*. I bet that had some influence as to why I question so much. And to be honest, I'm open to these concepts. I just haven't had much experience with dreams, visions, or past lives. Frankly, I find them fascinating and would love to know more. So where were you going with all of this?"

Hanif was about to explain when his wife reappeared with two full trays. She placed the heavier one on a table next to the couch. "I brought you some fresh coffee. Would you like a gullash? It's a filled dessert pastry—a specialty of mine."

Mudads jumped up to grab one. "These are my favorite."

Before he could get his fingers on the dessert, Rehema slapped his hand away. "Where are your manners, Mudads? Guests are first."

"But you make the best gullash in all of Cairo. They are hard to resist."

Rehema blushed from his compliment and waved her hand in front of her face. "Oh stop." Then she stepped forward again with the tray outstretched from her body to invite me to take some.

"You are right, though. Trust me, Michael, you will love these. You go first." Mudads stepped back and bowed to let his sister-in-law pass through.

Rehema made sure that I took a few, along with a coffee, and proceeded to serve Mudads and her husband. She put the second tray down and sat on the couch closest to Hanif's chair.

After taking a bite, I made a *yummy* noise and told her that her gullash was amazing. "The best in Cairo is not an exaggeration. They melt in your mouth. What's your secret?"

She laughed, "Ah, but if I tell you my secret, then it wouldn't be a secret anymore, would it?" We all chuckled at her quick wit.

"Speaking of secrets, Hanif, you were about to tell me something important." I looked at him hoping to make sense of the day's events.

"Yes, this is not really a secret, though, but something that has been foretold to us by our father, and our father's father, and so on. It's been handed down from grandfather, to father, to son for over one hundred and fifty generations, and it seems as if the *time* has come."

"What time? What are you talking about?"

Hanif got his brother's attention. "Did you bring the parchments, the ones that tell of Tumaini's return?" He nodded, got up, and walked toward the box that he'd brought from his shop.

While this was going on, Rehema looked at her husband with astonishment. She bent forward and whispered in his ear, "Is this Tumaini from another land?"

Hanif smiled and placed his hand on her knee. Then he gave it a loving squeeze as a silent way of saying *yes*. Rehema gasped, then her body went limp and flung back on the couch as if she had just fainted.

Being caught off guard, and not knowing what Hanif and she had communicated to each other, I leaned over and asked if she was alright. She just beamed at me with a huge grin. If grins could talk, it would have said: *We can all relax now. There is a brighter future at hand.*

Rehema regained herself and jumped out of her seat. In an excited and elevated tone, she gushed, "I must go and make preparations. There is so much to do. Please let me know when you are ready to leave. You are always welcome in our home." She placed her hands over her mouth to express her joy, and her eyes moistened with a few tears. Then she touched my hands. "It was such a pleasure to meet you, Michael." She turned and practically bounced out of the room.

Rehema's excitement had caught me off guard. Hanif saw my expression and explained, "She's a very compassionate person. That's even what her name means. I'm very lucky to have her as my wife."

"She is wonderful, I can tell—full of passion. I can see why you consider yourself lucky."

21

Mudads came back, sat down, and opened the plastic bag that contained the papyrus. After putting on his white gloves, he pulled out twelve large pieces of parchment and set them down on the bag. Picking up the first parchment, it had the familiar Egyptian image of a man holding a scepter in one hand and a scroll in the other. However, this man did not have black hair or a bald head, as all of the other versions I have seen; this man had gold-painted hair and blue eyes. The person's clothes were also painted in gold, and light rays were drawn emanating out from his body. A picture of a round planet was before him, and the light was shining onto the planet.

"Michael, these parchments have been in our family for generations. They were given to our forefathers by the person who originally made them. The translations tell a story about the return of a very important person."

Mudads looked at Hanif, then back to me. "We believe this person to be you. If we are correct, you are the rightful heir to these scrolls and parchments. You were the one who made them in a past life."

I broke out with a cynical laugh, stopped, and then laughed again. "What makes you think that I'm the person who made these? C'mon, let's be serious here. I'm just a simple guy who loves to teach. OK, if past lives are real, then maybe I could be the one who made them. But what's with all this Tumaini talk? What does Tumaini mean? What are the songs?"

"Michael," Hanif leaned forward and stated, "you gave us the signals that you could be the one who painted these pictures and hieroglyphs. It is also possible that we are both wrong, but we will go on our intuition and help you as much as we can."

He placed his hand over his heart to continue. "While you are here, our family will look out for you and protect you. Even when you return back home, you will be in our thoughts and prayers. We believe that you can help a lot of people with what you wrote in your scrolls. You can make a difference that we cannot. It is not our path, but we can help you along the way. That is how it is written, and that is how it will be done."

Mudads joined in, "What do you plan to do now, Michael?"

"At this time, I'm not sure," I replied. Then I abruptly chimed with a frightened and excited tone, "Time! What time is it? I need to get to the tour bus before it leaves. What time do you have?"

Hanif checked his watch. "It is 4:00 p.m. What time does your bus leave? We are less than a fifteen-minute walk from the Khan."

22

"It leaves at 5:00 p.m., then we're off the rest of the night to relax and pack for the next leg of our tour." I calmed down knowing that I had a little leeway.

"Then you could join us for dinner tonight if we picked you up at your hotel, yes?" asked Mudads.

"Now, that would be fun," I exclaimed. "And I have so many more questions. By the way, you still didn't tell me. What does Tumaini mean?"

Hanif was very encouraged and answered, "Hope, Michael. Tumaini means *hope*."

CHAPTER THREE

THE SECRET BOX

We still had forty-five minutes before we had to leave the store. Hanif asked if I would like to smoke the hookah with them, but I respectfully declined. I took a tiny sip of Rehema's coffee and raised my cup toward him. "My curiosity got the best of me, Hanif. I'm not much for alcohol, tobacco, or caffeine either, but I wanted to know what Egyptian coffee tasted like. It's the first coffee I've drunk in over twenty years."

"Do you like it?"

"Let me guess: It's a special blend that only a few people know and has been passed down for generations."

He caught my humor and laughed, "No, it's actually Viennese cinnamon. I get it from the grocer down the street. What do you think?"

I chuckled, "It's pretty good. I hope I don't acquire a taste for it. I'm also glad you didn't think I was mocking you."

Mudads joined in, "You know, Michael, not everything we do is a family secret. We live like everyone else. We just happen to have a purpose beyond making babies and running a business. Up until now—aside from keeping the scrolls and parchments—you wouldn't even know we had another calling. We serve customers with kindness, and hope to receive the same in return. Probably just like you have done, no?"

"Well, sure, I try to be kind toward others. I'm not as perfect as I would like to be, but I keep trying."

There were a few more pastries on the tray that Mudads gobbled up while Hanif prepared the hookah. He gave me a funny grin when he put a shot of alcohol in the water. With the tobacco and charcoal in the right place, he lit it and started drawing smoke in through the tube.

I motioned to him. "I can see that you have played hookah before." He started to laugh, which turned into a laughing cough. "Isn't that a sign you shouldn't be smoking?"

"When the time is right, I will stop. But for now, I will enjoy one or two nasty pleasures." Hanif took another long draw from the pipe, which made the water in the hookah bubble.

"I know what you mean. I haven't kicked the sugar habit just yet."

Hanif saw his brother with half a pastry stuffed in his mouth. "Mudads, at least save the last one for Michael. You can have Rehema's gullash anytime. Michael is only here for a short visit."

"I'll take the last gullash," I chimed. "They were tasty." I devoured the dessert in a second, and with a mouth full of flakey pastry, I mumbled, "Why thdid you and Hanif keep the boxtheth thepawate?"

"What did you say?" asked Mudads.

After swallowing the gullash and taking a sip of coffee, I answered, "Why did you and Hanif keep the boxes in two different places?"

"Oh, it was to keep your information from falling into the wrong hands. If someone took the boxes from Hanif's store, they wouldn't make any sense without the last box, and vice versa. It was written that all of the boxes are needed in order to bring peace to the world."

"Peace?" I paused for a moment. "OK, the world definitely needs some help with peace, but what are you talking about? What's in these messages that I supposedly left for myself? And even if I do make sense of the messages, what am I supposed to do? I'm just a teacher at a university. I'm not anyone special."

Hanif put down his pipe. "We will tell you more tonight at dinner, but you have to decide what you are going to believe and what you are not going to believe. We can only show you the path; you have to walk it. And if you walk the path, you won't be alone." He was about to take another smoke but paused to say, "And if you choose to believe that you cannot make a difference, then that is the path you will take. We cannot force you

25

to live your destiny, but we will encourage you, for we have a destiny as well, Michael."

Trying not to sound conceited, I remarked, "Well, I'm a teacher, and I've already made a difference in the lives of some of my students."

Mudads said to me, "Michael, from what has been passed down to us, you will do more than teach at a university. You and the others will give the message to the masses that needs to be heard."

"Others? What others? Now there are others?" I was a little frustrated. "Can I get a straight answer, please?"

"Tonight, Michael. Tonight," Hanif replied. "We will tell you the rest tonight. It's about time for you to meet your tour group, don't you think? I'll get Rehema before you leave."

Hanif took one more puff and began walking away with the empty pastry tray. "I need to tell Rehema that you will be coming to dinner and that the call should go out to the others."

While Hanif was gone, Mudads told me that he would walk me back to my group. "Where are you meeting them?" he asked.

"There's a large rectangular patch of grass in front of the bazaar. It's the one with a short metal fence that runs around the perimeter. If I remember correctly, there are also a number of palm trees inside the fence. It's where we are supposed to gather so we can walk to the bus."

"I know exactly where you are talking about. I also know a shortcut so we won't have to go through the crowded streets in the Khan. It will save us about five minutes. Tell me, Michael, are you going to take the papyrus with you?"

"Are you kidding?" I smirked. "If none of this is true, then you two get the award for best sales presentation *ever!* Of course I'm going to take the boxes with me. And don't forget the incense. I really liked that, too."

"Then it is settled. I will help you meet your group, and I will pick you up at your hotel at 8:00 p.m. sharp."

Mudads slipped me a piece of paper and a pen. "Write down where you are staying and your room number. If you are traveling with any other family members, we would like for them to come along as well."

As I scribbled down the information, I shared with him, "No, it will just be me. The rest of my family is at home. I took this trip during our vacation break to gather information for my next book. I was granted a sabbatical after this term, and I want to start writing after spring classes are over."

"A sabbatical?" Mudads asked inquisitively.

"Well, yeah," I smiled. "I call it a sabbatical from people, but don't tell my dean that. I like to travel the world and study cultures, teachings, traditions, and myths. I use that information for my classes and books."

Mudads wiped his hands on a cloth napkin and replaced the cotton gloves. He picked up the stack of papyrus and placed it back in the plastic bag. "Michael, these parchments belong to you as well. However, we need them for tonight's gathering. Will you bring them along with you?"

"Of course. Is there anything else you need me to bring for tonight?"

"Nothing else that I will give you."

I was curious about the papers he'd just packed. "Hey, Mudads, those extra parchments weren't with the papyrus pieces when we were back at your shop. Where did they come from?"

"Oh yes. When I went into the back room before we left, I added the parchments to the box. I had to keep them separate from the pieces of papyrus until I knew you were coming to meet my brother. I couldn't take the chance of them falling into the wrong hands. I hope you understand."

"I understand," I nodded. "Hey, are there any other hidden items in the boxes?"

Mudads hinted, "No, but I believe that Rehema might have something for you."

"Another gift? And it's not even my birthday."

Hanif returned and joined us at the couch. Mudads explained that I was taking the parchments with me and that I would also go to dinner. He mentioned, "Rehema will be down in another minute or two. She asked if you would please wait for her."

I chuckled, "So, men have to wait for the women here, too, huh?"

Hanif burst out laughing, "It seems that we are not so different, my friend. We like to say: *If you have a happy wife, you have a happy life.*"

"My wife, Constance, would love your philosophy."

Mudads finished sealing the bag and motioned with his head for us to go to the front. On the way, Mudads told the helper behind the counter that he could return to the back. Meanwhile, Hanif made a detour to the oil rack. He picked out a cute pink-colored oil burner and small bottle of almond oil for Hara. Then he wrapped both of them in about a half-a-mile of bubble wrap before coming to the counter.

Mudads replaced the parchments in the original box and began stacking

27

them—all except for the fourth box. I looked at all of the boxes piled up on the counter and wondered, "How am I going to get all of these to the bus, Mudads?"

"Hanif has a donkey and a cart. We could use that if you wish."

"Hmm…that would be interesting. No camel, huh?"

"No," Mudads laughed, "no camel. But the donkey will do just fine."

"Rats. I was really looking forward to my camel ride, too," I joked. "What's the donkey's name?"

"Donkey," is all he said.

I asked with a raised voice, "Donkey?"

"We rarely keep pets like other countries do. If you would like, though, you can name her."

I saw the window out front with all of the painted flowers. "How about Daisy?"

"For you, my friend, we shall call her Daisy."

Hanif finished his wrapping and was joined by Rehema. Both of them came up front with items in their hands.

Hanif was all business at this point. He went to the box for Hara and placed the bubble-wrapped gifts and incense inside. He sealed the box with tape instead of twine. While Hanif was working on the box, Rehema stepped toward me with two new boxes and placed them in my hands. One was very small, but heavy, and no bigger than a jewelry box. The other box was slightly smaller than a shoe box, but very light for its size. I knew it wasn't a pair of Egyptian sandals.

Rehema was glowing. "Michael, these are gifts for you. You can open the larger one anytime you'd like. The smaller box should be opened after you leave here but before you come to dinner. Will you do this for me?" She held my hands and shook them pleadingly.

"Of course, Rehema. I can't wait to see what's inside. And I didn't bring you anything."

"Oh, but you have, Michael, you have. You brought me hope. It was my wish that I would see Tumaini before I leave for the afterlife, and here you are," she gleamed.

"Talk about no pressure."

With my hands still in hers, she pulled me closer and kissed me on the cheek like I was family. "I must go again; there is much to prepare. I look forward to seeing you tonight." With purpose in her stride, she turned and walked to the back and up the stairs.

Having finished with his task, Hanif put his hands on the counter. "Michael, these four boxes, plus Mudads' box, are yours. I even wrote a receipt on our store letterhead stating that everything was paid in full. You can show this at Customs so you won't have any problems. The box for your daughter, with the incense and oil burner, I will let you have for two hundred dollars." He smiled to show me that he'd put on his business face.

I was shocked. "Do you really want me to haggle with you, after all of this? You can't be serious. Aren't you supposed to protect me?"

"Give it your best shot," he jested with a cocky grin.

After a fun round of haggling, which usually amounts to starting at half of the shop owner's suggested price, I ended up paying a hundred and ten dollars. In all rights, the papyrus pieces were garbage, but I wanted them for Hara. I didn't even balk at it while I pulled out five twenty dollar bills and a ten. The incense, oil burner, and almond oil alone would have cost me more than that back home.

"It was a pleasure doing business with you, my friend." He wrote a new receipt and gave it to me. Then Hanif shook my hand vigorously and bade me well. "I will see you tonight. All will be prepared. All will be prepared."

Mudads and I gathered all of the boxes, and he led me out the back of the store. Behind the shop was a stall for the donkey, the cart, and a small shed for tools and supplies. I greeted her, "Ah, there's Daisy. Hello, Daisy." I rubbed her rough coat and bristly mane. "I wish I had a carrot for you."

Since it's not uncommon for people in these parts to raise animals for their food supply, I asked, "Where are the chickens?"

"Oh, they are on the roof with the goats and some other birds." It was rather comical the way he answered so quickly. It didn't faze him at all, but I didn't expect the goats and livestock to be on the roof.

"You know," I reckoned, "these boxes aren't that heavy. Let's just walk and let Daisy rest. It looks like it would take more time to hitch her up than it would to walk."

"That's fine, but we should get going so we don't miss your group."

While we walked, a question popped into my head. "Mudads, what if I wasn't the one you were looking for? Would you still have sold me the papyrus pieces from your store?"

He looked sternly at me. "Michael, if you hadn't recognized the shape of the sphere and the cross, then I would have raised the price so high that *no one* would have paid for them. If you had agreed, then I would have raised the price again. And if I needed to be rude, I would have packed them away and said you weren't worthy of such a find. It wouldn't have been the first time that I had done that."

"You turned someone away before?"

"Once, and so did Hanif. The other people did not know anything about the shapes or songs and left in a huff. We knew what we had done was right."

"Do either of you know how to solve the puzzle?" I raised an eyebrow and continued, "Oh wait, it's my path, right?"

"Yes!" he exclaimed. "And no..." He paused for a moment. "Yes, it is your path; and no, I don't know how to solve the puzzle. You are the one who made it, which means you will know how to solve it when the time is right."

"And the songs?"

"The songs you know so well will unlock the power of the scrolls. That is all I can tell you at this time."

"And how did you plan to get me to Hanif's store if I'd bought yours but hadn't gone with you to get the scrolls?"

"I had faith that all would work out as planned. If you had left the country without them, the scrolls would have called you back. It was said that you used your powers to make this happen so you would be reunited with all of your clues. You were destined by your own hand to retrieve them to finish your task."

He stopped me and added, "It is also foretold that you might not succeed in restoring peace to our planet, but you will try with all your heart to do so."

"Peace to the planet is a pretty tall order, Mudads. Are you sure you've got the right person?"

We started walking again. "I can only tell you what has been told to me. You will hear the rest tonight when I read the parchments."

"Oh yeah, the parchments. Thanks for reminding me. Hey look, there's my group. Why don't you come over so I can introduce you?"

As we approached, they were buzzing with excitement over all of the touristy souvenirs that they'd bought at the Khan. A number of them were eager to show us their plastic statues and fake crystal pyramids.

"Who is this, Michael?" our tour guide inquired in a very pleasant tone.

"This is Mudads. He helped me bring all of these boxes to our rendezvous spot. You could say that we connected at his shop—which, by the way, is awesome. And when you come back to Cairo for your return flight, you should stop in his brother's store as well." I winked at Mudads. "He has the best perfumes and oils in all of Egypt."

More than one person wanted to see what I'd bought. I was hesitant, especially when Mudads gave me the *keep it secret* look. Not wanting to be rude, I pulled out Hara's box and laid it on the ground. Mudads gave me an *OK* grin and nod. I also pulled out the larger box that Rehema had given me and opened it first.

Mudads saw inside, and with a raised voice he burst, "Rehema gave you gullash?! I can't believe she gave you gullash to take home. She doesn't even give me gullash to take home. You must have really made an impression on her. You are so lucky."

One of the group members begged, "You are going to share, aren't you?!"

"Of course I am. Mudads, you go first and pass it around. If there is any left over—and by the look on your salivating faces and fangs, I doubt there will be—I'll take the rest back to my room. Here, help yourselves."

You would have thought that I had thrown a piece of meat into a pride of lionesses who hadn't eaten in a month. The box was torn apart as fingers flew in from all directions. This was followed by a chorus of people making *yummy* sounds. Mudads barely escaped harm and clung to the last pastry as if his life depended on it.

"I can see that you all liked her gullash. I'll have to tell Rehema how much it was appreciated," I chuckled.

The tour director asked, "What's in all of the other boxes? It looks like you made a great find."

I laughed, "There's no more gullash in these boxes, so please don't rush them. I found some papyrus scraps for Hara and some incense for me." I pulled open the tape while Mudads stood silently. He knew I wouldn't show them the other items, but he also did not leave yet.

"Wow, those look amazing," remarked the tour director. "You'll have to show me on the map where you got the incense. By the way, how did you find them?"

"Well, it's a long story, and I don't want to bore you, but I'll say that I found them by being lost." I said this partly to get a reaction, but more so to take their attention off of the other boxes.

Some of the group *oohd* and *ahd* at the papyrus, but most were unimpressed as the pieces were torn. After my little show, they returned to their small groups and resumed showing off their trinkets.

Once the last member of our group showed up, our Egyptian guide yelled out, "Yalla! Yalla! On to the bus."

Mudads shook my hand vigorously. "I will be in your hotel lobby at 8:00 p.m. to take you to dinner. Rehema asked me to give you this note regarding the smaller box. Read this in private when you get to your hotel. I will see you shortly."

I put the note in the same pocket as the small box. "I'm looking forward to dinner. Thank you for all you have done, my friend."

Calling Mudads a friend made him smile. He bowed to me, and I bowed in return. Then he turned and walked away briskly.

Our tour guide grabbed a few of my boxes and helped carry them to our bus. While in route, several members of our group kept pointing to the sky. There was a steady stream of white pigeons coming from the direction of Hanif's store. I thought to myself, "I should be surprised by this, but after today's events, I'm not."

CHAPTER FOUR

GUESS WHO'S COMING
TO DINNER

My eyes opened to a blurry vision of my hotel room. I was in a complete fog and had no bearings as to where I was or what I was doing there. Then it came to me. I sprang up like a frightened jackrabbit after I saw the clock. "I have to get ready. Mudads will be here soon. I don't think he'd like it very much if I were late."

I was still tired, though, and stretched my arms. "Boy, that nap felt great. I hope it's still today. I could have slept for a week."

The seven boxes glaring at me in my room reminded me of my day's excursion. The small box that Rehema had given me was still on top of Hara's. "Oh yeah, I was supposed to open that before going to the restaurant. I wonder if it's a different kind of pastry."

After picking it up, I put it right back down. "That's right! I have to read her note first. Now where is it? Pocket...it's in my pocket."

I pulled out the folded paper and opened it up. Inside the folded paper was a tiny envelope. "I didn't know they made them that small," I chuckled. "Wouldn't you think that the note would be in the envelope?" I rotated the paper to see the front and back. There was nothing written on it, so I flippantly tossed it aside.

Carefully, I pulled at the envelope flap. "Who knows? If I'm Tumaini, it could be rigged by an assassin." I closed one eye, turned and tilted my head back a little, and held the envelope far away from my body as if I were expecting a bomb to go off. After I peeked inside and found no poisonous asps, scorpions, or strange white powder, I pulled out a piece of blue paper that was folded in quarters. On it was written very neatly:

> *If Tumaini chooses to walk the path, please open the*
> *box and wear the gift to dinner. If he chooses not to walk*
> *the path, please keep the gift unopened until he answers*
> *the call.*
>
> *Lovingly,*
> *Rehema*

"I don't know if all this Tumaini stuff is real, but I'm game to see where this goes. If anything, it should make for an interesting chapter in my next book."

Without thinking, I picked up the small jewelry box and gave it a little shake. "Nope, no snakes in there." Then I shook it again and made a *hissing* noise. "Nope, still no snake. I'm so easily amused."

"Now, that wasn't smart," I scolded myself. "What if it was breakable? What if it was a special dessert? It could be all crumbs by now. Nah, she said it was something I'm supposed to wear. I'm sure she wouldn't want me to wear dessert."

I stopped my antics and looked inside. When I opened the box, there was a small amulet pinned to a thick piece of jeweler's cotton. A gold chain was attached to it and neatly tucked under the white fluffy stuffing. "Wow, this is impressive. Not what I was expecting at all, not that I knew what to expect anyway," I said in a matter-of-fact tone. "I hope it's not cursed."

Turning it over a few times to examine it, I laughed, "Well, here goes; red 'shroom it is." I put the necklace on and waited for a second. "Nope, still here, and the world's still turning. So much for any extraordinary events. I wonder what's so special about this amulet."

I took it back off so I could get cleaned up for dinner. There was just enough time for a quick shower and a change of clothes. Then I slipped it back over my head and buttoned my dress shirt. My collar covered the gold chain, and my shirt hid the amulet.

The door had just closed behind me when I remembered, "Parchments! I was supposed to bring the parchments!" I went back inside and picked up my travel briefcase. I had put the parchments in there so they wouldn't get damaged or be noticed. Then I went downstairs.

By 7:55 p.m., I was down in the lobby. My tour guide, Shannon, was talking with Mudads. "Hi, Michael." She waved. "I was just taking down Mudads' and Hanif's information. He was telling me how impressed you were with Hanif's special blend of incense. I'll have to put this on my future tour and take my groups there."

Mudads winked at me. "Yes, he bought several boxes of his finest incense. You should probably use it when you are in the temples at Luxor."

His cryptic wink and suggestion caught me off guard, and it showed on my face. "How did you know we were going to Luxor?"

"Shannon told me about the rest of your itinerary. We were trying to figure out a time when she could come into our stores before leaving the country. Weren't you, Shannon?" He looked at her for a friendly confirmation.

"Oh yes. And I am looking forward to meeting Rehema. I'd love to get her gullash recipe and share it with the group."

She turned to me. "Michael, Mudads tells me you are going to dinner with him. Will you be alright on your own? Do you need to take our guide with you as an interpreter?"

I glanced at Shannon, then to Mudads. "I feel perfectly safe with Mudads. He has taken extremely good care of me today. Besides, I can't think of anyone else I would want as an interpreter."

"Well, OK then. You are a big boy and don't need a chaperone. I just want to make sure you will be alright."

"I'll be fine," I smiled. "Thanks for looking out for me." Then I remembered something that I needed to ask. "Hey Shannon, just to be sure, what time does the bus leave for the airport tomorrow?"

She shook her head in disbelief, "Michael, Michael, Michael...how many times did I tell the group when we are leaving tomorrow? It's 8:00 a.m. Be there on time or you will miss all the fun and adventure."

If only she knew of the adventure I'd already had. "8:00 a.m. sharp. I'll be there."

Mudads motioned to me. "Michael, we need to be going. He'll be alright, Shannon, I promise. It was nice to meet you, and don't forget to come by my shop when you get back."

"Likewise, and I will. You two have a great night."

We both turned and left the building. Once outside the door, Mudads asked with a hint of sadness, "Michael, did you read Rehema's note?"

"Of course I did." Then I continued on to a new topic, "Where are we going tonight? I didn't have lunch today, and I'm famished. Rehema's pastries are delicious, but not very filling."

"Oh, it's a family-run restaurant near the Giza Plateau. The restaurant faces the Sphinx, so we should be there just in time to see the sunset between the pyramids. It's a breathtaking sight every time I see it."

"I can't wait to see it, too. We haven't been to the pyramids yet, so this will be an awesome preview."

After a few more steps, I checked, "Mudads, are you alright? You seem a little down."

"Oh, it's nothing. I'm glad that you remembered the parchments." He looked toward my hand. "Those are the parchments in your briefcase, aren't they?"

Holding it up to confirm his question, "Yes, I thought I should keep them protected. They're still wrapped up nice and neat in the plastic bag, too. I took a short nap at the hotel, so I didn't get to look at them. I can't wait to hear what they have to say."

Our hotel was less than a ten-minute drive from the Giza Plateau, so we showed up with plenty of time to see the sunset. After parking the car near the restaurant—which is a feat all in itself in Cairo—we walked a half a block to the front door. I could see off in the short distance that Hanif and Rehema were waiting outside. They were dressed in really fancy clothes, as was Mudads. I felt a little underdressed.

"It is good to see you again." Hanif held out his hand in friendship.

I returned the greeting and told them that they both looked amazing, which brought a huge smile to their faces. I also told Rehema about the ravenous tourists who loved her baked goods. I finished with, "You were a huge hit with our group."

She looked at me with wide eyes and gleamed from my compliment. "Michael, before we go in, did you read my note?"

I pulled out the amulet and held it by the chain. "Oh yeah, I did. Thank you for this lovely gift. You're incredibly generous. I don't know if I can accept it."

"Oh, don't you even think of returning it. It is yours." Then she asked, "Would you please wear it on the outside during dinner?"

"Of course, but"—I stopped tucking it inside my shirt—"you will have to tell me about the unique design. Is there any special meaning to the piece? Wait, let me guess; you'll tell me later."

Rehema laughed, "How did you know, Michael? We will tell you more inside."

Mudads' demeanor instantly changed when he saw the amulet, and his smile returned. "The restaurant is on the second floor, so we must get going if we are to catch the sunset."

Hanif opened the door, and Rehema grabbed my arm. "I knew you would put it on. I just knew it." She grinned and guided me inside.

As we walked through the door, Mudads turned back toward me and gave me a funny look. "You fooled me, Michael." He gestured to the amulet. "I thought you had decided not to take the first step."

"I'm sorry, Mudads. That wasn't my intent. I didn't even think about having to wear this in a special way. I just put it on and grabbed the parchments to meet you in the lobby. I hope you will forgive me."

"No harm done, my friend. Let's get inside. It is time."

There was a young man at the bottom of the stairs. He must have known Mudads, Rehema, and Hanif because he acknowledged them right away. "We closed the restaurant for you and your guests, as you requested. It will be a private gathering. Everything is in order. Please go upstairs and enjoy." He looked at my amulet and nodded in respect.

I thought, "This is going to be an interesting evening for sure."

———— ·•·•·•· ————

The upstairs restaurant was huge and could easily hold over two hundred people. It was as big as a ballroom with no separating walls, just pillars placed throughout to support the ceiling. Being a tourist area, the pillars looked like they belonged in the ancient ruins and had hieroglyphs on them from floor to ceiling. The south and west sides of the second floor were open-aired style walls with a balcony on the side that faced the pyramids. The other two walls were decorated with mini palm trees, mirrors, and paintings. A unique gold and red trim covered the lone corner and ran along the ceiling's edge.

The floor space, excluding the balcony, was filled with tables all decked out with the usual white table cloths, glasses, and silverware. What made this restaurant different was the napkins folded in the shapes of animals, birds, reptiles, and flowers. Most of the tables had the same eight shapes, but there were a few tables with other varieties.

Our quartet walked in and found a good number of people already seated. I asked jokingly, "I thought the young man downstairs said this would be a private gathering?"

Hanif replied, "It is a private gathering. I guess all of the pigeons didn't make it. The—"

I stopped him abruptly. "Pigeons?! Did you say *pigeons?!* What do pigeons have to do with dinner? They aren't on the menu, are they?" Hanif put up his finger and started to speak, but I interrupted again, "Oh, wait a minute, when we left the Khan, our group saw a stream of pigeons in the sky. Are you telling me...?"

"Yes, Michael, you guessed right," answered Hanif. "Not everyone has a phone or a computer. A lot of people don't even have indoor plumbing or electricity yet, so we still use pigeons to get the message out to a large number of people. Some make it, some don't, and some end up on somebody else's dinner plate."

"What did the message say? I mean, how did you keep others from knowing about the location?"

Rehema grabbed my arm. "Is it important to know everything?"

"Well, yeah. I'm a teacher...and a student. I like to learn new things," I chuckled.

Hanif continued, "The people who will be coming tonight already know where to go. We meet here once a year to renew our vow to help the souls of the world."

"So, what did it say?"

"It was a short message." He held up a tiny piece of paper for me to read. All it said was:

Tumaini
Tonight

"Remember, Michael. These are pigeons, not camels. They can't carry a whole book with them." Hanif laughed and laughed, and I laughed with him, too.

The light in the room changed color, and Mudads called me out to the balcony to watch the sunset. From our vantage point, the sun was setting perfectly between the Pyramid of Khufu and the Pyramid of Khafre, with the Sphinx sitting below as if it were guarding post. The Pyramid of Queens and Menkaure were barely visible off to the left, but they rounded out the mesmerizing scene rather nicely. As the sun began to set, it started off at first as a huge blazing yellow globe that levitated effortlessly between the two mammoth stone formations. As it sank a little more, the yellow ball turned into a massive red globe with orange highlights. It looked as if the sun had its own halo all around it. By the time it touched the edge of the sand, as if by magic, the once huge ball of flame lost its illusion of grandeur beside the pyramids and shrank to a tiny dot of yellow. But not to lose all of its magic, I could see light rays streaming from the tops of the pyramids and their rocky edges. The sand then seemed to swallow up the sun as dusk took over. Off in the distance, we could hear the melodic Muslim Salat al-Maghrib prayer over the loud speakers.

I was so entranced with the flourishing voice from afar, the sunset, and taking pictures, that I didn't notice that the restaurant had completely filled. Every chair, except for the four near the balcony, was taken. When I turned around, I burst out, "Whoa!"

Rehema held my hand to calm me. "It's alright, Michael. They all came to see you and to hear what was written on the parchment. Let's go in. They are waiting."

I was so nervous that you would have thought I was picking up my date for the prom and her father had answered the door with a shotgun in his hands. "Come, come," said Rehema, while Mudads and Hanif waited at the table.

Hanif pulled out the chair for her. "Rehema, you sit here." Then Mudads sat down, leaving a space between the two of them for me.

As I walked up to the table, every eye in the room was staring at me. It felt like the weight of an entire pyramid was crushing down upon my chest. I placed my bag under my chair and thought, "What did I get myself into?"

As if scripted, the napkin on my dinner plate was white with gold spun edging. It was in the shape of a *dragon*.

Dinner started right away, with scores of waiters coming in to light the candles on the tables. I took a picture of my dragon-shaped napkin and said to myself, "Constance is never going to believe this."

Rehema turned to me and spoke softly, "This must all seem very strange to you. Let me tell you, when I was first told about Tumaini, I, too, had a hard time believing. But as more and more events kept coming true in our recent history, I took a leap of faith. I knew that if I didn't see Tumaini in this lifetime, I would see him in my next incarnation."

She paused for a moment, then she continued, "If you haven't noticed, the world could use some help right now. All it takes is one person to get things started in the right direction. I'm not talking about a religious savior, a deliverer, or a prophet. I'm talking about a deliverer of answers, a deliverer of truth, someone who can deliver a message and let the people decide how they are going to live their lives. And this person will do it without condemning them for not following his or her creed. He won't use fear, oppression, or brute force to make people follow his ways. We've all seen what happens when our current governments and religions do that. This causes nothing but separation within the people. We need someone to bring us together, not to keep tearing us apart." She patted my arm. "Do you understand what I am talking about, Michael?"

"And you believe that person to be me?"

"Yes, I do."

Hanif joined in, "So do I, Michael. You have a way about you. You can talk to people without making them feel unworthy or inferior. You are logical in your approach. I noticed that when we bargained over the price for your goods. You just haven't realized your full potential yet. I know it. I can feel it."

"You do understand the kind of pressure you're placing on me, don't you?" I asked.

Mudads remarked, "That is why we are all here, Michael. You don't have to take on this path alone. And no one person can do it alone. That is what you said in your teachings so many lifetimes ago.

"You also said that you would come from across a great ocean when the world was at a crossroads. You would come to be reunited with your teachings and deliver a simple message to the world. You would deliver the truth that has been hidden from the masses for centuries. And if the people listen—and more importantly, *act*—then the world can be saved, along with all her children."

Before I could respond, a waiter entered at the back of the room and stopped in the doorway. He held up a small gong that hung from a gold-colored rope. He struck the gong three times, which got the attention of the entire room. We all quickly looked toward the back of the restaurant as a chorus of waiters, all dressed in black, entered with trays held over their heads. They were led in by two staff members carrying lit torches.

I looked toward Hanif and gestured at the parade with my head. Hanif mentioned, "It's how they serve dinner to large groups at this restaurant. Nice, huh? The tourists like it, so the owner keeps doing it."

I nodded again. "I'm glad it's not part of a dark ritual or ceremony. I'm famished. Let's eat."

———————

While appetizers were being placed in front of us, I was introduced to the four other people at our table. All of them spoke English, so it was easy to strike up a conversation.

It was refreshing to talk about something other than scrolls, secret songs, or destinies. We chatted about the simple parts of life. We shared what we did for a living and how we spent time with our family members. I truly enjoyed learning about these wonderful people and our similarities. They were like brothers and sisters to me who just happened to live a few thousand miles away. I could have easily been talking to a neighbor down the street.

As dinner neared the end, I asked Rehema to tell me about the amulet. She turned her chair toward mine and expressed with enthusiasm, "It would be my pleasure." The rest of the table went quiet and listened in.

"As the story goes, this is your amulet from the time when you made the scrolls. The outer gold circle with the line under it is called a shen. A shen is an Egyptian symbol for eternal protection. That which is within the shen is protected. If you look closely, it looks like a cartouche, but cartouches are taller, longer, and shaped like an oval. The bright red stone—the one that is embedded in the gold and shaped like a circle—is made of carnelian. This represents the sun, or Ra, to many Egyptians. To the Protectors of Souls, this represents the Creator and the Creator's infinite energy."

She pointed to the black shape that was embedded in the carnelian stone. The shape was made of two arms connected together where the shoulders would be, but with no body. The arms were bent at the elbows with the forearms pointing straight up at ninety degrees. It looked like two arms that were signaling a touchdown.

Rehema continued, "The arms are the symbol for your Ka. Your Ka is your consciousness, your soul. When you put it all together, the shen—which is us, the Protectors of Souls—are protecting the souls of humans and the light of the Creator. Do you understand?"

"I think so. Who are the Protectors of Souls?"

"Mudads will explain this to you when he reads the parchments. Tell me, Michael, what made you wear the amulet tonight?"

In a joking manner, I said, "Well, it was just like the scene from Hamulet: *To wear, or not to wear, that is the question.*" It took a moment, and some of them got my humor and laughed, but the others didn't. I tried to explain that it was a twist on a famous line from Shakespeare's Hamlet, but that didn't make it any funnier to them.

"OK, forget the bad joke. I'll tell you why I wore it." I looked back toward the group. "You see, a good part of me believes that I could be Tumaini. I knew the songs, right? And I have this feeling… I can't explain it, but what you are telling me feels like it's the truth." They all nodded. "The other part of me wants to believe, but it's not ready to commit to being Tumaini just yet. And a very small part of me doesn't know. The only way to find out was to wear the gift. That is why I put it on. I just want to know the truth. I believe in the possibility, but now I need proof."

Mudads patted my shoulder. "I understand, Michael, and I am glad that you took the leap of faith. You will have your truth soon enough." He pointed to my bag. "Would you hand me the parchments? It is time to address the group."

I slid my chair back and started to bend down, but before I could reach my briefcase, Rehema grabbed my arm and shook it vigorously. "This is going to be so exciting, don't you think?"

Hanif jumped in, too, "I've been looking forward to this my entire life."

While Rehema was still shaking my arm, I commented, "Rehema, I hope you don't take this the wrong way, but you don't act like many of the Egyptian women I've encountered. You are much more…much more… How do I put this? You express yourself more. You aren't as reserved and quiet."

"Oh, it's because I wasn't born here. I was raised in the States." She playfully patted my arm and sat backwards. "I even attended a college in New York and got a degree in world history. Then I came to Egypt to do research for my graduate degree."

She turned and pointed a finger at the Great Pyramid. "Right over there. That's where I spent many sun-baked hours doing research. I can tell you just about anything you'd want to know about the pyramids, the hidden doorways, secret chambers—and let's not forget the underground tunnels"—she leaned toward me and whispered with her hand beside her face—"the ones that the Egyptian government won't tell you about, the hush-hush kind."

My excitement got the best of me. "Secret tunnels? Hidden chambers?"

"Oh yes, and so much more—way above top secret. Because I spent a lot of time researching ancient religions and Egyptian ceremonies, I got to see more of the ruins than the tourists get to see. I even tried to duplicate some of the ritual ceremonies that were rumored to go on in the Great Pyramid."

She smiled at Hanif and gave him a loving look. "And that's when I met my husband. I bought some of his incense to use in the Queen's chamber. We both fell in love at first sight, so I stayed in Egypt."

Looking back at me, she continued, "My family and friends are still back in America. I miss them terribly, but I just couldn't leave Hanif behind. I've been here ever since. And as we say in my line of work, *the rest is history,*" she giggled.

I grinned at both of them, "Let me guess, the incense was—"

Hanif was already boyishly shaking his head *yes* before I could get the rest of the words out of my mouth. We both answered at the same time, "Incense from the Temple Gods."

"You must be psychic, my friend," he mimicked in an Indian-like guru's voice as he bobbled his head side-to-side. The table of people laughed together with us.

Mudads chimed in, "I hate to interrupt, but we really should get to the parchments."

"You are right, Mudads," his brother agreed. "Let us not keep the Protectors waiting."

I carefully laid my briefcase on the table and began to open it. The table went quiet when I pulled out the plastic bag. Then I leaned back toward Rehema. "Don't think you are off the hook yet about the tunnels and chambers. I want to hear all about them after dinner." She winked at me and nodded toward the parchments to keep me on track.

While this was going on, Mudads was putting on his cotton gloves. He held up both hands like a surgeon who'd just finished scrubbing. "These parchments are priceless, my friend, and cannot be replaced." Then he got a devilish little smirk on his face. "One can't be too careful with ancient Egyptian antiquities."

"Right," I said with a non-trusting tone. I still wasn't convinced about the whole Tumaini-I-own-the-rights-to-the-parchments spiel. "Mudads, I'm not going to jail for those. I swear to you."

He snickered, "Relax, my friend. You must not forget to stay lighthearted. Where's your humor? You won't go to jail."

"I think I left my humor back at the airport when they asked for my passport and a stool sample." The group laughed a little. "I'm kidding, you know. They only asked for some blood and a valid credit card."

I carefully passed the plastic bag to my right. "Hey, Mudads, I thought these parchments were written by me and only I could solve the puzzle. Isn't that what you said earlier?"

"Well, they are, and they aren't."

"You don't say," I zinged with a hint of sarcasm. "You don't like to give straight answers, do you? How 'bout a straight answer this time?"

Mudads gave me a calming smile. "Michael, I'm sorry for the confusion. If you are Tumaini, then you did write these parchments and the scrolls. You also made the symbols on the papyrus pieces. From what was told to us by our fathers, you encrypted the scrolls and the papyrus pieces. You did this because of the tremendous power that can be attained from these teachings. You also didn't want this type of power to fall into the wrong hands. The dark side is already powerful enough without this knowledge. They don't need any more help to keep the people enslaved beyond what they already are."

44

"Go on…"

He continued, "The first parchments were not encrypted. To anyone else, it could be a fanciful story. But to us, the Protectors of Souls, we look to them for inspiration. We know they are real."

At that moment, everything went still. My mind went blank, and I had the strangest feeling rush over my entire body. It was the strongest sense of déjà vu I'd ever had in my life. I knew what Mudads was going to say next because I'd already lived it. I was magically transported out of the current timeline, and I saw the room a few moments in the future. I saw the candles flickering on each table; I saw that Hanif was going to put more sugar in his coffee; Rehema was about to take another bite of her dessert; and Mudads was opening the bag and speaking to me. He was telling me something important about the scrolls.

I shook my head like someone who was clearing the cobwebs out of his mind. Then I became aware of my surroundings again. "So I understand this more clearly: The scrolls are messages from God; the pieces of papyrus are a puzzle I must solve to help the world; and the parchments tell of my life in Egypt and my return. The last few pages teach us how to regain our God-given powers. That makes it all seem so easy."

Rehema immediately held her hand to her mouth and gasped. Hanif was stirring his coffee and lost control of his spoon. The spoon went flying across the table and clattered on all of the dinnerware and glasses. And Mudads froze in his tracks with the parchments in both hands. His jaw dropped, and his eyes were wide open.

"Michael," Mudads exclaimed, "I never told you that the scrolls were from God. Where did you get that information? How did you know?"

I mimicked Hanif from a few minutes earlier and answered with a guru's voice, "I had a psychic moment, my friend. Seriously, though, I just had a major flash of déjà vu. Haven't you ever had déjà vu before?" He just looked at me. "Well, I saw what was going to happen next, and I just knew what you were going to say about the scrolls and the parchment pieces. I can't explain it any more than that. It felt as real as I'm sitting here right now."

Hoping that I had given the right information, I sheepishly asked, "Am I right? Are the scrolls from God? Didn't I scribe these a few thousand years in the past?"

"When you decode them and feel the light force flowing through your body; when you feel the truth of love and compassion being spoken in your words; when you deliver the words to those who would hear; then you will know that these are the Creator's words. These are the God Scrolls that you wrote many moons ago. Then you will remember who you are. Then you will remember that you are Tumaini."

Rehema put her hand on my arm and teared up. Hanif put his arm on hers and said, "This is a blessed moment, my friend. We are with you...to the end."

Mudads and Rehema echoed the same thing, "To the end."

CHAPTER FIVE

AND A PARCHMENT
IN A PALM TREE

Above Cairo, the sky was completely free of clouds. It was a moonless night, which allowed the stars to show off and twinkle a little more above the desert sands. Without heaven's main nightlight gleaming over the city, it was almost pitch black.

The tourists' light show at the Great Pyramid had just ended, too. The crowds had already dispersed, and the tour buses were well on their way back to the hotels. A few minutes after 10:00 p.m., the Giza Necropolis went completely dark. As the lights went out, a strange hum came from beyond the pyramids, and an eerie energy engulfed the land. It seemed there wouldn't be any more help from the stone watchcat that night.

From the alley beside the restaurant, a car engine turned over. With its headlights off, the car inched quietly out from the passageway and turned toward the front door. It moved so slowly that all you could hear was the crunching of gravel beneath the tires. The windows were tinted, so no one could be seen inside.

When the car reached the entrance, the passenger door opened, and a man dressed in a waiter's black shirt, black pants, and black apron exited the car. As he went inside, he held his right hand behind his back to hide a small wooden club. The club was in the shape of a fleur de lis.

The door to the restaurant creaked as it closed behind him. From outside, you could hear a short scuffle and a quick thud-like sound. The mysterious man quickly peeked his head out of the door and gave the driver a cryptic hand signal. It looked like a hand symbol that the Freemasons used, making this scene reminiscent of Hiram Abiff.

When the door closed, the man in black locked it, flipped the *Open* sign over, and barricaded the door with a chair. He also turned off the downstairs lights and the neon restaurant sign. Before going upstairs, he dropped a dead pigeon on the young man's body with a note:

Tumaini
Tonight

Upstairs, Mudads was about to address the group. As he picked up the parchments, a strong breeze suddenly blew in from the pyramids. The long red curtains behind us came alive and looked like blood-colored demons dancing in the wind. All of the candle flames in the room flickered mercilessly and made their own ghostly scene by casting shadows everywhere.

"OK, that was freaky," I declared. "Does anyone care to explain what happened?"

One of the guests across from me, Omar, insisted, "Supernatural, it must be. We've never had that happen at any of our gatherings before."

Rehema added, "Strange things do happen around the pyramids. I've heard the buzzing sound from far off in the desert, too. Something bad usually happens in the city when the buzzing starts." Her smile left for the first time that night and was replaced with a genuine look of worry. Hanif wrapped his arms around her to give her some comfort.

Mudads gave me a light touch. "It seems we are not alone, my friend. Would you like me to stop and put the parchments away? You can go back to your hotel and brush this under the rug as coincidence."

"Mudads"—I shook my head a few times—"I've lived through major hurricanes and tornadoes back home. A little breeze isn't going frighten me one bit. But for some unknown reason, I suddenly feel queasy…restless." I paused to find the right words. "Wait…agitated, that's it. I feel agitated, and for no reason at all. It seemed to have started right after the buzzing sound."

I put my hand on my stomach and head to see if I could alleviate the sick feeling. "You know, during the last few decades, the governments used psychological warfare on each other and their citizens. The Germans used it, the Russians used it—heck, the U.S. is still using it. Actually, I don't know who hasn't used it. Do you think it has something to do with the buzzing?"

"I don't know," Mudads replied with a concerned look, "but I can see the effect it is having on our guests. We need to do something to help calm them down."

Hanif agreed, "Yes, yes, let's do something. Why don't you address them, Brother?"

Mudads moved all of the tableware and glasses away from our place settings. When that was done, he opened the plastic bag and took out all of the parchments. I could see that he was also being affected and was having trouble concentrating.

Rehema asked, "Mudads, are you alright?"

"I'll be fine; just give me a moment." He sat down and put both of his hands on his face.

By this point, the dark energy had infected everyone in the restaurant. A few people were bent over like they were going to be sick, while others were groaning and holding their heads and stomachs.

Suddenly, the buzzing in the air stopped. I looked over my shoulder and briefly saw a bright light flash in the sky. Before I could focus and get a good look at the source, the glowing ball sped off at ludicrous speed in a southerly direction and went deep into the desert. This caused an instant vacuum effect in the room, and the atmosphere changed immediately.

"Did anyone see that?!" I pointed toward the balcony.

Rehema turned to look. "See what?"

"That light, out near the desert...did anyone see it?" They were all shaking their heads *no*.

Mudads investigated one more time over his shoulder. I told him, "You know, I'm not one who usually questions if something is coincidence or a fluke, but this one has me stumped." I gulped down some fresh air. "I'm starting to wonder what's going on here tonight."

The rest of the crowd began reviving themselves from the negative effects of the buzzing. Bewildered, they all looked toward our table as if we were going to make things right again. I slapped Mudads on the shoulder. "No pressure, huh? Go get 'em, tiger."

Mudads stood up and held the first parchment in his hands. This was the traditional signal for the start of the meeting. Since everyone was already looking in our direction, and for the most part quiet, he didn't need to do much to start his talk.

"Friends, we have just had an interesting experience together, one that binds us even closer as Protectors of Souls. We, like you, felt the dark, foul energy that harms the people of the land—the same dark energy that brings madness to people's minds and even drives some to commit despicable acts of violence." He raised his right hand and shook it. "But we are all here together, supporting one another, caring for one another, and loving one another. There is nothing stronger in the world than love, especially love in action." The crowd pounded their tables in appreciation of his words. The thumping was accompanied by the jangling of silverware and plates bouncing on the wooden tables.

"Hear me, friends: We have the upper hand over tyranny, for we do not use deceit or corruption to subjugate our neighbors; we have strength over the wicked, for we do not hide in the darkness and shadows to harm another; and we have the upper hand over the greedy because we show charity, kindness, and mercy to all." The crowd again pounded on their tables. It was akin to the knights of old pounding the table with their king.

While the crowd was still hammering their tables, I nudged Mudads. "Way to go, tiger. Nice recovery."

Without glancing at me, he continued, "We, the Protectors of Light, the Protectors of Souls, have seen the parchment that I hold. Some of you have even heard the tales of *hope* written on this parchment, a hope that would return to the land. But most of you have never seen or heard about the rest of the parchments. These are the parchments that were also recorded by a lost brother from so many centuries ago."

Mudads carefully picked up the rest of the old papyrus and held them up for the people to see. The crowd gasped, almost as if they were looking at a holy relic. He made sure to show the cover parchment, which was the same one I had seen before, the one with the man with golden hair.

———————

At the back of the room, the waiters were all in a line against the wall nearest the kitchen. One waiter in particular, the one at the end of the line, became angry when he saw the parchments. His face turned red, and his eyes glared of hatred. With his hands clenched into fists, he began to step forward, but he abruptly stopped and held himself back. It wasn't time to make his move yet, so he remained in his place.

"Tonight"—Mudads put down the stack of papers and picked up the first parchment again—"we will all hear the story that recalls the return of hope. Tonight, we will all hear the words that tell of hope's instructions. Tonight, we will hear the details that will wisely guide us in our future endeavors to bring peace and love back to our precious lands. Brothers and sisters, tonight we will hear about the return of..." He paused and looked at me. As he did, the man in black sneered at us. He continued, "Tonight, we will hear about Tumaini!" The entire place erupted in pounding and cheers—all except Hanif, who was putting on his white gloves. He walked behind me and stood by his brother. "Hanif will read what was written by Tumaini those many years ago." Mudads bowed toward him and placed the parchment in his hands before taking his seat.

"My friends, it is good to be with all of you again," addressed Hanif, as he glanced around the room to acknowledge the other Protectors. "Today has been a special day, an eventful day, and we have yet to hear the stroke of midnight. There is more to do on our quest to help others. That is why I will read what was written for the Protectors of Light, we the Protectors of Souls."

With one hand, he took out a pair of reading glasses and placed them on his face. They rested on the lower part of his nose. Then he adjusted the paper a few inches farther away so he could focus better. "My friends, here is what Tumaini wrote for the Protectors of Souls:

"This is my last writing before the temple guards take me away...

"The dark beings who live beneath the surface have corrupted the pharaoh's thoughts. They put living things in his head and body that slowly took over his mind. With the pharaoh's thoughts controlled and his will depleted, the dark beings were able to capture his ka: they captured his living soul. With his ka in their possession, they can control his mind and his body like a puppet on a string.

"We, the priests, the Protectors of Souls, can feel these things in our bodies, too. They thump beneath our skin and skull when we touch them. Humans cannot see these evil things—even our priests could not see them—but the priests could sense them with their special vision, the vision only possible through meditation and prayer.

"We fight these unseen demons with all our might so they will not possess our minds. Unfortunately, some of the priests have fallen to their dark magic and are now possessed to serve the dark side. But others have experienced great healings and have been able to push these hideous creatures out of their ka and bodies.

"The lizard people, insect men, and grey ghosts who live beneath the sands and fly in the sky can see those who possess our healing light and magical skill. They hate us with a passion and have tried to kill anyone who lives to serve others. But they have failed to wipe us out completely time and time again. Our white magic and prayers have protected us from these foul creatures. Now they come after our priesthood with the aid of the pharaoh and his military. There are too many of them and too few of us left to fight. The pharaoh gave the final order for all of the priests to be captured and executed. The few of us who are left are all that stand in the way of the desert beasts' and sky people's complete domination of the planet.

"With my visions of the future, I have seen our fate under these cabalistic bloodlines. It is complete slavery for all for centuries to come.

"We, the Protectors of Light, cannot stop these lizard and insect men at this time. We cannot stop the grey ghosts, either, although we have tried. But we can make a difference in the future. The future is the key. That is when we will return. That is when hope and the other priests will return to this Earth.

"Like the thirty-six stars in the sky, the Decans, thirty-six of our priesthood will remain suspended in the celestial realm. We will come back at a time when the offlanders and bloodlines can be overthrown. We will come when the world fails to unite in peace after two terrible wars. Then, with the help of our white magic, we will be born again and initiate our plan to overthrow evil.

"Our magic will call us back and reunite us with these teachings. Then I will come across a great ocean and seek my words once again. I am drawn to them as strong as the moon chases the sun.

"When I return, I will sing the verse that was not rehearsed. I will know two of five songs that give power to the children of the sun. I will also know the sign for eternal life. Only then will I be given the gift to help the future of man.

"Fear not, those who read this, for all bodies must die. The great ka and ba live on to right the wrongs of beast and men. Upon our return, the future of man will be placed on Ma'at's scale, and Ammit the devourer may feast or go hungry.

"To be a Protector of Light is to protect the souls of God. We protect the weak, the hungry, and the oppressed children of the Sun. This is only a small part of what was given to me by the Creator of Souls.

"I will bury these God Scrolls in the desert and bind a magical prayer to them. The jars will be found by the ancestors of future believers and providers. These ancestors will also pass down the amulet and stories for the Protectors of Light.

"I pray that mankind will awaken from the darkness, a darkness that corrupts the minds of men. To help their future, I will leave myself many hidden clues:

The future of humanity lies within the cross.

The scrolls will speak to the hearts of women and men.

And the parchments teach us how to rebirth our magical powers.

When you circle by threes, God comes to thee.

"I leave you now, but remember these words: I leave you with the thought that cannot be enslaved; I leave you with the thought that cannot be maimed; and I leave you with the thought that cannot be killed or devoured.

"Protectors of Light, I give you the word that moves both mountains and men. Hope is the word that inspires all to live. Hope is behind the soul that never gives up. Hope is the word that motivates men during the darkest of hours. And hope is the word that brings peace to all the lands.

"Remember, my friends, hope may stray from the narrow path of life for a short time, but hope will always return to those who seek to make a better life. Hope is always there for both women and men."

Hanif stopped and looked at the people's eyes. The room was silent for a few moments. Then he wiped away a tear and put down the parchment. No one moved or made a sound.

I thought to myself, "Did I write that? I mean, what do you say after hearing those words? I don't think I understood half of it. Lizard men? Grey ghosts? Sky people? What's going on here?"

After a few moments of silence, Hanif readdressed the group, "These words have been passed down through our families for centuries, and the story has not changed since it was written by Tumaini so long ago.

"To all who sit together in this room, we have survived the two great wars, but our lands have not united in peace yet. We still live as financial slaves to the bloodlines and greed-filled bankers. And we are still separated from our brothers in other lands by governments—governments who instill fear and create false borders for control. But no more! No more shall we accept their tyranny and oppression. With the return of hope, with the return of Tumaini, I swear to you, *we…will…be…free!*" The room erupted into cheers, applause, and table pounding.

Mudads stood up to share more with the group. After a few moments, the crowd began to settle down. "My friends, I have also brought with me the parchments that only a small number of you have seen. It is time to share this information with all of you, so you, too, can fulfill your vows as Protectors of Souls."

Mudads picked up the parchment that Hanif had been reading and turned it over. I caught a quick glance and saw that the page was filled from top to bottom with some form of hieratic writing. I leaned toward Rehema and pointed. "Those aren't hieroglyphs. That's an ancient form of Egyptian text. I remember seeing something like that in a student's dissertation on Egyptian and Greek philosophy."

She nodded and gave me a hush sign, so I focused back on Mudads. He had just started to explain that these parchments were from the Eighteenth Dynasty of ancient Egypt. As he did this, I grabbed a pad out of my briefcase. I wanted to take some notes so I could ask questions later.

Before he continued, he leaned down and told me, "Michael, I won't be speaking in English. I hope that won't offend you. This part has always been translated into Arabic, and I must keep this tradition."

"That's fine. Please go on."

As Mudads spoke in Arabic, I wrote down what Hanif had said about grey ghosts and other creatures. I penned a question about the hieratic writing and weighing of the heart—this was too important to forget—and I also wanted Mudads to translate the back of the page for me.

His voice rose and fell eloquently, giving emphasis to the information he was sharing. Meanwhile, I closed my eyes to focus my thoughts and see if I could remember anything else that I wanted explained.

Because I was being distracted with Mudads' speech, I did one of my concentration exercises. I formed an image of a candle flame in my mind and watched the hottest part of the flame near the tip. With my conscious mind completely focused, the subconscious part of my mind must have taken over because the flame started growing bigger and bigger all on its own. It grew so large that my entire inner sight was a white light that filled every corner of my mind. My conscious side was clearly no longer in control and must have gone on autopilot as I subconsciously followed the new vision.

Immediately, a brilliant, translucent, bluish-white light flashed and filled my head. Then the light shrank downward into a tiny glowing object. I could see that I was no longer in the same room as everyone else. This room was much darker and smaller, and it was lit by a single, small flickering light from an oil lamp. I could also see as if I was looking down at my hand, but it was not my present-day hand, even though it felt like it was attached to me. And this body was not dressed as I was, either. This person had on a white robe with a thick copper-colored rope tied at the waist.

The vision continued, and I saw the same hand with a thin, pencil-like brush in it. The hand dipped the bristles into a bowl filled with a black liquid and then moved toward a piece of papyrus. It was making these marks, almost like curvature drawings, from left to right on the page. And after a few more strokes of the brush, my vision stopped. I saw a flash of bluish-white light again and instantly regained my awareness of the restaurant. After the visions, I fell back in my chair and shook my head vigorously to clear my mind.

Rehema quickly leaned over and whispered, "Michael, are you alright? You were moving your hand so fast and writing furiously on your notepad."

"Rehema," I said as softly as I could, "you won't believe this. I hardly believe what just happened myself. I had something like déjà vu again. But it wasn't like regular déjà vu; this felt like it was from the past. It…it…it felt like I was about to write something important, and I was in a completely different body. Then, with a flash of light, I was right back here."

I looked at my notepad and saw the same style of hieratic writing that was on the back of the parchment that Mudads held. "Did I write this?" I asked. "I must have. It's on my notepad. I've heard about this before, too. It's like—what do they call it?—it's like remote viewing, but with writing."

Rehema suggested, "Automatic writing?"

"Yeah, yeah, that's it, automatic writing. It's when your subconscious connects with your conscious mind, like the so-called akashic records, or when you sketch an ideogram for remote viewing. From what I've learned, you can write down information without consciously knowing what's being written."

She looked toward my tablet. "It seems as if the parchments brought back a past memory and some of your latent abilities."

"Do you think that's what just happened? I mean, look at how much I wrote down in a short period of time, and I don't know this language."

She shook her head *yes* while smiling, "Most definitely. Do you not see that you have these abilities? You have the gift. We all do. And the more you use them, the stronger you will become."

"It all happened so fast. I don't know what to make of it, Rehema. It felt like I had to write down the words as if my life depended on it."

Hanif peeked behind Rehema's back and whispered, "This is no coincidence, Michael. You've experienced this for a reason. Your past is trying to communicate with you. Don't you see?"

Mudads glared toward his brother. He was a little perturbed because he was still speaking with the group. Our conversation had gotten loud enough that Omar and the rest of the table were listening to us instead of him.

Tapping him on the arm, I apologized, "Sorry, Mudads. Please continue."

A few more minutes passed, and Mudads finished the Arabic portion of his talk and switched back to English. "Friends, fellow Protectors, we are very excited to tell you that Tumaini has come." The crowd gasped in excitement. "My friend, Michael"—as he put his left hand on my shoulder to acknowledge me to the crowd—"has given Hanif and me the signs."

I wasn't prepared for that, and I gave Mudads a look that said: *What are you doing?*

He knew what he was doing and continued, "We believe that he is the one who can deliver a message, a message that all of us have longed to hear for so many years. We believe that with his teachings and guidance, he can offer the people of the world a new hope, a new way of looking at life, and a new way to live peacefully with one another. We believe that he can show us a way out of bondage and deliver us from the deception and lies that the bloodlines have used to manipulate and enslave the people for centuries. And with his insight and courage, he will deliver a message of truth that will make a difference for the entire world."

A member of the crowd stood up and confronted him. His name was Karim: a stoutly-looking man, maybe a few years younger than Hanif. He had been a member of the group for over twenty years. "Mudads, I've come to know and trust you. Your whole life has been spent preparing for Tumaini, just as your fathers have done. How do we know that this person is actually Tumaini? What proof do you have?" A few people in the room agreed with him and nodded their heads *yes*.

Mudads took a moment. He already knew that everyone would not accept this information without any evidence. He addressed the man who stood up, "Karim, you have always been generous and kind. No one here would argue with that. And your devotion to uncover the truth and live by it has always been a noble cause."

Karim stopped him from going on. "Mudads, I appreciate the compliments, but your words did not answer my question. How do we know this man is Tumaini? There are too many false prophets in the world already, and I won't align myself with—"

"Karim, please, please, give me a moment." Mudads was getting a little upset. "I will explain how we can—"

"No, Mudads. How can we verify your claims?"

I was feeling a little nervous and upset myself. I didn't like that Mudads was being challenged over me. Somehow, though, I got the courage to stand up and talk to this room full of strangers. I put my hand on Mudads' shoulder and gave him a look of growing confidence. He glanced back at me with a quizzical look when I told him, "I've got this. I'm used to addressing questions like this in my classroom. Trust me."

I gazed right at Karim. "Karim, hi, I'm Michael—or as Mudads and Hanif tell me, I'm also Tumaini. As you can tell from the tone in my voice, I also question this information. I just found out about all of this a few hours ago. And let me tell you, I'm not sure what to make of it all."

Karim gave me a gesture that said he almost empathized with me, and I continued, "First I was lost outside the Khan, and the next thing I knew I was being told that I'm a dead Egyptian priest. What I can tell you is this: I'm not a false prophet. In all honesty, I don't claim to be a prophet at all; I'm just a college teacher back home. But I've experienced so many strange things today that are rocking my foundations. I mean…look!" I held up my tablet and showed the crowd what I'd just written. "While Mudads was speaking to you, I had a flashback to being a priest, maybe even Tumaini. Then my hand started moving, and I wrote this. I can't write in hieratic. I don't even know what I wrote." The crowd was amazed, and a number of them stood up so they could see my paper.

Omar motioned. "Let me look at that. I was trained in hieratic writing." I handed it across the table to him, and before I could address the crowd again, he announced, "Mudads, that's exactly what you were telling us a few minutes ago. How does he know this?" The table and the room were still shocked from what was unfolding.

I chuckled, "That's a good question, and I'm sure there's a good explanation. I think."

Before I could continue, Karim challenged, "Strange writings do not make you Tumaini."

"Karim, I agree with you one hundred percent. I wouldn't put my faith into something I scribbled down a few minutes ago, and I won't ask you to put faith in me, either."

Mudads beseeched, "Michael, no!"

"Mudads, please, let me continue." I engaged the room again, "Karim, all of you who have gathered here, I can't bring proof from ancient Egypt that I am Tumaini. I don't have a brush, a sash, or any concrete evidence. But if I am Tumaini, all I can do is show you the same signs that I showed Hanif, Rehema, and Mudads. Then you can decide for yourselves what you want to believe. Well, let me just…" I put my head down and paused for a moment. I picked my head back up and looked at the group. Then I began humming the first tune. I only hummed a few notes and stopped.

The people were all very quiet. They were waiting for something magical to happen that would break the hostile energy. Then Omar urged, "Go on, finish it."

I requested, "Would you all join me?" I started humming again from the beginning, and almost everyone in the room sang with me. After the first four bars, I changed from a hum to toning vowel sounds and syllables with each note. When I did this, my body shook like I'd gotten an electric shock.

As soon as we finished, Karim questioned, "What did you just do? You changed the melody."

I had to think. Did I just change the melody? Then I answered, "I didn't change the tune, Karim. I...I added vowel sounds to the notes. Then my body shook."

"So you know the vowel sounds. And nobody taught you this?"

Shaking my head *no*, "I've never sung this before today. What do you think, Karim?"

"I think you might be Tumaini, but I'm not convinced yet."

Laughingly, I agreed, "Me, neither. But this has been a day that I won't forget."

Mudads stood up again. "Friends, whether you believe that Michael is Tumaini or not, we took a vow to help protect the souls of others. We *all* took that oath. Then we received our symbol of hope that peace would return to Earth. Would you all take out that symbol now and proudly show our solidarity to our mission of peace and protection?"

Hanif and Rehema started their pledge by standing and pulling out their amulets. Omar stood up next, followed by the rest of the room. Everyone, except for one person, took out his amulet and wore it proudly on the outside.

———————

At the back of the room, the waiter nearest the end of the line looked strangely at the man next to him. He didn't have his amulet out, nor did he sing or recite his pledge. He asked him, "Excuse me, but where is your amulet? Are you alright?"

The man's face showed his anger. "Stop bothering me! I left it at home!"

"That can't be. The only way you could get in tonight was to show your amulet to the man downstairs. What's your name again? Where is your amulet?"

Out of fear and rage, the man at the end pushed the waiter next to him to the ground, pulled out his assassin's club, and pointed it at the rest of the line. The other waiters were caught off guard by this sudden act and froze.

The tables near the back of the room turned their attention toward the lone imposter. As the other waiters attended to their friend on the ground, one of them shouted, "Stop that man! He doesn't have an amulet!"

In a panic, the infiltrator lunged at one of the tables. People scrambled in all directions to avoid being hurt. Then the man swung his arm around as if he were wielding a knife and jumped on top of the table.

A chorus of *Stop that man!* rang in the room as he jumped wildly from table to table. He was making a direct dash toward our group. A few men at the back dove toward him, but he was too quick as he jumped to the next table. One man leapt from a chair and flew in the air to tackle him. As he did, the assailant used his club and bashed the man's head before he could wrap his arms around his legs.

He jumped again and was only two tables away from our group. Hanif grabbed Rehema and positioned her behind all three of us. When the man flew onto our table, Omar pounced on him, but he could only grab his ankles. The mysterious man fell forward and smashed flat onto our dinner plates. His club rolled past us and landed on the floor.

In an attempt to get away, he kicked Omar in the face, which made him loosen his grip. Mudads tried picking up the parchments, but the man saw this, flung his hand onto the stack, and grabbed a sheet. Then he bounced up and snatched the candle from the table.

Hanif and I kept a barrier between the man in black and Rehema. We managed to back her to the side and away from the attacker. Mudads was on the other side and passed the rest of the parchments to Omar, who took them and ran behind a crowd of people.

Clutching the papyrus sheet in the air with the candle underneath, the assassin threatened to burn the valuable parchment. He abruptly jumped off the table and slowly backed onto the balcony, never taking his eyes off our group. Once at the railing, he peered behind him and downward to see if there was an escape route.

With his eyes diverted for a moment, we took a step toward him. When he turned back, he lifted the candle directly under the old paper. All of us instantaneously stopped our forward progress.

Without any warning, the man looked at me with contempt, threw the candle and parchment to the side, and jumped over the balcony. The next second seemed like ten years. Above the commotion of the room, we heard what sounded like a sandbag hitting the ground and the loud moan of a man in pain. The balcony became packed with our group looking downward over the rail. Below, we could see the man painfully rolling off of a red pickup truck that was filled with garlic plants.

The car that was parked at the front came screeching around the corner with the door hanging open. The man limped toward the car and jumped in. His legs weren't even in the car yet as it sped off into the darkness with the door still open.

Karim stepped forward, bent down, and picked up the oddly shaped club. He held it up for us to see. "This is no ordinary club. This is a weapon used by the bloodlines. It's meant to painfully bludgeon a victim to death."

Hanif piped in with a worried tone, "It's not like the dark side to come out into public like this. They usually stay hidden and work behind the scenes." He reached down and grabbed the crumpled papyrus. "One thing is for sure, he wasn't interested in the parchments. Otherwise, he would have taken the sheet with him. He was here for another reason."

He turned to me. "The dark ones must be extremely worried that you have returned, Tumaini—I mean, Michael. We will have to be more cautious from here on."

"They struck fast, too, and that is our fault," said Mudads in a dejected voice. "We should have been better prepared. It is not safe for you to travel alone on the rest of your trip. We will make arrangements for your safety. This is my vow to you, my friend. Are you alright?"

I replied with a shaky, adrenaline-filled voice, "Yes, I'm fine. A little stunned is all. Rehema, are you alright?"

"We're fine," she nodded.

"Tell me, Michael, do you now believe that Tumaini is real?" asked Mudads. "Do you think that you are only a myth?"

"Well, it seems the dark side doesn't think I'm a myth."

Karim joined in, "I have to tell you, Michael, that I am one step closer to believing you are Tumaini. Brother, I vow to you my protection, if you will have it."

I looked at him. "I appreciate your offer, Karim. I'm fine, though, really."

Hanif motioned to the group. "We should see if everyone in the room is OK, too."

Right after the man jumped over the railing, some of the guests went downstairs. They found the young man who had been knocked out. Luckily, he was regaining consciousness and rubbing his sore head. They helped him to his feet and brought him upstairs.

While our small party made our rounds through the room to give aid, the guests from downstairs reappeared. Two of the men were helping the young man, while a third held the dead pigeon and note. He came toward us and raised both of his hands. "They knew we were meeting tonight. Look!"

Mudads confirmed, "It's certain. We have been infiltrated, and the dark Order knows about you, Michael."

He nodded once toward Karim. "You know who to get. Bring her to Michael's hotel. Here's the name and his room number." After getting the information, Karim turned and left the group.

Hanif commented next, "Now that we know everyone else is safe, we should wrap up this meeting."

"Agreed," said the rest of us.

———◆———

As we walked toward our table, we asked everyone to sit down. After a few moments, Mudads looked around the room and spoke, "Friends, we won't keep you long. I am glad that you are all safe and unharmed. We all knew there would be risks with our assignment and pledge. And I know that I can speak for Hanif, Rehema, and myself: We won't give up or stop. We will protect the souls of others."

Omar stood up and vowed, "So will I!"

Hanif and Rehema rose and echoed, "So will I!"

Throughout the room, people stood up in a wave and pledged courageously, "So will I!" That sent chills down my spine.

I was the last one to stand. I didn't even think about it. I was caught up in the moment and declared, "So will I." Mudads put his hand on my shoulder and smiled.

He looked out at the masses who were standing and waiting. "Everyone return safely to your homes. Check in through our network. Use the codes. Your mission has just begun. You know what to do. Bit-tawfiq. Ma' al-salāmah. Good luck. With peace." Mudads bowed to the room, and they replied with the same goodbye.

CHAPTER SIX

A PRIEST'S TALE

It was a little after 11:00 p.m. when the restaurant had finally cleared. The only ones remaining were the cooks, and they said they would lock up behind us. We also made sure that the young man had been taken to a hospital to see if he had a concussion. He was still a little wobbly from his ordeal.

I said to all three of them, "You know, I have to leave at 8:00 a.m. tomorrow, and I have too many questions to ask you about the parchments and these bloodlines. Do you think you could spare me a few minutes so I can get a handle on all of this? I mean, I feel kind of lost at this point. I wouldn't even know where to start."

Mudads glanced at Hanif and Rehema for a sign of agreement, and they both nodded without hesitation. He smiled, "Of course we will help you. It's our life's mission. How about we go to your hotel and talk? I sent Karim to bring in someone who will tell you more than we can. Truthfully, Michael, I hadn't intended to just leave you stranded here. I know that I would want more answers."

"Great!" I picked up my leather bag with the parchments and we walked downstairs. On the way, I told Hanif where I was staying. He knew exactly where it was and said he would meet us there.

Mudads and I walked his brother and Rehema to their car. Then we hightailed it to Mudads' car. Fortunately for us, there weren't any more assassins hiding in the back of any pickup trucks.

As Mudads sped off toward my hotel, he mentioned with some regret, "Michael, what happened tonight has never happened before at any of our meetings. I don't know how to apologize for putting you in danger, especially since you haven't taken the pledge in this lifetime. It would be one thing if you had, but you were plunged headfirst into this without any warning or invitation."

"Mudads, don't even think of apologizing." I continued with a little smirk, "This sort of thing happens to me all of the time."

He laughed, "Good, I'm glad to see that you have a little humor left in you after what happened tonight. Nevertheless, I'm sorry, and we will take better care of you for the rest of your trip. I don't know what your future will bring you, but I have a feeling it will involve a great deal of challenge from the dark side."

"Mudads, you've never met my dean, have you? If you want to talk challenge and the dark side, try doing good things for your students while your hands are tied by the dean and the bureaucratic education system. Now, that's a challenge! Besides, this assassin had nothing on my dean. This guy only had an assassin's club. My dean can stare skin-ripping daggers into your flesh and shoot down any progressive idea better than a guided nuclear missile.

"Maybe I'm taking this too lightly. I'm sure it hasn't all sunk in yet, but I've been in a few tight spots in my life. I'll get through this one."

"You have a good spirit, my friend."

We pulled into the parking lot and walked into the hotel. Hanif and Rehema were already in the lobby waiting for us. Rehema had another white box with her and handed it to me. "Michael, here. I know you shared the last box of gullash with your tour group and didn't get to eat any. I thought you might like a few for yourself. I meant to give this to you after dinner, but, well, we got kind of sidetracked."

"Wow, thanks, Rehema. I don't know what to say." Mudads just rolled his eyes and mumbled something to himself.

"Just say thank you and be done with it." Her warm smile returned again. "It's nice to give a gift, especially when it is appreciated."

"Oh, believe me, my taste buds appreciate it. Hey, before we go upstairs, let me check the front desk for messages."

After waiting a few minutes at the counter, a man returned with a note. It was from Constance and read:

> Hope you are having fun with the mummies.
> Don't forget about your trunk.
> Hara sends her love.
> Kisses!
> I miss you.
>
> Love,
> Constance.

I flashed the paper toward them and laughed, "It's a note from my wife, and she started the message with *hope*. Do you think it's a coincidence?" They chuckled.

I thought about all of my new boxes. "Hey, this will work out perfectly." We were stepping into the elevator when I continued, "Before our trip, our tour guide suggested that we bring some clothes and gifts to give away. I filled a trunk with jeans, shirts, jackets, pens, and toys for the kids. Would you or your employees like to have them?"

Hanif accepted my offer graciously. "That is very generous of you. I'm sure we can put those items to good use."

"Great, that also solves another problem for me. I can use that trunk to put all of these boxes in. I was wondering how I was going to travel with them for the rest of the trip."

We walked into the living area of my hotel room. It had the typical hotel couch, matching chairs, tables, and refrigerator. I was mostly packed for tomorrow, but I still had a few loose items thrown around the room. "I'm sorry, guys. I wasn't expecting company." I speedily grabbed the clothes that I'd worn earlier and threw them into my open suitcase.

"It's OK, Michael. We weren't expecting to be here, either," Hanif laughed. "Here, you missed a sock." He tossed it to me with the same familiarity as a college roommate. Then he sat down.

"Thanks. Make yourselves at home. All I have is some water left in the fridge. How 'bout we order some room service while we chat? We can have them bring up some coffee, tea, and snacks. What do you guys want?"

Mudads replied, "We don't want to impose."

Rehema playfully slapped him on the arm. "Impose? Seriously? The man just had an attempt on his life because of us. I don't think we could impose any more."

She smiled at me, "I'd like some coffee, Michael."

"I can't argue with that." I looked at Mudads and Hanif for a response. "How about you two? Would you like something?"

"Sure, I'll have some coffee and a CLT," joked Hanif.

"A CLT?" I waited for the punchline.

"You know, a camel, lettuce, and tomato sandwich. And you are supposed to ask me, *One hump of meat or two?* Honestly, Michael, I thought you had played tourist in Egypt before." We laughed for a few moments. It helped to break up the leftover stress.

While we waited for coffee and snacks, I emptied the trunk and handed all of the bags to my new friends. They looked in each of them like kids opening a stack of birthday gifts. Then I put all of the other boxes in their place, except for the one that contained the parchments.

As they rustled through their goodies, I sat beside Rehema and pulled out the parchments and binder from my leather bag. "OK, it's time for questions, and I've got a lot of them. Let's start with this..." I flipped open my notepad to the page that had hieratic writing on it.

Mudads recalled, "Ah, yes, the part in Arabic. And strangely, you wrote it in ancient Egyptian. That's a first for me, too. I told our group that your amulet, the one you are wearing right now, was worn by the original Protectors of Souls. It was worn by the priests and scribes from the time of Tumaini. You wrote that the symbol should be copied and passed down to anyone who wished to serve the Creator and protect the souls of mankind.

"I also shared with the group about Tumaini's abilities. The priests, including Tumaini, trained in special skills that would be considered magic by most people today. You wrote that you were able to time travel, see potential futures, see the lives of others and their past lives, and heal people with your hands. It was also said that the songs unlock certain powers granted by God. These vowel sounds, and special combinations of vowels and consonants, have great power when sung the right way. Sanskrit, ancient Egyptian, Hawaiian, and Hebrew appear to have some type of mathematical code built into the creation matrix that gives them more power. This was encoded in our Universal Laws."

"Is that it?"

"No, there's more. When the scrolls were found, your amulet was found with them. When the first parchment was deciphered, your instructions were to pass down all of them together. But the parchments, papyrus pieces, and scrolls were to be kept in separate locations so no one person could benefit from the power and magic they hold. Only when Tumaini reincarnates should we bring them all together. That is why Hanif and I kept them apart. You need all of the boxes to complete your mission. And you already know that you had to pass the test by singing the songs and recognizing the symbol I showed you. If you hadn't passed the test, we wouldn't be here right now."

I laughed, "I don't know if that's a blessing or a curse, Mudads."

He laughed a bit, too, and continued, "Finally, I told the group that the scrolls were messages from God. Tumaini recorded these holy words that told the people how they could live peacefully with each other and the planet. The wisdom of God was to be revealed at the world's worst moments, when the world could no longer sustain the growing population of humans, when the people could no longer solve their problems on their own. Oh, and when the world was overrun by the dark side—let's not forget that one. These events would bring you and the other priests back from the celestial realms to reincarnate on Earth."

"Wow, that's some speech, Mudads. What else did you say—I mean, what else did I say?"

"That's it. The rest is waiting for you to decode and share with us and the world. I—we—are all anxious to know what you said in the rest of the material."

"This is amazing. As much as it sounds like a science fiction movie, it feels right. It feels real to me." I was pacing around the room at this point and throwing my arms in the air while I talked. "I know it's not my ego kicking in, either. I mean, who doesn't want to save the world? And I'm not saying that I can, but this just feels right. It feels like the next chapter of my life has already been written for me, and I've just gotten to read a few pages."

I stopped and ran my hand over my head. Then I got a little nervous. It finally started to sink in. "Whoa!" is all I exclaimed.

Rehema reacted, "Michael, what is it?"

"Guys, it just hit me. How the heck am I supposed to save the world? How can I make that big of a difference? I can barely balance my checkbook or change the bag in the vacuum cleaner. Constance has to do that for me. How am I supposed to pull off this kind of miracle? I don't think I can do that. I—"

Rehema stopped me and asked, "Michael, if you are Tumaini, do you know what that means?" She looked at me stubbornly and waited for my reply.

"No. What does it mean, Rehema?"

"Michael, all that means is that you bring hope: nothing more, nothing less—hope. And that hope can come in many different ways. Maybe you will influence one person, and that person will influence two, and those two will influence two more. Maybe you will bring a smile or some love where there was none before." She paused for a moment. "Being Tumaini doesn't mean that you will change the minds of the world overnight. Tumaini just means—"

I was nodding my head *yes* before she could finish and recited quickly, "Hope."

She grabbed my forearm and lightly squeezed. "Yes! All it means is that you will bring hope. And know this: Hope doesn't mean that you will be a savior of the world; hope just means that you can offer the people of the world another chance. That's what hope does, doesn't it? It offers people another chance, don't you think? Hope means you haven't stopped believing." I nodded my head *yes*.

"Does this help relieve some of the pressure, savior boy?" She grinned and shook my arm as a way to get through to me. Then she continued, "And who knows, Michael, maybe you could change the whole world, too. Just don't put any expectations on the how and why; put one foot forward and see what happens. Even if you don't believe yet, I have faith in you." She shook my arm one more time, smiled, and looked at her husband.

Hanif traded glances with her. "How can I put that any better? Rehema said it best: *Being Tumaini just means that you will bring hope.* And I, too, believe that is you, Michael."

Mudads put his hand on my shoulder. "And I, too."

There was a sudden loud knock on the door, which startled all of us. I guess we were still a little edgy from the attack at the restaurant. We looked at each other wondering which brave soul would answer it. Then we heard the familiar *Room service!* come from behind our trusty wooden shield.

"I'll get that," as I moved toward the door and squinted through the peephole. I comically turned and whispered to the others, "Coast is clear; no assassins." And I opened the door.

The waiter rolled in the service tray. All of the snacks, coffee, and pitchers were on silver platters. The cart also had a flower, two lit candles, and a full-length white table cloth. After tipping the young man, he left the cart and closed the door.

I fussed, "You know, I hate this already."

Hanif asked with a shocked tone, "What are you talking about? What do you hate?"

"OK, who wants to check under the table cloth for a bug or a bomb? Honestly, guys, I don't want to live my life in fear because of this Tumaini stuff. But I have to wonder, am I going to be followed and tormented the rest of my life because of an amulet and a few pieces of paper?"

"I can understand your feelings," empathized Hanif. "This is all new to us, too."

I walked to the cart and quickly lifted the cloth, put it down, then lifted it again. "Look, there is something under the cart. It's a piece of paper. Maybe it's a secret note." I ripped it off and focused on the words:

**Do not remove this label under penalty
of Egyptian Health Code 2C198.**

"Oh, great! Now the health code police are going to arrest me." They laughed as I put the sticker back under the cart and rubbed it furiously to make it stay.

"They won't arrest you over a sticker," chuckled Rehema. "Besides, the government needs your tourist dollars to dig up more mummies and draw bigger crowds."

"Speaking of buried stuff, how did you get these scrolls in the first place? Who dug them up?" I inquired.

"It wasn't so much that they were dug up, Michael," Hanif replied. "Our ancestors were led to them."

"Led to them?"

Mudads answered, "Yes, led to them. Let me tell you the story...

"While tending a herd of goats near the outskirts of Memphis, Onuris, our great, great, great, great, great, great, great, great grandfather saw a yellowish-golden light hovering far off over the grassy fields. He didn't know what it was at first. He squinted and put his hand over his eyes to shade them from the burning sun. It was hard to see because he was near the line between the fertile farm lands and the barren desert. In Egypt, they call this line the black land and the red land.

"As it was told, he felt compelled to go and take a look at this seemingly angelic sight. He even heard a soft voice tell him, 'Come, I have a mission for you, the *One who brings back the Distant One*.'

"He picked up his staff, left his herd, and walked about a quarter of a mile through the high grass toward the edge of the sand. There, floating at least fifteen feet off of the ground was the most beautiful outline of a human figure.

"The voice lyrically said, 'This is why you were born. You are to help the One who would bring hope to all of the oppressed people. If your heart is pure, follow me. I will guide you to your mission.'

"The glowing light led him into the desert for miles. He lost sight of his flock and his home, but he was not afraid. He felt comforted and protected by this saintly being.

"A huge sand dune towered in front of him. The voice instructed, 'Go now, over the hill. You will see what calls to you. You have felt this, have you not?'

"'Yes, I have felt this for many years. I have been waiting to know what this feeling was, and now I have found it. Thank you for your guidance.'

"With that said, a strong breeze blew and kicked up some sand. He blinked, and the floating light was gone. He quickly ran up the dune, stumbling a few times in his haste. Once at the top, he looked over the crest and down below. There before him were six clay jars half-buried in the sand.

"When he opened the first jar, he saw your amulet sitting on top of a white cloth. And underneath the cloth were the papyrus pieces you saw in my shop. The other jars were filled with scrolls and parchments. He buried the jars until he could bring his camel to fetch them.

"Once he'd brought all of the jars to his home, he asked the local priestess to decipher the first parchments. She read the story to all of his family and friends. They became the first generation of Protectors of Souls.

"We've been keeping the scrolls in our family until Tumaini's return— your return. We even kept the names you mentioned in your parchment.

Our names, Mudads and Hanif, mean *provider* and *believer*. Anytime there were two boys born in our lineage, they were named Mudads and Hanif. Do you remember Hanif saying that at the restaurant?"

"Vaguely. There was a lot of information, and I didn't really memorize what I heard word-for-word." After a moment of silence, I added, "You know, that was some tale you just shared. Is there any more to it?"

Mudads replied, "It is no tale if it is history, Michael. We are the descendants of Onuris, and we have honored him and your former self by keeping to our mission. We have fulfilled our vow, but we still have other vows to attend to. Our main work has just begun."

Hanif cheered, "Here, here! We have only just begun."

"Hey, while we are on the subject of Hanif's talk, you mentioned something about a devourer and the weight of the heart. What does that mean? It sounds like a nightmare in the making."

Hanif asked, "Have you ever heard about the *Egyptian Book of the Dead?*"

"I've heard about it, but I haven't read it yet."

Rehema jumped in and patted his leg, "I've got this, darling. This subject is my specialty.

"First off, the *Egyptian Book of the Dead* was really called *Book of the Master of the Hidden Place*. It has all kinds of spells for the afterlife and instructions for the soul's journey through Duat—that's the Egyptian name for the underworld. It also explains what Ammit is."

She used her hands to give details for the next part. "Ammit is an Egyptian beast made up of three animal parts. The back part of Ammit looks like the back half of a hippopotamus, the front part looks like a lion, and the head is a crocodile's head."

"Yeesh"—I grimaced with an ugly face—"now that's an image. Sounds like a science experiment gone wrong."

She continued, "The story goes that when you die you are to weigh your heart on the scale of justice in Duat. It's written that Anubis places your heart on the scale opposite of Ma'at's ostrich feather.

"You've probably seen hieroglyphs of Ma'at with a single feather on her head, right?" I nodded my head *yes*. "The feather is supposed to represent *truth*. Seems kind of unfair—a feather against a heart—but it's all symbolism.

"Well, while Ma'at and Ammit are watching over you and your heart, sometimes Thoth or a group of forty-two judges shows up. If your deeds were pure, your heart would be in balance, and the scale would not be tipped. If you were naughty, your heart was on Ammit's dinner plate. A few bites later, and then you had to be reborn to correct all of your wrongs and live a better life."

Hanif jumped in, "Or live your life in unrest and unable to move on to immortality, depending on who tells the story."

She winked at me. "I like my version better."

"Well"—I slapped both hands on my knees—"that helps explain that. Except, what does that have to do with me?"

"Why don't you pull out the parchment, and I'll read it to you again. Then you can answer your own question, since it was your information to begin with," Hanif chuckled.

I pulled out the wrinkled parchment. We were all a little sad because it had been kept in such good condition until the assassin got a hold of it. The good part was that it was still readable.

"I know," sighed Hanif. "It's not completely destroyed, and that is a good thing. We must not get too attached to the material world, but we can appreciate the knowledge and guidance that this part of the material world can give us."

He put his reading glasses on again. "So where is that section? I've read it so many times before. Ah, there it is:

"Fear not, those who read this, for all bodies must die. The great ka and ba live on to right the wrongs of beast and men. Upon our return, the future of man will be placed on Ma'at's scale, and Ammit the devourer may feast or go hungry."

"Oh, I get it," I stated. "It's not really about me. It's about the fate of the human race. It seems that humanity is about to be placed on the scales of justice, and from what we have seen, it doesn't look too good for humanity's heart. When is all of this to take place, Hanif?"

"It seems like it is taking place right now, since you have returned."

"And all I have to do is provide hope? That's no small feat in this me-me-me, self-absorbed world we live in. Now how am I supposed to provide help to a self-serving, brainwashed society?"

I looked at Rehema. "I know, just put one foot forward and don't have any expectations." She gave me a warm smile.

With my notebook in my hand, I leafed through my writing to see what else I wanted to ask, but another knock on the door interrupted me.

Mudads jumped up. "I have got this," and moved hastily to the door. When he opened it, Karim and an elderly woman stood in the entrance. Mudads greeted them and invited the two inside.

The elderly woman was dressed in a white cotton, floor-length robe. She had a copper-colored rope tied around her waist and a shimmery gold shawl draped over her shoulders and neck. Her feet had on modest Egyptian sandals, and her long silver and black hair draped down her back.

The other outstanding item was her staff. It was an ancient Egyptian Ptah staff. The top part was made of a shiny black stone that looked like an oddly-shaped canine head. Below the head was a golden ankh, and underneath the ankh was a four-tiered djed symbol that is commonly found in many ancient hieroglyphs. The rest of the staff was a polished piece of wood with black stain on it.

"Michael, this is—"

Before Mudads could finish his introduction, the woman took a few deliberate paces and came right into my personal space. She had the heavy smell of sweet incense on her, a combination of rose and sandalwood. Then she peered deep into my eyes. I was very uncomfortable from her encroachment, and the rest of our small party said nothing.

She circled my body, never taking her penetrating glare off of me. When she got back in front, she looked at my wary expression again and stepped back a few paces. Pointing at me with her staff, she proclaimed, "This is him. This is Tumaini. I am sure of it. He bears the energy of the *One who can*. But he...he is missing something. He is missing something very important." She kept her gaze on me as she shook her head slightly, "He is missing something. But what is it?" Concern now painted her brow and forehead. As she stared, she took one of the loose ends of her shawl and wrapped it around her front.

I stammered, "Wha...wha...what am I missing?" I looked at the others for some help, but they offered nothing.

She squinted, trying to see something hidden behind my Caucasian skin. Her eyes felt like they were piercing my soul at this point, almost as if she could read every page of my life and I couldn't stop her, even if I wanted to.

"Knowing. Knowing, Tumaini. That is what you are missing. You are missing your knowing. You don't know who you are yet. You think you do, but you have not taken the leap of faith. You have not believed and committed to that which is. Until then, your powers will remain weak and blunt as a dull blade." The woman turned and sat in one of the chairs like she owned the place, but without any arrogance in her stature.

Karim interjected, "So you *are* the one. You are the bringer of hope. If Ramla says so, then I do not question your authenticity anymore."

Ramla looked at Karim, then back to me. We both saw a look in his eyes that did not match his words.

Mudads continued his introduction, "Michael, this is Ramla. She is like a priestess to us. We seek her out for counsel and guidance. She has been a friend of our family for as long as we can remember. When we are lost, she sees our soul's purpose, our future, and tells us just the right words to put us back on our path again. She is like a prophet to the Protectors, but she won't call herself that."

Ramla put her gaze back on me. "I have waited for this for a very long time, Tumaini. My mother was the priestess who read the first parchment to the ancestors of believers and providers. She then passed down this knowledge to me when I was a very young girl. Since that time, I have kept this knowledge at the forefront of my soul for many incarnations.

"When I came back to Earth two lifetimes ago, I came back as a Hawaiian Kahu—a keeper of the secret—a kahuna. I had the abilities of the Egyptian priests because I knew the secrets of the sacred language. I knew the ways of the Creator's force and trained in the Energy of the Universe. I honed my skills before the Christians came and outlawed our practices."

She tapped her cane hard three times on the floor and scowled from her unpleasant memory, then she continued, "I stayed in hiding, using my skills to heal those who came to me. I also used my powers so I would come back when it was time for Tumaini's return. I would come back to add the last strand to the tapestry of my soul's journey. And here you are, standing there, helping me to fulfill my vow to you." She pointed her staff at me. "But you don't remember, do you? You don't know."

"Um, Ramla," I replied shakily, "I just found out about this today. I'm still trying to make sense out of all of this. I'm only a teacher back home, and—"

She briskly cut me off, "Yes, yes, I know. And you will."

"What?"

"You will *know*. Trust me." She motioned with her free hand. "Come here, Tumaini. I can help you if you are willing." I stepped toward her and stopped in front of the chair. I didn't know what to do next. "Down here," she pointed to the ground. "Don't make an old lady do all of the work."

I looked at the others. I still didn't know what to do. Rehema whispered, "Kneel. Kneel down, Michael." I put my hand on my knee and knelt down. I was a little skeptical about what was going to happen next.

She bent forward slowly. Her pointer finger was aimed at my forehead and traveled toward my skin on an eminent collision course. Her finger stopped just millimeters away from the spot between my eyebrows. My anticipation caused me to stiffen a bit. Then she rammed her finger forward and commanded with the jab, "Remember!"

When she touched the center of my forehead, I saw the brightest golden light of my life. It completely engulfed my vision and mind. What seemed like hours was only a second. I could still feel the heavy weight of her touch and the electrical surge that went along with her connection.

Then, the golden light magically transformed into bands of light that looked like a horizontal rainbow flowing by me: skinny at the center, and widening into a tunnel as it went by. In a wild light show, the streaks of colored photons started to blend together and formed images of people, places, and events from my past lives. These events moved by me at incredible speeds. I actually felt myself standing motionless in this time tunnel with these realistic events racing by. Interestingly, every few seconds a specific event moved by slower than the rest. This gave me the chance to focus on it a little more. Eventually, I saw every incarnation up to my present lifetime, and they all moved by in a matter of seconds.

Her finger pressure quickly receded, and I was forcefully snapped back to the present reality. I wobbled for a moment and put my hands out to balance myself from falling. "Wow! What did you do to me? That was incredible." I pleaded with an overwhelmed emotional state, "Can you do it again?"

She leaned in a little. "Tumaini, do you remember? Do you remember who you are?"

"I...I...I remember seeing a few key moments from some previous lifetimes, but I can't seem to recall any of them. It's like waking up and trying to remember a dream. I could see a few people and objects, but I don't know who or what they were. All I know is that I saw them."

"Good," she affirmed. "This will help you to remember more in the future. This will also help your confidence grow inside. The veil between lives and your timeline has been lifted a little. When the time comes—and you are ready—you will be able to see visions from your past that will help you in the future.

"Only the past is recorded like a book, Tumaini. The future is more like volumes of possibilities, but it has not been set in stone like the past. Your future is still uncertain because your actions have not created your next outcome. It's like waves of the ocean. Each movement of the water will create a new potential future. The waves can become large and violent, or they can be smooth and peaceful—just like human emotions, no? They can grow into great wars or heavenly moments of peace. Do you understand?"

"I think so."

"Good."

I was about to stand up when she added, "I have one more thing for you, Tumaini. Do not stand just yet. Your powers have been dormant for many lifetimes and need some help to be restored. Close your eyes and do not do a thing."

"OK," is all that I could muster from my dry lips.

I closed my eyes and waited. Ramla also closed her eyes, then she reopened them and began chanting some form of ancient prayer. Her body began to rock back and forth in short, fast motions. Her chanting became labored and heavy with each repetition. As her eyes rolled up in her head, she reached out with her finger.

When she touched my skin this time, my body shook like I had been hooked up to a Tesla tower and had received a hundred million volts of electricity. It wasn't painful at all, but I could feel the massive surge of power flowing through every channel in my body. My hands were hot and sweating, and my body temperature felt like it had gone through the roof.

Ramla stopped chanting and her body went still. Then she sat back and waited for me to open my eyes again. "Tumaini, I have done for you what you did for many when you were a priest so long ago."

I had no idea what she was talking about. "Ramla, can you explain, please? What did you do?"

"It is a transfer of spiritual power from a teacher to a student. Only those who are ready can send or receive this power. To others who are not trained, it could be deadly. In Hindu it's known as shaktipat. All I did for you was to jumpstart that which you already had. I helped awaken the sleeping giant from within. The rest is for you to cultivate and grow."

In my head, I thought, "Oh, I'm awake alright. That jolt almost made me pee my pants."

Also in my head, I heard Ramla's voice. "It is a good thing that you did not. That would be hard for the others to have seen, as this was not intended to bring any pain or harm to your body."

I instantly looked straight at her and didn't blink. In my head, I heard more. "Yes, you can hear my thoughts, and I can hear your thoughts, as we have linked to the Great Consciousness."

I replied in my mind, "How am I able to do this?"

She continued so only I could hear, "We all have this gift. Your past memories have brought this ability back to you. Just be careful; all voices are not to be trusted. Some are evil, some are deceptive, and others can be outright malicious. The dark voices can drive a person insane, especially the voices that do not stop.

"And then there are the highest and truest voices of love. You will know those because you will feel their righteous intention. You will feel their purest love. You might not even hear them speak, but you will feel an acceptance beyond words."

"And if I don't feel their righteousness?"

"Then you will have to decide if that voice is a voice of good or evil. Not all beings on the path of love can project their feelings along with their words. Some only have enough energy to project their thoughts. They cannot send their emotions through."

I tried an experiment. After closing my eyes, I focused all my intention on sending Ramla gratitude and love for her help. "Yes, yes, you see. You know how to do this. I felt your love. I felt your gratitude, and I share the same with you, my beloved Tumaini."

I saw a vision of her hand resting on my heart. Her hand was glowing with a divine white light about it. When she pressed more firmly, I felt the warmest love and acceptance that I'd ever felt in my life. Tears began streaming down my face. When I opened my eyes, I saw the other three staring at us with their mouths hanging open.

Rehema asked, "What was going on between you two? What just happened?"

"It was wonderful. I could hear Ramla's thoughts, and I could feel her love. It… Words can't even begin to describe."

The others remained silent. In my head, I heard Ramla again. "Tumaini,

Rehema has this gift ready to be opened, as well. You might even help her in the future. You will know when it is the right time."

I let that thought sink in a little deeper. And like many humans, I tried to see the future with me helping Rehema.

"Don't mess with the future, Tumaini. Let this unfold as it must. Your past self has already influenced this timeline for success."

I thought to her, "OK, I'll trust you on this. Thanks again."

Out loud I said, "I could use a drink and a snack. Hanif, is there any of that CLT left over?"

CHAPTER SEVEN

THE APPETIZER

Karim hadn't said much since he'd come into the hotel room. While we ate our snacks, he kept alternating his stare between his amulet, Ramla, and me. I could tell that something was on his mind, but I didn't know how to break his silence.

Being the natural hostess, Rehema waved to him. "Karim, why don't you come over and join us? We would love your company."

Politely, he declined, "I'm not hungry, thank you," and went back to his curious stare.

A few seconds later, Mudads put down his coffee. "Karim, this isn't like you to be so quiet. You speak your mind whenever something is on it, and we can all see that you have something to say. What is it? What do you want to ask?"

Mudads pulled out his amulet and held it toward Karim, rocking it on its string like a hypnotist swinging a watch. "You can ask anything. We are all friends here."

Emotionally, he questioned with his gaze directly at my eyes, "It's you, isn't it? You are the one. I want to believe this. I do. I want to believe so badly, but..."

Then he turned to Ramla. "I even said I would believe because Ramla believes it, but I don't know if I can put my whole faith in one man."

His frustration grew, but he didn't loose his cool. He focused on Hanif and Mudads. "I've dedicated a great portion of my life to serving others, serving this cause, pledging my assistance for when Tumaini returns. I don't know..."

Hanif asked, "What's really the problem, Karim? What don't you know? You're dancing around what you really want to say. Just say it."

He burst back and motioned toward me with both of his hands, "Look at him! Just look at him! There is nothing special about him. He's just a man. How is he going to stand up to the Order? The Order is all-powerful and controls the world with fear, greed, and vice. The Order uses violence without remorse to obtain ultimate power. And everyone knows that he who controls the guns controls the world—and the Order controls the armies, the governments, and the police. He didn't even stop the man at the restaurant. How will he stop the armies when they decide to enact the Order's final plan?"

Rehema countered, "That's not fair, Karim. Tumaini didn't even remember who he was until today. Not to mention that he helped protect *me* from the assassin at the restaurant. And he is just now starting to regain his powers. We all saw it. Michael and Ramla had a connection that we can only dream about. We can't explain it. Give him a break, Karim. Or better yet, at least give him a chance."

"Honestly, Karim," Mudads pointed out, "Michael never claimed to be Tumaini. It was Hanif and I who said he had passed the tests. It was Hanif and I who said he had given us the signs. The rest just fell into place when he addressed the group at the restaurant. So if you are going to be angry at someone, be angry at us. Don't take this out on Michael."

Hanif agreed, "It's true. Michael never claimed to be Tumaini. And I can see how you would be upset and untrusting if he did. I would be untrusting if a stranger claimed to be a reincarnated priest that would bring hope to the world, but that's not the case here. Michael is trusting in us—he is trusting in us a lot. And his faith in us has me trusting in him. I can tell you this: I will help this cause, and I will help Michael.

"Tell me, Karim, you know the tests he needed to pass. Did he pass them for you?"

"Well..." Karim struggled.

Hanif asked again, "Did he pass the tests, Karim?"

He huffed, "Yes, he passed the tests. He knew the two songs, and you said he recognized the symbols. So I guess he passed. It's just hard."

Ramla asked, "What's so hard, Karim?"

"All this time, I've been waiting…waiting to put a plan of peace into action. I've been waiting for a strong leader to show up and stand up to the Order. And maybe that is the problem. I've been so used to waiting that I don't know what to do next. It was easier when I was waiting. I just kept serving and protecting others while waiting for Tumaini's return. But what now? What am I supposed to do?"

I stayed quiet and let the others talk. There was nothing that a stranger would say to Karim that would settle his inner struggle. I could also tell that he was battling a fear that had not shown its ugly face yet.

Rehema walked over to where he was sitting and knelt in front of him. "Karim, how much more honorable could your life have been? You have always helped others. You've protected the weak, you've fed the hungry, and you've kept your faith that one day Tumaini and the other priests would return. Be proud of what you have done, and let's move to the next chapter of our service together.

She got up and stood by Hanif. Then she urged, "You've always talked about a plan for peace on Earth. Don't you want that plan to come true?"

"Of course I do. It's just…"

"Go on."

"It's just…I'm afraid, alright?! I'm afraid that our plan for peace won't work! I'm afraid that the Order is too strong. I'm afraid that the people won't change and wake up from being brainwashed. And I'm afraid that Michael—Tumaini—won't be able to…"

He got up from his chair and marched toward me. "What do you want me to do, Tumaini? What's our next step? Can you stop the Order?"

I engaged his stare for a moment, looked down to gain my thoughts, and then I stood up. "You know, Karim. Those who've changed the world, helped the world, given people a chance for freedom, have all been…well, they've been normal at some point in their lives. They all started out as regular people, had a vision, got help—maybe with some divine help—then made a difference in the world. I may not be the chest-thumping, testosterone-filled general that you'd hoped for, but I do want to help the world. I do want to make a difference. And I will do what I can to make that difference, whether I am Tumaini or not."

He gave me a hint of a smile, and I continued, "If I am able to make a difference, would you help me to make that change? Will you continue on your path as a Protector of Souls? If I need help, would you help me?"

"I will try. But what do you want me to do?"

"I'm not in a place to give orders, Karim. Besides, I don't think that's what I'm supposed to do—at least not yet. I'm still trying to believe that I am Tumaini. But I can tell you that I am a natural problem solver. And if I say so myself, I'm pretty good at it. So let's look at the problem."

I scratched my head while thinking. The others were all waiting for me. "You know, solving the world's mess is a pretty tall order, and it's not our job to solve all of the world's problems anyway. That would be pretty arrogant of us to pretend that all of the people want to live like us, don't you think? So let's focus on what we can do."

I walked around in a tiny circle, passing each of my new friends. "I guess the first thing we should do is know what we are up against. You keep mentioning the Order. Who is it? What are they? And why do they want me dead?" Ramla winked at me in approval. She knew that things were beginning to take shape.

Mudads chimed in, "That's the problem."

"What's the problem?"

"That's the problem, Michael. Nobody knows who the Order is."

"Wait a minute. I'm supposed to help you guys enact some peace-giving, miraculous Earth-saving plan against a group called the Order, and nobody knows who they are?"

"Well, we do, and we don't."

"Oh, great. Not this again. OK, do they have a name besides *the Order?*"

"No."

"OK, do they have an address that we can go to?"

"No."

"Alright then, what country do they live in?"

"We don't know."

"And do they run a business?"

"Not one specific business, no."

"Oh, so this should be easy then. All we have to do is stand up against an Order that has no name, no address, they don't live in any one country, and they don't have a specific job—but they control the banks, the governments, the military, and the police. This should be easy."

Hanif heard my tiny bit of sarcasm and asked, "Michael, do you remember the part in your parchment about the dark beings putting something in the Pharaoh's head?"

"Yeah, I remember. But I thought that was… Actually, I didn't let that sink in far enough when I heard it. Are you telling me that something or someone actually put some mind-controlling *thing* in the Pharaoh's head?"

"Yes, that's exactly what I am telling you. And they don't control everyone, just key people within the system. Some are bribed, some are blackmailed, and others seem to be under some kind of influence or magic spell. We often hear people talk about evil voices in their heads.

"And we know that something is not right with our leaders' decisions. They don't make any sense—or peace, for that fact. None of what the politicians are doing is solving any of the problems. They never look to the root or cause. They just keep pointing fingers and putting Band-Aids on huge lacerations. It's like they don't want people to be in peace. They want them in turmoil so they can keep the masses agitated and angry."

While shaking his finger in the air, Karim emphasized, "It's much easier to get an angry mob to kill and go to war than it is to get a meditating monk to pick up a weapon."

Mudads stepped up and walked toward Ramla. "Ramla, you know this information better than all of us. Would you mind telling Michael what you know about the Order? I think it's time that we laid all of the cards on the table."

Looking back at him, I jested, "Yes, yes, and let's not forget any cards that are up anyone's sleeve, either. I'm about to go on the rest of my trip here, and I still don't know what I am up against. Right now, I'm a ship without an oar, a sail, a rudder, or a chart. Any kind of direction will help."

Ramla asked, "Tumaini, do you remember how you were able to see your past lives?"

"Yeah."

"Well, we all have this ability within ourselves. We can—if we practice enough—look into the lives of others, and if permitted, ourselves. We can see any event that has taken place in our past. It takes a lot of time and practice, however, to do this."

She repositioned herself in her chair and leaned forward. "We have some who have started this work in our group of protectors. They have only just begun to open their inner sight. We call them the *seers*."

"I've heard about this. The Russians and United States engaged in huge psychic battles for decades with remote viewers. They would look in the past for lost planes, people, missile placements, secret documents, and look for assassination targets. Is this the same sort of thing?"

"It is very similar, but not exactly the same. And as I said, we all have this ability. Some are more natural than others, but we all can do it. Isn't that right, Rehema?"

"Yes, it is," she answered, but she wondered why she had been asked that question.

Ramla continued, "I understand that you had an event at the restaurant tonight. How do you think they got all of this information?"

"I thought it was just from the note on the pigeon."

"It could have been, but the Order also has its own version of seers. From what I have gathered, their remote viewers can only see small pieces, small glimpses of history and the future, and they are not able to watch an entire timeline. That is why they did not stop you sooner. They had to wait for one person to exhibit the energy that he or she was Tumaini.

"Up until now, it was like looking in a milk jug for a single drop of milk. Nothing stood out. They couldn't find one person amongst billions. But when you sang the songs, that must have sent the vibration into the ethers for the Order to locate you. You would have been like a rose petal on top of the milk.

"They won't always know your next move because they lack the skill. But you will need to be careful. They will be looking for you again, probably sooner than you think."

"You aren't helping me feel very safe, Ramla."

"I know, but you will always have help along the way. Isn't that right, Karim?"

He was caught off guard by Ramla's question and stammered, "Y-y-yes. As a Protector of Souls," he said with more confidence, "I will help protect your soul, Michael."

"And so will we," added Rehema.

I felt a little better, but not completely confident in what to do next. "So let's put things into order again—no pun intended. Who is this mysterious Order?"

Rehema cheerfully bounced in her seat. "I wish we had some popcorn. I always liked this part. It's nothing like they teach in school."

She leaned in toward me. "Michael, you're in for a surprise. What you've been taught about our history is nothing like it really is. You've been fed a lot of lies so far—all controlled by the Order. What Ramla is going to share is, well, it's eye-opening for sure."

"Great, let's get to it."

Ramla sat back in her chair and calmly began telling us about the real history of our world and the human race. Looking at all of us, she began, "I will tell you what my mother told me, and her mother told her, all the way back to the priestess who helped the first Protectors of Souls. My story is shared by many other peoples, nations, and tribes from around the world. All throughout history, our story has been told in fables, symbols, and metaphors so we could keep the truth alive. This is the history that the Order does not want you to know.

"Tumaini, to help you understand, I need to go beyond our current Earth's story. I need to include the origins of the Order, as well as the origins of the human race. You need to know that the Order came from beyond our timeline. They came from a Universe that is not part of our space and time.

"You see, Tumaini, this is the Creator's fifth Universe. From an older, parallel Universe, one group of consciousness who did not follow the path of love was a race of reptilian-like beings. They were not supposed to enter into this Universal cycle. They were supposed to remain in a different Universe that would give them the chance to heal their anger and war-like personalities.

"In their current state, their evil was too powerful and strong. If left unchecked, they would corrupt every planet with their hate-filled mind control before a consciousness could make spiritual choices for itself. They had done this through numerous solar systems in their old Universe and had become quite refined with their techniques.

"I am getting ahead of myself, though. Let me back up a bit.

"Five hundred million years ago, dinosaurs, insects, and plants were given a chance to grow and exist in love with one another on Earth. Those that grew aware of their God-self and began caring for one another graduated to the third dimension. Those that did not were transformed in the great cleansing, the harvest, and given a new chance to experience love on other planets. The goal has always been the same throughout all of the dimensions: to be aware that you are the Creator in many forms and to learn of love.

"However, there was one race of dinosaurs that adapted to underground living and survived the harvest of souls on the surface. These dinosaurs walked on two legs and looked similar to a velociraptor. They were taller than a human male, had long tails, and were extremely carnivorous.

"Being at the top of their food chain and without any competition, they evolved over countless millennia, giving them the opportunity to generate incredibly enhanced mental capacities. It is said that these reptilian beings evolved so much that they were able to control a human's thoughts or subjugate their prey with their mental powers alone.

"Since they only evolved as animals, they never developed emotions like humans have. They are missing the most important ingredient: love. They are completely void of an emotional body, so they remain evolved animals with nothing more than a reptilian brain.

"For the most part, they were not seen by humans because they were ground dwellers. There are stories throughout the ages about these lizard men randomly coming up from their tunnels and attacking villagers, killing them for food and sport. These reptilian-like humanoids are now part of the Order, which I will tell you about in a little bit."

She got my attention. "Do you understand all of this, Tumaini?"

"I think so. I'll ask questions when you are done, if that's OK."

"Of course it is. I am here to serve and to help you on your path. Now let me tell you more about the beginning of the Order.

"When a Universe is created, a Logos, a part of God, is placed in charge of a portion of the Universe. The more powerful the Logos, the bigger the assignment. Our Logos is in charge of the Milky Way Galaxy.

"When the Milky Way Galaxy of this Universe was formed, the fifth dimensional reptilians snuck into the creation matrix and influenced one of the star systems. You know of this star system when you look at the Big and Little Dipper. It is Draco, the dragon constellation. The fifth dimensional reptilians colonized one specific planet in particular. It is called Alpha Draconis, otherwise knows as Thuban.

"The Creator and Logos did not like that the destructive reptilians had forced their way into the Milky Way without permission, but the Logos followed the lead of the Creator and allowed the reptilians to stay, hoping that the reptilians might experience love before they destroyed another star system. And since the fifth dimensional reptilians forced their way in and were permitted to stay, they were given certain choices. One might even say they had free will."

I coughed in disapproval with my fist over my mouth.

"What is the matter, Tumaini?" asked Ramla.

"I don't believe we have free will. I'm sorry for interrupting, but I am very adamant about my belief on that flawed concept. We have controlled choice at best—forced, restricted choice, as a matter of fact—not free will. And individual consciousness does not equal freedom when you are controlled by laws that you did not create. So I don't believe we have free will. Not one bit!"

I bowed my head slightly. "Sorry, I just kind of react that way when someone even brings up those two words. Please go on."

"Very well," she said, without having her emotions rattled by my comments, "I will continue.

"Now let me give you a tiny taste—an appetizer—on how the reptilians and other aliens are involved with our planet.

"For the first four billion years, before the time of the dinosaurs, our planet was visited by numerous alien races. Some of these aliens were third dimensional, just like we are. Most of them had fragile chemical bodies and were affected by the Earth's atmosphere.

"You've probably heard about some of them. One species of alien was shorter than most humans, grey in color, had three to four fingers, and black, almond-shaped eyes. Another species had insect-like features and could pass as monster-sized praying mantises. The third most common race was the tall Nordic-looking aliens. They were humanoid beings that had an average height over six feet tall.

"Some of these aliens traveled here in spaceships that could move faster than light, while others came here in slower fuel-based ships. All of them came here with an agenda.

"The benevolent aliens who visited Earth were explorers. Their mission was to learn, help the upcoming population of dinosaurs, and to gather data for their scholars and scientists. For the most part, they watched the evolution of Earth without much interference. These loving beings believed that choice was a gift and should be respected at all times. Choice is what allows a conscious being to grow spiritually."

I rolled my eyes and scowled when she mentioned the word *choice*. In my head, I heard Ramla say, "I saw that, Tumaini. We will talk about your disagreement when I am through. I can see that this subject weighs heavily on you."

I replied back telepathically, "I hear you so clearly in my mind. How do you do this?"

"Just like you do. I focus my thoughts to you, and those who can listen will hear. Those who do not listen cannot hear. Once your gift awakens, it is as simple as that."

"That's some gift, Ramla. Can I ever lose this ability?"

"Oh yes, you can. If you turn your back against your destiny, if you turn your back against your soul, you can lose this gift and more."

"Yikes. That's good to know."

Karim shook his finger at us. "You are doing it again, aren't you?"

"Yes, Karim. Tumaini and I shared a moment together. And someday, maybe you will share a moment with someone you feel connected to."

"I don't think I can do that, Ramla. This is a gift that is only used by the chosen ones."

"I tell you again, Karim, this is a gift that all can use. We are no more special than you. One day, you may follow the signs. You will see beyond sight and hear beyond words."

Rehema piped in, "OK, enough with your magic show. I'm ready for the story. This is my favorite part—aside from the part where we are made into zombie-like slaves."

"Yes, it will be good to continue," Ramla nodded. "Before I tell you the story, though, I wanted to finish explaining a little about our dimensional alien friends.

"For those who came to our planet in non-fuel-based ships, they used their mental powers and combined them with their technology. Some aliens controlled their ships as a unit with their mental powers. By combining thoughts, they became a group consciousness. Others had only one being in control of their ship.

"You see, Tumaini, they were able to travel by thought alone. And thought is not bound to the laws of physics. They could be anywhere, any place, any time, and travel faster than light just by thinking their desire or command.

"Then there were the other aliens. They did not have this ability developed yet, so they used their mental powers to travel by angles."

"What do you mean, *travel by angles?*"

"They could move as an individual, a group, or an object like a spaceship and travel through space by jumping from space and time to time and space. When they found their desired location in time and space, they made their journey back to space and time again. This took incredible amounts of energy, which they usually stole from other people, planets, and suns. With this energy, they projected themselves out from their object at ninety degree angles.

"The angle was the key: ninety degrees out in front of them to time and space, and ninety degrees back to space and time. That is how most of the reptilians moved here, through what science now calls wormholes."

Ramla looked at Rehema and instructed, "Tell Tumaini about your theory."

She got really excited at the chance to share. "Michael, there are pictures in some of the old Egyptian tombs that could explain what Ramla is talking about. One of these pictures is in Senenmut's tomb. It shows how a soul leaves a body when it is dead. But I think it is a clue left behind by aliens to show us how we can move within dimensions while we are still alive.

"On the ceilings of these ancient burial rooms, there are four circles: two circles side by side, then two circles directly underneath. Beside the four circles are eight circles: four in the top row and four in a row directly underneath. The circles are the same size and have twenty-four spokes in each circle. The spokes are not all on the same angle, though, which is curious. I think they are coordinates for a specific place in time and space.

"My theory is that the circles represent different vibrations of sound. That specific sound matches a specific place in time and space, like coordinates on a map. I also think that it is the non-moving location of your higher soul, your higher self. The higher self seems to be in the pictures above the circles that are separated by stars.

"The ninety degree shift is one way to leave your body. While you are living, you can project your consciousness straight out in front of you. Then you instantly make your consciousness move upwards at a ninety degree angle. This will shift you from space and time to time and space.

"Of course, this is much easier when you are dead. You automatically go from your body to time and space to rejoin with your higher self."

"That's cool, but what's this time and space stuff that you are talking about?"

She explained more with her hands. "We live in space and time. Think of an old-fashioned movie film as space and time. Each slide is what we would call space. Turn on the movie projector, and you don't notice the individual slides whizzing by, the individual portions of space. When you watch a movie, like our movie of life, you only see a fluid, moving picture, not the individual portions of space.

"From your soul's perspective, time moves your consciousness from one slide to the next. You are in the flow of time, which we call space and time.

"Time and space are the opposite. When you are in time and space, you are not moving in time. You are stationary, and you can move to any part of space that you would like.

"It would be like rolling out the entire film on the ground. From time and space, you could go to any slide and spend as much spirit time there as you wish. You could also see the entire film at once and understand every nuance of the film. You could even jump back and forth on the same film strip. The combinations are immense, especially when you can see multiple film strips at the same time. Does this make sense, Michael?"

"Yes. It's like basic quantum physics. Who knew that spirituality and science could be joined together so easily? That's good stuff."

Ramla said to me, "Tumaini, there is another gift that the higher dimensions have and are able to use in third dimension. In the fourth dimension and higher, thoughts become things. What a higher dimensional being thinks becomes real instantly. Their thoughts gather energy and become thought forms."

"You mean, if I think of an apple and apply energy to that thought, I can instantly create an apple?"

"That's the general idea, Tumaini. When you add density—energy—to a thought, the thought becomes real. A fourth or fifth dimensional reptilian can add density to a harmful thought and direct it at a human. The human will experience this thought and feel the negative effects."

"So they could make someone sick and feel pain?"

"Oh yes, and more."

"Ramla, this is some pretty heavy stuff. And I need to know this, I'm sure I do—especially since my world just got turned upside down in one day. This hasn't sunk in one hundred percent yet. I think I'm still running on adrenaline.

"I don't think I still know what I'm up against. What else do you have for me? How did the reptilians put stuff in the pharaoh's head? Who are these monster insects? And how does this all fit in to the Order?"

Ramla answered, "Good, we haven't given you too much information to confuse you. Let me tell you about the alien agenda and the Order."

CHAPTER EIGHT

THE ORDER

Ramla straightened her back, pulled her feet up under her robe, and crossed them. Before saying anything, she pulled out her amulet and let it rest on her chest.

"Tumaini, this story is our real history, and the information I am going to share will help you fulfill your destiny. Before I begin, I will ask you to allow me to finish before you ask me any questions. Is that OK with you?"

"Of course. Know when to talk, and know when to listen, right?"

The others shifted in their chairs and assumed a seated meditative posture. I watched as Hanif and Rehema closed their eyes. Then Mudads and Karim did the same thing.

"I have to admit. I feel like a kid who just had his warm milk and is waiting for a bedtime story." No one said anything, as a calm energy grew in the room. I followed suit with the others and closed my eyes. It was a few moments before Ramla spoke again.

"The Earth has been home to many races and species. It was a little more than ten million years ago when a group of spirits saw the Earth as they were passing through our solar system. The blue waters, lush green landscapes, and budding new life forms seemed so intriguing that they had to stop and explore. It was surely a place where this group could gain more experience, so these souls decided to make Earth their temporary home.

"These spirits eventually settled on a large landmass that covered a huge portion of our Pacific Ocean. In time, this place became known as Mu, and the section of Mu where these souls lived was called Lemuria.

"The first souls on Mu were not humans as we know them today. They were more like floating thought forms of spirit called aku, and they had no physical bodies. If someone actually saw them, they would have looked more like primate ghosts than humans.

"Two million years went by, and the second race of aku came to inhabit Lemuria. At the same time, Earth's natural evolution of minerals, plants, and animals continued.

"While the ghost-like Lemurians grew in peaceful experience, the lands and seas continued filling with new life. Modern elephants, lions, gazelles, chimpanzees, and rhinoceroses roamed the Great Plains of Africa. Saber-toothed tigers, wooly mammoths, and deer owned the Americas. And the seas belonged to the whales, dolphins, and sharks. Trees grew, and the grasslands flourished.

"Mother Nature continued on her ever-slow path of change and mutation. The land mammals who'd bent forward and walked on their knuckles began standing upright and balancing on their heels. Some of the second density apes grew into the early stations of Homo erectus and Neanderthals. Early man had entered onto the stage of planet Earth.

"The Earth had been visited by many aliens during this time. The loving, benevolent aliens remained hidden and followed a philosophy of non-interference. However, not all aliens who visited Earth were of the benevolent order. Five races of aliens in particular were from the dark side. They came to Earth for conquest, domination, and ownership through enslavement.

"Around two hundred and fifty thousand years ago, the first evil race of aliens—the Anunnaki—came to Earth in their rocket ships. Long tails of fire spewed from behind the metal tubes. When these ships entered the atmosphere near Africa, their thunder was so loud that it shook the walls of man's caves and knocked down the surrounding trees.

"When the evil Anunnaki saw the development of early man, they jumped at the opportunity to ease their own burdens. They took the primate man and manipulated its genes to create a new slave race. These new slaves were engineered to be less aggressive than their earlier Homo brothers and to complete tasks without question. By enhancing their mental capacity just slightly above that of an ape, these slaves would be forced to work the fields, dig for minerals, and serve their new masters without any chance for freedom.

"As everyone knows, Mother Nature cannot be controlled. This new slave race evolved over time and grew in numbers far beyond the containment of its masters. Although not completely free from their slave programming, they were able to organize mass uprisings and turn against their alien enslavers.

"The Anunnaki, unable to restrain the large population of slaves, decided to destroy their creation and leave the planet. With the help of a few Anunnaki who cared for their workers, a small group of the genetically altered men and women were spared and left to evolve on their own.

———•—•———

"Two hundred thousand years ago, another group of souls came to stay on the planet. After circling the Earth many times, these souls found a large landmass between the coasts of the Americas and Africa to call their home. This was the birth of the Atlantean age.

"For the first chapter in their trilogy, the Atlanteans, who looked like present-day man, grew collectively in science and spirituality. Using the power of crystals for flight, building special healing rooms, and gathering local herbs and plants for medicine and food, they created a beautiful culture that benefited the planet.

"The problems began for them around fifty thousand years ago when the malevolent aliens started interfering with the Atlanteans. Patience finally broke, and anger grew. Thoughts of war split the people and divided the lands. By using crystals as an energy source for war, they broke the islands apart and caused the destruction of the first Atlantean race.

———•—•———

"For brief moments, peace settled back upon the lands. The remaining aliens took refuge on the islands and began intermingling with the surviving Atlanteans. Some of the Atlanteans remained true to their beliefs of love and peace and helped the aliens rebuild their cities. A few others, though, sustained great pains and emotional scars from the war and were unable to forgive them so easily.

"Twenty thousand years went by with many hard pains of life. A large number of aliens continued to use fear as a weapon to wear down the peaceful Atlanteans. In time, tensions boiled over again and erupted into another major battle. This next war lasted for tens of years, and more of Atlantis fell beneath the waters.

———•◦•———

"In other places around the globe, Homo sapien man continued to evolve and settled in the Americas, Asia, Europe, and Australia. The bodies of early man still carried the manipulations from the Anunnaki, but these new humans were not under any sadistic task masters. Their new goal was to see if they could reconnect with Source and grow beyond fear and control. Without daily torture and manipulation from the Anunnaki, these souls were given a chance to evolve mentally, physically, spiritually, and emotionally.

———•◦•———

"Back on Atlantis, the third root race had begun. Atlanteans and aliens were in full human form at this time. They had completely lost their ability to transform back to spirit and were bound to human bodies until death. And with the increased split in their cultures, language was also divided. Instead of one language, now there were many. True meanings were lost in translation, and this added even more tension on the remaining islands.

———•◦•———

"As Earth became more popular in the galaxy, four alien races took interest and began interfering with the Atlanteans and early man: Nordics, greys, and mantids. The fourth race of aliens was the one who forced its way into the creation matrix of this galaxy. They were not supposed to be here. And unfortunately for everyone on Earth, they were the cruelest and most sadistic of them all.

"These aliens were the same species as the second dimensional dinosaurs that had evolved beneath the surface, but these aliens were fourth and fifth dimensional beings. The majority of them came from Alpha Draconis. The others came from a bird race of reptilians, while the third group came from a star in the Orion constellation called Rigel.

"They had large, muscular, scaly, green bodies and stood over six feet tall. Some of their hybrid species were brown, red, black, shiny blue, and yellow. Their jaws were lined with razor-sharp teeth, and their eyes were like crocodile eyes—blood red with a black slit. These aliens were called the reptilians.

"The reptilians who landed on Earth had a huge advantage over the other aliens and Atlanteans. They had an army of evolved reptilian dinosaurs already living beneath the surface of the planet. With their telepathic abilities, alien reptilians could communicate with and control their earthbound relatives. To the reptilian dinosaurs, the alien reptilians were like gods, and they could not refuse an order from their gods.

———————————

"By this time, the Atlanteans had completely harnessed the natural power of the planet. The free energy found in the upper atmosphere and energy lines, called lay lines, had been collected with special crystalline cathedrals placed throughout the islands. Power beyond imagination was now at the hands of the Atlanteans.

"This new power drew the attention of the greys, mantids, and reptilians. If the Atlanteans were able to control the planet, this would interfere with the alien agenda. They could control the evolution of man and take all of the resources for their own. This was unacceptable, and each race took its turn attacking the Atlantean cities.

———————————

"The first attack was the bloodiest and most costly for the Atlanteans and greys alike. When the greys arrived with fifty of their ships, the Atlantean scouts had already seen them and alerted their entire armada. The cities were also alerted, and they erected domed energy shields.

"Five miles away from the main city, grey spacecraft and Atlantean war crafts fired plasma bolts at each other without mercy. Ships from both sides exploded in midair and rained metal over the ocean floor. A quarter of the greys' fleet took station over the protective domes. They began firing in steady streams trying to punch a hole in the Atlantean defensive shield.

"The Atlantean ground troops felt the shockwaves from each plasma bolt. Some of them were so strong that they knocked a few troops to the ground. With a signal from their commander, the ground troops activated the crystal obelisks that stood outside the city limits and shot pure streams of energy at the attacking greys. Within minutes, the obelisks destroyed all of their spaceships.

"Over the ocean, both sides had lost half of their fleets. The greys knew they could not win at this point and began to retreat. In an instant, all of the grey ships darted out of sight and flew into the upper atmosphere.

———————

"The second attack came from the mantids. Hearing about the failure of the greys, the mantids used a different approach. By using their telepathic ability, they learned about the defensive plans to protect the city from another aerial invasion. This gave the mantids a slight advantage. Instead of attacking from the air, they transformed a number of their spaceships to bore through the ground.

"With huge spinning blades that cut through the rock, the mantids made three large tunnels inside the perimeter of the main city. When they broke ground, an intense land assault ensued.

"Thousands of mantids poured through the tunnels. Using long staffs that emitted a stunning energy beam, they knocked out scores of Atlantean soldiers and civilians. Then they carried these prisoners down into the tunnels, never to be seen again.

"The Atlanteans changed their strategy within minutes. They activated the energy dome and launched all of their ships to attack the mantids. The ships raced to the three tunnels and hovered above them. With the tunnels surrounded, the Atlanteans unleashed their death-rays on the mantids, killing everything on the ground and in the tunnels. When the last mantid fell, the Atlanteans flew down the tunnels to rescue their citizens, but the tunneling machines were long gone.

———•—•———

"The last two battles used a great amount of resources and energy. To prepare for any new attacks, the military hired scientists to dig farther into the Earth. Their goal was to obtain enough natural energy to create a weapon that would stop the aliens dead in their tracks before they could wipe out Atlantis.

"The scientists dug deeper and farther than ever before and tapped into the Earth's core. Their work, however, was dangerously close to destabilizing the foundation of Atlantis. Many of the scientists warned the military about using this energy, as it could destroy more than just the aliens, but the military wouldn't listen.

"Meanwhile, the reptilians devised a plan to divide and conquer the Atlanteans once and for all. Their plan was to draw the Atlantean battleships hundreds of miles away from Atlantis. This would leave Atlantis vulnerable to a ground attack. Without their air support, the Atlanteans would easily fall to the reptilian dinosaur ground forces.

———•—•———

"On the day of Atlantis' most holy celebration, the greys attacked the outer islands. In a panic, the Atlantean military sent their airships to defend the cities and follow the greys to wipe them out.

"Taking the bait, the greys led the Atlantean airships hundreds of miles to the east and over current-day India. Waiting for them in the clouds were the reptilian battle cruisers and mantid destroyers. Outnumbering the Atlanteans ten to one, their plasma guns ripped through the Atlantean ships and disintegrated their entire fleet.

"Back on Atlantis, the attack was led by the second dimensional reptilians. They came up through the tunnels that had been left by the mantids and ripped through the ground forces with ease. The mantids followed and started collecting as many living Atlanteans as possible.

"With a complete loss in sight, the general of the Atlantean ground troops had no other choice but to use their new energy weapon against the invading forces. In a flash of intense heat and light that emanated from the central crystal obelisk, the directed energy beam burned all of the enemy ground troops to a cinder. Nothing was left of them but piles of ash. The new energy weapon had worked better than expected and saved Atlantis.

"The Atlanteans began to dance and cheer in the streets. They thought the war was over, but a loud rumble from under the Earth shook the ground. It started slowly, but picked up intensity with each aftershock. The birds all started squawking and flying away in massive droves.

"The shocks became stronger and stronger. The intensity grew, and sections of the outer islands began falling into the sea. A general announcement was made to all of the islands telling the people to gather what they could and head to higher ground. It was too late, though. Complete and total destruction was eminent.

"One final massive rumble shook the central island. All went silent for a few seconds. A deathly stillness hung in the air. Then an earth-shattering blast occurred beneath the surface. A mushroom cloud appeared over the island, followed by a disintegrating ball of light and heat. All of the Atlantean islands were blasted up into the sky from the destructive energy wave. Then they came crashing back down in an instant beneath the water.

"The power of the explosion changed the landscape of most of the Earth. What was once dry became wet in many places. Monstrous tidal waves crashed onto many of the shores around the globe and engulfed the landscape. This wiped out plants, animals, and much of early man. It was a major extinction that happened about twelve thousand years ago.

"Atlantis was now lost for good beneath the seas. Nothing remained of the once-peaceful people who had taken root on Earth many years ago. The only remains of indigenous Earth were a few tribes of early man who lived in the mountains scattered throughout the globe.

"The mantids, greys, and reptilians who had survived the cataclysm remained on Earth to begin an age of slavery for all human races. The Earth was now considered a dark planet.

"The reptilians had no opposing forces left to conquer. This was their planet to rule and own. Without much threat from the greys and mantids, the reptilians allowed the surviving aliens to stay, as long as they remained loyal to the self-proclaimed royalty of the reptilians. Now the plan was set, and an oppressive royalty needs subjects.

"The reptilians knew they needed to control the evolution of man—the only remaining third dimensional species on the planet. This would be the key to sustaining world domination. The only problem was that the reptilians liked to work from the shadows, from behind the scenes. They did not like to be seen by their prey. This would also protect them from any blame or revenge in the future.

"To the reptilians, man was nothing more than cattle: a food source. They needed a puppet ruling class that would work for the reptilians from the inside to control the human species.

"Going over the history of the planet, the reptilians found a potential answer. They were able to identify an interracial species of man left over from the Anunnaki occupation. The DNA from this cross species was unique and easy to identify.

"Their homo sapien-Anunnaki offspring had an evolutionary edge over the rest of man. They were more evolved physically and mentally. They could complete tasks much faster, solve problems with greater ease, and they had a creative edge over their genetic brothers. And their physical characteristics were close to the Nordic aliens—tall, blonde hair, blue eyes, and muscular.

————

"Besides eating flesh and drinking blood, the reptilians had developed a special taste for feeding on the energy of their slaves. The tastiest type of energy was sexual energy, but they truly craved the energy generated from human fear, anger, and suffering. Anything that caused emotional discomfort in a human's life had become a delicacy for the reptilians.

"Having done this on numerous other planets throughout the galaxy, the reptilians already had a successful and well-refined battle plan for global domination. This plan would allow them to stay in control and feast on human flesh and energy—especially children—whenever they wanted to. An unlimited supply of energy was now at hand.

"The number one rule that the reptilians followed to make this battle plan work was to never, ever, under any circumstance, let the humans unite around the world in peace and love. At all costs, the reptilians must keep the people afraid, angry, and separated. This was their ultimate goal to ensure success. They knew that if the people united in love and peace, they could free themselves from the tyranny of any sadistic leadership. The reptilians would be powerless against the awesome strength of love.

"By tempting and appealing to the greed of the Anunnaki hybrids and offering them power, wealth, resources, technology, and sacred knowledge, the reptilians could easily control the world from behind the scenes. The thirteen Anunnaki hybrid bloodlines who accepted the reptilians' gifts would be flown to the other continents to mate with the young human species in the Americas, Asia, Europe, and Australia. This would enable the plan for global domination. The Anunnaki who did not go for this plan were executed, used for sport, or tortured and killed in black magic rituals.

"Once the Anunnaki hybrids rose to power in each region—which was easy to do with the help of the reptilians, mantids, and greys—the next step was to have them control religion, education, and politics.

"A spiritual blindfold was placed around the world. Opposing religions with multiple versions of god were created, and the use of false prophets, guided by the aliens, was implemented immediately. Fear of displeasing the gods—who were really the aliens behind the scenes—was a major key to keeping humans afraid and separated. The only way to please the gods was by blood sacrifice and monetary gifts. Sacrificing humans and animals and tithing gold were to be accepted and taught in all religions for as long as possible.

"Because the Anunnaki hybrids would be in contact with the reptilians, it was taught that only the high priests, kings, and queens could communicate with god and the angels. It was made a sin for anyone else. This kept the people from realizing that all religious gods and angels were actually reptilians in disguise.

"Any human who portrayed natural psychic abilities was executed as a non-believer or a witch, unless they agreed to work for the dark side. This kept people from developing their natural psychic abilities. This also kept people from being able to see who was behind the enslavement of man.

"Once religion took hold in each land, rules and laws were controlled by the wrath of the gods. The right to rule and own land, animals, and people came directly from messages of the gods. Anyone who questioned a message from the false gods would be killed or ostracized. Torture, enslavement, and killing were approved by the false gods and permitted in most religions.

"Once ownership was granted by the false gods, barter, trade, money, and banks began to be used around the world to keep the people separated and controlled. A slave mentality had already been encoded in the humans by the Anunnaki, so this was not hard to establish. Coveting wealth—especially wealth gained by greed and fear—is a very effective tool to keep the people angry, afraid, and aggravated. These negative emotions created more food for the reptilians to feed upon.

"With ownership came names, titles, and pride. The reptilians knew that fear grows from the threat of invaders, intolerable strange customs, or being outnumbered by outsiders. By naming cities and defining countries and borders, separation and fear grew rampant. More food and control for the dragon race.

"The next phase in the evil plot was to keep the people entertained and distracted. Creating sports and entertainment kept the people from growing mentally and spiritually. Pursuing feats of strength and useless skills distracted both the players and the audience. And by having teams and competition, that created pride and more separation. Hate crimes and fear continued to grow with this hideous plan.

"Education had to be controlled, too, and the real history could never be taught. It was a privilege for the rich and the upper class. And when education was provided to all, it was completely controlled in order to dumb down the masses. The people were never allowed to learn what interested them. They were kept under a strict formula that created a slave class and an opposing wealthy class. And special treatment and favoritism was always given throughout the ages to those who showed a desire for self-advancement and greed.

"And finally, the slaves were controlled by politicians, who themselves were being manipulated by the reptilians. The governments were never to unite with peace and love as a goal. For centuries, borders were kept, armies grew in size, technology flourished, and the police forces enslaved the people to the laws of the reptilian gods.

"The police and military were given the right to bully, torture, and kill, and this infuriated the masses. The truth was kept from the people, and this infuriated the masses. And politicians were allowed to continue enforcing their made-up authority with violence and death, and this infuriated and separated the masses. With this plan in action, it was a smorgasbord for the reptilians.

"The failsafe to this plan was to discredit anyone who stood in their way, ruin anybody's life who tried to divulge the reptilian alien agenda, and to kill anyone who tried to overthrow the establishment.

"And this brings us up to today. We have been under this alien reptilian rule for the last ten thousand years. As our technology grows, the reptilians keep giving more of their technology to the government and military to institute complete global mind control.

"The people are growing more aware every day that something is going on behind the scenes, but they don't know what to do. They don't know how to break the cycle and regain their spiritual rights. So the people are frustrated, confused, and angry. Most want a change, and they will follow the right person or the right idea that will lead them to freedom.

"This is all we know to this point. The Order has developed three potential plots to take over the rest of mankind's will. We do not know which one they will use next. It's our theory that they have already tried two and have failed.

"Take your time to open your eyes, Tumaini, and you will see that what I have told you is true."

My eyelids fluttered open, and I said, "This feels so right. It feels so true. But"—I held up my first finger and shook it—"I have questions!"

CHAPTER NINE

BREAKFAST WITH THE BIRDS

The energy in the room had definitely changed. Before Ramla told her story, everything around us had been scattered, unorganized, and without purpose. There had been no direction to the atoms that danced in the air. But now, all of the energy in the room seemed to be gathering in a stream. It was like all of the atoms instantly knew what to do, and they all had a new direction and a purpose. They began moving like a parade of intention ready to embrace their destiny and take flight. The feelings inside me began mirroring these atoms.

With each second that passed, the waves of energy began coalescing into light, and the light began taking on form, and the form began taking on shape. The shape was structured, but with the ability to completely change at a moment's notice. It was firm, but with a hint of being pliable. The shape of this newly organized energy was not our history as we once knew it; it was now the shape of things to come.

———— • ————

Ramla requested of Karim, "Before I get to Michael's questions, would you go down to the car and bring my bag?"

"Of course, Ramla. I'll be right back."

Rehema chuckled, "I might have some questions, too. That's always an intense story for me, and it makes me think every time I hear it. Like, if the reptilians and the thirteen Anunnaki bloodlines did all of this without our knowledge, what else have they done that we aren't aware of? I mean, do we live on a *flat Earth,* or what?"

"I was thinking the same thing, Rehema," I exclaimed. "Who knows what other dark secrets are hiding in their closets? I've often wondered if the secret societies really do have a machine that can see into the future."

Ramla shared calmly, "Anything that promotes peace, health, and freedom is from the light. Anything that promotes domination, fear, and greed is from the dark side.

"Tumaini, who do you think it was that put fluoride in the water?"

I held up my tube of toothpaste. "Wasn't it the dental association?"

She practically scolded me with her sharp response, "No! This is not a time for jokes, Tumaini. You know what fluoride does to the body and mind, don't you?"

"Honestly, no. What does it do? I thought it helped your teeth."

"Those dark Order politicians and reptilians know that fluoride makes you extremely docile and submissive, and it affects the endocrine system in your body in the most harmful way. The Order doesn't want you fighting back or standing up to them; that's why they like fluoride so much. It dumbs you down and keeps you compliant. Think about that the next time you drink your fluoridated water."

I stammered, "I...I never thought about that before. What about the endocrine system, though? I thought it was just part of your body. What does fluoride have to do with it?"

She continued emotionally, "Your endocrine system is your chakra system, your spiritual energy system. Fluoride blocks your spiritual growth and access to your pineal and pituitary glands. Without psychic and spiritual access through your glands, you are cutting yourself off from God and your source of spiritual energy. That's why they put fluoride in the water. Don't you see?"

"Uh..."

"These are the same dark aliens and bloodlines who created a religious being called Satan. If people are brainwashed by religious fear and spend all of their time blaming Satan for the bad deeds in the world, then the people will never look for the real culprits who are behind our enslavement. Those are the real demons, not this made-up fairy tale figure.

"Surely you don't think that genetically modified food is good for you, do you?"

"Well, not really, now that you mention it."

"And who do you think it is that forces children to get immunized so they can go to school—which they are also forced to do? Fear of infection is their driving force. But those immunizations also affect the immune system and create even more harm to the mind and body.

"Tumaini," she said firmly, "the last thing that the corrupt corporate governments and the reptilians want is for anyone—and I mean anyone—to tap into their spiritual abilities. The more spiritual someone becomes, the less that person can be controlled by fear and greed, and this terrifies those who claim to be in power."

She lifted her cane toward me. "Don't you see the pattern here, Tumaini?"

"I'm starting to. But what do you want me to do? I mean, there're already so many finger pointers and blamers in the world. And anytime that someone tries to start a movement, that group always starts to argue from inside and eventually self-implodes. I don't want to do that. I've seen it happen too many times."

I held up my pointer finger. "Wait a minute, that's probably a set up, too, isn't it? I bet that the dark side sends in government and corporate plants to break up any organization that could bring them trouble."

"Now you are starting to see how they work, Tumaini. These are selfish, greedy, foul beings who don't care about anyone else but themselves. They only care about power, control, and domination. They are the true enslavers of mankind, and they will do anything in their power to keep us as slaves."

"Ramla, you didn't answer my question, though. What do you want me to do?"

"You are right, I didn't—at least not yet. Tumaini, tell me, what does the secret government do with finger pointers? We already know that they kill or imprison some of the whistleblowers."

"I don't know. But I do know that most of the finger pointers don't do anything but rile people up and get them angry. Most never provide any real solutions. I know that for a fact. I've been to some of these meetings before. It's all fire and brimstone with no plan to solve the problem—just like Sunday mass," I chuckled.

"Exactly!" she replied with great disgust. "That's why the government does not interfere with them, religion, or with the media—the other puppet arm of the dark side. The media is nothing more than a fear generator and instigator for violence."

"I know. I don't even watch the news or read the paper anymore—too much negativity."

"Tumaini, he who controls the media and entertainment controls the mood of the masses. And if you control the masses, you control the world. Get a person angry, and you increase the odds that you can get them to fight. Get a nation angry, and they will go to war without seeking the truth first. They will fight while being deceived and used for profit.

"So what are you going to do, Tumaini? Are you going to point fingers and blame those in power? Or are you going to make a difference some other way?"

Hanif leaned over toward his brother and whispered something. Then Ramla gave them a stern look. "No secrets at this time, you two. Now is the time for answers, not secrecy. What did you just say?"

Hanif replied sheepishly, "I'm sorry, Ramla. I told Mudads that Michael was a natural problem solver—at least that's what he told Karim. I said, 'I guess now is his chance to prove it.'"

"Ouch, I did say that, didn't I? Now the pressure is on, and I'm completely blank. That doesn't give you much confidence in me, does it?" I hung my head down a little.

Rehema chimed in, "Just because you don't act rashly doesn't mean that you can't solve problems, Michael. I'm sure you will come up with some answers. Who knows? Maybe some of them are in the scrolls that you wrote. But," she added humorously, "coming up with a solution would be better sooner than later." She followed up with a reassuring wink.

"Maybe you are right." I walked around pacing for a few seconds. No one else spoke. "I sure would like a good answer right now, though. Then I could use the line that I use with my students."

Mudads asked, "And what is that?"

"Somebody drank his epiphany juice this morning, didn't he? And I could use a good epiphany right about now... I know. It's funnier in class. It's more of a timing joke."

I looked at the clock. "Time! Holy cow, it's already 5:00 a.m.! I've got to get ready to leave soon."

"Wow," remarked Hanif, "it *is* that late. Or that early, I mean."

"I'm mostly packed, so there's not too much to do, and I showered before the meeting. I just need to tidy up before I check out. It caught me off guard, is all. Time has really flown by since I met you guys."

Mudads smirked, "I hope that will turn out to be a good thing for you, Michael."

There was a knock on the door, which Mudads answered. "Hi, Karim."

Karim didn't say anything and walked over to Ramla. "Here is your bag. Is there anything else I can do for you?"

"Oh, thank you, Karim. No, not at this time." She added mysteriously, "But I will have something for you to do in the next day or two."

Then she gestured to me. "Tumaini, come over here. You can finish packing later. This will help you with your spiritual growth."

Ramla reached in her bag and gave me two objects. One of them looked like a short shepherd's staff. It was made of a heavy bronze and covered with alternating strips of obsidian, blue glass, and gold from bottom to top. There was also a gold cap at the end of the staff with Tumaini's name etched on it. The other object was similar to the shepherd's staff, but it did not have the rounded hook on the end. Instead, it bent downward at the top like Ramla's Ptah staff. Hanging from the bent tip were three beaded sticks made of gilded wood flowing halfway down to solid bronze at the end.

Mudads was confused. "Why did you give him a heka and a nekhakha?"

I shook my head, "A what-a what-a?"

Rehema nudged me with her elbow. "A crook and flail."

"Oh, like the one on King Tut's coffinette? I thought they looked familiar. What are they for?"

Ramla replied back to me, "The crook will help you with your spiritual growth. The flail will help you to fertilize your cause.

"OoooohKaaaay. And I'm supposed to know what that means?"

"Shoosh, Tumaini. Let me finish. Do not be misled by their common appearance. These are two of the clues you left yourself…to remind yourself again. They do not stand for royalty, as the historians would have you believe. They are tools of life, the path that all must take on their soul's journey back to Source.

"Unfortunately, the royalty kept this treasure for themselves. They did not share this miracle with their peoples. They were selfish—fools! This was a gift for all mankind." Rehema nodded her head in agreement about the government cover-up.

"Take them, study them, and you will know God once again."

I laughed, "With all of this stuff, I could open my own museum." I waved the crook and flail in front of the others. "Now why couldn't I leave myself some simple instructions like: *Press this button and people will instantly be kind and loving to one another?* All these clues are going to take me a lifetime to decode."

Hanif grinned, "Maybe two."

"Oh great, Hanif. Thanks for building my confidence. It's not like the human race has a lot of time.

"Hey, what about Customs? How am I to report this and get this through Customs?"

"I'll take care of that," he reassured. "I'll print up another receipt and give it to you when you return to Cairo. Your name is on the bottom, so they are yours—even if it was from another lifetime. You do plan to meet with us again when you come back, don't you, brother?"

I gave him a bright-faced look because of his comment. He'd called me *brother,* and it already felt like I was a member of the family. "You'd better believe that I'll meet with you again. Besides, I know where your shops are. At least I think I do," I chuckled. "I'm sure I can get lost again and follow the voice in my head."

I stopped and thought, "Was that Ramla who told me where to go?" I put the flail and crook in my trunk and looked at Ramla.

She spoke in my mind, "It was not me, Tumaini, but I'm sure it was someone who had an interest in helping you with your destiny." I winked at her and smiled.

Karim shook both of his hands in frustration toward us. "How many times are you going to do that?"

Ramla reached out and softly held his arm. "The time will come when we may all be able to share our true thoughts and feelings with each other, Karim, with or without words. Just be patient; this is unfolding nicely. It's all beginning to take shape, and you will be a part of this, too. I feel it."

Karim stood there silently and pondered what she'd shared. Then he shook his head slightly and put his hand on hers, "Thank you for your words, Ramla. I will work on my frustration."

"Good," she replied.

"I've got an idea." I looked at all five of them and continued, "How about

I treat you to breakfast? The hotel has a fantastic restaurant, and we can have breakfast on the terrace by the pool. It's the least I can do, since you've spent so much time with me tonight."

Rehema looked at Hanif and Mudads while nodding her head in approval, "I could go for some breakfast. How about you two?"

Mudads agreed, "That is a great idea. Who needs sleep anyway?"

I gestured toward the other two. "Ramla, Karim, would you join us?"

Karim nodded, "I will join you."

Ramla bobbed her head *yes*, too, "We have much to do in a short time, Tumaini. I will be with you as much as you need during your stay. I know you have questions." She completed the rest in my head, "And you have something to resolve as well."

My face grimaced. It was a subconscious reaction from something she'd said earlier. I replied telepathically, "I remember. Yes, I have questions." I didn't want to dig up my sore spot just yet.

"The restaurant opens at 5:30 a.m. It's only a few more minutes, so why don't you go down and get a head start. I'll finish throwing my things in these suitcases, and I'll meet you down there."

Mudads said, "Sounds good. We'll be waiting for you."

Karim escorted Ramla out, followed by Hanif, Rehema, and Mudads.

Mudads turned before letting the door close. "We'll be waiting for you, my friend."

"I'll be there in just a few. See you then."

When I showed up at the restaurant, the others were already sitting at a large table that sat between the railing and the pool. A pitcher of water, coffee, and juice filled the middle, and a small tray of breakfast pastries rested beside them.

"Sorry I'm late, guys—and ladies." I gave both ladies a smile. "I decided to checkout now instead of later. The line at the desk gets really long after 7:30 a.m., and I didn't want to miss the bus. Our tour guide hates it when anyone is late, and I thought it would be better to get that out of the way first so I could focus on you and this mission."

Karim huffed, "Yes, that would be rude to keep people waiting."

I felt his negative remark pierce my chest. "I'm sorry, Karim. Checkout only took me a few minutes, and there was no line at the front desk. Have I done something to you in a past life? I'm trying my best here, honest."

"It's not you."

"It isn't?"

In my head, I thought, "It sure feels like it." Ramla reacted to my sharp, silent statement.

Karim continued, "No, it's the idea that it's you."

Hanif interrupted before I could speak, "And what does that mean?"

"Nothing," he spat shortly. "Let's get on with this. I'm tired and cranky. It's been a long night." Hanif wanted to say more, but Rehema put her hand on his knee to calm him down.

Mudads added, "Indeed. It has been a long night."

I took my seat between Ramla and Rehema and looked toward him. "It's OK, Karim. I understand. I'm a little cranky in the morning, too. I hope we can become friends someday."

Picking up my menu, I asked, "Did you guys order already? I could eat a whole CLT by myself. I'm starved."

Hanif laughed, "You learn quickly, my friend."

"Well, I had a good teacher."

Mudads motioned to the long tables near the hotel doors. "We saw the breakfast buffet on the way over, and they have an omelet station. We thought we would all start there first."

"Sounds good to me. I like the buffet."

I signaled to the waiter who was nearby. "We'll all be having the buffet. This will be on one check, too. I'd also like a stack of pancakes. Can you do that for me, please?" He nodded and walked to the kitchen to put in our order.

Rehema quickly called to the waiter, "Make that two orders of pancakes!"

She bounced a little. "I haven't had pancakes in a long time, Michael. That was a good idea."

When we came back to the table, there was a flock of about twenty sparrows eating all of the pastries left on the tray. Karim waved his arm frantically at them to make them fly away. "Shoo! Shoo! Get out of here!" Most of the birds flew off, but a few hopped across the table with crumbs in their mouths and finished eating. As we sat down, the rest flew to the next table and started devouring their pastries.

"Oh, I forgot to tell you about the birds. They're here every morning. If you go back to the buffet for seconds, don't leave anything on your plate that you want to eat. These little guys will probably carry it off. Except for the eggs, though. I think it makes them kind of squeamish."

Rehema giggled, "They're so cute. Look, that one has a yellow beak."

"Yeah, I even had to take my wallet with me. I thought they would fly off with it."

Ramla suggested, "Michael, why don't you ask me your questions?"

"Good idea, Ramla. Let's start with the simple one. Besides these reptilians, just who are the people behind the Order? Would I know one if I met him?"

"That's the problem, Michael," Mudads proclaimed. "No one in our groups knows exactly who is really behind all of this. We know that some are bankers, oil barons, land owners, media moguls, but we can't pin it down to any one person or family."

"Do they have a name?"

Karim harshly replied, "The Order!"

Rehema waved him off. "Don't pay him any attention." Then she continued, "The original bloodlines don't have the same names as when they were first recruited by the reptilians, so we can't pin them down through the long history. But we can look at the wealthiest people today and start to see if they fit the criteria."

"You mean, see if they use others for personal gain."

Hanif jumped in, "Well, it's hard to get rich anywhere in the world without using someone along the way. Let's face it, unless you inherit your wealth, you are taking advantage of a low wage earner. And that is something we are all very aware of here in Egypt."

"I get the point," I said with some sorrow. "I feel a little guilty buying a t-shirt because it might have been made in a third world sweatshop. But there is no way to know. The stores hide that from us and won't tell the customers the truth."

Mudads added, "It happens here, too. Honesty is not behind most corporate executives, mostly greed."

Karim asked, "So Michael, how do you feel about these corporate giants?"

"I want to help, but I need more information. It's no good going after a sergeant if there is a general hiding in the wings giving orders."

"Exactly!" He hit the table with his fist. "Do you hate them?"

"Well, I wouldn't go so far as to say I hate them, but I don't like what they are doing to other people. Do you want me to hate them?"

"Yes, I do!"

Hanif confirmed my earlier statement, "Michael, it's like you said. Going after the corporations is like going after the sergeant; they are puppets in a larger picture. The ones we need to focus on are the generals behind the scenes."

"I would agree with that, Hanif, but I don't think that would solve everything."

"Why not?"

"Well, I've been brainwashed by the same system, just like everyone else in most countries. We've been trained to go to school, pledge a flag, support your nation, get a job, earn money, and climb the financial ladder. Most never consider the little guy when it comes to personal financial security. And we never learned about reptilians, Anunnaki bloodlines, or secret governments in school."

Ramla squeezed in, "Go on, Tumaini, you are on to something."

"If we take out a general or two, I'm sure that the Order has just as many colonels waiting to take their spots. They must have thought this through, so that probably won't work."

She nodded excitedly, "Yes, go on."

"So it makes sense to change the system."

In my head, I heard her praise, "Good job!"

"And that seems to me to be the most logical step. Change the system."

Rehema burst, "I like that idea. Change the system."

Hanif added, "Yes, change the system." He reached behind Rehema and slapped me on the shoulder. "See, you can solve problems."

Rehema continued, "It makes sense, Michael. But how?"

Ramla joined back in, "And that will be your task, Tumaini. With the scrolls you left behind, you will find the answers."

"It's in the scrolls?"

"I feel it. The information is in what you left behind. That will be your destiny, your challenge. You will find a way. I know it."

Karim piped in with a better tone, "Now we are getting somewhere." I nodded my head toward him to acknowledge his new emotion.

With a little less sarcasm, he asked, "So, Tumaini, what do you want me to do? How can I help?"

"When I decipher the scrolls, Karim, I'll let you know. Until then, I still need to learn all that I can."

Rehema smiled at Karim, then turned my direction. "What else do you need to know, Tumaini?"

"Well, I've always believed in life elsewhere. Aliens aren't that far off my map. I've even—"

Hanif interrupted, "Wait a minute. You mean that you believe in aliens, but you question if there is reincarnation?"

"I know. I'm a complicated guy." I shrugged. "So back to the aliens. I thought that aliens existed, but I didn't know anything about the different races and their technology. What else can you tell me?"

Ramla explained, "Well, we've already shared that some can travel faster than light. Some can travel without using a ship, too: they call that bi-location. And some have extremely well-developed psychic abilities, while other aliens do not."

"Anything else?"

"Yes, some know the secrets of the Universe. They are well schooled in the use of black magic."

"Like witches?"

"More than just witches, Tumaini, they can manipulate time and space. That makes any Earth witch look like a kindergartener compared to them.

"When higher dimensional dark aliens want to manipulate the humans, they share their powers with the bloodlines and grant them favors. Anyone who accepts these favors is now under the control of the Order. It's like tying a balloon to your wrist. Once you have the balloon tethered to you, you can manipulate it, drain the life force out of it by sucking air from the balloon, or you can pop it—meaning that they can kill you."

"Wouldn't it be nice to just go *Pop!* and stop the dark side?"

"If only it were that simple, Tumaini."

"So what else should I know?"

Hanif explained, "From what our seers can tell us, the different aliens and dimensional beings all come from different levels of development. Some have psychic and magic skills, while others only have technological advancements.

"The problem is with the dark aliens who have psychic and magic abilities. They hate any human who can do what they do if they use it for the good of mankind. As a matter of fact, they hate those kinds of humans so much that they want them all dead."

"Is that why the pharaoh hunted down all of the priests back in Tumaini's time?"

Ramla emphasized, "Most definitely! The pharaoh was under the control of the reptilians. That is why he unknowingly killed all the priests. The pharaoh did not know about the organic implants they had put in his brain, and he was powerless against their ability."

"So he was a puppet for the dark side?"

"Well, yes and no. Originally the pharaoh was not interested in helping them take over the planet; he was more interested in protecting his people. When they put those things in his brain, he became a different kind of puppet, not like the banking puppets you are aware of today."

"That's some pretty scary stuff, Ramla."

"Yes, it is, Tumaini. The reptilians are ruthless—and the mantids and greys are not far behind them. They all have their agendas."

"Is this what they call the New World Order?"

Mudads corrected me, "Not really. There is no New World Order because all of this has been going on for centuries. It would be more accurate to call them the Old World Order. For us, we just call them the Order."

"I've heard of this conspiracy before back home."

Karim asked, "So, what do you think now? Is it still a conspiracy?"

"After what happened in the restaurant and meeting with all of you, no, I'm convinced. And that says something for a philosophy professor. I usually won't believe anything anymore until I get a chance to research it for a long time."

The waiter came to the table and gave us our pancakes. He asked if there was anything else he could get for us. "Well, guys, do you want anything else that's not on the buffet?" They all said *no*, and I told the waiter, "Just the check, please."

Hanif looked at Rehema. "Honey, we need to go when you are done with your pancakes. We still have to open our shop."

Mudads followed up, "Yes, I'll need to go soon, too. If I don't show up, my workers will get worried—or maybe clear me out."

"Then let me get to the most important question before you all go. I remember you saying that the Order had...what...three plans? And you think they've tried two and failed. What were they?"

Ramla answered, "With the help of the light side, certain people all throughout history have been given clues as to what was really going on behind the scenes. These were people who asked for help, so it did not interfere with—Michael, don't get upset—free will."

"Go on. I won't comment on free will for now."

"The Order's first plan was to keep everyone in the dark about their control and brainwashing of the people. They relied heavily on the reptilian dominance plan that I mentioned earlier: enslavement through made-up borders, ownership, taxes, laws, and paid thugs—the police and militaries—to make the rich richer. With those few brave souls who kept teaching that something was going on behind in the shadows, more people began to wake up and learn that an evil plot was taking place.

"The second scheme was set up only by the reptilians. Near the end of the Second World War, the reptilians were afraid that the people around the globe would rally for peace. In order to keep the world under their control and in fear, they telepathically gave scientists around the world the secret to the atomic bomb.

"At one point, the people came close to tipping the scales toward peace. The reptilians would have nothing to do with this and instigated the outbreak of five nuclear wars. If for some reason the two main powerhouses did not go to war, the people would still be afraid of the potential for nuclear annihilation. If they did blow each other up, the suffering from the survivors would also feed the reptilians. Either way, the reptilians would win if this plan worked.

"However, with the help of many benevolent spirits and aliens, the governments fell to the pressure of the people and the Cold War came to an end.

"The reptilians know that people in general don't want to fight. They would rather live peacefully together than blow each other up. That is why the Order continues to develop new ways to block the spiritual growth of the planet."

"So what is the third plan?"

Ramla continued, "Tumaini, we don't know all of the details, but we do know that it is far worse than anything conjured up by the Order to this point. This one is bad. All I can tell you is that it involves microchipping everyone on the planet."

"You've got to be kidding."

"I wish I was, but there's something more horrifying than that. We can feel it, but we don't know exactly what the other part of that plan is. I think you will be the one who figures it out when all of your abilities return. That is why you must pursue your spiritual path now.

"Use the parchments and the heka and nekhakha that I gave you. These will bring back your powers again, and the last few pages of parchments might tell of their plans..."

"Wait a minute. There's more than just the parchments and the scrolls. What about the pieces that Mudads showed me?"

"Yes, Tumaini, those will help, but I can't tell you how. You will have to figure that out on your own."

Mudads inquired, "Michael, do you think you have enough information to start with?"

"More than I bargained for. How am I ever going to explain all of this to Constance and Hara?"

Hanif kidded, "Very carefully, I imagine."

"Constance can always give me a call," offered Rehema. "I had trouble digesting all of this in the beginning, too, so it might help for her to talk with someone who's already been through this."

"That's very thoughtful of you, thanks. And I might take you up on it."

Hanif glanced at his watch. "Rehema, we need to go. Michael, we will see you when you return. We are always here for you."

"Let me walk you guys out."

Mudads put up his palm. "There's no need."

"No, I insist. Let me walk you guys out."

As we moved away from the table, another flock of birds landed and pecked away at our leftovers. "I was going to ask if you wanted to take any of the pastries with you, but that idea went out with the birds." After they groaned, I chuckled, "I know, I just couldn't help myself."

When we got to the lobby, Ramla asked Karim if he could stay for a few minutes. She needed to talk to me in private. He told her that it would be fine and that he didn't need to be at work until noon.

"Tumaini, I will wait for you here. You can see the others to their cars."

"OK." I knew there was something left to discuss when the others left, so I was not surprised by Ramla's request.

Mudads heard us and insisted, "Michael, stay here with Ramla. She needs to speak with you. We can say our goodbyes here."

Hanif and Rehema agreed. "Yes, stay here and chat," Rehema added, "We will see you in a few days when you return."

"I don't mind."

"I know, but stay here." She leaned in and gave me a proper motherly hug. "We'll miss you. And call us if you need anything. You do have Hanif's card, don't you?"

"Yes, I do."

"Good, then. Go have fun in Luxor."

Hanif and I shook hands, but he also gave me a quick hug.

Mudads included, "And don't forget the incense for the temple."

"Ah, yes, thanks for reminding me." We shook hands and bowed to each other before they left.

Ramla asked, "Tumaini, is there somewhere we can talk in private?"

"How about over there on those couches by the perfume shop? They don't open until 9:00 a.m., so there won't be much traffic."

"That will do. Come, let's talk."

Karim mentioned as we walked across the lobby, "I'll wait for you here, Ramla." She nodded to him as we walked away.

———— • ————

"Tumaini, do you believe in God? You're from America. Are you Catholic, Baptist, Methodist?"

"I usually don't share my personal beliefs right off the bat, Ramla."

"Well, we don't have much time, do we?"

"Alright, blunt it is. Do you mean the god of the Catholic or Christian religion? I was raised Catholic. I even went to Catholic school and was an altar boy. But when I got a little older—maybe around high school or college—I couldn't understand why people would accept the underlying principle of Catholicism or Christianity."

"And what was that?"

"That we were created as imperfect beings, but we are judged by these religious gods for our imperfections. It's a no-win scenario, so I left that religion. And I know what these brainwashed religious people say: Their rebuttal is that we were created perfect and that we fell from god. But anyone with any logical sense, anyone with a brain, knows that a perfect being can't make an imperfect choice, otherwise it was never perfect to begin with—even if it did have the myth of free will." I looked her straight in the eyes and stated, "I won't worship or serve an imperfect god who creates imperfection and then judges, deceives, or punishes its imperfect creations."

"Go on. I know there's something else."

"OK, anything that uses fear as a control factor, I won't follow—that's the dark side. Even Christianity uses fear, even though they claim they don't."

"They do?"

"Sure they do. Accept Jesus as your savior and messiah—or else! Color me fear, if you please."

"Are you saying that you don't believe in any God? Did you stop believing?"

"No. I think there is a Universal Power, but I don't know how to describe what that power is. Some have called it the Isness, some have called it Universal Consciousness, Divine Source—take your pick. But I don't believe in the god that is portrayed in most religions. And none of the religions agree with each other anyway, so what makes one religion better than the other? They all believe that theirs is the right one and everyone else's is wrong. And then they'll kill you for not believing in their god."

After a few moments of silence, I prodded, "Where are you going with this Ramla? Why do you need to know this?"

"Because of your reaction to free will. Most religions believe we have it, and your use of free will dictates whether you go to heaven or hell."

"And what if you don't believe there is a real heaven or hell? If you believe in reincarnation, then that kind of wipes out that theory, don't you think? And if there is no Satan, like you said, then the only real hell is living under the tyranny of the Order."

"I am not here to change your mind, Tumaini, just to ask you to stay open to new ideas. The information about the Order was new to you, and you seemed to accept this without much question."

"That's because I've *lived it* within the last twenty-four hours. I've also lived without free will for my entire life.

"Can you explain that to me, please?"

"Sure. As I said earlier, we are individuals who have forced, controlled, limited, restricted choice. Free choice is an illusion. You don't even get to choose!" I leaned over and joked, "*Whoever controls the menu controls what you eat. Your choice is an illusion because you aren't in control of the menu.*" I emphasized, "The restaurant owners have already chosen for you."

She had a look of wonder on her face. "I'm impressed. I've never heard anyone put it that way before."

"Let me share with you what I tell my students. The false teachings that we have free will go much deeper." She nodded that she was ready, and I continued, "Choice and control are the real illusions here. The forward motion of time places you in a new experience—that is usually not of your choosing—and forces you to react. And what happens, or does not happen, with your next time-induced, restricted choice forces your next choice. If you lack the ability, knowledge, technology, or if you don't have the power to control time and instantly manifest, then you are controlled by some other process, law, being, or system. There is no free will, just control. Oh, and let's not forget that we could all be hooked up to a machine and living in a holographic computer program. No free will there, either."

"Fair enough, Tumaini. Just know that this could become a block in your future."

"How so?"

"Love includes everything, including faulty creations."

"I'll have to think on that one, Ramla."

"I have something else I need to tell you, but I will share it with you when you return from Luxor. Do be careful. I have felt that they are coming for you."

"Can you tell me anything else?"

"Not specifically, but these are dangerous beings. The Order is not to be taken lightly. Please be careful, promise me that." She put her hands on mine. "Remember, *Tumaini* does mean *hope*. And the world needs hope right now—more than ever."

"I agree with you there. By the way, who's going to bring me a good helping of hope? I need some, too."

"Just be strong, Tumaini. You have a destiny that is ready to unfold, and we are here to help you as much as we can. We'll talk when you return. And now I must go. God be with you."

"I'd rather have a bazooka for protection, but I'll take your God as a last resort."

"You do like to have fun, Tumaini. I like that. Your humor will help you through the tough times ahead. Keep the channel open. I will speak with you while you are in Luxor."

I projected to her, "Thank you. I appreciate all you have done." She smiled, got up, and walked away.

CHAPTER TEN

BAD LUCK AT LUXOR

We got into the hotel in Luxor around noon. Most of the trip there was a blur. I slept on the bus to the airport, I slept at the airport while we waited for our plane, and I slept through the entire flight—which is unusual for me because I usually can't sleep in a moving vehicle.

Shannon was a saint and a devil during our four-hour trip. She knew I was up all night with my new friends, so she told the group to let me sleep. However, she decided she needed some funny photos for her slideshow at the end of our tour and played prankster on me.

While we waited for our luggage at baggage claim, our group took great delight in showing me pictures of myself asleep with all kinds of touristy t-shirts laid across my body. There was everything from panoramic shots of the Nile to hot air balloon rides. And one t-shirt with a cartoon camel in front of the pyramids read: *I came to visit the pyramids, leave me alone!*— which pretty much sums up the experience of a typical tourist who has been pestered to buy a camel ride near the pyramids.

I didn't care that much, though. I was so tired that they could have laid a ten-ton granite block on top of me and I wouldn't have felt it. And the sleep was some of the best I'd had on the trip so far. I was dead to the world. I didn't even care that they had taken a photo of me wrapped in a bunch of women's Egyptian scarves.

———————

We had the rest of the day to ourselves. For those who weren't too tired, there was a side trip planned to the Luxor Bazaar around 5:00 p.m. It's a lot like the Khan, but smaller.

I went with a group of eight people to see the shops and to get a bite to eat. On the outskirts of the bazaar was a tiny restaurant that served a traditional Egyptian dish called Ful Medames. We all wanted to try this poor man's supper—which consisted of salted, mashed Fava beans cooked in olive oil, and cumin—so we stopped in for a plate. Besides the Ful, we also split two orders of Fatteh: a dish made with broken toast topped with various vegetables and seasonings.

Dinner just wasn't the same without my new friends. My mind kept venturing to stories about pharaohs, invading aliens, and plans for world peace. Talking about tourist sites and bargain hunting lost all of its interest for me. I felt out of place with my travel group, and I felt distant from the normal activities that ensued around me. My life was changed, and I didn't know if it was for the better or not.

When we finished dinner, the others wanted to shop and walk along the Nile. I told them I would catch up to them later. I needed to write Constance a note:

Hi Honey,

My mind was blank on what to write next. I tapped the pad a few times with my pen, as if tapping would bring about the right words. I thought, "What do I tell her in a short note that I can send from the hotel? If only I had internet or cell service over here, I could tell her so much more."

I tapped again. "It's probably best not to share what has happened to me anyway, at least not until I get home. I don't want her to worry for the rest of my trip. I'd need at least a few hours to try to explain all of this."

Hi Honey,

I'm having an awesome time over here. I made some new friends, found some papyrus for Hara, and saw the sunset between the pyramids. You would have loved it. I took some pictures for you.

~~Got to run, I have an assassin chasing after me~~.

"Scratch that," I said out loud. "That wouldn't be very smart to say."

Gotta run. My group is waiting for me to go shopping in Luxor. See you in a few days.
Miss you and love you so much,

Michael

It was a short note, so the group was only a few shops away. I did my best to look interested in the alabaster vases and statues that Luxor is famous for, and I couldn't help but wonder if any of these people knew what was really going on.

———◦—◦———

Back in Cairo, the Protectors of Souls were busy preparing. While Mudads and Hanif ran their shops, Rehema took the reigns and sent messages out to the other Protectors. Using the codes to communicate, she sent messages across all of Egypt letting everyone know that the time to help was now. Hope had returned.

In the meantime, Ramla gave Karim an assignment that would help put things in motion. The network needed to be in full swing when Tumaini returned to Cairo. She also told Karim to get Omar to assist him. He was a part of the plan, whether he knew it or not.

———◦—◦———

The following morning, twelve of our group boarded a small tour bus with Shannon and our new Egyptian guide. The rest of our party disembarked in Luxor to take a four-day cruise up the Nile to see a few different sites. They would meet up with us again in Cairo.

The cruise offered more food, drinking, and relaxing than sightseeing. It wasn't what I was looking for because it didn't provide any research opportunities for my books. I also liked spending more time at the historic sites, and our small group gave us a lot of leeway when it came to scheduling and exploring.

Like most local guides in the region, ours felt obliged to tell us stories during our bus ride that had been approved by the Egyptian Antiquities. So, asking him *Who really built the pyramids?* got me a cookie-cutter response. I couldn't believe it! He actually said, "They were built by the Egyptians, of course." There was no chance that he would be open to other possibilities, so I politely closed my eyes and took another nap.

We were on our way to the West Bank to see the Colossi of Memnon, the Ramesseum, and the Temple of Hatshepsut. The brakes on our bus squealed at one of the roadside checkpoints and woke me up. I looked out the window and saw three Egyptian soldiers all dressed in black uniforms. Each of them carried a machine gun and a sidearm. Two were on the ground, and the third was in a tiny concrete box that sat on a column about twenty feet high. The box had a shingled roof with three small windows and an open door at the back. Checkpoints in Egypt are a common thing, so I wasn't fazed by this in the least.

As our bus moved through the gate, I saw the two guards on the ground scramble behind us. The guard in the tower started yelling at our driver to move faster. I popped my head out of the window to see what was going on as a small cloud of dust grew from our tires.

One guard knelt on the ground and put his machine gun in a firing position. The guard in the tower grabbed a rocket launcher, while the third guard ran to the gate and lowered it. Speeding in our direction was a black car, and it showed no signs of stopping.

The guards cocked their guns and took aim at the vehicle. When the guard in the tower poked his rocket launcher through the window, the black car slammed on its brakes and immediately spun around. Its tires twisted and dug into the dirt until it sped off in the other direction. There was a massive cloud of dust, so I couldn't see the car make its full getaway.

A few more of our party put their heads out their windows and watched the scene behind us. All they saw was a brown ball of smoke lingering in the air and the guards reacting to something bad. Before rounding the corner, I could see the guard in the tower grabbing his walkie-talkie and making frantic gestures with his hand.

Our Egyptologist looked at Shannon. She was more than a little frightened by the event. Before she could speak, he suggested, "It could have been anything—drug runners, smugglers... We've even had kidnappers come after busses. They take a few hostages for ransom or to get a political prisoner released from jail. We should be out of harm's way."

"I'm responsible for them, you know. I have to keep them safe," she worried.

"I'm sure the guards have already called this in to all of the checkpoints. As long as we stay on the main road, we will be alright."

"Just in case, I think we should hire some security when we get there."

"I'll see to it," he reassured.

The rest of our group huddled into small groups to talk about the event. They all had their own theories as to what had happened. I stayed quiet. I hoped that I would not bring any harm to my travel companions. In my mind, I knew it was the same black car from the restaurant.

When we arrived at the two seated stone giants in Memnon, our guide had us sit on the bus while he made arrangements. Shannon met him outside, and he reported to her, "We'll have a security person meet us at the Ramesseum. It's pretty open here, so we would be able to see anyone coming from a few hundred yards away. We'll be safe, I promise."

She came back on the bus and told us the situation. She then gave us the choice of going back to the hotel or continuing with our sightseeing. We all agreed that it was safe, and we wanted to continue.

One of our male group members joked, "No pain, no gain. Let's get off this bus and see some mummies."

His wife playfully nudged him in the arm. "There's no mummies here, honey, just a bunch of old rock guys on hard recliners."

"Yeah, I bet they're bored—no cable and no remote controls. What's an Egyptian statue to do?"

"Woohoo! Party time! Let's go... With your approval, of course, Shannon." We chuckled at their lighthearted banter and exited the bus.

The group, minus me, hung around our guide and Shannon. While the guide shared the history of Memnon, I wandered away and made my own adventure.

There really wasn't a whole lot to see at this site, so I spent my time walking around solo and wondering if I'd been here in a past life. "Did I visit here as Tumaini? Did I live near here as a boy, a girl, a mother or father?" Knowing that we reincarnate many times opened up a whole new world of possibilities for me. Philosophically, I was in heaven—so many options and opportunities for the mind to explore.

Unfortunately, I didn't get any psychic hits about this place. There wasn't anything that made me feel like I'd been here before. It was definitely missing the feelings I'd had when I saw myself writing ancient hieratic. Those felt real, so it made me wonder what brings about those feelings. Is there some kind of emotional residue left on past experiences?"

During my inner debates, the guide yelled, "Yalla! Yalla! Everyone on to the bus."

I laughed to myself, "Do all of the guides say the same thing when it's time to leave? Our last guide yelled that, too."

———————

We were met at the Ramesseum by our hired security. He was a young fellow, probably in his early twenties, dressed in a black suit, white shirt, and black tie. His open jacket showed his mini Uzi and extra ammunition clips neatly snapped to his gun straps. I introduced myself to him before we were let loose to explore, "Hi, I'm Michael."

"I am Gahiji. Pleasure to meet you."

"Thanks for being here. I swear, you look so familiar. Have we met before?" Before he could answer, I raised my finger to question. "Are you the same fellow who did security for us when we crossed the desert to reach the Sun Temple of Niuserre?"

"No, but it could have been my brother. He works for the same security company that is based in Cairo. We could pass as twins."

"I see you are packing. Do you have a vest on, too?" He opened his shirt around his midriff to show me his black Kevlar vest. "Smart man. It's good to be protected."

"I couldn't agree more," he smiled. "I have something else to show you, too."

That statement took me by surprise. "It's not something bad, is it? I swear, I didn't mean to rip that sticker off the food cart."

"Oh, no, sorry to give you that impression. It's this..." He opened his shirt up a little higher. It was the amulet for the Protectors of Souls.

"Holy cow! How did you...?"

"It was Karim and Omar. They sent me. Ramla—you know Ramla, don't you?"

"Yes." I just smiled.

"Well, Ramla saw something in a vision that worried her. She told Karim to contact the security company in Luxor and flag any request that came from Shannon's tour group. I was sent to be with you for protection."

"You've got to be kidding me."

"No, and she said you would say something like that. I will be taking care of you for the rest of your stay. I was hired to be with your group until you leave Luxor. It is my honor to be of service."

"Gahiji, the honor is all mine."

As we walked toward the stone pillars to catch up with the group, I mentioned, "And I have a favor to ask you."

"What is it, Tumaini?"

"That's my favor. I'd like to keep my identity a secret around these nice folk, at least for now. I don't want them to get caught up in all of this. I'm still wrapping my head around being Tumaini, and I'm not really ready to share this with them yet."

"If that is what you wish, it will be so."

"Thanks, I do appreciate that."

"Tumaini—I mean Michael—I do my best when I am not seen with the group. I'm more like a hunter who protects the village."

"Let me guess, that's what your name means, isn't it?"

"Yes. How did you know?"

"It's become a pattern recently. Go, do your thing. Shannon is waving me down. I think she wants me to be more of the party instead of on my own."

"Yes. I'll be watching you."

"Thanks."

True to his word, Gahiji stayed away from our group and patrolled the grounds like a skilled huntsman. We walked around the massive stone pillars knowing that we had our own version of a protecting angel. I don't think anyone really felt in danger anyway; the car was only a small distraction compared to the new experience of the ruins.

On one of the pillars inside the complex, I saw a symbol carved about fifteen feet from the ground. It was clearly done by an amateur, as it was sloppy, uneven, and terribly etched in the stone. I recognized the symbol as a Sacred Geometry symbol called the Seed of Life. I asked our Egyptologist what it was, and he said it was nothing but vandalism and should be ignored. He then called our attention to a huge sixty-foot wall covered with hieroglyphs reaching up to twenty feet.

On our way over, I thought to myself, "I'll have to ask Ramla about that when I get back."

In my head, I heard Ramla's voice, "Yes, we will need to talk about that." I snickered, which turned into a comical snort, and that caught the attention of the group.

Shannon leaned over to ask, "What is it, Michael? Did you see something funny in the carvings?"

"Oh, nothing. I just... It's nothing."

After spending another fifteen minutes at the wall, it was time to leave this site and head onward to the last one, so Shannon waved everyone along. "Let's get out of here, folks. There's a lot more to do today."

The man from the couple joked, "Yeah, let's get to it. Ramses is baked and done; on to the hat lady."

Shannon politely corrected him, "You mean Hatshepsut?"

"Yeah, that lady...the hat lady." We all laughed as we headed toward the bus.

———————

A row of tent-like shops that stretched about an eighth of a mile paved the way into Hatshepsut's Temple. I took advantage of the opportunity to buy Constance a set of purple Egyptian cotton pajamas. They had really pretty Mediterranean embroidery on them, which I knew she would like, and I also picked up some earrings and a few scarves.

Shannon smiled at me, "You are so thoughtful."

"Nah, could you imagine me coming home from a trip like this and not picking up something for my wife? I'm just playing it safe. I like sleeping in my own bed."

"Well, you can cover it up if you'd like, but I know different. You're a good man."

"Awww, thanks, Shannon. I appreciate that."

"C'mon, let's go see the temple."

While our group ventured inside, I left them once again to go and talk with the temple priests. I still needed research information for my books, and I knew if I gave them a handful of Egyptian pounds, they would give me an earful of information about the temple and how life was back then. It was well worth it, and much better than the standard tour.

Gahiji was still protecting us, hovering like a hawk just a few yards away.

On the way back to our hotel, Gahiji sat by Shannon at the front of the bus. I was hoping to get a chance to talk with him, but I knew he needed to focus on his job. When we got to the last checkpoint, he got off the bus and talked with the guards. They were the same three soldiers from before, so he was able to question them about the black car. When Gahiji got back on the bus, he moved to the very last seat, which was close to where I was sitting.

He sat upright and was very focused. He kept looking out the back of the bus and to the sides as if he was hunting for something. After we passed through the gate, I gave him a nod to say *thanks* for his help. That's when he patted his chest over his amulet and nodded back.

We drove for another ten miles. I took picture after picture of the crop fields and locals. As we got closer to the Nile, the farmlands turned into tiny two-story shops and houses. Some of them were built so close together that you could barely fit an ox on the tight streets.

Unexpectedly, our bus slowed down and came to a stop. There was a parade of women dressed in traditional black Muslim gowns and burkas. They were wailing and crying as they walked across the intersection in front of us. Our guide explained that it was a funeral.

"Would it be disrespectful to take a photo?" I asked.

He looked up and pointed to the sky. "No. Just pay your respects and ask for Allah's blessings."

I leaned out of the window to focus my camera and get a few good photos. I snapped about five pictures before I zoomed out to get a broader angle. From my view finder, I could see one of the side streets a block away.

At that moment, a black car pulled into the intersection, stopped, and a popping sound echoed through the concrete buildings. Then a small explosion occurred.

In a panic, all of the women went screaming through the streets in terror and ran for cover. Gahiji, being incredibly alert, pounced on me and covered my entire body like he was one of the president's secret service. As he pulled off two rounds from his sidearm, the car squealed its tires and left the scene.

Shannon panicked, "Is everyone alright?" That's when she saw Gahiji climbing off of my body and both of us coming back in through the window. "Michael, you have blood on your face. Oh my gosh!" she exclaimed.

Gahiji looked at me and saw the blood. "He's OK. It was a scratch from my gun."

I rubbed at the cut and knew it was nothing serious. "Thanks, Gahiji. I owe you one."

"No, you don't. They didn't even come close to you. But they hit one of the tires." The bus was drastically tilting toward the driver's side at that point. Our group was all in shock and in different stages of panic.

"What's going on here?" asked the man from the couple. "Are we cursed by the mummies or what?!"

Gahiji commanded, "Everyone stay here for a moment." He ran off of the bus and checked our perimeter. When he saw that it was clear, he ordered everyone to get off and go into the closest shop. After he called in the attack to his company, he told us that he and the driver would change the tire so we could get out of the area as fast as possible. Twenty minutes later, we were back on the road and heading home.

Shannon came over to me and asked, "Michael, why did he jump on you? I mean, don't get me wrong, but there was a bus full of people. Why did he protect you alone?"

I could tell that she was a little suspicious and suggested, "I think it's because I was the most exposed. Most of me was hanging out the window."

Shaking her head after a second, she agreed, "Yeah, that makes sense. I'm glad you're safe. Is there anything I can get you for your cut?"

"No, it's really just a scratch. Are you OK?"

"Yes, I'm fine."

"Don't you think you should say something to the others?"

"Yes, yes, I will, now that my blood pressure has come down." She stood up and apologized to everyone and assured them that this type of thing has never happened to any of her tour groups in the last twenty years. Everyone on the bus came to her defense and told her that it wasn't her fault and that she shouldn't take any blame.

The wife of the couple reassured her, "Don't think anything of it. There's no way you could have known. Besides, this is the most exciting trip I've ever been on." The rest of us agreed with her and did all we could to let Shannon know we supported her.

The last few miles to the hotel were abuzz with emotional talk from our troop. While we gabbed, Shannon followed Gahiji's advice and agreed to hire an additional security guard for the remainder of the trip.

At the hotel, Gahiji, Shannon, and our Egyptologist went off alone and spent about an hour going over the rest of the itinerary. Gahiji was all business and wanted to be prepared for anything that could threaten our tour. Since there was no chance that we would get to talk that night, I practiced patience and went to bed.

———————

The next morning, I decided to skip breakfast so I could sleep in. The bus was leaving at 7:00 a.m., and I walked out from my room at 6:45 a.m. sharp.

Across from the elevator was a small sitting area with two armchairs and a long coffee table that sat between them. In one of the chairs was a man in his late thirties. He was dressed like Gahiji, including the same Uzi machine gun bulge in his jacket. He stared at me intently as I walked down the long hallway, which made me feel a little uncomfortable. I hadn't expected anyone to be there, especially with a gun.

"Morning," I sang with a friendly tone.

He sprang up to greet me. "Good morning, sir."

I looked out at the blue sky through the windows. "Nice day out, isn't it?"

"Yes, it is. Did you have a good night's sleep, Tumaini?"

"How did you...?"

"I'm sorry. I should have introduced myself earlier. But it was late last night when I arrived, and you were in your room already asleep. I am Asim, your protector. Gahiji asked for me personally."

"Does your name mean—?"

Before I could finish, he affirmed, "Yes, it does. I am a protector, and I am also a Protector." He pulled out his amulet and nodded to me.

"You guys are everywhere. You weren't here all night, were you?"

"Yes, I was. It is my pleasure to be of service. Gahiji needed to do some advance surveillance, and I volunteered to take first watch."

"I don't know what to say, Asim. Thank you."

"I serve from the heart, and I don't require any gratitude, but I welcome it when it is offered. And you are most welcome, Tumaini."

"Asim, can you call me Michael? I don't want to let the others know just yet. I wouldn't know how to explain it to them."

"If that is your wish, it will be done. Shall we join your group?" He pushed the button, and the elevator arrived in less than ten seconds.

On the way down, he mentioned, "Gahiji filled me in about the two attempts on your life. Because the car was spotted, and you know what the assassin looks like, we both feel that this assassin won't make another attempt so soon. I imagine that they need to do some more planning, especially since Gahiji shot at them yesterday."

"I hope it's not like this every day. I don't want to see anyone get hurt, including me or you."

"The Order doesn't usually attack like this, Michael. Most of the time it is done covertly."

"That's what Hanif said."

"After what has happened these last two days, I have a feeling they will go back to their normal way of doing things, which is to leave no trail. We all think they are scared and they acted irrationally."

"Well, like I said, I don't want to see anyone get hurt."

"We'll do our best to make sure that won't happen, Michael."

"Great, and thanks again."

———————

Gahiji was in the lobby with Shannon and our guide. He nodded to us as we walked up.

"Morning, folks. How's it going?"

"Everything's fine, Michael. How did you sleep?" asked Shannon.

"Like a rock. And I think I had my own angel watching over me." Asim smiled.

I looked at my other Protector's friendly face. "Morning, Gahiji."

"Morning, Michael. I was just telling Shannon that I scouted the area and called in to all of the checkpoints. We should have a safe journey today. There has been no report of any terrorist activity."

"Well, I have to tell you that I feel very safe knowing that you and Asim are on the job."

Shannon's head snapped in my direction. "Who is Asim?"

"I am, ma'am. I was already casing the hotel this morning to look out for your guests. I was getting ready to report in to you. I am the second security guard."

"Wow! You two are amazing. I'm going to have to call your company and tell them how grateful we are for such wonderful helpers."

"It's our pleasure to be of service." Asim bowed.

"Well, it's time to get on the bus. We've got a fun day planned."

On the way out, Asim took position in the front, and Gahiji followed in the rear.

—————————

We were headed back to the west bank for the day. Our group was very cheerful and not even the slightest bit concerned about any terrorist attempts. We all looked forward to seeing Medinet Habu, which is the Temple of Ramses III; Deir el-Medina, which is the Valley of the Workers; and taking the donkey path from the Valley of the Workers to reach the Valley of the Kings.

Both of our guards remained on high alert during our bus ride there and back. The only thing that was of any concern was a tan minivan that seemed to be following our bus for a few miles after the first checkpoint. When Asim and Gahiji went to the back of the bus to get a better look, the van turned off at one of the main intersections and headed north.

For me, I was glad that our day trip was both boring and exciting: boring, in that there were no shots fired at us, and exciting because our donkeys were very feisty on the trail and kept veering off of the path to eat. As we rode, our new security team walked in a standard two-man formation.

I really wanted to talk with Gahiji and Asim, but I knew it would be selfish of me to distract them from protecting the whole tour group. It would have to wait for another day, or for a quieter time, so I spent my day gathering more information from the locals and temple priests.

———

We had to leave a little earlier the next morning to see the Temple of Hathor at Dendera. From there we would venture on to Abydos to visit the Temple of Seti I and the Osirian Temple located just behind it.

Today's trip was a little different in that we traveled in a large convoy of tour buses and taxi cabs that were protected by the Egyptian military. There must have been over twenty buses and a handful of cabs that were sandwiched between two armed vehicles at the front and two armed vehicles at the rear. Because we had extra protection, Gahiji and Asim didn't have to be as watchful.

Asim sat closer to me than Gahiji, so I showed him the photo that I'd taken at the Ramesseum. He acknowledged, "Yes, I know of this symbol. When we get to Abydos, I have something to show you."

"What is it?"

"It's too hard to explain. You need to see it and just be mindful of it. Do you know much about Sacred Geometry?"

"I know a little about it. When you travel the world and look at the large monuments, it's hard not to notice the Phi ratio that was used to create such beauty."

"Well, there may be more to Sacred Geometry than just the Phi ratio."

"What do you mean?"

"I'm not quite sure how to go about this, Michael. Some say that Sacred Geometry"—he bent closer to my ears so only I would hear—"was developed by the reptilians and used by the Order. It's said that the Order uses Sacred Geometry in a lot of their rituals and buildings. Others say that it was Creator's tool for manifesting light, sound, colors, and our Universe."

"What do you believe? I mean, is it good or bad?"

"I don't know, Michael. I kind of look at it like intention and energy. Intentions can be good or bad. Energy—great power—can be used for good and for evil, too. It's all directed by the quality of the soul. So, in my humble opinion, I think that Sacred Geometry can be used by both sides."

"I like how you put that, Asim. The same thing could be said about magic."

"Yes, exactly. There can be white and black magic. It all depends on the intent."

Gahiji looked back at Asim and gave him a hand signal. "Michael, excuse me for a moment. We are coming to a main intersection up ahead, and I need to keep an eye out."

"Of course. You do your thing, and I'll catch up with you when we get to Abydos."

——————

The Temple of Hathor was interesting. The Dendera light bulb was in a tiny, hot, cramped crypt. We saw the restored ceilings that portrayed the magnificently painted hieroglyphs, and we also saw the Dendera zodiac.

It was when we were in the Temple of Seti that Asim showed me the carvings near the ceiling that looked like a helicopter, a submarine, and a UFO or a fighter jet.

"Now those are interesting," I exclaimed. "Having just experienced everything that I have in the last few days, that doesn't surprise me in the least—especially the UFO carving. I bet that the Egyptian government won't acknowledge that one."

"Those are interesting. And you are right, no government wants to admit there are UFOs, especially since most of the governments are working with them and are under their influence.

"Come, we should go to the Temple of Osiris. I will show you another symbol called the Flower of Life. I'm friends with some of the guards back there, so they will let you go down and take a few pictures."

"And what if that symbol is a deception, too? You know, set up by the Order."

"Michael, I guess time will tell. But for now, let's go take a look."

——————

The temple itself was a mess. There was a deep pool of standing water around all of the stone columns. The water had a slight smell to it, and algae covered most of the surface. There was a set of wooden stairs that led down to a platform near one of the pillars in the middle of the complex.

On that pillar were a few symbols that looked like they were painted on the stone. All of the symbols were based upon the Flower of Life, including a Seed of Life that was close by. None of the other pillars had anything carved or drawn on them.

"So, Asim, why are you showing this to me?"

"Ramla wanted me to. She said it would open your mind to other possibilities. She didn't say if it would be bad or good, though. I'm sure she had her reasons."

"Oh, man!"

"What, Michael?"

"Mudads kept telling me to meditate in a temple while we were in Luxor. I totally forgot, and we are just about out of time here."

"Relax, I know of a place in Karnak where people do some meditating. I can show it to you tomorrow, if you wish."

"That'd be great. Just out of curiosity, do you meditate?"

"Yes, I do. And I use Hanif's special blend."

We both recited together, "Incense from the Temple Gods."

"Yes, I picked up a few boxes myself. I'll use some of it tomorrow."

"It will be a good journey, I'm sure. And speaking of journeys, it is time to head back to the hotel, Michael. Did you get all of the pictures that you wanted?"

"I did, thanks."

"Good. Let's go, then. Tomorrow should be an exciting day."

CHAPTER ELEVEN

EXCUSE ME, HAVE WE SEKHMET BEFORE?

The sun was already blazing on the horizon when we arrived at the Temple of Luxor. As we were walking off of the bus, our guide told us that this temple was an important place of worship and was built to honor the creator god Amon-Ra. He also said that this city was called Thebes back then and was the capital of Egypt during the New Kingdom.

To get into the main entrance of this complex, we all had to pass through two gigantic walls called the pylon. Both of them were over seventy-eight feet high and two hundred and thirteen feet wide. In front of each pylon were two thirty-foot statues of Ramses II—or Royal Ka statues, depending on whom you talk to. They were accompanied by a single remaining pink granite obelisk that towered on the left. The statues were built to guard the complex, as only priests, pharaohs, and other officials were allowed in.

I could just imagine them asking in a deep, foreboding voice, "What is the password? Only the chosen may enter."

I looked at the Ramses twins and playfully joked, "Scarab."

I didn't expect anyone to hear me, but Shannon asked, "What was that, Michael?"

"Um…I said *scarab*. I imagined those two statues as bouncers at a nightclub, and you had to say the correct password to get in. I was just having fun."

"Oh, OK."

The woman from the couple giggled, "That was funny. I like that." Then she imitated in a deep, manly voice, "Scarab. You may pass."

We laughed a bit, and then her husband chimed, "Well, we got the password right. Let's go in."

———◆———

Our guide was deep in his talk telling us how Akhenaten's father, Amenhotep III, was the first to begin building this temple, and how it was finished years later by the boy king, Tutankhamun. Then other conquerors, like Ramses II and Alexander the Great, came and added to the complex.

When we walked into the Outer Courtyard, we saw Amenhotep's colonnade: two rows of very tall, open-flower papyrus columns that connect Ramses' courtyard to Amenhotep's courtyard. I looked over toward Asim to see if this was the place he was talking about for meditating. "Not here, Michael. The place I was thinking about was in Karnak. However, I don't want to stop you if you want to meditate here. This is a place of worship to many."

"No, I'll take your advice and wait until Karnak. Is there anything special that I should know about? You know…" I patted my amulet that was under my shirt.

"What does your heart tell you?"

"That this place feels familiar to me, like I've been here before."

I closed my eyes and took a breath. Then I saw a quick glimpse of the outer pylon as it was centuries ago. The walls were pristine and smooth, with vividly colored hieroglyphs and murals painted from the sandy ground to the top. There were also six brightly colored gigantic-sized statues of Egyptian men standing beside the Ramses twins. Three were on the outer left of the seated Ramses II, and three were on the outer right. Rounding out the picture were four flagpoles that spanned the height of the pylon with streamers dancing in the wind.

"That was cool," I marveled. "I just got a flash of the outer temple in its heyday."

"That is interesting. Were you there at that time?"

"I don't think so. I'm not sure. I don't know if I just saw it from history or if I was really there. But I can tell you that it was from the past and not my imagination. That vision was too vivid and real. I couldn't see anything like that until just a few days ago."

"Ramla was right, you are progressing. She mentioned that you would."

"How well do you know Ramla?"

"She has been our teacher since I took the oath to protect others. Both Gahiji and I have met with her more than once. She has especially been an inspiration to me for spiritual growth."

"Yeah, she made an impression on me, too. Hey, Asim, is there a place where I could have a few moments to be by myself? I don't have to stay with the group the entire time."

"Yes, there is. To the south, just past the Hypostyle Hall—the one with thirty-two pillars—there's an antechamber called the birth room. You might be able to have a few minutes alone. Not many of the tourists seem to go there because it's not in great shape."

"I think I'll do that. Do you mind?"

"Not at all."

I tapped Shannon on her shoulder and told her I was heading on my own for a few minutes.

"Why don't you take Gahiji with you? I'd feel better if someone went along."

"Shannon, I'm a big boy. I can take care of myself, honest."

"I know, but would you do it for me? I don't want to worry about you."

"Only because you insist, but I'm sure I'll be alright."

"I know." She winked at me. "Thanks for taking him."

She went over to Gahiji and asked him if he would walk with me. He nodded, looked at me to catch my attention, and he started walking toward the south end of the temple. I thought he might walk with me, but I remembered that he preferred keeping a distance.

When we got to the antechamber, I complimented him, "Gahiji, you are good at your job, no question about that. Thanks for watching out for us."

"You are most welcome, Tumaini."

"You remind me of a well-trained sniper: always watching from a distance, yet so dedicated to your job."

"You honor me with your kind words."

"No, seriously, you and Asim are excellent Protectors. Your dedication is quite admirable. Do you want to come in and meditate with me?"

"I would love to, but I should keep a watchful eye for now. Maybe we could meditate together at another time."

"I'd like that."

"Go in, Tumaini. I will keep watch."

"Thanks, Gahiji. I won't be long. I just want a few minutes to myself."

Asim wasn't far off in his description. Compared to some of the tombs and other temples, these rooms were more like an old musty cellar. A few carvings were on the walls, and they were not in great condition.

I sat down for a moment and then shifted to a half-lotus position. It didn't take long to quiet my mind, and when I did, I caught glimpses of ancient Egypt again. More than the images, though, I could feel the emotions of that time. It was very festive: lots of people in celebration, with a huge parade of people carrying statues of deities. They were moving down the Avenue of Sphinxes and into the temple complex.

This was a new experience for me. I'd never felt emotions from my past visions, but this one felt full of life. I enjoyed it and reveled in the happiness from the festivities.

Then it hit me. I felt other emotions, like the walls were talking to me. I felt death. I felt cold. I could hear the screams coming from the walls themselves. It was fear. My breath shortened and sped up immensely. My skin grew cold, and I could feel the terror from something in pain.

It was animals. I could feel the fear and pain from animals. Then I saw the herds of cattle being driven into the temple to be sacrificed by the pharaoh. I screamed out loud, "Nooo!" I saw men slashing their throats without any remorse. The cattle were writhing in pain on the floor as their life flowed out of them. There were piles and piles of dying cattle all around. Then I opened my eyes in horror.

Gahiji ran into the room with his Uzi drawn. "Tumaini, are you alright? What's wrong? Who was here? You are as white as a ghost."

"Oh my gosh, Gahiji. It was horrible. I felt...I felt the emotions of this place. At first it was wonderful; then it turned into death and blood. I saw a festival, but then I saw hundreds of cattle being slaughtered to honor a made-up god. It was horrible. The gore was overwhelming. How could someone be so inhumane to so many innocent animals?"

"Are you sure you are alright?"

"Yes, yes, thanks. I just need a moment. That's not a feeling I ever want to relive again. That's why I'm a vegetarian. I don't like killing things. It's not the loving way."

"I'm going to take a look outside, anyway."

"Seriously, Gahiji, it wasn't a person. It was this place. The emotions were in this place. It's like the walls had a soul and that soul reached out to me. I felt its happiness and its agony. I only wish I had a way to heal it."

"What?"

"I wish I had a way to heal it. Nothing should have that much pain stuck inside it. This temple should be able to be healed."

"That sounds strange, Tumaini. Can you heal this place?"

"I don't know. I've never even considered doing anything like that before. What could we do to heal this place? If only Ramla were here."

In my head, I heard Ramla say, "Michael, raise your energy and heal its pain."

"What?" I asked.

Again, she repeated, "Raise your energy and heal its pain."

"Gahiji, did you hear that?"

"Hear what?"

"It was Ramla. She spoke to me. I didn't know if you could hear her, too."

"You can talk with Ramla without speaking?"

"Yes, we…we share a connection. I can sometimes hear her thoughts when I mention her name."

"Are you joking with me, Tumaini?"

"No, I'm serious. I can hear her thoughts sometimes, and she seems to be able to hear my thoughts just fine. Maybe I can communicate with her when I say her name. That's happened a few times since I met her. Maybe that's the key: I have to mention her name to make the psychic connection.

"So, how do we heal this place?" I thought to myself. "She said to raise my energy. What does that mean?"

Asim showed up inside the antechamber. "Michael, are you alright? We heard a scream and came running."

"Yes, I'm fine. Everything is OK. I had a new experience is all, and I paid the price for it."

His facial expression showed his confusion. "What are you talking about?"

Shannon and the others came into the room before I could answer. "What's going on in here, Michael?"

"Shannon, you wouldn't believe me if I told you." They all stood there looking at me. "Guys, I'm sorry. I didn't mean any harm. Do you mind if I spend a few moments with Asim and Gahiji? I think they can help."

Shannon said with some frustration, "Michael, I'm not sure what is going on with you, but I sure hope you can fix it."

I could tell that she was a little perturbed with me. "I'm sorry, Shannon— and you guys, too. I'll be fine. I just need a minute." They looked at me as if I had a virus or something. "Seriously, guys, I'll be alright. I...I...well, I'm sorry. I'm fine. I'll join up with you later."

The husband hollered, "C'mon folks! Let's give him some air! These places can play tricks on the sanest of people."

As they walked away, I added, "Thanks for understanding. I promise that I won't cause any more trouble."

The crew walked out of the room, and I heard from a short distance, "There's not a whole lot to look at here. Let's go back to the columns and do some bowling." Their laughter got softer as they walked away.

"Well, now that we are alone, guys, I'm sorry."

Gahiji explained to Asim, "Tumaini had a vision, and he felt great pain from the walls. Then Ramla spoke to him. She told him to heal its pain. Do you know what that means?"

"Heal its pain? How?"

"I have an idea." I glanced at both of them and walked up to one of the walls. "There is power in focus and meditation. And from what I have learned, the more people who meditate together, the stronger the intention becomes."

Gahiji asked, "Do you mean like prayer? What do we pray for?"

"Love, healing, forgiveness, releasing... Those words just popped into my head."

"Those sound good to me."

"What do you say? We can take a moment and focus our thoughts to this temple. Maybe, just maybe, we can make a difference."

"I would like to help," offered Asim.

"So would I," added Gahiji.

"Great!" I exclaimed.

"I don't know why, but I feel like we should touch the walls"—I nodded toward the left—"then focus on sending love and healing to this land."

Asim agreed, "Yes, yes, that sounds good. I have the same feeling."

We positioned ourselves at each of the three walls inside the antechamber. Then Gahiji spoke:

"Divine Creator, we thank you for sending your love to heal this land; we thank you for strengthening our love to heal these walls; and we thank you for guiding us to help one another. We will continue to protect as needed, love each other more, and show mercy at every outcome. We, the Protectors of Souls, thank you for this opportunity to express our love and help those who are in pain. With this, we pray."

After a few moments of silence, we stopped touching the walls and looked at each other. "That was well prayed, Gahiji."

"It was from the heart, Tumaini. Do you think it helped?"

"I don't know. But the intent was sincere, and that should say something."

Asim replied, "That it should. Let's get with the others and head back to the hotel. We'll be going to Karnak later tonight. You should rest now and meditate when you are there."

"You've got to be kidding me. Today's meditation didn't turn out that great, and I scared half of our group. Are you sure?"

"I think you might have a different experience there. You did not have an intention here, but there you can set your intention. That's something that Ramla taught me."

"Yeah, that's some good advice. When I meditate there, I'll set an intention for a better experience. I'll have to think on that one."

"Good, let's be on our way, then."

———•——•———

We were the last ones on the bus. I could see that they were all looking at me differently. When I sat down, the man from the couple counted, "One, two, three!" Then they all started singing:

"For he's a ghostly good fellow,
For he's a ghostly good fellow,
For he's a ghostly good fellow,
Who scared us half to death."

They all laughed and laughed. Then he said comically, "It was the best we could do on such short notice. We're glad you're OK."

I grinned as he slapped my shoulder, and then he continued, "Don't take it too hard. You're not the first person to have a ghostly encounter on this trip. Why, the Mrs. and me saw something spooky at the Valley of the Kings. It scared the *you know what* out of me. I'm just glad that no one saw *us* freaking out."

His wife added, "And Shannon said she saw the famous dead pharaoh riding his chariot there a few years back, so don't feel bad."

Shannon nodded her head to acknowledge that it was true. "Is that what happened to you, Michael? Did you see something?"

"Actually, I felt something horrible."

"See, you're not the first. Laugh it off, dude," jabbed the guy with a beer in his hand. "Nobody here's judging ya." *Skoosh!*

"You guys are great."

The wife leaned over toward me. "Next time, take a picture so we can all see it. Hey Shannon, you can turn this into a ghost hunter's tour. What do you think?"

"That would be awesome, and we could end the trip with a haunted Halloween party."

The husband put his arm around his wife. "You should be Cleopatra, and I'll be the mummy and chase you around the room."

She held his hand and kissed his cheek. "Oooh baby. Can I unwrap that present?"

Shannon groaned, "Hey, get a room...or at least a coffin and a tomb."

The rest of the ride was filled with playful jabs and jokes about ghosts and goblins. Nobody brought up anything else about my encounter.

After our dinner break back at the hotel, we all gathered on the bus to head to Karnak. I sat across from Gahiji and asked him, "Do you know anything about the parade that I saw back in the temple?"

"It could be many things, but my guess is that it was the Opet festival. There was a mile and a half procession from Karnak to Luxor to celebrate renewal and fertility. From what I know, they paraded a statue of Amon-Ra through the Avenue of Sphinxes and celebrated for almost a month. That would explain the good feelings that you felt."

"Yeah, those feelings were good. Let's not bring up the other feelings."

"If you wish, but you can learn from them."

"You know, for a young guy, you're pretty smart."

"We all have gifts and our destiny."

"Yes, and it seems that mine are just starting to arrive."

"Better late then never, right?"

"Right, and they say that destiny catches up with you, whether you want it or not."

"Consider it a blessing, Michael, and it will be so."

"Good advice, Gahiji. Hey, it looks like we are here."

"Yes, it is a short trip from the hotel. Wait on the bus. Asim and I will check things out for you."

Besides what had happened earlier in the day, I was actually looking forward to meditating again. I bypassed Shannon and asked Asim where I should go. He mentioned that it might be best for me to stay with the group until sunset. He also said that after the usual tour was over—which lasts for a few hours because the complex is one of the largest holy places in the world—he would stay and take me to a special temple for meditating. He went on to say that he knew a temple guard who would let me remain after hours and meditate without the crowds. And because we were so close to our hotel, we could easily catch a cab back without any problems.

"That's a great idea, Asim. Thanks for putting this together."

"Michael, I must warn you. It's rumored that seven children were killed in the area by a cave-in at the temple. They call it the Infants' Grave. If you are that sensitive to feelings, you might feel their pain."

"Thanks for the warning. I was thinking about that during dinner, too. I'm going to have to learn how to handle those dark emotions when I feel them. I can't run from them forever. Where would I go? People die all over the planet."

"That's a good point. Do you have a plan?"

"Yes. It's called *try, try, try again until I succeed*."

"Well, let me know if that works. I don't have a better suggestion for now."

———————

Asim was right. The tour took a few hours, and before we knew it, it was sunset. I saw him walk up to Shannon for a short talk, then he came over to me.

"Everything is good, Michael. I will stay with you while Gahiji goes back with the others. Once he is done escorting them, he wants to come back and meditate with you. Is that OK?"

"That's more than OK. Do you want to meditate with us, too?"

"I might. It all depends on my friend. If he will stay and watch, I'll come in for a bit."

"You're more than welcome, Asim. I know you are security for our group, but I look at you more as a friend."

"Me, too, Michael. I wish we had more time to visit. So far, it's been mostly work."

"Yeah, I know. I've wanted to spend more time with you and Gahiji, but I didn't want to be selfish."

"Selfish?"

"Sure. You were hired to watch the group, not just me, so I didn't want to pull you away from protecting the others."

"That's pretty considerate of you."

"Not all Americans are selfish, Asim."

"I didn't mean it that way, Michael."

"I know. But I also know that many countries look down at the U.S. because of its greedy, capitalistic nature. We aren't all greedy, just a small portion of Americans are."

"It's the same all around the world, don't you think?"

"I do. I guess that is why the Order still operates the way it does. Do you know much about the Order?"

"I know they exist, and I know that aliens are behind the scenes working with them. Other than that, I don't know any details. As a Protector, I'm just here to help where I can."

"That's a pretty noble cause, Asim. You should be proud."

"I'd like to think I'm more humble than proud."

"Oh, you are. You are."

As the others left for the bus, Asim and I began walking toward the northern wall of the complex. There was nothing but rocks, sand, and debris along our three hundred yard jaunt. It was a rough path, so we had to keep our eyes glued to the ground.

The sun had completely disappeared by this time, too, and we were only able to see because of the portable light towers that were run by generators. The generators weren't terribly loud, but you could hear the mechanized chugging and hum from each of the gas-powered machines.

"Where are we going again, Asim?"

"To the Temple of Ptah. There is a three-room chamber there that we can meditate in. It's just up ahead."

As we came to the outer pylons, we were met by a short man in a grey gallibaya and kaftan (a traditional full-length shirt and a floor-length gown worn over it). He also donned a traditional white turban worn by many of the temple guards. Asim greeted him, and he indicated that everything was ready.

"Hey, Asim, I brought my own incense. I know that some places allow us to use it in the temple. Would you ask him if it's OK?"

The temple guard said in a heavy accent, "I understand English. Here, let me see." After smelling it a few times, he asked with a lifted tone, "Is this *Incense of the Temple Gods?* Hanif's shop, right?" I just laughed and nodded to him. "This will be just fine," he smiled. "Come, come. You can meditate in peace. I'll keep watch."

———————————

A sliver of the moon was already visible as we walked down the six gateways toward the altar and sanctuary. As we entered the small building, we were immediately greeted by an incomplete statue of Ptah in the central chamber. To the left was an empty room with only a few reliefs on the wall of Tuthmosis III. It was in the third room where we would do our meditation.

The temple guard led us in and motioned. "This is the lion goddess

Sekhmet. Many people pray and meditate here. I will light your incense and leave for a while."

The statue of Sekhmet was at least six feet tall and made of black granite. On top of the lion-headed woman was a flat sun disc. In her left hand she held a wadj scepter with the flowering lotus, and in her right hand she held the ankh of life. Above her was an opening in the ceiling. The light of the moon shone through it and gave a strange glow.

"Do you want to wait for Gahiji?" I asked.

"It would be nice. I know he wanted to meditate with you. He should be here any minute."

"Is the temple priest one of the Protectors?"

"No, he's just a friend. But we have many who have taken the pledge. Some remain, and others fall away. We have also been infiltrated before. I can recall three different times when a new member joined, kept quiet for a while, then he or she started causing all kinds of problems. They would instigate dissention and fighting amongst the group. You could tell that they were trying to break us apart."

"I told Ramla that I've seen that happen before in other peace movements. It seems like a common tactic used by the dark side—the Order. What happened next?"

"Unfortunately, a few members left. But our determination to serve others kept the Protectors in unity. We did not, nor will we ever, disband because of the Order's vile tactics."

"Are the Protectors just in Egypt?"

"Oh no, we have members all over the world."

"How is that so? I've never heard of this group before."

"It's because we do not advertise, Michael. We aren't a secret organization, not in the least. We…well…we accept all who choose to serve others. When someone makes the decision to help people on a global level, beyond self-aggrandizement, religion, or political reasons, they tend to find us."

"That doesn't make sense, Asim. I try to help others and make a positive impact by teaching. I wasn't drawn to your group."

"Ah, but you were, Michael, you were. Why do you think you are here right now? You were drawn to serve at a different level than you were before. This is help on the universal soul level, not just on the human level. That is the difference, I think."

"Maybe, I'll have to think on that. I wouldn't buy into the fact that everyone who helps other souls is drawn to this group."

"I would agree with you. Maybe I can't explain why some are drawn and others are not."

"I can think of a few examples why some would and others wouldn't. Maybe part of it is past life stuff. I mean, if I'm here because of past life commitments, maybe others are, too. It's also like someone being drawn to help in one non-profit over another. There is a calling of some type."

"It's possible. All I know is that I am glad to be here and to be of service."

Gahiji and the temple priest walked in. "Hi, Gahiji. I'm really glad that you were able to make it." Then I looked at the temple priest and told him, "I want to thank you for staying late tonight. Here…" I reached into my pocket and pulled out a handful of Egyptian pounds. I didn't count what I pulled out and handed it to him.

Gahiji commented, "That was nice, Michael. You know about our custom to tip the temple priests."

"I've played Egyptian tourist more than once in my life. I just forgot to do it when we first arrived."

The temple priest smiled and blessed me with gratitude. He added another stick of incense to the pile, bowed, and made his way out of the tiny temple.

"He seems like a nice fellow."

"He is," replied Asim.

"You know, Mudads kept telling me to meditate in the temples in Luxor. I wonder what will happen. I hope it's better than the last experience."

"That will be my intention for you, Tumaini," smiled Gahiji. "I will pray and meditate that you have a better experience."

"Thanks, Gahiji. But you don't have to do that."

"But I want to. It is my service to you."

"What can I do for you in return?"

"I can't think of anything, but I want you to know that I am not doing this for any return favors."

"I know, but let me know if there is something I can do to help you."

"I will."

"How about you, Asim? Can I do anything for you?"

"You are already doing it. You have trusted us with your very life to meditate in this room, to remember who you are, and to help in service of others. I can't ask for anything else at the moment."

We all sat down in the small room facing toward the statue. I felt a little uncomfortable about our position. "Hey guys, it feels like we are giving homage to this statue. I hope you don't mind, but I want to change where I am sitting. I only serve the Divine Source, not a statue."

"It's fine with me, Michael. We can all change if that makes you feel better."

"You don't have to do it for me. I want you to be comfortable. I'm going to go and sit in that corner."

On the way over, I asked, "Hey, Asim, why did you want to meditate here anyway?"

"It's not because of the room or the statue, Michael; it's because I know the priest who works this part of the temple complex. If I knew a guard at the other buildings, we would be meditating there instead."

"OK. That's a simple answer."

I looked at the statue and smirked, "Excuse me, but have we ever *Sekh-met* before?"

Gahiji laughed, "Funny, Michael."

Asim's body jiggled. Then he gave me a single head nod. "We should probably start meditating. My friend said we could stay a few hours, but not all night."

"You're right, Asim. Let's see…what do I choose to meditate about? I know, something that will help me to help others. That's what I want to receive information on."

"That sounds good, Michael—I mean, Tumaini. That is a great way to put it. I hope you get some new information that can help the world."

"Me, too. Let's get this meditation started. Should we *Aum* or something?"

"Shoosh, Tumaini. Just close your eyes and let it happen."

"OK."

The smoke from the incense gave the room a foggy haze that shifted effortlessly with the breeze. The little bit of moonlight that shone on the smoke trails gave the illusion that others were in the room with us, especially since there was a tall statue against the back wall. It was interesting to watch the shadow figures dance in the mist, but I knew it was an illusion.

I closed my eyes, took in a few deep breaths of incense, then the visions started happening in my mind…

CHAPTER TWELVE

TUMAINI LEFTOVERS

The smoke from the incense was extremely intoxicating and made it easy for me to focus on my meditation. When the smoke cleared, I could see my two friends—Talibah, a young woman in her twenties, and Bes, a young man in his late teens—sitting beside me. They both wore the traditional white priest's robe accompanied with a copper-colored sash.

Talibah bounced excitedly. "Did you make it, Tumaini? Did you complete the challenge?"

"I did, and I was able to go farther this time."

"What did you see? How far did you get?"

"I was able to get out of my body this time. I created my body double, my aku, just like Master Baniti taught us. Then I was able to use my aku to travel around our temple. I could see everything. I saw you, I saw Bes, and I even passed through the stone wall behind us and went outside. It was incredible."

Bes perked up. "You saw me? What was I doing?"

"Yes. I saw you meditating, but you weren't doing any traveling yet. Your aku was just forming, and it stayed directly over your head."

"That's right. I was working on creating the energy fields so I could transfer my meridians to it. Wow! You really did go out of your body!"

"I did, and I know I can go farther next time. And so will you, I can feel it."

Talibah tugged on my sleeve. "Did you see what I was doing?"

"You are kidding, right?"

"No. What was I doing?"

"You know because you saw me from your aku. You were floating around the room, too. I saw you by the oil lamps and those two hieroglyphs that were carved into the wall."

"I was! I was! I got out and floated. I was out of my body."

Just then, Baniti entered the room. "What are you so excited about?"

Bes answered right away, "We did it, Master. We were able to create our body doubles and move about. Well, those two moved about. I was still creating my aku and hovering."

"Very good." He gave a small bow. "Did any of you complete the task I gave you?"

Talibah pointed toward me. "Tumaini did. He went around the temple. He even went outside."

"You did, Tumaini? Excellent! And what did you see?"

"As I passed through the temple rooms, I saw some of the priests in meditation, some of them were praying, and the other students were making incense."

"And, what else?"

"Well, I went through the walls and traveled outside."

"Hmmm," is all he said.

"I'm sorry, Master. I know I should have waited until you told us to travel farther, but I thought about the sand dune that was beside our walls, and I instantly appeared there. Then I thought about our other temple building next door, and I appeared there, too."

"And that is why you must continue training to focus your thoughts. Where you think, you will eventually go. Tell me, Tumaini, did you protect yourself?"

"My shield! I forgot to make my shield! I am sorry, Master. I know you taught us the steps, but I forgot that one."

"It may be a hard lesson for you if you forget and travel beyond the temple grounds, Tumaini. We are protected here, but beyond this place you may not like what you encounter without a shield around your aku."

Bes was curious. "What will we see, Master Baniti?"

"I will not tell you everything because everything is what you could see.

But I will tell you that in the lower spirit realms, there are evil monsters who would love to attack an aspiring student who forgot his shield." He gave me a teacher's glance. "But it is possible to travel anywhere in space."

"Anywhere?" Talibah questioned.

"Well, you can travel anywhere in the past, you can travel anywhere in the present, and you can see potential futures."

I chuckled, "Is that it, Master Baniti?"

"Tumaini, if you practice enough, you can even travel to places that are not bound to time and space. It is said that some masters can even reach the mind of the Infinite Creator, but that takes years of dedicated practice in service to the One."

"That would be a worthy cause, Master."

"I could think of some other worthy causes, Tumaini. Can you?"

"Well, yes, Master Baniti." I paused. "I'm sorry, I lost my train of thought."

He looked at Talibah. "You are a seeker of knowledge, Talibah. What else would be a worthy cause?"

"Ooo, ooo, I know that one, Master. We could serve others, a lot."

"Yes, yes you could. And is that all you could do?"

"No, Master Baniti. We could serve others with a loving heart and a humble spirit."

"Very good, my child. And Bes, is there anything else you could do?"

"Um, let me think. Yes, yes, we could serve as a living example of love, truth, and honor, Master."

"Yes, my children, very well said. You are progressing nicely."

I inquired, "Master Baniti, what should we do for the rest of the day? Can we travel again?"

"It's best to take small steps at first, Tumaini, but I do have something for you to do."

"What is it, Master?"

"The upper rooms need sweeping, and you are to meditate on love, service, and kindness. You can either meditate first, then sweep, or you can meditate while you sweep. The choice will be up to you."

Bes mumbled with a disgruntled tone, "I notice that eating lunch was not one of the options."

"Bes, you are fasting while you practice spirit travel. Did you forget?"

"No, Master, I didn't forget. But my stomach keeps reminding me."

"Very well, then. Off to do your chores. We will train again tomorrow."

For the next few months, the three of us practiced as a group. We learned to shield our aku bodies and travel with them well beyond our temple walls. We experienced healing energy on ourselves, and we learned how to use our hands to heal others. And the best part was time travel. We took our first trip into the ethers to experience a part of our past.

Bes was always so happy in his work, as long as he had food in his belly. He told us that he saw his mother and father holding him just after his birth. He was always smiling back then as a child, and he brought tears of joy to his parents. He never lost this trait, and his happy, infectious spirit inspired everybody he met.

Talibah traveled to a previous lifetime and saw herself in Atlantis. She was an expert with healing crystals. She told us how they would fill a room with these crystals to create a vortex that instantly healed people. Atlanteans came from all over to visit her because of her friendly nature and her natural skills.

She asked, "Where did you go, Tumaini?"

Master Baniti walked in at the same time. "Yes, Tumaini, where did you go?"

"You wouldn't believe me if I told you. I'm still trying to make sense of it myself."

Bes jumped in, "Don't make us wait, Tumaini. Where did you go?"

"I…I was on Mars, and it was just like Earth. It was green and lush, with rivers and oceans. But the people were not happy where I was. War was just breaking out. I tried to keep them calm. I tried to get them to work toward peace. But too many people were angry at each other, especially the governments on different parts of Mars.

"Then I saw the militaries from both sides unleash the fury of their weapons. It was terrible. Instead of killing their enemies, these weapons killed the entire planet and everyone on it. The planet was an inferno, and the atmosphere completely burned away. Nothing was left but a dry, red planet.

"Afterwards, I saw this from space with all of the other Martian souls. We were all sad."

Talibah looked up. "Are you talking about the same red planet that we see at night in our skies?"

155

"Yes. I believe it is the same one."

Baniti suggested, "I think you saw this for a reason, Tumaini. You tried to help those people save themselves, but they chose war instead. Perhaps you came here to help this planet choose a different path."

"My gut tells me that you are right, Master. I think I have unfinished business, and that is why I came to Earth."

Bes added, "My gut tells me that I'm hungry."

"Oh, Bes"—Talibah rolled her eyes—"you are always hungry. Can't you let Tumaini finish his story?"

"There's not much else to tell, Talibah. I didn't see any more than what I've told you."

Baniti complimented us, "I think you did very well for your first exercise in time travel."

"Thank you, Master," replied Bes.

"What I want you to do for the next few months is to practice more time travel, but I want you to focus on the past. Do not venture into the future, yet. I will let you know when it is time."

Talibah giggled, "When it is time? Were you making a joke, Master?"

He grinned at her, "Keep your spirits high, young one. You will need those high spirits in the future."

"What do you mean by that, Master Baniti?"

"You will see. For now, practice your healing and time travel. There is much to do in the coming months, and you must be well honed in our arts to help others."

I raised my hand. "How will time travel help others, Master?"

"You will see, Tumaini. You will see." Then he turned and walked out of the room.

———•———

Months went by. We did as Master Baniti told us and developed our healing skills. We were good enough that we were given the opportunity to see people from the town and offer our assistance.

Talibah was a natural at healing. I think her gift from Atlantis helped her immensely in this lifetime. Bes was also very good with his hands and mental projections. They both helped scores of people instantly mend broken bones, brought sight to the blind, and helped some of the crippled walk. My gift of healing came in a different form.

Talibah had a confused look on her face. "Tumaini, how did you do that? You didn't use your hands to heal anyone, but they were completely healed when they left your table."

"I'm not sure how it all works, Talibah. I created an energy field around my body with the intention of being whole and complete. When people came to me, I told them that they could accept being whole again if they wished, or they could refuse and remain sick. I let them know it was up to them. It just seemed to work."

"That's interesting. Can you show me how to do it?"

"I can, but I think we should ask Master to see what he says."

"Maybe you are right."

"There's one other thing that I can do, too, and it seems to work just as well as sending energy."

Bes walked over to join in. "What is it?"

"Well, I seem to be able to talk with people and help them heal their own emotional pains. Over time, those emotional pains manifest into ailments in the body. I guess if they heal their emotional pain, they can also heal their bodies on their own."

Master Baniti interjected, "That is interesting, Tumaini. Good for you." We all turned around shocked.

"Master"—I bowed—"when did you arrive?"

"Just in time to hear you explain your gift."

"Should I teach this to the others?"

"Not just yet. Each of you should develop your natural talents. Besides, it is time for you to learn the art of magic."

Bes took a small bite of his roll and queried, "Master Baniti, isn't magic bad? Why are we learning magic?"

"Energy is neither good nor bad, Bes. Magic is just putting energy to your intention. Your intention is what makes it good or bad. Love and service to others creates white magic. Hate, fear, and greed are the ways of the dark side."

"So healing like we are doing is already white magic, isn't it?"

"It is, Bes. But some would call your healing just magic—even black magic."

"How could they call it black magic? We are helping others."

"Some people are afraid of things that they don't understand. Others are jealous because they have not developed their natural skills. Their anger can fester, and then they will take their anger out any way they can, including accusations and aggression."

"Master," I prodded, "what will we be learning to do with magic?"

"The first lesson is to respect the power of magic. Magic can do many wonderful things. But also know that if it is used for selfish reasons, it can backfire and take you down a path that is full of trials and pain."

Talibah quipped, "Well, that doesn't sound very fun, does it? Couldn't we just stick to healing?"

"You may, but there are other things you can do to help people besides healing. That is why, as students, you must learn the other laws about energy."

"I'm ready, Master," I affirmed. "When do we begin?"

"Tomorrow, Tumaini. Tomorrow."

Weeks flew by as we learned the basic skills in the art of white magic. Weeks eventually turned into months, and months turned into two years of dedicated practice and service. We also continued healing the sick, helping the poor, and cleaning the temple.

My favorite part of magic training was the prayer songs. We would sing those songs as we helped the sick and poor. The healings happened much faster, and our intentions came about almost effortlessly when we used these songs.

Our time traveling skills improved as well, and it was time to add the final lesson before we could become full-time priests.

Bes spoke up, "Master Baniti, what is our final task?"

"Now that you have shown your respect for life, your respect for energy, and your respect for the Creator, it is time to learn about the future."

"The future?" Bes quipped. "I can tell you about the future. The scarab pushes the sun through the sky until nightfall. Then it does it all over again the next day. In between pushing, the beetle stops for breakfast, lunch, and dinner. That's the future. And I'm hungry."

"Very funny," giggled Talibah.

Baniti continued, "He is not far off, Talibah. That is the predictable future. However, it is possible to have more than one future. It is possible to influence the future in many ways to create a specific outcome. It is also possible that many futures can grow from special events in the past.

"So, my students, it is time to learn about the unpredictable futures."

I proposed, "You mean, like if Egypt's armies win a war, it creates one timeline, and if they lose, it creates another timeline?"

"Yes. And all of those timelines exist at the same time. They sit one on top of each other like layers of sand."

All three of us reacted, "What?!"

"You will understand more when we start our new lesson. All times exist at the same time. And the actions of the many can influence, change, and create a new future."

Talibah inquired, "Does it always take a lot of people to change the future?"

"No, and yes. Usually it does, but it depends more on the actions of the people, their determination, intention, and focused energy. That is what makes a future event grow more than another. And every once in a while there is an anomaly: someone with enough energy to create a massive change on his or her own. But that is very rare."

I was curious about his answer and raised my hand. "Can one person really make a difference?"

He looked at me with a strange face. "Why do you ask that, Tumaini?"

"I don't know. It seemed like the logical thing to ask."

"Do you want to change the future?"

"I just want to help, Master."

"That is very noble of you, Tumaini, and you may just get that chance."

"What are you trying to say, Master? Do you know something that I don't?"

"I will tell all three of you that something is on the horizon, something dangerous and very bad for all of humanity. We will all need to do our best to help our brothers and sisters of the world survive, whether it is in the present or in the distant future."

He looked at me again. "Do you understand, Tumaini?"

I felt a little uncomfortable from his stare. I had no idea what he was talking about. "Master, I'm not sure, but I will do what I can to help."

"Good. Then it is settled. We will begin your final lesson soon. You will all be needed to help one day, and you must be prepared."

Talibah vowed, "We won't let you down, Master."

"I know you won't, Talibah. Go and rest. Your lesson begins tomorrow."

—————————

We sat in a semicircle around Baniti. He lit a stick of incense and began teaching. "Do you remember how you time traveled to the past? Each of you was told to think of an instance and place that would bring you the best information for your soul's growth. Then, you were taught to pinpoint specific events in the ether with coordinates and send your aku there. Do you remember?"

Bes answered, "Yes, Master. We had to locate the event with time coordinates and three space coordinates."

"Very good. Well, the same principle applies for going into the future. You will set your intention to see a specific time and place in the future. You will set the coordinates and project your aku to that place. What you will see will be a potential future based upon your beliefs and current events."

I asked, "Can we also see other future timelines, Master?"

"Oh yes, and you can also influence the future timelines with your aku and positive energy."

Talibah was a little confused. "Are you actually telling us that we can rewrite the future from the past?"

"No, I'm not saying that, but it was smart of you to ask. I am saying that you can influence a future event from the past. Depending on the current timeline and those events surrounding it, you can leave yourself breadcrumbs, hints, suggestions. Your future aku will pick up on those feelings and present them as instincts and voices. The stronger the impulse, the more you will follow your gut instincts."

I mused to myself, "So that's why I joined the priesthood."

Baniti raised an eyebrow toward me. "What did you say, Tumaini?"

"Nothing, Master."

"Come now. Share your thoughts, Tumaini. It is important for your training."

"Master, while you were explaining what to do, I had a flashback to my youth. I remembered hearing a very loving voice say something to me as I saw a temple priest help a poor man. The man was being ridiculed by others, then the priest gave the man a loaf of bread and a new blanket. I heard the voice say, 'Remember this.' That expression of kindness had a huge impact on my life. Years later, I decided to join the temple. Do you think that voice was my own voice?"

"I believe so. And now you know that you can leave your future selves breadcrumbs.

"Here is your assignment. After I leave the room, you will start your meditation. I want you to go one day into the future and leave yourself a clue that only you would know. If the timeline is not altered, you will be able to feel this breadcrumb very strongly in your mind tomorrow. If the timeline is altered in any way, you won't feel the influence as much.

"Here is a piece of papyrus. I want you to write your intention on it before I leave. I will take it with me and we will review it in a few days."

Talibah stared at the paper. "What should we tell ourselves, Master?"

"I will leave that up to you, but I would hope it would be a positive suggestion."

Bes joked, "Master, if we leave ourselves a loaf of bread instead of a breadcrumb, would the influence be stronger?"

He snickered, "The stronger the energy, the stronger your magical influence, the stronger the feeling. Do you understand?"

I nodded, "I think so. But Master, if we leave ourselves a clue today, won't we be looking for it tomorrow?"

"You might, but you can also suggest that you won't remember it. That will be your choice as well."

"I want to see if I am able to do this, so I will suggest that I won't remember it."

"As you wish. Now write your intention so you can begin."

We all took a moment and scribbled our thoughts onto the papyrus. Then Master Baniti collected them, bowed, and left in silence.

We closed our eyes, and the room went dark. The only noise was Bes' stomach growling in hunger. "Sorry guys. All that talk about bread got me hungry."

"Shoosh, Bes."

He whispered, "Sorry."

Our first attempt was not as successful as we'd hoped. I only got a small hint the next day, and Talibah and Bes didn't get anything. We were determined to make this work, so we spent the next few months in intensive practice. It took more than two seasons before we could send ourselves multiple signals. When we passed this test, we were now ready to become priests of the temple.

―――・◆・―――

Our ceremony was simple. For the first time, we were permitted to meditate with the other priests. We prayed together, and then we offered our services to the Infinite One. After that, each priest came up to us and recited a magical prayer. These prayers were meant to help strengthen our abilities in the service to others. The more we helped others, the stronger our abilities would grow.

When the festivities were over, we were given our priests' robes and a box full of blank scrolls. Baniti came up to us and smiled, "I am proud of all of you. Welcome into the service of the Creator."

I started to address him, "Master—"

He stopped me from continuing. "I am no longer your Master; I am only a humble servant in the name of the Creator. I may share teachings with you from time to time, but we are one and the same."

Talibah sniffled, "It will be hard not to call you Master anymore. I still look up to you."

"Ah, but it is I who looks up to you as well. You are an encouragement for the future of humankind and our priesthood. You serve without asking for anything in return, you offer your assistance when asked, and you strive for spiritual growth over making your pockets and ego grow fat with money and fame. We are all very proud of you." Talibah's eyes watered a little.

"Mast—" I stopped myself. "Baniti, thank you for all of your help. I could not have asked for a better teacher."

"You honor me, Tumaini."

"Tomorrow, we have an important meeting with all of the priests. I will show you to your new living quarters near the temple grounds. After morning prayers, we will meet in the great hall. Come, let's enjoy our celebration meal."

Bes jumped up. "It's about time. I'm starving."

During dinner, I got Baniti's attention. "Baniti, would you tell us please? What are the scrolls for?"

"They are for you to record spiritual insights and messages. Because paper is scarce, we only record what will help people the most to grow in love, peace, and wisdom."

"Thanks, Baniti."

"You are most welcome, Tumaini."

———•◦•———

Our morning prayer was simple. We remained outside our temple and thanked Source for the opportunity to live in the Spirit of One. Then our temple leader gave a short message to everyone in attendance:

"We believe that all things are the Creator in one form or another, and we treat others with love and respect. Our challenge in this lifetime is to balance love with wisdom. In our earlier teachings, we were taught that the highest form of love could lead one to martyrdom, but this is just one of many goals.

"In our next lesson of life, we learn that it is not wise to pursue martyrdom. Wisdom, especially wisdom combined with love, chooses another path. It does this so love may continue to be expressed in all ways.

"Keep your hearts and minds pointed toward love and wisdom, and we will all flourish together."

The head of our temple welcomed all of the new priests and bowed in our direction. There were ten of us, and this made our total well over a hundred. We bowed in return, and all of us walked into the great hall.

The instructions were simple: We were to meet with our former teachers, and they would inform us about a threat that was invading Egypt. We gathered around Baniti to hear him speak again.

"For years, we have been able to protect our lands with our white magic. However, a dark and evil force—an evil beyond imagination—has broken through our magic shield and threatens all of Egypt.

"There are evil aliens and dark spirits who have been here since the dawn of man. You have already seen some of these aliens in your out-of-body travel. You have also met some of the dark spirits when you have time traveled. Our priests are even aware of an advanced race of dinosaurs that live beneath the Earth.

"Somehow, these aliens have found a way to infiltrate our priesthood and penetrate our protective shield. There are cracks in our energy lines, and they can now control the minds of the pharaoh and his family. We believe that they may also control other government leaders, military officials, and select priests. One of our own even saw these aliens placing living creatures and strange devices into their minds and bodies. That is how they are controlling them so easily."

Talibah gasped, "That's awful. Who are these aliens?"

"They are known as the reptilians, mantids, and greys. There are also advanced dinosaurs that are in the reptilian family. Together, they control a group of humans called the Anunnaki. This malevolent Order is a formidable force, and they are completely focused on keeping the entire planet enslaved. If they succeed, Earth will remain a dark place for all souls for a very long time."

Bes was hunting for an answer. "How can we stop them?"

"We are working on a plan, but we fear our time is very limited. It is rumored that the pharaoh is losing his mind to them. And since our priesthood can see these reptilians with our powers, we might be in grave danger."

"Tell me what to do, Baniti, and I will do all that I can," I vowed.

"I will let you know when we come up with a plan. In the meantime, we suggest that you meditate, pray, and continue serving others."

"Since they have cracked our magic shield, can we still travel with our aku?"

"You can, but be extra careful. These aliens do not show mercy to unprotected souls."

"Thanks for the warning, Baniti. I'm sure that we will all be careful."

Our life in the priesthood changed drastically from that day forward. Aside from our daily duties, we were requested to meditate on messages of love, hope, and peace. What we learned from these meditations was to be written on our scrolls and gathered in the temple.

My messages seemed to come more in the form of instructions, more like guidelines that would help people to create communities of peace. The voice that gave me these messages was not my own. I could feel that they came directly from God, the Infinite Creator, because they focused on love and how to share love in all forms of life.

This same voice encouraged me to use my gifts of time travel to bring hope to an enslaved people. I had to think about this request because I did not know how to accomplish such a monumental task.

———•◦•———

When seven suns had passed beneath the sands, I came up with an idea. I used my skill, as the voice had said, and I began traveling to future time-lines. I saw the Earth already in many different stages of slavery. Most of these timelines were already doomed, and the human race was completely at the mercy of the reptilians and Anunnaki bloodlines. Some of the time-lines I saw were even more horrible than the first. I saw one version of the Earth that was completely destroyed from wars between rival governments. Nothing survived, as the atmosphere had been burned away.

Since I could not help those timelines, I decided to focus on the ones with the most chance for freedom and success. I saw one in particular that entailed two world wars. If the world survived those wars, that timeline would support a chance for freedom.

I began sending messages of hope and instructions to my future self. I used my white magic to continue urging that future part of me to travel to Egypt so I could reunite myself with my parchments and scrolls. I even gave directions to one of my future selves to enter the shop of a Protector. He would lead me to his brother, which would start a long series of events toward possible freedom. I focused all of the positive energy that I could to make this timeline the most successful.

In one of those timelines, I also saw myself in a temple with Sekhmet and two other men. I could see their soul essence, and I knew they were the reincarnations of Talibah and Bes. I hoped that I would end up in that timeline so I could be reunited with my friends once again.

When I finished my travels, I began writing instructions that I should follow to complete my task in the future. I also created two coded symbols, made up of smaller symbols, which would help me complete my destiny of serving the world.

———•◦•———

By this time, the pharaoh, under the influence of the reptilians, had killed most of our priests. Less than half of us remained alive, and we travelled at night to escape the terrible slaughter. I was informed that the soldiers had also found the scrolls of the dead priests in the temple and burned them all. I was still working on mine, so they were not destroyed in the fire.

To keep my scrolls safe, I took them and buried them in the sand. I placed a prayer on the vases so they would be found by a farmer in the near future. This farmer would be guided by a projection of my aku to those same vases. With the guidance of a local priestess, she would help this farmer to reform the Protectors of Souls. My last possession on Earth was an amulet that was given to me as a graduation gift. I put this amulet in the vases to act as a symbol for hope.

———————

Baniti, Bes, and Talibah were able to escape with the other priests. There were only thirty-six of us left out of one hundred and nineteen. We decided that we could not stop the Order at this time, so we all made a pact with magic to reincarnate on Earth when we could make the most change for freedom.

The pact said that if we were killed by the Order, our magic would place us in suspended animation together in space. We used our skills and created an energy bubble that would protect our souls until the time was right to reincarnate as a group.

Within two months, the remaining priests were found by the pharaoh's guards. We did not put up any fight as they rushed toward us with blades drawn. I looked at my friends and encouraged them, "Have hope. We can make a difference in the future if we don't lose hope."

———————

That was the last thing I remembered. I opened my eyes and found myself back in the Temple of Ptah, with Gahiji and Asim staring intently at me.

CHAPTER THIRTEEN

FOLLOW THE
YELLOW BRICK PYRAMID

"Tumaini, what just happened?! Why did I get the name Talibah in my meditation?!" demanded Asim.

"Yes, and why did I get the name Bes in my meditation?!" echoed Gahiji.

"Guys, you aren't going to believe this. First, take your fingers off your triggers."

"Oh, sorry." Asim loosened his grip. "When I came out of my meditation, I felt like someone was coming after me and I had to protect myself. It must have been a subconscious reaction."

Gahiji added, "Me, too. Sorry." He pulled his hand out from his jacket.

"Well, believe it or not, we were together in a past life. I was with both of you in ancient Egypt, and we were priests.

"Gahiji, you were Bes. You brought joy to everyone you met. And Asim, you were Talibah. You were... Wow, you were so skilled with healing others. You were amazing. And you had an insatiable appetite for learning. You were always asking questions.

"To make this short, we discovered a plot by the reptilians and the Anunnaki to take over the world. We were eventually hunted down by the pharaoh's guards and killed so we couldn't expose them."

Gahiji reacted first, "I was a priest?"

"Yes, and you knew how to time travel. We all did."

"Tumaini, this sounds like the parchment that is read at our annual meetings. Are you saying that we…?"

"It seems so, Asim. We are three of the thirty-six priests who came back to help bring peace and freedom to Earth."

Gahiji shook his head in disbelief, "This can't be happening. I'm not a priest. I'm not even religious."

"Gahiji, we weren't really religious back then, either. We focused more on love and helping others. Actually, our priesthood didn't fit in with the others because we didn't honor their gods. We gave thanks to the Creator, not to the god of the Nile. They kind of hated us for that."

Asim was still hung up on something I'd said earlier. "We could time travel?"

"Oh yes, and much, much more."

"Why can't we do it now?"

"We can. I mean, my abilities are just starting to come back, and it seems like yours are, too. You got a name in meditation from a past life. That's an ability."

Gahiji agreed, "He's right. I never got anything like that before. And during my meditation, I felt very…I felt hungry."

I laughed, "As Bes, you were always thinking with your stomach. See, you do have abilities.

"I think we are the first of the priests to awaken. That means there are others who will come to help. At least that is what I wrote as Tumaini."

The temple guard came into the entranceway and stood there. Asim waved him in. "I do not want to intrude," he insisted.

"No, you are not intruding. We are just finishing."

He started cleaning up the ash from the incense. "Did you have a good experience?"

"I can't speak for the others, but I gained a lot."

Gahiji added, "I'd have to say that I had an interesting experience."

The guard didn't actually say that we had to leave, but I knew he was waiting for us. I looked toward Asim's watch. "How long were we in there?"

The guard answered first, "Over three hours."

"You're kidding! Three hours? I didn't know I could meditate that long."

Asim suggested, "Well, let's catch a cab and go back to the hotel. We can talk more on the way."

I reached into my pocket and gave the temple guard some more money. "Thanks for letting us stay extra. I am grateful."

He replied, "It is an honor to serve. Asim told me that your group might come back early in the morning. Will you be back to meditate again?"

My initial feeling was that I shouldn't. I had a twinge in my gut, but I couldn't tell if it was just my stomach or if it was something else. "I'm not sure. I might."

We walked out of the temple, and the guard escorted us to the front of Karnak. We hailed a cab and arrived at the hotel within a few minutes. "Guys," I yawned, "I'm a little tired. We can pick this up tomorrow. How about you join our group for the morning meditation?" I got another funny feeling in my stomach. I wondered, "What was that?" I dismissed it as they both replied, "OK."

"Great. We are supposed to leave here at 5:30 a.m. I'll see you then."

Gahiji hollered on the way out of the hotel, "Don't forget the doughnuts!" I snickered to myself.

———•+•———

My wakeup call came way too soon. I dragged myself out of bed and started packing. We had just a few hours at Karnak before we'd be heading back to Cairo.

Only three other people joined Shannon and me on the bus. Gahiji and Asim came along, too.

Shannon closed the bus door. "I think this is it. The others must all be sleeping in today. Let's get rolling. We only have an hour or two before the crowds show up."

Shannon had some great connections in Egypt and had arranged for us to get inside Karnak before hours. "Michael, we are going to meditate by the Sacred Lake. Do you want to join us?" she invited.

"Actually, I had a really good meditation in the Temple of Ptah last night. Would you like to join me?"

"I don't know. What do you guys think?" The other three said that they wanted to be outdoors near the water, so they politely declined. "Michael, if it's OK with you, I think we'll stay by the lake."

I was having second thoughts about the temple and had a small glimpse of the lake. "You know what? You guys go to the lake. I might join you later."

"I'd like that. We've missed you on this trip."

She asked Gahiji and Asim to split up. I could see in their eyes that they were hoping to join me again with Sekhmet. Gahiji reluctantly volunteered, "I'll go to the Sacred Lake with you, but I will keep my distance—with your blessing, of course."

Shannon replied, "Of course, Gahiji. I know how you like to work. She smiled at Asim, "It looks like you get to be with Michael." He nodded back and gave me a grin.

The same temple guard met us by the columns again. "I see you came back. I already put the incense you left last night in the temple. You should have an hour by yourself before they open the gates."

He offered to Asim, "Do you want to go in? I will keep watch for you."

"Yes. I would like that, thanks."

Asim's friend pulled back a large piece of plastic that covered the entire doorway. After we dodged the generator by the main wall and ducked under the plastic, we noticed there was no light coming through the man-made holes in the ceiling. They were closed off by roofing tarps.

"That's odd. The holes are covered. And what's with the plastic door?"

The temple guard pointed to the tarp and told us that they were doing restoration work all over Karnak and that maybe this was something they'd put there last night after he had left. Then he went behind the statue, lit the incense, bowed, and started to leave. I was putting my hand in my pocket when he motioned to me to wait until afterwards. I thanked him as he left.

Asim hesitated, "Maybe I should wait outside, Tumaini. Something doesn't feel right."

"I'm fine either way, Asim. I'd like your company, but I understand if you want to go. I'm not expecting a marathon meditation today. I'm just hoping to get another glimpse from my past. Besides, I wouldn't mind going to the Sacred Lake in a bit."

"Maybe you are right, and I am overreacting. If you only plan on being here a short while, we can meditate together."

"Great. I'm going to sit where I sat last night—creature of habit and all." He laughed and sat down in the same place he'd meditated in last night, too.

I was doing my best to quiet my mind, but something kept me from going into a deep trance. My body kept itching unexpectedly, and I kept humming those prayer songs. It was like someone or something was keeping me from reaching my subconscious state.

After about five minutes, I heard one of the generators start up near the entrance. I did my best to drown out the noise, but my focus was completely gone. Then things started getting really hazy. Ten minutes later, I heard a small thump on the floor. Then everything turned black.

Gahiji arrived just in time to save our lives. He ripped down the plastic, turned off the generator, and dragged our bodies out into the fresh air. My eyelids began to flutter, and with my blurred vision I saw the temple guard lying on the ground. "Wha…what happened, Gahiji?"

"Someone knocked out the guard and left a rotting pigeon on his chest."

"But…but, why?"

"While I was watching the others at the lake, I had a premonition that someone was suffocating in the hall. I ran over here as fast as I could, found the guard on the ground, and the generator was running inside the plastic."

Asim was regaining consciousness. "What happened?"

"There was an attempt on Tumaini's and your lives. This has to be the Order. This is one of Hanif's pigeons. It has his markings on its wing."

The guard was coming to and rubbing his head. Asim instructed, "We should leave here immediately. You take point, and I'll follow in the rear." He asked his friend if he could stand, and he said that he was fine.

On the way to the Sacred Lake, Asim explained to his friend what he thought had happened. Surprisingly, the temple guard had already deduced that something out of the ordinary was going on with Asim, Gahiji, and me. Three hours in the temple last night gave him a small clue.

I tapped Asim's arm. "He isn't mad at us, is he?"

The guard replied, "No, I am not mad at you. You weren't the one who hit me with a club."

Gahiji inquired, "A club?! Did you see who hit you?"

"Yes, he was a thin Egyptian man. He held a blunt wooden object that had an odd shape to it."

"Was it like a fleur de lis?" I drew the same shape in my palm. "Did it have something that looked like flower petals on it?"

"How did you know?"

"I've seen this club up close before. It's the man from the black car. He also attacked us at a restaurant back in Cairo."

The guard continued, "He must hate you terribly, especially since he has chased you all the way from Cairo."

"Unfortunately for me, yes. He seems to hate me with a passion."

"I will pray for you and your family. No one should be hated that much."

"Thanks. Will you be alright?"

"Yes, I will be fine. I am going to report this to the temple security and see an aid." He rubbed his head for a moment and reacted to the pain. He also saw blood on his hand.

"Here, let me look at that." Asim tilted his friend's head closer. Then he pulled out a handkerchief and applied pressure to the cut. Instinctively, he closed his eyes, hummed a melodic tune, and then his body shook for a second as if someone had touched him with an electrical wire. When he removed his hand, the cut was gone.

"Asim, what did you do?!" Gahiji blurted.

The temple guard reacted, "My pain is gone. What did you do?!"

I asked excitedly, "Asim, what did you do?!"

Asim replied, "I don't know!"

"I do," I exclaimed. "Your ability spontaneously returned, Talibah."

The guard asked, "Who is Talibah? Did you do black magic on me? Stay away!"

Asim tried to explain, "No, no, I didn't do any black magic on you, honest. I wanted to help you, that's all."

"Then it was a miracle. You must have performed a miracle on me. Praise Allah." He started to supplicate, but Asim stopped him.

"I'm no miracle worker. I just wanted to help. Please don't kneel."

"But you healed me. I am grateful."

"I think you healed yourself. Maybe my energy helped. I don't know... From what Michael has told me, we all have this ability."

The guard looked at me and emphasized, "How do you know?"

"It was from a vision I saw last night. Asim was a great healer in ancient Egypt. He must have tapped into a latent ability."

"What ever he did, it is still a miracle to me."

Gahiji was scouting the grounds while we were talking. "Michael, we should meet up with the others."

Asim asked, "Can we walk you to the security room?"

The guard politely declined, "No. I will be fine from here." He took Asim's hands in his and shook them in thanks. "I would like to speak with you on this, though."

"We can, but later. I need to keep watch for now."

"I understand. Thank you, my friend." We bowed and said goodbye as he walked away.

As we got closer to the lake, I could see that the others were still meditating. "Let's not interrupt them, OK?"

Gahiji agreed, "That's fine with me. Besides, you are leaving in a few hours, and I think we should talk."

I asked jokingly, "What do you want to talk about?"

"You know: life, art, instant healing, time travel—the simple things."

"Your light sarcasm is duly noted," I smiled.

Asim gazed at his hands in wonder. "Did I really do that?"

Gahiji replied, "You must have. I didn't do it."

"I think it's fascinating. Both of you did something unique. Gahiji got a premonition, and you instantly healed someone. That's just awesome. It seems your abilities were triggered from your meditation."

Asim suggested, "Or maybe it's because we are close together. Some people are able to do things because others can, too. I've seen this before, this sympathetic resonance. The first person makes it easier for the second, and so on. You have your abilities, Tumaini, and because you have yours, you made it easier for us to have ours."

"I think you're right. When I was around Ramla, my abilities seemed to come alive."

Gahiji snapped his finger and pointed at each of us. "So maybe that's what we are supposed to do, then. When the other priests start waking up—I mean remember who they were—then we can help them activate their abilities."

"I couldn't have said it any better, Gahiji."

173

"You know, Tumaini, I don't think the Order is going to stop coming after you—us. From previous encounters, it's said that they work in threes. The first attempts are human, the second attempts are alien, and the third ones are dimensional. We've also heard that sometimes the attacks never stop."

"What do you mean by alien and dimensional?"

"I can't explain it. I just know that there are attacks on those levels."

"Well, that's not very comforting."

Asim pointed toward the pylons. His friend was coming, and he was accompanied by two soldiers. "I think they'll want a statement from us. Let's head over and tell them what happened."

Asim was right. We were grilled with numerous questions about the incident. The soldiers were very much to the point with their investigation and didn't want to know anything extraneous. Before we parted, they asked how to get in touch with me if they captured the assailant.

Gahiji informed them, "You can contact our security team. We know how to reach him." That seemed to satisfy the soldiers, and they started to walk away. Asim's friend smiled at us and wished me a safe journey.

I mentioned to Gahiji and Asim, "Speaking of contact, I think we should stay in touch with each other."

Asim replied, "I couldn't agree more."

We exchanged emails and phone numbers. I also wrote down my address and joked, "I'm sorry, guys, I don't have any pigeons. This will have to do." They both smiled and shook my hand, saying that it was a pleasure getting to know me.

In a few hours, we were well on our way to the airport. It was hard saying goodbye to my new friends, but I knew I would see Gahiji and Asim in the near future. When we landed, I was met by my other new friends that I'd left back in Cairo.

———————

Rehema practically tackled me with a hello hug at baggage claim. "Michael, it's so good to see you."

"Rehema, what are you doing here? I didn't expect to see anyone at the airport."

"Hanif sent me. He thought it would be a good idea. I hope I didn't startle you."

"Not one bit. I'm actually glad to see you. How did you know I was here?"

"It was Mudads, remember? He talked with Shannon about your itinerary before you left. By the way, where is she? I have something for her."

"She's right over there."

I introduced the two of them, and Shannon introduced me to our new Egyptologist, Ehab, and our new security guard, Jabari. We all exchanged handshakes and greetings.

"Shannon, I have something for you." Rehema gave her a small box with a piece of paper on the top.

"Oh my gosh. Thank you, Rehema."

"Are those what I think they are?" I asked.

"Yes. And Shannon, I wrote out the recipe for you." She ripped open the box and saw all of the goodies inside.

"So much for keeping it a secret recipe, huh?" I laughed.

"Well, life is too short to keep me from sharing."

"You are a doll. Hanif is a lucky guy."

She smiled back, "Yes, he is."

We chuckled for a moment while Shannon gave her thanks again. As she shared her pastries with the others, Rehema pulled me aside. "Michael, we have much to talk about. I heard that you were going to dinner first, then the pyramids, and then to check in at your hotel. Is this correct?"

"As far as I know, our schedule hasn't changed. Do you want to join us?"

"I was hoping you would ask. You stay with your group, and I'll meet you at the restaurant, OK?"

"Sure. It will be fun to talk. And I have a lot to share with you, too."

"Excellent. By the way, you will be in good hands with Jabari and Ehab."

"What do you mean?"

"They are one of us."

I glanced over toward them. They nodded in respect and patted their chests. I could only imagine that they had on their amulets. I returned a nod and patted my chest, too."

———————•◆•———————

Dinner was actually at a stand-and-grab falafel joint near the pyramids. Rehema and I were lucky; we snagged two of the few chairs available to sit and talk. "Michael, I want to tell you that we have our network in place to help you as much as we can."

"I know. I heard that Karim and Omar sent Gahiji and Asim to help me, and let me tell you, those two guys are awesome! Not only did they save my life—twice—but they are also two of the temple priests from the parchments."

"They are what?!"

"You know, the parchments, the ones that are read at the annual meeting. There were thirty-six priests that would reincarnate to help the world. Well, they are two of the priests. Does any of this ring a bell?"

"I'm shocked. I don't know what to say."

"I know what to say. Thanks! Thanks for all of your help. I wouldn't be here if it wasn't for you guys.

"And Rehema, I have so much more to tell you. I've remembered some of my gifts. When I was at Karnak, I saw myself as Tumaini. I was able to time travel. I even told myself to go into Mudads' shop. How's that for some interesting news?"

"That's wonderful. What else happened?"

"You mean, besides the attempts on my life?"

"Yes, I heard about them from Gahiji, but he failed to mention that he was a priest...hmmm. He called me while you were in flight." I motioned for her to go on. "That's why we set up Jabari and Ehab to go with us. Jabari is his brother."

I laughed, "He mentioned that he had a brother who worked security.

"You know, Rehema, I'll only be here for one more day, and then it's back to the States."

"I know. We also have some friends in the U.S. Not as many as in Egypt, but if they can help, they will."

"You're a peach."

"I thought I was a doll."

"Well, you're both."

She blushed and asked, "Anything else I should know about?"

"Well, from what happened in Luxor, I believe even more—that I'm Tumaini, that is. And just to let you know, our friend in black from the restaurant gave me a couple of personal visits. I think he was trying to get me to join his personal club. No pun intended."

"We're trying to find out who he is, Michael. When we do, we'll let you know."

"Hey, Gahiji said that the Order tries to kill with people first, then aliens, and then dimensional beings. Do you know anything about that?"

"No, but I'll try to find out for you."

Shannon yelled out, "Everyone to the bus! It's pyramid time!"

"You know, I'm actually excited to go to the pyramids again. I saw them when Constance was with me on our last trip."

"Good, I have something to show you when we get there. I saw it when I was doing my graduate work. I think you'll like it."

"Are you going to give me a clue?"

"No, it's best seen. Words can't describe it."

"Alright, I'll wait."

"Michael, I'm going in my car. Why don't you talk with Ehab and Jabari? I know they are anxious to meet you. They were at the Protectors meeting at the restaurant."

"They were? I'd love to talk. Who knows? Maybe they are priests, too."

"Great. See you there."

It was rush hour in Cairo, which looked a lot like a semi-controlled demolition derby. There were almost no lines painted in the streets, barely any stop signs or traffic signals, more honking than a flock of geese, and a ton of angry drivers cutting us off from every direction. We all had white knuckles from clenching the armrests, and we prayed that we got through each intersection alive. What was supposed to be little more than a ten-minute commute turned into a sixty-minute drive.

Despite our state of panic, Ehab remained calm and did an awesome job of entertaining everyone on the bus. He was funny, full of knowledge, and much more personable than our last guide. I told him that it was better than winning the lottery.

He beamed, "My name actually means *a gift*. Will that do?"

I chuckled, "Why am I not surprised?"

Jabari got up from the back of the bus and sat beside me. "It is an honor to meet you, Tumaini."

"Mine, too. Tell me, have we met before?"

"I was your guard when you crossed the desert at Niuserre."

"I thought so. And Gahiji?"

"He's my brother. He speaks very highly of you."

"Well, I think very highly of him, too."

"He told me that he was a priest with you."

"Yes, and so was Asim."

"Do you think that I was one of the priests?"

"I don't know. There were thirty-six in total that made the commitment. If all of this is true, then there are thirty-three who have yet to remember. If you are a priest, then you might experience a special ability."

"Like what?"

"Well, Gahiji was able to astral project his spirit anywhere he wanted, and he could heal the sick with his hands when he was Bes."

"I would like that. I like helping others."

"I do, too.

"Jabari, is there anything that you can tell me about the Order?"

"They are everywhere...and nowhere. As an example, your attacks weren't done by those in charge. You might never meet them. This man was nothing more than a foot soldier, an expendable. He means nothing to those with power, and they'll use him until they have no more use for him."

"That's a pretty cold life, don't you think?"

"It is how they operate, Tumaini. These are selfish, greedy people. If you aren't in their inner circle, you are a commodity, nothing more. You either provide slave labor for them, or you are their muscle."

"I'm starting to get that picture more and more. They really don't care about other people, do they?"

"Well, the humans don't. They'll blow up large buildings full of people and start wars just for profit. The aliens are another story. I think there's something more going on with them."

"Like what?"

"I've heard rumors. I think it has to do with an alien machine, something about capturing souls when people die."

"What?!"

"I don't know any more than that, Tumaini, and it's just a rumor. I haven't been able to get any more information."

"If you do, I'd like to know about it. That sounds pretty important."

"I will do all I can for you."

Before I could probe any further, we pulled into the tourist parking lot and got off of the bus to rejoin with our friends from the Nile cruise.

Rehema was also waiting for us and looking at her watch. "What took you guys so long? I've been waiting here for almost half an hour."

Ehab joked, "You must have taken the shortcuts, and we decided to experience a Cairo traffic jam. It was very surreal—lots of honking."

"Ha-ha, funny."

Shannon made her announcement. "Are you guys ready for our horseback ride into the desert?" They all screamed in excitement.

I gibed, "What, no camel ride?"

"No, silly. You know we are going on horses tonight and camels tomorrow."

"Oh yeah, I forgot."

Shannon continued, "Then we are going to hang around the Sphinx until the light show. C'mon, our horses are waiting."

Rehema said, "Michael, I had something to show you, but I didn't know about the horse ride and light show. I'll have to show you tomorrow."

"That's alright. I actually forgot about it."

———————

The horse stables were near the Sphinx, which allowed us to catch a glimpse of the old cat while we saddled up. Since it's a two-hour ride into the desert and around the pyramids, they gave each of us a bottle of water. The tour also supplied its own guide, so Ehab didn't have to work for a bit.

"Rehema, do you want to come with us?" invited Shannon.

"Yes, I would, actually. I've been here so many times, but I've never seen it from a horse."

I piped in, "I've already paid for her fee, so she's all set."

"You did?" Rehema gushed. "That was nice of you."

"I figured you would go with us, and I took a chance."

A stable hand was already walking another horse toward our group. He helped Rehema into her saddle, and off we went.

Jabari, Ehab, Rehema, and I stayed at the back of the group. This gave us a chance to talk about last week's events and what might materialize in the future. Ehab was especially interested in the part about the reincarnating priests. He had a feeling, just like Jabari, that they might be part of that group.

After an hour or so, our talk eventually shifted away from the Order to more personal thoughts. "I love being in the desert." I sat up on my horse and looked around. "It's so relaxing out here. I wish I could stay and meditate for a bit."

Jabari offered, "Maybe when everyone goes back to the hotel, we could come back for a moonlight meditation."

"I'd like that, Jabari."

"Me, too," added Rehema.

———————

The sun was setting, and the group was *oohing* and *ahing*. When the sun cast its last few rays on the pyramids, a ball of light shot across the sky and flew deep into the desert. It hovered for a moment and disappeared into the sand. Then a low buzzing noise filled the air and caught the attention of everyone, including our horses.

Shannon was in a panic, "Did you see that? What was it?"

Other members started commenting frantically, "I saw it, too. It was a ball of light. What was that?"

The horses were the first to feel the effects. They began snorting and pawing at the ground in fear. Two of them began bucking like they were in a rodeo and threw one of the riders to the sand.

Jabari, Ehab, and the new tour guide told everyone to get off of their horses immediately. "Get down! Get down!" commanded the tour guide. "Everyone off of the horses. Lie down. They will not hurt you."

The buzzing noise happened once again. This time, we could feel the vibrations in the sand. A few people immediately began wheezing and gasping for air, while others grabbed their stomachs in pain. One of the men started yelling at his friend and got into a pushing fight. The two of them wrestled to the ground screaming angrily at each other.

Surprisingly, Jabari, Rehema, and Ehab were not as affected by this attack and went from person to person to offer aid.

As the air cleared a little, I saw the light ball float up into the sky about one hundred yards. It hovered for a moment, then it started spinning. A laser-like beam of light shot from the ball and hit my head.

The light beam looked eerily like a glowing arrow. As it struck my head, I got a piercingly loud, high-pitched sound in my left ear. I grabbed my head and made a grunting sound, "Ugh!"

Rehema rushed over. "Michael, are you OK?"

"Ow, that hurt. Did anyone else get that high-pitched sound?"

Some of the others replied in a confused state, "What high-pitched sound? What are you talking about? I didn't hear anything except the buzz."

I don't know what came over me, but I addressed the group and began telling them about the Order. "This has happened before, about a week ago—honest! I saw a UFO, a buzzing sound occurred, and people began to get sick and angry. This is the secret government, the Order, the government behind the government. They're working with the evil aliens."

"What?!" a lot of them reacted.

Shannon asked, "Michael, what are you talking about? What secret government? What Order? What's happening here?"

"All I can tell you is that there is a group of people all around the world who believe they are superior to everyone else, and they don't care about hurting other people. These are bad dudes. All they care about is power, money, control, and domination."

One of the guys in the group denounced what I said right away, "Our government doesn't hurt people. You must be crazy. The United States are the good guys."

"All I can tell you is that this happened before."

Rehema backed me up, "It's true. This happened about a week ago, and it has happened many times before that. Some people go crazy and hurt each other when this buzzing sound occurs."

One of the guys who had wrestled with his friend commented, "I don't know what came over me. I just felt this intense anger. Then I heard voices in my head telling me to fight. I've never been that angry before." He turned and apologized to his friend.

Jabari pointed toward the sky. "The UFO is gone. Let's walk the horses back. Then you can decide if you want to stay for the light show or go back to the hotel."

Ehab, Rehema, and Shannon checked out the rest of our group. Everyone seemed to have recovered and said they wanted to continue.

Shannon reflected on the events and shook her head, "This has been the weirdest tour I've ever been on."

The wife and husband cheered, "This has been the best. Let's do it again. We're ready to sign up."

The horses were back at the stable, and our group was buzzing with chatter. Four members said they had changed their minds and wanted to skip the light show. Ehab mentioned he would get a cab and escort them back to the hotel. The rest of us waited for the show near Khafre's Temple. Except for Jabari and Rehema, they all kept their distance.

"Guys, do you see how they are all looking at me? I feel awful. I never wanted anyone to get hurt."

Rehema pointed out, "Michael, you didn't hurt them. This is all because of the Order. They are the ones behind this, not you."

"You know what? You're right. I didn't hurt them. And the Order has been hurting people for centuries."

Jabari added, "And they'll continue hurting people long after we are gone."

"Unless we can find a way to stop them."

"Ooh, nice going there, Tumaini," snickered Rehema. "What do you have in mind?"

"I guess some of those answers are in the parchments and scrolls."

"I bet you're right."

The others began walking around the small temple and moved out of sight. As they moved away, an Egyptian guard took post on one of the empty statue mounts about ten feet away. He kept staring at us with an ominous look in his eyes.

Jabari noticed him first and put his hand in his jacket. The guard reacted and swung his machine gun off of his shoulder, but he did not point it at us. Instead, he held it in front of his body on an angle in an offensive position. His face grew angrier by the moment, and then it changed.

"Holy cow, did you see that?!" I shouted. I could instantly feel his dark energy.

The guard's face suddenly shifted into a reptilian-looking head. It was green and scaly, with blood-red eyes. You could see its pupils change from a black round shape to a black slit. It hissed at us and showed its lizard fangs.

Jabari warned us, "It's a hybrid reptilian! Run!"

He tackled the guard like a charging linebacker and knocked him down before he could shoot. I pulled Rehema behind me and shielded her. Then the others came running toward us and saw the guard. He kicked Jabari, struggled free, and ran away.

"What was that thing?" asked the wife.

"It was a thief. He was posing as a guard and wore a mask," answered Jabari, as he picked up the soldier's gun. "I think it's best that everyone goes back to the hotel tonight."

"I couldn't agree more," said Shannon. "I've just about reached my limit."

Jabari spoke to Rehema so only she could hear, "I think you should take Michael. He's not safe with this group. They know all of our movements now. You know where to take him. And don't use your car, either. I'll go back with the others to the hotel. I'll tell them that you wanted Michael to stay with you. When I'm done, I'll get your car and meet you at the predestined location. Don't think about this. Go!"

"OK," and she tossed him her keys.

She grabbed my hand and started pulling. "Follow me. I know a safe passage out of here. Let's go before anyone asks any questions."

Jabari got the others' attention and told them to walk to the bus. As they walked away, Rehema guided me to the back of the temple. Then she went behind one of the stone pillars and pointed to the wall. "Michael, do you remember me telling you about secret tunnels?"

"Yes…"

She pushed a large stone on the back wall and it moved inwards. A latch behind the stone made a clicking noise, and this released a door beneath it. When she pushed the lower stone, it swung inside the wall on its hinge.

"Come on," she whispered.

She knelt down, crawled inside, grabbed a torch from the inner wall, and lit it. I ducked my head and followed her. Then the door swung shut behind us.

"Careful with these stairs. They can be treacherous."

"Where do they lead?"

"They lead down, silly. Come on."

CHAPTER FOURTEEN

ALL ROADS LEAD OUT OF EGYPT

"Rehema, wait a minute. Don't go down the stairs yet. What was that thing? Did you see its face? It looked like a real reptile, but with a human body."

"I did. I couldn't believe my eyes, either. It changed from a human's face to a snarling monster and back again. Did you see its teeth?"

"Yeah, they looked like shark's teeth. Tell me that's not what we are up against."

"I'm afraid so."

"So now we've gone from human attacks to aliens. What's next? Attack of the killer mummies? Zombies? Flesh-eating camels?"

"After seeing that alien, I know we need help—a lot of help."

"I think the whole world will need a lot of help."

"Let's get going. We have a long walk ahead of us."

"Hey, Rehema, who built this tunnel anyway? Where does it go?"

"It depends on whom you ask. Some say it was Khafre, some say it was Ramses—supposedly he built this as an escape route—and others say it was built by smugglers or aliens. It runs all the way from the Sphinx to the other side of the Nile. Then it branches off."

"It goes under the Nile?"

"Yeah, I guess if they could build a pyramid, they could build a tunnel under the Nile."

"Who else knows of these tunnels?"

"We do, the government, and the black market."

"Look, here's another torch. We'll make better time if we can both see."

Rehema lit the torch and we walked for another twenty minutes. Up ahead, we could see a light that was coming toward us at a fast pace.

"Rehema, what's that up ahead?"

"I don't know. We should douse our light and hide."

"Hide? Where are we going to hide? It's a tunnel."

"I don't know, but let's do something. That light is getting closer really fast." We doused our torches in one of the puddles and crouched down.

"They're going to see us," I whispered.

"Michael, I'm scared." She grabbed my arm tightly. "What should we do?"

"Stay here, I'm going up ahead. Maybe they haven't seen you."

"I'm going with you."

"No. You stay here. It'll be safer." I ran through the dark as best I could. Then I stopped because I heard a lot of footsteps up ahead. It sounded like a mini stampede.

"Whoa!" yelled a voice in a commanding tone. The footsteps began to scuffle.

"Tumaini, is that you?"

The light was right on top of me, and all I could make out was a donkey with a cart strapped to it. It was trying desperately to stop before we crashed. "Who is it? Who's there?!"

"It's me, Hanif."

"Hanif?"

"Yes. Where's Rehema?"

"I'm right here, hon," as she darted past me. They hugged and kissed for a moment.

"How did you know we were down here?" I asked.

"It was Jabari. He called me and told me what happened. I strapped up the donkey and got here as fast as I could."

"This is Daisy?"

"Yes."

"Hello, Daisy. Boy am I glad to see you."

"C'mon, Michael, help me get Daisy unhooked so we can turn the cart around. We need to get out of the tunnels as soon as possible."

In a few minutes, we were back on our way. The lights weren't bright enough for the speed we were going, so Hanif stayed focused on the tunnel ahead. When we reached a spot where the tunnel branched off, Hanif asked me to help. "Michael, come here. Help me push this wall."

"We're not going down the other path?"

Rehema replied, "No, this is our secret tunnel entrance. The Protectors built this decades ago."

I started pushing on the wall, but it didn't budge.

"Wait a minute"—Rehema jumped down and walked past us—"I almost forgot." She pushed a panel on the wall, and the door cracked open.

"Boy, you sure know where the secret compartments are."

"It goes along with the territory. We archeologists know all the secrets," she giggled.

After we pushed the door all the way open, we angled the cart to make the sharp turn. Once on the other side, we closed the door and heard the click of the latch.

"What, no hi-tech security panel?"

"Who needs a security panel when you have a Rehema with you?" he chuckled.

Daisy trotted along for another fifteen minutes or so and stopped at a dead end. "Now what do we do?" I asked.

"We go upstairs." He paused for a moment. "Strike that. You go with Rehema upstairs. I have to take the donkey up the ramp."

"What ramp?"

Rehema was reaching for the wall. "This one." She pushed on another panel, and a door exposed a basement filled with incense boxes, glass-making supplies, and other trinkets. The stairs were on the left, and the ramp was on the right. At the top of the ramp were two storm doors that led to an alley.

"Michael, come with me. We are home." She started up the stairs.

"Home? Where are we?"

"Follow me."

When I walked through the doorway, I saw a stone furnace in the middle of the room with all kinds of glass-making tools. There was a small pile of red coals still smoldering amongst the ash. I looked to the right and saw a familiar archway.

"Here we are, Michael."

"Wait a minute. This is Hanif's shop."

Mudads walked into the room and smiled, "Yes, it is. I'm glad you made it here alive. We were worried about you, my friend."

I gave him a fast hug. "It's good to see you, too."

"Let's go into the other room. I know some people who are anxious to see you."

I was met by Omar, Karim, Ramla, and Ehab. They were sitting on the familiar red sofa and chairs. "You guys are incredible. I don't know what to say. Thanks for all your help."

Omar got up to shake my hand. "We heard about what happened in Luxor and the desert. I'm glad you are alright."

"I am, thanks to you and Karim—and you, of course, Ramla." She smiled back at me.

Karim added, "We did our best. I understand that the assassin tried to kill you more than once."

"Yes, and it was Gahiji who saved me twice. He really lived up to his name. Asim was a great help, too."

Ramla prodded, "Tumaini, what else happened?"

I walked over and sat down next to her. "Ramla, I time traveled back to ancient Egypt. I saw myself as a young priest. It seems as if the parchments I wrote were real. There are thirty-six priests who are supposed to come back."

"Yes, there are, and you already met two." In my head she shared, "And there are more in this room." I looked around at everyone, trying to figure out who might be a priest.

Ehab spoke next, "Michael, I know you didn't get to check in at the hotel. Ramla thought it would be a good idea to bring your luggage here." He pointed to the pile by the front door.

"Actually, that's a great idea. I was thinking about the parchments and how they were written in ancient hieratic. I haven't had any time to decipher them. And Omar, I remember that you can read hieratic."

"I can, for the most part. Some of it I still struggle with. But if I'm given time, I can translate most writings."

"Great, that would be a huge help." I turned to see Hanif coming through the archway. "You walked in just in time. Do you have a copy machine?"

"Yes, I have one in my office."

"Can we use it to copy some of the parchments? Omar can help me translate them."

"That is a great idea. Rehema and I can do that for you."

I walked over to my trunk, unlocked it, pulled out my leather bag with the parchments, and handed it to Hanif. He motioned for Rehema and Omar to follow him. They left and went upstairs.

"Guys, I also had a run-in with a reptilian hybrid. If it wasn't for Jabari, I think I would have been lizard food. He was incredibly brave. As soon as he saw the reptilian shape shift, he lunged at it before it could kill us."

Karim agreed, "He is very brave. That's why we sent him to be with you."

"Again, thanks, Karim. You've been a big help."

My compliment must have broken a barrier between us because he walked up to me and put his hand on my shoulder. "It was my pleasure to serve you."

"Wow, thanks, Karim. I'll do my best to serve you, too."

Mudads asked, "Michael, did anything else happen in Luxor that we need to know about?"

"Yes, there was. It seems that some of my abilities have come back and strengthened over time. And when Gahiji and Asim were with me, they were able to do things that they couldn't do before."

Karim's curiosity was piqued, "Like what?"

"Asim healed a temple guard. His cut instantly disappeared. And both Gahiji and Asim got names while they meditated. I think it was because they were near me. My abilities helped theirs to manifest, just like Ramla helped mine. I think that will aid the other priests when they come forth. Whoever has an ability can help the new ones develop theirs."

Ramla thumped her cane on the floor. "That's an excellent idea, Tumaini. We'll help the ones who are here, and you help the new ones that you meet."

"I will."

Mudads inquired, "What else can we do to help?"

"I think what I've said is a great start. We need to identify and help the priests. When I get back to the States, I'll work on the scrolls and parchments. I have a feeling that more answers will come from them."

Ramla nodded, "You may be right, Tumaini. That will be our plan for now."

Mudads joked, "And staying alive. Staying alive is always a good idea."

While I laughed, Jabari came in through the front door. "Jabari! Are you alright? I didn't get to speak with you after the reptilian showed up."

"I'm fine, Michael. Just a small bruise on my elbow—barely even noticeable."

"Well, I'm sorry that you had to even endure that."

"Really, it's nothing. What did I miss?"

Mudads informed him, "We were going over a plan of action. Michael's going to work on the scrolls, and we'll help the awakened priests."

"I can do that, no problem. By the way, where is Rehema?"

Karim pointed behind him because he heard their footsteps. "She was helping Omar with some copies. And there she is! What timing."

"Rehema, here's your keys. I checked your car, and there were no explosives."

Hanif reacted, "Explosives?! What do you mean, explosives?!"

"Well, because of the attack, I didn't want to take any chances. I thought I should check her car for tampering. I might be overreacting, but it's better to be safe than sorry in my line of work."

"I'm glad you checked. Thanks for bringing my car back."

"Glad to be of service."

Omar walked over and gave me my bag. I checked inside for any hidden pastries. There weren't any that I could see, so I sighed, "Do you have everything you need?"

"Yes, this should give me a lot to do in the next few days."

"You are going to be a big help, I can tell. It would have been pretty challenging to do the translations all on my own."

"Is there anything else you need me to do?"

"Not that I can think of."

Hanif remembered, "Oh, and I put the receipt for your new stuff in your bag. It's in the bottom under the stack."

I thanked him, then I looked at Ramla. "Ramla, you've been pretty quiet so far. Is there anything you can share that would help?"

"Yes, there is. I've been waiting for the right time to bring this up. Do you remember when we had breakfast together?" I nodded, and she continued, "You asked me about the Order and their three plans."

"Yes, you said that they've attempted two, but failed—well, kind of failed."

"I was wrong about that, Tumaini."

"What?" The others all turned and listened in.

"From what our seers have told me, there weren't three plans. It's all been one big long plan." She shook her head in disgust. "The bloodlines were waiting patiently for the time when technology would catch up with their sinister plot. They want to microchip every human being." She hit her cane on the floor really hard. "And they don't just want microchips that monitor your movements and your spending accounts; they want to put mind control implants into every living soul. They want to create a race of mindless drones to serve their selfish needs."

Rehema gasped, "Surely, you must be joking!"

"I wish I was. And there's more."

"Please tell us," I urged.

"From our intelligence, it seems as if the reptilians are doing something far worse than this. They now have the technology to trap living souls."

Mudads objected, "How can they do this?"

She gave him a quick glance. "Everything is energy. Our souls are energy, and our souls vibrate in a certain way when the soul leaves the body. Supposedly, the reptilians found a way to capture the energy waves of the soul right at the moment of death, just before the soul can move on to its next stage of development."

I burst in anger, "Why would they do this?! What do they gain from it?!"

"If they can capture a soul, they can place it into another human body and torture that soul for an entire lifetime. Then they can feed off of all the negative emotions, agony, and suffering. If they are successful, they can ultimately keep a soul in a perpetual cycle of painful reincarnations. The soul will never be able to return to the Realm of Souls."

"Those dirty...reptilians!" cursed Karim.

Ramla went on, "This goes further. When the reptilians put a soul into another body, that body will be chipped in the future by the Anunnaki. It essentially becomes a slave to the Anunnaki, and the Anunnaki serve the alien agenda. It's a vicious cycle that will never end."

Jabari countered, "Unless we can do something about it."

Ehab joined in, "Yes, unless we can do something about it. But what can we do?"

Ramla looked at me. "I think that is why Tumaini and the other priests—including you two—have come back. Maybe you and the others can change this terrible cycle."

I asked, "But how do they capture a soul? I mean, I understand the energy part, but there must be some type of mechanics to all of this."

"They have a machine in outer space that borders the physical and the spirit worlds. That machine is what captures and holds the souls."

"This is a plot far more devious than any Bible story I've ever read."

"Remember, Tumaini, the Bible was influenced by the aliens. They aren't going to put their plot in writing for everyone to see."

"That's a good point, Ramla. Let's get back to the part about the micro-chips. Won't people reject the idea of being chipped?"

"That's part of the plot, Tumaini. The Order doesn't want an uprising, so they are using fear as a way to get people to accept being chipped."

Mudads asked, "You mean, if people don't get chipped, they can't buy things?"

Rehema answered, "Exactly. But there is more to it. The Order is try-ing to brainwash everyone that being chipped is the safest way to protect people's money."

Omar added, "It's already started, too. The governments have chipped our licenses, passports, and credit cards. They've even brainwashed people in other countries to chip their pets. It seems like we're next."

Karim angrily pointed out, "You mean *the Order* has done this. The governments are nothing but puppets."

"Yes, thank you for correcting my error." Then he addressed the group again, "Furthermore, the Order uses the media to drive people into a frenzy with fear. We can all see the handwriting on the wall, too. The media will get the people demanding to be microchipped so they can protect their cash and bank accounts. And the banks will gladly play along and force you to get chipped just to open an account with them." He huffed, "Get people afraid, and you can control them like a herd of sheep."

Karim nodded, "That was eloquently put, Omar."

I asked, "So if you guys know all of this already, how come you haven't solved the problem? What do you need me for?"

Jabari retorted, "It's because the people are brainwashed, and they are taught not to question. And with all of our efforts, we can't get the people to change. Besides, you're labeled a terrorist or anarchist if you challenge the government"—he looked at Karim—"I mean, *the Order*."

"Again, what does that have to do with me?"

Ramla pointed at me with her cane. "There must be something in your destiny that can give people a chance, Tumaini. Give people a little hope, and they can change the world. I think that is what you are here to do."

"I'll do my best to help, honest. So what happened from the time I left up till now? Where did all of this new information come from?"

Hanif responded, "Our seers have been working around the clock since you left. After you met with Ramla, they have been able to see things in the near future that they weren't able to see before."

"I get it," I nodded.

"What?" asked Ehab.

"It has to do with the timelines. When people work toward the same goal, that future gets stronger. Then, the seers can distinguish it from all of the other possibilities because it is more predictable. I experienced the same thing as Tumaini when I time traveled and talked to my future self. That's how I ended up in your shop, Mudads. Maybe that's why the seers could see this new information."

Ramla agreed, "I think that must be so. The future solidifies with intentions and actions."

"Great," I exclaimed. "So now we have to wait, which seems odd, but it's true."

Karim asked angrily, "Why wait? We've already waited long enough. Now is the time to act!"

"I know, Karim, but it will take me some time to decipher all of the clues from the scrolls and parchments."

Omar added, "That's where I can help."

"And what do you want the rest of us to do?" inquired Hanif.

I glanced at Ramla, then the others. "Keep living. We've been doing this up till now. We're all being forced to practice patience."

Karim spat, "I hate patience."

"I know, but I can't ask any more than that. When I get new information, I'll pass it along as soon as possible."

Ramla spoke in my head, "Faster than thought, I imagine."

Ehab mentioned to Jabari, "We have to get to the hotel soon and finish our duties."

He gibed, "Yes, we still have to live. The sheeple aren't done being led around yet."

"Now, now, give this some time," implored Rehema. "We've made huge progress in one week. This will change."

I asked Hanif, "Do you have a shower I can use? It doesn't make sense for me to check in to the hotel for just an hour or two."

"Sure, you can stay here as long as you'd like."

Rehema came over and told me, "Michael, I'm going back to the pyramids with you. There's something that you must see."

"Great. It doesn't seem like we can do any more, unless someone has some other secret to share."

We all looked at Ramla. She smirked defensively, "Don't look at me."

"It's settled, then. Let's live our lives and keep in touch. Now I have to figure out how to break all of this to Constance and Hara."

Rehema reminded me, "Don't forget, I offered to help."

"I won't. Hanif, I could use that shower about now."

"I'll show you where it is."

"Hey, Ehab and Jabari, I'll meet you guys at the pyramids. Please tell Shannon that I've been here all night so she won't worry."

Ehab gestured. "No problem, my friend," and they walked toward the door. Ramla, Omar, and Karim said their goodbyes and followed behind them.

"I'll miss you guys," I shouted.

Ramla replied, "Don't worry. We'll see each other again."

―――――•+•+•―――――

We were in line to enter the Giza Necropolis at 7:20 a.m. We saw our tour bus and waved hello. Once we got inside, we parked and walked over to our group. Jabari was standing guard, and Ehab was deep in a humorous tale about the pyramids.

Shannon walked up to me and asked, "Michael, I hope you don't take this the wrong way, but some of the group wants to know what you will be doing."

"Why do they want to know?"

"Well—and please don't shoot the messenger—they want to go where you won't be going."

"Honestly, I'm not surprised. I feel really bad about what's happened on this trip."

"Some of them actually think you are cursed. Did you spit on a pharaoh's wife in a former life?"

"Believe it or not, you're not that far off. And I can't explain to you what is going on. It would take more time than we have left."

I looked toward Rehema. "What's the agenda for today?"

She held up a small piece of paper. "We are going into the Great Pyramid as soon as it opens. I have a special pass that will take us anywhere we want to go."

Shannon called to Ehab and Jabari, "Michael is going into the pyramids first. How about, Ehab, you go with the camel riders. We'll let Michael have the pyramids all to himself. Jabari, you go with him. When he is done, we'll all switch."

I jested, "I thought you said there were *some*..."

Rehema squeezed my forearm. "I think it's best this way. Let them go."

I didn't argue with Rehema or Shannon. As Shannon walked away, I hollered, "Have fun! Watch out for the camels—they spit!"

Climbing the enormous stones of the pyramid to get to the lower entrance is an experience all in itself. It gave me a glimpse into what it might have been like when these towering monuments were built.

"I wonder if I was here as Tumaini?"

Rehema answered, "It wouldn't surprise me. Did you move that stone into place?"

"No, I was in charge of the twenty-third floor. You must be thinking of my twin brother, Two-few. He's the opposite of hope."

Jabari laughed, "Do you mean despair?"

"Yeah, despair. That's a good one, Jabari."

"Well, I do have my moments." We all chuckled and kept climbing toward the guards.

When we reached the opening, Rehema showed them her pass. They studied it for a long time. I felt uncomfortable because they kept looking back and forth between her and the paper.

She leaned over and whispered, "Don't worry, they do this sometimes. They have to check the paperwork since it is an all-inclusive pass. Everything is in order. Besides, the guard on the left knows me."

He gave his approval with a blank tone, "Go ahead." We thanked them and went inside.

"Hold on, guys. I want to take some pictures." I pulled out my camera and turned into a tourist again. I snapped photos all the way down to the first intersection. There was a casually dressed guard standing at the metal gates that continued to the subterranean chamber below.

Rehema pointed to the left. "This is where we are going, Michael. Are you ready to climb down?"

"I've never done this part before. Last time I was here they had it locked, even though we had permission."

"I know; it's inconsistent at times. Tell me that you didn't leave because the gate was locked."

"Oh no, we still went up to the Queen's chamber and the King's chamber."

Jabari patted my shoulder. "My favorite is the Grand Gallery. That will give your calves a workout."

"I remember that. Thanks for the memory."

Rehema added, "Well, this will give you a different kind of workout. Down to the Well is easy; *up* is the hard part. Your hamstrings and glutes will be screaming at the end."

I looked at how steep it was. "You aren't kidding, are you?" About every ten steps or so, I kept asking, "Are we there yet?"

Rehema playfully answered, "Shoosh, Tumaini, or I'll turn this pyramid right around."

"Ha! That's what I've said to Hara more than once. But seriously, are we almost there yet?"

"Yes, see for yourself. But don't get too excited. Now we have to play commando."

"Commando?"

Jabari chimed in, "Yes, now we have to crawl on our hands and knees for about thirty feet through this tiny tunnel. Hope you aren't claustrophobic."

"Not a chance. Let's get moving."

———————

At the end of the tunnel, we stood up inside a medium-sized cave that had been dug out of the foundation stone. To the left, there was a round, beat-up barricade that encircled a deep pit filled with garbage. To the right were stone platforms with lights which barely illuminated the room. And at the back of the Well, we saw a tiny tunnel cut into the limestone that was only big enough for one person to squeeze through at a time.

"Rehema, what are we doing here?" I asked.

"Come here. It's behind this wall. Geez, it's really tough to get back in here." Rehema was up on a stone ledge and crawling into a tiny crevice that was barely big enough for her body.

"What's back there?" inquired Jabari.

"What are you waiting for? Both of you come here and look."

I took a few photos and joked, "I forgot my spelunking hat."

"Michael, stop that and get over here!"

"Yes, ma'am."

Rehema was grunting and forced the last of the big rocks to one side. "Hardly anyone in the mainstream knows about this. Only a handful of Protectors have seen it. We are trying to keep this hush-hush until the time is right."

"What is it?" I tried looking over her shoulder to get a better look.

"See for yourself." Fused in the stone was a shiny piece of black metal. It resembled a handle from a walking stick, with a button under the curve and a long piece that disappeared into the rock.

"Fascinating," I mused.

Rehema gestured. "Here's the best part." She took one of the smaller rocks and held it near the stick. Then she simultaneously pushed the button and let go of the rock. Surprisingly, the rock didn't fall; it levitated just inches off of the ledge. "We think this is how the aliens built the pyramids."

"Wait a minute. Aliens built this?"

"Well, we believe that the aliens genetically made slaves to do the grunt work, and they used this device to levitate the massive stones into place. For whatever reason, this was left here, and we can't get it out of the rock. Even Arthur of Camelot couldn't pull this out of the stone."

I exclaimed, "This has to be the archeological find of the century. Why can't we tell people?"

"Because the Egyptian government and the Order won't allow it. Anyone who has tried has been killed."

"So why show it to me?"

"I wanted you to know that the pyramids were built by aliens, and here is the proof."

"I already knew it wasn't built by slaves who used copper tools and wooden hammers. We're not as dumb as they think we are!"

Jabari was nodding his head as he looked in amazement at the suspended stone. "And this pretty much cinches it. I'm a believer."

I asked, "Do we know which aliens built it?"

Rehema suggested, "We think it might have been the mantids or the reptilians, maybe even both. All we know is that it wasn't humans who were in charge."

"I think I hear some people coming." Jabari peered around the corner. "We'd better cover it back up." He crawled back off the shelf and walked to the entrance to take post.

Rehema went to work and placed all of the stones over the stick. Then she moved the heavier rock and wedged it firmly back in place.

"I don't know what to say, Rehema. Thanks for showing that to me."

"I thought it might help, since you are Tumaini and all."

A few tourists came into the Well. They only stayed for five minutes, took some photos, and left.

I looked back at both of them. "There is something about this place. The energy has changed. Do you feel it?"

"I don't feel anything," answered Jabari.

Rehema pointed near the pit. "I feel it. It's coming from over there."

Then Jabari added, "Wait, I do feel it. It's…it's…I've never felt anything like this before."

"Whoa, do you see that?!" I yelled.

"What is that?" asked Rehema.

"It looks like a portal. And those aren't humans on the other side."

Jabari put his hand on his gun. "They look like aliens to me, but they don't see us. What do you want to do, Tumaini? Do you want to go in?"

"Not on your life, and we need to watch out for Rehema. Hanif would never forgive us if we went in and didn't come back out."

Rehema nodded, "That's some good advice. Let's get out of here."

We didn't waste any time and left the Well behind us. Once we were out of the tunnel, Rehema said, "I've never felt anything like that before, and I've been in that Well more times than I've been in my own kitchen. What made the difference this time?"

"Don't you get it?" I asked.

"What don't we get?" inquired Jabari.

I think your abilities just manifested to see and feel new dimensions. We had to go through this when I was training as a priest. I think that you two are priests."

Jabari laughed, "You've got to be kidding. I'm not even religious."

"That's funny. Your brother said the same thing."

"Tumaini, this is going to take some time to sink in."

"Take all the time you want, but I'm convinced. And this makes five of us. Rehema, don't you have anything to say?"

"I'm a reincarnated priest from ancient Egypt? No wonder I was drawn here. Now it all makes sense. Thank you, Tumaini. I don't know what else to say."

"I do. I'm encouraged now more than ever. And you two get to help all the other priests who keep waking up."

I thought in my head, "If only Ramla were here to see this."

She replied back, "I am, and don't forget to help Rehema with her telepathy."

I was about to tell Rehema and lifted a finger, but Ramla included, "However, don't tell her just yet," and my hand dropped.

Rehema saw my hand gesture. "What was that all about, Tumaini?"

"You'll see...you'll see," and we began the long climb back outside.

Shannon was waiting at the entrance to check on us, while the rest of our tour group waited below. "Michael, will you be going to the camels now?"

I shook my head *no*. "I've got a better idea. I'm already packed, I'm not going back to the hotel, and I think I've seen enough here. I'll just meet you guys at the airport."

"What about our end-of-the-tour lunch at the hotel?"

"If I join you, I might jinx your order. You guys enjoy the luncheon. I'll be fine."

Rehema mentioned, "We'll take care of him, Shannon. Hanif, Mudads, and I want to see him off anyway."

I looked at Jabari, who was still in awe from his experience. "It's been my utmost pleasure. We'll be in touch."

He replied, "I know. I'm looking forward to it."

From a distance, I waved. "Goodbye, guys!" Then Rehema and I walked away.

CHAPTER FIFTEEN

A PLANE STATE
OF EMERGENCY

Tears were flowing like the Nile at the airport. "Mudads, Hanif, Rehema, I don't have the words to tell you how much you have come to mean to me in such a short time. I'm more than lucky to have met such wonderful people like you. No matter what happens in the future, I will always be grateful. Thank you."

Mudads choked up for a second. "And we feel the same, Michael. Is there anything we can do for you?"

"Yes, tell every one of the Protectors that I am honored to be a part of such an admirable group."

"It will be done, my friend."

Rehema took my hand in hers. "Just remember, the network is up and running. They know about you and are ready to help. And we're just a phone call away."

"You mean, just a pigeon away." Hanif and Rehema grinned, and I added, "I'll be sending you updates as soon as I can."

They walked me to Customs and helped me get through. Hanif and Mudads vouched for the items in my steamer trunk. Since they were the store owners, the Customs officer didn't give me any trouble and let me pass without any problems.

"Well, this is where we say goodbye, my friends." We all hugged, and I did my best not to break down in the middle of the airport. Mudads did his traditional bow, and they walked away.

———————

I met with our tour group and they began boarding the plane. Instead of going on right away, I went to the counter to see if I could upgrade my ticket with my frequent flyer miles. There was one first class seat left which would pretty much wipe out my balance. It was a long flight over the Atlantic, and I didn't feel like answering a lot of questions from the others, so I took it.

"Welcome aboard, Mr. Whyse. First class is up the stairs. Can I take your bag?" asked one of the attendants.

"No, thanks. I'll keep this with me for now."

"The first class attendant will take your drink order when you get there. Enjoy your flight."

"Thanks again. By the way, is there an in-flight movie?"

"Yes. *Mantis Men Conquer the World*, or my favorite, *Attack of the Killer Reptile.*"

"I think I'll pass on those."

"Are you sure? They are free."

"I'm very sure."

Shannon and the others watched me walk up the stairs. I could see a few of them move toward their seat neighbor and whisper. When one of them pointed toward me, I thought to myself, "I bet they were hoping I would miss this flight."

I got to my seat and declined the complimentary drink. I had a lot of catching up to do on my sleep, so I closed my eyes and thought of Constance and Hara.

———————

I woke up a few times during the flight, made small talk with my neighbor, had a surprisingly good vegetarian dinner, and I did my best not to watch any of the movies. We'd been in the air for about eight hours, and there wasn't much else to do, so I closed my eyes again and went back to sleep.

Suddenly, I felt the plane jerk wildly, and this woke me up from my slumber. Then the plane violently bounced up and down for ten seconds straight. The captain announced, "Ladies and gentlemen, please fasten your seatbelts. We are experiencing severe turbulence."

The stewardesses were scrambling to get people seated and buckled up. A person three seats up from me was frantically pointing out the window. "Did you see that?! Did you see that?!" The plane instantly dropped down a few dozen feet. Both attendants fell to the ground, and all of the oxygen masks burst into the cabin and jangled in the air.

From the other side of the plane, another person warned with a frightened voice, "Here it comes again! It's heading straight for us," followed by another sudden drop.

I did my best to lean forward and look out the window, but I kept bouncing around like I was riding a mechanical bull. "What was that?" I asked the other person.

"It was a light...a ball...a spaceship!"

The plane shook even more violently this time. Over the loudspeakers, the pilot stressed, "Ladies and gentlemen, we are experiencing extreme turbulence. Please remain calm and put on your oxygen masks."

The man up front blurted, "Turbulence my ass! Who's he trying to kid? That's a UFO!"

The light ball came at the other side of the plane. This time we tilted in the same direction and turned like a fighter jet making an attack run. Our nose started diving, and we were picking up speed.

Another woman screamed, "It's following us down! We're all gonna die!"

Luggage was shooting out of the overhead bins, and people were hysterical and crying. Two people across the aisle were knocked out by flying suitcases. The plane continued picking up speed as we headed toward a watery grave.

Over the speakers, the pilot broadcast, "Ladies and gentlemen, please brace for impact. Place your head between your knees and clasp your hands behind your neck."

Almost everyone was in a panic. I kept looking out the window to try and see the light. The woman beside me grabbed the armrest and pinned my arm down. She squeezed so hard that I yelled, "Owww!"

The plane tilted from the left to the right this time, which finally enabled me to see the light ball. It was still traveling down with us as our plane accelerated. Then it suddenly stopped and hovered.

The pilot came back on with fear in his voice, "Ladies and gentlemen, brace for impact." Some of the people began to pray and beg for help.

The loudspeakers were left on, and we could hear the pilots reporting, "Mayday! Mayday! Flight 641 heavy is going down into the ocean. Mayday!"

"Pull up! Pull up! Don't give up, Stan. Pull up!"

"Loudspeakers—turn them off! Now!"

The light ball flew off, made an instant ninety-degree turn, and disappeared behind the clouds. When all seemed lost, the plane slowly started to level out and regain altitude. We climbed a little more, and the shaking finally stopped. After another minute of flight, the pilot came back on. "Ladies and gentlemen, thank you for your patience. We've regained control of the plane, and all of our instruments appear to be functioning normally again. You can remove your masks now. Please remain seated until we turn off the overhead sign. We'll give you another update in a few moments."

The plane erupted into cheers, while attendants and passengers were busy helping those who were injured.

I turned to my neighbor. "Are you alright?"

She removed her hand and gasped, "I'm so sorry." I could see her handprint on the back of my arm. "Do you know what that was?"

"I think it was a UFO."

"A UFO? I thought those were a myth."

"What do you think it was?"

"I don't know, but I don't believe in little green men. This must have been a problem with the plane. How is your arm?" She touched it lightly.

"I'm OK, thanks."

The rest of the passengers were deep in discussions about terrorist plots, engine failures, and other conclusions. One of the passengers in front of me turned around and asked, "I heard you say UFO. Do you believe it was a UFO?"

Before I could answer, the woman beside me shook her head *no*. Then I replied, "I saw the light fly away at an incredible speed, then shoot off at an angle. After it was gone, our plane regained control."

"Oh, my," is all she said. Then she turned around.

The woman beside me retorted angrily, "You should stop saying it was a UFO. You're scaring the other passengers."

I was confused. I wasn't trying to scare anyone at all, so I queried, "How do you explain a light ball instantly changing directions and defying our current technological abilities?"

"Maybe you didn't see it correctly. Besides, our government would have told us if UFOs really existed."

I was a little perturbed by her accusation and asked sincerely, "Do you really think our government tells us everything?"

"Yes, I trust them. Don't you?"

In my mind I thought, "This is going to be rough. She's brainwashed to trust them, and she doesn't even know it."

I enunciated slowly, "I don't trust our government—not one bit."

She snapped back, "Well, you don't know how lucky you are to be a U.S. citizen and protected by the government. They gave us the constitution. We live in a free world."

"I'm sorry, I was just being truthful. And we certainly are not free."

"Well, you should be more grateful anyway."

A wall instantly came between us, and she didn't say another word. That effectively ended our conversation for the rest of the flight. Luckily for me, the pilots came on and helped cut the tension. They said that everything was working fine and we would land as scheduled.

For the rest of the flight, I kept mulling over how hard this shift in consciousness was going to be. I was still surrounded by people who never questioned the government, were separated by religious beliefs, and lived for themselves. Greed, fear, and selfishness were still very much a part of life in our country and others. This was going to be a tough transition.

Two hours later, we were rolling in to our gate. One of the attendants announced to us that the airlines had arranged paramedics and counselors for anyone who needed medical assistance. We were also told that the media would be waiting at baggage claim for anyone who cared to make a statement.

On parting, the woman beside me grumbled, "I think you should have your head examined."

"Have a nice day, ma'am," is all I said.

I didn't need medical attention, and I certainly didn't want to talk to the puppet media, so I made my way as fast as I could through the crowds.

At baggage claim, Shannon came up to me and pleaded, "Michael, please don't sign up for our next tour. I don't think I could handle it."

The married couple came over to me and gave me their phone number. "She might not want you, but tell us when you are taking your next trip," the wife beamed. "This has been one of the most exciting times of our lives." I thanked them, collected my bags, and put them on my baggage cart.

When I wheeled up to the Customs checkpoint, I filled out the necessary paperwork, pulled out all of my receipts, and prepared to wait in the long lines. Twenty minutes later, I was face to face with a young man sporting a goatee and black metallic rings in his ears. The portions of his arms that weren't covered by his white dress shirt were painted with tattoos all the way down to his wrists.

"Do you have anything to declare?" he demanded.

"I'm glad to be home."

He didn't react and said bluntly, "Passport and paperwork."

I handed him my passport and the list of items I'd brought back with me.

"Do you have any fruits, vegetables, or animals to declare?"

"No, sir."

He looked at the list, looked at me, then looked at the list again. "Sir, I'll need to see what's in the trunk."

"OK. It's full of the papyrus and other gifts for my family."

"Just open the trunk, please." He was all business and not very friendly.

"Sir, you'll need to open these boxes."

I was getting a little concerned. I hoped he didn't think I was bringing in ancient artifacts. I asked him, "Do you need me to open all of them?"

"Yes. Open all of the boxes." I did as he instructed and opened everything in the trunk. "Do you have proof of purchase for all of these items?"

"Yes, yes I do. Where did I put those receipts? Ah, here they are. There is a receipt for everything."

He took his time checking between the list and all of the contents in the box. He was nothing if not thorough. "I see that you have an amulet on your list that is not in the trunk. I don't see a receipt for it, either."

My palms were getting a little sweaty, and I thought, "He's much tougher than the guys in Cairo. Where're Hanif and Mudads when you need them?"

"Sir, where is this amulet?"

"Oh, I didn't keep it in the trunk. I wore it on the plane. Here it is." I pulled it out and showed it to him.

His face changed instantly. "Where did you get this?!"

"It was given to me as a gift from the store owner's wife."

"No, I mean, where did you get this?"

I was confused and stammered, "I...I got this in Cairo, at an incense shop. Is everything OK?"

His personality flipped, and he became extremely inquisitive. "I've been looking all over the internet for this symbol. Can you tell me what it means? I saw a guy wear this on his chest a year ago. He was helping an elderly woman who had just fallen. It inspired me so much that I had it done as a tattoo. Look!" He pulled up his sleeve and showed me the symbol for the Protectors of Souls. "You've gotta tell me what this means. It's been driving me crazy. Can I see it?"

"Sure." I pulled it off and handed it to him.

"That's so cool. Wait till I tell the guys. Do you know what it means?"

"Yes, and it can change your life, too. This is a symbol for the Protectors of Light, the Protectors of Souls. The gold outer circle with the line at the bottoms is called a shen. Everything inside the shen is given eternal protection. The red stone represents the energy of Source, and the touchdown-looking arms are a symbol for your Ka, your soul."

"I don't know what that all means, but it sure looks cool. Thanks dude, you can pass." He helped me to rebox my stuff and handed me all of my paperwork. "Thanks again, dude. You rock."

"Glad I could be of help. Hope you have a great day."

As I walked away, I heard him whisper, "Protectors of Souls...huh."

———————

Constance was waiting for me just outside of the security gate, the place where it says *Point of no return*. I thought that was ironic and maybe a message for the rest of my life. She ran up to me and jumped into my arms. "I'm so glad to see you, and I was worried half-to-death. They said that your plane almost crashed." She kept kissing me on my lips and cheek. "Oh, I'm so glad that you are home." She squeezed me tighter than I could ever remember and kissed me again.

"Constance, you have no idea how much I missed you. It's wonderful to be back home. I love you."

She got a little teary-eyed, wiped her face, and kissed me one more time. "I love you, too, honey. Do you have all your bags?"

I counted everything on the luggage cart. "Everything's here."

"Good. Let's go home."

We were walking toward the parking garage, and I asked, "Where's Hara?"

"Oh, she's with her friend, Tammy. I think they are planning something for her birthday party tomorrow. By the way, I got your note. Did you get her the hieroglyphs?"

"I did, and I got her some almond oil and an oil lamp."

"How much did you have to bargain for that?"

"Believe it or not, I came out way ahead. Hanif was an expert in haggling, but I won more than money."

"Who's Hanif, and what are you talking about?"

"Hanif is the store owner. Actually, he may have beaten me in price, but I won something far more valuable—I won his friendship."

"That's nice," is all she said. "So what happened with the plane?"

"All I can tell you is that I saw a strange light outside of the window, and the plane took a nose dive. The light darted off, and we regained altitude. I think it was a UFO."

"A UFO? Are you sure?"

"I know it sounds crazy, but I'm pretty sure."

"What happened next?"

"That's it. I didn't get hurt, and the plane made it back safely. The only harm I endured was from the overreacting lady who sat beside me."

"Well, I'm so glad you are OK. I was really worried."

"Everything's alright, dear, honest."

"What did it look like?"

"Do you know your Aunt Elma's Christmas ornament?"

"Which one?"

"It's the plug-in one that looked like Saturn with its rings. But the UFO was all white, and the rings spun around. That's what it looked like."

"That's cool. I wish I could have seen it."

"I don't think you would have liked seeing it like we did."

"Oh, sorry, that must have been horrible."

"It's alright. Dinner at your Aunt's house is just as frightening."

"That's not funny."

"I have something to compare it to, so, yeah, it is."

"OK, you have a point."

———————————

We finally got the car packed, and we were ready to get on the road. It's a ninety-minute drive from the airport to the 'burbs, so we'd have plenty of time to talk.

"Honey, you've been flying all night. Why don't you let me drive?"

"I'm going to take you up on that, thanks," as I opened the door for her.

"After fifteen years of marriage, you're still such a gentleman."

"Well, I like looking at your legs. It's a win-win."

"Oh stop it."

"I can't help it. I'm excited to see you. Besides, you look much better than the camel I saw at the pyramids."

"Did you get to ride the camels?"

"Funny you should ask. It was at the *tail* end of the trip, and it wasn't *hump* day, so I didn't make the camel ride this time."

"Oh, that's a bad joke."

"Wait, there's more."

"OK, smarty-pants, get in. Morning rush hour is terrible here, you know that, and I want to beat the traffic."

"Alright, keep your pantyhose on." I smiled, ran around the car, and jumped in.

"So, what did you do while you were in Egypt? Did you get a lot of material for your next book?"

"Do you want the abridged version or the director's cut?"

"I'm feeling adventurous. What's behind door number two?"

"Are you sure you want to know?"

"Yes, tell me everything."

"Just remember, you asked. Seriously, though, can't this wait until we get home?"

"No, no, I want to know now."

I took a moment because my hands started to sweat. "Honey, make sure your seatbelt is on because this is going to be one heck of a ride."

———————

It took me a few moments to get going, then I said, "I don't know where to begin."

"Did you see the Colossi of Memnon?"

"Yeah, it was pretty boring, actually. Two tall men sitting in chairs, not much else to see."

"And did you see the Ramesseum?"

"Yes, that one was a little better. I didn't get much research material from that site, though. But I did see an interesting piece of graffiti that was carved onto one of the stone columns."

"Graffiti?"

"Yes, but it wasn't done very well. That person could have taken lessons from these guys." I pointed as we passed a bunch of graffiti on the overpass walkway.

"What was the carving?"

"Do you remember when I was doing research on sacred codes for my last book?"

"Yes."

"It was one of those symbols: the Seed of Life."

"I remember that one. It was part of the whole *Flower of Life* chapter."

"Exactly."

"What else did you see?"

"I saw the same symbol at the Osirian Temple. Now that one was cool. I took a couple of photos for you."

"I wanna see."

"How about when you aren't driving? By the way, I picked up a couple of presents for you."

"You didn't! What did you get? Where are they?"

"They're packed in the back. You'll have to wait until we get home."

"Awww, you're such a tease."

"I know. Will you forgive me?"

"I don't know. Teasing me with presents that I can't open is a fineable offense."

"Ha, good one. I think you'll like them. I found them at the vendors

208

outside of Queen Hatshepsut's Temple."

"I remember that place. Didn't we see that on our trip?"

"No. You're thinking of the vendors near Abu Simbel, Kom Ombo, and the Temple of Isis. We didn't do any of those on this trip."

"Oh yeah, now I remember. We had to take the train down to Abu Simbel. The bathrooms were disgusting." She made an ugly face.

"They were, weren't they?"

"So what's wrong? You don't seem too excited about this trip."

"Oh, this was a very exciting trip."

"Are you talking about the UFO and the plane?"

"No…well…I mean, yes. But there's so much more."

"Then why don't you tell me?"

"Because I'm afraid. I'm afraid you'll think I'm crazy."

"Honey, how long have we been married? I'm behind you no matter what. Wait a minute. I know you. You're setting me up for a big joke."

"No, I wish I were."

"Then what is it? You're starting to scare me."

"Well, it all started when I got lost at the Khan…"

CHAPTER SIXTEEN

VISITORS IN BLACK

Constance pulled over and stopped the car. She looked mad. She wouldn't face me, either, and kept staring out the front window. And for the first time in our marriage, I had no idea what she was thinking.

"Constance, say something, please."

With a short tone, she huffed, "What do you want me to say?" The atmosphere was very tense, and it seemed like an hour before she spoke again. "Why didn't you tell me?"

"I wanted to, so bad, but there was no way to tell you everything in a telegram. And I didn't have access to a phone or internet. Everything just happened so fast. I'm sorry."

She thumped the steering wheel and looked at me angrily. "You should be."

"Again, I'm sorry. What did I do that was so wrong?"

"You almost got killed—more than once—and you kept it from me. That's what's wrong! What were you thinking? How could you? Don't you know how much Hara and I care about you?"

"I'm sorry."

"You've had an assassin chase you all over Egypt trying to kill you at every turn. How do you think that makes me feel? I'm your wife. I should know these things." I was speechless, and she went on, "You were almost

210

shot, beaten—oh, and let's not forget...*suffocated*—and I'm thinking you're having a great time. And don't tell me that I'm overreacting." Constance started crying hysterically. I wanted to help her, but I didn't know what to say or do.

Then she sobbed, "And what's worse, you kept going and trying to help—for perfect strangers. I don't know whether to be proud or angry. Promise me you'll never do that again."

I handed her a tissue and apologized, "I can't do that."

She slapped me on the arm. "You mean you can't tell me when you almost get killed?"

"No, no, that's not what I mean. I mean that I can't stop helping others."

"That's not what I'm talking about, either. Don't you know anything about women?"

"Apparently not," I mumbled.

"How can I help you if you don't tell me when you are in trouble?" Another wave of tears erupted.

"I'm sorry that I hurt you, honest. In a million years, I never intended to hurt you. I thought if I told you it would make matters worse. I didn't want you worrying about me."

"But that's what I'm supposed to do. You're my husband, and I care about you."

"I know. I'm sorry." I reached over and gave her a hug.

Her tears were softening, and she sniffled, "I love you so much. Please let me help you when I can."

"I will. Will you please forgive me?"

"I'll think about it." She squeezed me hard and kissed me on the cheek. "OK, I forgive you."

I wiped away her tears and asked, "Do you want me to drive the rest of the way?"

"Are you telling me that I'm too emotional to drive?"

"The tears do kind of give it away."

"Alright, you drive. But don't think you are off the hook, mister. You have some explaining to do." We switched seats and I began driving.

"Did I tell you that I bought you something in Egypt?"

"Yes, yes, you are already forgiven. There's no need to bribe me."

"So, we're good then?"

"As long as you aren't hiding any assassins in your luggage. Are you?"

"No, I left the assassins at Customs."

"And what about the alien attacks, this reptilian thing?"

"I'm still learning about all of this. Remember…me…simple college teacher before my trip? I'm going to have to do some research. And I promise you that I will tell you what I find."

"What can I do to help?"

"At this very second, I can't think of anything. There's a lot to do in the next few days, though. I've got to unpack, we've got Hara's party tomorrow, and I start back to school in a few days. There'll be some things coming up, I'm sure of it."

"Can I help you right now?"

"Do I need help right now?"

"Yes, you just missed our exit."

"Oh, shoot! I'll catch the next one. It's only a couple miles up the road."

"I *hope* you can get us home on time."

"You're sassing me, aren't you?"

"Maybe just a little, but I do love you." She blew me a kiss in the air.

"I'll take one of those on the lips when we get home."

"You've got it, mister."

———————

I got back onto the right street and prodded, "I know there's a question brewing in your head. What is it?"

"So where's this special amulet that you were talking about?"

"It's right here." I pulled the chain over my head and handed it to her.

"Wow! This is beautiful! And look at the colors. Is this real gold?"

"As far as I know, it is."

"And you supposedly left this for yourself from a past life?"

"I'm starting to believe I did."

"You know, this would go with my red and black dress really well." She turned the amulet over and looked at the front and back a few times.

"I don't think that is supposed to be a fashion accessory."

"Of course it is. Add a belt and matching earrings, and I'm ready to go out on the town."

"You would look hot in that."

"Steady big boy. Keep your eyes on the road."

"What? It's been a long time since I've seen you."

"Flattery will get you everywhere." We both chuckled a bit.

After a few more minutes of small talk, we stopped at a red light and I asked her, "So please tell me what you think about all of this."

"You know me. I'm open-minded about a lot of things."

"Yes…"

"And this…" She paused.

"Yes…"

"I'm trying to find the right words."

"Take your time."

"Well, it's like this: I trust you, I believe in you, and I'm behind you all the way."

"But…?"

"It's going to take some time to let all of this sink in. You've had a few days to process it, and you had help. I've had, what, about an hour?"

"I know, and I'm not trying to rush you. I just wanted to know if you thought I was crazy or not."

"I don't think you are crazy. Silly at times, but not crazy."

"I can't deny that."

She turned to me and asked with a little enthusiasm, "And what do you think? Do you believe you are this reincarnated priest?"

"To be honest, I had a hard time digesting all of this myself. I still question it, but not near as much as in the beginning. I've had too many coincidences to make this a farce."

"And who are these people back in Egypt?"

"Some of them have become good friends in the last week. And others I only met for a day or two. But I can tell you that they all believe in this. And some have laid down their lives for me. I mean, what do you say to something like that?"

"It is pretty wild."

"And boy, if you could have experienced these abilities…like when I meditated in Luxor. I saw myself in ancient Egypt. I saw my friends Bes and Talibah. And then, to meet them in the future…it was very surreal. I've never experienced anything like this in my entire life. It almost seems like it was preordained."

"Are you talking about destiny?"

"Yes…no…maybe. It feels like things are unfolding. But…"

"But what?"

"It feels like I have to make them happen, that they won't just happen because someone calls it destiny."

"So the future isn't written yet, and we aren't robots in a play?"

"Not from what I've experienced."

"And we have time?"

"Yes, we have some time, but I think time is starting to run out."

"That's scary. So what's next?"

"Well, when we get home, I'll show you all of the stuff I brought back. Then I have to decipher it."

"I can help with that."

"That'd be awesome. I've needed help all along the way, so I won't turn it down now, either."

"Do you think I might be a priest?"

I hit the breaks really hard at the stop sign. "What did you just say?"

"If the others woke up as priests, who knows? Maybe I'm a priest too." She had a sly smile on her face.

"Did you get a sign or something?"

"No, but it could happen." Just then, we passed a car with a bumper sticker that read *Trust in Destiny*.

"You know, if you were a priest, it wouldn't surprise me in the least. Especially after the week I just had."

"Honey, if I'm a priest, then you just broke about a thousand sacraments with me in the last year alone." We laughed and laughed.

"OK, let's get home. I've got to pick up Hara in about a half an hour."

"Alright."

As I sped down the home stretch, I kept turning between Constance and the road. "I know there is more to this, honey, so don't feel like you can't ask me any questions. And I still have to play Michael in the so-called real world. Boy, that's going to be tough. I still have to teach in a few days."

"Yes, and we have a party to get ready for, too."

"Yes, we do. And I miss Hara. I can't wait to see her again. How is my wiggly worm?"

"You haven't called her that in years."

"I know. I was just having a nostalgic moment."

"She's just fine. She's anxious for tomorrow."

"I'll bet she is."

We pulled into our driveway and parked. "Honey, I promise you, I will do all that I can to make things right. I promise. And what I do to help others will…well, it's bigger than me. I'm just hoping to do the right thing."

"I know you will. That's one of the many things I adore about you. You try hard to serve others. Better than I do at times."

"I don't know about that. You're pretty awesome yourself—in a class all by yourself."

"You're so sweet. Hmm…do you want to give me a private tutoring lesson?"

"Are you looking to get an *A* on your assignment?"

"You bet, professor. Let's get inside."

"You're on." I dragged my bags in the front door and laid them to the side. Before closing the door, I turned to look around our neighborhood. There weren't any black cars tailing me, so I sighed, grinned, and closed the door.

Forty-five minutes later, Constance straightened up her clothes before heading out the door. "I'll be back in about an hour. Tammy's mom wants to ask me some things about the party. I think she's planning some type of surprise for Hara."

"That's cool. I'll just be here unpacking. Hurry back."

The door closed, and I had the house all to myself. I flopped onto my couch and closed my eyes for a moment and thought, "Oh, it's so good to be home. Hello, couch. Boy I missed you."

I woke up to the sounds of Hara running across the living room screaming, "Daddy!" She pounced on top of me and gave me a huge hug.

"Oh, how's my little ragamuffin?" I picked her up and spun her around a few times.

"You haven't called me ragamuffin since I was a kid."

"What are you now?"

She announced with an animated lift in her voice, "I'm going to be a preteen."

Constance sang, "Not until tomorrow."

"Well, don't grow up too fast. I like you just the way you are."

"Before you know it, Daddy, I'll be driving."

"And dating," Constance teased.

I groaned, "Stop it, you two. Just let me enjoy the moment."

Hara was hopping up and down with excitement. "Did you bring me anything from Egypt?"

"I don't know. Why don't you ask your *mummy?*" I poked her side and she giggled.

"Ha-ha, very funny."

"Good girls get all their presents on their birthday, so you'll have to wait."

"Nooo, don't make me wait." She hopped up and down some more.

Constance asked, "Honey, did you pack that camel like I asked you?"

"You brought me a camel?!"

"No, they had a one-hump limit on the airplane, and the guy in front of me brought his camel first. Besides, you don't want a camel, they spit."

"Eww!"

"And I hear that boys spit on their dates, too."

"Eww!"

I muttered, "Maybe that will stop you from dating."

Constance assured Hara, "Boys don't spit on their dates." Then she playfully scowled at me, "Stop it."

"What? She's too young to date anyway."

"I know. But don't give her any ideas."

Constance already knew, but she asked anyway, "Did you get your unpacking done?"

"No, I got reacquainted with my old couch here. Those plane seats aren't very comfy. I'll get to it in a little bit."

Constance hopped up and down and mimicked Hara, "Well, hurry up. I want my presents, too."

"OK, OK, I'll get on it. By the way, what time is it?"

"Oh, sorry, I was at Tammy's place for a couple of hours. It's lunchtime."

"How about we go out for lunch and I'll unpack later?"

Hara screamed, "Bongo Billy's Pizza House! Bongo Billy's Pizza House!"

I grinned, "Does that mean you want pizza?"

She bobbed her head once and excitedly said, "Yesss!"

Constance pulled Hara in to her side. "What do you say, honey? Can you do pizza for your daughter?"

"After a week of CLT, I could do anything." Hara smiled and ran upstairs to get ready.

"A CLT?" She had a confused look on her face.

"Oh, yeah…camel, lettuce, and tomato sandwich."

"What?"

"It was an inside joke between Hanif and me."

"Oh, one of your new friends?"

"Yeah." I thought to myself, "I miss them already."

⎯⎯●◆●⎯⎯

After losing to both girls at putt-putt golf and pizza crust tipi making, we made our way home, and I began unpacking. Constance walked in and hinted, "Am I allowed to look?"

"I'm not hiding any secrets." I knew full well that she wanted her gifts, so I gave her my camera and told her to scroll through the photos. This would stall her until I was ready.

I rummaged around Hara's box, along with the rest of the scrolls and parchments. Then I got to Constance's gift bag and held it out for her. "Here you go, honey. I hope you like it."

"Oh, you didn't have to."

"Of course I did. I'm a husband. I know better."

"Well, you still didn't have to." She kissed me on the cheek. "Thanks!"

She draped the embroidered pajamas across her body and spun around. "These are beautiful."

"So you like them?"

"Oh, yes! And the cotton is so soft. Where did you get them again?"

"Outside of Hatshepsut's Temple. There's more in there, too."

She practically ripped the bag to get at the other presents. Then she pulled out the scarves like she was doing an Arabian scarf dance, followed by her dangling the earrings next to her ear. "These earrings are perfect. I love them. And the scarves are wonderful. This one will go with my new dress."

"What new dress?"

"Hara and I did a little shopping while you were gone, and I can wear these for the birthday party."

"Do I have to get a second job to pay for this shopping trip?"

"No, silly. Here, let me show you my dress." Constance ducked into our closet and pulled out a clear plastic dress bag. "Do you like it? I got it on sale."

"You'll look stunning as always."

"Cha-ching! You just got some hubby points. Oh, speaking of stunning, I made Hara an appointment to get her hair and nails done. It's a little mini spa day—kind of an early present for her."

"I know she'll like that. What time do you have to leave?"

"I made the appointment for 4:00 p.m. Do you think you can mow the lawn before tomorrow? It's getting pretty high."

"Sure, I'll do it while you two are gone."

"Great. I'm going downstairs to start making some of the snacks. Let me know if you need any help. And put your laundry in the washroom. I'll take care of that tonight."

"OK. I'll be here unpacking."

I looked at all of the boxes from Mudads' and Hanif's shops. "You know, I'm just not getting into this tonight. It can wait until after Hara's birthday party." I pulled out Hara's gifts, closed my trunk, locked it, and dragged it into the closet. "I'm going to be a regular dad for a day. Then I can get back into this Tumaini stuff before school starts."

———•———

I had just finished cleaning the mower when the girls returned. "Don't you just look like the prettiest birthday girl?"

Constance agreed, "She does look pretty, doesn't she?"

Hara blushed and smiled, "Thanks Dad. Can I go call Tammy?"

"Sure, but don't get into the cookies. Those are for tomorrow." She scampered up the stairs, and the door slammed behind her.

I looked at Constance. "Man, these kids look so much older these days. I don't remember us looking that mature when I was a kid."

"Me, neither. Do you think it's the growth hormones they're putting in our food?"

"Probably. They grow chickens faster than my students write their midterm papers. And the cows today don't look like anything like the skinny Bessie from the old dairy farm."

"Maybe we should start eating cleaner food."

"I'm all for it. And maybe you and Hara can think about giving up meat altogether."

"I don't know if I can give up meat that fast. I grew up as a meat-and-potatoes girl. You know that."

"I know. But you can always go slow if you want. We could have a meat-less day or two every week. I hear it's better to make the change slowly anyway. What do you think?"

"Maybe. But can we wait until after the party tomorrow? You're supposed to cook all of the burgers I have in the fridge, and we don't want a house full of hungry fourth graders."

"I can wait, but maybe you could think about it."

"Are you really serious about me giving up meat?"

"If you'd like. I'll support you either way."

"Well, I'll have to think on that one. In the meantime, can you help me in the kitchen? I have a lot of work to do."

"Sure, just let me get cleaned up. I'd hate to deal with a screaming kid who found a grasshopper in her punch."

"Alright. But don't take too long, and leave the grasshoppers outside."

"You got it. Hey, I'm going to wrap Hara's gifts that I brought home. It'll take me a few more minutes."

"OK. She's going to love them."

"I hope so."

"I know so."

———•◦•———

The next morning, the DJ was knocking on our door at 10:30 a.m. to set up. The inflatable bounce house we rented also arrived, and the guy showed me how to set it up. I called toward the house, "Hara, come here. We're going to blow up the bounce house."

The man mumbled with a cigarette in his mouth, "Back in my day, we used to call this the moonwalk."

"I remember those days. Why did they change the name?"

"Why does anybody change anything these days? You know, repackaging, and bigger and better advertising. It's all about the greenbacks."

"Ain't that the truth?" I nodded, "It could also be the Mandela effect." Then I tilted my head once in the direction of CERN.

He gave me a funny look, then he asked, "Are you all set here? I need to deliver three more of these by this afternoon."

"I'm fine."

"Good. I'll be back in six hours to pick this up."

"Sounds great." As he left, Hara came walking out to our backyard. "Oh, Hara, you look beautiful. Happy birthday, sweety."

"Thanks, Dad. Are you going to blow this up right now?"

"Yep."

"How does it work?"

"Do you see that tube right there? Well, you stick your head in it and blow as hard as you can for about ten hours. If you're not passed out at the end, you go inside and have a blast."

She giggled, "That's not how they inflate those."

"I know. These things come with a high-powered inflator. Do you want to push the button?"

"Can I?"

"You're the birthday girl. You get to do what you want." Hara pushed the button, and two noisy minutes later the multi-colored castle was up and bouncing.

Constance yelled out the door, "OK, you two, the guests have started arriving. It's time to come in."

Hara ran ahead of me and bounded up the stairs. I passed Constance and asked, "Are you ready for this?"

"It'll be fun. Thanks for putting up the castle."

"That was the easy part. The next few hours are the challenge."

"I know. Maybe after this is all over, we can go to Hawaii and build some sand castles of our own."

"Now you're talking my language. Should I repack?"

"You just got home. Let's stay here for a few days."

"But then we can go to Hawaii, right?"

"Come on, our girl is waiting."

"By the way, you look stunning. And I see you wore the scarf and earrings."

"Thanks, sweety." She gave me a kiss as she sashayed past me.

———————

For the next hour, I played door greeter and let in twenty-five kids and fourteen parents. When the last child arrived, I walked past the guest room and peeked in. It was packed from floor to ceiling with gift bags, wrapped boxes, and a few pink baskets filled with girly items. I thought to myself, "Hara is going to have so much fun unwrapping all of these. And we're going to need an extra room just to put all of this stuff in."

I walked up to Constance. "Did you see all of those gifts?"

"Yes, I did. But that's nothing. Don't you remember Tammy's birthday party? She had twice as many people and twice as many boxes."

"Now that you mention it, I do. It must have taken a full hour for her to open all of her presents."

"It felt like two."

"It did, didn't it?"

"Hey, will you help me pass out all of the little guest bags?"

"Sure. Where did you put them?"

"They're still in the kitchen next to the cake."

While the DJ played all of Hara's favorites, I handed out little bags stuffed with cookies, party hats, poppers, and small toys. The kids went berserk for the next thirty minutes shooting confetti and streamers all over our living room and backyard.

"They're having so much fun, honey. I'm glad you made it home for her party."

"I wouldn't have missed this for the world."

Constance gave me a look that said: *You almost missed this.* I grimaced because I knew what she was thinking.

She yelled out the back door, "It's time for presents!" We both ducked out of the way just in time to avoid the oncoming stampede.

"That was a close call," I laughed. "Next time, give me a little warning."

"You've had worse. Suck it up, big boy."

"Yeah, yeah."

I kissed her cheek, and Hara ran up to us. "Is it time for cake?"

Constance answered, "We're going to open presents first, baby doll, then we'll have cake."

"OK," and she ran into the other room.

"Do you want me to pass out the second round of bags?"

"Sure. And don't forget the camera."

"I won't."

To keep the kids from getting too bored, I gave them another bag filled with more poppers and confetti. Constance began ushering boxes and bags from the guest room, and I played proud papa and took dozens of photos. As Hara opened her gifts, our living room turned into a New York City tickertape parade.

Constance came in one last time and gave Hara two more boxes. I whispered over, "Are those ours?" She nodded *yes*.

Hara ripped into her mother's gift first and yelled, "Makeup! Oh my gosh! Makeup! I'm allowed to start wearing makeup? Is this for real? And a jewelry box, too. Thanks, Mom!"

She ran up and gave her a fast hug. "Am I allowed to start wearing makeup?"

"Of course, dear. And I'll help you if you want me to. Now go open Dad's gift."

"OK. Thanks, Mom." She ripped into the last box like she was digging for buried treasure.

"Peanuts?! You gave me packing peanuts?"

"Dig down a little farther, darling. And don't be tidy. Have some fun."

She showered the room with packing peanuts and found two wooden boxes. "Are these what I think they are?"

"Yes, one of them is a camel."

"Oh, Dad!" The room broke out in laughter.

She pulled out the first box and opened it. "It's so pretty. What is it?"

"It's an oil lamp from Egypt. I'll show you how it works later."

The next box was heavier and harder to get out of the gift box. When she finally opened it, she got tears in her eyes and ran up to me. She hugged me hard. "This is the best present ever. Thanks, Dad!"

"Do you like it?"

"I love it. Thanks for the puzzles."

"That's real Egyptian papyrus, too." The kids came up and looked in the box. They were *oohing* and *ahing*.

"You'll have to let me know what they say, birthday girl."

"Will you help me?"

"Yeah, we'll do it together. Don't forget to thank everyone for their gifts."

"I won't." Then she yelled, "Thanks for all my gifts!"

"Good girl. Now don't forget to thank everyone individually before she leaves."

Constance stood up and announced, "OK, everyone, time for cake!" and the kids erupted in cheers.

Tammy's mother came up to me. "Mike, this is a great party. You are a special dad."

"Thanks. I try to be. But Constance is the one who put this all together while I was away. She's the awesome one."

"Well, you both are."

"Thanks."

"I made arrangements for an ice cream truck to come by after cake. I told Constance that the kids could each get one cone and eat it in the backyard while they played. Do you think you can go out and see if it's here? He should have shown up by now, and I forgot his phone number."

"Sure. I'll check in a moment. I want to take some pictures of Hara blowing out her candles."

"Of course. You go be Dad for a bit."

"Thanks."

It was fun watching her spit on the cake as she blew out the candles. When the chorus of *Happy Birthday* ended, I went out the front door to watch for the ice cream truck.

I looked down both directions and didn't see anything that resembled ice cream, just a bunch of parked cars and minivans for the party. I walked down our yard and onto the pavement. From a block away, I could see a black van parked on the left. It pulled out slowly and came toward me.

"That can't be ice cream," I thought to myself.

In a second, the van sped up, and then it stopped like a brick just a few feet away from my body. Two men wearing black suits and black sunglasses jumped out and walked straight toward me. "Are you Michael Whyse?" one of them asked.

After my trip, I could sense that something was wrong. "Who wants to know?"

"Did you see anything strange while you were on flight 641 yesterday?"

"I'd like to see some identification before I say anything to you."

The first one repeated himself, "Did you see anything strange while you were on flight 641 yesterday?"

Both men took two more steps closer. And with emotionless faces, they both threatened, "It would be wise for you to cooperate."

I didn't realize it, but I was blocked by one of the minivans, and I couldn't escape backwards. "You guys need to back up. I don't have anything to say to you."

Again, they warned, "It would be wise for you to cooperate."

"That's it. Back up, now!" I tried to move past them, but they grabbed my arms and pinned me against the van.

"Did you see a UFO yesterday? It would be smart for you to tell no one about this."

"Hey, let go of me!" I commanded. Then I tried to struggle free, but it felt like I was wrestling with mannequins made of steel.

They both lifted their arms and picked me up off of the ground without any effort. My feet dangled helplessly. "You will come with us. You are being uncooperative."

I hit them in the face with my elbows, cracking one of the guy's glasses, but that didn't faze them. "Let go of me!"

"Did you see a UFO while you were on flight 641 yesterday?" asked the man on the left.

I made another attempt to get away by pushing my legs off of the door. I couldn't move and yelled from the pain.

The man on the right stated, "You will come with us."

As they started carrying me to the opened door of their van, the ice cream truck music began blaring at the end of the street. I could also hear the kids reacting in the backyard. Instantly, both men dropped me to the ground and ran to the van. They closed their doors and sped off.

By that time, the ice cream truck was right in front of our house, and the kids were running from the backyard. The young driver asked, "Dude, are you alright?"

"Yes, yes, I'll be fine. Please don't say anything to anyone, OK?"

"Sure, dude. It's your nickel. Are you sure?"

"Yes, I'm fine."

Children were swarming the driver like ants on honey, followed by a chorus of *I want...! I want....!* Some of the other parents came out to help the defenseless driver.

I thought to myself, "I don't know what is worse, what happened to me or what's happening to the ice cream man."

Constance walked up with her hands on her hips. "What's wrong? I know that look."

"Not now, honey. I'll tell you after the party. Let's take care of Hara and our guests first." She stared at me and knew something bad had just happened.

"I'll tell you, honest. No secrets. This is Hara's day. Let's not ruin it for her."

"OK, but you promised. I'm keeping you to it."

"Yes, I promise."

I dusted off my pants and looked down the street. There was no sign of the black van, so I walked toward the house and did my best to enjoy my girl's party. On the way, I thought to myself, "Those had to be the Men in Black I've heard about. That would make this the third alien attack. I wonder what's next."

CHAPTER SEVENTEEN

TED TALKS

I asked Constance, "Is Hara finally asleep?"

"Yes. She could barely keep her eyes open. She had a great day."

"Thanks to you."

"And thanks to you, too."

I pulled her in for a sideways hug and smiled, "Yeah, we make a pretty good team, don't we?"

"We do, don't we? When do you want to tackle the house cleaning?"

"How about we skip cleaning and just sell it like it is?"

"I'm up for that. Let's have Tammy's mom put it on the market tomorrow."

"Great, but you'll have to dial. I'm too tired."

"Me, too. Are you going to tell me what happened today?"

"Yes, I'm glad you brought it up. Have you ever heard about the Men in Black?"

"You mean the ones with the UFO stuff?"

"Yep, those same ones. I think I had a visit from two of them. And the strange thing is they didn't act like real men. I could swear they weren't human. They acted really weird, like they couldn't hold a normal conversation. And their strength was incredible."

I checked for Constance's reaction. All she said was, "Go on."

"They were trying to scare me, I think. They kept asking me if I'd seen anything strange on the airplane. Then they threatened me about telling others it was a UFO."

"Did they hurt you?"

"No, not really. They didn't have any knives or guns, but I think they were trying to take me with them. The ice cream truck came, and then they dropped me and ran. That's when you showed up."

"I'm doing my best not to get upset."

"I know."

"This is getting close to home, Michael. Hara was just a few feet away. What if they'd come after her?"

"I know."

"Well?"

"I know!"

"Stop saying that."

"I'm doing what I can, Constance. I didn't plan for this to happen. If either of you are threatened in any way, I will protect you. You know that, don't you?"

"I'm sorry. I'm a little emotional over all of this."

"I don't blame you. It's still all new to me, too.

"Tell you what... Ted—you remember, Ted, from my department—well, he's really into all of this UFO stuff. I'll talk with him and see if he can offer any suggestions."

"You're actually going to listen to Ted talk about aliens? I thought you didn't like him."

"What gave you that idea? He's OK. I just didn't want to get into all of the conspiracy stuff with him. But now, it doesn't seem like he's too far off."

"Does he still wear the tinfoil hat in his office?"

"Not that I know of. I think that was a rumor started by some students."

"Well, any help that you can get is a blessing. I'm just a little scared at the moment."

"I know."

"You're saying it again."

"I know," I grinned. "Do you want to go and check the street with me?"

"OK. But I think we should call the police."

"And tell them what? Besides, the police are in on all of this, whether they are aware of it or not."

"What do you mean?"

"Can we talk about this at another time? I'm really tired."

"Alright, but let's check the house and the street. I'll feel better that way."

"I'll grab the flashlight out of the drawer. Do you want to take the point or the rear?" I thought about Gahiji, Jabari, and Asim doing the same thing.

"How about I hide behind your shoulder with a bazooka?"

"How about we go one better? You stay in the house with Hara, and I'll go take a look. If I see something, I'll make a noise."

"Like what?"

"I'll make an owl sound: *hoo-hoo, hoo-hoo.*"

"Ha-ha, funny."

"No, *hoo-hoo, hoo-hoo.* I'll be back in a minute. You go in and check on Hara. Don't forget your bazooka." She gave me a pseudo-smile.

After I came back in the house, I reported, "Coast is clear. Is everything alright in here?"

"Yes. Hara's still sleeping, and I'm ready for bed, too."

"Good. We'll clean up in the morning."

"Do you feel any better?"

"Yes. Thanks for going outside and checking."

"Keep letting me know what I can do to make this better."

"I will."

When I woke up the next morning, Constance was already out of bed making breakfast, and Hara was up playing with her makeup kit. I walked over to the closet and dragged out the trunk. "Hello, Tumaini stuff. I didn't forget about you." I let out a little sinister laugh. "Are you ready to reveal your secrets? Let's see…"

I pulled out all of the boxes and laid them on the bed. I thought to myself, "I shouldn't put them here. Where should I put them? I know…"

After putting the boxes back in the trunk, I walked down the hall and stopped in Hara's room. "Don't you look pretty? You're just like a little princess."

"Dad, don't look!"

"Why? You look beautiful."

"I'm not finished. Can you close the door please?"

"Sure, but we'll be eating in just a few minutes."

"OK."

With the door closed, I continued down the stairs to meet Constance. "Hello, dear, breakfast smells fantastic. Are those Belgian waffles?"

"They are."

"You know those are my favorites."

"I know. I thought it would be a nice welcome home breakfast, even though it's two days late."

"You are awesome. I couldn't have asked for a better wife."

"Yeah, I am pretty good, aren't I?" she chuckled.

"Better than good, you're great—even if it is two days late!" I gave her a loud smooch on her cheek.

"Do you have any plans today? I'm taking Hara to a friend's house for the morning, and I need to do some work in my office."

"Actually, yes. I need to run a small errand after breakfast so I can start doing research."

"Is this UFO research or school research?"

"It might be both. I won't be long, though. I'm just heading to the local market."

"What do you need? Maybe I can pick it up for you."

"I need something to put all of the Egypt stuff on—you know, something safe. And I have an idea of what to do, so I kind of need to be the one who shops for it."

"I know. I'll just mess it up. You go get what you need. By the way, where are you going to put them?"

"In my study. I already have most of my reference books and computer in there, and they might help me solve some of these clues I left myself."

"Clues?"

"Yes. When I get everything set up, I'll show you. And you offered to help, and I'm not going to turn it down. You're stuck, missy."

"I'm actually looking forward to helping. I want to know what you've gotten yourself into. Can you call Hara and warm up the syrup?"

"You betcha." I wrapped my arms around her and gave her a hug.

"C'mon, get the syrup. We can visit later."

"Hara, breakfast! Time to eat!"

An hour and a half later, I was in the car and running my errands. "Let's see, I need at least three six-foot tables, cotton gloves, wooden tweezers, white table cloths, and clear plexiglass sheets for coverings. That oughta do it."

Another two hours went by and I was pulling into our driveway. Constance came out the front door to meet me.

"Is everything alright?" I checked.

"Oh, everything's fine. I just thought I would come out and help."

"Great. If you grab the bags, I'll grab the tables."

"What is all this stuff for anyway?"

"It's for the papyrus I brought home. When I get it all upstairs, I'll show you."

It took five trips to get the tables and plexiglass into my study. To make room, I dragged my couch and two chairs out and put them in the upstairs game room. Then I pulled the trunk in and put the boxes on the tables.

"Are you going to show me what all this is for?"

"Yes. Help me open the boxes, but don't touch anything inside yet."

"Why? Is something going to jump out and grab me?"

"No, I left the junp-out-and-grab-me box back in Egypt. What's in these boxes is very old and fragile. Here…" I tossed her a pair of cotton gloves and wooden tweezers.

"Let me guess, I'm checking for dust."

"Ha-ha. Those are for handling all of the papyrus."

"I thought you gave Hara the papyrus."

"I did, but these are the clues I left behind for myself. You wanted to know what the clues were. Well, here they are."

"Are there any hidden treasure maps?"

"I don't know yet. I haven't deciphered anything. And a lot of it is in ancient hieratic. Do you know how to decipher ancient hieratic?"

"No, but I can solve a Sudoku puzzle."

"I don't think that will help, but maybe. Who knows what kind of primer I'll need."

We spent the next forty-five minutes carefully laying out all of the parchments and papyrus pieces on the table cloths. Constance clapped her gloves together once. "What do you want to do next?"

"We need to put the plexiglass on top of each table to protect the papyrus."

"What about the other box of stuff? Don't you want to put those on the table?"

"There isn't enough room for all of the scrolls. I'm going to leave them in the plastic bags for now."

"Ooo, this scroll is cute. It has a scarab on it."

"Supposedly, that's a special one. When I picked it up in Hanif's shop, both Mudads and he pegged me as being Tumaini."

"Just from picking up a scroll?"

"Well, there was more to it than that."

"Good thing you didn't pick up a call girl. They would have called you too-many-nights-in-jail."

"Ha-ha. Very funny."

The front door opened and closed, and we heard Hara's familiar footsteps running up the stairs.

"Hi, honey. I was just getting ready to come get you. Did they drop you off?"

"Yeah, they had to change their schedule. They're going to the store or somethin'." She got a huge smile on her face and sang, "Whatcha doin'?"

I motioned. "Well, come here and take a look."

"Wow! You've got papyrus, too."

"I do. Maybe we can help each other."

"They don't look anything like mine. What are they covered for?"

"It's because they're very old, and we need to keep them protected."

"Like the sneeze guard at the salad buffet?"

"Yeah, something like that."

"Mom, I'm hungry. Are we going to eat soon?"

"Yes. Come downstairs and help me make some sandwiches. We'll let your father finish up here."

"OK." She ran out and bounced down each step of the stairs.

———————

When lunch was done, I went back up the stairs. Hara saw me leave and ran to catch up. I mimicked her tone from before, "Whatcha doin'?"

"I wanna come help."

"I think you should help your mother clean up after lunch. Don't you think?"

"How come you're not helping Mom?"

"Because I clean up after dinner. We take turns."

"But I wanna help you instead."

"You can, in a minute. Go clean up lunch, and then you can come see me."

She grumbled, "OK."

"That's a good girl."

I put on my white gloves and looked down at the papyrus pieces. "What the heck do these mean? There are no pictures, there's no text, just symbols repeated over and over. How am I supposed to solve this?"

I sat down on my swivel chair and did a three hundred and sixty degree spin. When I stopped, Hara was looking at me through the doorway. "Whatcha doin'?"

"Taking a spin. Did you help your mother already?"

"She was done and said I could go play."

I spun the chair again. "Wanna join me?"

"Sure." She bounced on top of my lap. "I'm ready."

"OK, buckle in, and keep your arms and hands inside the car at all times."

"You sound like a roller coaster ride."

"I am a roller coaster ride. Hold on!"

We spun around a bunch of times. Then I snickered, "Hurry up. Get off, stand up, and look straight at the ceiling." We both looked up and could barely keep our balance.

Hara giggled, "I'm so dizzy. Let's do it again!"

"No, no. I don't want my lunch to come up."

"Eww!"

"Alright, do you really want to help?"

She nodded once, "Yesss!"

"Put on these gloves and come here."

"What am I gonna do?"

"I don't know yet. Wait a minute, I do know what we're going to do. I have a picture of this when I was in Egypt. These pieces form a shape, like a puzzle."

"What kind of shape?"

"I'll show you in a minute." I grabbed my camera and downloaded the pictures onto my computer. "Where is that photo? Ah, there it is. Come here, Hara. This is what we are going to make."

"It doesn't look like anything."

"Well, it's a puzzle, and this is where we start. We have to find the exact matches from all of those pieces and put them precisely as they are here."

"I can do that."

"Then you'll be a good helper."

She smiled, "I like being a good helper."

We spent about an hour matching pieces to the picture on the computer, then putting them in place with the tweezers. I gave a little cheer, "There, it's finished."

Hara yelled out, "Yea! But it doesn't look done."

"You're right, it doesn't look done. But this is where we start." I covered the papyrus again with the plexiglass and thanked Hara for all her help.

"Dad, can you help me with my puzzle later?"

"Of course I can. Do you want me to do it now?"

"No, I want to go play now."

"OK. We'll do it later."

Constance walked in as Hara left. "What did you guys come up with?"

"Well, we matched up these papyrus pieces to the picture and made these two symbols."

"Oh, interesting. What does it do?"

"I don't know yet. I've never seen anything like this before."

"Are you still going to call Ted?"

"Yeah, I was going to do that next. What are you going to be doing?"

"I'm going to go downstairs and work in my room for a couple hours. Can you keep an eye on Hara?"

"Sure."

"Hi, Ted. This is Michael Whyse. Am I catching you at a good time?"

In an unfriendly tone, he answered, "Hello, Michael. Why are you calling me? School's not in session for another three days."

"I know. This isn't school related. I had something that I wanted to ask you."

"This is unusual. You don't talk to me at school too much. What do you want now?"

"Well, I need your expertise."

After a few moments of silence, he went on, "OK, shoot. But make it quick. I have to get going."

"Thanks. I'll get right to the point, then. It's in regards to UFOs."

He was quiet, and then he replied angrily, "Who put you up to this, Thompson over in psychology? You guys are too much. I'm hanging up."

"No! Don't hang up, please. I'm not making fun of you. I'm not like the other guys."

"You aren't?"

"No. I believe in UFOs, and I don't have anyone else to talk to. I thought maybe you could help me."

"I'm not convinced yet, but go ahead."

"I don't think I know where to start."

"Are you pulling my leg? Do you really need my help? I'm not in the mood for another prank."

"I'm serious, Ted. I wouldn't call up and make fun of you. I had a few encounters over spring break, especially when I was in Egypt. I—"

He interrupted, "You were in Egypt?"

"Yes. And then I had another encounter when I was on the plane coming back home. And then two guys in black suits showed up."

"They what?"

"Men in Black. They showed up at my daughter's birthday party and tried to kidnap me."

"Michael, we shouldn't talk about this over the phone."

"What do you mean? Why can't we talk on the phone?"

He enunciated very sternly and slowly, "Because the government is listening."

"OK. I get the point."

He did it again, "The government is always listening."

"I'm starting to understand."

"How about we meet somewhere safe and quiet?"

"Could you come over for dinner tomorrow?"

"I could do that."

"Great."

"Where do you live?" I gave him my address and said we would eat at 6:00 p.m. "I'll be there. Is there anything you want me to bring?"

"No. I'm just glad you are willing to help."

"This isn't a joke, is it? I swear to you, I've had enough ridicule at school."

"I promise; this is no joke."

"Alright, 6:00 p.m. I'll be there."

"Thanks, Ted. I'm looking forward to it."

He hung up without a reply.

I peeked into Constance's office. "Ted's coming tomorrow at 6:00 p.m. for dinner. I hope that's OK."

She nodded, "That's fine. I need to get back to work. Can we talk later?" I nodded back and walked to Hara's room to check on her.

"How you doin', short stuff?"

She whined, "Daaaad, I'm not short stuff. I'm almost four feet tall."

"You're right. You're honey bunny."

"Daaaad, I'm not honey bunny, either."

"Are you getting too old for nicknames?" She didn't reply, which told me that times were changing, and my little girl was growing up.

"Since you helped me with my project, do you want to put together your papyrus pieces?"

"Can we wear the white gloves again?"

"Of course we can. I'll go get them. By the way, let's put them all on the card table in the game room. It'll give us more room, and we won't have to move them until we are done. Why don't you meet me there?"

"OK."

She grabbed her box, and we worked until it was dinner. From dinner until the next evening, I worked on my lesson plans for the last six weeks of school. Ted was due to arrive any moment, so I closed down my computer.

Ding-dong! "I'll get it!" I yelled to Constance.

"Hi, Ted. You're right on time. Come on in."

"I took the liberty of bringing you some wine. I didn't know what we were having, so I brought red and white." He handed me the bag and I pulled out the wine.

"Aw, thanks, Ted. You didn't have to do that."

"I thought it might help the evening go smoother. I still didn't know if this was a joke or not. I almost didn't come."

"This is no joke, and we are still having dinner together. Why don't you come in and make yourself at home? I'm not much of a wine connoisseur. Do I let any of these breathe?"

"It's a good bottle of aged red wine, so it doesn't need to breathe. But if you want, you can open it now and let it stand for thirty minutes. The white doesn't need to sit at all."

"Thanks for the info. Come on into the dining room. Constance is just finishing up dinner."

There were three place settings and Ted asked, "Is it just going to be you and Constance? Don't you have a little girl? I'm sorry, I don't know her name."

"Hara's her name. We thought it might give us more liberty to talk, so she's spending the night at a friend's house."

"That's probably a good idea. Didn't you say on the phone that she just had a birthday party? How old is she?"

"She just turned ten."

Constance walked in and smiled, "Hi, Ted. It's been a long time. It's good to see you."

"Thanks for having me over to dinner. Can I help with anything?"

"No, you just stay there and chat. I'll bring out the salads and bread in a moment."

"Honey, Ted brought us some wine."

"Wow, thanks, Ted. I'll get some glasses and the corkscrew, too."

"Are you sure that I can't help?"

"I'm sure. Make yourself comfortable. We're not that formal for dinner."

"Thanks. I'm not used to being a house guest."

She winked. "Well, consider yourself a friend and not a guest."

His face changed from her gesture and he smiled, "Thanks, Constance. I will."

She walked back into the kitchen, and I asked, "Ted, did you have a good break?"

"I did. How about yourself? Sorry, that's why I'm here, right?"

"Well, to put it bluntly, *yes.*"

"Do you want to skip the small talk and get right into it? I mean, we can talk about school all you want, but that's not going to solve your problem."

"Sure, but I'd like Constance to be here. This is as much for her as it is for me."

"How so? Did she have an alien encounter?"

"No. Well, not that I'm aware of. She's worried about me, though."

"So what happened?"

Constance brought in the bread, salads, and glasses. "Here you go."

"Honey, is everything set in the kitchen? Ted's ready to talk with us."

"Yes. The only thing left is to open the wine. We're having veggie lasagna."

Ted grinned, "I've got this. Red it is." He picked up the cork remover and popped the plug like a pro. "Constance, are you having any?" He picked up a glass and tilted the bottle.

"Yes, I think I will."

"How about you, Michael?"

I picked up a glass and handed it to him. "I'll have a snort."

He gave me a glance that said: *You won't snort this wine.*

Constance put her glass down and headed toward the kitchen. "The lasagna's already done. I'll get it so we don't have to wait. I'm anxious to hear about your experience with aliens."

"Hurry back!" I yelled. "I'm anxious, too!"

"You've got a great wife. Hang on to her."

"Thanks. We've been together for fifteen years, and I couldn't imagine being with anyone else."

"I can tell. Both of you have this energy about you, like you're more than just a husband and wife."

"I've never heard anyone say something like that. But you're right; I don't feel like a husband to Constance. I feel like we are connected on a deeper level."

"Would you say a spiritual level?"

"Actually, I would."

"Here's the lasagna," she sang with a cheerful voice.

"That smells wonderful." Ted sat up and opened his napkin. "Thanks for inviting me over."

"It's our pleasure. And don't stop on my account. I'll serve this up, and you two just keep talking. By the way, Ted, don't be shy. Take as much as you want, and don't skimp on the garlic bread."

"I won't," he smiled again.

"So, Michael, tell me what happened."

After I gave him the highlights about my run-in with the Men in Black,

UFOs, and the reptilian hybrid, I asked for his opinion, "What do you think?"

He hesitated, and then he got serious. "This is some pretty intense stuff. Not too many people have these types of encounters. Just so I'm sure I didn't miss anything, did you get abducted?"

"No, I was never abducted, just accosted and affected by this negative energy pulse thingy."

"Not to mention the plane incident," he added.

Constance blurted with a hint of sarcasm, "No, you can mention it. I want to know what's going on."

He continued, "For whatever reason, my best guess is that you have been targeted by the reptilians and dark aliens. And how did you put it—the Order? They must want you out of the picture in the worst way."

I threw up my hands. "But why? Scratch that. I know why. Well, kind of. I'm not going to join them, and that they don't like."

"Is there something that you left out?"

I looked at Constance. She tilted her head back at me and urged, "Don't leave anything out. He's here to help."

"Well, it turns out that I might be this reincarnated priest that can help bring hope to the world. I don't know how yet, but they seem to want to stop me."

"Before you go on, that's not too farfetched for me, so you aren't going to frighten me away with reincarnation."

"That's good," I sighed with some relief. "Do you have any advice?"

"It depends. Exactly how much do you want to know?"

"I want you to share as much information as you can that will keep Constance and Hara safe."

He looked at Constance. "Do you want me to be blunt or give you fluffy answers?"

"Don't hold back on my account. Let's hear it."

"Constance, this Order that Michael is talking about doesn't care about you, Hara, or anyone else for that fact. They only care about themselves and how much power they can accumulate. And the aliens are helping them. That I know as a fact."

I inquired, "How do you know this?"

He turned over his arm and showed me a scar. "Because I had a number of alien implants removed. The aliens and military put these in me years ago to control me, but I discovered them and had them surgically removed."

Constance was frustrated and threw down her napkin. "But this is our military. How could they do such a thing?"

"Most of the soldiers have no idea what's going on. They are just following orders. But there are those who are deep into the alien agenda—those who don't care if the world becomes a *slave world* for the soulless cabal. Those are the ones we are talking about. They don't serve a country—as they would have you believe—they serve themselves."

"That's horrible," she fumed, "just horrible. This isn't anything like they teach you in school."

"Don't get me started. I've spent all my time outside of teaching to learn about these aliens and their agenda. And none of this will be taught in school as long as money and the Order control the curriculum."

I quipped, "Believe me, I know all about that."

Constance asked, "Is there anything I can do to protect Hara?"

"My advice is to get her out of public school. The last thing you want her to do is to have the establishment continue to brainwash her."

"You mean, homeschool her?"

"Yes. You do the teaching. The government doesn't want free-thinking people, so they dumb kids down in school with useless tasks. It's much better if you are teaching her about love, kindness, sharing, and serving others. They don't teach that in school. They only prepare you to be a worker bee and fit into their mold of control."

"But you're a teacher."

"True. But there are a few of us who stand up against their mind control tactics. People like your husband and I teach free thinking. And no offense, Michael, but that's why the dean hates you with a passion, just like he hates me."

"You know about that?"

"Yes, it's one of the reasons I respect you. You don't go along with the crowd when it comes to teaching. You do everything that the dean can't stand. You don't care about the money aspect or the alumni fundraising. You get your students to think outside of the box and challenge the rules."

"He's got a point, honey. You know the dean doesn't like me."

"I know. But I don't have to be happy about it."

"Constance," he said, "this has been going on for centuries. There has been this plan that the cabal have put in place that is leading the people into complete mind control, and anyone who stands in their way will probably get hurt. I'm sorry to be so cold about this, but that's how it is for them. These are cold people."

"Ted," I concurred, "I actually know some people who confirm what you're saying. There is a plan for global mind control that *is* in the works. They want to microchip every human being."

He nodded, "I have a lot more that I can share with you, too. Do you want to talk about HAARP, microwave weapons, satellites and direct energy weapons that target individuals, and flicker rates on the TV? All of these are set up to control the people."

She replied, "I don't even know what any of those are."

"I'd be happy to explain it to you, if you want."

"I do, but I'm not hearing any solutions so far. What can we do?"

I raised my hand. "I think that is where we come in. I think that some of what I brought home could show us how to change the world, or at least give some of us a chance."

Ted had a confused look on his face. "What are you talking about? What did you bring home?"

"After dinner, I'll take you upstairs and show you. Maybe you can make heads or tails out of it."

"I'll help where I can."

Constance picked up her fork. "We can keep talking, but let's not forget to eat. Dinner's getting cold."

I added, "Yes, let's eat. Ted, can you stay for a bit?"

"I'd love to stay and help. Could I get a garlic roll?"

Constance handed the basket to him. "Eat up. There's plenty."

"Thanks. I'm anxious to see what's upstairs."

———•—•———

During dinner, Ted filled us in on all kinds of techniques that the government was using to institute mass mind control. I could tell that Constance's head was swimming with all these new ideas. She was also having a hard time believing that any government would do such horrible experiments on people. She prodded angrily, "Are you telling me that MKUltra is for real, and they used civilians as test subjects?"

Ted answered, "I know you don't like hearing this, Constance, but yes, they used people just like you and me. The government, politicians, and the military are not who you think they are—especially groups like the CIA, FBI, DARPA, and NSA. They're supposed to serve the people, not hurt and enslave the people. And I won't even go into the other countries' psychic warfare programs and military dictatorships."

"They can't all be bad."

"Well, parts of the government might not be involved, but everyone who works for the government is still part of the agenda, whether they deny it or not. The government we have today is all about control, not freedom."

"I can't argue with you on that, but do you have any proof?"

"Actually, I do. Some of the MKUltra information has been declassified by the CIA. Just look up McGill University and Allen Memorial Institute. You'll read about some horrific experiments that were done on innocent citizens, and it was funded by the CIA. And other experiments were declassified as well, but you know they aren't telling the whole truth. The governments and militaries are hiding so much stuff that it's not even funny."

"Can we get back to the UFOs and aliens, though? That's what I'm most interested in at the moment."

"We can, but they are intertwined. Right, Michael?"

"From what I've learned from my friends in Egypt, they are. You can't talk about one without including the other."

"Exactly!" He lifted his glass toward me, then he took a sip of his wine. "You know, Michael, I didn't think that you and I had much in common. I thought you were like the others who made fun of me because I believe in some of these conspiracies."

"To be honest, Ted, I never disliked you. I knew you believed in UFOs, but I wasn't into the conspiracy stuff at the time. It's not really that I wasn't into it; it's because, I guess, I wasn't aware that most of it was going on. What I've learned in the past week, though, could fill a journal."

"I have a bit of advice for you, if you want it."

"Sure."

"Don't tell the guys in the physics department. They don't think any of this is real, particularly the spiritual stuff. It's all quantum-this and Einstein-that. That's how I got my reputation for wearing tinfoil hats. They started it." Constance looked away with a guilty face.

"I'm sorry about that, Ted. I never believed what they said about you."

"Well, it doesn't matter. I'm not trying to change how they think. I just wish they were more open-minded. There's more going on than just equations and theorems in the world."

"I couldn't agree more." I checked with Constance, "Are you OK, hon?"

"Yes, and no. I like learning new things, but this is a hard pill to swallow. It's not easy thinking that your government is so twisted and callous. And I still am not comfortable about Hara."

Ted pointed out, "If no one does anything about this, Constance, then there's no protection for Hara anyway. She's going to be used, just like the rest of us."

"But I don't want that to happen."

"Then something needs to be done."

"But what?"

"If the people don't wake up and realize what's going on, then the Order is just going to keep doing what they're doing."

"I agree, hon, the people just aren't aware. And nobody seems to have a plan yet."

"Then make a plan, and I'll be behind you all the way."

Ted asked, "Do you have a plan in mind?"

"I just might. And the answers might be upstairs."

"Then what do you say we go take a look?"

"Sounds good to me. Are you coming, honey?"

"Yes, I'm a part of this, whether I want to be or not. And there's no going back now."

Ted clapped, "That's the spirit, Constance. Let's go make a difference."

CHAPTER EIGHTEEN

TAU CROSS OR NOT TAU CROSS, THAT IS THE QUESTION

On the way to my office, Ted pointed to Hara's table. "Are these the pieces? They shouldn't be that hard to assemble and decipher."

"I wish it were that easy," I replied. "I got those from a friend's shop in Cairo. They are ancient Egyptian poems that were headed for the trash at one point."

"Bummer, we could have knocked that puzzle out in a couple of hours."

"They're back in here, Ted. Come take a look."

He reacted, "Ooo, I like the other table better. Can't we go back out there?"

"Sure, if you want to serenade your class with love poems."

He just about pressed his nose onto the plexiglass and stared at them for a while.

"Do you want a magnifying glass or something?" I offered.

"To be honest, I don't think it would help. I've never seen anything like this before. Tell me, why are they in these odd shapes?"

"The person who gave them to me laid them out this way. Do they look like anything to you?"

"They don't resemble any languages that I know of."

In my head, I laughed, "He must not be the one. He didn't recognize the shapes."

"Michael, what are these? They aren't hieroglyphs or hieratic."

"That's what I'm trying to figure out."

"And why are they separated? There're a ton of loose ones over here to the left, and only a handful in these shapes."

"I took a photo of the original layout and matched it up. I put all of the extra pieces in rows beside it to make them easier to look at."

"So there's nothing to the other pieces?"

"There might be. I imagine that they must have some importance, or I wouldn't have left them for myself."

"You left these for yourself? When did you do that?"

Constance chimed in, "This could get a little confusing, Ted. I'm still trying to wrap my head around it."

"Supposedly, when I was a priest"—I gestured at everything on the table and shrugged—"I left these for myself to find in the future. I also wrote about it in this parchment." I had him look at the other table with the parchments on it.

While studying them, he remarked, "These are incredible, and this guy with the blonde hair kind of looks like you. Do you know what they say?"

"I heard my friend, Hanif, translate the first page at a gathering. It was a pretty intense story. The pharaoh was under the control of the reptilians, and he ordered all of us priests to be killed."

"That sounds like the reptilians all right. They hate anyone involved in spirituality."

"Back then, I had certain talents, and those talents helped me to be reunited with all this stuff."

"What about those two pieces over there?"

"Oh, another friend of mine, Ramla, she gave those to me. She said that I was the original owner."

"They look like a heka and a nekhakha."

"Wow! You know your history."

"Well, it is part of my vocation."

Constance leaned in to hear better. "What did you call them?"

"A heka and a nekhakha. It's a fancy way of saying a royal crook and flail."

"Ohhh. This is a little out of my league."

He laughed, "Mine, too," which also made Constance laugh with him.

He glanced back toward me. "Michael, I'm not sure how I can help you with these. But if I run across anything like this in my UFO research, I'll be happy to pass along the information."

"I'll take any help that you can give me. If I'm right, these items could help tip the scales in the battle with the Order."

"I'm not sure how, but I'll keep an open mind."

We were about to head back downstairs when he stopped and sniffed. "Hey, what's that smell?"

Constance was worried. "What smell?"

"Oh, sorry. It's nothing bad. It's a unique scent, like incense."

"That would be *Incense from the Temple Gods*," I grinned. "It's a special blend I got in Cairo."

"It smells amazing."

"Would you like some? I know the store owner personally."

"I'd love to meditate with this. Do you mind?"

"Not at all. Here, take a bundle."

"You know," I continued, "I haven't meditated since I got home. I need to start again."

"Do you meditate often?" he asked.

"I used to meditate for health reasons, but on my trip I meditated to get more information about my past life."

Constance sighed, "And that's when the problems started."

"What problems?"

"Oh, like someone trying to kill him," she shared with a not-so-happy tone.

"The Order tried to kill you?"

I nodded, "Yes, more than once. First there was an assassin who tried to bludgeon me with a fleur de lis club, then I was shot at, and the last time they tried to kill me with carbon monoxide poisoning."

"You didn't mention that on the phone."

"I thought it wasn't time yet. We were just getting to know each other." I gave him a sly grin, "Besides, the government is always listening."

He smiled back, "That they are."

Constance was a little upset. "Guys, I'm going back downstairs to start cleaning up. Do you want anything else, Ted?"

"I'm stuffed, Constance, but thanks for asking. Dinner was great." She thanked him and left the room.

"She's still a little troubled by all of this. She didn't like me getting shot at."

"Who could blame her? I wouldn't like you getting shot at, either."

"Well, I wasn't too keen on the idea myself. I like not having extra holes in my body."

"You know this isn't over yet, don't you? You're still in their crosshairs."

"Any advice?"

"You could always stop doing what you are doing."

"You mean, don't pursue this anymore?"

"Yes. They'll know if you've stopped. If you don't bother them or pose a threat to their plans, they move on to the next person."

"I can't do that, Ted. I feel like I have an obligation now."

"What about your obligation to your family?"

"You said it earlier: There's no safe place for Hara or Constance in their world. They're going to enslave us anyway."

"You mean, they've *already* enslaved us. We're just trying to break free at this point."

"Yes, that's what I meant," and we started walking down the stairs.

Constance met us at the door and handed him a bag filled with food. "Here, Ted. I packed you some lasagna and rolls. I also corked the wine and put it in the bag."

"Aw, thanks, Constance. You didn't have to do that."

She smiled, "And you are welcome here anytime."

"Why don't you keep the wine?" He lifted the bag towards her.

"We hardly ever drink, Ted. You finish it with the lasagna."

"I will. And thanks again."

He shook my hand. "Michael, I'll be in touch if I find out anything else."

"Great. Do you want me to keep you informed, too?"

"Are you kidding? This is right up my alley. I want to take down the Order as much as the next guy. Keep me posted about everything."

"I will. Thanks for coming. See you in a few days."

After the door closed, Constance commented, "That was pleasant. Ted's a nice guy."

"I agree. Once he warmed up—thanks to you—it turned out to be a great evening."

"What do you mean, *thanks to me?*"

"It was your warm welcome when he came in the door. You treated him like he was a friend right away, and that softened him up. He's never acted this sociable at school as far as I can remember."

"Who could blame him, after all of the ridicule he's received?"

"I know. Hey, let me clean up. It's my turn anyway."

"Are you sure? There's a lot to do."

"I don't mind. And after I'm done, I think I'll do some meditating with the incense I brought home. Do you want to join me?"

"No. If you're going to do the cleanup, I'm going to do some research on the computer."

"Is this work research or UFO research?"

"More like UFO and secret government research."

"Interesting. Let me know what you find out."

"I will. You can bet on it."

———•+•———

An hour later, I was up in my study with my incense burner. "Hmm, I'd better move the scrolls. Don't want them catching on fire." I moved the box back into our bedroom and put it in the trunk. After rechecking the parchments under the glass, I surmised that they would be safe and lit the black incense stick.

"Now this brings back memories." My mind flashed to Hanif's shop and to my meditation with Sekhmet. "Boy, I miss those guys. I need to call them and see how they are doing. I should tell them about the UFO attacking the plane and the Men in Black. Oh well, not right now. Let's get to meditating."

I closed my eyes and started my deep breathing. As I was expanding my abdomen, I remembered that I should set an intention. "How about love? I can send as much love as possible to everyone I know and wish them good intentions. That sounds like a good one to start with."

I continued in my mind, "Now how do I do that? I've never done this kind of meditation before." I figured that the answer might come to me while meditating.

After minutes of useless mind chatter, I had a revelation. "They say that love comes from the heart. How about I focus on my heart and send out love energy to the Creator and the world?" For the next ten minutes, I did all of my mind exercises to focus on sending love to Source and others. I could feel my chest beginning to expand, like a huge balloon of energy was filling it up. I thought, "This is interesting," and went back to sending love.

The more I kept projecting good thoughts, the more I felt energized. The energy in my chest continued to get stronger and built up a slight pressure.

My mind wandered, and I thought, "How long do I do this for? I know; I'll build up all the energy I can and send it out in one big blast. What's the worst that could happen? It's love, right? Then I'll call it a good night."

I added my breathing exercise to my thoughts and kept packing all of the love energy in my chest that I could. When I felt like I couldn't hold the pressure anymore, I held my breath and mentally said my intention:

"I send my love to the Divine Source and to all of creation."

I instinctively pushed the energy out from my chest and up through my head. Immediately after doing this, my mind flashed white and I felt a huge soothing feeling come over my entire body. I stayed there with my eyes closed for the next ten minutes to enjoy this new feeling.

From off in the distance, I could hear a low rumble interrupting my silence. It was heavy sounding, like a lawn mower the size of a truck coming our way. As the sound came closer, it grew in volume and intensity. It completely broke my focus, and I wondered, "What the heck can that be?" The sound grew so loud that I couldn't hear Constance calling to me.

"That's a helicopter. What's it doing buzzing our house? That's never happened before."

Constance ran up the stairs and hollered, "Did you hear that?! Did you hear that?!"

"How could I not?"

"That was a helicopter. It sounded like it was right on top of us. They're not supposed to be that close. What did you do?"

"What do you mean, *what did I do?*"

She looked at me, and her gaze said: *You know exactly what I mean.*

"I was just meditating, honest."

"Well stop doing that!"

"You want me to stop meditating?"

"Yes! What did you do in your meditation, call to the helicopter gods?"

"No. I sent out a bunch of love to everybody. Do you want me to stop sending out love—seriously?"

"Well, no. But what just happened?"

"I don't know. I'll look into it though. Maybe it has to do with love energy."

"Good thing you didn't send out hunger energy. We would have been hit by a pizza delivery guy."

"Ha-ha, funny."

"Is this going to be like a daily thing—Men in Black, helicopters in our attic?" She threw up her arms and bleated, "What's next?"

"It would seem that they don't like love energy, whoever it was."

"Well, you've got their attention—and mine. Tell me what to do, Michael. I'm trying my best to be supportive here."

"I know, and I appreciate you more than you know."

"What do you want me to do? I want to help."

"Just keep supporting me; that's all I can say at the moment. Keep researching and learning, too. The more you know, the less surprised you'll be."

She took a moment, then admitted, "That makes sense. I hate it when you make sense," and came over to wrap her arms around me.

"I'll try to be more confusing in the future."

"I think you're doing a pretty good job of it right now."

"Are we good?"

"I'm calming down. I'll be OK. Do you think Ted will want to know about this?"

"I think that's a definite *yes*. I'll let him know later."

"Alright, let's get ready for bed."

"You go ahead. I want to look at the pieces for a bit and see if I can figure anything out. I'll be in in a few minutes."

"Fine, but don't call any more helicopters."

"OK." We kissed each other, and she headed into our room.

———— ·◆· ————

As I walked into my study, I saw that part of the incense had broken off and was glowing red. I thought, "That can't be good around a bunch of old paper, especially the irreplaceable kind. I need to get a different type of incense burner, one of those metal boxes with a lid. I'll go to the metaphysical shop tomorrow and look for one. Now to the table..."

I studied the two symbols for well over ten minutes. "They still look the same to me. It looks like part of a tau cross and an incomplete circle. Nothing's changed. And what's with all of the other pieces? Are they supposed to make another shape? What do they do?"

I paced around the room thinking, "What is all of this? Well, let's do what I do best: solve problems. I'll make a list of everything that it could be, and then I'll eliminate what it isn't until the answer remains."

With pad and pencil in hand, I started listing all of the obvious things these two shapes might be. After filling up two columns, I thought, "You know, I could easily scratch all of these off the list right now. None of them feels like the answer. Think...think...the answer is here somewhere. The bookshelf... I have tons of books with symbolism and religious figures. Maybe the answer is in one of those books."

Thirty minutes passed, and ten books were scattered on the floor. After an hour, I had twenty-three books piled on either side of me. Sixty more minutes flew by, and I was surrounded by stacks and stacks of books. It was just past 2:00 a.m. when Constance came into the room. "What's all this? Aren't you coming to bed?"

"I'm on to something here. These books are helping."

"What are you looking for?"

"Those two symbols. I want to know what they are. I've seen tons of things that resemble them, but no exact matches yet."

"Are you going to keep looking? It's late."

"I'm almost done here. I'll be in in a minute."

"That's what you said a few hours ago."

"I know. I'm sorry."

"I'm going back to bed. I've got to get up early and pick up Hara."

"Do you want me to get her?"

"No, you keep doing what you are doing. This is how I can help."

"Thanks, dear. Thanks for understanding."

I had fallen asleep on a massive pile of books when Constance woke me up in the morning. "Did you sleep here all night?"

"Wow, I must have. The last thing I remember was looking at the clock around 4:22 a.m."

"Did you find your answer?"

"Not yet, no. Lots of possibilities, but nothing that matches both of them."

"Have you looked online?"

"A little bit, but without knowing where to start, I was being led in all kinds of directions. My gut tells me that these symbols don't work as a pair, and a lot of online symbols put the cross in the middle of the circle. I'm not writing it off, but I don't think that's what it is."

"Well, I know you. You'll figure it out."

"Thanks."

"Do you want me to pick you up any breakfast? I'm going to get Hara."

"I'll get something from the kitchen. I might be going out later to get a different incense box. Do you want to go with me?"

"Maybe. I have a deadline to meet today for work. If I get done by noon, I'll go with you."

"Great. See you in a bit."

———————

Constance was in her office, and Hara was playing in the game room. "Honey, I'm going to call my friends in Egypt. I need to fill them in on what's been happening."

"I think you should call Ted, too, and tell him about the helicopter."

"I will. Thanks for the reminder."

"Will you be able to reach them? Isn't it too late in Egypt?"

"It's only midafternoon there. It should be fine."

"Let's see, where did I place Hanif's card? Ah, I bet it's right next to the incense in my office." I took the phone with me and dialed his number.

Hanif answered, "Hanif's Incense Shop, finest incense in all of Cairo. How may I help you?"

"Hanif, my old friend, how are you? This is Michael—Tumaini."

He practically shouted, "Michael! It's so good to hear from you. We heard your plane almost crashed, and we were worried sick."

"I'm fine, I'm fine. The light ball seemed determined to take us all the way to the ocean floor, but the pilots regained control of the plane just in time. We all made it home safe and sound."

"Light ball? What light ball? What are you talking about?"

"I'm pretty sure the light ball was a UFO."

"A UFO! Was it like the one Rehema and you saw at the pyramids?"

"Exactly like that one."

"I'm so glad you are safe, my friend."

"Me, too. How is Rehema?"

"Oh, she's doing well, thanks for asking. She's been extremely busy over here."

"And yourself, how are you?"

"I'm good, too."

Hanif called out to Rehema, "Rehema, Michael is on the phone! Come quick!"

"I have much to tell you. Since you left, we've had a surge of people joining the Protectors."

"That's wonderful."

"And there is more. Seven more people had instant rememberings about their life with you when you were Tumaini."

"Seven? Holy cow! Or should I say holy camel?"

He laughed and continued, "Gahiji, Jabari, and Asim have been helping them with their meditations. Some of them have recalled many skills from when they were priests."

"Like what?"

"Some can heal others, two are able to time travel, and one can communicate with animals."

"Really? What do they say to him?"

"Apparently, they don't like to be eaten."

"Now that's good incentive to go vegetarian."

"We've already made the switch."

Rehema got on the phone, "Michael, it's so good to hear from you. We've missed you. Wait a second; let me put this on speaker phone. Can you hear me?"

"I can hear you just fine."

"Did Hanif tell you about the other seven priests?"

"Yes, he did, and I think that's fantastic."

"Ramla's been helping them, along with Gahiji, Jabari, and Asim."

"That's what Hanif was saying. Has she been helping you?"

"Yes, but none of my abilities have surfaced yet. She keeps telling me that they will come in time."

"I'm sure they will."

"So what else has happened?"

I filled them in about the Men in Black and the helicopter strafing our house. I also told them that I had a friend who was helping me out. They were glad and said they would help any way they could.

I asked, "So how are Mudads and the rest?"

Hanif replied, "He's fine. He asks about you often."

"Well, please tell him that I miss him, too."

"I will."

"Can you also pass along to the group that I am busy working on the parchments and clues I left myself? Apparently, I did a really good job of encrypting my information."

"What do you mean?" inquired Rehema.

"Let's just say that I haven't cracked anything yet, but I'm working on it. I stayed up most of the night working on this."

Hanif mentioned, "Speaking of encryption, Omar has been working with Rehema on the parchments."

Rehema chuckled, "You encrypted those really well, too. What we translated doesn't make much sense. At lease it doesn't sound like helpful information. We've already sent you a number of pages in the mail. You should receive them any day now."

"Thanks, guys. I don't know what to say. You've been such great friends and helpers since we first met."

"We feel the same way about you, Michael."

Hanif added, "We sure do."

"Hey, Hanif, my new friend liked your incense. Can you send him a box to this address?" I gave him Ted's school address and a credit card number.

"Sure thing. How much do you want me to send?"

"I don't know. Make it a good sized box."

"I'll do that for you."

"Perfect. If you don't mind, I'd like to keep in touch more often."

Rehema replied enthusiastically, "That would be a great idea. The others are anxious to help."

"As soon as I have more information, I'll call you. Is there anything else you can tell me that might help?"

"We are all praying for you, Michael. We know you are doing all that you can."

"And I'm keeping you in my thoughts, too. I should get going. I'll call in a few days."

Hanif agreed, "That's good, my friend. And keep an eye out for the mail."

"I will. Thanks, guys."

Rehema and Hanif both said, "Goodbye, Michael. We miss you."

———◆———

For the rest of the morning, I spent my time working on the papyrus pieces. I added more possibilities to my list, then scratched off more than two-thirds that didn't lead to anything. After lunch, I asked Constance if she wanted to go to the shop with me.

"Honey, I'd love to go, but I'm swamped. I have all of these purchase orders to fill before the end of the day. I don't think I have the time. Do you mind?"

"Not at all."

"Do you want to take Hara with you?"

"Not on this trip, but I can take her somewhere when I get back to give you some alone time."

"I'd appreciate that."

"Do you need me to pick up anything on my way home?"

"Yes, there's a small shopping list on the refrigerator. Can you stop and pick up some groceries?"

"I'll take care of it," and I gave her a quick goodbye peck.

———◆———

On the way to the metaphysical shop, I decided to switch my errands around. "There's nothing frozen on this list, so I'll start at the grocery store." I thought of Constance and how wonderful she'd been. "And I can stop at our florist, too, and get some flowers for her on the way home."

Once inside, I picked up a few more items that weren't on the list. It was too much to hold in my hands, so I went to the cart area and grabbed a buggy. On the way back through the doors, I spotted the magazine rack filled with free apartment guides and auto trade magazines. Stuffed in one of the slots was a magazine for this month's horoscopes. The cover was a shade of dark purple with the complete circular zodiac sign printed in white.

"Now that's odd. I don't remember seeing anything like that in this area. Maybe it's a sign," I chuckled.

I picked it up and placed it in the cart. While I finished my shopping, I kept staring at the zodiac sign on the front of the magazine. "Nah, there's no cross there. Must be a coincidence." After grabbing the last two items, I went to the checkout.

At the metaphysical shop, I was greeted by the familiar smells of incense and oils. "Welcome, can I help you find anything?" asked the clerk. She was a middle-aged woman dressed in a floral-print blouse, with very large dangling earrings and a wooden beaded necklace.

"Actually, I'm looking for an incense burner that's a box. Do you have anything like this in the store?"

"We might. Let me show you what we have." She walked me through a few rows of books and crystals, which ended at the essential oils and incense area. "Here's all of our stock. Is there something in particular?"

"Yes, I need something that will burn incense but will keep the ashes from being exposed."

"How about this one?" She picked up a plain black metal box with slits for the smoke to come out. "This one is twenty dollars."

"That might work. Do you have anything else?"

"I think this is all we have. I could check in the back if you'd like."

"If you don't mind, thanks."

"Sure, I'll be right back. We're having a sale on essential oils today." She pointed to the racks nearby. "Feel free to smell the samplers."

"Thanks." I thought to myself, "It's not Hanif's shop, but it has some potential."

The door to the storeroom was open, and I could hear her shuffling things around. I didn't see anything else on the shelf, so I picked up the metal box and went toward the books. When I got to the shelves, my sight was immediately drawn toward a book about tarot cards. On the cover were all different pictures of tarot spreads in unusual shapes. One of the pictures looked like one of the symbols I had at home.

I was so excited that I almost dropped the metal box. I grabbed the book and started flipping through the pages. When I spotted the photo of the tarot cards in the shape of a cross, I yelled out loud, "This is it! This is it! It's not a tau cross. It's not a tau cross at all. It's a magic cross spread. I know it. This is it! I've got to get home and check this out. It's a magic cross spread!"

I picked up the box, and without thinking I started heading toward the door. The clerk was coming out of the room and was momentarily oblivious to what I was doing. She called out, "That's all we have." I barely heard her because I was so excited.

Before I reached the door, she shouted, "Hey, wait a minute! Are you going to pay for those?"

"Oh, yes, sorry. I kind of lost my senses there. Here's fifty bucks. Keep the change."

I checked the back of the book to make sure that I didn't underpay her, and then walked out the door. As the door was closing, I heard her say, "Are you sure you don't want the change?" I gave her a friendly wave and walked to my car.

"Constance is never going to believe this," and I drove away.

CHAPTER NINETEEN

THE DECANS

Constance yelled to me as I ran up the stairs, "Where are you going?!"

"I'll be in my study. I have to look at something, quick."

"What about the groceries?"

"They're on the dining room table."

I could hear her in the background say jokingly, "Sheesh, you could at least put them away."

"I'll put them away in a bit. Don't touch them. I need to look at something."

I was so excited that I nearly missed the chair as I sat down. The pages were blurring by as I frantically looked for the magic cross spread. "There it is." I grabbed the crook and flail off of the nearby table and pinned the pages down. "This looks like the same thing, only mine is missing a few key pieces."

Constance came in the room. "What's going on? You ran up the stairs like you found something."

"I did! I did! Come here."

"What is it?"

"I think this is a match for one of the symbols. It looks like a cross, but without all the religious stuff."

"I still don't understand."

"I haven't read about this spread yet, so I can't tell you any more. Take a look and tell me what you see."

"It looks like a cross. What makes you think it's a match?"

"I just had this feeling, like I knew. I think I created this when I was Tumaini and told the others to pass this down until I returned."

"You what?"

"I've done this before, with the parchments, and Hanif and Mudads continued the tradition."

"You're not making any sense."

"Sorry, I'm having trouble putting my thoughts into words."

"I can tell. Take your time and tell me what is going on."

"When I was Tumaini, I left instructions for the Protectors of Souls to help me when I returned. They've been doing this for hundreds of years. You remember Mudads and Hanif? Well they've been doing this, too. They've passed down the prayer songs, the amulet, and these pieces. And now it's my turn to help."

"I still don't get it. If this is a cross, doesn't that make it a Christian symbol?"

"Not exactly. Wait a minute...here." I dug into the pile of reference books beside my desk and handed one to her. "See, this symbol predates Christianity by thousands of years. It was an Egyptian symbol used in the ankh, a letter in the Jewish and Greek alphabets, it's a pagan symbol, and the Masons used it. It's everywhere. That's why it was so hard to pin down."

"How is this in the ankh?"

"Let me show you." I took the book and flipped back a few pages. "See, the tau cross under the circle? In ancient Egypt, the gods carried this with them, and the tau represented a sacred gateway or a sacred opening."

"I thought the ankh was the sun rising and setting over the horizon."

"It all depends on whom you talk to. I tend to go with the hidden meanings more than the general interpretations. You know what they say: *Hide your secrets in plain sight.* I think this cross is more than just a piece of wood, don't you?"

"What are you going to do next?"

"Figure this out. If I'm right, this might unlock the keys to one of these symbols."

"What can I do?"

"You are already doing it."

"You mean, asking questions?"

"No, you are taking an interest and want to help. And you are being extremely supportive. I couldn't ask for anything else. What can I do to help you?"

"Put away the groceries."

"You got it. Then I'm going to read this and see if I'm right."

"OK, groceries are away, and the flowers are in a vase." I checked those off my mental list. "Let's get back into the book."

It wasn't a very long chapter, so it didn't take long to read. I stood at the table and looked at the pieces in the cross. "According to this book, I'm missing six pieces. That would be four, seven, nine, eleven, twelve, and thirteen. If this is the magic cross spread, then the big mysteries are the pictures on the papyrus. They don't resemble any tarot cards, playing cards, or languages. Maybe I'm going in the wrong direction."

Just in case I had missed something, I went page by page in the book to see if there was a resemblance to the odd geometric shapes. When I didn't find anything, I went back to the computer to search the internet. "Nothing. Not one thing that looks like these shapes. This is frustrating."

"Don't give up now," I heard from behind me.

"I'm not giving up, honey. I just hit a small roadblock."

"Well, if anyone can figure this out, you can." She gave me a kiss on the cheek. "And thanks for the flowers. They're beautiful." I smiled, and then she motioned to my desk. "What did the book say?"

"This is cool. The cross is made of thirteen cards: five across horizontally, two on top, and six on the bottom vertically. You start numbering the cards from the left to right, that's one through five." Next, I pointed to the vertical row. "Then you number from the top down from six to thirteen."

"Wait a minute, you skipped the third one on the vertical row."

"I know. That's part of the secret to this symbol. According to the book, there are thirteen cards, and thirteen is the cross of death. Watch this... What's hidden is that you count *all* of the cards in the vertical and horizontal rows without skipping a card." This time, I pointed at the horizontal row and counted from one to five. Then I pointed at the vertical row and counted from one to nine. "When you add it up, it equals fourteen. Fourteen is seven doubled. And seven in esoteric literature means regeneration. So, you doubled your regeneration. The book says it's the symbol for eternal life."

"Five plus the nine… I get it. So you count the third card twice on both rows?"

"Yes. From what I've read, there are a number of ways to read them as tarot cards, too. What seems to be most common is the left horizontal represents the past, card number three on both rows is the present, and the right horizontal are your obstacles. The top two vertical cards are your fears and dreams, and the lower vertical cards are the future."

"But you're missing quite a few cards in your cross. Look…"

"Yeah, I already figured that out, too. It feels like I'm on the right track, though. What do you think?"

"I say, go with your gut. If it feels right, keep doing it."

"That's what I say."

Constance went to the computer and sat down. "Whatcha doin'?" I asked.

"I had an idea about the symbols."

"By all means, go for it."

While she browsed through her search, I looked at the pieces on the table, including the partial circle, and closed my eyes. I said to myself comically, "Reveal to me your secrets."

Constance's fingernails kept clacking on the keypad, and I tried to focus my thoughts. "This isn't going very well. I can't concentrate on anything." I tried again and put my focus on my breathing, and then I drowned out the environment.

For some strange reason, my mind went back to the night Hanif was telling the crowd the story about Tumaini. A word kept repeating every few moments.

Constance didn't know I had my eyes closed and started talking, "Honey, there's a word here that I've never seen before. It's—"

At that exact same moment, I recited with her, "Decans."

"How did you know that I was going to say that? You're way over there."

"I kept hearing it in my mind. Where did you see it?"

"Right here. I was looking up Egyptian symbolism and saw that very word. It tells about—"

Before she could finish, I asked, "When I came home, I had a magazine with the groceries. Do you know where it is? It wasn't with the bags."

"I do. I was reading it in my office. I'll go get it."

She left the room, and I went to the table and looked at the incomplete circle. "I think I might know this clue."

When she got back, she handed me the book. It was folded back a few pages, so I turned it to the cover. "Look. I think this could be the outer circle." I pointed to the zodiac sign.

"That's what I was going to tell you. When I looked up Decans, it referred me to a page about thirty-six celestial formations." She showed me the circular chart with all kinds of astrological information. Then she continued, "The Egyptians used to follow them in the sky, and a new formation showed up every ten days. The website said that our current astrologists follow a similar pattern, but they don't use the Decans anymore."

"Exactly. And I think that this circle represents the thirty-six priests who would rise again to help change the world."

"I think you might be on to something."

"I won't know until I figure out these geometric shapes. That's a big stumbling block."

"Hey, look at this. I went to the other webpage and found a circle with more information on it. This one talks about kings of swords and queens of cups in the Decans circle. Isn't that like the tarot?"

"It is. They use those names for each card in the deck. Now I know we're onto something."

"Cool. I got to help."

"Yeah, you did great. Thanks, hon." I walked over and gave her a quick kiss.

"You're welcome," she sang energetically.

"By the way, I forgot to tell you... While you were gone, Ted called. He wanted to know how things were going."

"Yeah, he's on my to-do list for today. I need to talk to him about the helicopter."

"I'd like to know what he has to say on it."

"Me, too. Thanks again for all of your help."

"It's been my pleasure."

"Hi, Ted."

"Hi, Michael. Constance tells me you had another encounter."

"You could say something like that."

"So, what's up?"

"This may sound strange, but we had a helicopter fly overhead and it nearly took off our roof. Do you know anything about them? We think it was another attempt to scare us."

He fired back unexpectedly, "You know, you're not the only one who gets helicopter flybys and attempts on your life."

"I know. I'm not even insinuating that." I stammered a little because of his tone, "I...I'm just trying to get to the bottom of it all."

He was very agitated and started preaching, "Michael, let me tell you something. If you create waves for the dark side, they will come after you. Anyone who makes a self-sustaining battery, discovers a source for free energy, or finds a cure for a disease either gets bought off by the big oil and pharmaceutical companies or they get killed mysteriously. What you are doing is no different."

"Ted, did I do something wrong? I'm on your side, remember?"

"Oh, sorry. I'm just tired of the harassment I'm getting from school. There was another prank call. You just caught me at the worst time. And the people just don't want to wake up and see what's going on. It gets to me at times. I'm sorry."

"It's OK, I completely understand frustration. Do you want me to call back?"

"No, I'm sorry. I shouldn't have gone off on you. I just read some more of what the government is not telling us. These politicians pretend they are on our side, but they just keep getting bought off by the corporations. Another black act just got passed about genetically modified food."

"This keeps getting bigger and bigger each time we talk. What do you know about the helicopters?"

"From what I have deduced, they come around when there is an energy surge that they can't identify. They seem to be able to detect this power source, and then they investigate it with these black, unmarked helicopters. Usually, they only investigate the power used by UFOs, but sometimes other things catch their attention."

"Can a human catch their attention?"

"I guess... If a human can generate enough power and it gets noticed on their machines. Why?"

"Because I did this."

"What?"

"During my meditation, I generated a lot of love energy and sent it out to the world. Then I had a flyby."

"You're pulling my leg, right?"

"No, I wouldn't do that."

"Did you research this on the internet?"

"Not yet. I spent most of my time going over the items I brought home. Constance told me that you called, so I picked up the phone."

"Anything new come up?"

"Yes, I think I identified the symbols."

"Really, what are they? Scratch that. I'll come over in a few days and we can talk. Better not say too much over the phone."

"I've been thinking about that. I don't want to involve you and get you in any danger, but I'm also not going to run from them because they listen in to everything we say. We've already talked about helicopters and UFOs, what else could we say that would get me in any more trouble?"

"You've got a point." He paused. "I didn't even think to stop talking when you asked me a question. So what did your research bring up?"

"I think the tau cross is really a magic cross spread and the circle represents the Decans. Do you know anything about them?"

"Not one bit. Actually, I've never heard of those terms before. Maybe you can show me."

"That'd be fine. You can come over on Tuesday, and we'll compare notes."

"I'd like that. Hey, I am sorry about jumping down your throat. I really do want to help."

"No offense taken. Is there anything I can do to help you?"

"Not at the moment, but if something comes up, I'll let you know."

"Great. Are you ready for tomorrow, Ted?"

"What do you mean?"

"School...college...we start back up tomorrow from spring break."

"Yeah, it's just another day for me. I'm looking forward to summer break. There's a lot of research I want to do on Antarctica. Did you know that the governments of the world banned people like you and me from going into Antarctica? There are soldiers there just waiting to arrest anyone without proper papers."

"I didn't know that at all."

"They're hiding something down there, I know it. And they are so pomp-ous about it. One of these days there will be a reckoning. All of the truth is going to come out, and they aren't going to be able to hide."

"I'd like a good cup of sincere truth right now. I can tell you that since my trip, I've lost all faith in the government and the military. I guess you could say that I've seen the light. They really don't care about people, just power and more power. They have cover-ups to hide their cover-ups."

"Now you can see why I get so upset."

"I'm starting to."

"I'd better get going. I have to do some prep for tomorrow."

"Alright. Maybe I'll see you on campus."

"Bye."

———————

A couple hours went by. In that time, I played a game with Hara in the game room, I finished my preparations for the last few weeks of school, and I helped get dinner ready. We were sitting down to eat when Hara mentioned, "Tomorrow we have to take some type of test for the whole grade."

Constance put a plate down in front of her. "What type of test, baby?"

"It's supposed to tell us what kind of job we would be good at when we grow up. And next year they place us in these learning blocks to prepare us for it."

"When did this all happen?" I was a little perturbed. "How come we weren't informed?"

"I don't know. They're just doing it."

"Did you know anything about this, Constance?"

"I haven't heard anything about it. I can tell you that I don't like it. A child shouldn't be locked into a job at the age of ten. And we should be able to have a say in this."

Hara glanced over and told me, "They said our test would be tracked. This would help them know what we can and can't do."

"This sounds like prep for that Common Floor initiative. It's just another failed attempt to fix the education system, but it's really nothing more than brainwashing. They don't want free-thinking kids; they want subservient worker bees."

Constance shook her head, "I haven't heard any parent say that they like this Common Floor education. Supposedly, it was all pushed by the government, even though the parents didn't want it."

"What's brainwashing?" Hara started playing with her silverware.

"It's when someone teaches you to accept their beliefs and way of thinking without you being able to think for yourself."

I motioned for her to put her fork down and look at me. "You like the hieroglyphs, don't you?"

"Yes."

"Brainwashing's something like this: I'm going to teach you that hieroglyphs are evil and people get hurt when they read them. Do you want people to get hurt?"

"No," she answered concernedly.

"Then don't play with hieroglyphs or people will get hurt."

"They will? How?"

"You just have to trust me. You trust me, don't you?"

"Yes."

"Then do you agree that hieroglyphs can be bad?"

"I don't know, maybe..."

"Hara, first thing I want to tell you is that hieroglyphs are not evil. I just made that up to show you how someone could *start* to manipulate your thinking. It's the same as brainwashing. This is what's going on in your schools right now. Do you see?"

"Kind of, but I don't like it."

"We don't like it, either. The schools are getting worse and worse. They are brainwashing you."

"But I like Mrs. Telly and my other teachers."

Constance started sawing the main course really fast. "Honey, she has to earn a paycheck, and she has to do what her bosses tell her or she'll lose her job. They use fear to make her do what they want."

Hara made a serious face. "That doesn't sound fair."

"It doesn't, does it?"

I got Hara's attention again. "Hara, did they ask you if you want to take this test?"

"No, we just have to take it."

"Why?"

"Because they said so."

Constance beat me to the punch. "And that is submissive brainwashing. You're not allowed to ask or question why. You just have to do it."

I added, "I even heard that some of the people who created Common Floor education wouldn't sign off on their own program because it hinders kids from thinking for themselves. But the government is pushing it through anyway. It's all about money and control to them."

Hara frowned, "I don't like the government. They're mean."

Constance nodded, "I agree with you. And what you just said told me that you are too smart to take that test."

I leaned in toward Constance. "We need to do something."

"Like what?"

"We need to think about homeschooling. It's time that we teach Hara instead of allowing the government to brainwash her."

Hara asked, "Is taking this test that bad?"

Constance replied quickly, "It is! I don't want you forced to choose your career at this age."

"It's still bad, Hara." I used my hands to help emphasize. "And they are still brainwashing you. Were you taught to pledge the flag in your school?"

"We all do it every day."

"Why do you do it?"

"I don't know. We were just told to do it."

"Then you were brainwashed. They told you how to think before you had a chance to think for yourself." I made a puppeteer gesture with my hands and face. "They made you into a patriotic puppet."

Constance slapped both hands on the table. "You just convinced me. We need to talk."

Hara grinned, "Do I have to take the test tomorrow?"

I shook my head vigorously, "As far as I'm concerned, *no.*"

"Really?"

Constance added, "This is one test that I'm telling you that you don't have to take."

Then she meekly said, "I don't want to get in trouble."

"Honey"—I held her hand—"if you don't take that test and they say you'll be in trouble, you call me. I'll come right down there. As a matter of fact, I'm going to tell them that you aren't taking that test. And if they don't like it, we have other options."

"Can I skip my spelling test, too?"

"We'll see. But let's just start with this test first."

She bounced a little in her chair. "Can we eat now? I'm hungry."

Constance started dishing out our servings. "Sure, let's eat."

For the rest of dinner, we talked to Hara about the possibility of home-schooling her. She didn't like the idea of leaving her friends, but we told her that we were just talking for now. We also told her that she could always see her friends after school. Dinner ended, and Hara went to go play.

I grabbed a few plates to help clean up. "I'm going to write a note to her teacher that under no circumstance is Hara to take this test. If she has any problem, have the principal call me."

Constance rubbed my back. "I'm behind you all the way."

"And I'm behind you. We definitely need to deprogram our child. I'm in favor of homeschooling her right now."

"I agree. But can we give it a few days? This is a big step, and we need to make sure this is the right thing to do for Hara's sake."

"We can give it some time. I can already see the writing on the wall, though."

"What's that?"

"She'll be home before you know it. They're all plugged in at the public schools, and they aren't going to change because of us. It's controlled with money and fear."

"Wow, I've never seen it that way before. You're right. Just give me a few days, and let me wrap my head around this."

"OK."

———————

I cleaned up from dinner and stopped in Constance's office. "I'm going upstairs to meditate. Do you want to join me?"

"Another time. And I'm not just saying that; I want to start meditating with you. I'm looking up information about Common Floor brainwashing. You're right—it's all about mind control, who's getting rich from this, and power. It almost seems hopeless. Our kids are being dumbed down and trained to be a zombie work force for this power-hungry cabal."

"That's why we need to get her out as soon as possible. The only way we can make a difference is if we take action."

"I agree. I'm proud of you, honey."

"And I'm proud of you, too."

"We'll give it a couple of days to prepare. Then it's time."

———————

"Where's that new incense box? Did I bring it upstairs?" I searched everywhere and couldn't find it. "Did I leave it outside?" I walked to the car and opened the door. "There it is. It must have slipped down the side somehow." I picked it up and took off the sticker. "This'll work just fine."

I moved the old burner and put the new box in its place. I filled it part way with some of the smaller pieces and lit the pile. They took to the flame very easily, and I shut the lid. "Wow, those slits work well. Just look at all that smoke pouring out. I'd better close the door and open a window so the smoke detectors don't go off."

I sat back down and adjusted my posture. "Now for my intention... There's so much I could meditate on: the papyrus, Hara's homeschooling, helping others. I could start a new system for myself. I'll send out love to everyone, and then I'll focus on my goal. That sounds good for now."

I started to gather love energy in my heart. Like before, the feeling in my chest grew, and I felt a slight pressure. The pressure wasn't uncomfortable at all, and it gave me a confirmation that I was doing something right. In my mind, I set my intention to love the Divine Creator and all of Its creation. I pictured all that I could: the birds, the fish, the bugs and animals, the people, the land, the grass and plants, the sky, the clouds, and beyond into space, all of the stars, planets, suns, galaxies, and all beings living and dead. When I couldn't think of anything else, I sent out my love to everything.

I thought, "I like that one. I might tweak it some, but I like it. OK, let's focus. Let's focus on getting information that would help the most with my mission."

Deeper down I went. I followed my breath—abdomen out, abdomen in, abdomen out, abdomen in. As usual, the mind chatter began. I didn't get any visions, so I followed my thoughts from one to the next. I remembered that this is what they call mindfulness meditation: following the flow of thought without condemning one's self for having thoughts.

This lasted for a good ten minutes or so. In the distance, I could hear the low hum of an engine, followed by footsteps pounding on the stairs.

Constance came bursting into the room, and instinctively I opened my eyes. "I know; it's coming again. Don't be scared. They aren't doing anything."

Hara also came into the room. "What is it, Dad?"

"I bet it's a helicopter. Let's take a look out the window."

We jammed our heads out the opening, Hara below, and Constance and I above her. I pointed to the north. "There it is." An unmarked black helicopter flew right over the housetop with a deafening rumble.

Hara jumped up and down. "Wow! That was cool!"

"It was, wasn't it, honey?" I remarked.

"Too close for my comfort." Constance pulled her head back inside. "Is this going to be a regular thing?"

"I hope not. It interrupts my meditation."

Hara put her arms out and swirled around us. "Why did they fly so close?"

"'Cause they wanted to see my honey bunny."

She smiled and whined, "Daaaad, I'm too old to be your honey bunny."

"Too old for the nicknames, huh?"

"Why did they come so close?"

"I think they're curious about something."

"What?"

Constance replied, "We don't know, but they're looking for something."

I looked at Constance. "Everything's alright. See…nothing happened. Why don't you take Hara downstairs and have some chocolate milk."

"Chocolate milk?!" Hara cheered.

"I'd like to finish my meditating."

Constance put her hand on my chest. "OK, we can have some chocolate milk, but no more helicopters."

"I'll see if I can make it a blimp next time."

"Ha-ha."

"Alright Hara, back downstairs."

"Yippee!"

With the girls gone, I closed the door again and resumed my meditation. I reset my intention and did my belly breathing. As my mind drifted in and out, the mind chatter started shifting from the helicopter to my life as Tumaini. Eventually, I no longer thought about helicopters, and I found myself entranced by the incense. In a flash, I was no longer in my body; I was reliving part of Tumaini's life again.

"Baniti, I'm finishing preparations for the future. Do you think this will work?"

"Did you leave yourself clues to follow?"

"I did. In the timeline that seemed to have the most success, I reinforced the voice that spoke to my future self in Cairo. I made the messages louder so it would be heard in his head. What I saw next was this man walking in the direction that I had suggested."

"Good, good. You have learned this skill very well. Did you follow through with that timeline?"

"Yes. Eventually, my future self was reunited with the papyrus that I haven't written yet."

"Do you understand paradoxes, Tumaini?"

"Yes, Baniti. If I don't write the parchments and scrolls, then this timeline might never happen."

"Correct. So you know what you must do then."

"Write the scrolls and parchments."

"There is something else you must consider."

"What is that?"

"You must find a way to keep the information from falling into the wrong hands. If the dark side comes across your writings, or if someone who does not respect power finds it and uses it for personal gain, then these parchments could cause even more harm than good in the future."

"What do you suggest, Baniti?"

"Find a way to encrypt the information so only you will understand it. If someone else finds your writings and they can't decipher them, then it will be useless to them. But if you use your powers and knowledge to make it known to yourself, then you will be able to bring hope to the world."

"I have an idea, but I'm not sure it will work."

"What do you have in mind?"

"In our history lessons, you taught us that the tarot was not originally used for divination, but in the future it is used in this manner. What if I find a way to leave myself a clue using one of these forms?"

"That's pretty clever. Do you have one in mind?"

"I do. It's a common symbol used all around the world, and the tarot spread will give my future self much help."

"And how will you deliver this information to yourself?"

"In pieces. I'll hide the future that I saw in these pieces. When my future self finds them, he will know that it should take this shape." I took a stick and drew a cross in the sand, and then I tapped each section. "With these pieces, I can tell my future self what's happened, what will happen, and what might happen."

"I like this idea. How will you encrypt these pictures?"

"In the future, I saw a way to hide a picture within a picture. I'll use this form to draw all of the pieces."

"And how will your future self solve this puzzle?"

"When I saw my future self with his child, he was looking at a book filled with pictures in pictures. I'll use the cover of this book for the first tarot card. This will teach him how to discover all of the images that I'm hiding."

"That's pretty ingenious."

"Thank you, Baniti. Now I must start drawing these clues."

"Yes, I will leave you to finish your task. I am very proud of you, Tumaini."

"Thank you, Baniti. Would you like to see them when I am done?"

"I would like that very much. Tell the keeper of supplies that you are to be given as much papyrus as you need for this task."

"Yes. Thanks again for your help."

The vision of my former self faded and I regained consciousness. "I've got to tell Constance. Wait till she hears this."

CHAPTER TWENTY

RELIGION, POLITICS, AND SEX

There was a soft knock on the door. "Honey, it's getting late, and you have to teach tomorrow."

"Wow. What time is it?"

"It's almost midnight."

Constance opened the door slowly and let in some light. The smoke from the incense gave the illusion that she was standing in a thick morning fog with a spotlight behind her. "It smells great in here."

"Yeah, I like this scent. Hanif better have restocked his shelves. I'm going to get more of this."

"How did your meditation go?"

"I saw myself as Tumaini again. This time travel stuff is cool. I just wish I could control it like Tumaini did."

"But aren't you Tumaini?"

"I am…at least I'm pretty sure I am. Unfortunately, I don't remember how to do everything he could, but some of it is starting to come back."

"What did you see?"

"He, I mean me, err…this is confusing. My past self was putting together these puzzles for me to find in the future." I shook my head, "I mean now."

"I get it. Did you see the puzzles?"

"No, but he—me—said he was going to use a cross shape for clues. He didn't actually create the entire magic cross spread in time for me to see it, but I know this is what it turned out to be. This isn't easy to talk about when you are talking about yourself in a former life."

"You're doing great. I can understand everything you've said."

I snickered, "At least that makes one of us."

"What about these geometric shapes?"

"It has to do with a picture in a picture. Does that ring a bell?"

"Nothing comes to mind, but I'll think on it."

"Is Hara in bed?"

"She went to sleep a few hours ago. Are you still going to write that note for her teacher?"

"I did it before I came upstairs. It's in her backpack. Will you help me to remind her in the morning?"

"I'll leave myself a note to remind you about the note in a former lifetime."

"Ha-ha. Good one."

"Well, if Tumaini's ready for bed, I need to get some sleep."

"Sounds good to me. I'll be in after I clean up."

I took the embers to the bathroom and put them in water. When I returned to my study, I noticed something odd. "I could have sworn that I left this book open with the crook and flail on it. Why is it closed?"

I turned toward the window. "There's no breeze, so that wouldn't have closed the book." When the window was shut and latched, I walked back to the book and flipped it open to the page with the magic cross spread. As soon as I pinned down the pages, I felt a sharp jab on the bottom of my left foot and a black mist flew out the window.

"Ow!" I yelled, and I picked up my foot to see what I'd stepped on. There was nothing on the floor, and there was no blood on the sole of my foot. "What the heck was that?" I bent down and searched the floor again to make sure there wasn't a pin or splinter sticking up from the carpet. "Nothing's here. What caused that?" I didn't feel it again when I put my foot in the same place, so I brushed it off as a coincidence and went to bed with Constance.

"Morning, Hara."

"Morning, Dad."

"Are you ready for school today?"

She smiled, "Mom packed me a peanut butter sandwich."

"That's good. I put the note for your teacher in your bag."

"What if she makes fun of me for not taking the test?"

"I don't think she'll make fun of you. She might not understand why, though."

Constance interrupted and whispered with her hand to her face, "Because she's brainwashed."

I grinned, then continued, "But she won't make fun of you. And remember, just call me if you have any problems."

"OK. Mom, do you really think she is brainwashed?"

"Does she pledge the flag?"

"Yes."

Constance sang with a lift to her voice, "She's brainwashed."

"Ohhh."

"Hara, grab your stuff. I need to drive you in a little early, and Daddy needs to get ready for college."

"Dad, do you say the pledge at college?"

"No, dear, and I don't think I'll ever say it again."

Constance asked, "Will I see you before you leave?"

"I have to head in early, too. I have my 101 and 201 class before noon and my second 101 class in the afternoon."

"Are you doing the same thing for your 201 class as last year?"

"Yes, but with a little twist. I'll tell you later."

"This oughta be good."

I gave her a wink. "Trust me, it'll be good."

"It's not going to get you fired, is it? Your dean already hates you."

"I won't make any promises, but it will be fun—fun for, me at least. I can't promise for my students."

"Just don't be too hard on them. Your advanced class likes you."

"I know. I like teaching them, too." I kissed both girls as they were leaving. "Have fun at school, Hara." She smiled and walked to the car.

My Intro to Philosophy 101 was packed as usual. Since this class is an elective, and it fulfills part of their core curriculum, I get a lot of students. Some of them think it's going to be an easy ride, but I make them work for their grade. We don't spend much time in books, either. Most of our class centers around discussions on current events. And because I don't do what the other teachers do and make them read boring philosophical tripe and test them on their memorization skills, I get a lot of students signing up for my advanced courses. That's when it gets really fun.

With that class over, it was time for the next. The last of my 201 students came in and my teaching assistant gave me the all-are-in-attendance signal.

"Welcome back, everyone. I see that some of you are glowing a little more bronze and a little redder than when I last saw you." A few chuckles filled the air, while other students looked around to goggle at the suntans and sunburns.

"I know that some of you have heard the rumors—the rumors that say for the last part of the semester you get to pick the final topic. Well, I'm glad to say that this rumor is true. I'm turning over the reigns to you, so to speak, and you get to choose how you will sink or swim." I gave them the classic fingers-pinching-the-nose-as-I-went-under-water routine. Another round of laughs echoed in the room.

In a game show manner, I walked over to the main board and presented their choices. "Do you want to choose what is behind screen number one? Ooo, this one could be scary. Do you want to choose what is behind screen number two? Only the brave enter this category. Or do you want to choose what is behind screen number three? This one is the most arousing of all," I chuckled to myself.

After their initial reactions, my students started yelling out numbers. "Number one! Number one! No, number two, number two! Number three! Number three!"

"Well, I can see that we are divided in our choosing. Maybe we should see what's behind the screens and you can change your mind. But first, I must ask my traditional philosophy question for the day." They settled back down and waited in silence. I looked at my TA, and he just smirked because he already knew the question. I addressed the class, "If a rocking chair is nailed to the floor and never ever rocks, can it still be called a rocking chair?" The laughs were a little harder than before. "OK, I have a bonus one for you. Why do they call it a yard sale if nobody ever sells their yard?" More laughs filled the room.

One of the students hit his head comically. "I've never thought about that before."

Without missing a beat, I punned, "And that's why you are in philosophy class."

Another student yelled out, "Touché!" followed by a lot of laughs.

One of my no-nonsense students raised her hand. "Can we please see what is behind the screens now?"

"Of course, Rochelle, I'll get right to it. Just for you." I gave her a teacher's wink.

"Robbie, could you come over here and help?" My TA came to the board and put his hands on the first sliding screen. I announced to the class, "Your final choices are...drum roll, please..." They pounded on their desks, and Robbie slid the panel. "Your first choice is...U.S. politics!"

Some of the students cheered, while others moaned and groaned, "Boring!"

I turned and faced all of them. "Steady class. We don't want to rock the boat too much. Are you ready, Robbie?"

"You betcha."

"Our next topic is..."—he slid the screen as I yelled—"religion!"

A number of students exclaimed with intrigue, "Oooo!"

"Ah, I see this one has piqued your interest. OK, class, final drum roll." They pounded one more time, and I gave them a gesture to pound louder. "The third topic is..."—Robbie slid the last screen, and the room erupted into cheers—"sex!" I laughed with them and confirmed, "I knew that would get your attention."

After all of the catcalls quieted down, I thanked Robbie and came back to the podium. "OK, I see that the independent vote has a strong run in the preliminaries. But to make this fair for everyone, I've already decided to eliminate one of the choices. I have in my envelope a number written on a card that matches a screen. If Robbie gets the number right..." I looked at Robbie. He was caught off guard by my statement, and he looked worried. "If he guesses the number on this card, we get to keep it as a choice. If he guesses the number wrong, it gets eliminated."

Some of the frat boys started chanting, "Rob-bie! Rob-bie! Rob-bie!"

One of the girls near the front winked at him. "Don't let me down, Robbie."

He walked over to me and pleaded, "Can I decline?"

"Do you want to graduate?" I replied jokingly.

"Alright, but I do this under protest." He went back and forth. "Three... one...two...one...three... Which one do I choose?"

Impatiently, Rochelle barked, "Just choose one, Robbie."

He stammered, "I choose...I choose...number one."

Without any pause, I pulled out the card which had a red three painted on it. "I'm sorry, class, sex is out of the question for you." They all started yelling and booing at Robbie.

The girl who had winked at him said dejectedly, "No sex for you, Robbie."

He turned to me and whispered, "They're going to hate me."

"Probably. Thanks for playing along.

"OK, moving on. We have to choose between politics and religion."

One of the students interrupted and yelled, "Let's go back to sex!"

"I'm sorry, young man. You have to get permission from your parents first." They laughed a little.

"So, class, which is it going to be? If you want politics, you have to raise your fingers in a V sign and say *I'm not a crook*. And if you want religion, you have to make the sign of the cross with your fingers over your chest and say *A-men*. Ready...? Go!"

There was a jumble of *Amens* mixed with a chorus of *I'm not a crook*— including a few slobbery cheeks shaking in the air. I laughed out loud, "Now that was funny. Well worth going through the torture of getting tenure. Seriously, though, that didn't work at all. We'll have to resort to raising hands. Robbie, you count."

The girl who had winked playfully scolded, "Sit down, Robbie."

He glanced at me with worry in his eyes. "I'm never going to live this down, am I?"

"Probably..."

I looked at the group and pointed to the first board. "If you want boring debates, monotonous recountings of politicians lying through their teeth, and you want to talk about broken promises from every president who never fixed anything in this country, you'll raise your right hand." I yawned dramatically and covered my mouth.

"If you really want to sink your teeth into some juicy, philosophical, expand-your-mind and help you get an *A* in my class, with saintly verses, fire and brimstone, and death and damnation debates, then raise your left hand. And I want you to know, I'm not peppering this at all. Vote any way you want." I winked at them suggestively. "OK, raise your hands."

Robbie began counting appendages in the room. "It's a close one."

"What were the numbers?"

"Twenty-three wanted religion, fifteen wanted politics, and two guys in the back abstained and said that they wanted to reinstate sex."

"Well, there you have it, folks. Religion it is." Most of the class cheered, with a few *boos* mixed in.

"Are you ready for the truth?" I gestured.

One of the male students, who dressed more like he belonged at Yale than in my class, asked, "Can we really know the truth in a philosophy class?"

"We'll save that one for next semester, Todd." And I continued, "The truth is, we were going to talk about all three: sex, religion, and politics. I just wanted to choose a focal point, which is now going to be religion. But back to my question, can anyone tell me why we were going to talk about all three?"

No one raised his hand at first. Then my 4.0, soon-to-be-valedictorian student raised her hand. "It's because they are intertwined."

"Correct, Stacey. Do you want to tell us why they are intertwined?"

"Because you can't talk about religion without talking about politics. A few hundred years ago, religion was the political force in many European countries. And today, politicians try to garner certain religious voters to back them."

"Exactly! Go on. What about the sex part?"

"That one is obvious…"

Another student jested, "Not to me," and the class laughed.

"Go on, Stacey." I motioned.

"Sex is as much a part of politics—" The class broke out in instant laughter and stopped her from continuing.

"Easy, folks. Let her finish."

With a little frustration, Stacey continued, "As I was saying, sex is as much a part of politics as it is of religious faith. Sex acts are permitted or considered illegal based on the ever-changing laws of the land and laws of religion."

"Very good, Stacey." She smiled and wiggled in her chair with that knowing feeling.

Rochelle burst in with a perturbed tone, "Then why did you have us vote?"

"Did you see the looks on your faces when you made your choices? It was priceless." Except for Rochelle, they all laughed. "And to be honest, I wanted one subject to have more weight than the other.

"So now, let's go over the grading and rules. You'll be happy to know that there are no tests or long papers that you have to write." There were a bunch of cheers and table pounding. That brought a quick flashback to Mudads standing at the restaurant and the Protectors cheering him on. "Glad you like that part. Let's see if you like the rest." I walked to the other side of the room. "You will have assignments to complete and reports to turn in. I'll explain those when we get to them. You will also be graded on your classroom participation. Robbie, here, will be keeping track of everyone's contributions in class."

The girl who had winked at Robbie pointed back and forth between them. "We're good now, huh, Robbie?" He smiled and nodded back.

I continued with one finger in the air, "Rule number one: Since our main focus is on religion, you cannot use your speaking time to recruit someone into your religion. This is not a free speech zone at an airport."

With two fingers in the air, I stated, "Rule number two: There will be no reciting of scriptures, verses, stanzas, prayers, or religious laws of any kind." I gave them a comical look and pointed to my podium. "This is my pulpit, not yours. Besides, nobody wants to be preached to in this class, especially me. I've heard it all before. If we want to know a scripture, we'll get a religious book and read it on our own."

A few kids cheered, "Here, here!" There were also a few students with frowns and furrowed eyebrows.

"You've been with me long enough to know that I don't want to know what someone else said you should believe in. I want to know what your thoughts are. This is your opportunity to think for yourselves. So we are going to leave religious rules and policies to the policy makers."

With three fingers in the air, I included, "Rule number three: If you are going to say something negative about another person's religion, you also have to say something positive. As an example, if you say something negative about the Jewish faith, then you have to say something that you admire or like about the Jewish faith."

I waved four fingers in the air. "And the last rule: To the best of your ability, don't take anything that is said in this class personally. Once you leave this class, you are still you. You still have your faith, and you still have your choice—however limited it is."

I looked around the entire room. "Are there any questions? And before you ask, we are way beyond the withdrawal period, so you would take an incomplete grade at this point if you dropped my class."

Stacey's hand shot up. "Are you serious about not quoting scripture?"

"Yes. With one exception, though. My experience with this type of open debate is that a very religious person will use a verse or a commandment to back up his or her belief. As I said before, I want your thoughts, not someone else's. However, I will bring up a religious belief every now and then so we can philosophize about it and see if it is actually attainable or true." She nodded in agreement, and I looked to the rest of the class. "Are there any other questions?"

Todd joked, "Just so we're clear, sex is *not* off the table?" A few guys snickered and made lewd comments.

"It's not my position—" They laughed. "Wait a minute, let me rephrase that. Sex is still a topic we will discuss, but it will be in the context of *sex* as it relates to religion."

He replied, "OK."

"We have two more things to do today, and then we'll be done. I would like to take a poll from the class on your current religious beliefs. If you choose not to participate, nothing will be held against you. Just raise your hand when the time comes." I turned to Robbie. "Robbie, will you tally the results again?"

"Sure." He stood up ready to count.

I went through the most known religions and had the students raise their hands. I also asked about those who were spiritual, metaphysical, New Age, pagan, Scientologists, Wiccan, not decided, atheist, agnostic, undecided (but they believe in something), and those few who did not want their answers recorded.

"What about Satanists?" asked Rochelle curtly. "You didn't ask if there were any Satanists in the room."

"You're right, I didn't, and it wasn't from being insensitive. Are there any Satanists in the room? It is recognized as a religion." No one raised a hand. "Are there any other religions that I didn't ask about? We covered most of them, but I won't say all. Here's your chance to speak up."

One of the students looked angry. "What is it, Beth?"

"I don't want to break one of your rules."

"Say it, and I'll let you know if you broke a rule or not."

"Well, I don't have anything nice to say about it, but I don't think Satanism should be considered a religion."

"Really? Why do you say that, and can you back it up? And before you answer, what do you know about Satanism? Were you actually a member, or are you going to comment based upon your own viewpoints and morals?"

"It's just not right."

"What's not right about it? And to the class, I'm not condoning or condemning any religious belief system. This is a class on philosophy, not a class on banishment or punishment." I looked back at Beth. "Were you ever a member of that religion?"

"Certainly not! I'm a Christian. I believe that Jesus is the way to salvation."

"OK, your belief is honored. Can you find something nice to say about Satanism?"

She answered quickly, "No! They worship the devil and perform human sacrifice."

"Then this would be a good example of breaking the rule."

One of my quiet students, Phillip, inquired, "What do you believe in?"

A couple others chimed in, "Yeah, what do you believe in?"

"Are you sure you want to go there? I said that only the brave choose door number two."

A chorus of *Tell us! Tell us!* echoed in the room.

"Alright, but you asked. And besides, I was going to tell you anyway. This happens every year, so it's best to get it out of the way so the rest of the semester can be focused on you guys.

"Before I tell you, though, let me ask this: How many of you were born into your religion? Meaning, how many of you did not choose your current religion; it was chosen for you by your parents or guardians?" More than half of the class raised their hands.

I nodded my head, "Like many of you, I was also born into a religion. I was raised Roman Catholic. I was even an altar boy for many years and was encouraged to become a priest."

Phillip prodded, "Why didn't you?"

"Because I didn't like the idea of celibacy. And by that same time, I didn't agree with a lot of things that the church had done in the past, or what it stands for now."

I paused for a moment. "I'm going to share this with you because it may give you something to chew on tonight—food for thought. In no way am I trying to dissuade anyone in this room from his or her beliefs. If you don't agree with me, that's fine. I honor your beliefs. If you choose to put a wall between us—which has happened in the past—just know that I hold no malice against you, and it will not go against your grade. What I share is for teaching purposes only. Are we good?" Most students nodded or indicated *yes*. "Good..."

I walked over to the other side of the room and re-engaged the class, "When I was in Catholic school, I did what I was told. I tried my best to be a good boy"—I looked at them and jokingly shook my head humbly—"but I didn't always succeed." After the laughter died down, I continued, "But something never felt right to me about many of the messages we were taught in church. We were supposed to love everyone and cause no harm, which includes sending negative emotions. Well, fear is a negative emotion, punishment is a negative action, and war is an extremely negative action that harms millions." I used my hands to gesture. "Guess what the Catholic faith does a lot of? It uses fear as its main control factor over people: *Do this, or you are going to hell for all eternity*. And God and the church punish those who don't follow the rules."

I walked back to the board and wrote the word *rules*. "But here's the kicker: The rules of many churches change all of the time, and Catholics and Christians have engaged in countless bloody wars since the inception of Christianity. For myself, I couldn't abide with this constant rule changing and blatant hypocrisy. Instead of unifying people in love, it separated people in fear and doubt."

Beth asked angrily, "How does it separate? My church doesn't teach that."

"Good question. And this will turn into your first assignment...but I'll get to that in a bit. Here's an example of how religion separates. When my wife and I were walking Hara in her stroller, we came across a nice man in our neighborhood. We struck up a conversation with him, which led to church and faith. He asked us if we went to church, and I said I didn't belong to a specific church, but that the world is our church. He instantly shut us down, and the conversation was over. Because we didn't believe in the same thing, he ostracized us. Instead of loving and accepting us, which is what is taught, he turned us away. I've encountered this all of my life, and so have you."

Stacey contended, "We don't do that."

"I'll get to that, Stacey. It's your first assignment."

Todd raised his hand. "I'm confused. What religious rules have changed?"

I pointed out, "Just look at Galileo. He was under house arrest because he went against the church's belief regarding the solar system. Now the church has changed its mind, and the solar system idea is hunky-dory. A lot of us today would have been burned at the stake or tortured in the Spanish Inquisition for openly talking about science and sex."

One of the guys in the back blurted, "Ooo, I don't like that."

"Exactly. Twenty years ago, it was bad to eat meat on Friday, but now it's OK. Do you see how the rules change to meet the masses and science? If you believe in heaven or hell, your entrance could have been determined on the decade that you born in and not on how loving you were." My statement got mixed reactions in the room.

I told them, "It's a tough pill to swallow if you've been raised this way, but there's no denying that the rules have changed throughout history."

Rochelle asked, "Is that what made you change your faith?"

"No, it was this: It didn't feel right to me that I was going to be saved because I was born—by chance—into the right family, and those who weren't born into the right religion were going to be condemned for all eternity. That felt wrong to me. Saved by chance? Well, that and the myth of free will."

Robbie shook his head and mumbled, "Uh-oh, not the *F* word again."

Phillip mentioned softly, "Free will? What's wrong with free will?"

"I'm glad you asked that, Phillip. The number one reason that I do not follow most fear-based religious belief systems is that they all use free will as the rationale for who is good or bad, saved or not saved, or who is going to heaven or going to hell. According to them, your supposed *free will* actions will damn you or save you."

Robbie shrugged. "Here we go again."

"Alright, I'll make this short. Free will implies that you get to choose. First mistake is: We don't get to choose. And before you react, hold your thoughts. Second thing is: We don't get to be perfect. Would you agree with that, that we are not perfect?" Everyone agreed.

"OK, here it is. For whatever reason, we are not allowed to be perfect—even if we choose to be perfect. How many of you would like to be perfect, or at least be perfect at something?" Everyone's hand went up. "See, we all want to be perfect, but we are not allowed to be. In regards to religion, you are judged on your imperfections. If you are too imperfect, you are going to hell. Do you see the problem here?" Nobody said anything.

I was about to continue when Stacey interrupted, "But we can choose."

"I'm so glad you brought that up. Now we go into our assignment." Before I could continue, they were opening up their notepads and computers. "Take this down for your philosophical reservoir: As a human being, we do not have free will or free choice, we have forced, controlled, limited, restricted choice. Your abilities and power dictate what you can and cannot do with choice."

Phillip murmured, "That sounds so limiting."

"I agree with you, Phillip, but it is not meant to be limiting. What we are involved in is the simple pursuit of truth.

"Let me ask all of you this question. You just came back from spring break. Do any of you have any regrets about what you did?" A few girls blushed and covered their faces, while a couple of guys nodded *yes*. "I'd like for you to undo your choices and redo them the way you would like. Can any of you do that?" They were shaking their heads *no*. "Then you don't have freedom of choice. You have restricted choice based on your power, energy, and abilities."

I looked at Phillip. "Phillip, let's take this a step further. Can you control time?"

He answered, "No."

"Can anyone here control time? And I'm not talking about time travel, I mean, can you actually stop time?" No one raised a hand. "Then consider this: If you cannot completely control time, then the forward motion of time forces you to choose. It forces you to be in a new, uncontrolled experience. This, in turn, forces you to react to that new, uncontrolled experience. And when you develop the ability to control time completely and alter any event—past, present, and future—then you could say you have some choice over time. Until then, you don't even get to choose because you are forced to choose by the forward motion of time."

Todd questioned, "What if you can time travel?"

I snickered, "I actually have a little practice at this. When you time travel, you are still in the forward motion of time. The event that you see or participate in, whether in the past or future, is still in the forward motion of your current life. You would have to stop all time from moving—past, present, and future—in order to create power over time."

Rochelle put her hand on her head. "That's some pretty deep stuff."

"It is. Take some time—ha-ha—and think that one over."

I could see the haze in some of their eyes. "I'm not going to go over each part of my earlier statement because I want to get to your assignment."

I looked at Stacey and asked, "Stacey, do you remember what you said earlier about turning people away?"

"Yes, but I have a feeling you are going to prove me wrong."

"I just want to open your mind to other possibilities. You can choose if it is right or wrong."

"I'm ready. Shoot away."

"I'll direct this to the entire class. In my viewpoint, religion separates people. That is why I will never join a religion. A simple look at the history of the Middle East validates this fact. We could spend weeks going over all of the power struggles, enforced borders, and wars that are a result of religious differences. If you don't commit yourself to any one religion, then you lessen the chance you will argue and fight.

"So let's take this back to Stacey. Most religions focus on love, and love supposedly accepts everything. OK, I have to back up a minute. Let's go back to choice. This is an in-class assignment that we are going to do in a few moments. I couldn't say right now because now is over, and that would be another time joke. But it's not *time* for that."

Rochelle muttered, "Get on with it."

"I want you to prove to yourself that you have control over the most simple of human attributes. Choose to control your emotions."

Someone in the back yelled out, "What?! You've got to be kidding. The terrible twos and puberty already prove we can't do that."

One of the girls whispered, "You've never been pregnant or had a period before."

After the laughter died down, I continued, "And I'll make it even simpler. Choose to focus on one emotion, and that emotion will be love. Choose to focus on nothing else but love. And as soon as your mind focuses on anything else, raise your hand. If you focus on breathing, raise your hand. If you focus on the person sitting in front of you, raise your hand. If you experience any other emotion, raise your hand. Ready or not, go!" Seven hands went up immediately.

"For those of you who have not put your hands up yet, keep focusing on nothing else but love." More hands kept popping up like daisies.

"The rest of you keep going. And to the two guys in the back who voted to reinstate sex, what did you think about?"

They both laughed and recited in unison, "Sex!" which made more people raise their hands.

I asked Todd, "Why did you raise your hand?"

"Because I thought if I don't pass this class, my parents won't pay for my tuition anymore." Six more hands went up.

"Rochelle, your hand was the first one up. What did you think about?"

"I'm hungry, and I hope I still have money in my meal plan."

Only one hand was left at that point.

"Stacey, you look mad," I observed.

"I don't think that was a fair challenge."

Rochelle countered, "Why? Is that the first time you ever failed at something? He just proved to you that we don't have control over our emotions." Stacey just sneered at her and fumed in her chair.

Phillip's hand was the last to go up.

"Wow, Phillip, you lasted the longest. Congratulations. What did you think about besides love?"

"I thought about time travel, and that blew it."

"Alright class, put your hands down, and let's put this into philosophical perspective. I think this experiment proves that you don't have the free will or control over choice that religions would like you to believe. It's not easy focusing on love, for even just a short period of time. And with all of your daily distractions and expectations, being all love seems almost impossible. That means no one is going to heaven." Beth's face showed a lot of confusion.

"Now, love is all-accepting. Would you agree to that as a possible definition? I'm not saying it's a complete definition, just possible. What do you think, Stacey?"

"I agree with that."

"Good. Back to earlier, you stated, 'we don't do that'. Meaning, we don't separate ourselves from others based upon likes, dislikes, habits, religion, political preferences, sports, and so on. Tell me, class, do you accept everyone in the room? Do you love everyone unconditionally? Isn't that one of the most common messages for the popular religions?" There was an uncomfortable silence.

Todd urged, "What are you getting at?"

"I'm just pointing out philosophical options. It's up for you to decide."

The guys in the back joked, "Can't we talk about sex now?"

"Not just yet. Now that I have you thinking, let's solve a problem instead of pointing out a problem."

Robbie nodded, "Ooo, I like that."

"I've done this experiment before, and it has changed my life. I admit that I have judged others based on their looks, beliefs, and personalities. I wanted to know how I could stop judging and start inviting others into my circle. So I came up with this idea: Every time that I saw a new person—before I could make the slightest judgment about their appearance, clothes, hair, makeup, whatever—I said in my mind as I looked at them, *I love you.* When I started doing this, I started focusing on love and other positive attributes of love. I started asking myself: How could I serve you? How could I be kinder to you? How could I help you? And not once after I said *I love you* did I say: They don't meet my standards. They don't look right. They don't like what I like.

"What happened was that I began loving more, and more, and more, and judging less, and less, and less. I became more of a servant to mankind instead of living for myself. Basically, I began accepting everyone for who they were and not what they did, how much money they had, or what their outward appearance was. In my mind, I changed for the better.

"So here's what I want you to do for your assignment. Before our next class, you are to engage in this *I love you* experiment ten times while you walk around campus and see if you notice a change. You'll write down your observations and turn them in to Robbie. There's no right or wrong about this, just do the experiment.

"We're done for today, so I'll see you on Wednesday. Class is dismissed."

Beth came up to me and expressed, "I like this idea, Professor Whyse. You've already changed me."

"Thanks, Beth. But you are the one who changed yourself." She smiled and walked away.

CHAPTER TWENTY-ONE

BOTTLE OF DJINN

On the way into the house, I picked up a large mailer that was balanced against the door. When I looked at the address, it was from Mudads. "I bet these are the papers that Omar deciphered for me."

I became really excited because I missed my friends. As soon as the door clicked behind me, I ripped open the flap, and that's when Constance walked up. "How was school? Did you surprise your advanced class?"

I stopped opening the envelope to get my hug. "I did. It was fun, too. I played a game with them, and they had to choose the main topic for the rest of the semester. They were bummed that they didn't get to choose *sex*."

"You're joking, right?"

"Not at all. Sex was one of the topics. Unfortunately, Robbie axed that for them, and we ended up with religion."

"Nooo! Poor Robbie. How did he do that?"

"I gave each topic a number, and Robbie eliminated one of them without knowing it was sex. He made the best of it, though. He's a good kid. He'll make a fine professor one of these days."

"Make sure you tell him that."

"I will."

The phone rang, and Constance started running. "I'll get that."

She stood in the doorway to the kitchen, and I waited to see if I needed to get on the phone. I mouthed to her, "Who is it?"

288

"It's Hara's school." She put up a finger to have me wait. After a few minutes, she pointed to the phone and whispered, "Principal." Then she made an ugly face.

She continued, "Uh huh, I understand. We'll be there first thing tomorrow morning."

I got angry and walked over with my hand stretched out. "Give me the phone. I want to talk to her."

Constance stopped me and confirmed forcefully, "Eight o'clock. Believe me, we'll both be there," and she slammed the phone.

"Before you say anything, you are going to be very proud of your daughter."

"Why, what's up? What did she do?"

"She did what we told her. She gave the note to her teacher, and she chose not to take the test."

"Is that all?"

"Well, not exactly. It seems that she made a ruckus right as the pledge was being said."

"So?"

"She told everyone that they were being brainwashed into zombies. The teacher tried to stop her, but she ran around the room and kept screaming, 'Don't brainwash me! Don't brainwash me! I don't want to be a patriotic zombie!' It caused such a disturbance that they sent her to the principal's office for the day."

I was stunned for a moment. "I don't know how to react. I'm extremely angry at her school, but I'm even more proud of Hara."

"I'm angry, too. But did you expect anything different from them?" She threw up her hands in disgust. "I bet that most of them have never even heard about the Order. They don't even know that they've been used. To these administrators, this is just how life works, and they accept it."

"Wow, you're starting to sound like Ted and me."

"I know. Scary, isn't it?"

"I'm still mad, though. I can't wait until tomorrow morning."

"What do we do about Hara?"

"We're going out to celebrate. That will show her that we are behind her all the way and that we are rewarding her for being truthful."

"Bongo Billy's Pizza House?"

"You read my mind. But we need to talk with her and let her know this behavior is not appropriate everywhere. You have to pick your battles."

"Ooo, good one. I like that."

———•—•———

It wasn't long before Hara was dropped off by the bus. When she came in, she looked dejected. Both of us went up and gave her a hug. Constance consoled her, "Are you OK, baby?"

"No," she muttered.

"We know, dear. We spoke with the principal today."

"Am I in trouble?"

I knelt down, looked her in the eyes, and adamantly reassured her, "Not one bit, Hara. We are so very proud of you. We couldn't be any prouder."

"Really? But why? I got in trouble. They said what I did was wrong."

Constance gave her a squeeze. "No, your principal said you were in trouble and you were wrong, but we are very proud of you. And we disagree with your principal; she's the one who is wrong. You stood up for yourself and spoke the truth, even though they couldn't see it yet, and you acted on your truth. That should be rewarded, not punished."

I winked. "I have a surprise for you."

"What is it?"

"You're getting rewarded."

"Really?"

"We're going to Bongo Billy's Pizza House."

"Twice in one week?"

"You betcha. And afterwards, we're stopping for—"

"Ice cream?!"

Constance grinned, "Two scoops, with hot fudge and cherries."

"Yea! This is the best getting in trouble *ever!*"

I popped into teacher mode. "Well, there is more to this. We need to talk about when it's right to do this and when it's not right to do this."

"You mean, I shouldn't tell the truth?"

"You should tell the truth, but sometimes it's smarter not to volunteer the truth if the truth is going to put you in immediate danger. It's not the same as sitting in the principal's office. Do you understand?"

She looked confused. Then Constance added, "Hara, we're going to talk about this more at dinner. And we might talk about homeschooling again. Why don't you get ready, and we'll leave right away."

290

"Mom, Dad, I'm sorry if I got you mad."

I shook my head, "We're not mad at you one bit, pumpkin. We're mad at someone else. It's your—" Constance grabbed my arm before I could finish. "OK, we'll talk about this at dinner, but we're not mad at you."

"Are you sure?"

"We're both positive."

I looked at the envelope from Mudads. "I'll get to this when we get home. Come on, girls, let's go."

———◆———

Hara felt much better after dinner, and she let us know that she felt more comfortable with homeschooling. We were home pretty early, so Constance helped Hara with her hieroglyphs. I decided that it was time to look into the envelope and read what Omar had to report.

There were five pages in the envelope: a short note from Mudads and four pages of translation.

Dear Michael,

> We all miss you and are looking forward to hearing about your successes. Omar has been working on your project. He has had much difficulty with everything beyond the first parchment that we read to our group. He said that the dialect has changed, so it is taking him longer than expected. Also, what he translated didn't make much sense to him, and he questioned if he was doing it right. He thought it must make sense to you, since you wrote it, so he sent it along. Karim has been helping him when he can.
>
> Hanif and Rehema send their best. And Ramla, Gahiji, Jabari, and Asim are working with the reincarnated priests. You would be surprised how many have awakened and remembered their past life with you.
>
> We are all excited about the possibility of returning hope to the land. Please keep us informed, and let us know what else we can do to help.

Allah Ma'ak,

Mudads

"Boy, I miss these guys. I can't wait to get back to Egypt sometime and visit. Maybe when this whole thing is over, we can just enjoy each other's company."

I set down the letter from Mudads like it was an emotional treasure. Then I spent the next fifteen minutes looking at the first two pages that Omar had sent. It was word-for-word the first parchment that was read at the meeting. "Constance is going to love this," I thought. "So what did Omar come up with for the other pages?" I lit some incense, opened the window, and began to read:

The prince was excited. He had finally found someone who would lead him to the hidden treasure and control over all of Egypt.

The man who spoke to the prince wore a simple short-sleeved white robe that was cut just above the knees and a pair of sandals made from rattan.

The prince asked, "Are you sure that I will have all of the riches I seek and power to rule over man?"

"Yes," he affirmed, "if that is what you seek."

"And will I be able to smite my enemies and claim what they possess without drawing any blood?"

Again, he replied, "Yes, if that is what you seek, it will be done."

"And if I choose to have authority over the kingdom, will they bow to me and acknowledge my dominion?"

"When the work is done, all will come to your bidding. But only if the work is done."

"Then tell me, please, what must I do?
How may I gain this power, and soon?"

"You must face the challenges one by one.
Seven in all, before the one hundredth sun.
Your experience from one will lead to the next.
Your first challenge comes from the allure of the opposite sex."

"Is there a chosen path that I should take?
How will I meet my lovely new flame?"

"Follow the Nile, it will lead you on the way.
Start at the basin to meet your new flame.
She will be in the waters waiting for you.
With her, your trials will see a debut."

"Thank you, wise one, I will heed your words.
I will seek this woman out at the base of the Nile.
When future challenges come, may I seek out your guidance?
You honor me with your knowledge and vibrance."

"As all rites of passage, this is no different.
You must face each challenge with courage and innocence."
He bade me goodbye and walked into the sun.
"For now," I thought, "I am on a journey of one."

The woman was beautiful, fair skinned, and tall.
We ate, drank, and danced without thinking about anything else at all.
Our minds were filled with lust and celebration.
I had completely forgotten about my prize and our nation.

It didn't take long before I saw my own faults.
There is only so much food one can eat, and drink to be drunk.
Not even flesh could satisfy my quest and desire.
It was empty of course, and no longer began to matter.

This path I was on must not stop at the basin.
If I lingered here, my growth would not hasten.
I would be bound to the earth if I didn't change my ways.
I had already lost much more than twenty-one days.

I traveled by boat with the flow of the Nile.
The words from behind me were filled with curse and vile.
They flung arrows at me to sink my wooden float,
But they could not stop my strong renewed hope.

My second challenge came with thoughts from my past.
"Do I harbor ill feelings toward my friends and my lass?

Do I forgive my former self and my brethren, too?
Can I love them?" I thought, "I sure hope I do."

The word spread I was coming, challenge two was not over.
My friend's brothers were at the next port of order.
I was more conscious of my thoughts and my behavior.
I was turning into my own personal savior.

I sent them good wishes and shared my coin with them.
They were concerned with their greed and fear and remission.
They struck me down hard and called me a thief.
I was hurt and bewildered, shocked beyond belief.

With no money left, my clothes were in tatters.
I told them I was a prince, my pride had been shattered.
They laughed and scoffed at me, "Your title means nothing here.
Get out of here now, or you'll be buried up to your ears."

For days I wandered with no shoes, food, or drink.
The pain in my belly made it hard to even think.
I came upon a man who was also robbed and beaten.
I could be concerned for myself, or I could stop, help, and greet him.

I offered my hand and tended to his wounds.
He said, "Thank you, sir. You have not come too soon.
The men over there were harsh and mean.
They came one blow from sending me to the world that's not seen."

Something inside me changed, I wanted battle no more.
I was abhorred by violence, ridicule, and scorn.
It was my new path to help others prosper and thrive.
There was much, much more than money could provide.

From that day forth, I made it my vow.
Help others as needed, don't belay, do it now.
Do it for nothing, and show love, mercy, and compassion.
This is the path of God's will, and my new life's passion.

The man whom I'd helped came up to my side.
He wanted to help me get back toward the Nile.
My boat had been taken, I had nothing to ride,
So he helped me to build something that would flow with the tide.

Challenge two won't soon be forgotten.
Up the Nile I went to fields filled with cotton.
The people lived by laws unusual and strange.
I wondered if I should help them make a loving change.

I asked, "Tell me, sir, why must I pay taxes?
I own no fields or sheep or axes.
Is it love that makes another man toil
For the riches of others' greed and their spoils?"

"Don't argue now, just do as you're told.
Pay your tax and duty, hand over your gold.
You can fight our system, or spend time in jail.
Maybe you should go and put wind in your sail."

This was a hard lesson learned. I sat and I wondered,
"What would love do? They'll just take and go squander.
Do I make my stand for justice and what's right
Or give in to greed controlled with their might?"

I asked the man if my love he'd accept.
I surely didn't want to make them upset.
"I will tell you again, if you stay you must pay.
It's better that you go and be on your way."

I chose not to linger, not even for a night.
I didn't want violence or to put up a fight.
I wished the man well and floated up stream.
I believe I was done with challenge number three.

The next forty days I spent giving thanks.
I loved my life, the land, and my new romance.

I was back in my homeland of pyramids of stone.
My new personal goal was to never be alone.

I reveled in love, but had lost my goal's sight.
My prize still waited for me, it was deep in the night.
The material world still owned me. I had trouble giving it away.
There was more meaning for love that lay in the spiritual way.

More days flew by as I struggled in fear.
Do I give up my quest? It's not even near.
To move toward my prize, I must love more than men.
My love must grow strong in God, more than every now and then.

My fourth challenge has kept me many days from the Nile.
Upward I must go or be in denial.
I left my friends and homeland as we shed many tears.
This journey I must complete or be stuck here for years.

With memories tucked deep in my treasure chest's hold,
I flowed with the river to seek more than gold.
What lay ahead gave me more fear than most.
The Nile forked in two. "Which way should I go?"

I anchored my boat and asked myself this:
"Do both paths lead to love and God and bliss?"
I must make my choice true and hold to my fate.
One hundred days approach soon. I don't want to be late.

Instincts rang true, "Go left without a doubt."
I moved my sails to the left to make them fill out.
In one day's time, I reached the Nile's throat.
There was much more to do. I knew not to gloat.

Speak truth and enter the Mediterranean Sea.
Speak false and sink to the rocks beneath thee.
Onward I went. I didn't know what would happen to me.
It'd all become such a grand mystery.

The Sirens, who charmed both women and men,
Thrashed waves at my side to put me in a water's den.
They sang and shrieked with great determination.
I almost fell for their evil aberration.

I regained my thoughts and focused my speech.
"Be gone, foul ones. Return to your beach.
My goal is more precious than just staying alive."
Speaking my truth had conquered challenge number five.

Eight more days gone, I was terribly lost at sea.
I knew no one would be looking for me.
The only company was the voice in my head.
The voices wouldn't stop, not even if I was dead.

Maybe I should follow my thoughts all the way through.
Seek out the silence amidst all this blue.
Calm the mind and be with the One.
When you conquer this, your task will be done.

I floated and waited for the seas to be still.
They rocked and waved as big as a hill.
They rolled and crashed and kept me at bay.
I thought I would not live to see another day.

When morning came, the seas were serene.
I pondered, "What does one's life really mean?"
I closed my eyes and found peace at last.
My thoughts were still. Number six had just passed.

A new wave grew and splashed water on my face.
It reminded me that I should quicken my pace.
I had one day left to reach my goal.
It was not for me, it was now for my soul.

I looked back at my life and saw nothing to hold.
It was barren and selfish and fully controlled.

It was time to turn my life to the One,
To let go of fear and become the humble son.

Into the water, I had left my boat.
I lay on my back and began to float.
I gave myself to the holy Creator.
It was to time learn from a new educator.

I rolled my head back with ears under water.
The sun was ablaze, it was getting much hotter.
It came to me what I must do.
Let go of it all, no longer accrue.

I offered my senses to be with the One.
When this was done, I knew I had won.
No sight, no sound, no thoughts to think.
My body let go, and I began to sink.

This was not death, it was the start of life.
I was held in a void, not the afterlife.
My lessons came quick with seas full of knowledge.
I had just begun in a new sort of college.

I thought the Mediterranean Sea was so grand,
But connected to it were oceans without sand.
Infinity had shown her graceful attire,
Songs were sung by the heavens' saintly choir.

I had made it back home, my prize lay before me.
I was asked by the One, "What would you be?"
I offered myself to serve in God's ways:
To love and honor and thank and praise.

In life you'll encounter a reflection of you.
What will you see? What will you do?
How will you greet your shadow self's son?
I hope it's with love. We are all made from One.

I put down the letter from Omar and joked, "What the heck was I drinking back then? One too many hits in the head with a sand wedge."

At the bottom of the page, Omar wrote:

Michael,

These were a challenge to translate. I hope I did it correctly. I tried a number of different languages, too. The only one that made sense was the rhyme in modern-day English, so that is what I went with. Maybe Tumaini knew Michael would be from the West and wrote these specifically for you.

When you figure out your riddle, will you please tell me? I'm anxious to know what the hidden meaning is. There is a hidden meaning, right? I asked Ramla about it, and she told me that only you would know.

I have already started working on the next section of parchments. They are also in a different dialect. It may take some time. You hid your messages well.

I laughed to myself, "Too well."

Omar's letter ended with a pleasant goodbye. I thought, "I wish I'd had more time to get to know him."

The incense was still smoking, so I decided to do a short meditation. "I'll focus on this new riddle. Maybe I'll hear Tumaini telling someone about it."

All throughout my meditation, I kept getting flashes of the Nile and human skeletons. The skeletons were floating on the water with their spines beneath the waves. "This didn't make any sense," I thought. "I'm not as deep as I would like to be, either. Is this my subconscious going berserk? Is it a simile? I'm probably just thinking about this because of the story."

I tried to stop thinking, but my thoughts kept showing me strange images. The next flash was a skeleton being sucked down in a whirlpool. "Alright, I'm not asleep, so I'm not dreaming. And I'm not on acid or ayahuasca. What does all of this mean?"

Instead of fighting my thoughts, I went with them. In a few moments' time, I was having more visions. Instead of skeletons, I saw bodies on the water covered with hundreds of water beads. These beads kept sparkling like constellations in the sky. I swear that I could just about make out patterns and lines in the sparkles.

I thought to myself, "OK, spirit, subconscious, Easter bunny, Creator... tell me more. What do I need to know?"

I noticed that I was slouching, so I straightened out my back. My belly began to burn with an intense heat. It wasn't hurting, but it did catch my attention as it grew in intensity. Then the palms of my hands and feet began to have this strange tingling feeling about them. I could feel something that felt like a ball of energy in each hand.

My body was getting hotter and hotter. Sweat began to form under my clothes. Just as I was about to go deeper into meditation, I felt an intense, cold energy envelop me and wrap around my neck and back.

Having never experienced this before, I didn't know what to do. Then I felt like my life force was being drained from my soul. I opened my eyes and saw a black mist in front of me. When I looked down, the mist was over my legs, hips, and stomach. My arms were covered in this dark, hazy bubble of soot-like fog. I raised my hands around my head and felt the coldness on my face. I was completely engulfed in this black, endless mass.

Evil feelings began to flood my mind. I could hear voices telling me to kill others. Fear overcame all of my other emotions. I was under attack from this mist, and I felt completely helpless. My vocal chords would not work, either, and I struggled to speak. It almost felt like the wind had been knocked out of me.

I was gasping for air and fell to the floor, while the black mist stayed on top of me. I could tell that this presence was trying to harm me. It felt like it was trying to take over my mind. I was in a struggle for my life, and I didn't know what to do.

My voice still didn't work. In my head, I screamed, "Help! Help me! Help...me!"

I was fading and losing control. I struggled to move, but I was held down by this dark force. Ramla's name popped into my head. Desperately, I called out, "Ramla... Ramla... Hear me. Help me, Ramla! Where are you?"

The sweat on my skin was gone, and it was replaced by uncontrollable shivers and spasms. It felt like I was dying, and fast. The black mist was wrapping around me tighter and tighter, entering my nose, mouth, and ears.

With one last attempt, I called out, "Ramla, I need your help."

I was almost to the point of blacking out, when a jolt of lighting flashed from inside my body and began attacking the mist. It sparkled and popped every part of darkness it touched and began breaking it apart. The tightened strands loosened their grip, and the intrusions in my mouth retreated.

The lighting intensified in another wave of fury. It was like the white energy had a consciousness to it and knew exactly where to hit. More lighting bolts flashed and concentrated on the upper portion of the mist. I could finally make out a form to this evil being. As I saw a black head appear, the white energy flashed at its skull and stunned it.

A large white plasma ball came from inside me and projected at its chest. It knocked it off of me for a moment and staggered it. I made a long gasping sound for air, "Mduuuhhhh!"

The mist came back toward me for a final attack. White lightning surrounded me and formed a protective shield around my body. Again and again, the smoke monster lunged at me, and every time it did, it was shocked with a lightning bolt.

I could see and feel the anger in its eyes. It flew around the room blowing over books and loose papers. It circled twice at an incredible speed, and I did my best to keep sight of it.

On its second pass, it flew above my head and hovered for only a second. Then it came crashing down like a knife trying to pierce into a melon. Black spokes splintered to the side and white sparks exploded in the air. I could see an umbrella of white covering my head a few feet up.

In an attempt to end this, I regained my composure, stood up, and focused my energy. I threw my hand toward it, and a ball of light came from my palm and struck it head-on. As I did this, I commanded angrily, "Get out of here!"

I was about to throw my hand at it again when the dark entity gathered in front of me, glared, and then flew out the window. I fell to the floor, completely exhausted.

In my head, I heard, "Tumaini, are you alright?"

"Ramla, is that you?"

"Yes, this is Ramla. Are you alright?"

"I'm OK. Thank you. You saved my life."

"That was a djinn, and from what I could tell, a very powerful djinn. It must have known that your powers were growing and tried to stop you."

"A what?"

"A djinn—a dark spirit with magical ability. They hate anyone who tries to grow spiritually. If given a chance, they will possess a weaker body and take over its mind."

"I felt that. That's what this thing tried to do. If you hadn't stopped it, I think I would have been a goner."

"I didn't stop it, I only distracted it. It was you who made it leave."

"I did? How did I do that?"

"I put your shield up, and you stopped it. Do you remember?"

"It all happened so fast. I felt this white bubble form around me. Then I commanded it to leave and saw an energy ball fly out of my hand. It hit it and knocked it backwards."

"Yes, that was you. I helped in the beginning, but you finished it. Together we sent it back to its lower dimension."

"Dimension? What dimension?"

"They come from the lower realms of the fourth and fifth dimensions, and these dimensions overlap ours. All of the dimensions exist one on top of the other, and at the same time.

"Tumaini, these are foul beings who work with the dark side. They are as evil and as cunning as the reptilians and other aliens. They are not to be underestimated, and they work with the Order."

"I won't underestimate them again. What did you say earlier? You mentioned something about a shield."

"Yes, did you protect yourself?"

"Oh my gosh, I just had a flashback to being Tumaini. I was warned by Baniti about protecting myself when I traveled. So, I need to shield myself? That's what he was saying."

"Every day, especially if you are doing spiritual work to help others. Any type of white magic needs shielding from the dark."

"And this bubble? Is that my shield?"

"Yes, it is. And it will grow stronger with practice. Your shield can also help protect others, too. Be aware of this."

"I will, thanks."

"Tumaini, they know about you, and I fear that the attacks will not stop. Do not be afraid to call out for help. I will do what I can."

"You've already done a huge amount."

"It is my honor to serve. Have you uncovered any information from the items you took with you?"

"I'm working on it. Actually, I just finished reading what Omar sent."

"You are on the right path, Tumaini."

Constance knocked on the door. "Honey, are you OK? Did a bat come in again?"

"No, honey. I'll be out in a second. Everything's alright."

"Ramla, I should go. I need to share this with Constance. Is there anything she needs to know?"

"Tell her the truth, and the rest will follow. She is a strong spirit and can handle most things, as long as she knows the truth."

"I'll do that. I'll be in touch as soon as I find something."

"Good. Be with God. Go get some rest."

"I will. Thanks."

I called Constance into the room and explained what had happened. I told her how Ramla and I sent this djinn packing back to the dark side. I could see the concern on her face, and I felt her tears as she hugged me.

"Are you going to be OK?" she asked.

"I'm fine. This is getting weirder and weirder, though. And don't worry about yourself or Hara. I'm going to put a shield around both of you. You should be safe."

"I don't feel too safe right now."

"Can't say I blame you, but I am going to work on this shielding thing."

"Should I do this, too?"

"Considering what has happened, I would."

"You'll have to show me."

I pulled her in for a hug. "It would be my pleasure, baby. Let's go to bed; we have to go see the hag tomorrow."

"Don't say it that way. It wasn't very nice."

"I know. I never said I was perfect. I'm going to stay here and energize my shield, and then I'll do yours and Hara's."

"Can I do it with you?"

"Sure, I'd like that."

She laughed, "School's in session. Show me what to do."

CHAPTER TWENTY-TWO

PRINCIPLES, PRINCIPALS, AND CROSSES

We checked in at Hara's school just before 8:00 a.m. As we waited in the main office to see the principal, one of Hara's friends walked by and waved to us.

Hara asked, while swinging her legs under the chair, "Can I go to my class?"

Constance answered, "No, honey. We need to go in together."

The secretary came over and announced, "The principal will see you now."

The principal was an elderly woman with grey hair, an extremely long nose, and an unusually bony figure. She sat behind the typical administrator's desk adorned with plaques and trophies to imply how important she was. She greeted us snidely, "Hello, Mr. and Mrs. Whyse. Why don't you take a seat?"

I replied with hint of sarcasm, "Hello, Principal Snout."

She corrected me, "That's Principal Snoot."

"Whatever..."

Constance grabbed my arm. "Be nice."

I looked in Snoot's black eyes. "I can already tell by your tone that you didn't like our note or Hara's demonstration of truth. So let's get down to it."

She stated matter-of-factly, "We don't condone rude, disruptive behavior at our school."

I countered, "But you condone brainwashing and slavery."

"We do nothing of the sort. We prepare students to contribute to society."

"Spoken like a true brainwasher. You mean that you subjugate students to become little minions for the bankers, corporate owners, and the cabal, don't you?"

"Mr. Whyse, we—"

"Save it. I'm going to tell you how this goes."

"Mr. Whyse, I must—"

"I said save it! I'm well aware of all the false platitudes and training that you receive to try and take control of every conversation, but that's not going to happen here. I'm going to tell you how this goes, so listen up!

"This country was started by slave owners. The New World Order made a slave owner and Indian butcher the first president of the U.S. And if that wasn't enough, they elected thirteen more slave owners as presidents in America—eight of them owned slaves while they were in office. I bet you didn't know that, did you?" I didn't give her a chance to speak and continued, "And if you didn't like how they ran things, they sent their military and police to arrest or kill anyone who stood in their way. And these presidents and politicians don't care about you, me, Hara, or anyone else. They only care about power and money. It's evident in all of the laws that protect these seedy leaders and their mind-robbing education system. By the way, if you don't believe me about the greed and slavery, just ask the early Mexicans, Indians, French Canadians, and the African slaves who were here in the beginning."

Like a typical administrator, she responded, "This is a great country, Mr. Whyse. What does this have to do with Hara? We live—"

I stopped her abruptly, "People are forced to give up any freedom to govern and rule themselves by the public education system and the very government that you worship and pledge. We went from racial and gender slavery to educational and financial slavery. Not a great bunch of role models, if you ask me. How does this make it a great country?"

I looked at Hara and patted her knee. Then I looked back at the angry face behind the desk. "What Hara did should be applauded, not condemned by manipulative, brainwashed, don't-challenge-the-system administrators like you. She spoke the truth, and you couldn't handle it, so you kept her in the office for the day, didn't you?"

She was stunned and didn't respond.

"You don't have to say anything. We already know." I looked at Constance, and she gave me a glance of approval.

"Mr. Whyse, I can assure you that no one is being brainwashed here."

Constance scoffed, "Surely, you must be joking. Even I can see what's going on in the schools. They are all being dumbed down and turned into compliant, subservient workers. Even your test yesterday proved that. Hara didn't have a say in this. And she was going to be locked into a program next year to prepare her as a slave worker."

The principal declared, "That test is a proven tool to determine what skills a child can contribute to society. It's beneficial for our country."

I laughed sarcastically, "Our country was started by greedy land-grabbers and butchers. They wiped out the Indians and took all their land. Is that what we should be teaching our children, that we live in the *Land of the Greed, Home of the Slave*? Should we teach them to be butchers? This was never a great country!"

It was clear that she was not going to change her position. "Mr. and Mrs. Whyse, if Hara does not take this test, then she will not be blocked correctly next year. That is a fact."

I retorted, "Well, let me tell you a fact. You need Hara for funding. I know this. Without students, you don't get the precious money that you covet. And without your patriotic puppets sitting in their desks swallowing the garbage and false history that you feed them, you might just lose some of those prized trophies that you hide behind."

"Mr. Whyse, I—"

"Save it. There is nothing you are going to say that will change this."

I motioned to Hara. "Hara, did they ask you if you want to take this test?"

She shook her head, "No..."

"And did they ask you what you want to be when you grow up?"

"No..."

"And did they tell you that you can choose what you want to learn next year?"

"No... They said we would be placed."

Constance added, "Do we need to say any more about this? You don't teach freedom here. You don't let students grow and learn and choose their futures. You brainwash them to accept working for others. *Here's your diploma. Now go out and look for a job to make the corporate owners rich."*

The principal glared at me. "Aren't you a teacher, Mr. Whyse?"

"I don't brainwash my students. I teach free thinking, and I encourage my students to stand up against the establishment."

"Well, I can see where your daughter gets this from."

Constance fired back, "Yes! And there should be more people like him, too."

"Thank you, hon." I smiled at her. Then I scowled at Snoot. "Here's the bottom line: I know you aren't going to change your system, so we are prepared to take Hara out of your system and teach her the true meaning of serving others for love—not for money or power. And since you can't see this past your nose, we are withdrawing Hara from your school right now."

She didn't say anything for a moment. "She will have to be properly withdrawn, and you will have to do the paperwork."

I looked at Constance with a smirk, grabbed a pen out of my pocket and slammed it down on her desk. "Here's a pen. You do the paperwork. That's your system, not mine. Consider Hara officially withdrawn. Good day, Principle Snoot.

"C'mon, Hara, it's time to start your real education."

As we walked out, Constance grabbed my arm. "Wow! I've never seen you like that before. You were on fire in there."

"I'm just getting warmed up. I knew she wasn't going to change; she's too plugged in. She's a compliant cog who's keeping their machine going. And the worst thing is she doesn't even know it."

"Well, I'm proud of you, honey."

"Thanks, and I'm proud of you, too. You told her."

"I did, didn't I?"

I smiled at Hara, "It's official. You're with us now."

She grinned and asked, "Am I really going to be homeschooled? Can I still have recess?"

"You betcha. And no more pledging the flag, either."

"Yippee!" She skipped out of the school holding her mother's hand.

———————

We were on the way home, and I told Constance, "We need to get Hara some new books and supplies for home. Do you want to stop at that educational supply store that's near the mall?"

"Sure. And if you don't mind, maybe we can go in the mall, too. I saw a great puzzle book that would be good for her. It's in one of those kiosks by the shoe store."

"I know which one you are talking about. What book do you have in mind?"

"There's a series of them. These books teach about geography, maps, ecosystems, and math. I really liked them.

"Hara, do you remember those puzzle books?"

"Yeah, those were cool."

I laughed, "It sounds like we are going to the mall, then."

Constance turned around to the back seat again. "Hara, do you want to start drawing and painting at home? You were looking forward to taking art next year."

"Can I get one of those painting aprons that the kids get to wear?"

"Sure. Maybe we can learn how to make one instead of buying one. Would you like to sew one with me?"

"But I don't know how to sew."

"Then I'll teach you."

"Can I pick out the fabric myself?"

I snickered, "I guess we'll have to go to the fabric store, too, huh?"

We loaded up on anything educational that hadn't been influenced by the Order. I motioned to the small stack. "Wow, there's not as much as I thought there would be."

Constance put another book on top. "I'm sure we'll find more. I'll research this and see what I can come up with. I saw a number of sites that gave information on homeschool curricula."

"Don't you think that will be contaminated, too?"

"It might be. We'll just have to be more hands-on about teaching her the truth."

"You know, this might be a good time to restart our garden in the backyard. Hara, how about we grow our own corn? You like corn on the cob, don't you?" She shook her head *yes*.

"I like that idea of growing our own food. That way we'll know that there are no pesticides in it or any of that GMO stuff that Munchmanto and Blayuer put in there."

"What's GMO?" she asked.

"Poisonous food." I made a sour face.

"Ohhh, yuckhhh!"

———————

At the kiosk, Constance spent time with Hara leafing through stacks of puzzle books. She had already found six of them that she liked and wanted to take home.

"You two seem to have a good handle on this. I'm going to browse over here." I walked to the other side of the kiosk and started my vertical gaze over the shelves. About halfway down, I spotted a book with a strange bluish-gold backdrop on the cover. I picked it up and gawked in disbelief. "I know this picture. This is…this is…this is one of the parchment pieces! Holy cow!"

I ran around the corner and blabbered excitedly, "This is it! This is it! This is the key to the parchment pieces. I know it."

Constance reacted, "Slow down, Michael. What are you talking about?"

"This book cover, it's one of the parchment pieces. Don't you remember? I think it will tell me how to decode all of those geometric patterns—the ones in the magic cross spread."

"Are you sure? What is it? What kind of book?"

I showed her the cover again. "It's a 3D stereogram book. You know, the picture behind the picture stuff. You have to stare beyond the picture to see what's behind it. I used to spend hours looking at these when they first came out. I can't believe that I didn't recognize this before."

"How could you? I would have never guessed it was a stereogram."

Hara took the book from me. "I like these, Daddy. Can we get it?"

"Sure, and you can help me look at my pictures at home, too." I nodded toward the checkout counter. "Honey, we need to get home. I need to check this out."

"We're just about done here. Let's go home." We paid for our items and sped off to do our homework.

Taking three stairs at a time, I raced into my study. "There it is! It's a perfect match for card number three. How could I have not seen this before?" I stared and stared at the piece of parchment on the table. "C'mon, please let there be something behind this picture."

Constance and Hara stumbled into the room. Constance asked, "Did you see something?"

"Not yet. Help me look."

All three of us crowded around and looked at the parchment piece. Hara saw something first. "I see it. It looks like three people holding a book."

Constance saw it next. "It does look like three people. Do you think it's us?"

Hara exclaimed, "This is so cool!"

"Wait a minute"—I squinted at the papyrus—"I'm getting something, too. I think you guys might be right. It *is* us looking at the book we just bought. And card number three is the present moment. That would make this a match. And if this is the present moment, this would make these two the past. Let's look at these and see if it works again."

We put our focus on the left two pieces of the cross. I pointed to the first one. "Now, if I've read this right, this first card is from the furthest point in the past. And the next card is supposed to be another important event in history."

Hara complained a little, "These are harder to see, Dad."

"Well, these are pretty old paintings. It might take longer." We stared intently for another minute.

Constance shifted to another angle. "I'm not getting anything. Are you sure this will work for all of these pieces?"

"Not exactly sure, but if it works for one, maybe it will work for the rest. Besides, I don't have any other ideas."

Hara stamped her feet. "Oh, I almost had it!"

"What was it?" asked Constance.

"It was round-like."

I yelled, "Aha! I got it! Wait right here."

I ran to the bedroom while they kept looking. When I came back in, Constance pointed to the object in my hand. "That's it. That's the first piece. I saw it as soon as you left."

Hara asked, "What is it?"

"It's the amulet that I brought back from Egypt."

Constance grabbed my arm. "This is so exciting."

"I wanna see."

I handed the amulet to Hara. She studied it and then went back to the parchment. "Now I get it. This looks exactly like your jewelry, Dad. How did you do that?"

"I don't know, baby. It must be magic."

"Magic?"

Constance looked at me with a face that said: *Do you want to go there?*

"Yes, baby, magic. There are things that some people can do that others can't do because they haven't practiced."

"Wow, I wanna learn how to do magic."

Constance echoed, "Me, too."

"When you get a little older, maybe. For now, Daddy needs to keep figuring out these pieces."

"Can I wear the amulet?"

"Sure, but only while we work on this."

She put it on and went back to our puzzle. "Which one do we do next?"

"Let's do the second one."

A pattern started to emerge. When one person was able to see the hidden drawing, the others started to see them faster, too.

Constance got the next clue. "It's WWI and WWII. Why would you draw that one? I get the amulet part, that's when you started this whole thing. But why war?"

"Do you remember the story I told you when you picked me up at the airport? Well, that whole story is right here." I held up the translation from Omar and handed it to her. "This is what Tumaini wrote and what the Protectors hear every year at their meeting. Go ahead, read it. Right here, it says:

"Like the thirty-six stars in the sky, the Decans, thirty-six of our priesthood will remain suspended in the celestial realm. We will come back at a time when the offlanders and bloodlines can be overthrown. We will come when the world fails to unite in peace after two terrible wars. Then, with the help of our white magic, we will be born again and initiate our plan to overthrow evil.

"Our magic will call us back and reunite us with these teachings. Then I will come across a great ocean and seek my words once again. I am drawn to them as strong as the moon chases the sun."

Constance put the translation back down. "You know, up till now I was doubting this Tumaini stuff, but I'm really starting to believe."

"Thanks, hon. That gives me a boost of confidence." I pulled her in and kissed her cheek.

Hara gave us a funny look. "Who's *too-many?*"

Constance answered, "Someone from Daddy's past."

I winked at her, and then Hara grinned, "I figured out number six."

"What is it?" I bent down quickly to look.

"It's a man being led by a rope around his neck. Another man is pulling it."

Constance bent down beside me. "What do you think that one symbolizes?"

I suggested, "Number six is hopes and fears. I think that one is definitely fears. If we don't do something to change the way we live, we are all going to end up as slaves to the Order."

Hara asked, "What does that mean?"

"Imagine no more recess—*ever!* That's what that means."

"Oooh, I don't like that."

Constance agreed, "We don't like that, either. The Order are bad people."

"Like my principal?"

I blurted, "Worse."

In the next twenty minutes, we figured out the number five and number eight pieces. Number five is the obstacle that's not ready to be faced yet, and that was spelled out as the *Order*. Number eight was a little more cryptic. It was a future card that looked like a spaceship hovering over Earth, and it appeared to be collecting human souls. The last card was number ten, and we were completely stumped by that one.

"It kind of looks like a futuristic black box with an open door," speculated Constance. "But what are those rows of dots near the top?"

I nodded, "I agree with you, it does look like a black box. I counted the dots, and there was no pattern to them." I tapped my forehead with my finger. "What is this?"

Hara gave up. "I don't know. Can I go play now?"

"Sure, hon. But before you go, can you hand Daddy the amulet, please? And then maybe we can go to the fabric store and sew your apron after you play." She disappeared behind the door, and we heard her going down the stairs.

Constance pointed to the magic cross spread. "Did you see anything like this in your meditations?"

"No, nothing like this at all. This is the first I've seen this."

"I say that we keep looking for clues. What about the circle over here? Do you think there's anything to this one?"

"I bet there is. All of those pieces are like the ones in the cross."

"Didn't you say this was like the zodiac sign?"

"Yes, the Decans. You found the Decans on the computer, too. There are supposed to be thirty-six priests, and that matches the thirty-six constellations that the Egyptians used to follow."

"But there are only twenty pieces in the circle," she harrumphed.

"I figure we're missing sixteen more. I'm sure I'll figure this one out."

"Let's look at the top one and see what we get." We both peered at the apex of the circle for a number of minutes, then she nudged me. "Are you getting anything?"

"I'm starting to. I can make out a man. Give me a moment; I think I've got this. It's definitely a man, and there is a name beneath him. It's... Oh, come on!" I was fighting my frustrations and stared beyond the outer picture once more. "It's...it's...it's Baniti. The name is Baniti. He was one of my teachers back when I was Tumaini."

"And if he's Baniti—"

"Then the rest might be names of all the other priests who pledged to come back."

"It sounds logical to me," reasoned Constance.

"Me, too."

We looked at the next three cards and saw two male figures and one female. The names were Talibah, Bes, and Tumaini. "That pretty much

314

cinches it for me." I drew my finger around the circle. "These must be the names of the priests. Well, I would guess that these are twenty of the names. The rest must be in all of these other pieces over here."

"I need a break, and my eyes are starting to hurt. What do you say we tackle more of this later? I also need to take Hara to the store."

"You go ahead. I'm going to stay here and do what I can." Before she left, I thanked her sincerely, "Thanks for all of your help and for not thinking I'm completely crazy."

She smiled and held her fingers in a *tiny* gesture, "I only think you're a little crazy. But honestly, I'm very proud of you. And believe it or not, I'm starting to get some hope from this, too. Thanks."

<hr />

I grabbed a notepad and pencil and started recording everything we'd found up to that point. After all of our findings were jotted down, including the corresponding color patches for each piece, I verified, "OK, we have seven parts of the cross figured out, but not all solved yet. And we've got four pieces of the circle identified. That leaves six more here"—as I waived my pencil at the cross—"and thirty-two there"—as I pointed to the circle. "What to do next?"

I looked at the large number of pieces that were to the left of the circle and the cross. "I'm not ready to get into those just yet. There're too many of them." Then I thought about the scrolls in the other room. "I'm definitely not ready to tackle those. Let's finish the circle first, and then I'll start chipping away at the rest."

Before starting into the Decans pieces, I glanced at the poem-like riddle from the other night. "Yeah, yeah, I know you're on the list, too. Wait your turn."

It took over two hours before I finished getting the other sixteen names that were already in the Decans circle. I rubbed my eyes and groaned, "I can't keep doing this. I'm getting a headache."

I took the tablet with me downstairs and showed it to Constance. "I got all twenty names, so I'm more than halfway there. Only sixteen more to go on the circle and five on the cross."

"That's great, honey. Hara and I were just getting ready to leave. Do you want to go with us?"

"No, I'll leave that as a girls' outing. I need to grab a bite to eat and look over my class assignments for the next three days."

"By the way, Ted called while you working. He asked if you were teaching today, and I told him that you don't have anything scheduled for Tuesdays. I also told him you would call him back later."

"Thanks. Did you two already eat?"

"No, I thought we would get something while we are out. Did you find anything besides names for the priests?"

I shook my head, "Just names."

"Well, we're off. Give me a call if you crack the code."

"I will. Have fun."

I laughed to myself, "Maybe we should call this the Tumaini code." I tilted my head. "How about *The Freedom Code*? Nah, we'll just stick with the Tumaini code. I think someone already wrote a book with that other title."

———————

With my college work out of the way, I called up Ted and invited him to come over later that evening. Then I went back to the cross and circle. "Maybe there's something on the backs that I missed." I put on my cotton gloves and lifted off the plexiglass. Using my tweezers, I picked up the amulet parchment piece and examined it with a magnifying glass.

"There's no paint on the back, no markings, no X-marks-the-spot, just papyrus from what I can tell. Is there something hidden here that I haven't found yet? I could take this to the lab at school and have them look at it with their microscopes."

I flipped it over about a half-dozen times to look for any new clues. "Nope, nothing. That's a bummer."

I set it down on the cross, but I accidentally put it back in the number eleven spot. Then the phone rang, and I made a mad dash to answer it. "I'll fix it when I get back."

———————

"Hello, honey," I said half out of breath.

"Hara and I are on the way home. Did you get to eat?"

"I did, thanks. I'm working on the cross right now."

"Anything new?"

"Not yet. Hey, Ted's coming over later. I hope that's alright with you."

"That'll be fine. I need to get some work done myself. See you in a bit."

"'Kay. Bye."

———•◦•———

When I got back to the study, I looked at the cross again. "Hey, isn't that…? I don't remember… Didn't I put that down here?" The amulet card was back in the number one spot. "How did that happen? I didn't move it there."

My natural problem-solver mode kicked in. "There's no black mist in the room, and the windows are closed. What made it do that? Let's move it back down and see what happens."

After placing the card in the number eleven spot again, I waited and watched. My stare was unmovable and fixated on the entire cross. After a few seconds, the edges of the card visibly started to vibrate. Then the vibrations grew stronger and stronger until the entire card was jiggling on the table. In an instant, it flew into the number one spot.

"Whoa! What was that?! Let's see that again." I picked up the card with the tweezers and replaced it in the eleven spot. In another few moments, the card started to vibrate, jiggle, and flew back into the correct spot.

"That's so cool! Let's do that again! I wish Constance was here. I wonder what will happen if I move it to one of the other spots?" In a scientific manner, I put the card in all of the other available slots. Each time, the parchment piece vibrated and flew back into the number one spot. No matter what I tried, the card would always return to its correct location.

"Hmmm. What if I disassemble the cross? Would the card return to that spot?" When all of the cards were scattered, nothing happened.

"OK, maybe the cross has to be assembled for this to work." I reassembled the cross in its original order and did my experiment again. Sure enough, the card flew back into its appropriate spot. "This is crazy. How is this working?"

I backed away from the table and thought, "I've got to try this." Then I stepped forward and shuffled all seven pieces to different positions and waited. This time, the table started vibrating violently and jiggled every piece on its surface. Instantaneously, all seven parchment pieces flipped through the air and landed accurately in their original order in the cross."

At that point, I was scratching my head. "This goes way beyond the normal behavior for a simple piece of paper."

The door opened and closed downstairs. I hollered, "Girls, come up here, quick! You've gotta see this!"

Constance yelled back, "Is everything OK?!"

"Yes, yes, hurry up. You've got to see this." Both of them stomped their way up the stairs, and I was met by two huffing women.

"Come here, come here! Watch this!" I moved the number one card into a different place and told them, "Just watch."

"Oh my gosh!" exclaimed Constance.

"Whoa!" gasped Hara.

"What did you just do?" begged Constance.

I responded, "Look. I moved this card into a wrong spot, and it magically moved back to its destined location."

Hara pulled on my sleeve. "Daddy, do that again!"

"I will, but look at this…" I moved all of the cards around and motioned. "Step back. This one will knock your socks off."

They stepped back cautiously, and both of them grabbed my arms. "What's going to happen next?" implored Constance with a shaky voice.

"Here it comes!" The table vibrated just like before, and all of the parchment pieces flipped into the right spots.

Constance's mouth was agape, and Hara was jumping up and down excitedly. Constance tried to speak, "They uh, they…they…they all moved. How did you do that?"

"I didn't. They moved all by themselves."

"But that's impossible."

"You saw it, so it must be possible somehow."

"But that's impossible. I don't…"

Hara sang, "It's magic!"

"You're right, honey. It's magic. And this is a magic cross. I must have used some of my powers when I was Tumaini to make this work."

Constance looked at me, and then looked at Hara with a concerned face.

"Cat's out of the bag, Constance. She might as well know."

I explained to Hara, "Honey, your Daddy can do certain things, and I'll tell you all about them later."

"Can you make Tommy disappear? He keeps tugging on my hair."

"I don't think so, but we'll talk about this later on."

Constance urged reluctantly, "Michael, I'm not sure..."

"Honey, we need to tell her the truth. If we don't, what kind of role models would we be?"

She stopped to think. "You're right. We need to tell her. Promise me you'll keep her safe."

"I'll do all that I can, you know that. But let's have some more fun. Do you want to see it again?"

Hara shook her head briskly, "Yesss!"

"OK. Step back. Let the magic cross begin..."

CHAPTER TWENTY-THREE

TED TALKS 2

We spent another hour on the cross. When the girls exhausted all of their experiments, I got Hara's opinion, "What do you think?"

"I think this is amazing!"

"Do you understand that your school would never have taught you this? They hide the truth from you, just like the government. That's why Mommy and I took you out of school."

"Why do they hide?"

Constance answered, "Because they are afraid, baby."

I added, "That, and the government won't allow it. I heard from Tammy's mom that a teacher got pulled into Principal Snoot's office for talking about UFOs. She was told that she wasn't allowed to talk about such things with her students, even if they asked. Talk about hiding the truth."

Hara wondered, "Do UFOs exist?"

"Yes, honey, they do," I replied.

"Have you ever seen one?"

"More than once. I've seen two in the last month."

"I wanna see one."

"I can't promise that you will, but I can tell you that they exist." I knelt down to make my point. "But not all UFOs are nice. Do you remember that boy, Tommy, who pulled your hair?"

"Yes." She gave a yucky look to me.

"Well, some UFOs are like Tommy—they aren't very nice. Some can be mean. I'm not trying to scare you, but think of them like kids at recess. Some are kind and polite on the playground, and some are mean and want to fight."

"I don't want to see any of the fighting kind. Have you seen any good ones?"

"Not that I can tell. The only two I saw were the mean kind. Do you understand what I am saying?"

"Yes, Daddy, I should watch out for UFOs on the playground." She giggled to let me know she was joking.

"Good girl. Now why don't you go and play and let Mommy and me talk."

She started walking out of the room, but before leaving, she turned to say, "Thanks for showing me, Dad. That was cool."

I winked at her. "You're welcome, honey."

When Hara left, Constance went back to staring at the cross. I leaned over to join her. "Thanks for supporting me, and for helping me figure out these clues. Your belief has meant a lot to me these last few days."

"You don't have to thank me. But thanks, I'm glad to be a part of this. What you are doing is…well…it's going to help. And maybe it will help a lot of people." She smiled at me, "You've already helped me, so anything beyond this is gravy."

"How did I get so lucky to have you as my wife?"

"Oh, it wasn't luck. I trapped you, remember? It was my legs." She winked at me.

"It's true, you are the looker. But I got the whole package, though, and that is what I appreciate the most."

"You're sweet." She gave me a quick kiss. "So what did you want to talk about?"

"I think we should talk to Hara about reincarnation and tell her that this one-life concept was created by religions under the Order so they could control people with fear."

"Do you think she's ready for that?"

"The only way to know is to talk with her. She's got a good head on her shoulders."

"I know. She gets that from my side of the family." We both chuckled. "If you think she's ready, then we should talk with her."

"I agree. You already told her that Tumaini was from Daddy's past, and I think we shouldn't keep this from her. Telling her about reincarnation will help start the deprogramming process."

"This is all happening so fast, Michael."

"I know. And I like how you handled the *Daddy's past* stuff. That was some quick thinking on your feet."

"I do have my moments, savior boy."

"Hey, that's what Rehema called me. How did you...?"

"How did I what?"

"How did you know?"

"I didn't. I just called you savior boy."

"Well, anyway, Rehema—she's Hanif's wife—she said that you could call her anytime if you wanted to talk about this."

"That's nice of her. And I might take her up on that offer. It would be nice to hear a woman's perspective."

"I'm sure she would be glad to hear from you."

"Maybe I'll call her while you are at school tomorrow. You do plan to go to school and teach, right? I know how you college professors like to cancel class at the last minute."

"I'll be there. I'm actually anxious to hear how the students did with their *I love you* assignment."

"The *I love you* assignment?"

"Yeah, you remember. I used to look at people and say *I love you* before I could judge them in any way."

"Oh yeah, I forgot all about that. I didn't know you'd turned it into an assignment. That's great thinking. I'll have to start doing that again."

"Me, too. I liked how I felt. I was more connected with other people instead of separated."

"For me, it reminded me to be kinder to others."

"That's the kind of reaction I'm expecting to hear tomorrow. Maybe that little change will help some of my students. There's so much selfishness and me-me-me-ism in the world right now, a little love toward others might help turn the tides."

"It just might. When is Ted supposed to arrive?"

"He should be here after supper. Do you want help in the kitchen?"

"Sure. I was going to try one of your veggie burgers. Do you mind?"

"Really? I think that's great. What about Hara?"

"I'll ask, but you know how she is about veggies."

"I bet she'll like them. Besides, they don't taste anything like vegetables. And if she goes down from eating one, I'll get my cape and turn into"—I jumped into a superhero pose—"savior boy! Da-daaah!" She laughed.

"I'll put my stuff away and meet you down there."

"Kisses. Love ya."

"Kisses. Love ya' back."

Ding-dong! "That must be Ted. I'll get it!" hollered Constance.

"Hi, Constance. Is Michael here? He invited me over."

"Hi, Ted. Of course, come on in. He's in the kitchen."

"I wanted to thank you again for the extra lasagna and rolls. They were delicious."

"Oh, you're welcome. That's one of Michael's famous veggie lasagnas. He packs on too much cheese for my taste, but don't tell him I said so." She winked at him and smiled.

"I thought it tasted great. It was a perfect blend of mozzarella and ricotta. One can never have too much cheese, you know."

"I thought that was for chocolate."

"Well, that too."

"Hey, Ted. How are you?" I walked up and shook his hand.

"I'm doing great. And thanks for the incense I got in the mail. You didn't have to get me a whole box."

"It was my pleasure. Have you used any of it?"

"I did. I like that brand. I kept Hanif's card, too. Who knows? Maybe I'll start meditating on a regular basis again."

"I've been trying to do more meditating myself, but..." Constance glanced at me with her special look.

Ted asked, "But what?"

"Well, it seems that every time I start meditating, I either get the helicopters in my attic or this new thing that happened."

"What happened?"

"The last time I meditated, I was attacked by this evil, black, mist-type being. My friend told me it was a djinn."

323

"I've heard of those from my research. They are Arabian and Islamic demons."

"Yes, they are—well, dimensional beings, from what I was told. And the one that attacked me was quite adamant about killing me."

Constance's tone changed. "I'm worried about him, Ted. Do you think we should call the authorities?" Ted's eyes got really big.

Before he could speak, I said, "Honey, do you remember after the Men in Black attack you wanted me to call the police, and I was hesitant about it?" Ted's eyes got even bigger. "I didn't want to call them for a reason."

Ted finally burst, "Don't even *think* of calling the police! They are as dishonest as they come. They lie in court. They lie to protect other officers. What do they call that…the blue wall of silence, or blue code, or something? There's no such thing as an honest cop! And to top it off, they are on the payroll of the Order. They protect the rich by upholding the laws that the rich created. They're too dumb to even get that they are nothing more than paid thugs who protect the oligarchy—the greedy bad guys."

I added, "Also, the police won't trust anyone. They bash that concept into their new recruits' minds. Officer Wash told me that when I called up to file a complaint last year. He boasted, 'In the eyes of an officer, you are guilty first, and then you have to prove your innocence in the legal system.' He flat out told me, 'We don't trust anyone.' The police care about you as much as the Order does—which amounts to about nothing. That's why I didn't want to call them. They are worse than the criminals."

"I remember," replied Constance. "You nicknamed him Officer Wash-my-hands-of-the-whole-thing."

Ted pointed out, "Think back to all of the police brutality videos and the police shooting innocent people. Those are not the good guys. They are sadists in black and blue suits."

Constance sighed, "I know. I've experienced a policeman on a power trip, and he bullied me because I accidentally went over the speed limit. There's no call for that kind of behavior. Do you remember that, honey? I was in tears the whole day." I nodded. "I just thought that they might be able to help in some way."

Ted continued, "All you have to do is look at the system, Constance. He who controls the money and media controls the system. The Order controls the police with fear. If the police don't do what they say, they'll get fired. And the police are too afraid to really stand up against the bad guys who rule the system. They're terrified of losing their jobs. They're only thinking of themselves and their paychecks. Selfish bastards!"

"They've been brainwashed, too," I tapped my head. "They've been indoctrinated like the rest of us. And Ted's right, the greedy rich created the laws to protect the greedy rich, and the rich use the police as their muscle to stop anyone who tries to change the system. Too many police have been paid off by these corporate owners and politicians."

Ted angrily joked, "If there was a police officer and a thief that were both going to drown, and I could save only one of them, I would save the thief and let the officer die. You know where the thief stands. You never know where the police stand."

I reacted, "Wow, Ted, that's pretty rough."

"What do you expect? The police and military use fear, threat, violence, and force to get what they want. And let's not forget coercion, too. These are not men of honor; these are cowards in uniform." He threw his hands up in disgust. "Who needs terrorists when you legalize terrorism and slavery in your own city?"

He looked at Constance sternly. "The police will kill you, and then the police chief will cover it up to save their own skins. Is that who you wanted to call?"

"I don't know. I just wanted to get some help. I was scared."

"Well, forget calling the police. You won't get any help from them. It will be the smartest move you've ever made."

"I think she's got the point, Ted. What do you say we go upstairs? I have something to show you."

Constance nodded, "I got it. Don't trust the police anymore. Hey, Ted, did the police hurt you? Is that why you hate them so much?"

"It's not hate, Constance. It's that I don't respect anyone who enforces slavery, and the police enforce slavery on the people. You aren't allowed to choose how you want to live, and the police make sure that you don't. They follow the puppet legal and political system that was set up by the greedy cabalistic Order. I swear to you, they have no integrity and are complete hypocrites. And I don't like saying it, but it's a numbers game. For every dead police officer, dead judge, dead politician, dead banker, dead CEO, or dead military person, there's one less enslaver you have to deal with."

I whispered and shook my finger, "And don't forget dead lawyers."

She giggled a little, "After what Michael's told me, and from what I've experienced lately, I'm starting to believe you. I don't like the killing part, but we are slaves, and the police and dirty politicians make sure of it."

He gave her a look of agreement. "I'm glad you are starting to see the light."

"C'mon, Ted, you've gotta see this," and we walked up to the study.

On the way up, Constance suggested, "We could try the *I love you* experiment with them, but I don't think it would work. They're too plugged in, aren't they?"

I added, "I agree, and they are plugged in. Saying *I love you* to the police won't stop them from beating you up or bullying you, either."

"It's sad, but you are right." She stopped on the stairs and came to a realization. "We'll never hear a president, general, banker, or police officer say *I love you,* will we? If they did, they couldn't hurt us and still mean what they said. They would be hypocrites." She shook her head, "Their enslavement and brutality are proof of this."

"It is sad. And both of you are right." Ted also shook his head in agreement.

———•—•———

When we got to my study, Ted asked, "What happened with the djinn? How did you escape it?"

"I had help from a friend. Between the two of us, we were able to put up a defensive shield around my body, and then I sent it packing with an energy blast."

"An energy blast? How did you do that?"

"I'm not quite sure, to be honest. During the battle, I put my hand up, and a plasma-like energy ball shot out of my palm and hit it. The djinn stopped attacking me and flew out the window. I must have developed this ability in the past."

"That's some pretty intense stuff. Can you do it again?"

"I'm not sure. I haven't tried to duplicate it. The only attack I've had since then was from the garlic spread on my bagel. It seemed like overkill to use a plasma bolt for garlic breath." Both he and Constance laughed. "You have a good point, though. I think I'll try to duplicate it in the future."

"Why not now?" He gestured to my hands.

"I don't know." I closed my eyes, lifted my right arm, and waited. Nothing happened. There was a deafening silence in the room.

I felt a little embarrassed. "Wait a second. I have an idea. Let me try this again." I put my hand up a second time and waited. My body shook for a second. Then a small stack of books and a bunch of papers on the corner of my desk went flying off and slammed into the wall. The force was so strong that it knocked a picture down and broke the frame. The broken glass scattered and flew under the desk and tables, along with some of the papers.

"Holy cow! I didn't know I could do that!"

"Holy cow!" exclaimed Constance. "I didn't know you could do that!"

"Holy cow!" yelled Ted. "I didn't know you could do that, either!" He comically stepped behind Constance for protection.

"Honey, that was amazing. How...how...how did you do that?"

"Yeah, Michael. How did you do that?"

"I thought about Ramla and when I was fighting the djinn. This warm feeling, like a tiny fire, grew in my belly. And then I felt the ball of energy leave my hand. The next thing I knew is that I had a stack of books to clean up."

Without missing a beat, Constance joked, "And glass."

Ted added immediately, "And paper."

"Well, I don't think I'll be doing that again in the office. I don't want to destroy the house for target practice." We all laughed.

I walked over to start cleaning up, and Ted commented, "That's the darndest thing I've ever seen. I don't know what to say."

Constance snickered, "You haven't seen the half of it."

"What do you mean?"

"Wait until Michael shows you the magic cross."

"Magic cross? What magic cross?"

"It's this one." I pointed to the partial cross under the glass.

"Show him what you found," suggested Constance.

———

After ten minutes of explaining to him what I had discovered, I removed the glass and moved the first parchment piece. Just as before, the papyrus jiggled a bit and jumped back to its original resting place. Ted stood there with his mouth wide open. "Say something, Ted," I said. He remained quiet and didn't move a muscle.

Constance asked, "Are you OK, Ted?"

"Yes," he replied. "I don't know what to say. Can I see that again?"

"Of course." I moved the piece to a new spot on the cross, and we all watched it flip back into the number one spot.

"Michael, this is…this is—"

Constance and I finished his sentence. "Magic."

"This is magic," he managed to say in a confused voice.

Constance gave me an elbow bump. "Show him *the event*."

"The event? What's next, dancing girls and marching bands?"

"Just wait and see," she grinned.

With gloved fingers, I rearranged the cross. "Hold on to your horses." The table became energized, bounced around, and each piece flung into its rightful spot.

"Michael, I'm an open-minded guy, but what you are showing me is… well, it's beyond my understanding."

"It turns out that I used white magic to create this cross when I was Tumaini. I left it as a clue so the other priests and I could help the world."

He pondered for a moment, then asked, "How could a bunch of trained, bouncing pieces of paper help the world?"

"It's like I explained earlier: this cross formation defines moments in time." I pointed to each part of the cross. "These are the past, this one is the present, these are the future, and these are obstacles, hopes, and fears."

"I don't get it. There's nothing on these cards that makes it the past or future. Why would you leave yourself these?"

Constance jumped in, "That's where this book comes in." She grabbed the stereogram book and showed him the cover. "Have you seen these before?"

He took it from her and fanned a few pages. "Yes, I used to look at them when they first came out a few years back. But what…?"

I told him, "There are hidden pictures behind these geometric shapes."

"C'moooon," he replied with a hint of disbelief.

"Honest, Ted, see for yourself." I handed him the tweezers and told him to look at the second parchment piece. "Take a second and tell me what you see."

It took him a minute to identify the first image. "It's WWI and WWII. Wow! You weren't kidding. There are hidden pictures behind these things. How did you discover this?"

"One thing just kept leading to the other, and here we are." I pulled out the paper that had all of the images that we'd found and showed him. "Except for the blank spots, here is what I"—I stopped and looked at Constance—"here is what *we* found. Constance has been a huge help in all of this, and so has Hara."

He nodded once toward her. "You saw these, too?"

"Yes, and Michael also decoded twenty of the returning priests' original names."

"Yeah, those took me a few hours to do."

"I'll bet," he remarked. Then he pointed to the cross. "Do you know what all of these mean?"

"We figured out all of the pieces except for one. It's this one, the number ten card."

"Do you mind if I give it a try?"

Constance gave him the tweezers. "Not at all. That one has us both stumped."

He stared and stared at the papyrus piece. "I'm not getting anything yet. Sometimes I need to stop looking, focus on something else, and then try again." He looked at me for some help.

"I get it. Let me tell you what we've found on the cross." I mentioned the amulet, the Order, slavery of mankind, and the reptilian ship taking souls.

"Michael, none of this surprises me. Let me take a look again. Now that I have a better understanding, maybe the image will pop up."

He gave it another go and saw the same black box that we had seen. "I see the rows of dots, and I can see where you'd think they are lights. To me, if this card is in our timeline, I'd bet it could be a computer mainframe."

"A mainframe! That's it. How come I didn't see that?"

Constance encouraged him, "I think you are on to something."

He continued, "If it's a mainframe, I think it might have to do with this." He reached into his pocket and pulled out a wad of folded white papers. "Michael, from what I have seen, I'm not sure that what I brought you even comes close to matching your stuff."

"What did you bring, Ted?"

Constance asked jokingly, "Did you bring me anything?"

He smiled at her, "Well, I hope it will help both of you, and Hara, too." He handed me the folded papers. "After our dinner the other night, I spent a few days researching reptilians and mind control implants. Why don't you read this out loud for Constance?"

I started reading:

Reptilian and Cabal Information
Mass Mind Control Technology

"Catchy title, Ted."
"It's the best I could come up with on such short notice. Go on, read it."
"OK, here goes."

<u>Implants</u>

- If a man or a woman is hearing voices in his or her head, these voices are most likely projected into that person's mind from the psychic government/military programs—such as the CIA, FBI, NSA, black budget programs, and DARPA in particular—other psychic warfare programs in other countries, reptilians, other dark aliens, djinn, and demons. The Order can control your thoughts and implant voices at will, and you won't even know it's them. Mass hypnosis technology has been around since the early 1970's. These voices can also be projected into the brain by targeting the bones near the ears or the entire cranium.
- A massive display of this technology was used in the Iraqi war in 2003. Iraqi soldiers thought they heard the voice of Allah in their heads. This voice—which was actually the U.S./Order military using a Voice of God device (synthetic telepathy, voice to skull-V2K, microwave hearing, subliminal communication, and electromagnetic technology through HAARP)—told them to throw down their weapons and surrender. The soldiers, believing it was Allah, surrendered in large numbers without putting up a fight. This war was a fake. It was manufactured to test these mind control weapons, to induce fear in people around the world, and to generate wealth for the Order.
- Alien Artificial Intelligence Implants that are placed in a human's brain are programmed to learn your thought patterns and speech patterns. These AAI implants will mimic your own voice as if it were your own thoughts and control you to commit destructive acts like suicide bombings, mass shootings, and targeted assassinations. These

AAI implants will also get you to argue with their/your false thoughts so you are in constant turmoil and anger.

- Ringing in the ears—especially the left ear—means that you have implants in your head and body, a reptilian is attached to you, a djinn is attached to you, or you might be possessed by a different type of demon or dimensional being. This is also an indication that you are being monitored and attacked by the Order through the secret CIA, FBI, NSA, MKUltra, and DARPA programs. This is a classic sign of electronic stalking and electronic torture.

- Clicking in the ears means that you have negative implants in the auditory cortex, or your temporal bone has been targeted with electronic torture technology. These are used specifically for brainwashing. Right ear clicks mean: trust this, do this, accept this as truth. Left ear clicks mean: don't trust this, don't do this, don't accept this as truth. These clicks are controlled by AAI, aliens, world militaries, CIA, and the Order. These clicks are also used to induce fear in the victim.

- Vibrations in your groin, hands, and bottoms of your feet are caused by implants. These vibrating implants create negative energy fields around the body which induce anxiety and other harmful effects.

- Physical and etheric implants are generally placed in the temporal lobe, base of skull, top of head, around the ears, in the ears, nose, sinus cavities, hands and fingers, feet and toes, spine, and back. Smaller implants in the body are attached to the acupuncture meridians.

- Implants draw energy from sexual energy and negative emotions: anger, fear, frustration. Some implants draw energy from the three dantian centers and chakras.

- Some implants look like a jellyfish or octopus. Tentacle-like streamers run through the body and take over the nervous system. These can also keep a person in an addiction cycle: sex, alcohol, drugs, sugar, negative emotions, etc.

- Wernicke's commands. These are hidden subconscious commands implanted in the Wernicke's section of the brain. These are used for brainwashing and mind control.

- Brainwashing Agenda: keep the masses dumbed down with technology and implants. Global satellites, HAARP, cell phone towers, and personal electronic devices—such as cell phones, smart phones, and personal computers—can now target individuals and shoot negative energy beams to harm a person's mental and physical health anywhere in the world. These same satellites, cell towers, and electronic devices will also control most of the government implants that control the evil voices and other destructive commands.

- Electronic stalking, electronic torture, and mind control agendas are coordinated by the reptilians, greys, mantids, world militaries, psychic warfare programs, governments, and law enforcement agencies. If you are under attack, you have a satanic Illuminati handler orchestrating your torture. These satanic, human handlers are under the control of the reptilians. Do not go to the authorities or government. They are the enemy!

I glanced up at him with a look that said: *I'm shocked that someone could be that evil, but I'm wrong. They are that evil.*

He motioned. "Keep reading. You're almost done."

"OK."

Reptilians

- When you find out about the reptilians, and you are on a spiritual path, they go berserk on you and attack you without mercy. They block your chakras, your heart energy, and they hook you up to an etheric machine that will keep you from raising your vibration.
- Reptilian dominance move: one-second sex rape. When a reptilian does this and you don't stop it, they consider you to be inferior and they now own you.
- Reptilians will lie on top of you at night while you are sleeping. It will feel like heaviness on top of your body. This is a dominance move.
- Aliens and reptilians use dream manipulations to induce fear.
- Black magic is used by the Order and the reptilians to attack anyone who stands against the dark alien agenda.

Constance asked, "Why are people being targeted like this? Why do they want to hurt us so bad?"

Ted replied, "It's because people like your husband, me, you, and anyone else who does not support the Order are identified by this prediction software that the world governments and military use. It was given to them by the aliens."

"What does this prediction software do?"

"From what I've read, it's an artificial intelligence program with specified algorithms that will find people who are not swayed by greed and corruption. It also identifies people who show abilities that might disrupt the Order's plan for complete technological domination and slavery of the people. Basically, if you aren't being dumbed down and controlled by them, then you have a good chance of being on their hit list. You can bet that's when the electronic torture and psychic attacks begin."

"I can attest to that." I hit the papers in my hand. "These guys mean business. Just look at what happened to me the other night with this djinn thing."

Constance shook her head, "I can't believe that I used to look up to the government, police, and military to protect us. Now we need protection from them."

Ted affirmed, "You're right. This is a sad state of affairs we are in right now."

"I couldn't agree more," I added.

Constance asked, "But I still don't understand. How did they do all of this?"

Ted answered, "We've been under this information gathering grid for decades. Why do you think the government demands national testing in schools? It's just another way of gathering information and identifying students who would stand up to the Order."

"And all of our shopping habits, travel plans, voting patterns...those have all been tracked, too?"

"Yes. And they now have the capability of scanning a person's mind"—he pointed at her forehead—"so they know your thoughts. They couldn't do this twenty or thirty years ago, but today they can identify a person just by what he or she is thinking."

"We never saw this coming, did we?" I said with disgust. "And from what I have learned, this was orchestrated long before we were ever born. I never thought our governments could be so twisted."

Ted came back with, "It's all about power and greed. These are people who do not care about the population. And to be honest, this isn't the first time that the governments and military have used people to experiment on without their consent. Do you remember? I told you about this at dinner a few nights ago. This has been going on for well over a century. One of the presidents... Who was it? I don't remember. But one of the U.S. presidents gave a useless apology back in the 90's for the nonconsensual experiments done by the CIA and other programs on unknowing citizens. Nobody got punished for it."

I sighed, "And nobody will, either."

He walked over to the table and pointed to the last card. "I bet this mainframe is what will control all of the implants. If it's already placed in the future, that means that they have it developed, but maybe not turned on yet."

"That's a good deduction. I haven't completely figured out all of the pieces or how this cross works, but that makes sense."

Constance remarked with a worried tone, "I hope it's not true. I don't want to be controlled by some sick reptile alien."

"If we have any say in these future slots"—I looked at her—"then maybe we can make a difference."

"Then what are you waiting for, savior boy?" She was still worried.

"I'm working as fast as I can, honey."

"I know. I'm just a little rattled by all of this."

I pointed to the paper. "Hey Ted, you have something on here about chakras and dantians. Do you know what those are?"

"As a matter of fact, I do." He took a piece of scrap paper off of my desk and drew a rudimentary human figure with a bunch of circles running up the middle. "These are supposed to be energy centers in the body. If it's true, it would make sense why the reptilians and the Order attack them. Weaken your energy supply, and you can't fight back."

He started writing some additional information on the paper and stated, "I wrote down the title to a few books that might help. I think you should read up on these."

I glanced at his list. "I will, and I know just the place to find these books."

"Great!" He looked at the Decans circle next. "And what about these twenty priests Constance mentioned?"

"Actually, there are supposed to be thirty-six in total. Wait a minute." I picked up the decoded papers that Omar had sent. "These will tell you more about priests and my past life as Tumaini. Maybe it will help."

"Are these your only copies?"

"Yes, now that you mention it. How about I copy them and bring them to your office tomorrow?"

"That'd be great. Is there anything else? It's starting to get late."

I laughed, "Haven't I shown you enough?"

He laughed, too. "You've got a point." He looked at both of us, to the table, and back to us again. "You know, I'm not one to get too attached to other people. I'm kind of a loner and have never been part of the regular crowd. But what you are doing...well... I want you to know that I'm with you on this. I want to keep helping you. If you'll have it?"

Constance smiled, and I said, "Ted, you've already been a big help"—I pulled Constance to my side—"just like Constance. We're in this together, my friend."

He smiled back, "To the end. To the end."

CHAPTER TWENTY-FOUR

KEYS TO THE SCROLLS

Ted had just left, and Constance commented after closing the door, "You know, Ted is starting to warm up some. I think you've made an impression on him."

"I think you've made an impression on him, too. He has some good intentions. I can feel it. It's a shame that he's gone through so much."

"Maybe that's why he relates to you. You've gone through some stuff yourself there, mister." I didn't say anything. I just nodded in agreement.

Constance asked, "Do you have anything else planned for tonight?"

"Do you have anything special in mind?" I hinted with a suggestive tone and an over-the-top wink.

"Yes. It's called preparing for Hara's homeschool. That is, unless you want to enroll her back in public school again."

"Can't we give her an early vacation and forget the planning?" I raised my eyebrows toward the bedroom. "She's learned enough."

She smiled and patted me on the shoulder as she walked by. "There'll be plenty of time for that after you figure out the rest of your clues, savior boy." Then she playfully slapped my butt and ran away.

I chased after her, wrapped my arms around her waist, and gave her a tight hug. "Alright, but we need some you-and-me time, too. Homeschool isn't a twenty-four-seven event."

"You've got it. Let's make a date night this weekend."

"A real date? You mean, like you and me going out alone? Are you asking me out, Mrs. Whyse?"

"Why yes, I am. And you'd better say yes if you know what's good for you." She gave me a quick kiss on my cheek. "Now let me get some stuff ready for Hara's lesson tomorrow, and we can plan a date later." She took a few steps away from me.

"I haven't said yes, yet." She turned around with her hands on her hips. I played along and joked, "Yes, dear, I'd love to go out with you. It would be my pleasure, Mrs. Whyse."

"Good boy. What will you be doing the rest of the evening?"

"I want to look over the parchment stuff again. There's so much to figure out. I have to just keep chipping away at it until I figure out the answers."

"Anything else?"

"I'm going to meditate again." She glared at me. "I know, take care of me, you, and Hara before I start. I've got it."

"Just be careful."

"I will."

I slumped down on my office chair, leaned over, and covered my eyes with my palms. Shaking my head a few times, I muttered, "Too many clues and too little time. What was I thinking back then? How am I ever going to find these answers?"

After getting up, I walked over to the table. "I know there is more here." I looked at all of the pieces that weren't in the cross or the circle. Using the tweezers, I pulled out one of the unidentified pieces. "Maybe this one is the hidden key." I stared at it for a few minutes to find the picture behind the picture, but nothing became visible. I couldn't make out a thing.

I thought, "Did I use my magic on this card to keep me from seeing it? That wouldn't make any sense. Why would I keep this from myself? There has to be another explanation." I put the piece back and paced between my desk and the table over and over.

"It's elimination time," and I bent over the table. "If I find all of the Decans pieces, that would leave just the ones for the cross. That makes perfectly logical sense to me. But it's late. I can't start that project tonight;

it would take hours. And what about the scrolls? Hmm...the scrolls... I haven't touched those since I came home. It's time to add them to the mix. Maybe *they* will unlock everything."

As I walked toward the bedroom to get the trunk, I kept hearing that phrase over and over in my mind: *They will unlock everything*. It was like a mantra. I tried to stop thinking those words, but my mind wouldn't cooperate and kept repeating that sentence: *They will unlock everything. They will unlock everything. They will unlock everything.*

"Gloves, I need my gloves." The mantra of *they will unlock everything* came right back and continued echoing in my head as I walked into the study. I grabbed the gloves and returned to the trunk. After repeating the message at least thirty times, it stopped. "Boy that was a persistent thought. What brought that up? It sounded familiar, too. Where did I hear that? Think, Michael, think..."

It was a distant memory that wouldn't surface just yet, so I knelt down and picked up the box of scrolls. "It's time for you to join the party," I mused.

On the way back, Hara peeked her head out of her room and asked in a sleepy voice, "Whatcha doin', Daddy?"

"I'm working on my project, pumpkin. What are you doing up? You're supposed to be sleeping."

"I heard you in your bedroom. It woke me up."

"Sorry, hon. I didn't know I was that loud." I kissed her forehead. "Now, go back to sleep. Mommy's getting your lessons ready for tomorrow." She rubbed her eyes, turned with a smile, and closed her door.

"That smile gets me every time," I thought. "I'm a lucky Dad."

Constance reached the top of the stairs. "Was that Hara I just heard?"

"Yes. She's going back to sleep now."

"What woke her?"

Lifting the box of scrolls, I replied, "These."

She said laughingly, "Those are some pretty loud scrolls. Can you tell them to keep quiet next time?"

"I will."

She nodded toward the box. "What are you going to do with them? It's getting late, and I'm ready for bed."

"I thought I would take them for a *scroll* around the block. You know... get to know each other." We both chuckled. "Seriously, though, I was going to check them out before calling it a night."

"Really? This late? Are you still going to meditate?"

"I'm planning to. I won't be long. Don't wait up."

She patted my chest twice. "You're a big boy, do what you want. 'Night, hon," and she walked to our room.

———————

With the box beside my chair, I pulled out the first scroll with care. I thought to myself, "I've never actually seen what's on any of these scrolls, except for the one in Hanif's shop. I wonder what's so special about them." I was very excited and bouncing with anticipation. "I need a place to put them, too. Where can I put them?" I looked at the table with all of the papyrus pieces. "No, can't put them there. And the other table is filled with the parchments. I'll just need to get more tables tomorrow so I can keep these laid out."

I rocked back and forth in my chair. "The only other place is my desk. But it's a mess." Glancing that direction, there were stacks of books and papers everywhere. "It's the desk or nothing. So here goes."

The scroll was placed back in the box while I moved all of the books. I made sure to keep them stacked in order, and I positioned them under the other tables. "Now I have some room to operate." I took one of the extra white table cloths that I had and lined the top of my desk to protect the old paper. "Let's see what's so important about these."

I recognized the outer edgings of the scroll I had already seen back in Egypt. It was a little more torn than the rest and had darker brown edges. "I've seen this one already. How about this one?" The scroll I'd picked up was tightly rolled and had a simple tan-colored string wrapped around the center. It was the lightest color papyrus in the bunch, so it caught my attention the most.

The knot was easy to unravel, and I put the string to the side. I moved the scroll to the far left of the table and gently placed my hand on the edge of the papyrus. Carefully, I took my time to unroll it. With each turn of the paper, my eyes got bigger, and bigger, and bigger.

I paused for a moment because I was completely dumbfounded. "Nothing! There's nothing here! What the heck is going on?! There's nothing on it!" I was confused, and a little furious. "How could there be nothing on it?" I picked it up by both edges and turned it over numerous times while looking at the front and back. "Nothing! This is unbelievable!" I flipped it over again three more times. "There's nothing on it. This can't be!"

Angrily, I gently slammed the papyrus onto the cloth. The padding of the fabric muffled any loud noise that would have been made. The table nearest my desk had a stack of books close by, so I grabbed two of them to hold down the edges. I flipped part of the cloth over the ends of the papyrus to protect it from the books. Then I grabbed my magnifying glass. "There'd better be something here. Those guys made such a big deal about these scrolls." I was so close that my nose was fogging up the magnifying glass. I couldn't see a thing on the paper.

"Alright, maybe there's something on a different scroll." I reached into the box and pulled out another one with the same tan-colored string. "This one had better not be blank." With a little less care, I pulled the string and unrolled the curled-up parchment. I sat there staring at another blank piece of paper. A bit of fear grew inside my belly, and my hands began to sweat inside my gloves.

One after the other, I picked up a new scroll and examined it for writings, markings, or pictures. "Nothing, nothing, nothing." I picked up a scroll from the white cloth hoping to see something that I had missed. "Nothing." I picked up another off of the desk. "Nothing." I picked up a third one. "Nothing." Partially rolled scrolls were now covering my desk.

"There're only three scrolls left in the box, and one of them I've already seen. There'd better be something on it still." My fingers were trembling at this point because my adrenaline was at an all-time high. "Finally, there's something here. It's the same writing that I saw in Cairo. At least I'm not totally crazy." I moved the other papyrus away and used the books to hold down the edges. "One clue found—I hope. What's going on here?"

The second to last scroll had a black string around it. "Maybe you have a clue. Different string means new information?" I was calming down some and took my time with it. The slip knot gave way easily and allowed the tension on the rolled paper to come undone. With renewed hope, I opened the paper on top of the other scroll. My head slumped immediately and I expelled all of my breath in a sigh of despair, "Nothing."

A few moments passed as I remained in that position. "There's only one left, the one with the scarab on it." I rubbed my face with my gloves. They were wet from perspiration. "I can't pick this up with these gloves. It will ruin the papyrus."

I got up, changed gloves, and stared into the box. "You're the last hope that I have." I gave it a tiny point. "Maybe I should call you the Tumaini scroll. Maybe you can give *me* some hope."

The silk ribbon came right off, but the scroll didn't open because of the wax seal. Not wanting to miss any clues, I grabbed my camera out of the drawer and took a few pictures of the seal and scarab. "It's a guess, but this might be important." I finished my photo documentation and put my camera back in the drawer. Then I pulled out a pair of scissors. "I can use the edge to pry the wax off."

Carefully, I put the scissor blade under the wax. I wiggled and tilted the blade multiple times to loosen its grip. "Just a little farther to go." The clump of wax and scarab were almost off. I could also see a colored stain left on the papyrus. "There, that should do it." I moved the gold-embedded scarab to the side of the books. The moment of truth came, and I was almost afraid to look. "If this scroll was so important, there must be something on it."

I unrolled it a little, and there was nothing there. I unrolled it a bit more. "Still nothing." It was one-third unrolled. "Still no writings." Half of it was exposed for me to see. "This is getting ridiculous." My right hand ratcheted until I unrolled the rest. "I don't get it. Why is there nothing here? I can't believe I went through all of this for a bunch of blank, empty scrolls."

Leaning back in my chair, I stated, "There has to be some explanation for this. Why would I leave myself blank scrolls?" After a few moments of sitting in frustration, the thought from before resurfaced: *They will unlock everything.*

Springing out of my seat, I spun around to see if anyone else was in the room. Nothing moved, made a sound, or breathed. "That has to be my own thought. It was in my own voice, I'm sure of it. OK, maybe not that sure." I looked around one more time, but I was completely alone.

While standing in front of my desk, I noticed Omar's papers lying on the parchment table. "There's something about scrolls on it. I remember this from the meeting at the restaurant." I set the scroll down and picked up the translations. Using my pointer finger, I raced down the page until I found the right place:

The future of humanity lies within the cross.
The scrolls will speak to the hearts of women and men.
And the parchments teach us how to rebirth our magical powers.

I thought to myself, "The scrolls aren't speaking to too many women or men right now, not to mention their hearts. There's nothing on them. Well, unless all of the messages are on the only one with writing—that I can't read yet." Again, the thought came back: *They will unlock everything.*

"Yeah, yeah," I replied sarcastically. "Great, now I'm talking with myself again." I shook my head in disbelief.

"If I'm going to do any meditating tonight, then I need to clean this up." I rerolled each scroll and retied the strings. All of them went back in the box except the one laid out on the table and the scroll that had the scarab on it—the God Scroll.

The next ten minutes were spent examining both of them. "I can't make anything out on this one. I don't know how to translate it. And there's nothing but wood fibers on this one. And that phrase..." I caught a glimpse of the memory again, but not enough to make it completely known to my conscious self. "Where did I hear that before? I know I've heard it. I know it." Instead of focusing on the scrolls, I turned my full attention toward that memory. "I know I can bring it up again if I just give it more time."

Flashes of Cairo were filling my head: plane trip, Customs, hotel, the Khan, and then Mudads. "Mudads! It was Mudads! He told me. Wait...it's coming to me. He told me that outside of Hanif's shop on the way to the Khan. That's where I'd heard it. What was it that he said?" I scratched my scalp. "He said...he said... Focus, Michael. He said, 'The songs you know so well will unlock the power of the scrolls.' That's it. The songs you know so well will unlock the power of the scrolls. The songs will unlock the power of the scrolls. I wonder if that's what this thought was saying to me over and over again? That must be it. That must be what it was saying."

With the blank scroll in hand, I joked, "Here goes everything." I took in a long breath through my nose, held it for a second to get my pitch, and then I hummed the tune that I knew so well. When I finished the short song, I looked at the old paper. "Blank." I collected my thoughts for a moment. "Wait, that's not it. There're vowel sounds to that song. I remember."

I filled my lungs until I couldn't hold another gulp of air. Then I involuntarily started to intone the vowel sounds, which came out as some sort of guttural noises and vocal buzzing. As I sang each note, something miraculous happened. My body shook as it had done in the past, and then gold letters started to appear on the scroll. I sang a few more vowels, and more letters appeared out of nowhere. I took another breath and sang again, and row after row of words appeared on the scroll. It was completely filled from top to bottom with gold hieratic writing.

"Aha! That's it. I remember now. I did this as Tumaini. I hid them this way. That's why these songs were so important. They unlock the power of the scrolls."

A soft tapping sound came from the other side of the door. "Michael, is everything OK? Can I come in?"

"Yes, honey. Come here. I have something to show you."

She opened the door and whispered, "You're going to wake Hara again. What's going on?"

Without looking down, I flipped the scroll around and held it up in front of my face. "Look!"

"Ha-ha. Very funny. What am I looking at?"

"What do you mean, *what are you looking at?* Don't you see it? Look!"

"See what? There's nothing there. Are you kidding around?"

"What?! What do you mean there's nothing there? I'm not kidding around."

"Exactly what I said: there's nothing there." She pointed to the papyrus sheet.

"Wait a second." I flipped it around. "What's going on here? There was gold lettering all over the page just a second ago. It was completely filled, honest."

"Well, it's not filled now. What did you do?"

"I don't know. I sang one of those songs I told you about, and the letters appeared. I showed you, and now they are gone."

"I didn't do anything."

"I know. I'm not blaming you. Come here, close the door, and sit down."

"I'm tired, Michael. Can't this wait?"

"Just give me a second." I inhaled and sang the tune. The golden words reappeared and were even more vibrant than before.

"Wha...wha...?! How did you do that?"

"I don't know. I must have made this work in the past when I was Tumaini."

"What does it do?"

343

"I don't know," I replied with a little louder voice.

"How…how are you doing all of this, Michael?"

"I don't know," I echoed with a full voice. "But I'll tell you when I find out."

"Great. You can tell me in the morning. The sun's almost up, and I can barely keep my eyes open."

"You mean, you're not even going to stick around and help? Aren't you even a little impressed?"

"I wouldn't know where to start." She rubbed her eyes and yawned. "You know, before today, I would have been completely shocked by all of this, but with all that has gone on in the past week—"

"Don't say any more. I'm right there with you. A few gold letters appearing on a page doesn't shock me as much, either. But I am curious. I can tell you that."

"You just did," she snickered. Then she turned and walked out.

Before closing the door behind her, I agreed, "You're right. Why don't you go to bed? I'm still going to meditate. And then I'm going to hit this hard tomorrow after class." She blew me a kiss just before the door clicked.

"I can't wait to show this to Ted tomorrow."

———•+•———

My emotions were finally calm again, my shield was up, the incense was lit, and my intention was set. "It's *go* time," I chuckled to myself. I closed my eyes and started into meditation rather easily. Before completely reaching my place of Zen, I made sure to protect Hara and Constance. For extra measure, I did the same for Ted and everyone back in Egypt, too. Then my mind became still. I could feel that I was slipping back in time, and I felt my body was becoming Tumaini again.

———•+•———

Talibah came into the garden where I was meditating and sat beside me. My thoughts were stirred ever so slightly by her gentle presence. I knew it was her because of her familiar walk. When she grabbed her robe to kneel, the heavy fabric created a small breeze that brushed against my warm skin. It taught me a good lesson about distractions and about losing my focus. I didn't say anything to her, and I did my best to return to my mindful state.

With my eyes closed, I could hear another person coming into the garden to join us. Aside from the loud footsteps, it was the chewing noises and smell of fresh bread that told me Bes was here. I couldn't see him, but I could hear him licking each finger multiple times before he knelt next to Talibah.

He leaned over and whispered, "Hi, Tumaini. Do you mind if I meditate with you?"

I thought, "It's kind of hard to meditate when people are asking you questions, not to mention the smell of yeast in the air." I didn't get upset, though. I was glad to have my friends beside me. I nodded and gave him a welcoming smile.

Talibah had already closed her eyes and started meditating, which was also interrupted when Bes whispered to her, "Hi, Talibah. Can I meditate with you, too?" Without opening her eyes, she nodded with a smile.

The sun was warm, but not too hot. The smell of wildflowers came on the next breeze and captured my attention. We were taught by Baniti to use smells, mantras, and visualizations to aid with our meditations, so I used the sweet smell to guide my thoughts back toward nothingness. My last fading thought was, "Bes must like using the smell of food for meditating: *Incense of the Temple Cooks*." I smiled and drifted inward.

My intention was clear. I was not going to time travel, explore the ethers, or to project myself around the world. Instead, I was going to the place of my origin. I was going to go home. I was going to be one with the Source. My sole intention was to commune with the Creator.

With every breath I went deeper than I had ever gone before. I was losing all sense about myself. I no longer felt my clothes, my body, or my surroundings. I no longer heard the wind, the birds, or my friends' breathing. I journeyed beyond the shallows of myself and became engulfed in nothingness. It was there that I stayed: no time, no thought, no senses.

For the first time in my life, I knew what it was like to be as God. I was in the void. Nothingness existed. It was the beginning before the thought. Complete consciousness!

A blazing light flashed in the middle of my forehead. My mind was instantly filled with information about the entire creation process. Concepts and thoughts become things. Things become light. Light becomes reality. The journey from one thought to another creates time. Time exists right alongside no-time. Paradoxes grew and faded, and I felt at one with everything.

A voice rose from within and said, "I am you, and you are Me. Our separation is an illusion. You and I are all that exist. Do you understand, Tumaini?"

Because I had this miraculous download of information, I knew exactly what this heavenly voice was saying. "Yes. I understand completely. All are as One."

"You understand perfectly," the voice affirmed with a loving tone.

I had no desires at that point and waited patiently. The voice returned and asked, "Do you know your purpose?"

"I do. To experience that which was once as concept and thought, and to do this through light and reality."

The voice agreed pleasantly, "Correct. You are also here for another reason, Tumaini. Do you know your purpose?"

"To serve others, as we are all One."

"Yes. And you know that there are others who have forgotten this original thought. They have forgotten their ways and serve only themselves."

"I have experienced them many times here on Earth."

The voice continued, "Tumaini, your Earth is in jeopardy. The dark forces are taking over your world and will add this planet to their collection. If they are not stopped here, the dark forces will conquer more galaxies in the same way." The heavenly voice showed me visions of past galaxies that were decimated and lifeless because of these dark aliens. The voice also showed me future galaxies that would be enslaved if they were not stopped.

"What can I do?" I implored. "I am here to serve."

"I will share concepts and thoughts with you for peaceful living, where service to others will thrive and bring joy to all of the land. Then you can share these concepts with others who will listen."

"And how will I do this? What must be done?"

"In words of gold on scrolls you will write. Use them in your future when times may be right."

"I will do as you ask as a humble servant of One. I will." I paused for a moment. "Will they listen to me at all? Can I really make a difference?"

"Tumaini, before this is done, you will be called a traitor, a heretic, and a dreamer. Many will turn their backs on you. But the few who will listen may turn the tide and begin a new way of life that brings freedom to all."

"I will teach all that I can, this is my vow. But what of these treacherous beings? The pharaoh has already passed the order to kill all of the priests. How will I see these words of gold in the future?"

"When you hold the God Scrolls and sing words of praise, the memory of the words will produce the letters to stay."

"Sing words of praise? I can do this. How long should I sing?"

"It is not the length, but the intent." The voice added, "When you circle by threes, God comes to thee."

"Do you mean that the song needs to be sung three times?"

"Yes. The golden words will remain seen when sung the third time. The songs call upon Me."

"Will I hear your voice again?"

"If you permit, My voice will come through you when you hold the first scroll. I—We—together we will find the right words to convey a message of service and peace."

I asked, "Do you have a melody that you like best?"

The voice replied lovingly, "Your body lights up when you sing with consonance. Dissonance is harsh and dimming to all living souls."

"Will you help me with the melody for the songs to be sung?"

"I will give you five if you like. They can be sung with the Vowels of Creation. These will awaken your scrolls and bring forth our message."

"I appreciate your help. Really, I do."

"It is I who appreciate you. You and the others like you can bring hope to the people once again. The people are searching for a way out of bondage, but they don't know how to do it on their own. Our messages will give them a way. It will give them guidance to free themselves from the darkness that rules your planet."

"How many scrolls shall I write?"

"You were given ten scrolls when you took your oath to serve others as a priest. We will do one scroll for the songs and nine for the teachings. That will be a fine start."

I thought, "How did you know...?" Then I laughed, "Of course..."

The voice resumed, "When you meditate, have your parchments and gold ink ready. I will help you write *Our* words. The first song will only work on the first scroll. The remaining four songs will uncover two scrolls each."

"I understand. Will you share the songs with me before you leave?" A flash of light beamed onto my head, and I instantly knew each of the five songs.

The voice came back and continued, "Add the vowel sounds as you choose. Write them down as the keys for the rest. You will know what to do as your future self."

For a moment, bluish-gold waves of light and sound filled my head. They flowed like waves of the ocean: growing and receding, growing and receding. A feeling of acceptance filled my entire body, and then I began my journey toward consciousness.

Before leaving the void of my mind, I heard, "I am with you...always."

———————

When I opened my eyes, Bes and Talibah were staring at me.

"What?" I asked.

Talibah pointed to the sun. "You were in meditation for over four hours. We came back to check on you."

Bes had a snack in his hand. "Are you going to tell us what happened?"

"Yes, but give me until tonight. I need to go write something down... and fast. I don't want to lose this." I started running toward my sleeping quarters, and I was followed closely by my friends.

Bes yelled out while jogging, "Where are you going so fast? Can't this wait until after dinner?" He was having trouble keeping his sandwich together.

Talibah playfully slapped his arm. "Stop that. We're here to help. C'mon!"

I reached my room and made a dash for my brush, ink, and scrolls. I looked at them and struggled to say with an out-of-breath voice, "I need to write down these songs before I forget them. Then I'll tell you everything." I began writing furiously until all five songs were copied.

Bes swallowed his last bite. "Now are you going to tell us?"

"Yes. And more than tell you, you need to help me remember these songs. Are you willing?" They both nodded *yes*. "Good. Now, repeat after me..."

We spent the next twenty minutes rehearsing the short little tunes. Then I instructed, "We need to pass two of these songs on to the local farmers that we help each year, and we need to ask them to pass the songs down until our return in the future. Will you help me do that, too?"

Talibah inquired, "What's going on, Tumaini? What's so important about these songs?"

"In my meditation, I visited with the Creative Principal, the Source, God. I was asked to help, and these songs will help."

Bes blurted out, "Help what?!"

"When the time is right, they will unlock the secret of the scrolls."

Talibah leaned in and whispered, "What scrolls?"

"The ones that I haven't written yet, but they will help us when we return to help the world in the future."

Bes laughed, "So, let me get this straight: We just learned a bunch of songs to help us"—he pointed to all three of us—"after we die and supposedly reincarnate, and they will unlock secrets to scrolls you haven't written yet?"

"Exactly. Any other questions?"

He replied, "Nope. I'm good."

"Me, too," added Talibah. "Now tell us what God said..."

———— • • ————

Two weeks went by. During that time, I spent most of my days meditating and copying down word-for-word the information I had received in gold ink. When I wasn't meditating, I worked diligently on a poem that would help me remember some of my magical powers. The other powers would come when the time was needed.

I also used my magic on the scrolls. First I made the letters disappear until the songs were sung again. Then I added another spell: my future self had to be holding the scrolls while the songs were sung or the letters would not reappear.

Bes and Talibah were a big help and went to the surrounding farms. They shared the two songs I had chosen from the five. Everyone was extremely supportive, and I had a good feeling about the future timeline when we would all return.

———— • • ————

I came out of my meditation in my study and exclaimed, "I remember the other three songs!"

349

CHAPTER TWENTY-FIVE

LET THE GOD
DEBATES BEGIN

Morning was right upon me. The sun lifted above the horizon and spread its light in the room. I thought to myself, "That was one long day." Then I gave my body a good stretch and walked toward my bedroom.

I could hear that Constance was up already. She saw me from the bathroom and asked, "Did you get any sleep last night?"

"Sleep? What's that?" I yawned and scratched my chest. "I don't need any sleep. I can teach with my eyes closed."

"Sure you can," she replied with a hint of sarcasm. "Did you get to meditate? I didn't hear any helicopters."

"I did. And you're right, there were no helicopters. That's strange."

"What? Do you want the helicopters to come?"

"No, but it's strange that they come sometimes and not others." The word *energy* popped into my mind. "Maybe it's because I didn't send out any energy."

"Would you send out for some breakfast instead? Hara would like some pancakes this morning. Can you do that in your meditation?" she giggled a little.

"I'll see what I can do."

She emphasized with her hands. "So?"

"What?"

"Did you get anything in your meditation?"

"I did. I remembered the other three melodies. I remember writing the God Scrolls when I was Tumaini. And I remember...the...the smell of bread." I smiled from my memory of Bes.

"God Scrolls? Is that what you are calling them now?"

"It's interesting that you should ask. When I was Tumaini, I visited what I think was God, and God gave me advice to help bring peace to the world. Then I wrote it down on the scrolls. That's what the gold lettering was for."

"Peace to the world. That's a pretty tall order for a piece of paper."

"It goes along with the pancakes," I laughed. "But seriously, I think I was given a roadmap for people to follow if they want to live...well...to live with more peace and freedom."

"And what did this voice tell you? What's this miracle roadmap?"

"I wrote them on the scrolls. I think I have some decoding to do."

"You mean, besides finding the rest of the magic cross and all the other stuff."

I yawned again, "Don't remind me."

"You know I'm joking with you. You're making huge amounts of headway. Just look at all of the things you've discovered in the past week alone. I'm proud of you. It'll come."

"I know. Thanks, and I'm proud of you, too. You've been extremely supportive."

Hara came out of her room in her bunny slippers and polka dot pajamas. Constance gave her a morning smile, "Are you ready for your first day of home school?" She was still sleepy and rubbed her face. Then she gave a tiny nod.

I laughed, "Glad to see all of the excitement hasn't gone out of that idea."

She walked by us and went into her bathroom. "It's too early to be excited. I wasn't even excited about going to the other school this early."

Constance held her finger up. "She's got a point there."

Before she closed the door, I joked, "Let me know when you're ready to catch the bus."

That made her think for a moment. "Bus? But I don't need a bus."

"Sure you do. How else are you going to get down the stairs for school?" She grinned and closed her door.

351

Constance asked, "What about you? What do you have planned for the day?"

"Teach, give Ted the copies, get more tables, stop at the metaphysical shop for the books Ted mentioned, and come back home and work."

"We also need to set up a rotating teaching schedule for Hara. You know, when you will teach and when I will teach. I have a bunch of work in my office to catch up on."

"I know, I was thinking about that yesterday. Let's go over that during dinner, OK?"

"OK. I'm going to go down and start breakfast. Do you want anything?"

"Yeah, I'd better eat something to get my energy up. Then I'm going to clean up and get an early start. I still need to make copies for Ted."

"Give me a call if you need anything."

"Will do. Thanks, hon." Before she walked downstairs, I inquired, "By the way, are you going to call Rehema?"

She nodded, "Yes, I think I will. Is the number still downstairs?"

"Yes. And can you fill them in on everything that's happened here since my last call? Oh, and get any updates from them, too."

"Sure. Pancakes will be ready in twenty minutes."

"Great, I could use some pancakes."

Knock, knock!

I waited outside Ted's office, but no one answered. I checked his office schedule and saw that this was his reserved time for student conferences. I was about to leave him a note when I heard someone coming around the corner. "Michael, thanks for stopping by. Did you bring those copies?"

"I did. Is this a good time?"

"Yes, yes, come on in. None of my students signed up for any help, so I went to the cafeteria for a quick snack. Do you want some?" He held out a bunch of red grapes.

"No, thanks. I just had breakfast with the girls."

"How is Hara?"

"She's doing just fine. Today's her first day of homeschool."

"I'm so glad you took her out of..." He was having trouble opening his door. "It sticks sometimes. I've got to give it a little..." He lifted the handle

352

and forced the door open with his whole body. "There. Now what was I saying? I'm glad she's at home with Constance."

"So are we."

"What's in the fancy box?" He rounded his desk and took a seat.

I put the box on his desk and opened the lid. "Here're the copies. Let me know if you find anything."

"Thanks, I will." He lifted up off of his chair and saw the other contents. "What are those?"

"These are the scrolls I wrote when I was Tumaini. I thought you might like to see something."

"Like what?"

"You're going to like this." I did my normal protection routine with the gloves and cloth.

After unrolling the scroll, he remarked, "Um, there's nothing on it."

"Just wait..." I breathed in, looked him in the eyes, then I looked at the scroll and sang the first few lines. The letters began appearing one by one. Ted's eyes were fixated on the golden words that were appearing out of nowhere.

"Michael"—he put his hand on his cheek in amazement—"this is magic. Isn't it?"

"Let me finish." The first few words remained on the scroll, just as I had remembered they would. When I finished singing, all of the words filled the papyrus and stayed visible.

He was astonished and shook his head slightly, "You're doing things that are way out of my league again."

"I can only do this because I was taught how. I'm no more special than you are."

"Well, I was never taught how to do that in school. So, what do the scrolls say? Do you know?"

"It has to do with a plan to help people live in peace. I just discovered this last night after you left, so I haven't gotten any further than this."

"I'd say that's pretty far." He scratched his head. "You keep doing these things, and I don't know how to help."

"Ted, you are helping. Trust me."

"What happens to the words? Do they disappear again?"

"From what I remember, they stay after the third time I sing. This was the third time, so I guess it worked."

"I'll say. What about the rest of these scrolls?"

"I haven't done the other songs yet. I didn't have time. I didn't get any sleep last night, either."

"That would explain the sags under your eyes," he smirked.

"Hey, I'm not that old. I just worked long hours."

"I know. I'm kidding."

I looked at my watch. "I've got to get to my 201 class. I'm glad you got to see this. Can you give me a call if you find anything from those copies?"

"Sure. And thanks for showing me your new discovery."

I packed up and headed off. "I'll have just enough time to get to class if I bypass my office."

------◆------

It took me fifteen minutes to cross campus. When I walked into my room, Robbie gave me the sign that everyone was there. I set my box down on the table near the podium and jumped right in.

"I hope that everyone turned in his *I love you* paper to Robbie. I'm looking forward to reading all of your observations." A number of students scrambled to find their assignments and scurried toward the front of the room. As I watched the frantic parade, I added, "In the meantime, does anyone want to share an experience or two?"

Beth raised her hand. "I did the experiment more than ten times, like you said."

"That's good, Beth. What happened? And before you ask, no, you don't get any extra credit for doing it more than ten times"—Beth and a few students laughed—"it just makes you a better person." I smiled toward her, "Go on, Beth."

"Well, I did like you told us. As soon as I saw someone, I said, 'I love you.' I...I...liked it."

"What did you like about it?"

"It felt good. I felt more loving, like Jesus used to teach."

"OK. Thank you for your observation—and your faith has been duly noted. Does anyone else want to share something? What about you, Todd? Did you do the assignment?"

"Yeah."

"Good. Would you mind sharing?"

He waited a moment to get his thoughts together. "It was cool. I saw some chicks on campus—" Some of the girls immediately *hissed* at his comment, and Rochelle turned around and gave him a mean look. "OK, sorry." He bowed his head with his hands in a regretful position. "I saw some *women* on campus and did your experiment."

"And?"

"I noticed what you said last time. I wasn't as judgmental."

"Anything else?"

"Yeah. I didn't look to see if they were hot or not. And I admit that's what I would usually do. But when I said *I love you* first, I saw them for who they were. It was different. It caught me by surprise, actually."

"Thank you for your honesty, Todd." I gazed at the entire class. "How about one more person?" No one's hand went up.

Robbie mustered up his courage and leaned over to get my attention. "Well, since nobody else is going to share, I did your assignment, too. Is it OK?"

"Of course." I motioned. "Professor Robbie, you have the podium." This reminded me that I needed to tell him he would make a great teacher someday. Then I stepped aside.

That statement also seemed to ring a bell for him. He smiled extra big and raced toward the podium. "I said *I love you* to twenty-six people: fourteen women and twelve guys. Each time I said it, I felt more open to them. It didn't matter if it was a man or woman, either. I had no problem saying it to both sexes. I was actually quite surprised by that, too. It was after I said it that I noticed something peculiar."

The girl who had flirted with him in the last class asked, "What was it?"

After recognizing her, he answered, "It happened right after I said it. I noticed what I would have judged about that person if I hadn't said *I love you* in the first place. Then I made the decision that it wasn't right to judge any person by his or her appearance. I mean, no one is perfect. And it seemed, well, wrong to segregate people because they're too tall, too short, or not attractive enough. That assignment really made a big difference for me. I liked how I accepted others more." He got a few claps from the room.

"Excellent. I'm glad this little experiment had some positive feedback. Let's get to the next part of class, which will still focus on religion first." The guys in the back *booed*.

"Instead of the usual philosophy question, it's fitting for today's talk to focus on speech, inflection, hidden meanings, suggested meanings, and cultural influences. It's not good for students of philosophy to assume that we were all taught the same social interpretations as each other. So, with that said, here's the first question of the day: You walk up in someone's yard and you see a fence. On that fence, you see a sign that says *Dogs! Keep out!*" I moved one of the screens to show the students the same sign. "Now think about this…" I joked, "Is this sign telling *all dogs* that they must keep out of the yard?" A few students chuckled, but the majority kept silent. "Or is it a sign to warn you that a dog is behind the fence?

"OK, you already know it's a warning sign about a dog. But I want you to think for a moment and tell me three instances where this assumption wouldn't work."

One of the girls near the back spoke, "If you aren't afraid of dogs, that sign wouldn't have the same meaning. I'm not afraid of dogs, so it wouldn't work."

The girl beside her added, "Yeah, that sign might tell you that a testosterone-filled guy might be trying to show you he's got a big dog to compensate for his—"

"Steady now," I stopped her before she could finish. "Let's keep this friendly." The class broke out in laughter.

Phillip answered next, "What if you came from a desert island and you didn't know how to read, or you'd never seen a dog before? That sign wouldn't make any sense to you."

"Very good, Phillip. Good thinking."

Stacey raised her hand, and I acknowledged her, "Stacey?"

"It's a sign used to incite fear, or to show that the person using the sign is afraid."

"All great answers." I nodded toward her. "And Stacey, can you elaborate on yours?"

She liked getting to speak more and wiggled in her chair. "Yes, either someone is hoping to make someone outside of the fence afraid; someone might be afraid of a lawsuit if a person got bitten by her dog and she hadn't posted a sign; or that person might be afraid of being attacked or robbed, and she hoped the sign would scare off any burglars."

"I like your answer, Stacey." She wiggled again with confidence.

I walked to the other side of the podium and leaned on it with my elbow. "This takes us to a popular notion shared by many religions. Before I tell you what that notion is, does anyone care to take a stab at one of our religious topics for today?"

Rochelle suggested, "Fear?"

"Well, yes,"—she was happy about her correct answer—"and no," I finished, which also upset her. "Let me explain. Rochelle is half right. Fear is a popular control tool used by most religions and governments. But as philosophy students, one must look at the other side, too. Rochelle, what's the other side of fear? What's the opposite of fear?"

"Love?"

At the same time, another student yelled out, "Courage!"

I pointed at Rochelle. "You're right. They go hand in hand. It's often been said that the opposite of fear is love, and vice versa."

I pointed toward the other student and said jokingly, "Wait your turn." I looked back at him after a quick moment of silence. "You're right, though." He smiled.

I walked to the board, grabbed a marker, and wrote the word *love*. "We all know the nice things that love can stand for: kindness, mercy, compassion, and acceptance." I wrote those under the word love. "But what is another definition for love that would not use any positive words? And before you answer, think about using an opposite approach, one that would not use the word fear, either."

A girl on the right side of the room answered, "A romantic feeling?"

"Nice. But romantic would fall under a positive term. Think folks. Define *love* without using any gushy words."

One of the fraternity guys answered, "I've got it. Tolerance!"

"I like this one...tolerance. It's not the usual fluffy word used for love, and it can go either way: positive or negative." I asked him to elaborate, "Bruce, tell us what you mean."

"It's like, you know, when you no longer tolerate someone, and they fall out of favor. Like when the pledges don't clean up after the party. They fall out of favor with the rest of the fraternity. So I guess they wouldn't be loved as much."

"That's a great point," I remarked. His buddy slapped him hard on the shoulder. "I've often thought of love in this manor: How much imperfection will you tolerate before that person falls out of favor?"

After walking around my podium, I added, "Here is another point about tolerance that I would like for you to consider. This will go along with a famous religious statement—since we are focusing on religion. I'm sure you have heard this popular phrase: *Do unto others as you would have done unto you.* Can you give me an example where this would not work as an expression of love and is actually terrible advice?"

Stacey perked up right away. "Each person's tolerance level is different, and each person's tolerance level changes moment by moment and day by day."

Bruce added, "Yeah, just ask my girlfriend. I never know if what I'm saying will make her happy or sad." His response got a lot of laughs.

Stacey continued, "It would be impossible to gauge everyone's tolerance level and to know what is loving at one moment and insulting in the next. I, for one, would not follow that religious statement."

"Good point, Stacey. Well done."

After acknowledging a new hand being raised, one of the football players added in a more serious tone, "I could take a slap on the back and not care. A teammate could slap me on the butt and call it sportsmanship and support. But if I slapped a hemophiliac, that person could bleed to death. When I was growing up, I had a friend who died from an extreme hemophiliac reaction. He died from an accidental hit to his body. He couldn't tolerate what I could tolerate physically, even if it was a sign of sportsmanship or love. So, to do unto others as you would have done unto you could kill you."

I looked at the young man and the rest of the class. "These are all excellent responses. You guys are really sharp today. Tolerance can be a positive word for love, and it can have an extremely hazardous effect due to individual circumstances. So, it seems that some religious statements need to be looked at more carefully before they are taken as law. After our findings and personal experiences with *tolerance*, would you agree?" The majority of the room responded by nodding *yes*.

"Class, I can belabor this point longer, but we have a lot to cover today. So let's get to your assignment, and then we can use the rest of our time for discussion. Your assignment will be on another form of love. And this one will be *service*. With love—and with religion, politics, and sex—you can serve in two main ways: you can either serve yourself and not care about anyone else, *or*, you can serve someone else and not ask for anything in return. You serve someone else because you love them completely." I tilted my head and joked, "Or you love them for the moment because you tolerate their imperfections." After a few laughs, I added, "And since this is considered by some to be the highest form of love, this will be your assignment."

I continued, "It's easy to serve one of your personal friends and do what they request, but we are going to make this more challenging. If you accept this challenge, you will be paired with a partner from this class."

I turned to my TA. "See Robbie at the end of class for your pairings." He nodded.

"Then, for at least one to two hours, each of you will serve your partner and not ask for anything in return. Then you will write one paragraph about your experience and turn it in on Friday."

Holding up a finger, I emphasized, "If you don't feel comfortable serving someone else, this is your time to speak up. You will be excluded from this experiment without harming your grade. Is there any objection?" No one raised his hand. "Good. Let's go over the rules."

I walked to the board and slid the screen. "Rule number one: You cannot ask your partner to do anything illegal or that will get you expelled from school."

One of the fraternity guys smirked, "So much for hotwiring the dean's car and robbing the bank."

"Exactly! We'll have none of that." The students laughed.

"Now, for rule number two: You cannot ask your partner to do anything sexual without his or her complete—and sober—consent."

The two guys in the back both whined, "Awwwww!" I didn't say anything. I just nodded and pointed in their direction.

"And rule number three: You cannot ask your partner to do anything that would go against his or her moral or ethical standards. And if you don't have any of those, see Robbie for a list of approved activities."

He looked at me very confused. "I'm only kidding, Robbie."

I readdressed the class, "If there are no questions, we'll continue."

One of the guys in the front rubbed his thumb and fingers together. "What about money?"

"That's a good question. Money is off limits for this assignment, too. You can't ask someone to serve you by asking for money, using his or her money, or asking them to work your job for you."

Stacey inquired, "What are we supposed to do then?"

"There are many ways to serve someone without breaking these rules.

Your partner will guide you. Let them ask, and you'll decide if what they ask is acceptable, or even doable. If it isn't, then ask them to make another request. The main focus here is not on the rules; I only set those up for your protection. The main focus is on love and service so you can experience serving someone without asking for anything in return. That's all."

She replied, "I can do that."

"Good. Let's get to our next religious topic."

Phillip's hand went up right away. "Yes, Phillip?"

"Professor, in the last class, you never mentioned what you believe in. I mean, you kind of danced around it and never told us. I'd like to know, if you don't mind sharing."

I thought back to Monday's class. "You know what, Phillip, you're right. I never explained myself. I kind of went with the flow of my talk to get to the assignment. It wasn't deliberate, I assure you. You guys are the main focus here, not me."

He mulled around what I said, and then he raised his hand again. "Yes, Phillip?"

"Will you tell us now?"

"We have a lot to cover today. Can't this wait?"

His hand went back up for a third time. "Phillip, you don't have to keep raising your hand. I get the point. You really want to know, don't you?" He nodded *yes*, and so did a number of other students.

I sighed, turned toward my desk, and saw the box of scrolls. Instantly, I heard a voice that started speaking in my head. The words weren't completely audible, so I couldn't make them out. They were off in the distance, softer than a whisper. But it was a voice, I was sure of it, and that voice wanted my attention.

Looking toward the class, I continued, "As you know, I don't follow any one religion. In my lifetime, and even recently, I have experienced something that…well, the best way I can explain it is that it is an energy and a consciousness."

The voice inside my head came back and was much clearer this time. It was not my voice or the voice of Tumaini. This voice came from deep within my being. The voice filled my head with one phrase, "The God Scroll will help you."

I walked to the box, opened the lid, and picked up the God Scroll. My body felt connected to the energy emanating from the golden words. I could feel their thoughts flowing through me. The thoughts were me, and I was the thoughts. I was as connected to them as I was connected to my own consciousness.

Phillip prodded, "So, Professor, what are your thoughts on our world religions?"

The voice responded through me, "Your religions were created by evil aliens and the Anunnaki for the purpose of separating all people. All religions that use fear to control their congregations were created by aliens, humans, or evil spirits." Then I put the scroll back down.

My own thoughts rose above the voice, and I questioned myself, "Holy cow! Did I actually say that out loud? It's time for damage control." I quickly said, "Class, I want you to—"

Todd interrupted, "It's OK, Professor. We know all about aliens and government cover-ups. You didn't say anything upsetting." Some of the students shook their heads in disagreement, though.

I stammered in the beginning, "My intention…my intention was not to insult anyone for his or her beliefs." I looked at the scroll. "As a professor of philosophy, I am here to share new ideas and to help you nurture your own ideas and beliefs."

The voice stopped me and said, "The God Scroll will help you."

I overcame my apprehension and picked it back up again. I felt a new strength that I hadn't felt before. "It is time for you, My children, to hear the truth that has been withheld from you for many of your years. You have been deceived by your leaders. It is time to hear the truth."

I came to the conclusion that I might be channeling Source at that point, but I didn't tell my students yet. I was almost sure it was a voice I'd heard before, the voice of a loving, old friend. I paused and waited for it to continue. When nothing happened, though, I carefully set the scroll back down in the box.

One of my New Age students, Daphnee, offered, "I'm not here to disagree with you, or anyone else, but I don't believe we are being deceived. I was taught by my mother that there is no right or wrong, there is no evil."

I thought this was a good way to get the class back toward a regular discussion. "What do you mean, Daphnee? Can you elaborate for us?" Phillip looked a little perturbed.

"I was taught that there is no good or bad. There is no such thing as an evil person, which also means there would be no deception"—she looked toward Todd and added—"or deceptive governments."

Rochelle didn't like her comment and retorted abruptly, "There's no good or bad? There are no deceptive governments? You've got to be kidding me. Who taught you that?"

"My mother. She follows many of the New Age teachings."

I took over. "I am going to ask you something strictly for the class's benefit. Is this OK?"

"Yes," she replied a little sheepishly.

"I have studied most of the known religions, including a great deal of New Age teachings. I have heard that many in the New Age community believe there is no right or wrong. Am I correct in this statement?" She nodded in agreement.

One of the guys in the back interrupted, "But there is right or wrong. There are facts. Two plus two does not equal three thousand six hundred and thirteen pink fuzzy slippers and a quart of ice cream. You *can* be factually wrong."

I acknowledged his contribution, "I concur. I don't agree with this New Age philosophy, either. There is factual right and wrong, which bleeds over to moral right and wrong. There are moral rights and wrongs."

I addressed the entire class, "Think about this, folks. If there weren't moral rights and wrongs, there would be no such thing as regret, remorse, guilt, or shame. Those emotions would never have been created at all if the New Agers were right about this concept."

I glanced back at Daphnee and asked, "I am not trying to bully you or push my beliefs on you, but would you answer this for me? Here is your chance to convince the class."

"OK," she replied.

I waited just a few seconds and continued, "If there is no right or wrong, as you say, and if I'm wrong about there being no right or wrong, then I just proved your statement to be...factually wrong. Would you agree to this?" She had to think and did not respond.

Rochelle spat, "Just say it. You know he's right about that statement." I gave her a look to be more kind to the other students. Then she turned to the class. "Besides, if there weren't moral rights or wrongs, we'd have no such things as whistleblowers telling the truth about our horrible governments, military, and police. Right and wrong exists!" She received a bunch of support from the class.

I motioned to Daphnee, "Daphnee, is my statement correct?"

She didn't like saying it, but she agreed, "Yes... But that's not what I was taught. It made so much sense until you had me question it."

"Please tell us what you were taught," I announced to the room, "and *all of us* will be open to your teaching—including me."

She explained, "I was taught with this example: There is no good or bad. It's like looking at a magnet. One side of the magnet pulls things in, and the other side pushes away. Neither side is good or bad, it's just what they do. Everything is—"

Todd interrupted, "But the negative side of the magnet doesn't try to kill the positive side of the magnet for being the wrong color or rob it for more money. This is the most ridiculous thing I've ever heard. There is evil in this world. All you have to do is turn on the news or look at how our government operates."

Beth asked, "Isn't that a violation, Professor? Shouldn't he say something nice about the New Age community?"

"She's got a point, Todd. Can you think of something positive to say about those who follow the New Age belief?" I laughed in my head, "There's nothing positive to say about our world governments."

"Um...this isn't easy." He took a minute. Then he said sarcastically, "I appreciate how New Agers can devote themselves to all of these spirits, aliens, and so-called ascended masters who don't seem to do anything about the problems in the world—even though they pray to them every day."

"Todd," I cautioned, "I think you missed the point about saying something nice. Would you care to try again?"

"I...I appreciate their tenacity to believe"—cough—"even if nothing happens."

"We'll need to work on that, Todd." He got the message and nodded back to me.

Phillip asked, "What do you believe about polarity, Professor?"

The God Scroll called to me. I followed my urge, picked it up, and the voice spoke through me, "Love has no polarity, and love serves all. There is no negative aspect to love. Your examples of dual polarities were given to you by an evil group of souls who had a selfish agenda. They did this so you would accept all harmful actions from others, and they influenced you to believe it was a gift. Their hopes were that you would accept this false teaching so no one would stand up to them, retaliate, or resist. Guilt was their effective weapon, and it worked very well. Hear me now: This is not the way of love. Love would not harm another and call it a gift.

"I tell you, My children, love gives freely. Love gives without asking for anything in return. Love gives, and gives, and gives.

"But know this, too. Love is not blind and *will* also accept gratitude in its many forms."

The voice paused for a moment, and then continued, "A loving mother never hands a bill to her grown child for all of the care and nurturing she shared. A loving father never sends a past due notice to a son or daughter for all of his care, nurturing, or attention. Hear me, My children: Love gives freely and does not harm another.

"Fear, on the other hand, abandons love, and ownership is completely based upon fear. Ownership creates monetary value, monetary value creates laws, then laws create the need for enforcement. The police and military are a product of fear, and they continue to incite fear on behalf of those few who created the fear-based laws. Your kings, queens, dictators, oligarchies, presidents, and politicians live to create fear, and they use this to control you.

"Consider this, My children: Love needs no laws. Love only needs guidance and cooperation, not laws. And many words can describe love: acceptance, unity, togetherness, service to others. When you separate yourself from your brothers and sisters, you are no longer in the realm of love. This includes laws, borders, and nations that the authorities have created. Your laws and nations separate and divide, but service to others unifies and brings people together. Service to others requires no laws and creates no borders. When you serve one another, you are expressing love. Love always accepts with open arms and open hearts."

The class was stunned. I was not speaking with my own voice. Another voice was speaking through me every time I picked up the God Scroll.

The voice continued, "I tell you, My children, no one owns anything. Throughout all of history, men and women who were overrun with fear have claimed ownership to parcels of land and bodies of water. Their arrogance grew, and they claimed ownership to God's animals and peo-ple—which they said I gave them permission to do, but this is false. Then their arrogance grew even further, and they claimed free air, free energy, and free space—including outer space. Beyond this, the arrogance of the people grew so enormous that they claimed ownership to words, thoughts, and music—which I gave freely to all souls. Even today, your people claim legal trademarks and punish those for speaking My free words.

"But when all is said and done, when these people die, they take none of their money, land, or possessions with them. If they truly own these things, they would take all of them to the Realm of Souls when they pass on, but they do not. They take nothing with them but their memories and their emotions. They leave all of the rest behind with their human bodies. And what is even more arrogant, My children, is when they say they have the right to pass these possessions, these things, My creations, on to their heirs.

"I tell you, My children, no one owns anything in this world—including your nations. You are stewards of a soul, and your soul came here to share and to love, not to live in fear and covet physical possessions. It is your memories and emotions that are your soul's possessions. It is your kind deeds and love that your soul gives honor to. Nothing else!

"Think of this, My children: If the people from your past really owned the land and water, and they had taken it with them when they died, there would have been no world left for you to live on. If it worked their way, with every death of a landowner, a piece of the world would have flown off with his soul. Chunks of earth and water would have simply disappeared. Animals would have vanished. Words would have simply faded away from your vocabulary because someone said he owned them.

"This is just preposterous! I did not make this planet to be carved up amongst your greedy, fearful, selfish peoples. I made this planet for you to experience love, charity, sharing, compassion, and forgiveness. I made this planet as a place for you to choose kindness over fear, sharing over fear, caring over fear, mercy over fear, and love over fear.

"You are all born free, and you remain free until someone begins to govern you. You are free until someone, or some group, says you must follow his edicts or laws. Those who govern for their own selfish beliefs and agendas create the laws, and they create organizations that will use force to bend you to those laws. Governing always uses fear, force, coercion, punishment, torture, imprisonment, and death to make someone bow to the wishes of those who govern. Love does not do this.

"A loving parent may stop a child from running in front of a speeding car, but that parent is looking out for the well-being of the child's soul—not governing his or her life. However, your governments do not care about the souls of others. The governments use the police, military, and other organizations to control the souls of others for their own selfish purposes, agendas, ideals, and morals. This is *not* why I created your planet!

"I tell you this, My children: Love also stands up for those who cannot stand for themselves; love cares for those who cannot care for themselves; and love is standing up against oppressive governments for those who are enslaved. Courage is love in action, and your courage is needed if you wish to see a change in the world. You, and all of your people, all of your souls, are enslaved by those few people who claim authority over you. If you show courage, if you show love, you can change this world before it is too late. And I am telling you lovingly—not with fear—that your time is running out. It is almost too late. The sands of freedom and love are running out. Your planet is dying because of these evil people and evil aliens."

The voice coming through me stopped speaking. Everyone remained quiet.

Beth broke the silence, "I'm confused. Are you acting, Professor Whyse? And why do you sound so different? Are you trying to tell us something? I mean, we live in a democratic society. We have the right to vote."

The godly voice continued through me, "A president, an oligarchy, or a democratic government can enslave a people just as easily as a king, queen, or dictator. All forms of government institute slavery of the people—including democracy! Either *all* of the people are enslaved under a monarchy system, or *portions* of the people are enslaved under a democracy. You have been slaves to presidents, monarchies, and oligarchies on this land since the creation of presidents, monarchies, and oligarchies. If you are being governed, you are being controlled. There is no freedom in that.

"Think back to your past, My children. A president can initiate a nuclear war and destroy the entire planet over fear, greed, or lust. No human should have that much power. Your world was almost lost forever, blown apart, killed, with no chance of survival for anyone, because of the actions of two arrogant people and their parliaments. I say again: No human should have that much power on your world.

"Instead of being governed, look for ways to live together in peace. Look for ways to conquer your fears with courage. Look for ways to live with love of one another, despite your supposed differences. You are all souls wearing different colored suits. You are all souls wearing different sized garments. You are all souls with an incredible body to give you the chance to love. You forgot that you are souls of God. You forgot that you are loving children—the Creator in human form. And this is not your fault. You were genetically modified to be subservient slaves to evil aliens and select humans.

"I tell you, My children, love is not a rule. Love is not a law. Love is but a way of *being*. Love just *is*. And do not, for the love of God, do not make a law out of what I have said. Instead, use love as a guideline. Love your neighbor, and love yourself. Live freely with one another, and know the peace and love that I share with you. With this, I take my leave for the day." The voice stopped, and I put the scroll on the table.

Robbie was looking at me strangely. "Professor Whyse, should I...should I hand out the pairings?"

"Not just yet, Robbie. I need to wrap up first." I thought about picking up the scroll again, but I followed my instincts and asked for reactions from the room, "I know I said a lot. Was there anything that struck a chord with any of you?"

Todd was the first to speak. "I like what you said: You are born free until someone says you must follow his laws. And in my opinion, politicians are not good enough to say what we can or cannot do. I'm tired of them acting superior to us. They didn't go to any politician school. There are no qualifications to being a politician except for having money, a name, or some charisma. They have some gall telling us what is morally acceptable and what isn't. And once they're in office, they do like you said: They have an agenda, which usually means doing what it takes to keep their job and not serving the people. I like your message."

I thought, "Maybe there is some hope, and it lies with these students."

Rochelle added, "I like where you mentioned that people who love each other don't need laws, they only need guidelines. It makes sense."

"Rochelle," I smiled, "I'm shocked...and pleased. Do you have anything else to add on that?"

She shook her head *no*, "Not really. Maybe later."

"OK, thanks for sharing. Anyone else?"

Phillip offered his thoughts, "This is what made a huge impact on me. You mentioned something like: You keep looking to a government to tell you how to live instead of looking for *a way to live without a government*. I liked that a lot. I'd like to hear more about this and how to do it. What's going on in this world is clearly not working." A number of students clapped and pounded on their desks. "If we don't change, I'm not...well... I'm not looking forward to life after graduation. It's just getting worse out there." More students clapped.

A different student ranted, "I don't like what you shared. This was a great country. We need to get America back to being a great country again."

Rochelle stood up and burst back, "When exactly was this a great country?! There has always been slavery, prejudice, and killing for profit." She pumped her fist and thundered angrily, "Women are still looked at as objects, and everyone knows that we are owned by the corporations and bankers. And we have more laws that tell us what we can't do instead of saying *you are free*. When exactly was this a great country? Give me a decade. Hell, give me a year. Give me a month. Give me a day! I dare you!" He backed down and didn't say anything else.

She continued while shaking her finger at him, "Just tell the American Indians who lost their land that it was a great country. Just tell the African slaves who were ripped from their homes and brought here on slave ships that it was a great country. Tell the women who've been oppressed for hundreds of years by egotistical, ape-like men that this was a great country. Don't you dare say America was great! You sound like a politician running for office! It's like Professor Whyse has taught us"—she looked at me, and then back to him—"stop being brainwashed and think for once in your life!" She got a round of applause from the class. When she sat down, she was so mad that her face was red.

She stood up one more time before I could speak and yelled at him, "And one more thing: This America that you like so much will kill you and never think twice about it. The U.S. goes to war with anyone, or any country, that they don't like. Haven't you got the sense in you to see that? This is not a great country! They'll take your land, your money, and your resources, no matter where you live! America goes to war or gives aid only when it serves the rich. It's time for you to see the pattern. Wake up!" The class went berserk with applause.

"Rochelle," I smiled, "that's a whole new side to you I've never seen before. Thanks for sharing." She was huffing very hard at this point.

"I have to bring this back to our original topic, which was religion. A lot of your comments were on politics, but what about your religious views?"

One of my Muslim exchange students answered, "I like some of what you said, but I cannot leave my faith, or my belief in the Koran. I would not join a city or country like this unless it adhered to my religion and the laws of Allah. Allah is the only one who can give us guidance, or who can decide who is righteous or an infidel. When I get my degree, I am going back home to help my people and my religion."

"That's an honest answer. I respect this."

I looked toward the class. "Is there anyone else who would like to share a religious perspective?"

Beth raised her hand. "What you said sounds...well...too good to be true. And unless it is taught that Jesus is the Lord and Savior, I wouldn't be a part of it."

"Again, I respect your opinion. And I notice that we have enough time for everyone to see Robbie. Get your partner and meet with him or her before you leave the room. Set up a time when each of you can serve each other before Friday. Bring back your papers. Class is dismissed."

Phillip came up to me and asked, "Will you tell us how to live like you said?"

"I will, Phillip. Friday's class. I will."

CHAPTER TWENTY-SIX

AN OLD FRIEND RETURNS

With three more tables, new white linens, and more plexiglass in the car, I made my way toward the metaphysical shop. I was only five blocks and three turns away when I saw a man dusting off his pants and looking toward the sky. I thought to myself, "Now that looks strangely familiar." I was still heavily distracted by the day's events and couldn't place where I had seen that before, so I put my attention back on the road and drove onward.

Maverick Priestly, a Jamaican man in his late twenties, with dark brown skin, shoulder-length dreadlocks, about six foot one and one hundred seventy-five pounds, was walking with a purpose. He didn't know where he was walking to. He was following a clue, a hunch, a feeling that he'd had for the last week. He was following a voice in his head, and his purpose was to find out why he'd kept hearing a word repeated over and over for the past seven days.

"This is driving me nuts," he spat with a light accent. "I've got to find out what is going on. I can't keep living like this."

He walked to the corner and became agitated. "Now what?!" He stood there and looked down all three directions. Then he threw his hands up in the air and turned around behind him. "I'm lost. I don't know where I am going, and I can't ask for directions. Who's going to help me get to *nowhere?*" The spring heat had come early this year and he began to sweat. This added to his frustration.

When he faced forward again, a soft voice in his head told him, "Turn left here."

He complained to the voice, "You know, I'm getting really tired of this. I demand some answers. Who are you?" The voice gave no response. Maverick wiped the sweat from his brow, turned left, and walked down the next street.

I was in the shop and headed toward the book area when the woman behind the counter recognized me and asked, "How's the incense burner working out?"

"Oh, it's working just fine, thanks." She smiled and went back to helping the next customer in line.

There was a special event at the store that day, and I passed a number of people on the way to the back. The store owner came over and inquired, "Can I help you find something?" She was a middle-aged woman, thin and fairly attractive, with long, straight, ash-brown colored hair and huge brown eyes. Her personality was soft, but she exuded with confidence.

"Yes. Do you know if you have any of these books?" I handed her Ted's short list.

She glanced at it for a second. "I know these books. Let me see if we have them in stock." In a methodical order, she gazed up and down each of the shelves. "Ah, here it is." She grabbed the first book and handed it to me. "Are you studying energy systems of the body?"

I flipped open the book to peer inside. "You could say that. I know a little about chakras and stuff, but I've only just scratched the surface. I was hoping that these books might help."

She skimmed the list again and then handed it back to me. "Do you mind if I make a recommendation? These are pretty rudimentary for you."

"Not at all. Any help you can give me is welcome."

She moved toward another shelf and used her finger to guide her sight.

"It's this book..." She was still looking. "The books on your list are rather basic. If you know anything about chakras or the Chinese energy system, you won't need them. What you want is..." She picked a thick book off of the shelf. "You want this one."

The book fell heavily into my hands. "Wow, is there a whole car battery in there? This book is huge."

"Trust me. Everything you want to know about the human potential is in there. I haven't found any other that's as comprehensive, and I've been studying for twenty years. If you want to know about the energy systems, this is the one."

"Thanks. Can you still show me the other books, though? I'd like to compare them."

"Sure. What are you studying for?"

"I've had some experiences lately with energy and..." I stopped speaking. I wasn't sure that I wanted to explain everything.

She prodded before I could continue, "And what? You aren't going to shock me. I've seen pretty much every type of energy healing out there." She paused looking at the shelf and stared at me. "I'm also pretty psychic—clairvoyant and all—and I can tell you want these for something big"—she looked up to the right to get the correct words—"some kind of battle."

I was caught off guard by her comment. "How did you know? I didn't say anything."

"I told you: I'm clairvoyant. I can sense things about people. And you"—she pointed at me—"you have a purpose beyond your teaching job, don't you? It's in your aura." I stood there motionless, and she continued, "You don't have to say anything. I know." She leaned in and whispered, "I won't tell anyone." I still remained motionless.

"I usually don't read people when they come in the store, but you have something about you. You have a strong purpose. It hit me when I started looking for these books. Hasn't anyone taught you about shielding?"

"Um..." I thought back to being Tumaini and my harsh lessons.

"There are too many negative spirits out there just looking to zap an unprotected soul like yours. You should know better."

Not knowing what else to say, since I'd just been scolded, I muttered, "Thanks for the reminder," and I put up my shield again.

"There, that's better." She acknowledged the protective bubble I'd just made. "Now here are the other two books on your list." She handed them to me and motioned toward a table and two chairs at the far wall. "You can look at them over there if you wish. Call me if you have any questions, Michael."

"How did you...?"

"I'm clairvoyant. Weren't you listening?" she answered with a sweet laugh. Then she walked away.

I sat down and started paging through Ted's recommendations first. I was going to ask her name before she left out of sight, but she turned around and shared, "Laura. My name is Laura." I smiled because she knew. I bowed my head towards her and gave her my teacher's point.

Maverick was walking toward the metaphysical store when the voice returned, "I am from your past. It is time for you to remember. Go into this shop, now. Tumaini will help you."

He turned toward the storefront and saw it was a metaphysical shop. "What am I doing here? I don't need any of this stuff."

The voice instructed softly, "Go into this shop." He opened the door, smelled the heavy scent of incense, and walked inside. He couldn't see much because a young couple was walking out at the same time and blocked his view. Once they were past, he examined the main room.

The woman behind the counter saw him and was immediately taken aback by his physique. She tried to hide her interest and quickly looked away before he saw her. She lifted her head again in a more business-like manner and greeted him vibrantly, "Welcome! Can I help you find anything?"

He shook his head *no* and walked in farther. "Now what am I supposed to do in this place?" Since he didn't hear anything, he began to walk around. As he made his way through the aisles, he picked up a talisman that he recognized from his country and commented out loud, "What's a duppy doing here?"

Laura came by and overheard him. "It's a Jamaican ghost. Are you familiar?"

"Yes. I grew up hearing all about them back home. I didn't expect to see one here."

"Well, we carry a lot of exotic things. Look around. What you are looking for *is* in this store." He gave her an inquisitive look. "Just give me a call if you need any help."

"I will." He was still reeling a little from what she'd just said.

The voice in his head spoke very clearly, "Say the name."

He thought to himself, "I'm not going to say the name. You say the name!" He was agitated by this and put the duppy back down. "Great, now I'm arguing with myself."

Across the room, at that exact same moment, I stopped looking at the books and thought about Laura's abilities. Somehow, by thinking about her, I tapped into her psychic connection and I heard another person say, "Great, now I'm arguing with myself." That made me think back to Cairo. I wondered, "That's what I said outside of the Khan. How come I'm thinking about Egypt?"

Back in Maverick's head, the voice repeated, "Say the name out loud."

"Grrrr! I can't believe I'm doing this. OK, here goes." He looked around the store full of people and became a little nervous. Then he loudly appealed, "I'm sorry, folks, but is there someone here who knows what the word Baniti means?" Almost everyone stopped what he was doing and looked in his direction. He asked even louder this time, "I'm looking for some help, please. Does anyone know what Baniti means?"

A few people shook their heads *no* and replied, "Uh-uh," and then went about their business.

I, on the other hand, threw the books onto the chair behind me and raced over to the young man. "What did you just say?!" I asked with great exuberation.

He looked at me with a little confusion. "Baniti. I keep hearing a voice saying Baniti in my head. Please tell me you know what it means. It's driving me crazy."

"Don't worry. I know all about the voices."

"You do? You hear voices, too?"

"Well, not as much as before. But when I was in Cairo, I heard voices that helped me—"

He added at the same time, "To remember."

"Exactly. The voice told me a few minutes ago that it was time to remember. Just what's going on?"

"I might be able to explain a little. That voice might be trying to help you. This is a friendly voice, isn't it?" He nodded *yes*.

I looked around and saw some of the people staring at us. I pointed toward the chairs. "Why don't we go over there and sit down? We might have a little more privacy." I led the way, and Maverick followed me.

After getting comfortable, he reached out his hand. "My name is Maverick, but everyone calls me Rick. Well, Ricky, for short."

While exchanging handshakes, I smiled, "Nice to meet you, Ricky. My name is Michael. I was a friend of Baniti in another place. If it's the same person, I might be able to help you."

"I sure hope so. Some person named Turmeric is supposed to help me in here."

I smirked hard, "Do you mean, Tumaini?"

His eyes got very big, and he leaned back like he'd seen a real duppy. "Yeah!" His body language and speech instantly became cautious. "How do you know all of this? Is this voodoo or something? Are you the voice in my head?"

"Well"—I sat back so he wouldn't feel so threatened—"I'm Tumaini, and Baniti was a close friend of mine. Actually, he was my mentor a very, very long time ago." His look told me that he wanted more information. "Baniti made a vow to come back and reconnect with a number of priests to bring a message of hope to the people."

"A priest, huh? I don't know anything about this."

"Yes, there were a number of us—thirty-six to be exact."

He shook his head, "This is getting weirder and weirder. My last name is Priestly, but I can assure you that I am no priest."

"I can understand that. I was told something similar when I was in Egypt a few weeks back, and I had a hard time adjusting to what I was told."

He got a little excited from what I'd said. "Egypt, what's up with Egypt? I keep seeing stuff all over the place about Egypt—pyramids here, ankhs over there. Look"—he pointed to a few ankh necklaces—"there're some more of them. I can't get away from this Egyptian stuff."

I nodded, "I think someone is trying to tell you something."

He relaxed a little. "You bet they are. So where do I fit into all of this? Why am I hearing this name? And why was I led here?"

"Can I ask you when you started hearing Baniti's name?"

"It was about a week ago, maybe two." He looked down and saw the books that I'd put on the table. He got a strange chill and shook it off. "Since then, I've had strange dreams about ancient Egypt—ceremonies and stuff. None of it has made any sense, though."

He nodded toward the book. "Do you get into all of this?"

"I have some experience with it." I thought to myself, "I wish Ramla were here. She could help." I looked back toward him and asked, "Do you remember anything about the ceremonies?"

"Not a lot. I kept seeing a number of people in short white robes. Sometimes I had the same three people following me around like I was important or something. It was strange."

I thought to myself, "It's possible that he really is Baniti, but he doesn't remember it yet."

He continued, "So, how is it that you have two names: Michael and Tumaini?"

"Maverick—sorry, Ricky—how much do you know about reincarnation?"

"I've heard about it, but I don't know if I believe in it or not."

"I know what you mean. I felt the same way." He relaxed a little more because we shared a number of beliefs. "I had an experience a while back... Well, the experience is still going on, and it has to do with reincarnation— my reincarnation. It turns out that I was a priest called Tumaini back in ancient Egypt."

Laura had walked by to check on us. She leaned in toward Ricky and whispered, "I told you what you were looking for was in the shop. Do you need anything else?"

I looked up at her and replied graciously, "No, Laura, thanks." Ricky shook his head *no* as well.

"Alright, but when you are ready, let me know. Hope is just a stone's throw away."

I laughed at her *hope* comment and also thought, "I hope he doesn't actually throw a stone at me."

Before leaving, she comforted Ricky, "You're in good hands. Trust him." He smiled really big for the first time that day.

A friendly voice in my head spoke, "Tumaini, help him like I helped you. You have the power now."

It was Ramla, and she told me exactly what I thought I should do. "Thanks, Ramla," as I projected my thoughts to her. "You know just when to come in."

"It is my pleasure to serve. We miss you, and we may need your return soon. I must go for now. We will speak shortly."

"Bye, Ramla. Thanks."

Maverick was staring at me with a quizzical look. "Do you want to tell me what just happened?"

"I have this ability…and if I'm right, so do you. It's to speak with others telepathically. I was talking with a friend back in Egypt."

He became a little skeptical. "Yeah? What did he say, mon?"

"Well, he was a she, and she said to help you."

"Help me. How? Are you going to give me any real answers?"

"It would be my honor to serve you. But to do this, you will have to trust me."

"I don't have any reason not to trust you, and that nice lady said I was in good hands. What are you going to do?"

"With your permission, I'm going to help you remember. Would you like to know who Baniti is?" He nodded his head slightly.

"Just to be sure… I'm going to touch your forehead in a moment. You may get a jolt. Is it OK?"

"Yeah, sure, as long as it isn't going to hurt."

"It won't hurt—at least I don't think it will. But you will remember Bes and Talibah."

"Who are Bes and Talibah?"

"You're about to find out. Are you ready?" I leaned forward with my pointer finger aimed at his forehead. He was a little apprehensive and leaned back a bit.

"Trust me"—I winked—"and close your eyes. You're in for a ride."

He leaned forward slowly and bent halfway to my finger. "Go on…" Then he closed his eyes.

I touched his skin and an electrical shock zapped both of us. There was an audible *Zzzzt!* sound.

Flashes of Ricky's past flowed for a second before he leaned back and broke contact. He jumped back in the chair with his feet on the cushion. "What did you just do to me?" He was a little panicked. "I saw…I saw…I saw me. But I wasn't me. I saw me, and I was a woman, a man, a cat, and I think an alien!"

All I could think to say was, "Are you OK? Did I hurt you?"

He took a second. Then he shook his head *no*, "You didn't hurt me, but what did you do to me? I could see part of my life, well part of what I think was my soul's life." He rubbed his forehead where I'd touched him. "Ow, that stung."

"I'm sorry. I didn't know it would zap you."

"It's just a tingle. I'm alright." He rubbed it again furiously with his palm. Then he looked more seriously toward me. "I need to go through with this…please. I need to know more. I need answers to this voice that I keep hearing, and I can't stop now." He leaned forward again. "Do it! And don't stop this time."

"Are you sure?"

"I'm positive." He grabbed my arm and pulled until my finger was close to his head. He closed his eyes and urged, "Do it!"

"I am at your service." I regained my focus and felt the energy rise in my belly again. When it flowed down my arm, I uttered, "Here goes." Another electrical zap sparked loudly in the room when I connected with his skin. *Zzzzt!*

Lifetime upon lifetime flashed quickly inside of Ricky's mind. He saw everything from when his soul was created up to the present. Then his visions took him back to Baniti's life.

———————

"Tumaini," Baniti asked, "did you finish your parchments and scrolls?" He was working on his scrolls while we talked.

"Yes, I put them all in vases and buried them in the sand. I also used my magic to reunite me with them in the future. Would you help reinforce the magic that I used? I don't want to make a mistake. This is too important." I bowed to honor him.

"It is my honor to serve you. What you are doing is extremely admirable. You have worked very hard to ensure our success in the future." He looked at me again with his usual teacher's stare. "But don't you trust your own powers?"

I didn't answer right away, even though I knew I was being schooled. "I…" Then I looked down at the stone floor. "I don't know if what I am doing will work. I guess I needed some reassurance."

"Your intention is what is most important, Tumaini. Whether the future receives any hope or not is not entirely up to you. Others must also want this hope. You can't do it all for them." His words helped to heal my fear. "But I will add my powers to yours. From what you have shared with me about the future, *hope* could use a little extra help." He laughed, and I laughed with him.

He put down his brush and wiped his hands. "I've visited the timeline that you saw. When you finished your scrolls, I could see it more clearly. Your work has solidified it in the time-space continuum. What you have done is not just possible"—he paused and smiled—"it's now very probable."

"How do you know this?"

"I added my magic to your timeline already, but I will add more to the scrolls that you buried."

"Thank you. But what did you do before?"

"Do you remember when you visited all of those timelines and you found the one with the most chance for success?" I nodded *yes*. "And you also told me how you found your future self in Egypt and guided him to go into a store to be reunited with your parchments?" I nodded again. "I, too, visited my future self. I gave him a one-word message over and over again to follow as a clue. Then I saw your future self pass him in a horseless carriage. I guided him into a store where you were waiting for him. That is how we will be together again."

"You did?"

"Yes. And to be honest, what you have done is rather ingenious. All of the priests are talking about you and your efforts. Those who took the vow to wait amongst the stars have begun preparations for reuniting with your future self. The power of the Creator shines upon your plan, Tumaini."

"I don't know what to say, Baniti."

"You don't have to say anything. As a matter of fact, it is we who share our gratitude with you." He bowed toward me.

"Please don't. I'm just trying to help."

"We know. And if you wish, I can ask the others to strengthen this timeline and our chance for success."

"You don't need to ask me for permission. I want this to work. Let's do what we can to help."

"You are a good soul, Tumaini."

"Well, I had a good teacher."

He acknowledged my compliment and added, "It's settled, then. I'll get the others to set our final intentions for *hope's* return."

Bes and Talibah walked up. Bes asked, "Are we interrupting?" Talibah wiped away a few crumbs from the corner of his mouth.

"Not at all," I replied. "Baniti and I were just having a discussion about our future."

Talibah asked, "Can you tell us what we can do?"

I looked toward Baniti. He motioned. "This is your plan. You tell them how they can help."

"I will. Any other advice?"

"Yes. Don't forget to reactivate our powers"—he paused and looked into the future—"for those who forgot they had them."

"I'll do that."

Then I turned to Bes and Talibah. "Let me fill you in on the plan..."

After his vision, Ricky's mind made one more stop. He journeyed to the Source and made contact with the Creator. He felt the love of the Universe flow through his entire body. It surged through his veins and cleansed his soul completely. Since he had never felt so much kindness and love in his life, and because he wasn't prepared for it, the godly feeling overwhelmed him emotionally. He burst into uncontrollable tears of joy, and he wept.

I broke my contact with him and let him sit. He bent over, covered his eyes, and continued to weep.

Laura came by with a box of tissues. "Here, he might need this"—she bent down and whispered in my ear—"and I need to talk to you before you leave."

"Sure...and thanks." I grabbed the box and waited for Ricky to open his eyes again. A few people walked by with stares of curiosity, but no one else stopped or interfered.

When Ricky finally came back, he straightened up slowly. He was physically drained from his experience. "I don't know what to say."

"When you are ready, you can tell me what happened."

"I can tell you now. I remember. I remember everything. I remember all of it. I remember my lifetime with you. I remember all of my other thousands of lifetimes—some good and some bad—and I know why I am here right now. I even connected with Source again, and that's when I broke down into tears. I've never felt that kind of love before—at least not in this lifetime—and I feel healed. It completely caught me by surprise." He took the box and wiped his face with a tissue. After blowing his nose, he mentioned, "Just give me a minute. Then I have something to say to you."

He cleaned up a bit and regained his composure. "That was incredible. I'm me, but I remember myself as Baniti. I am Baniti, but in a new body. This is going to take a bit of time to…to…assimilate. I need to adjust to this. I don't know how else to explain it."

"I think you are doing pretty good right now. Take your time. I went through the same thing a few weeks ago."

"And what did you do?"

"I did what you are doing. I took my time to assimilate everything. And here I am."

"We need to contact the others. Are the others awake—Bes, Talibah—do you know?"

"As a matter of fact, yes. Well, some of them are awake. And I should be getting a report from Constance when I get home. Maybe all of them are awake."

"Constance? I don't recognize that name."

"She's my wife. I'll introduce you to her later. She's going to love this."

"How many others… This is strange. I'm Baniti, mixed with myself, in the same body. It's very confusing, you know."

"I know how you feel."

"Yes, you do, don't you?"

"At least I think I do. I'm still me, but with memories of my past. I'm not really Tumaini in the sense that Michael no longer exists. Tumaini is a part of me, but not all of me."

"That makes sense," he agreed. "So, I shouldn't let Baniti take over?"

"I don't think it works that way. Unless you lose yourself to your past, you are still you, and you are still living in the present. To me, you are Ricky with the memory of Baniti. Baniti had his life, and you have yours."

"That makes even more sense. Thanks."

"It helps to have someone who has gone through this before."

He stopped and shook his head to try and get a grip on what had just happened. "How many others are awake?"

"At last count, there were twelve of us. Except for me, they are all back in Egypt. And I left myself a clue about the other twenty-four. Excuse me"—I looked him right in the eyes—"twenty-three."

He acknowledged my correction, which helped him to believe in himself even more. Then he recalled, "Wait…let me…the Decans. There were thirty-six of us left before the pharaoh killed us. You mentioned that earlier." He grabbed the back of his neck. "I can still feel where the blade pierced my skin." He rubbed his neck some more. "That smarts."

"You must have remembered more than I have. I didn't feel anything like you did until I started time traveling."

"Who helped you to remember?"

"Her name is Ramla. She's the person I spoke to right before I helped you."

"I don't recognize that name, either." He was still rubbing his neck.

"I'll introduce you to the others. They've become really good friends to me."

"You were a good friend back then, too, Tumaini."

"You were a good teacher." He smiled from my compliment.

"I hope I can live up to my former self."

"I don't think you'll have any trouble with that, Ricky."

He closed his eyes again and scrunched his face. When he opened them, he reacted, "Whoa!"

"What is it?"

He reached his hand out like he was touching the air near my body. Then he curled his fingers and pawed as if he were trying to grab something.

"What are you doing, Ricky?"

He enunciated very slowly, "I…can…see…things. How…how did this happen?"

"What things?"

"This is freaky." He scrunched his eyes again. "I can see this energy-like stuff emanating from your body. It's almost like liquid, but it doesn't feel wet." He kept pawing at the air playfully. "That's so cool, mon."

"I never saw anything like that when I remembered."

"I think this is one of the advanced teachings from when I was Baniti. I can see your body."

"My body?"

"Yes. I can see the energy lines, your meridians that make up the body. You are all lit up."

"My what?"

He pointed at the books on the table. "Those. Do you see the acupuncture lines on the cover? Those are your meridians. And you have other energies emanating from you, too. You're one big massive glob of colors with streamers of energy flowing up and down your body."

"I think you have more teaching to do. I don't see what you are seeing."

"You will…in time." He kept playing with the air.

I yawned unexpectedly because I was tired, "Ricky, I need to get some sleep. I've been up for over thirty hours."

"I'm a little tired myself. That crying kind of wiped me out. I feel a little emotionally spent."

"I think I can help you out with that."

"You can?"

"Yes. Do you trust me?"

He gawked at me strangely. "Trust you? Are you kidding? You just helped me to remember who I am. Of course I trust you." I was going to speak again, but he continued, "Ah, I know what you are going to do. Go on. I'm ready."

I laughed, "I'm not sure I know what I was going to do."

"Yes, you do. You were going to give me a boost and help me regain some of my abilities. It's what Baniti would have done." He looked to his past. "Actually, it's what I told you to do when you were Tumaini."

"I was, wasn't I? I vaguely remember that, too." I started to move my hand and finger, but I stopped. "I wonder why I didn't have to do this with Gahiji and Asim."

"Gahiji and Asim?"

"Yes, they were Bes and Talibah."

"Oh, so they came back as Gahiji and Asim? I remember those names. I knew them. They were good souls."

I nodded, "They were—*are*," I chuckled. "But I didn't have to give them a boost." Then I remembered that Ramla did this for me when I first met her. "Hmm…strange. Maybe we all need this boost? Who knows?" I shrugged my shoulders. "At any rate, I'm going to send you as much energy as I can to help your powers. Take as much as you need."

He laughed, "I'll take what ever you give. I trust you."

I started to center myself and let the energy naturally build in my abdomen.

"Whoa! Now that's freaky."

"What?!" I exclaimed. "I didn't even touch you."

"I know. Your body"—he expressed with both hands—"it just lit up with energy. This massive ball of light grew in your stomach. I've never seen anything like that before. Well, at least not in this lifetime."

"Phew! Good. I though I did something bad."

"No, not at all." He pointed at my chest. "By the way, I can see that you are low on your B vitamins. You need to take some supplements."

"How did you...?" Then I remembered his ability to see my energy field. "Never mind. Are you ready?"

"Ready as I'll ever be." Then he said jokingly, "Throw the switch."

"OK. Here goes..."

He closed his eyes and bounced a little in his chair in anticipation. I reached over and felt a massive energy ball fill my entire body. When I connected with his forehead, all of the light bulbs in the store began exploding. Sparks went flying everywhere with loud *popping* noises echoing in the store. Some of the people reacted and immediately panicked. Some screamed and covered their bodies from the sparks and glass, while others dashed for cover. Where my finger was touching his skin, tiny purplish-white lightning bolts flew off in a three hundred and sixty degree fashion.

Laura was watching off in the distance. She saw what I had done and began running across the store toward us.

I kept my finger on Ricky's head. I could feel him accepting the energy into his entire body. As he filled up with power, I actually saw his aura glowing. Then I saw the streamers coming to life up and down the length of his body. They looked like moving street lights. "That's amazing!" I exclaimed.

When the last of the light bulbs popped and the sparks faded, Ricky opened his eyes, and I removed my finger. "Wow! What a rush!" He shook his head, and all of his dreadlocks spun in the air. "I feel super...mon."

Laura took her last few frantic steps and fell into a kneeling position by the table. She grabbed my arm. "You...you...you did shaktipat! You blew the entire store out. Who are you?!"

The emergency lights kicked on and the small amount of smoke provided an excellent backdrop to the scene. I smiled at her, "I am Tumaini, and this is Baniti. We came back to help bring hope to the world." Then I added jokingly, "I thought you were psychic?"

"Clairvoyant doesn't mean all-knowing," she said with a hint of defensiveness. "And whoever you are..." She stopped for a moment and collected herself. "I don't know what you are doing, what your purpose is, but I can tell it is good. I want in. You're the real deal! You have real powers!"

I just grinned. Then I thought, "It has begun."

"Laura, this is Ricky. Ricky, this is Laura."

She was confused and asked, "I thought you were...?"

"I know. Just call me Michael. It'll be easier." I turned my head to hear something better. I swear I could make out a low rumble off in the distance.

"Michael, who are you? How do you know how to do shaktipat?"

I thought of Ramla. "I had a very good teacher"—then I looked at Ricky—"two good teachers."

He replied, "If Baniti were here, he would be very proud of you."

I laughed, "He is here."

He smiled back, "Yeah, he is here," and he laughed with me.

The rumble was getting louder. The familiar sound of rotor blades slicing heavily through the wind was unmistakable. I glanced at Ricky and motioned to the door. "C'mon, I've got to see this."

Most of the people had already cleared out of the store in a panic. Some of them were hanging around outside and talking about what had happened. When Ricky and I stepped onto the sidewalk, followed by Laura, a red, unmarked Agusta helicopter flew into sight. It was the kind that looked like one of those corporate helicopters, and it was flying just above the power lines.

The noise was growing exceptionally loud. I looked toward the street and saw that it was empty, so I ran out to the middle for a better look. As the helicopter flew overhead, I did my best to look for numbers or markings, but there was nothing on it. It kept flying fast and low over the street for another block. Then it stopped abruptly and hovered in place.

Ricky and Laura were now beside me. He asked, "What's it doing?" Laura grabbed his arm for comfort.

While hovering, the helicopter slowly started to rotate ninety degrees to the left. When it stopped moving, it was broadside to us. I could see the pilot clearly through the window. He had on a white bubble-shaped helmet with black sunglasses. The window slid open, and he put his hand outside. He was looking directly at me, and I knew I had just been spotted.

Ricky shouted, "He's pointing something at us! Duck!"

Before we could run away, a low buzzing noise filled the air. We grabbed our ears and were immediately in pain. It hurt so badly that we fell down onto the street and were curled up like little babies. Everyone around us was screaming from the torture.

Ricky reached out and touched my arm. Amidst his agony, he managed to say, "Do something, mon! Please!"

My protective energy shield was weakening, which allowed the suffering to increase. I struggled, clenched my fists, focused on my abdomen, and felt an immense amount of energy filling my body. I tried to stand but couldn't get completely upright. I refocused one more time and got all of the way up, but the pain was too much. I fell into a kneeling position.

My body was trembling at this point. I pulled my right arm back like I was going to throw a punch. Then, instinctively, I flung it out and upward toward the helicopter and released everything from my stomach. I screamed, "Aaaaaaaaauuuuuuhhhhhh!"

An energy bubble blew from my body and expanded all of the way around the neighborhood. The shockwave instantly cleared out the negative effects of the pilot's weapon. At the same time, an energy ball flew from my hand and hit the pilot dead on, which caused him to drop his raygun. As my energy bubble continued to expand, the helicopter began violently rocking around in the sky from the shockwaves. It spun around helplessly for a good ten seconds like a furious rodeo bull and barely missed clipping some of the electrical wires. As the turbulence dissipated, the pilot regained control of his ship. He glared at me with his lifeless glasses, and then he flew out of sight.

I struggled to stand and muttered, "I was wrong. Now it has started."

Laura was scared. "What's started? Who are you? Just what's going on here?!"

Ricky stood up and reiterated, "We are Baniti and Tumaini, and we are here to help the world." He put his hand on my shoulder. "And I am with you, my old friend. It seems that the bad guys haven't given up."

I put my hand on his shoulder as well, "And I am with you. I'm glad you are back."

He mustered a laugh and said, "This is some welcome home party. I would rather have had some cake."

"I'm sorry for this, Ricky, but this is what I have been dealing with since I remembered a few weeks back."

Laura burst in, "Remembered?! Remember what?! Are you going to tell me what's going on?"

"It seems that the Order has made its presence known. C'mon guys, I want to get a good look at that gun, and then we need to get inside. There's a lot of work to do."

Ricky looked up to the sky for a moment. "Maybe I should rethink this and go back to sleep."

I started running toward the gun, followed by Ricky and Laura. She announced while panting, "Well, whoever you two are, I want in. Nobody attacks my shop and gets away with it."

"That's the spirit," I thought. "Maybe the sheeple are starting to wake up and will make a stand."

CHAPTER TWENTY-SEVEN

ABDUCTED BY THE ORDER

Laura's helper had already put up the *Closed* sign and was sweeping up the glass near the back. We walked in and crunched down on some of the remaining shards. In the people's panic, they had also knocked over some of her shelves and display racks. I picked up one of the racks and put it back in place. "Laura, I'll pay for any damages."

"Michael, don't you even think of it. You didn't do this. It was that guy in the helicopter." After bending down again, I held the bottom part of the light bulb and showed her that it was my fault. "OK, you broke the light bulbs, but you didn't do the rest of this."

I gave her a look that said: *Yes, it was my fault.*

"Alright, you blew out the light bulbs and scared my customers half to death, but I'm not going to charge you for it." After she picked up a clothes rack, she gave me a big smile. "Seeing you perform shaktipat—for real— was worth every light bulb." Ricky was helping her to upright another rack, and she continued, "Now, are you guys going to tell me what is going on?"

"I'm going to tell you the short, short version." I paused for a moment to get the right words. "There are some bad people and aliens out there who want to implant all of us and capture our souls."

She had a disappointed look on her face, which threw me off. "What?" I asked with my shoulders shrugged and hands outturned.

"I thought you were going to tell me something new. A very small number of us in the psychic community already know about this."

Ricky asked, "So this is nothing new to you?"

"Well, not to us. But we're just a tiny number—barely noticeable—and we can't make a difference on our own yet. No one will take us seriously. It's the... What did you think outside, Michael? Oh yes. You said 'the sheeple' in your mind." She looked at me and grinned, "Yes. I'm psychic. I heard your thoughts." Then she continued, "It's the masses who need to learn about this and wake up." She picked up the last clothes rack. "Is that what you two are doing? Is that why you came back?"

I sighed in relief, "Thank goodness we don't have to try and convince you. And to be honest, I think we are here to do more than just tell people. I think time is running out very fast, and telling the people won't do anything. We have to stop them. Now!"

Ricky asked, "Stop them? How?"

"I left myself clues, remember? Whatever I'm supposed to do—whatever *we* are supposed to do—could give the people a chance to change how they are living."

Laura shook her head, "Michael, these people are really plugged in to this fake life that the aliens and governments created. It would take something drastic for them to change."

"I agree with you. But I can't give up hope. We have to try something."

Ricky added, "Yes, we do. So, what's your plan?"

"First off"—I held the parts of the gun toward her—"do you have somewhere to keep this? We can research this later and see how we can dismantle their weapons—or at least find a weakness."

"Yes, I can keep it locked up in my safe." She took them from me and set them on the counter.

Ricky nodded, "Yes, dismantle their weapons. That's a good hunch. I like that plan. Then what?"

"I need to find out if there are any updates from Egypt. What's going on is connected there, I think." I saw the time on my watch. "Speaking of updates, I need to get home soon. Constance is going to get worried."

"But we aren't done here yet," exclaimed Laura. "What can we do? We need some guidance before you leave."

"Yeah, what can we do?"

I thought back to the clues. "Some of this has to do with the scrolls, I know it. I know there is a plan penned on them to help the people rebuild the world."

"Your scrolls. I remember those scrolls."

"What scrolls?" asked Laura.

"They're called the God Scrolls. They have messages to teach the people about life and how to live peacefully together."

"And what does this have to do with Egypt? I don't understand."

"I think we have to learn from modern-day Egypt." I paused to gather my thoughts. "Do you remember when the people rose up against the government in Cairo and it fell? Well, the people didn't have a plan to rebuild their political system before they toppled the government. Then it turned right back into a military state. If the people don't have a plan ahead of time—a plan that leads toward peace—then the same thing will happen all over again. Egypt is a prime example. The aliens and the military have this thing locked up."

Ricky agreed, "That makes sense, but the people need to be able to..." He stopped. "These people aren't ready yet, Michael. And they don't have a chance if the aliens and the military are in on it."

"I know. That's where we come in. It's up to all of the priests. I have a feeling that we will be able to do something that will help."

Laura implored, "This all sounds encouraging, but what can we do?"

"Ricky, where do you live? Are you here in town?" I inquired.

"No, I came from upstate. I kept following Baniti's voice—my voice—until I got here."

"Laura?"

"I live here."

"Right..." I knew it was a stupid question. "Can you help Ricky while I get some rest? We can meet at my home in the morning before I have to teach, say around nine o'clock?"

"Sure, and I can help find him a place to stay."

"Great, I can come over tomorrow." He winked. "Besides, what else am I going to do? I came back to help you, Tumaini. I'm sure not going to stop right now."

"Thanks for your support, old friend."

Laura looked at me. "Old friend?" She pointed back and forth between the two of us. "But you are older than he is."

"That's another story for another time. But to give you a clue, he was my former teacher in another lifetime."

"Back in ancient Egypt, right?"

"Right," I nodded. "Are both of you OK? Can I head back home?"

Ricky answered, "Sure, I'll be fine."

Laura added, "And I'll help him out."

"Good. Before I go, let me write down my address and phone number. Give me a call if anything important comes up." I handed them both a piece of paper.

"I know where this street is. I shouldn't have any trouble getting there." She offered to Ricky, "I can give you a ride, if you'd like."

"That'd be great."

With some renewed hope, I said, "I think we can make a difference, team. Let's call it a day and meet up tomorrow."

Ricky put his hand on my shoulder. "Tomorrow it is. We can make a difference."

Laura agreed, "Yes, we can."

"Hi, honey, I'm home!" I yelled. "Where is everyone?" I walked to the kitchen to see if there was a note. "Nope. No note."

The door to the backyard was ajar. Right when I reached for the handle, Constance and Hara walked up.

"Hi, dear. I didn't know you were home."

"I just got in." She kissed me hello.

"Hi, Hara." I gave her a quick hug.

"Mommy and me were outside. We planted a new tree."

"You did?!"

Constance added, "Yes, we put it in the back corner. I thought it would give us a little bit of shade for our flower garden in the summer. It was part of our homeschool project."

"That's a great idea."

"Hara, go wash up for dinner."

"OK," and she scampered up the stairs.

"You look exhausted. Did your class go well?"

"I had a great class. And…"

"And what?"

"I don't know where to begin." I yawned really big, "I showed Ted the scroll, and the letters appeared again."

"Wow! What was his reaction?"

"Just like the other night. He was excited, and then he felt like this was out of his league."

"I know how he feels. This is way out of my league, too."

"And then, I used the scroll in class. When I held it, I think I was channeling some higher consciousness—maybe even God."

"God?"

"Yes…maybe. It's hard to know. The voice never said who or what it was. All I know is that it gave some pretty incredible advice. My students were stunned."

"I'll bet they were. Can you tell me what the voice said?"

"Yes, but I need to tell you something else first."

She glared at me with a little concern. "What?"

"I met my old teacher from Egypt—Baniti. He showed up at the metaphysical shop."

She exclaimed, "You're kidding!"

"No, and there's more. I helped him to remember, just like Ramla helped me. And then…"

She stopped preparing dinner and looked up. "Then what?"

"I gave him a jolt of energy, and a red helicopter came." Her eyes got big. "Then the helicopter stopped, turned—I saw the pilot—then he shot something at us. It was like Egypt all over again."

"Oh my gosh! Are you alright? Did he hurt you?"

"I'm fine. We're all fine. But something new happened."

"What? Are you sure you're OK? You look awful."

"I'm just tired, honest. I was able to fend off the helicopter. I think my powers are getting stronger. I sent out an energy blast, and the shockwaves almost made the helicopter crash."

"You're kidding!"

"No. And we even recovered the weapon he fired at us. Laura has it in her safe."

"Who's Laura?"

"She owns the metaphysical shop. She's coming over tomorrow morning with Ricky."

She asked a little louder, "Who's Ricky?"

"Sorry, he's Baniti. Real nice fellow, too."

"Hon, this is getting really strange."

"Getting?" I chuckled.

"It's hard to keep up with everything. So much is happening so fast."

"I know. But everyone is alright. No one suffered any real harm."

"Good. Is there anything I can do?"

"Yes, just keep taking care of Hara for the day. I'll take over on the weekend as much as I can. I need to get some rest."

"Are you going to have any dinner?"

"No, I'm too exhausted. I think I'm just going to go upstairs and go to sleep."

"Do you need me to wake you for anything?"

"No, but thanks for asking."

Before I walked away, Constance added, "By the way, I spoke with Rehema today."

"Yes?"

"She's a wonderful person. She speaks very highly of you. And we had some great girl talk."

"She is wonderful, isn't she? She also gives me way too much credit."

"I think she's spot on. Don't sell yourself short." She went back to preparing dinner.

I yawned really big. "I can barely keep my eyes open, I'm so tired." I yawned again. "Did she say anything else?"

"She did. I wrote it all down so I wouldn't forget. She mentioned more priests were awake. And they think they've found something important, but they want you to call them so Hanif can explain it—something about their seers."

"That's nice." My mind was already shutting down and not comprehending everything that she was saying. I still asked, though, "Did you fill them in on the news from here?"

She saw the fading look in my eyes. "You're exhausted. Why don't you go upstairs and sleep? I'll tell you everything in the morning."

I yawned one more time, "I will. Thanks, hon, you're a peach." I leaned over and gave her a quick peck on the cheek. "'Night," and I stumbled off to bed.

I was under the covers when I remembered something that Ramla had said. I was supposed to help Rehema with her telepathy. "How do I do that?" I struggled to think. After reviewing what I had learned so far, I snickered, "Time to ring the bell. All I have to do is focus, think of her, call her name, and send a message—simple." I was already half asleep, but I wanted to help her with her abilities. Breathing in deeply, I called in my mind, "Rehema, hear me. Rehema, hear me. Rehema, hear me. This is Tumaini. Hear me, Rehema." I waited, but there was no reply.

My body was physically wiped of energy. I knew I had used most of it while helping Baniti and fending off the helicopter. I was extremely weak, and I felt it. I was so tired that I didn't remember to re-energize my shield. Then I drifted off and all went black.

My soul, my ka, left my body and went to the place where all souls go when we sleep: the dream world, the space between the physical and the Realm of Souls. This is the place where reptilians and other demons troll to inflict nightmares and harm to the souls of men.

———•—•———

Across town, students from my 201 class began meeting with their partners. Phillip was paired with Bruce for the service assignment. He arrived at Bruce's fraternity house at the scheduled time. He stood patiently in the main room and waited about ten minutes for him to show.

From the upstairs balcony, Bruce yelled down, "Dude, what's up?!" He briskly and loudly trumped down the steps because he was a few minutes late. He slapped the side of Phillip's shoulder hard. "Sorry about the wait, dude. I just got off the phone with my girlfriend." His face changed to a sour look. "Well, now my ex-girlfriend."

Phillip was a little disturbed by the hard hit on his arm. That's not the usual greeting he was used to, or liked. He wasn't as physical with other guys, never played sports, and didn't seem to fit in with most rough activities. "What happened?"

"It's nothing. It was bound to end. She was all moody and stuff and complained that I didn't pay enough attention to her. Can you imagine that? I called her every chance I got and took her out at least once a week. Women! Who knows how to please them?"

He hit Phillip's arm once more, which made his body tilt to one side.

"C'mon, let's go upstairs and do this assignment." Phillip frowned and rubbed his arm.

Bruce led the way, followed closely by Phillip. He turned and asked, "Is this the first time you've been to a frat house? We're having a party tonight."

He nodded meekly, "I was never asked to pledge or anything."

"Well, most frats don't go after people—that is, unless they are hurting for members. We're doing pretty good, so you'd have to come to us."

"That makes sense."

Bruce changed the subject. "So what do you think of that last class? The professor sounded pretty strange when he held that paper."

"I liked it. I thought what he had to say was brilliant. Somebody needs to make a change in this world, don't you think?"

"Yeah, I like what he said. It just sounded...well...not like his voice. I couldn't tell if he was serious or not. He was acting weird."

"I think he's a great teacher," he countered a little defensively.

"Oh, don't get me wrong; I like his class. That's why I signed up for it. It was just different. I've never seen him do that before."

"Me, neither."

Bruce turned to him outside of his room. "Hey, what about this assignment? Have you thought about what I could do for you? I need to get a good grade in his class to keep my GPA up." He unlocked his door and they both went in. "Have a seat." He pointed to the chair at the desk while he flopped down heavily on his bed. Then he clasped his hands behind his head.

Phillip hesitated, "Promise you won't laugh?"

He gave a Boy Scout sign to him. "Promise." Then he returned his hand behind his neck.

"Well, I've never had a girlfriend before, and I don't have too many guy friends, so I need some help."

"What kind of help?" he laughed hard. "Do you mean that you want me to hook you up or somethin'?"

"No. Well...nothing like that. I just need someone to talk to. I could use a guy's advice."

Bruce sat up on his bed a little. "Don't you have a dad?"

"Nah. My dad left us when I was about four or five. It was me, my mom, and my two sisters."

"Sorry, dude," he stressed with some remorse, "that must have sucked."

"We did OK. My mom did the best she could to raise us and all, but I never had a guy friend to confide in or ask questions to. I don't even know where to start with a girl."

"Well, shoot, I can help you some. But after what happened today, I'm not sure I'm the right person for the job." He laughed in light of his situation.

Phillip nodded his head in acknowledgement. Then he picked up his backpack and pulled out his notebook from class. "So, what is it that I can do for you?"

"For starters, you can put away your notebook. Let's just chill and hang out for a bit." Then he sat up completely and chimed with that I've-got-a-new-idea voice, "I know…when my roommates get back, we'll hang out with you and give you all of our best moves and advice for picking up chicks and stuff. We'll tell you all the things we did that worked, and everything that didn't."

"I don't know," he said with a little reservation. "This assignment was supposed to be between the two of us."

"C'mon, dude, nothing to be embarrassed about. All of us had to learn sometime."

Phillip thought for a moment. "OK, but please don't tell them that I don't know what I am doing. It's tough enough confiding like this as it is."

"I think they'll know anyway. Don't you think?"

"Probably." He paused and tilted his head. "You've got a point." He put his pad back into his pack. "So what do you want me to do for you?"

"Just hang with me for the night at the party. I may look all tough and stuff, but I have feelings, too. It sucks being dumped by your girlfriend. The guys here are cool and all, but they can be really cruel at times. Just hang with me, and maybe we can pick up some girls together."

"Alright, I can do that."

"Great. Let's talk about girls."

———— • ————

Hara was in bed by 8:00 p.m., and Constance called it an early night and followed right behind her. By that time, I had already been in and out of sleep for three hours. I could tell that something wasn't right, but I was too tired to react to the warning signs I'd been feeling. I kept having visions of men in military uniforms and very tall beings in heavy black cloaks in the astral realm. I was completely surrounded.

In my stupor, I heard, "He is the one." It looked like they were staring at a monitor of some type. The screen had four sections to it. One of the pictures had the red helicopter with me standing on the street; another screen had the plane with the UFO flying by; a screen below it showed the desert with our tour group on horses near the pyramid; and the screen beside it showed me holding the God Scroll in class.

One of the cloaked figures growled ominously, "Hsssss. He is the one. We need to implant him now and hook him up to the machine." The military officers agreed. Then two of the cloaked figures started touching buttons and sliding green, clawed fingers on a control panel.

What seemed to be the leader of the reptilians commanded in a low, raspy, hissing-like voice, "Hsssss. He is a strong one. Not easy to control. We will need to attach them directly to his ka." After a few more buttons were pushed, they placed me in an energy bubble and used a voice inhibitor. This stopped me completely from being able to call out for help.

One of the military men was new to the procedure and asked, "What are you going to do?"

A reptilian at the monitor turned toward the leader with his scaly finger over a button. The leader nodded and gave its approval. "Hsssss. We have just placed Ring of Torture implants on the crown of his head. This group of implants will cause him agony day and night and will drain his resistance. It will feel like a constant, painful pressure to him."

It looked at the reptilian on the left and gave a guttural command. The reptilian followed the order and turned a knob to the right. In my sleep, I groaned in pain, but not loud enough to wake Constance.

"Hsssss. We can fluctuate this with an artificial intelligence program. When he meditates or does anything spiritual, it will activate the machine to make him angry and hateful. It will keep him from becoming godly. Hsssss."

The new recruit gulped, "Have you done this before?"

"Hsssss. Yesssss, to many of your spiritual people, those not working with greed or money. Hsssss. We keep all of them from reaching their full psychic potential."

I tried to fight them off and scream for help, but I was incapacitated somehow by the energy bubble. I was helpless against their evil efforts.

The commanding reptilian made a new sound, and the reptilian on the right maneuvered a different set of knobs.

"Hsssss. Implanted his stomach, gall bladder, and bladder meridians, we did. This will amplify his fear and control his thoughts."

One of the older military men tapped the new recruit. "They are very thorough at this. Keep watching."

The new member whispered, "These guys are really sadistic."

"You haven't seen anything yet. Keep watching."

The reptilian leader gave another guttural command, and the reptilian on the right touched more buttons. "Hsssss. We have just applied two psychic inhibitors: one to stop his frontal lobe from becoming more activated and the other to block his endocrine brain. He will not be able to reach full power with these in place."

The new guy motioned to the older man, "These reptilians are going full out. Why is this guy so important?"

The head reptilian overheard his question and answered, "Hsssss. He is the leader of the priests. If he fails, the others will fail. He is the key to their success."

Then the reptilian leader turned toward the ranking officer. "Hsssss. Is your mainframe ready to control the people on your planet?"

"We are close. Another two weeks to work out all of the problems, then we will be ready to initiate the takeover of the world."

The new recruit asked, "Why don't you just kill him now?"

"Hsssss. We want him to suffer. We feed on suffering. Then we will send him back for more suffering. Your human implants will control him even more. He must suffer for us to feed."

The reptilian gave a clicking command to the two at the console. "Hsssss. When we are done, we can control his movements easily. Normally, we can do this to a weak soul, but his is strong. We need implants to control his muscles." It continued after another command. "We will attack his family and vulnerable students. It is up to you to discredit him on your planet."

The ranking military officer said to the new recruit, "We *are* the military. We're experts at lies and deception. And if there is one thing we know how to do well, it's to discredit, kill, or buy off those who won't join us." He turned toward the reptilian. "He won't be a problem."

The reptilian hissed in anger, "Hsssss. Do not underestimate this one. He is strong."

"Don't worry. We can handle a college teacher."

"Hsssss." It raised its claws at him. "Do not be a fool! You have not dealt with this type of magic before. He is powerful, this one."

The officer was worried by the anger from the reptilian. "We will handle this. I assure you." A bead of sweat formed on his forehead.

"Hsssss. Do not fail us. If he is not stopped, he could disrupt all of our plans."

"He will be bought off, just like the rest. We've paid scores of professors and scientists to do contract work for us at DARPA. He'll take the money. If he doesn't, we'll make up something and completely destroy his reputation. He'll be in jail before you know it."

"Hsssss! He is different. Control of energy, he has. Can hurt us if we are not careful."

"Then we will dispose of him."

"Hsssss. Not until he suffers. We must feed." The new recruit was a little scared. He'd never seen this type of behavior from the other alien contacts.

"Hsssss. What will you do to discredit him? Tell us now!"

"If you locate his vulnerable students, we will get them guns this weekend and use our voice and brain control technology to turn them against this guy. We have done this rather successfully in many schools. You know this. You have seen it on your screens."

"Hsssss. Yesssss, we have seen this work at times. Do not fail with this one. He must be stopped. Hsssss."

"It will be done."

The military men stood by while the reptilians began their final attack. Thousands of etheric, web-like strands were coming out of their soul-catcher machine and surrounding my body. They were attaching to every chakra center, acupuncture point, nadi, and the entire spine on my ka. I mentally tried to pull them off of my body, but there were too many. I was too tired and lacked the energy to get free. Eventually, I had thousands of tiny hair-like strands connected to me.

The officer said to the new guy, "The intent is that these energy strands will capture his soul and return it to the reptilian machine when he dies. Then they can put his soul in a new body on Earth. When the baby is born, either they will implant the brain, or they will instruct us to implant the baby with our implants. Either way, it will be under our complete control—docile, submissive, and subservient, just like they need to be."

The new guy grimaced, "That's one effective system."

"It's almost in place. Once we turn on our mainframe, nothing will be able to stop us. Not to mention, we have an upgrade for their soul-capture device in the works. It should be ready within days."

"Who's behind this? I mean, I know these reptilians are, but who's running the show on Earth?"

"The Anunnaki bloodlines. You won't ever see them, but follow the money...if you can. They are very good at keeping themselves out of the public eye. They hide their faces as well as their money." He continued after a short pause, "And don't ever get on their bad side. If you do, they'll send one of their Illuminati handlers or henchmen to mess up your life. Those are some sadistic people."

He had a look of fear on his face. "I'll keep my nose clean. I saw what they did to those two skyscrapers."

"Fear! That's what does it every time. Remember that. Control with fear."

"I will."

The reptilian turned to the men. "Hsssss. We must initiate the artificial intelligence programs. They will learn his speech and thought patterns to control his mind over the next few days. He will be under our complete control soon."

"This is insidious," the new guy thought.

They all turned and left my view. I felt my ka being returned to my body, and I fell into a deep sleep.

The music was blaring through the speakers in the frat house, and the subwoofer created a low drone throughout every room.

Bruce shouted, "This is a great party. Just look at all the girls." He pointed to two who were hanging out at the wall with drink cups in their hands.

Phillip put his hand to his ear because it was so loud and screamed, "What?!"

Bruce waved to him. "C'mon. Let's go mingle."

He walked Phillip over and introduced him to the girls. "Girls, this is Phillip. Phillip, this is the girls. He needs some company tonight. Can you help him out?"

One of the girls giggled and handed him a cup. "You look like you could use a drink."

He screamed back, "Thanks, but I don't drink!"

"Oh, c'mon," she smiled. "It's a party. Liven up some!"

Bruce added, "Yeah, Phillip, liven up some." He winked at the girl. "You wanted to know how to serve me. Well, have a drink with me. I could use the support. Remember…my ex-girlfriend and all."

"Well, I really don't like to drink."

The girl moved his cup to his lips and tipped it to make him drink. "Just one sip. It won't hurt." She winked at him. "I promise." He gulped down the sour beer and winced.

"That's the spirit. Have another." She tipped his cup again.

After coughing and wiping the beer from his chin, he asked Bruce, "Is this what guys do to get girls?"

She laughed and answered before he could reply, "No, silly. We choose the guys." The other girl nodded in agreement. She took a sip and continued, "If we don't like the guy, there's no chance we'll go out with him."

Bruce grinned at Phillip, "Take some notes, dude. She's right."

"I can't. I don't have my notepad."

The other girl laughed, "He's cute."

Then the first girl added, "Now that's what we like. Making a girl laugh is a good start."

"So, I did good?"

"Well, it's a start. Do you dance?"

"I'm not very good at it."

Bruce stated, "I like to dance. Let's all go downstairs and dance."

"I don't think I should," Phillip protested shyly.

The first girl stroked his arm. "Don't be shy. I'll show you how. It's easy. Just move your hips to the beat…like this." She wiggled and danced with her hands up in the air. Then she squealed, "Woohoo! Dancing is fun."

Bruce leaned in to his ear. "If you want to get the girl, do what she wants. Dancing is a great start."

Phillip took another drink, winced, and sighed, "Here goes nothing."

The girls screamed and grabbed his arm. "Let's go dancing!" His drink spilled some on the way.

For the rest of the night, Phillip and Bruce kept drinking and dancing with the girls. By midnight, everyone was drunk, flirting, and laughing. Bruce leaned over to Phillip and lisped in a buzzed voice, "Thankth, man. I appreciate you." He pushed him hard with his finger. "I needed a friend tonight. You can write down that you therved me."

He yelled back in a drunken slur while pushing Bruce with his finger, "You...you...you therved me thtoo!" The girls laughed hysterically.

"He's drunk off his butt," the first girl giggled.

"Yeah, he's toasted," added the second girl. "Let's get him another drink."

Bruce took Phillip's cup away. "Nah, he's had enough. One more and I'll have to carry him home."

"Party pooper," she teased, and playfully slapped his arm.

"Hey Bruthe, I can't feel my legth." The girls laughed again.

"You can sleep on the couch in my room."

The first girl asked, "What about us?"

"You can sleep on the couch, too." She leaned over and gave Bruce a kiss on the cheek. He grinned and nodded upward, "Let's go upstairs."

Both girls looked at each other. They gave the secret signal that it was OK and followed the guys up to Bruce's room.

———————

Meanwhile, on the reptilian ship, the head reptilian sent out a number of djinn to search for any students whose defenses were down. They were instructed to tag the targets with tracking devices so the military could use their mind control weapons on them.

The only two students who were incapacitated that night were Phillip and Bruce. After the girls had given the guys their numbers and left, the djinn attacked the boys without mercy, tagged them, and reported back to the head reptilian. Then the order was given to the military on Earth to immediately start the enhanced CIA MKUltra assassin programming.

Both Bruce and Phillip had no idea what had just happened. They passed it off as a terrible nightmare from drinking too much. Unfortunately for them, the subconscious programming had already begun.

The military were back in the room with the reptilians and watched the attack through the djinns' eyes. The older military officer reported, "In a day or two, they'll start hearing voices telling them to hate, torture, and kill anyone who stands against their country. They'll accept all commands to assassinate any target given to them by their Illuminati handlers."

The new recruit asked, "How do you do this?"

"This programming is projected through a voice frequency modulator with embedded hidden commands. To the victim, it sounds like tinnitus at first—ringing in the ears. And with the advanced technology we have, we can turn that signal into audible words. The human brain eventually entrains to this frequency, so there is no conscious defense against this weapon. We've broken thousands of people this way and made them perform mass killings and other nasty stuff. We do this mainly to induce fear in the people or to take out self-empowered individuals."

"Do you mean like students opening fire in schools and movie theaters?"

"Yes, that was us. We want the people running to the police and military for protection instead of *realizing* that the police and military are the bad guys behind all of this."

"That's like a living nightmare."

"It works, and that's all that matters to us."

"Glad I'm with the Order." The older man just nodded.

———————

The attack also heightened in my bedroom. One reptilian dimensionally shifted inside of our room and lay on top of Constance. The reptilian hissed in her ear while taking great pleasure in dominating her with its mind and body. It left after ingesting all of her fear energy.

On the ship, the commanding reptilian gave the order to initiate the body-control program. The programmer used the new brain implants to induce specific muscle movements. The sadistic being kept me in my dream state while making me form a fist. Then, the evil reptilian raised my arm and slammed my fist down on Constance's chest. We both woke up instantly.

"Oh my gosh! I'm so sorry. I had no control. I was manipulated in my sleep. I'm so sorry!"

Constance was still trying to come out of her enforced sleep state. When she realized what the reptilian had done to her, she rolled over into my arms and started crying.

"I'm so sorry," I kept repeating. "They were controlling me."

"It violated me!" she sobbed some more. "It violated me and took my energy." She made a fist into the covers, pulled it to her face, and she screamed.

"I'm sorry for hitting you. I was forced to do it. Are you OK?"

403

"It violated me!" she cried even harder. "You didn't do it. It was them. Those dirty...I hate them!" Tears were streaming down her cheeks.

"What can I do?" I was frantic.

"No woman should ever go through that. Promise me you'll do something. It was a reptilian. It held me down and stole my energy."

I held her tight. "I promise, Constance. I promise."

I didn't go to sleep for the rest of the night. I tried to re-energize myself and put up a shield around her, Hara, and our house, but something was wrong. While I was doing this, I could feel tiny muscle spasms all over my body: my hands, knees, underarms, elbows, nose, and temples flinched uncontrollably. I knew something else was wrong, too, but I didn't know what it was or what to do. All I could do was hope that I could make a difference.

CHAPTER TWENTY-EIGHT

TAG, YOU'RE IT

Constance was quiet when she got up. I could tell that she was still upset from the reptilian attack. "What can I do to help, Constance?" I asked with partially closed eyes. I was holding the side of my head from the immense pain I was feeling.

She didn't respond right away. When she finished making the bed and slapping the pillows extra hard, she cursed, "They are evil...pure evil. I can't believe you've gone through this kind of stuff for the last few weeks." I knew she was extremely angry because her vein was pulsing on her temple. "They need to be stopped. Better yet, they need to be killed."

The pressure on my head was growing in intensity. It felt like a vice with long metallic, barbed spikes poking into my eyes, ears, and skull. The pain was becoming excruciating, and I fell on the bed with both hands covering my face. This was accompanied by a loud single pitch ringing in my left ear.

Constance noticed me holding my head. "What's wrong? What did they do to you?"

I struggled to speak. "I was attacked last night. When I was in the astral realm, they attached things to my body. My head feels like it is on fire. The pressure is intense."

On the ship, the reptilian turned a knob on the panel.

———•◦•———

I screamed, "Aaarrrrgggghhhh!"

Constance ran to my side. "Michael! What? What? What can I do?"

"I don't know. The pain is… Aaaaahhhh! It hurts!"

"How can I help you?" She knelt down trying to get me to look at her.

"Something is piercing my flesh. I feel these jabs all over my head and body, and this ringing won't stop."

Constance held my hands and noticed the muscle spasms on the side of my head. "What is that? Your skin is pulsing."

"I think it's muscle spasms." I groaned again, "Aaaahhhh!"

"I'm going to call a doctor."

"No. They won't know what is going on. They'll think I'm crazy."

"You aren't crazy. I'll tell them that."

I bent over again in pain. Then I grabbed one of the small pillows and put it on my stomach and crunched down. "They won't care what you say. They don't believe in this stuff. They'll just say I'm losing it and put me on heavy medication." I grabbed the back of my head. "Don't trust them. They work for the pharmaceutical companies."

"Who should I call?"

"I don't know." I rocked back and forth from the pain. "Just don't call them." She began rubbing my back trying to relieve the discomfort.

———•◦•———

The reptilian on the ship was satisfied with the results. It turned the knob and the pain receded slightly. Then it initiated the artificial intelligence program and turned to its commander. "Hsssss. Priest is now controlled by the machine."

The head reptilian ordered, "Hsssss. Set the level on low and have it increase every day when he wakes up. Then power the machine down while he sleeps. Add this to his program." The reptilian at the monitor touched the control panels and made the adjustments.

———•◦•———

I gave one last groan, "Something just happened. The pain isn't as intense as before. It's like someone flipped a switch, and all of the sudden it's not as bad."

"Are you OK? Can you stand?"

"It still hurts. There's something on the top of my head. I can feel it. It's like it is invading my brain. I can feel these *things* moving down into my skull." I grabbed my head and tried to pull them off, but nothing came loose. When I grabbed again, I could feel an energy field surrounding my body. I told Constance, "It's like I'm covered in a terrible static electricity. I can grab at it, but I can't pull it off." I tried again. "I…can't…get…this…off!"

"Can I try?"

"Yes…please…" She mimicked what I did and pulled around my head. Nothing came off.

"Did I do anything?"

I felt around my body to check. "I can still feel this thing on my head. I don't know…" I looked up at her. "Thanks for trying."

"I feel so helpless. I hate that you are going through this."

"I think that's what they want us to feel—helpless. I think it makes them feel powerful." I could tell I wasn't helping her with my statement, so I asked, "How are you doing? Is there anything I can do for you?"

"I'm not in pain like you are."

"Good, but what about the other thing?"

"I'm coping." I looked at her because I knew she was holding back. "OK, I'm mad—mad as hell! If this is what it is going to be like in the future under this Order *thing*, then they have to be stopped."

"I agree." I grabbed at my temple when I felt the next spasm. "What is this thing? When I pulled at the skin in that area, it made something in my second to last toe move."

"What?"

I did it again. "When I pull here, it makes something move on my foot." I reached down and put my hand over my toes. Nothing happened at first. Then I felt something bumping around on my toes and in my hand. I quickly pulled my hand off to look, but I couldn't see anything."

"What is it?"

"I can feel something bumping around on my toes." I reached down again and covered them. "There. It happened again." I pulled my hand off.

"I can feel them in my temples and feet, but I can't see them."

The word *bumping* brought back a memory. "I have an idea." The pain in my head increased slightly at that exact moment. I put my hand on my crown for relief, and the pain lessened some. "I think I've read this before."

I walked to my study and looked at Omar's letter. "Here, look." I pointed to a section of the paper and read:

> "The dark beings who live beneath the surface have corrupted the pharaoh's thoughts. They put living things in his head and body that slowly took over his mind. With the pharaoh's thoughts controlled and his will depleted, the dark beings were able to capture his ka—they captured his living soul. With his ka in their possession, they can control his mind and his body like a puppet on a string.
>
> "We, the priests, the Protectors of Souls, can feel these things in our bodies, too. They thump beneath our skin and skull when we touch them. Humans cannot see these evil things—even our priests could not see them—but the priests could sense them with their special vision, the vision only possible through meditation and prayer."

I told Constance, "This is what they did to me last night. I'm sure of it. I remember feeling this as Tumaini, too, but I don't remember how we removed them."

"Maybe Rehema can help."

"It's possible, but her abilities haven't started yet, at least not that I know of."

"What about Baniti? Can he do anything?"

"Ricky? It's possible, too. He knew about these things when he was Baniti." I bent down a little from another shot of pain. "I can feel a ring-type thing on my head. It's piercing into my brain, I swear it is." I grabbed the sides of my head again. "The pressure is almost too much to handle. I need to go lie down."

Constance walked me back into the bedroom. "I think you need to cancel your class today."

I curled up into a tight fetal position with my hands still on my head. I noticed something and explained, "When I put my hands here, it seems to interfere with whatever it is they are doing. It lessens the pain somehow."

"Can you keep doing it until Ricky comes?"

"I don't have a choice." Another piercing wave hit my brain and I winced.

Constance picked up the phone. "I'm going to call Ted. Maybe he knows what to do."

"Yes, call Ted. He might be able to help. Call him quick, please."

"I'm on it."

For the next two hours, I stayed on my bed and battled with the pain. I tried to send energy balls to disintegrate the ring on my head, but I felt that my power had been stopped somehow. I couldn't even put up my shield. It was like someone had completely turned off all of my abilities and powers.

Bruce and Phillip were waking up to Bruce's alarm clock. Phillip said with a severe case of dry mouth, "I feel awful." He smacked his lips to get some saliva going. He also noticed that his head was buzzing and asked, "Is this what a hangover feels like?"

After stretching his arms, Bruce mumbled, "You had a little too much to drink last night. But hey, you got the girl's number." He threw his pillow at him and hit his head. "Way to go, champ!"

Bruce put his finger in his ear and wiggled it a number of times. He couldn't figure out why it was ringing so loud.

Phillip moaned, "I'm never going to drink again. My head is ringing. It's like someone's playing a single note in my ear and it won't stop."

"My head's ringing, too." He popped the side of his head with his palm. "I've never had a problem like that after a party."

"Maybe it's from all of that loud music."

"No, this is different, trust me. I know what that sounds like, and this isn't it."

The ringing in both of their ears changed some. It grew in intensity, like someone had turned up the volume on a stereo slowly. It remained loud for ten seconds, and then it diminished back to its starting volume.

"Whoa, my ear did something funky," exclaimed Bruce.

"Mine, too. That ringing got louder."

"Yeah, that's strange," he said a little more angrily. "Do you think the girls put something in our drinks?"

"No, those were nice girls. They wouldn't do that."

Bruce shook his head hard with his loose cheeks slapping in the air. "I hope this stops soon. It's hard to concentrate on anything else."

Phillip's answer was a little sharp for his personality. "Can you stop talking so loud? Sheesh!"

That threw Bruce off some. "Sorry, dude. I must be talking loud so I can hear myself over this ringing." He didn't really feel angry toward Phillip, but he didn't have control over how he responded to him next. "Maybe you should go, dude, if I'm too loud for you."

Phillip jerked his head back in surprise. "Well, if you're going to be that way about it. I thought you were becoming my friend." He picked up his backpack and started heading toward the door.

After realizing what he'd done, Bruce took a step toward Phillip with a stop gesture. "Wait, Phillip. I didn't mean to say that. Something weird came over me."

He was already opening the door and turned around. He felt something strange, too, and thought for a second. "Yeah, I snapped back at you as well, and I didn't want to say anything mean. Do you think it has to do with this pitch in our ears?"

"I don't know, could be." He walked over to Phillip. "Sorry, dude, I didn't mean it. You can stay if you want. I think someone is playing a trick on us."

"No, I'd better be going. I have a class in an hour, but thanks. I had fun last night."

"Yeah, me, too." He walked up to hold the open door. "You can come back any time. We're having another party this Saturday. We can invite the girls."

Phillip smiled, "I'd like that. Hey, see you in class tomorrow."

"See ya', dude," and he closed the door.

Constance came back up the stairs to check on me. "How are you doing?"

"I'm hanging in there."

"I called Robbie to cancel all of your Thursday classes and to send out the notification to your students."

"Thanks."

"I also called Ted. He's on his way over. He cancelled his class as soon as

I told him what happened."

"He what?"

"He's becoming a good friend. He'll be here any minute."

"Thanks, hon. I don't know what I'd do without you."

"You just rest. I'm going to take care of Hara."

"OK."

Within five minutes, Ted was at the door. Constance pointed to our room. "He's upstairs and in pretty bad shape."

"Let me see if I can help. I brought some things with me." He held up a black canvas bag bulging with weird shapes poking the sides.

"I've never seen him in so much pain before, Ted. I don't know what to do." He briskly followed her up the stairs.

Hara was in the game room, and Ted waved. "Hi, Hara."

She replied in a soft voice, "Hello."

"Hara, this is Mr. Ted. He came to talk with Daddy. Can you go downstairs and play while we help him?"

"OK, Mom." She packed up her game and left the room.

I was still curled up in a ball on the bed. "Michael, Ted's here. He brought some things that might help."

I groaned, "Hi, Ted."

"Man"-he put the bag on the bed and opened up the drawstring—"you look worse than yesterday."

"Gee, thanks."

"Here, hold this." He handed me a round disk made of clear glass filled with a bunch of copper and steel shavings and some other items I couldn't recognize.

"What is it?"

"It's called orgonite. Some people say it helps, and others get nothing from it. I thought it was worth a try."

I held it and shook my head, "Nothing. I'm not getting anything, just ringing in the ears and pain in my head and body."

"Ringing in the ears?!" he blurted. "Do you remember the list that I gave you?"

Constance piped in, "Yes, it's in the study."

"I wrote something on it about ringing in the ears."

I held up a finger. "I remember. It's implants, a reptilian or djinn attached to you, or—"

Ted reacted, "Uh oh!"

"What?" asked Constance.

He pointed at me. "You've been tagged."

"Tagged? What's that?"

"I've done some reading on this. Besides being implants, or having some nasty beast clinging to your soul, you could be tagged. A lot of people who are being attacked by the Order call it electronic stalking." He rummaged around in his bag and pulled out a new item. "Here, hold this." He turned on a black box with a light on top and a meter gauge.

"What's this?"

"It's a fancy device I picked up that might block the signal. Did it stop the ringing?"

"No, it's still there. What's tagging?"

"The Order is able to locate you somehow anywhere in the world, either by implants in your body, etheric implants in your energy body, or by using some sort of global GPS tracking system. There're a lot of theories out there. Then they can zap you with brainwashing programs through cell towers, HAARP, military drones, or even individual targeting satellites—and they can cause a lot of pain from what I hear."

He took the box away and pulled out a box of aluminum foil. "Have you tried this?"

"Ted,"—I winced painfully—"that's not going to work. They took my astral body last night and hooked all kinds of implants and wires on me."

"What about your powers? I mean, I saw you blast the books off your desk the other day."

Constance told him, "They've blocked his powers somehow."

"Yes," I added, "I think they put some type of psychic inhibitor on me. I thought I remembered them saying that while I was held in this energy bubble. It feels like it is on my frontal lobe."

"Wow, they can do that?!"

"It seems so. I can't even put up my shield. I swear I hear them doing things on their ship."

Constance nodded, "He's not making this up, Ted. I was held down by a reptilian last night, and they made Michael hit me."

"I remember you telling me that on the phone. It makes me angry just to hear about it. I'd like to strap them all to a bomb and press the button."

"The way I feel right now, I'm ready to join you." I put my hand back on my head. "The ringing just got louder."

"What do you want me to do, Michael?" He lifted his bag. "Nothing I brought is going to help."

"I know this may sound silly, but I want to try something."

Constance asked, "What is it?"

"I want to try sending them love, and—"

Before I could finish my statement, both of them chimed in total disbelief, "What?!"

"I know, it sounds silly, but I've heard from the New Agers that sending sincere love stops them. Supposedly, they can't handle emotional love."

Constance sat down beside me and put her hand on mine. "I don't know if I can do that. Look at what they are doing to you."

"It's worth a shot." I shrugged. "I don't know what else to do. And *I can* honestly say that I can send them love and forgiveness. Would you help me?" Ted gave me a strange look. "Ted, I'm asking for your help. Can you please love them and forgive them? It's worth a shot."

"I'll try."

"And it has to be sincere love. You can't just love them to send them away."

"Honey, this sounds ridiculous. If you loved me, I wouldn't leave."

"I know, I wouldn't either, but I want to try. If anything, it will let me know if it works or not."

She added more, "Think about this, hon. If I did something to hurt you, whether it was intentional or unintentional, and you forgave me and loved me with all your heart, I wouldn't leave. The New Agers have this completely wrong."

"I know. Everything about that doesn't feel right. Love has to matter to the other person for it to work. But will you still try? I'm almost out of options."

"OK, I'll help you." She squeezed my hand.

"It sounds crazy. I never bought in to any of this New Age stuff," remarked Ted. "But alright, here goes nothing."

"OK, on three, send them all the forgiveness and love that you can send. Do it for as long as you can."

We all closed our eyes. After a few seconds, Ted opened one of his eyes and looked at both Constance and me, then he closed his eye again. After a minute or so, Constance and Ted stopped. They waited for me, and I stopped a little bit later.

On the reptilian ship, one of the reptilians at the console reported, "Hsssss. We are picking up love vibrations emanating from his body. Human fool doesn't know we don't respond to love. What should I do?"

The reptilian commander huffed, "Hsssss. Love is folly. Won't send us away. Hsssss."

The new recruit asked his commander, "They really don't respond to love?"

He replied, "No, that's a New Age concoction that we planted years ago. Emotional love doesn't stop these guys, only force. Love only works that way for those who care about each other, and we don't care about them."

The reptilian leader ordered, "Hsssss. Ask the human priest if he wants us to stop."

The reptilian at the panel pushed a button and sent a telepathic message. "Do you want us to stop?"

In my head, I heard the message very clear. Not knowing that it was deception used by the reptilians, I thought, "Of course I want you to stop."

The reptilian told its commander, "He acknowledged and gave his permission."

"Hsssss. Good. In ten minutes, drop the pain one level and send the black ooze. We have permission to add more suffering."

Constance opened her eyes. "Did it work?"

I shook my head *no*, "The pain is still there."

Ted smirked sarcastically, "I knew that wouldn't work. Love me and see if I leave the house." He looked at both of us. "You two are way more loving and positive than I am. I wouldn't leave because you cared about me. I'd want to hang around you more."

"It was worth a shot, Ted. Thanks for doing it."

On the ship, the recruit asked, "Why even ask permission and then use deception? Why not just do it anyway?"

The older officer responded, "It's supposed to be one of their Universal Laws or something. You have to ask permission, or you are going against free will." He turned to whisper in his ear, "I think this is a bunch of crap. There is no such thing as free will. It's all about power, agendas, ability, and technology—who has it, and who doesn't. I think this is a reptilian law that they made up so they won't feel so guilty for using deception in front of their one-eyed reptilian god."

The young recruit nodded. In his mind, he thought, "It still doesn't make sense."

He questioned the other guy, "The reptilians didn't ask permission to attack anyone else before. They took over this planet when they found it, and they didn't ask permission to attack this guy last night."

He spat agitatedly, "Look, do you want to ask them why they follow this silly law and aren't consistent about it? We never asked permission when we wanted to take something from someone else, or go to war for that fact; we just did it—and so did they. Now stop asking me about this, or I'll tell them to put it on you."

He gulped, "OK."

The reptilian commander turned to the two military men. "Hsssss. Boys' programming. Did it begin?"

The older officer stepped forward. "We started it as soon as they were tagged by the djinn. They've already had four uploads and verbally attacked each other this morning. It is working perfectly. By Saturday, they will begin hearing voices."

"Hsssss. Discredit the priest. It must be done."

"Relax. It will be done. We've already initiated a plan to have a police officer who works for the Order bring one of the boys a gun by Sunday."

"Hsssss. We want him stopped."

"So do we."

The reptilian commander gave a guttural command to the one at the console, "Hsssss. Prepare the black ooze and send it."

The young recruit tapped his superior on the shoulder. "Black ooze?"

"Boy, you are new. Where did they dig you up from?"

"Sorry, I just started in the Order. My father has a high rank, so they are pushing me through fast."

"Ah, so you are on the fast track. They must want you ready for something big, and soon."

"Probably."

"OK, I'll help you out some. But remember, you owe me. The black ooze is an insidious biological weapon that can't be seen by humans, only felt." The young guy was looking for more. "I know, it's strange. The ooze is not third-dimensional—meaning, we can't see it. It's a fourth dimensional silicon-based life form with living technology built in. Once the Order got a hold of it in its raw state, we were able to integrate artificial intelligence into it. Now it's programmable. It attacks like a wild beast and won't stop unless the program is changed."

"It sounds like science fiction."

"It's not. It's actually science reality. Our scientists are the top developers in the world. Now listen up; you need to learn this. Once the black ooze is sent to a victim, it attaches to the crown of the head, the chest, and the forehead like a parasite. The human becomes the new host. As it grows, it penetrates over and under the skin."

"Yuck!"

"It learns the person's weaknesses and feeds on them. If it gets on you, you'll know it. You will feel it on your chest, head, back, behind your eyes, on your cheek bones, and at the back of the skull. It pretty much takes over your mind if not stopped. I've never seen anything so hideous in our arsenal."

"How does it sustain itself?"

"Like I said, it's a parasite. It sends some kind of feeding tube down the person's throat and taiji pole—that's the energy pole that runs through the center of the body—and then it attaches to the lower dantian. If it's not detached there, it will just keep feeding."

"Anything else?"

"Yes. It can also attach to the acupuncture points on the body. Basically, I think it can attach anywhere, but some places are more effective than others."

"Why the acupuncture points?"

"It can attack and control a person's organs and health by taking over the acupuncture system. With enough time, it can even kill you." He put his hand on his shoulder. "I'm telling you, this is one of our most terrible weapons. Be glad you are on our side."

"Believe me, I am. All hail to the Order."

"All hail to the Order."

———•+•———

It was 9:00 a.m., and Ricky and Laura rang our doorbell. *Ding-dong!*

"I'll get it," as I struggled to stand.

"You'll do no such thing. Stay here with Ted. I'll be back in a minute."

Ding-dong! On the porch, Ricky asked, "He did say to be here at 9:00 a.m., right?"

Laura nodded, "Yes, we're right on time. I wonder where he is." She got a psychic hit when she searched for me, and she grabbed her head. "Ow, that hurts."

"What?" he asked.

"Something's not right. I felt a jabbing pain when I thought about Michael. I guess I'm a little clairsentient also."

The door opened, and Constance greeted them, "Hi, you must be Ricky and Laura. I'm Constance, Michael's wife. It's so nice to meet you. Please, come on in."

Hara came out of the kitchen and ran up to her mother's side. "Mommy, who is it?"

"These are Daddy's friends. This is Ms. Laura, and this is Mr. Ricky."

"Hello," she greeted them politely and gave a tiny wave.

Laura bent down at her waist and shook her hand. "Well, hello there. Aren't you just a beautiful girl?" Then she smiled at Constance. "She looks just like you. She's adorable."

"Thanks." Then she told Hara, "Hara, please go run along for a bit. I'll be back down to start your lessons shortly." Hara turned and went back to the kitchen.

Ricky asked, "Where's Tumaini? Is he OK? I can sense something, too."

"You must be Baniti. Michael's told me so much about you." She pointed to the bedroom. "He's upstairs. They did something bad to him last night."

From the second floor, there was a yell. "Get...off...of...me!"

All three looked at each other for a second, and then they frantically ran up the stairs. When they got to the bedroom door, Ted was by the closet

417

and as white as a ghost, while I was deep in a struggle with this unseen creature. I was pulling at my face like I had a cat wrapped around my head with its claws digging in.

Constance started running toward me, but Ricky grabbed her hand. "No! Stay out of the way. I've got this. I can see it."

He stood facing directly toward me. Then he put his hands out to each side and drew them into his mid-chest. I could see that he was gathering energy. The air in the room actually began moving with his motions.

I was still struggling, and Constance took a step. Laura grabbed her. "No! Let him finish!" She was still trying to get to me. "He's going to help him. Just wait."

Ricky threw his hands out one more time and gathered in another round of energy. Wind was moving in the room in a circular fashion. The curtains were blowing around, along with any loose items on the dresser. A white mist was now visible in the circulating air.

His third round of energy gathering was intense. I could see his entire abdomen glowing with a concentrated light ball. It was so bright to me that I almost forgot I was struggling for my life against this hideous beast. I was pulling hard to keep it from moving down my body.

I yelled, "Baniti! Now!"

He lunged forward with his left foot and threw both hands upward toward my head. Streams of purple, white, and gold electric bolts were shooting out of his hands and fingertips and struck the pulsating beast.

He pulled back one more time, circled his arms around his head to gather even more energy, and then brought his hands to his chest. With as much intensity as he could muster, he lunged again with his left foot stomping forward. This time, the lightning bolts lit up all the way from his shoulders down to his fingertips and struck the black ooze hard. Everyone in the room could now see the outline of this nasty creature because of the added energy.

I yelled again, "Now, Baniti! Now! Hit it again! It's almost gone!"

He pulled in energy one more time with his entire body. He was grunting and clenching his fists, and white mist was flowing into his chest and stomach with ferocity. With one last lunge, he screamed, "Aaaaaaaaarrrrrrrrhhhhhhhhhh!"

An enormous white ball shot out of his stomach and hit the black ooze. It instantly evaporated the main mass with an explosive flash, leaving small, black, wavy clouds that dissipated behind it. I collapsed onto the bed, and Constance ran up to me.

Ricky gasped with an exhausted voice, "Is it gone?"

I grabbed my head and chest. "I think so. What was that?!"

Ted was still in shock from what he'd seen. "Who are you people?!"

"Ted, this is Ricky and Laura. Ricky was the priest who taught me back in Egypt."

Ricky leaned over and shook his hand. "Hi, nice to meet you, mon."

I felt around my head and body again. "I think that last blast killed it. I can't feel it anymore."

Constance gave me a really tight hug. "I'm so glad you're OK."

While Laura introduced herself to Ted, Ricky scanned my body. "It's not gone. There're all of these tiny pulsing things on your head and body. What are those?"

"No, no, that thing is gone. Those are the implants that they put in me last night. That last thing was new." I felt again. "It's gone. I'm almost positive."

Hara was standing in the doorway. "Mommy, what's wrong with Daddy?"

I motioned to her. "Hara, come here. I'm fine. I was—"

Constance interrupted, "Your daddy's OK now, pumpkin."

She ran up and gave me a hug. "You were really loud. What was all that noise and screaming?"

"Daddy was getting help with a bad thing in the room. It's gone now, thanks to Mr. Ricky."

She looked at him scared, which made him a little uncomfortable. "Hello..." he said, and waved to her meekly.

Constance put her hand on her shoulder. "Honey, why don't you go back downstairs? I'll be behind you in a minute."

"Go on, honey," I nodded. "I'll be alright." She slid off the bed and walked out the door.

Ted was still in shock. "Does anyone want to tell me what just happened?"

"I was under attack by this thing. It was trying to clamp down on my body. I don't know what would have happened if you hadn't shown up, my old friend."

Ricky made clawing gestures with his hands. "I saw that monster attacking you. It was like a black glob of smoke, but it had substance and tentacles."

Ted reacted, "Holy cow!" We all turned toward him, and he continued, "I thought that was only a rumor."

Constance asked, "What, Ted? Tell us."

"There's this new weapon that's rumored to have been used in the last year called the black ooze. No one's been able to see it to say for sure, but from what I just saw, with those bolts lighting it up, I think that was it."

———•—•———

On the alien ship, the commanding reptilian got the report that the black ooze had been destroyed. It hissed in anger and gave the command to turn the implant machine up to full at once.

———•—•———

I felt a searing pain and immediately curled up on the bed with my hands on my head. "Aaaaahhhhhhhh!"

Constance was looking at Ricky, and pleaded, "Help him, please!"

He asked, "What is it?"

"They turned up the implants. It...it hurts. Aaahhhh!"

"I can see them. They are all glowing blood red."

Ted asked, "See what? I can't see anything."

Laura commented, "They must be the etheric kind and not the physical implants used by the military."

Ricky opened his arms to clear a path. "Constance, I need you to move. I think I can grab this one near the surface."

I implored, "Trust him." She stopped holding me and moved away.

Ricky moved in and used both of his hands toward the back of my head. He warned, "Brace yourself. This may hurt."

He could see what no one else in the room could see. There was a tiny, red, glowing sliver sticking out of my energy body. It was attached to a ring of other sliver-like implants on my skull. "I'm going to grab this and pull it real hard. Then I'm going to hold it and destroy it with an energy pulse. Are you ready?"

"Do it, please. It hurts."

He turned to the others and cautioned, "Stand back."

He pulled with a quick, sudden jerk and ripped the ring of implants right off of my head. I screamed like I'd had my first hot wax job and wasn't prepared for the pain, "Yeeoooowwwwww!"

420

While I yelled, Ricky pulled the ring into both of his hands, his stomach glowed, and then the energy went up his body and down his arms. His arms glowed with the same electric lightning bolts as before. We all heard an audible popping sound as he destroyed the implant's central brain.

Constance asked, "How did you do this?"

He turned to her and replied, "I did this when I was Baniti. We had a terrible time removing these nasty implants from inside our priests back then, too."

Laura looked interested. "I want to know more."

"I can remember this like it was yesterday." He turned to me and smiled, "When I was Baniti, Tumaini and the rest of the surviving priests worked on our vision to see dimensional objects. We could see these implants with our inner-sight. Then we figured out how to remove them. Some are easy, but the ones they put in Michael are… Well, let's just say that they went all out on him. This is going to take more than one try."

"I could feel a little relief when you ripped out the ones on the crown, but I still hurt from the others."

He suggested, "Then we'd better get a move on."

I looked at Constance. "I think you should take Hara somewhere so she doesn't hear her daddy screaming all morning."

"Good idea. I'll pick up some food for all of us."

"Thanks, dear. I'll be OK." I nodded toward Ted, Laura, and Ricky. "I trust them with my life."

She smiled at them and added, "So do I." She walked over to Ricky and kissed his head. "Thank you."

He held her hand. "It was my pleasure to serve."

I pointed to my temple. "Hurry, it's going to jolt me. I can tell from the spasm." My toes were scrunched from the pain.

Laura mentioned, "I know this. That's your gallbladder meridian that they've attacked. It runs from the corner of your eye down to your toes. I can sense it."

Ricky asked, "Do you have something to bite down on?"

"No, just do it."

He turned to Laura and verified her comment. "Your psychic skills are right on. This is one of the main ones the reptilians used."

Constance hadn't left yet. There was concern all over her face. "Can I do anything?"

"Just help Hara." I turned to Ricky and gave the go-ahead, "Rip away." He grabbed the etheric implant on my temple and pulled hard. It ripped around to the back of my ear, up to my forehead, back down my scalp, and then it ripped off down to my second to last toe. I screamed again, "Yeeooowww! That smarts."

Ricky finished blowing up the artificial intelligence brain of the implant with another jolt of energy. "We've got a few more to go."

Hara came back to the door again with a frightened look on her face.

Constance looked back toward me. "It'll be OK. Take Hara for something special."

"Alright, but please call me if there is an emergency."

"I will. Hara,"—I blew her a kiss—"go with Mommy. I'll be fine. Ricky's taking things off of me."

Constance grabbed her hand and took her downstairs. Just before leaving the house, there was another yell of pain from upstairs. "Yeeoowww!"

She squeezed Hara a little. "He'll be OK. He's in good hands." And she led her out the door.

CHAPTER TWENTY-NINE

MISSING PIECES

Constance came home two hours later with her arms filled with bags of take-out. Hara was only holding a cupcake. She opened the door for her mother, and they both walked in. Ted, Laura, and Ricky were downstairs sitting in the kitchen.

Ted came over to help Constance with the bags. "Michael's upstairs. He needed some sleep."

"What happened?"

Laura gave her the good news. "Ricky, the master implant remover, took out fourteen different implants, removed his psychic inhibitors, pulled out the tracking tag, and destroyed all of those nasty-looking threads that were hooked to Michael's soul."

"Threads to his soul? What?"

"That was one of their plans. Remember, the picture upstairs on the cross?" Ted made a cross with his two fingers. "It's the soul-catcher."

Ricky nodded in agreement, "It took a while. He was really hooked up bad. But he should be fine now."

Ted snickered, "Yeah, when the psychic inhibitor was removed, he got so mad from the pain that he shot an energy bolt across the room and put a hole in your rattan hamper. Good thing your laundry was already done."

Constance gave him a funny look. She was trying to comprehend all of the news. Then she pictured a hole in her hamper with burnt clothes flying everywhere.

Ricky continued, "He was able to put his shield back up without any problems before going to sleep. I also put up a shield around him and your house. We should be safe for the time being."

Constance put the bags she was holding on the counter. One of the bags slipped and hit the floor. Laura rushed over. "Here, let me help you with that." They both picked up the containers and put them on the table.

I walked into the kitchen and mumbled groggily, "Hi, guys. Hi, hon." I walked over and gave her a hug. "I'm feeling much better now. Did they tell you the good news?"

Ted joked, "Yes, you need a new hamper."

I was rubbing the side of my head when Constance wrapped her arms back around me. "I was so worried about you, and so was Hara. I don't know what I'd do without you."

"Well, you have these guys to thank for coming to the rescue."

She turned and expressed to all of them, "Thank you so much!"

Ricky humbly bowed. "It was my pleasure to serve."

Ted and Laura added, "Ours, too."

"What did you bring home?"

"I thought some Chinese might do. Is that OK?"

"It's great. I'm famished. Are you guys going to stay and eat?" All three commented *yes* in one way or another. "Great. I could sure use the company right now."

Ted slapped my shoulder. "That's what we're here for."

"Laura," I asked, "what about your shop? Are you going to open today?"

"My helper is going to run the store. After you left, Ricky and I did some more cleaning up. Then he filled me in on all kinds of fun stuff, and he showed me a trick or two." She lifted up her pointer fingers and ran a little lighting bolt between the two of them. "It's not very powerful yet, but I'm working on it."

Ted and Constance looked at Laura's new ability. Constance pointed to her fingers and exclaimed, "I wanna learn how to do that."

Ted echoed, "Me, too. That could come in handy some day."

I looked at all three of them and grinned, "It just might."

Laura wiggled her fingers when the energy stream stopped, and then turned to Ricky. "Last night, I tried to help Ricky fine-tune all of the skills that he remembered, but he was such a natural that I barely had to do a thing. He was manipulating energy in ways that I couldn't even imagine."

He nodded in appreciation towards her, and then he asked me, "Is the ringing in your ears gone?"

I checked to make sure. "Yup, no more ringing. Phew, that's a relief! You're going to have to remind me how to remove all of those things. I remember us doing it back then, but I can't recall how to do it now."

"Sure, and you'll have to catch me up on what's been happening in this timeline with all of our priestly friends." He glanced toward the ground, and then back to me. "Tumaini, this will go much faster if...well...if I connect to your thoughts. It will catch me up much quicker than asking a lot of questions. I never showed you how to do this when you were in training, but I remember how. This was an advanced technique that only a few priests learned after years of service. Can I connect with you?"

"Sure, anything that will help." He put his hand out and pressed it flat onto my chest. He breathed in slowly until his lungs were full. When he exhaled, he confirmed, "There, that'll do it."

"Do what? What did you just do?"

"If we have time, I'll show you. I just connected to your soul's record in the Realm of Souls. It's not that hard, but we have work to do. The Order—that's what they are called, aren't they?—the Order has grown beyond anything imaginable to the priesthood of old. If what you have in your memory is correct, the world is in terrible danger again."

"That's why we are here to help. How about some food first? We can talk about this over egg rolls."

We all helped get the table ready, while Constance made Hara a plate to take to her game room. "Here, honey. Thanks for eating upstairs. We adults need to go over some things."

"OK," and she bounced away.

Ted nodded once toward Hara. "Watching Hara with the two of you, and how much she loves you, I can see why you want to make a change for the better. She's precious."

We both replied at the same time, "Thanks, Ted." Then I motioned to Laura and Ricky. "Let's eat."

After talking about the state of the world over lunch, Ricky was distraught. "This is worse than ancient Egypt. Why aren't people developing their God-given gifts and developing their psychic powers?"

Laura answered angrily with a mouth full of noodles, "The governments of the world don't want anyone growing spiritually or developing their psychic skills." She stopped to swallow and took a sip of water. "Imagine if everyone could read the politicians' minds. They wouldn't be able to keep all of their deception and lies from the people."

Ted sang, "Ooo, I like her."

She continued, "If the people really knew what was going on behind the scenes—I mean, really knew what shady deals are going on behind closed political doors that kill or enslave innocent souls for greed and power—they wouldn't put up with it. They might even rise up against the governments and overthrow the Order."

Constance asked, "Why don't you tell people what they are doing?"

"Some of the people, thank goodness, are waking up to the deception all on their own. But if a psychic tells them, they don't believe us as much. The people were taught by the government, scientists, and religions that we are woo-woo stuff and not to be trusted."

I added, "That makes sense. The Order controls the governments and religions, and the religions say that psychic stuff is the devil's work. If the people only knew it was the Order that put that in their religions, they would leave those made-up faiths in a heartbeat."

Ted shook his finger. "And let's not forget, the government runs its own psychic programs—and has been for decades—but for its benefit only. They won't teach these skills to anyone else. They believe in psychic abilities because it gives them power, but they'll discredit any psychic who stands against them."

"Exactly!" I enthused. "The government is all about control and fear. They don't want anyone developing abilities that they can't control. Imagine if we could move objects with our minds instead of being forced to use fossil fuels. It would topple the control they have over the people, and it would destroy their economy. We wouldn't be enslaved to use their made-up money system anymore, and that terrifies the dark side."

Ricky sighed, "I thought it was bad when I was Baniti; this timeline is worse. The people need real help."

"That they do," I replied. "So what's the plan?"

"Michael, in this timeline, you are the leader, not me. This is your show. I'm just the helper now."

All of them were looking at me for an answer. "Well, you know me. I'm all about finding simple solutions to life's major challenges. We need an update from Egypt, and—"

Constance interrupted, "Got it." She went to get her note from the phone call.

"And then we need to solve the clues upstairs. They've helped so far, and I'll bet more of the answers are tucked away in them."

Laura asked, "What clues?"

"Ricky knows about them. Don't you, Ricky?"

He nodded in agreement, "Yes. Those were very well-thought-out clues, from what I remember."

Ted hinted to Laura, "You're going to love these."

"What are they?" she asked with curious excitement.

"I'll show you after Constance comes back. There're a bunch of them, and a lot left to answer."

Constance came into the room with her paper and handed it to me. Before I read it, I looked at Laura. "You know, I took a vow to help this timeline when I was Tumaini, and so did Ricky. We've already reincarnated with a number of priests. Constance is already helping"—I put my hand on hers—"and Ted"—I looked toward him—"I appreciate all of your help, but I can't ask any more of you without you willingly—"

Ted gave me a stop sign. "Say no more. I'm in."

"But you could be in danger, Ted. You could get hurt."

"Michael—or should I call you Tumaini?—after what I've seen in the last week, I'm in more danger if I don't do anything. I don't want to be implanted and hooked up to that machine to suffer for God-knows-how-many lifetimes."

Laura added, "Me, too. I'm in all the way. It's a future that I don't even want to imagine. Consider this my pledge."

Ricky planted his hands firmly on the table. "It's settled, then. What did we call them? Oh, yes…you are now Protectors of Souls."

Ted laughed, "I don't know what that means, but do we get a badge or something?"

"Oh, man!" I exclaimed. "I wish we had more of those amulets to pass out."

"Amulets?" Laura perked up.

"It's upstairs. It's really cool, too. More like a fancy novelty piece. The pledge is what's most important, though."

She sat up straight in her chair. "I want to see it."

"We will, I promise. Let me read this for a minute." I read down a ways and shared, "Wow, there are seven more priests awake back in Egypt. That puts the total up to twenty, just like the pieces I found in the Decans circle. They all traveled to Cairo to meet up with the others. It says here that Ramla is helping them to practice their powers." I put the paper down for a second. "You've got to be kidding. Omar, Karim, and Ehab are priests? I should have known."

Ricky remarked, "I don't recognize any of those names." Then he got it. "Those are their current names, right?"

"Yes, and I found their Egyptian names upstairs. I wonder who they were."

"Me, too."

"Interesting…Rehema still hasn't gotten her full powers yet." I looked at all three of them. "This is important, give me just a second. No, wait. I've got a better idea. Let's amplify my call."

Constance asked, "Who are we calling?"

"It's Rehema. Ramla told me to help her open her telepathic ability. If we all concentrate on her name and send the same message, we could help. What do you say?" They all agreed. "Perfect. Let's keep it simple. Say *Rehema, hear me* three times, and that will be it."

Laura patted her heart. "Can we add *love* to the message?"

"Sure, we'll add it to the end. We'll all say *I love you.*" She smiled with the new addition.

"Alright, close your eyes and send the message. Go."

We all focused on Rehema and recited our greeting. I was about to open my eyes and say something to the group when I heard in my head, "Hello, Michael. Oh my gosh! I can hear you. This is so wonderful." It was Rehema's voice. "I can hear you! Oh my gosh, I have to tell Hanif."

"Hello, Rehema. It's good to hear your voice again," I communicated telepathically.

She responded in my mind, "It's so nice to hear you. I miss you so much."

"I miss you, too. I'm glad you can hear me."

"Ramla said that you would help me with my gifts. I swear that I heard you call yesterday. I thought it was in my dream state. Did you call?"

"I did. It was me."

"Call me on the phone soon. Hanif and Mudads need to talk with you.

It's important—about the Order."

"I will. How about this weekend?"

"Good. I will tell them. And by the way, your wife is a gift from the gods."

"She is, isn't she? I feel the same way."

"Thank you for helping me. This is so wonderful. I need to tell Ramla."

"It is my honor to serve you, my friend. Why don't you tell her telepathically?"

"Great idea. Bye for now, Michael."

"Bye, Rehema." I opened my eyes to four people staring at me.

Ted spoke first, "Let me guess; it worked." I nodded *yes*, and he added, "Why am I not surprised? The guys in the physics department would never believe this, even if they saw it."

"Probably not."

Laura smiled, "This is so cool. I'm glad I met you yesterday."

"Thanks, Laura. That was nice of you to say." I laughed, "Not many people would think that after being shot at by a helicopter."

"Well, this sure beats selling books about Feng shui," she laughed, too.

Ricky inquired, "Is there anything else in the note?"

Constance answered, "Yeah, something to do with ghosting and finding the mainframe. Does anyone know what that means?"

Ted piped in, "Ghosting is a term used by the government psychic and remote viewing units." He shook his head and said disgruntledly, "Go figure. They'll use psychics to spy and target people, but they won't teach it."

He glanced at all of us. "Sorry, got caught up there. Ghosting is when a number of psychic agents, like the army's remote viewers, would hide a target with another target—like hiding a nuclear missile silo with an image of an ice cream truck over it."

I gave him a puzzled look. "Do you want to explain that one a little more?"

"Sure. Let's say that you want to hide a missile from the other guy's remote viewers. What they do is take a picture of an ice cream truck and actually put it on the missile. Sometimes they'll just put a picture on top of a picture of the missile. It works either way. I don't know how. But anyway, when the picture is on top of the object they want to hide, they do some type of mental focusing to hide the real object. That way, if someone looks for the missile with remote viewing or psychic powers, they'll see the ice cream truck instead."

Laura was stunned. "Really? I didn't know they could do that."

"It fools most of the amateurs. If someone has more ability, they might get the cross between the two—like a nuclear Bomb Pop," he chuckled to himself. "But those with real talent can get through their ghosting techniques. It's really quite interesting. I wish I knew more."

Constance remarked, "That's more than what I knew."

Ricky and I added, "Me, too."

Ted continued, "The remote viewers don't like being labeled with the psychics, but they are tapping into the same stuff."

I nodded, "Yes, the *ethers*. It's all the same thing—that stuff that holds all of the information."

Laura agreed, "He's right. We tap into the same source. They have their methods, and so do we." She looked at Ted. "They just don't like us because of the methods we use, right?"

"Sad, but true. Calling a remote viewer a psychic is insulting to them. They prefer to be known for their"—he made quote signs with his fingers—"scientific protocols and methods."

"Whatever," she huffed. "We all get results, and we all make mistakes."

I added, "It seems that this ghosting thing could throw off the best of them."

"From what I've read, you could be right."

"Interesting…ghosting," I thought. "I have to remember that." I raised my head toward the study. "What do you say we go upstairs and look at the clues? We've got more work to do."

Ricky replied, "Right," while the others nodded.

On the reptilian ship, the commander was furious at the two reptilians who manned the console and had them painfully executed for failing to make the black ooze work. Without the implants or black ooze, and with the extra shielding that Ricky had provided, they could no longer get to anyone in the house.

The military officer commented, "We still have Plan B. We'll focus on his two students and bring him down that way. The improved CIA MKUltra assassin program is working better than expected. With our algorithmic updates and new software, we've caused both of them to lash out uncontrollably at their roommates in less than a day. One nearly got into a fistfight because of our control methods. Trust us. We'll get the job done."

"Hssssss. Do not fail us." The head reptilian used its mental power on the officer and sent a piercing jab to his chest. He clutched his sternum in pain. "Hssssss. The next one will be at your heart. Go finish your plan."

Gasping for air, the officer stumbled out of the bridge angrily. He was jabbed again because the reptilian could hear his thoughts.

Ricky's first reaction was fun to watch. He was like a kid in a candy shop. "Wow! I remember all of this stuff." He went from table to table, and then he turned to me. "I was there when you made all of this. Your plan really worked. I'm thoroughly impressed."

"Well, you helped me."

"It's like being back home again." He went to the table with the Decans circle and looked around.

Laura was astonished. "This is better than an Egyptian exhibit. Where did you get all of this stuff?" She had also walked up to the tables and was bent over staring.

"I left it all for myself when I was Tumaini. With a little magic, and some good guidance, I was reunited with it on my last trip to Cairo."

"Are these the clues? What does it all mean?"

I pointed to each table and explained, "This circle contains the twenty priests' names that we've discovered so far. Those loose pieces over there will fit into these holes over here. And this…this is the magic cross spread. It—"

She interrupted, "I know about this one. Well, kind of."

"Good, then maybe you can help me with it." I motioned to the rest. "These tables have the parchments on them. And the last tables will have all of the God Scrolls." I picked up the crook and flail. "Oh, and this is another clue."

Constance patted her upper chest. "Show them the amulet."

I opened my desk drawer, pulled it out, and handed it to Laura. She gushed, "This is beautiful."

Ricky commented, "I remember that piece. It looks as new today as it did thousands of years ago. Good job, Tumaini."

Looking around the room, I concluded, "I think that's all of it. Did I miss anything?"

Ted lifted his finger. "There's that riddle poem thingy and the decoded pages from Omar."

"Oh, yeah. Thanks, Ted. I completely forgot about those."

Laura chimed, "I like riddles. Do you think I could take a look?"

"Sure. The more help the merrier." I handed her the copies, and she buried her face in them.

I got Constance's attention. "Speaking of poems and pages, are you sure that Omar didn't have anything new to share? He was supposed to be working on the translations still."

"That completely slipped my mind, sorry. I should have let you read the entire note from the call." I pulled it out of my pocket and unfolded it, and she added, "He said he could only make out one more thing from the parchments. It was another riddle."

Ted jabbed, "Good going, Tumaini. Did you purposely try to make saving the world so hard?"

I snickered, "Well, I guess I was thorough in that lifetime, too."

Constance continued, "It was something about falling down and getting back up again."

"Close, hon. It pertains to the riddle clue. You wrote, 'You must go down to go up.'" I repeated it quieter to myself, "You must go down to go up. What the heck does that mean?"

Laura asked, "Michael—or do you want me to call you Tumaini?"

I shrugged. "I don't know who I am at any particular moment anymore. Just go with the flow."

"OK, I can do that." Then she held up the papers I had given her. "Do you think I could take these with me and study them? I have a hunch I could solve them if I had more time."

"Those are the only copies I have. Maybe I could—"

Ted interrupted, "She can have my copies. I have them in the bag. I couldn't make heads or tails out of them anyway."

Laura smiled, "That'd be great."

"Here, I'll get them for you." He went to the bedroom to grab his bag.

Ricky was hunched over the magic cross. "Do you remember how this works, Michael?"

"Partly. I found a book in Laura's shop that told me the basics."

She walked over and professed, "I know how to do this with playing cards, but not like you have it laid out."

"Well, this is the next clue."

Ted came back in, handed Laura the papers, and pointed to the magic cross. "Show them the table trick."

Hara was right outside in the game room and overheard. She came running to the door. "Can I see the table jump again?"

Constance motioned. "Of course, honey. Come on in." Hara came up to her mother's side and held onto her fingers.

I was getting the plexiglass off, and I asked Ricky, "Do you remember much about this?"

"Give me a moment. It'll come to me."

"Daddy, make the table move again." Hara was jumping up and down a little.

I told Laura and Ricky, "You guys are going to love this. You might want to back up a bit." They moved back beside Constance, Hara, and Ted.

"So, here's what happens: Each piece of papyrus seems to be locked in with magic to this timeline. When I rearrange them in the wrong order, they go nutso. Then—*whammo!*—they are all forced back into their right spots. Just watch…" After moving them all around, the pieces and the table started bouncing. In a flash, they all flipped into their correct places.

Hara was jumping up and down even more. "I like the bouncing table."

Constance nodded to her, "Me, too."

Laura laughed, "My cards never did that. And my customers would've run out of the store if the Queen of Hearts had jumped in the air. Are you pulling my leg with this, like those fake séances?"

Ricky answered, "Not one bit. I remember now. What Tumaini did…it's a masterpiece. Here"—he pointed to the table—"I recall how most of this works." We all walked forward.

He looked to me for approval. "Do you mind?"

"Not at all. I don't remember everything, either, so don't keep us waiting."

Hara left the room and went back to play. Ricky used the tweezers and picked up one of the pieces. "Do you see these images? Tumaini time traveled to learn how to do the picture behind the picture technique."

Laura chirped, "Do you mean like those stereograms? I loved those. We used to carry them in the store."

"Precisely." He winked at her knowledge. "If I remember this right, when he made the cross for me, each piece would gravitate toward a given spot. If a card wasn't going to be used, it wouldn't move. But if a few cards could go into a time slot, they would all be drawn to it."

I burst, "I get it! I remember now! The future is being set by what we do today. More than one card can move toward a slot based upon the possible outcome."

Constance reacted, "Wow! That's incredible. How did you come up with that?"

"I got that clue from when I did all of my time traveling to find the best possible chance to beat the Order. The more things I did to ensure that future, the more it solidified in the space-time continuum."

Ted postulated, "So, if we all move toward the door, we add more chances to the future that one of us will walk through it."

"Yes. And since there are five of us, there are still five different futures—one future for every person walking through the door first. You see, each one of us plays a small part in the future. So, five cards could gravitate toward that slot."

Constance raved, "That's pretty intense."

"So, it is true"—Laura nodded her head—"we can influence the future."

Ricky replied, "Well, to a point. There's more to it than that."

"Exactly," I agreed. "I added energy to this timeline—and so did you and the other priests—so there is more energy to make it work." I looked at the others. "Think of it like two cars in a race. The car with more energy will cross the finish line first. With my energy, and your energy, we can influence which event will become our next reality."

Ted got excited. "This makes total sense. I get it. But why won't some of the pieces stay in the slots when you put them there? I mean, I saw you put pieces in the open slots, and they flew right out."

Ricky explained, "It's because he used his knowledge of time, space, and magic. If an event isn't close to being in the future timeline, it won't gravitate toward a spot. It will be repelled by the actual event that belongs there."

Constance bent over the pile of papyrus. "And all of these extra pieces... are they future events?"

"Well, some of them are," I replied. "There're still the other priest's names, and two of the other slots on the cross aren't about the future. This one is about hopes and fears."

Laura pointed to the number four spot. "And this one right here; I know this one. It's reserved for hidden obstacles."

"Right you are." I gestured.

Ricky scratched his head. "Can you fill me in again on these other pieces? I have a good memory about being Baniti, but I don't remember *all* of the specifics."

"Sure, I have them written down over here." I got the paper and asked Laura and Ricky, "Can you guys see the image in this first card? Take a moment." While they looked, I told Ted and Constance not to say anything.

They both saw it at the same time. Ricky motioned. "Ladies first."

Laura answered, "It's the amulet you showed me. This is amazing. How you did this, I'll never know."

"It's the amulet for the Protectors of Souls." Ricky was encouraged. "You did it, Tumaini. You really did it. What's behind the others that you found?"

I filled them in on the other pieces, "Here's what we need to do next. We need to find the piece for the hopes and fears, hidden obstacles, and the remaining priests' names. That will leave all of the potential future cards."

"That's a great plan," Ted concurred, "process of elimination. I can see why you're the leader in this timeline."

"Guys, I'm making this up as I go along. The pieces are just falling into place."

Ricky snorted, "Pieces falling into place. That's a magic cross joke, right? Good one." He snorted again.

Laura shrugged. "So, what do you want us to do?"

"If you can stay, we need to look at these stereograms and find the clues. It'll help us to locate the cards for the future time slots. If we can see what might happen next, we could potentially swing the future in our favor and defeat the Order."

Constance grabbed my side. "Great plan, honey. I'm so proud of you."

Ricky exclaimed, "That is a great plan! And I'm not going anywhere else. I'm here to stay."

"So am I," grinned Laura. "They can run the shop without me."

"I'm all in, too," added Ted. "Hand me some gloves. Let's win this thing."

Ricky busted with excitement, "Ya, mon!"

By dinner time, we'd located the sixteen remaining priests' names, along with the other two cards.

I placed each of the papyrus pieces in the Decans circle, and they all remained. "That's it. Now we have that clue finished. A perfect circle of thirty-six priests. My friends"—I looked at Ricky—"and yours, too." He smiled.

Constance said, "Now the real test remains. What about the other two?"

"If they stay in the cross, we'll know we have the right ones. Hand me the number four card."

Laura carefully passed me the papyrus piece and mentioned, "The obvious obstacle for number five was the Order, and the hidden obstacle in number four is—"

I finished her sentence, "The ones running the whole show from behind the scenes. Who found that one?"

Ted raised his hand. "I did. It was a picture of a reptilian standing on a human. Nasty little sucker. So they've been the ones behind this all along."

I added, "That they are, and I have the implant scars to prove it." Constance rubbed my back to comfort me.

"Here goes nothing…" I placed it in the spot, and it stayed.

Ricky cheered, "Cool! Now let's get the *hopes* card."

Constance yelled out, "I found that one! It was the number seven card. It had four humans holding hands in peace. I think it symbolizes all of humanity living in harmony."

Laura sighed, "We can only hope."

Ted laughed, "That's what Tumaini is here for—to bring us hope."

"Well, that, and a veggie burrito." They all chuckled from my short joke.

I picked up the piece and placed it in the cross. "There, that does it. Nothing like peace on the planet for a great sign of hope. That leaves four open spots for the future."

Ricky pointed out, "A future that hasn't happened yet. And we can help to shape it."

Laura nodded, "Yes, we can."

Constance squeezed my side again and had a small tear in her eye. "I don't know what to say, honey. You really amaze me. I couldn't have asked for a better husband."

"I'm the lucky one. I couldn't have done this without you"—I turned to the others—"without any of you. Thanks."

Ted responded first, "Stop being so emotional. I'm hungry. What do you say about those veggie burritos?"

"Ya, mon. I could do one of those."

"Burritos it is. Let's call it a day. I need some rest, and we both need to teach tomorrow."

"Yes, we do. Let's eat."

I was the last one to leave the room. I turned back and looked inside. "It's coming together." I nodded, knowing there was hope in these clues, and I walked downstairs.

CHAPTER THIRTY

GOD CAME TO CLASS

It was the best night's sleep I'd had in a while. I could feel the reptilians try to attack me and Constance again, but they couldn't get all the way through Ricky's and my shield. All I felt was some slight pressure on my body, and Constance didn't feel a thing. I made sure to re-energize everything in the morning to keep both girls safe.

"Morning, hon," I whispered.

She rolled over and grumbled, "Five more minutes. Rrpphhng."

I kissed her and then slid out of bed. "I've got Hara's breakfast this morning. You stay and sleep." She mumbled something that I couldn't understand, and I went downstairs.

A little over half an hour later, Constance showed up to a ready-made breakfast. A stack of warm blueberry pancakes and fresh fruit were taking up the middle of the table.

"Wow!" she gushed. "Hara gets pancakes twice in the same week. What's the occasion?"

"Nothing. I just wanted to help out since you've done so much lately. I made the batter last night so I could whip them up fast this morning."

"That was nice, dear, thanks." She looked upstairs and called, "Hara! Breakfast is ready!"

She came stomping down the stairs. "Pancakes with blueberries! My favorite."

"I need to work in my office this morning. Can you watch Hara?"

"Sure. I can do her next assignment."

"That would be a lot of help. What else do you have planned today?"

"Well, you know, teach, help Hara, and battle some more aliens," I joked.

"Can we leave out the aliens for today? I need a break."

"I'll see what I can do."

Hara blurted out, "I don't like the mean aliens. They hurt Daddy."

"We don't like Daddy being hurt either, pumpkin."

I glanced over. "Constance, I know we'd talked about creating a teaching schedule for Hara. How about I take over all of the times when I'm not at school? It seems to make the most sense."

"That was easy. I'm sold. And leave the evenings free?"

"Done. Couldn't have said it better myself."

"We sure did a lot yesterday. Do you think we'll find more answers soon?"

"Laura took the riddles home, and Ricky's going to help her today. And all three of them are coming back over tomorrow."

"Are we still going out on a date?"

"Can we leave that one open for now? I have a feeling that a major breakthrough is about to occur."

"Well"—she flirted with her shoulders wiggling—"I don't want to get in the way of a good feeling. Just remember that you owe me a date, mister."

"I won't. I want to go out with you, baby." I kissed her passionately.

Hara groaned, "Yuck, you're ruining my pancakes with that mushy stuff."

I licked my lips. "Extra sticky kisses with syrup are the best."

"Yuck!" as she scrunched her face.

"Hara, after breakfast, I want you to go do your reading assignment that Mommy gave you the other day. Then I'll come up and talk with you about it. OK?"

"Yes, Dad. Is it the story with the cats?"

"Yes, it is."

She sat up fast and leaned forward with both hands on the table. "And then can you help me with my Egypt puzzle? I'm almost done."

"Absolutely! And we can start to decode it, too."

She bounced in her chair with her legs swinging wildly beneath. "This'll be fun."

I smiled, "Yes, it will."

———•—•———

I had finished Hara's work and my first 101 class. It was almost time for my 201 students to show, so I went to my classroom a little early.

Robbie welcomed me into the room, "Hi, Professor. Glad you're feeling better today."

"Thanks, Robbie. Were there any problems from yesterday?" I set down my briefcase and the box with the God Scroll in it.

"No. This late in the year, everyone's glad to get an unexpected break. A lot of the students said they were going to meet in the quad and get some sun."

"Good. And by the way, I meant to tell you this on Wednesday: I'm really impressed with your work and findings as of late. You're going to make a great teacher someday."

"Wow! Thanks, Professor. That means a lot coming from you." He perked up from my compliment. "Is there anything you need done for today?"

"Just keep doing the great job that you've been doing."

"Will do."

The students were trickling in for class. In the midst of the pack, I saw Rochelle and another student coming in holding hands. "Isn't that Allen, the same boy that she yelled at in the last class?"

Robbie whispered, "Yeah. They got paired up before they had their altercation. I guess something good came about from it."

"Interesting. I can't wait to hear about that one. Sometimes it's nice to be shocked from a service assignment."

"I can't wait to find out, either."

As the last rush of students came in, I heard Phillip and Bruce harshly speaking to one of the girls in class, and they both tried to pinch her butt.

"That's odd," I thought to myself. "That's not their usual behavior, and those were some awfully rude comments."

Robbie motioned with his head. "That was another pairing."

"And sometimes it's *not* nice to be shocked from a service assignment." I leaned over a bit. "Any more surprises?"

The girl who had flirted with Robbie during the last two classes came in alone and winked at him. Then she sang seductively, "Hi, Robbie," and sashayed to her seat, looking back over her shoulder once.

He turned to me in a panic. "I can explain." His face turned beet red.

"No need. You're a big boy. There's no law against teaching assistants and students dating, at least not in my room."

"Honest, I can explain." He struggled to get beyond his nervous reaction and stammered, "There...there were no more partners available. One of the students opted out, and Brandi wanted to serve someone."

"Uh huh, I get it," I replied in a teasing manner. "Just be careful. There is a fine line between teachers and students."

"Honest, I didn't plan it that way. There were no more partners!"

"Relax, Robbie. It's OK."

"Are you sure? I don't want to cause any problems."

"You aren't responsible for giving them grades, I am. So, just be professional in class, and it should be fine."

"Thanks, Professor."

"No problem. Just let me know if everyone is here."

He was sweating a little. "Sure."

After the signal was given, I started right in, "Good to see everyone today. I'm looking forward to reading your summaries from Wednesday's assignment. If anyone else has one to turn in, make sure you see Robbie."

While waiting for the rush to the front to be over, I thought, "I didn't read the last batch, either. I'll have to do that this weekend."

Bruce and Phillip flung their papers at Robbie. Bruce laughed sarcastically, "Here you go, teacher's pet." Robbie wasn't offended, but he looked strangely at him, and so did I.

"So, who would like to share something about their experience...anyone?"

Allen's hand shot up immediately. "I have something that I would like to say, Professor."

"The floor is all yours, Allen."

He enunciated slowly, with a lot of enthusiasm and arm motions, "That... assignment...was...awesome! I mean, it totally woke me up to what was going on in the world." He smiled at Rochelle, "If it wasn't for Rochelle and you helping me, I think I would have gone through life like a patriotic puppet." Bruce and Phillip received an instant left ear *zing*.

"Would you care to elaborate for us?"

"Well, I admit, I grew up like most Americans…I think. I was taught to support the U.S. no matter what—small farm town and all. Heck, the only thing to do where I grew up was to play football, then join the army or go to college after school. We never had any discussions in high school that made us question our history." He made a big hand gesture. "They didn't teach history at our school. And then"—he motioned to Rochelle—"she opened up my eyes even more with your assignment."

Rochelle winked at him. "Tell him about Hawaii."

"Oh yeah, that was interesting news, but in a terrible way. Did you know"—he turned to face the class—"that not only did the U.S. government continue to kill Native Americans, Mexicans, and the French Canadians for land and money since it was created, but 300 Marines were used to take over Hawaii before it became a state. Heck, the U.S. minister to Hawaii knew about the takeover plans before it even happened. And after the Marines arrested the queen—with no charges or reason—two different presidents did nothing about giving the land back to the Hawaiians. It was all about money and greed."

Rochelle interrupted, "Yeah, then one of the recent presidents gave an apology to them. But did *he* give Hawaii back to the Hawaiians?"

Allen answered her sarcasm, "No, he did not."

"Tell them about ARSOF, honey."

Stacey inquired, "What's ARSOF?"

Allen turned to her. "Oh, you're going to love this one. Basically, there's this paper written by the U.S. Army Special Operations Command called ARSOF Operating Command 2022. If you read it, there's a part in there that says self-empowered people are now a target of the Army—well, basically the CIA, NSA, FBI, and the lot of them, even though it doesn't say it that way. After you read their definition of what a self-empowered person is, well, if you pose a threat to the American money-driven system, you are now a threat and an enemy to the U.S. Can you believe this? If you show any sign of resistance to the bankers or corporations, you are now labeled by the Army as a traitor."

The steady tone in Phillip's and Bruce's ear got louder, then softer after hearing this.

Todd asked, "Why the sudden change, Allen? I mean, you were totally supporting America last class."

"It's like I said, they never taught us this stuff in school. I was completely unaware about most of the atrocities that the U.S. had committed against innocent souls. It took Rochelle"—he turned to me—"and the Professor to wake me up. I'm glad I did the assignment." Rochelle nodded and held his hand after that.

"Thanks for sharing, Allen. Is there anyone else who wants to contribute?"

Brandi gave a sly look to Robbie. In a worried fashion, he shook his hand ever so slightly to say *no*.

In Phillip's head, he had an extremely violent thought. He didn't hear any voices saying it; it just appeared as a random thought. "Kill him. Kill him now!" He was scared about this and replied in his mind, "I'm not going to kill him." He received another loud tone in his ear. "I'm not going to kill anyone. Leave me alone! Stop putting thoughts in my head!" There was no reply.

"Very well, then," I announced to the class, "let's get to the question for the day. It will lead right into our religious discussion." Most of the students pulled out their notepads and fired up their computers. "This is a simple one, but extremely important when talking about any version of a religious deity. It has to do with *life* and *time*. Any takers? No? So, here it is. Is it possible"—I paused so everyone would look at me to focus—"to kill an immortal being?"

Hands went up everywhere. "Daphnee?"

"It would be impossible to kill an immortal. If an immortal could die, then he or she would have always have been mortal, not an immortal."

"Exactly. Thanks for your answer. Does anyone disagree with this?"

Bruce mumbled softly, "Can we kill a teacher?" Phillip smirked from his joke. Both boys were losing to the CIA MKUltra assassin programming.

Nobody's hand went up. "Good. Then we have a mutual consensus. This leads us to lessons of futility and a very common word used amongst almost every religion. Extra bonus points for anyone who can guess this word that ties in directly with religion and futility."

Stacey's hand was the only one that went up. "Stacey?"

She declared very confidently, "It's *belief*."

"Right, as usual. Robbie, can you mark that down for me?" I looked over and saw that he was distracted. Brandi was rocking her leg with her stiletto heel dangling from her toes. "Robbie? Can you record that for me?"

He snapped out of his daze. "Oh…sorry, Professor. Right away."

I just laughed and thought, "Ahhh, young love."

One of the girls near the front asked, "How are futility, religion, and belief linked together?"

Stacey's hand shot up like a rocket. I whispered to her, "Let's see if anyone else can answer."

I directed my attention to the class, "Can someone reply to her question? It's a good one."

Brandi looked at Robbie while curling her fingers in her hair. "Is there any extra credit?"

I thought, "The hormones are so thick between the two of them, I could cut it with a baby spoon."

Todd's hand went up. "Todd?" Stacey frowned and looked toward him to see if he could answer it correctly.

"I'm guessing, but doesn't it have to do with being all powerful and stuff?" I gestured for him to continue. "I'm not religious or anything, but I hear that God is supposed to be all powerful."

Bruce poked sharply, "So what's your point? Get to it already."

Todd made a face that brushed off his rude comment, then he added, "It seems to me, that if God is all powerful—and God could not kill an immortal, or be killed as an immortal being—then even *belief* wouldn't make a difference."

He looked down in disappointment about himself. "I know I'm not making much sense. Give me a moment..." He gathered his thoughts, looked back up, and continued, "It's not just religions that say to believe, either; a lot of rah-rah motivational speakers tell you to believe. My basketball coach says to believe. But belief can't do everything. It takes more than just saying *I believe* for something to work. And some things just can't be done. That ties futility in with religion and belief." He looked to me. "Am I making any sense?"

Stacey turned around and practically begged me for her chance to speak, but I replied, "You're on the right track, Todd. I think you've done really well for such a complex question." Then I nodded to Stacey. "Go ahead."

She was so ready to answer that she nearly burst. "Thank you," she huffed. "Belief requires more than just thinking something and it will happen; you have to meet certain criteria for anything to work. There is a checklist that must be followed." That made a lot of students' heads perk up.

"Stacey, I want the students to write this down. And I have to say that I'm very impressed that you know about the list."

She smiled, "Thanks. Shall I go on?"

"Please do. I'll add or subtract something if it's wrong." I gave her my teacher's wink because I had a feeling she knew the list already.

"Well, first, you have to make sure it's even possible, like your question of the day. If you can't kill an immortal, then any attempt to achieve that goal would be a lesson in futility. It would never happen. So even with belief, God could not kill an immortal."

"Right," as I looked to the class. "Here's another example where belief would not work, and this ties in with the three religious O's: omniscient, omnipotent, and omnipresent. I want you to consider this: Is it possible for a being to know *everything* and know *nothing* at the same time without creating any paradoxes?"

One of the guys in the back shot his hand up. "What's a paradox?"

"I'm glad you asked," I smirked to myself.

Robbie moaned and put his hand on his head, "Not the paradox joke again."

I continued, "It's when a parrot is in the soul realm and says there's no such thing as death. Then the parrot reincarnates as an ox and gets hit by a truck, dies, and goes back to the Realm of Souls and merges with the parrot's soul. That creates a parrot-ox. Get it? A parrot-ox, a paradox..." The students groaned.

The guy in the back chuckled, "I get it—parrot-ox. That's a good one." He laughed some more to himself, "Funny!"

"Thank you." I bowed. "I'll be here every Friday, and don't forget to tip your waitress." They laughed at that joke.

"OK, let's get back on track, shall we? Part of knowing all experiences would also include the experience of knowing nothing at all. You can't know *nothing* at all and still know *everything*. The experience would cancel one or the other out. It's a lesson in futility. Even belief could not make that work. Right, Stacey? Would you like to continue?"

She nodded in agreement, "So, as I was saying, there is a checklist. And the first thing is to see if it's even possible. Then you have to have the energy, power, resources, and ability to do it."

She got Todd's attention. "You can't make a free throw in the third dimensional world without some kind of hoop and some kind of ball, right?"

He clapped. "Stacey's right. That's why I questioned my coach, and he didn't like it. He made me run laps for days."

Looking toward the class, I acknowledged, "Her list is spot on. First, it must be achievable. Then you have to have all of the parts needed to make it work. If your goal is to make a house out of playing cards, don't you think that you would need to have a deck of playing cards?" They all nodded. "No playing cards, no house. And before you say *You could build it out of something else,* you have to look at the goal. The goal was *house out of playing cards*—which leads me to the missing part of belief." Stacey was stunned that she'd missed one part. "Belief seems to have a built-in goal at the beginning of the list to guide the entire process, don't you think? The rest is exactly what Stacey explained." She was still shocked that she had missed a part, and her mouth was hanging open.

"For the next class, I want you to consider the three religious O's for yourself and see if it works within your faith. We'll talk about that on Monday. Use Stacey's checklist and my small addendum to see if it's possible to be omniscient, omnipotent, and omnipresent—and don't forget about parrot-oxes." The guy in the back laughed again. "Please write down your assignment before we go on."

While they were writing, I had my own epiphany. "As much as I believe loving the Order could change things, I'm sad to say that it won't. If they don't care about love, compassion, or kindness toward others, then nothing I do in that manner will help. They won't respond to my love; they don't honor it. It's as plain a lesson in futility as it gets. They'll just laugh at me and continue to enslave the world with their implants, mainframe, and soul-catcher ship. They'll kill and destroy everything just to keep this world under the Order's control. The only way to help these students and everyone else is to make a stand."

Another thought followed. "I love these people so much that I will do what it takes to give them a chance to work toward freedom for all souls. Love may not work with the Order, but my love for others could make a difference. It's settled, then. I know what I must do."

Bruce and Phillip had another zing in their ears with the brainwashing signal. Then Beth raised her hand. "Professor, can I ask you a question, please? It's a religious question."

"Sure, Beth. We are here to philosophize about religion."

"Well, I've been confused lately. I was at my youth meeting last night at my church, and I brought up some of the things you were talking about and told them to my priest. Then my priest brought up some good points in favor of our religion." She smiled confidently. "Then he asked me to ask you a simple question."

"Go on. You can ask."

"He wanted to know why you won't accept Jesus as your Lord and Savior."

"Beth, you know that I said there would be no recruiting in this class"—I looked around to the entire room—"to anyone's religion."

"I know, and I'm not trying to recruit you. I—"

Rochelle interrupted and chastised her, "It sure sounded like it!" A few students nodded and agreed.

Phillip said with an uncharacteristically sarcastic voice, "Yeah, Professor. Why won't you accept Jesus as your Lord and Savior?"

Bruce gave him a punch in the arm. "Good one, dude." Phillip smiled evilly at him and laughed. Then he wiped his arm.

I looked toward Phillip and Bruce with concern. I knew something wasn't right.

Beth was still looking at me for an answer. "Well…?" she pursued smugly.

I took a second, and then responded, "I think you should write this down for your priest. I'll give you three examples." She got her pen ready. "And before I begin, I've done this for years, and I have answered many questions like this. I know that most people—in any religion—will have a rebuttal for my response to try and prove me wrong based on his or her religious teachings. Before you refute me, please listen to what I have to say. I don't want to be saved or given some response that was taught to you by your religious leaders. If you are going to give me your own thoughts, I welcome them. OK?" She nodded *yes*.

I took another moment before starting. "As I've said numerous times, I won't follow a religion that uses fear to recruit or control anyone. Both Christianity and Catholicism use fear as their main control method, along with Judaism, Muslim teachings, Baptist, Methodist, Lutheran, and many other offshoots of those religions not mentioned."

She looked up at me with concern. I continued, "To paraphrase, your teachings say to accept Jesus or you are going to hell, right? It's commonly known that this is taught in all of your Bibles and Catholic schools. It was taught to me when I went to Catholic school. And clearly…well, that's very plainly a fear-based teaching."

I looked to see if she was done writing, then I added, "Second, the rules to get into any religion's supposed version of heaven keep changing throughout history. One century you are going to hell for doing something not accepted by the church or some temple god, including believing in science, and the next century it's OK and completely acceptable." She was writing furiously.

"Third—and this is strictly for any Jesus-based faiths—there are major contradictions about Jesus alone."

"Like what?" she asked, hoping to stump me.

"Here's one great example, out of many—and there are many." I made a big sign with my hands and arms. "You've heard that Jesus said to invite in your enemies. You are supposed to love your neighbors no matter what, right?"

"Yes," she replied. A number of students nodded, too. "I hear that all of the time in church and our Bible study group."

"Here's the contradiction: One minute, Jesus is saying to love everyone. 'OK, everyone into the pool. We are going to have one big party.' The next minute, Jesus—and this is reported throughout many Christian and Catholic texts that I've read—is said to have cast out many demons and performed countless exorcisms." Her eyes got big from what I'd just said because she had just realized there was a major contradiction to her faith that she couldn't deny.

I continued with emotion, "So, one minute, Jesus is saying, 'Everyone is invited into the pool.' Then Jesus says angrily and points, 'OK! Someone peed in the pool. Everyone, get out of the pool!' Beth, you can't have it both ways and not be called a hypocrite. You can't say to love your enemies and invite them in, and as soon as they are in your pool, you perform an exorcism to remove them. That's as clear a contradiction as it gets.

"And to add one more, according to many fear-based religions, there's supposedly an invisible Saturnian old man sitting on a cloud who loves me unconditionally, but will judge me for my imperfections—that I'm not allowed to be in conscious control of—and will cast me to hell to suffer for all eternity. That's not a loving act, nor would that be an all-loving god—and certainly not a god that I would worship. And we already proved in Monday's class that no one is perfect or able to love everyone for every second of the day."

I re-emphasized, "We are not allowed—for whatever reason—to be perfect." I looked at the entire class and gestured. "Everyone would be going to hell, based on this reptilian-induced, man-made, favoritism-based religion. And please don't quote the Adam and Eve myth about falling from perfection. That was set up by the reptilians and evil organizations so women would be punished and controlled by men. So no, Beth, I won't put my faith into a Saturnian-based belief system filled with contradictions, fear, subjugation, and control. The major religions just keep fighting amongst themselves, and with others, to prove whose religious belief is right, and I don't want to be a part of that."

She was extremely upset and had a tear in her eye. I calmly added, "Beth, in no way am I trying to pull you from your religion. I support your quest for knowledge so you can strengthen your faith or change your mind. I am behind you in your search either way. If you wish to stay in your religion, I support you. Stay…stay for as long as you like. And if you decide to change your belief, I support that, too." She was still upset, and I finished, "I did my best to answer your question so you and your priest would understand." She wiped away a number of her tears.

Bruce practically bit my head off, "Why did you have to be so mean?!" A number of students turned around in shock to his question.

Phillip followed right behind and repeated the same thing, "Yeah! Why did you have to be so mean?!"

Stacey said defensively, "He wasn't mean. She pushed her question on him, and he answered her honestly. There wasn't anything mean about his answer."

Todd added, "Yeah, he didn't say anything mean at all. And he didn't offer his beliefs until she asked. What's gotten into you two?" Almost everyone was either visually or verbally showing their agreement with Todd and Stacey.

Bruce raised both of his hands and answered sarcastically, "What?!"

One of the guys in the back asked, "Can we talk about sex now?"

"No, we can't talk about sex now, although I appreciate your tenacity." I gave them a forced smile.

"Beth," I urged, "are you OK?"

"I'll be fine. I just have to think about what you said."

"If it would help, you can always set up a meeting with me and your priest during student conference time. I'm here to help you."

"No, I'll be alright. I just need to think about this."

I looked at the entire class and reiterated, "Folks, I want you to be crystal clear on this. I don't want this class to be about me. I want it to be about you."

The girl up front spoke up, "But we learn from your experience. I, personally, want to know about what you think. It will save us a lot of headaches in the future, especially if we've really been brainwashed." That caught me by surprise, and I smiled.

A girl at the back left added, "Yeah, what she said." A number of students were nodding their heads. "I want to know what you came up with. No one else is bringing up this many great points about life, not even my parents. You've been the best source for me so far. I don't care if it contradicts what the U.S. government or religions teach. I want to know the truth. That's why I signed up for your class." She got a number of students clapping.

Phillip and Bruce got another zing in their ears because someone had talked negatively about the government. Phillip immediately held his head to try and block out the signal. He fought the negative urges and apologized sincerely, "Professor, I'm sorry about earlier."

"It's OK, Phillip. Do you have a question?"

He was struggling to ask due to the programming. "Can you please tell us about living together without being governed?" He received another upload in his left ear.

I saw him grab the left side of his head. I realized he was getting a signal from the Order. "Sure, I can tell you about this system."

Bruce started to mumble something, but Rochelle turned around and yelled at him, "Can it, Bruce!" He didn't say anything else for the moment.

The voice grew from my soul and resounded in my head, "The God Scroll will set them free. Together, We will speak to the hearts of women and men."

When I picked up the scroll, my body became filled with a loving, powerful energy, much more powerful than I had ever felt in either lifetime. This time, I heard the thoughts before I said them. I also recognized that it was the same voice that Tumaini had heard in Egypt, and the same voice that had spoken through me on Wednesday. The message was picking up from the last conversation.

"My children, it is good to speak with you again. I return with a continuation of My message, and then we shall talk about true freedom for the world. I say this with love and the hope of returning that which was taken from you so long ago.

"I give applause to those among you who live with courage, to those who live and speak his truth, to those who bare their souls for all to see. For those courageous souls in this room, you are the sun that will shine brightly in the future of days. You are the ones to give hope to the new masses. You will be the ones who will pave the way for a world of peace, love, and abundance.

"You, My children, are the strong ones, for it is the weak who must lie and use deceit to gain their power. It is those who hide behind the shadows who lack the courage and strength that you show. When you speak the truth about your thoughts, desires, and emotions, you will be stronger than any pyramid ever built."

While these godly thoughts were being channeled through me, I envisioned the power-based control pyramid that the Order uses. Then I saw it begin to crumble and fall.

The voice continued, "When you look at the world around you, you see great divisions amongst your people. It almost seems that peace would be impossible with so many different thoughts. But I tell you, My children, that peace is at hand for those who choose the path of the brave.

"As I have shared in your days past, you must realize that the separation of your nations and religions was strategically planned by a small group of selfish leaders and aliens. They did this with the sole purpose of dividing you. If you have the courage to forgo what was given to you as truth, and look to the real truth, then you can begin your way toward peace and freedom for all men and women, for all living souls—plants, animals, birds, and trees alike. All souls on your planet can be free from this day forward.

"As I have said, My children, fear creates many things. Fear creates ownership, laws, borders, names, and nations. You were taught to accept this as a way of life by your elders, and you were taught to cling to them as if your life depended on it. I will tell you, as you already know deep within yourselves, your life does not depend on a name, a border, a nation, a law, or ownership to live and thrive. None of this creates life or sustains life in any way. These concepts break the hearts of nature and your souls. See the pattern of destruction, and choose a new path toward life for all.

"Hear Me now, My children: Not I, nor any loving being, would force you to remove your beliefs and personal identities. We would not strip them from you and bend you to Our ways. That would be a repeat of what you have already experienced up until now. But, My children, what if you gave up your identities freely for a higher goal of peace and love? Could you imagine such a place? Could you see yourself living in a world without division and enslavement? Could you experience a world that was meant for life, love, growth, and experience?"

The voice paused for a moment. Some of my students' heads were nodding in approval of this thoughtful message.

"There is a way to attain such a life. There is a way to reach beyond your current plateau. The way is simple, and it is to accept your fear and move beyond it. Work to transform your fears into love and courage. I tell you, My children, when you transform your fears, you remove the need for borders. Transforming your fears removes the need for nations and national pride. Transforming your fears dissolves the need for competition. Quite simply, transforming fear disintegrates the need for coveting possessions and allows you to give openly and freely to all.

"I know these concepts may seem new or strange to you, as you were taught that competition was good and that only the strong survive, but this is not the very nature of your souls. If you look at your natural state of being, your soul would not think twice about giving aid to the sick, your soul would not blink at comforting those who hurt, and your soul would not pause when it comes to feeding the hungry. That, My children, is the very nature of your soul."

One of the football players chimed in, "But competition isn't bad. It can show you how to rise above adversity."

"Yes, My son, but what is the very nature behind competition? It is fear, fear that you must prove to your friends and self that you are worthy or good enough. What do you need to prove that is greater than love? Can you forgo your need to compete and show compassion in its stead? Can you alleviate shame and love your neighbor over proof? Competition is always about separation, pride, and the concept of *us against them*. This is not the way of a loving soul. A loving soul does not divide itself based upon fear. Love unites. Love brings together. Love grows and shares and asks for nothing in return."

I watched his reaction. He sat in confusion from the words that could not be denied.

"My children, upon this wonderful planet you call Earth, did I not give you food to eat, water to drink, raw materials for shelter and clothing to wear, medicine to heal, and creativity for entertainment—and all without the need for gold or coin? Were you not given the ability to learn and to educate yourself and others for free? There is no task that cannot be done without your need for exchanging golden trinkets. You have everything handed to you that you need for life, free of charge, and free it should remain. It is only those with fear who say they have not enough and accumulate worthless piles of numbers for self.

"My children, you were taught to be subservient to those who create the laws. You were taught to respect the authority given to those who protect the rich. My children, when you are ready to stop being treated as slaves and inferior beings, you will stand together, liberate yourselves, and reclaim that which I gave to all souls—freedom."

Beth inquired, "Professor, I still don't know if you are acting or not, but how does this all work? All we have ever been taught is that we grow up, get an education, then get a job and pay taxes. I feel like a worker bee already."

"A good question, My child. Remember, I gave you everything you need to sustain life without asking for anything in return. No one person owns the air, land, space, or seas. If you held true to concepts of love, courage, and freedom, everything you do would be a gift given to another."

"So let me get this straight...I would do a job, and then give everything I do away for free?"

"Yes, My child. And all things you need would also be given to you *for free*. This was the plan before the reptilians changed the Matrix of Being."

"I don't know about these reptiles, but wouldn't that be like barter or trade?"

"To barter or trade still claims ownership of the things I gave all souls freely, and ownership is a creation of fear. To live in fear is not the way of the soul.

"Ask yourself these questions, My children: If your coins disappeared and all money systems dissolved, would the fish stop swimming? Would the cows stop producing milk? Would the apple trees stop bearing fruit? Would the wind stop moving, the sun stop rising, or the air no longer be breathable? I tell you again, My loved ones, life exists, and will continue to exist, without the need for coin or profit. You have the chance to free yourselves from this cycle of tyranny, or you can remain as slaves. But you must do it, and do it together, for the freedom of all—including your children's children's children. Your future relies on your deeds and actions of today."

The voice stopped, and a flash of light completely filled my mind. I had just received a massive download of information directly from Source. I was told lovingly, "You now have the information you need, Tumaini. Teach them in your own voice. They will listen, and most will hear. I am with you...always." Then the voice faded within.

I put the scroll down in the box and engaged my students, "Who has a question?" Like a startled covey of quail, hands went flying into the air in all directions. I thought to myself, "I've got this."

I looked at them and motioned. "I'll answer all of your questions, promise. Just put your hands down and give me a second to explain first." They all complied.

"OK, to explain this, you will have to do something challenging. You will have to forget *everything* that you've been brainwashed with up to this point by the aliens, religions, governments, and schools. Not an easy task—not even for myself—but it will help you to understand how this works." My body language added to my excitement. "And boy does it work well!

"Imagine waking up as an adult in a town. There are no financial obligations of any kind. There's no paycheck needed because everything is free. There are no taxes, fees, interest rates, collection services, credit cards, bank accounts, or annoying salesmen. All there is is a desire to serve others with your best God-given talents. I haven't said a lot, but is everyone with me so far? There's no money whatsoever." There were a lot of confused looks, but no one raised a hand.

"Here's how this works. When you are a kid in this new community, you won't be forced or taught to go to school to be trained like a brainless monkey just to make other people rich. There is no trying to outdo the Joneses, either. When you are in school, you would learn at your pace, and you would learn what interests you. If you like to paint, you learn to paint. If you like to garden, you learn to garden. If you like to build, you learn to build. And who are your teachers, you might ask? Well, they would be the best gardeners, painters, and builders in the world. They would be the masters at their craft because they would have been given the opportunity to master a trade in service to others, instead of being forced to work for someone else where they hate their jobs."

Allen raised his hand. "I think I get this. Because people like what they are doing, and they aren't forced to do it, they would do a better job. They would produce better things—things that have better quality. I hated flipping burgers when I was sixteen and didn't care how they came out. I'd even pick a few up off of the floor. But, if I liked to cook and serve that way, I would make the best burgers for others."

"Exactly. You are starting to get it." I looked around the room. "And why would someone make the best burgers for others to eat?"

Rochelle answered, "Because if I liked sewing—which I do—I would make the best shirts, blouses, and dresses to give away, knowing that I would receive the best from others in return." She turned to Allen and winked. "Including the best burgers from you, sweety."

"That would be the goal in a town like this," I affirmed. "You would learn from the masters of each trade. Essentially, you would apprentice and learn all that you could. Then you would take your skills and provide for others, knowing that they are providing for you.

"Think of it with numbers. Let's say you live in a small town of only one hundred and fifty people. When you wake up, you ask one hundred and forty-nine others what you can do for them."

Phillip tried to sabotage the talk. "It sounds like slave labor. You are forced to work for the town."

Stacey countered immediately, "That's not what he is saying at all. Aren't you listening?" She was angry at him. "It makes perfect sense. If you wake up and serve the community, one hundred and forty-nine others are serving you, too. You would have more people asking you *What can I do for you?* than you would know what to do with. How many people do you have serving you right now?" He didn't reply. "I bet you can't even count them on two hands. This is an awesome idea. Please continue, Professor."

"That's a great point, Stacey. In our current system, you are taught to look out for yourself, and maybe your family, if you are lucky. No one in your neighborhood is trying to make your life better every day. But in this system, the entire community serves each other. You would wake up to more people helping you than you would ever experience in our money-driven society."

A girl near the back contributed, "It's like that barn-raising concept. When everyone pitches in, they raise a barn in a day instead of hiring contractors to do the same job in six months."

Allen added, "And it would be a quality barn because it was made by people who liked doing it, and they would care about you, instead of caring about making a buck."

"That's the idea!" I applauded both of them.

Daphnee commented, "It sounds like some of the communes in the sixties."

"To a point, but a lot of communes were either sabotaged, or they lacked a binding belief system."

"Do you mean like a religion?"

"Sort of…" I took a few steps before continuing. "Think about this folks, if you use a religion as a binding belief system, it separates people. I grew up in Amish country, and the Amish separated themselves quite well from anyone who didn't follow their beliefs. And if I recall correctly, some of you in the last class said you would do the same thing.

"So what could be a potential binding belief system that would bring people together instead of separating them—where people of all races, sexes, or creeds could live?"

Brandi asked, "Love?"

"Yes. Good answer." Robbie smiled at her.

"But you have to have something else, something that also strengthens love to make this work. Think folks. What is it?" A number of answers were given, but nobody hit the nail on the head.

"Alright, I'll give it to you. The binding belief system must be based upon peace—with love—above all else. Peace and love overrules personal pride, ego, fear, and greed. If these two concepts are taught above any religious belief, then a community like this would have a better chance of cohesion. Peace and love would be the glue that holds it all together."

Bruce spat angrily, "This is crazy. If I go to a car dealership, they aren't going to say that they love me and give me a car for free!"

"Yes," I acknowledged him. "In the old money-driven, greed-based system, you are correct. They would laugh at you because they've been brainwashed to use money by the reptilian and Anunnaki Order. But in this new system, if you want a car—hopefully that doesn't use fossil fuels—then you would receive one for free. And not only that, you would receive the best car possible because the car makers would love doing what they are doing. There would be no taxes on the car, no deposit, no slick car sales-man ripping you off for a commission, and your vehicle won't depreciate thousands of made-up dollars as soon as you pull it off the lot just so the insurance companies can get rich."

"I don't like what you are saying," he retorted. "I came to college to get a degree in finance and become rich."

Rochelle barked at him, "Nobody gets rich without using a lower wage earner, stepping on someone's back, or hurting someone to get to the top—no one! If you aren't receiving equal pay to what your boss makes, then your boss is using you for his or her own greed. Is that the type of person you want to grow up to be?"

"Yes! Don't you?!" I could feel the anger in the room, and a number of students were fidgeting uncomfortably.

"This is a great debate," I contended. "This type of community would not happen overnight—although I wish it would. And it's like you heard earlier: You have the chance to free yourselves from this cycle of tyranny, or you can remain as slaves."

Robbie spoke up, "I like this new money-free system. Can we talk about it more?"

I looked at the clock, and then to the class. "Here's what we are going to do. I am going to add one more point—even though there are many to cover—then we'll list pros and cons to this idea. Sound good?" All but two in the room agreed.

"I know what some of you must be thinking: it sounds too good to be true. And you are right, we are still human, and with human flaws and emotions. But isn't this better than being treated as slaves by the cabalistic Order?" They were nodding and wanting more. "Here is one of the points that needs to be covered. What about the jobs that nobody wants to do—say, sanitation?"

Stacey piped in, "That's simple. Everyone does it on a rotating schedule. With a normal-sized town, you wouldn't be doing sanitation but once, maybe twice, a month."

"OK, I'll add another point beyond this one, and then we'll do pros and cons. There still has to be a standard for certain occupations, like medicine. You don't want a three-year-old performing open-heart surgery with his pacifier. And what would make this work is that a person would not volunteer his service until he knew for sure that he could do it without causing intentional harm to another. And this would work if peace and love were taught from infanthood instead of people being controlled to live in fear.

Pride would not be as big an issue.

"I can see we need to talk about this more on Monday, but let's get the list going. What are some of the useless jobs that would become antiquated with a money-free society?"

Rochelle mentioned, "Anything to do with money or advertising. They were useless to begin with. They create nothing but a pain in the—"

"Rochelle, be nice," I chuckled. Bruce was extremely angry at all of this talk because of his programming, but he didn't say anything to her. "Can you give me a pro or con, Rochelle?"

"Yes. When you give money power, you become powerless. Money now controls everything. And you also make those with money powerful. It's time to take back our power and tip the scales back to the people."

"I like that one. Who else has a pro or con?"

Stacey proposed, "It seems, after everything you've taught us in the past week, that any argument you would have against a no-money system or serving everyone in the community for free is just an expression of your own personal greed or fears. So the only con to this community would be those who can't stop living in fear."

"Based on the information provided lately, I would agree with you." Looking to the room, I instructed, "Let's list at least ten to twenty benefits to a no-money society and call it a day. I'll start with the biggest one: *time*.

"Money, or the pursuit of money to barely survive, has taken away our personal time—time away from family, time away from friends, and time away from love, peace, and community"—I raised my finger for emphasis—"and doing things we enjoy. This is one of the objectives of those in power: destroy the family unit and make both parents work long hours just to survive. How about another?"

Todd volunteered, "My dad hates taxes. He's makes just enough to be stuck in the highest tax bracket, but not enough to do what the rich do. So he gets hammered every year. With your no-money system, that would mean no more taxes—ever! And this goes directly with the other things I wrote down while you were talking: no more inflation, no more deficits, no more recessions, depressions, stock markets, global economic collapse, credit scores, world banks, U.S. Federal Reserve, separation by economic class, and no more third world countries. It also wipes out greedy stock brokers and lawyers because there would be no more stupid lawsuits for money. Oh, and no more IRS! My dad hates them with a passion."

I nodded, "I can understand why, too. They aren't on anyone's favorite list. And that was a great summation, Todd." He smiled.

Rochelle couldn't help herself and blurted out, "You forgot a big one. No more men controlling the pay scale." She turned to Todd. "Would you like to add that one to your list?"

He pointed to her like I would have. "Got it!"

I mentioned to Robbie, "There's a lot to write on the board. Would you grab a marker and help me out?" He stopped looking at Brandi and got up.

One of my quietest students, a young man up front raised his hand and shared, "There would be no more unemployment. If there is no more money, there is no need to fire someone because of a profit and loss margin. And to add to this, there would always be something to do in a community to help out. This alone would wipe out most of the job stress out there."

"Great point!" I praised. A number of students clapped for him.

Brandi joined in the conversation, "With no more money, there wouldn't be any more homelessness. You wouldn't need a mortgage from a bank. If you needed a home, the community would pitch right in and build you one."

While I was writing, Robbie added, "And you could have the best architects design you a home that is pretty to the eye." I knew why he said that, but he was right about the best architects part.

One of the guys in the back shouted, "Since we *still* aren't talking about sex, I'll add some." A number of students laughed at his comment. "If there are no mortgages, then there wouldn't be any loans, either. I mean, there wouldn't be any kind of lending or obligations to someone. Oh, and no foreclosures that force people out of their homes. That happened to our family when my dad lost his job."

His friend added, "So, no more bills of any kind. And no need for food stamps, Medicare, Medicaid, welfare, social security—"

The other guy took over again. "This would be cool. No need for banks, which also means no more bailouts for bankers or banker bonuses that the people paid for." The class broke out in applause.

Rochelle appended to his statement, "And did you notice that none of the bankers went to jail or were punished for what they did? The useless president and government did nothing." She got more applause.

"I have to tell you, this is better than I had expected. How about a few more?"

The girl who had talked about not being afraid of dogs exclaimed, "This is amazing. If everything were free, and if we really could make this work, there would be no theft. How could you steal something if everything is free and you are already getting the best from your neighbors? Why would you steal something that they want you to have?" She paused for a brief moment, and then continued, "This would wipe out so many crimes, it would be awesome! Theft, bribery, scams, and counterfeiting would all be a thing of the past."

Phillip was struggling with the thoughts in his head and replied to her, "It doesn't stop someone from killing."

"Yes, but the majority of crimes behind killing would be gone, too. I think this is a great idea. I'd love to live there." Then she addressed the class, "This no-money system is a gift to humanity, whether it was created by God or not. Think about it… The problems of the world have existed ever since the creation of ownership and money. Why keep repeating the same mistake over and over again? The governments sure aren't going to fix anything. They just keep perpetuating the problems to keep their jobs. This would be a way to break the cycle. And it might not be perfect, like the professor said, but it sure beats living in financial slavery." She got a bunch of applause.

Allen spoke next, "I've got a few." I gave him the gesture to go ahead. "If there isn't money, and no one is controlled by fear, that would annihilate the insurance companies. They all rely on fear to sell you things."

Rochelle reached over and squeezed his hand. "Wow, Allen. Good one."

He continued, "And if there are no insurance companies, nobody could be denied health care. Everyone would be treated by the best physicians. And the doctors could focus on prevention and their patients staying healthy, instead of writing prescriptions for pain management. I would think people would be healthier in a society like this—less stress and all."

"That's a good supposition," I commended. "The pharmaceutical companies of today would hate this type of town." I shook my head in disappointment toward their greed. "Let's add one more."

One of the guys in the back announced, "I have to say this. The politicians would never go for it because it would wipe out prostitution. They wouldn't be able to pay for sex anymore, and nobody else would sleep with those scumbags."

"Nice, but that's not a benefit for this type of community. There would be no government in its current form. So how about one last example?"

Todd responded, "I still like that there would be no need for lawyers, but I'll add to the list I said earlier. This one is personal. No more Ivy League schools that only grant higher education to the rich. Everyone in the community would be given the best education possible by teachers and masters of the trade who love to teach."

"Excellent," I clapped. "And I'll add to your list, Todd. No more bankers, judges, lawyers, multi-billionaires, politicians, or any of the one percenters controlling your choices, moral standards, or your life—ever again!" The class erupted into cheers.

"This is an awesome list, folks. You did great today. Let's not forget about Monday's three O's assignment. Oh, and I want you to consider this over the weekend, too. Think about your parents' jobs. Were their jobs created only because of money? And what about your future profession? Was it only created because of money? Would your profession still exist in a community that does not use money? And with that, class is dismissed."

I looked directly at Phillip and Bruce. "Would you two mind staying after? I'd like to ask you something." I knew they'd been tagged by the Order, and I wanted to help them remove it.

Everyone left except for Robbie and the two boys. I started to say something, but Bruce stood up and began walking out in a huff. "I'm not staying here. I didn't do anything wrong. But wait until my father hears about this class. He's a major contributor to the university. He won't like that you just put down my major." His look was of pure anger. "See you next class, dude!" Then he walked out the door.

"Phillip—" I didn't get any further.

He burst back, "Stay out of my personal life." He ran out of the classroom before I could tell him about the ringing in his ear.

Robbie asked, "What got into those two? They've never acted like this before."

"I'm worried about them, Robbie. Something bad happened to them. Just keep them in your good thoughts."

"I will. Do you need me anymore?"

"No, I can see that Brandi is waiting outside for you. Go have fun."

"Thanks, Professor. Great class today. I was inspired."

"Me, too, Robbie. Me, too."

CHAPTER THIRTY-ONE

WEEKEND BOOT CAMP: SATURDAY A.M.

Constance kissed me passionately on our doorstep. "That was a great date tonight. I'm glad we changed plans instead of waiting for Saturday." She gave me one more quick kiss. "Thanks for being flexible."

"Well, flexible is my middle name," and I gave here a suggestive wink.

"No, it's not. You have to stretch every time we—"

"Hey now, I'm not that old. I just like to stay limber."

"OK, limber boy, let's go pay the sitter and see how Hara is doing."

I pulled her in one more time for another smooch. "Do you want to see how limber I am?"

"Do you want the neighbors watching?" She turned and opened the door, and then she whispered, "At least wait until we're upstairs."

I whispered back, "OK. I don't think they could handle any more than us kissing anyway."

She walked in while doing her best sexy walk. Her dress swished with each step. "Will that hold you until we go to bed?"

"Can I see that again?" I laughed.

"If your heart can handle it." She winked. "And don't drop the leftovers." I actually bobbled them for a second.

Constance stopped just in time for the sitter to meet us. We asked if everything was fine, and she told us there were no problems. After paying her, we checked in on Hara. She was sleeping, so we didn't wake her.

"Shall we?" she asked.

"No need to ask me twice," and I closed the door.

———————

Just after 2:00 a.m., Constance woke up, and I opened my eyes with her. We were both still partially asleep. She quickly sat up. "Do you hear that noise?"

In the bedroom, we both heard a mechanical whirring sound near her side of the bed, but up toward the ceiling. We couldn't see anything, but it was definitely loud and audible, as loud as a high-pitched blender on low speed.

"What is that?" I asked. "Do you hear it?"

"Yes, do you think...?"

"It's something." The noise continued for another few seconds. It moved slowly toward the foot of the bed, like it was scanning us, and then the whirring sound stopped abruptly. Neither of us was in any pain or danger, but we both knew it wasn't a bad dream.

Without any notice, the door flew open. "Mommy! Mommy! There's a noise in my room!" Hara jumped on the bed and scurried into her mother's arms.

Constance held her tightly. "I know, baby, we heard something too, but there's nothing to be scared of."

I bounced off the mattress to turn on a light, and Constance gasped when she looked at the window. She immediately covered Hara with her body to protect her.

"What is it?!"

She pulled the blanket up over Hara so she couldn't be seen and pointed at our window. "Look! Out on the balcony!"

Through the partially-opened curtains, we both saw the shape of a very tall humanoid-looking figure. It had a black outline and was at least eight feet tall. The only facial feature we could see was a pair of glowing red eyes.

I flicked the switch, jumped onto the bed to get across, hurdled Constance and Hara, and threw the curtains open. By the time I got them completely moved, the figure was gone.

Constance was entirely over Hara's body. "What was it? Did you see it?"

Hara pleaded in a muffled voice, "Mommy, you're hurting me."

"Oh, sorry, baby." She got off and lifted the blanket. Hara put her arms around her.

"What ever it was, it's gone," I affirmed.

Hara asked, "What was it?"

"I don't know, sweety, but it's not there now. You must have frightened it off." She knew I was only saying that to comfort her.

"Michael, did you shield the house?"

"Yes, I did." I had to think if I really had or not. "Yes, I'm sure of it." I refocused my energy and put more force into the protective bubble. "Maybe that's why nothing hurt us. I think someone was just trying to scare us."

"They did a pretty good job of it." She was looking at Hara's face, then she looked at me with concern.

"If they were going to do something to us, they would have done it by now. Are both of you OK?"

Hara lifted her head. "Was it the mean aliens again?"

She replied, "It might have been. But we're OK. Daddy's going to take care of us." She put her hand on her head to comfort her more.

"I'm going to check outside. Both of you stay here."

"I'm not staying here. I'm going with you."

"Me, too," added Hara.

"Alright, but both of you stay behind me."

I grabbed my flashlight as we were heading out the back door. There were no clouds in the sky, and some of the stars were visible. I checked everywhere with the beam of light, while Constance and Hara were clutching onto the back of my robe.

"There's nothing here," I assured them.

"Do you think it's safe, Daddy?"

"I think we'll be just fine, pumpkin. What do you say we all go back to bed?"

Constance was looking at the sky. I nudged her softly. "Do you see something?"

All three of us were now looking at a group of stars. One of the stars was twinkling brighter than the others in the cluster and flashing opaque colors. "Do you know that constellation?" she asked.

"If I'm right, that's Ursa Major, that's Ursa Minor, and that brighter star over there is directly where Thuban would be—Alpha Draconis."

The star kept getting a little brighter, but not any bigger. Then it moved slightly, revealing the real star directly behind it. It floated toward the right to show that it wasn't a star at all. Immediately, it shot vertically in the sky, which made all three of our heads jerk backwards. And in an instant, it changed directions and flew off horizontally and out of sight—again, making all of our heads move in tandem to follow its flight path.

Hara was excited. "Whoa! Was that a UFO?!"

"I'd say that's a pretty good guess. Either that, or the government is hiding secrets again."

Constance stammered, "I… I…don't know what it was."

"That star, Alpha Draconis, is where some of the reptilians are supposed to come from. Ramla and the guys taught me that back in Egypt."

Hara asked while phonetically saying, "What's a rep-til-i-an?"

Constance answered, "Very mean aliens."

I looked at Hara. "She's got that right."

"Was that really a UFO?" Constance grabbed my arm.

"Your guess is as good as mine. But with all that is going on lately, I'd say you're right."

"And that thing in the window?"

"I think it was one of them."

"Them?" Hara chirped.

I nodded toward her, "Very mean aliens."

"Ohhh."

"Luckily, there's nothing else going on out here. Let's all go back to bed. If something happens, I'll take care of you."

"These aren't books that you can just blow off your desk with an energy ball. Can you handle one of those things?"

"I think so, and I'm starting to formulate a plan. It might be something that can help all of us."

"Well, just be careful. I don't want to lose you."

"I will." I pulled her in for a sideways hug. "C'mon, I have a feeling that they won't be back tonight."

Hara scowled, "Good. No mean aliens. Yuck!"

"I couldn't have said it any better, baby," I replied. "Now let's all go to bed."

The rest of the night was uneventful, and so was breakfast. At 9:30 a.m., Ted showed up with a cup of steaming coffee in his hand. By the time he was on the porch, Laura and Ricky pulled up behind his car. He turned, nodded, and waited for them to join him.

"Morning, Laura. Morning, Ricky. Good to see you again."

Ricky waved back, and Laura walked up and gave him a hello hug. "Hi, Ted. It's good to see you. What's been cookin'?"

"Oh, the usual research stuff about the Order—nothing major as of yet. How about you two? Did you discover anything?"

Ricky answered, "I think Laura figured out the riddle poem."

"I might have. I want to run it by Michael to get his opinion."

"Well, let's not keep his opinion waiting, then." Ted smiled, and then he rang the doorbell. *Ding-dong!*

Hara opened the door after peeking out the side curtain. "Hello," she said in a cheerful voice. "Daddy's upstairs with Mommy. They told me to let you in."

Laura greeted her first with a soft palm on her head. "Good morning, Hara." The other two gentlemen nodded and waved.

She jumped up and down a little bit. "Guess what?! We saw an alien and a UFO last night."

Ted asked with a raised tone, "You did?"

"Yes. I didn't see the alien, but I saw the UFO. Daddy chased away the mean thing in the window."

Laura knelt down to talk. "What did the UFO look like?"

"It was cool. It flashed all kinds of colors, like a blinking Easter egg. And there was this weird sound in our house right before it happened."

Ricky exclaimed, "I want to see a UFO."

Laura got a psychic hit. She saw a small glimpse of Ricky standing on a metallic-looking floor. "I think you just might get your wish." He turned to her with a quizzical look. "I'm just saying. There're no guarantees." She put her hand on his shoulder to get him moving. "Come on, let's get upstairs."

Ted leaned down to Hara. "Can you tell me more about the UFO?"

"It moved fast, so fast that it hurt my neck watching it."

"Did it have a shape to it? Was it like a flying saucer or a cigar shape?"

"It was too far away to see a shape. It was a ball of light," she answered with such innocence.

"Interesting…"

Hara jumped to the front of the line to take them up the stairs. Ted touched Ricky's shoulder to get him to look at her. "If you want to know what we are doing this for, there's your answer."

"It's a good answer, mon."

Constance greeted all of them as Hara rushed by her, "Morning. It's good to see all of you. Thanks again for coming."

Laura gave her a fast hug. "It's our pleasure."

Ted called to me, "Hara tells us that you had a visitor last night."

"Hi, Ted, Laura, Ricky. Just another event-filled night at the Whyse house. We should start selling tickets," I chuckled. "We could be the new alien deportation center comedy show."

Constance snorted, "Is that another *Whyse* crack?" We all laughed from her quick wit.

"Good one."

"Well," she said coyly, "I do have my moments."

"That you do. That you do."

Laura got my attention. "What's the plan for today?"

"These right here. When I took the glass off of the table this morning, a few cards moved toward the cross."

Hara rushed over. "I wanna see."

Constance and the rest echoed, "Me, too."

"If it does like before, we should be able to duplicate it. Can some of you put on gloves and help to hold the pieces down while I replace the glass?" Ted, Constance, and Hara put on the cotton gloves. "Great, you two hold these down over here"—I pointed to the other side of the large grouping of papyrus—"and Ted, you hold your piece below the grouping. When I count to three, put it down quickly and remove your hand."

Constance replied, "Got it."

"Are you ready, Hara?" She nodded. "Good. One...two...three!" They all let go of their pieces. As I was laying down the plexiglass, all four pieces of papyrus had started to move to the magic cross spread. One moved so far that it went into the pile of extra parchments. It only stopped because of the weight of the glass.

Ricky was astonished. "Will you look at that?" He pointed to the cross on the right. "They sure want to get over there."

Laura added, "I think we already know what will happen next."

Hara bounced a little. "Can I help lift the glass?"

467

"Sure, honey. Go grab that edge at the end." We lifted the cover, and all four pieces instantly wobbled and glided across the table. The one piece that was in the stack actually moved a few other pieces of papyrus with it.

With a hint of sarcasm, Ted cracked, "Just another plain ol' day at the Whyse house."

Constance teased, "Do you think you could muster up some of your old magic tricks and teach the dirty dishes to get in the dishwasher by themselves?"

"Yeah," I answered. "And I'll get the laundry to separate itself and jump into the washing machine, too."

"Good idea," she giggled.

"I hate to break up the Home Cleaning Network," joked Ted, "but do you know what these four cards are?"

"I haven't gotten that far yet. Whatever they are, they are the next possible futures in this timeline. It looked to me like they were heading for the number nine spot."

Ricky added, "It does look that way. And you've already experienced the soul-catcher ship."

"And the mainframe is locked into number ten." I pointed to the card. "We have an idea what the mainframe will do, but we don't know what the actions are that match up with the card yet."

I was scratching my head. "I have a thought. The soul-catcher happened recently, and with the events that happened yesterday, they opened up the possible events for number nine. It seems that the soul-catcher and the mainframe are controlling card number nine."

Laura burst, "That's so cool. The past and the future are now controlling what will happen next."

Ricky piped in, "Well, from what I know of this tarot spread, Tumaini set it up correctly. Only one event in the future"—he pointed to the mainframe card—"will control what is happening in the number nine spot. The last three events will grow from the actions of the present moment."

Constance remarked, "This is getting confusing."

Ted was looking concerned. "So let me get this straight. Eight and ten control number nine, right?" Ricky and I nodded. "Then eleven, twelve, and thirteen will happen from number nine?"

I corrected him, "You're close. Eight and ten control nine. That's the way I saw it when I was Tumaini. But the mainframe event still has to happen after number nine. So eleven, twelve, and thirteen build from the outcome of the mainframe."

"I think I've got it," as he scratched his head.

Constance pointed to the table. "I understand now. I got it, I got it, I got it. These two create the one between them, and this one has to manifest in the space-time continuum to create the last three."

Laura complimented me, "That's really ingenious, Michael. Way to go."

"Way to go, hon." She patted my chest. "Tumaini did a great job." I just nodded because I was surprised that it was working.

Ricky mentioned, "Michael, we need to figure out what the images are behind these shapes, and then see if we know what each of them means."

Ted agreed, "Let's get to it, then."

We all gathered around the four cards and looked for the clues. I wrote them down as they were discovered. "So, we have the number thirty-six, another thirty-six with a dash beside it, a burning building, and a planet exploding. Does anyone want to take a stab at it?"

I looked to Laura. "Are you getting anything?"

"Strangely, no. I'm not getting a thing. Do you think it's too far in the future for me to see?"

Ricky stated matter-of-factly, "It's not that at all. There's not enough energy put into that future to make anything stand out above the rest. That's why you can't feel one future stronger than the other three."

Constance asked, "So, there're four possible events, but nothing has set them in motion yet?"

"I still think the mainframe in number ten is the key to making number nine happen," I insisted. "We won't know what will go there until something is done with the mainframe."

Ted stood there with his thumb and finger to his lips. He was thinking, and then shared with us, "Based on what you've said, it all seems to make sense. My gut says to go with what Michael is telling us."

Laura perked up, "Are you becoming psychic, Ted?"

"What?"

"That's how some people open their psychic abilities. They go with their gut feeling."

Ricky confirmed her statement, "She's right. That's how we taught the young priests back in my day."

I laughed, "'Back in my day.' That sounds funny coming from someone younger than me."

He laughed, too, "I know, mon. This is some ride."

"That it is, my old friend. That it is."

Constance grabbed Hara's hand and asked, "Do you want to go down and help me prepare some lunch while Daddy works?"

"OK. But if the table jumps again, can I come see it?"

"Yes, hon," I answered. "We'll call you if something weird happens again."

"Cool!" She went out, followed by her mother.

Laura was looking at the crook and flail on my desk. "Michael, I took a long look at your riddle yesterday, and I think I have a good idea why you were guided to the books in my shop, along with the crook and flail."

"Great! That's wonderful news. Do you want to tell us?"

She pulled out the papers that Ted had given her. "Why don't we all have a seat?"

I chuckled, "Is it bad news?"

"Oh, no," she grinned. "I'm tired of standing, and this may take a minute to explain." We all grabbed a chair and waited for the answer to be revealed.

"I spent time meditating on the riddle. I was getting bits and pieces, actually, but none of it made sense until I put all three clues together." We were all doe-eyed waiting for more. "I have to start with the riddle first. And I must say, you were very creative in hiding all of this. We know some of this knowledge today." She motioned with her head and hands. "You can't keep a secret forever. But what you wrote gives the final touch to a complete and fully functional energy system. If I'm right, you two are going to max out your energy bodies and reach your full potential. And the rest of us will have a guideline to follow."

Ted made a levitation gesture. "So I could move books, too?"

"With this, you'll be able to do more than that."

Then she got all of us to focus on the paper. "Look at this. The beginning part talks about control over Egypt, power to rule over man, authority over the kingdom, and work that must be done." We all acknowledged her. "Well, that is a metaphor. Egypt is your mind, body, and soul. And this right here, 'Are you sure that I will have all of the riches I seek and the power to rule over man?' That's talking about the same thing. It's all one big hidden message. The power over man is the power that both you and Ricky have shown, it's the power to control yourself and generate energy. And *the riches* refers to the spiritual growth for the well-being of mankind. When

470

you do the work and control your urges, you gain in ability." Ted was lost.

"Here, Ted, Ricky, I made some copies for everyone yesterday." She dug in her purse and handed them out. "Just follow along, and I'll tell you what I think it means. Then we'll have to test it out." I grabbed the originals off the other table.

Ted expressed with an unsure tone, "If you say so." Then he began to read, "So, the part where it says, 'And will I be able to smite my enemies and claim what they possess without drawing any blood?' Is that the same thing?"

"Yes," she replied. "Your enemies can be your thoughts, your urges, your lusts...anything. And you can do it through meditation, focus, and determination. That doesn't draw any blood. That's what he meant by smiting your enemies."

I had a small flashback into Tumaini's thoughts. "I'm starting to remember this. I know where you are headed."

"Great."

"But continue doing what you are doing. It will let me remember as we go along."

"Are you sure? You're the one who wrote this."

"I'm positive. I just had a flash into Tumaini's mind, and what you are doing is helping me to remember."

"OK. If you insist." She went back to reading. She used her hand and mimicked speaking to get to the next main point. "*Zuuuhh, zuh, zuh, zuh. Zuh, zuh, zuh, zuh. Zuh, zuh, zuh, zuh.* There it is." She read out loud:

"You must face the challenges one by one.
Seven in all, before the one hundredth sun.
Your experience from one will lead to the next.
Your first challenge comes from the allure of the opposite sex.

"This is talking about your seven chakras, starting with your first chakra all the way through your seventh." We were nodding in agreement. Then she read:

"Follow the Nile, it will lead you on the way.
Start at the basin to meet your new flame.

471

"This is the base of your spine. And anytime that you refer to the Nile in your poem, you are talking about the energy pathways that lead up to your brain."

Ted remarked, "I studied some of this chakra stuff. I didn't get that at all when I read it. Good job, Laura."

"Me, too, Laura. Good job," I added. "I know about the basic chakra stuff, but I didn't put any of it together when I read it. Well done."

Ricky nodded with a smile towards her. He knew she was spot-on with her analysis so far.

"Thanks, guys. That means a lot."

I emphasized, "No. Thank *you*. Please continue."

"Well, I don't need to reread the entire poem. I just want to hit the highlights. To sum up the first half, anything dealing with the lower chakras is dealing with personal issues. Negative issues like lust, fear, gluttony, greed, shame—well, anything that deals with the physical world—those would be a block to your energy moving freely up your spine. Too much lust or food, you're blocking your root chakra. Too many fights with others, or problems with greed and money, you're blocking your second and third chakras."

Ted asked, "I get the first three chakras, but what about this?" He read out loud:

"The next forty days I spent giving thanks.
I loved my life, the land, and my new romance.
I was back in my homeland of pyramids of stone.
My new personal goal was to never be alone.

I reveled in love, but had lost my goal's sight.
My prize still waited for me, it was deep in the night.
The material world still owned me. I had trouble giving it away.
There was more meaning for love that lay in the spiritual way."

She explained, "That's a block in your heart chakra. If you still love relationships with the material over the spiritual, you can block your energy there, too." She looked at all three of us and continued, "That's the tough one for a lot of people on the spiritual path to understand. If you idolize the material world, you get stuck here. If you live for third dimensional things and relationships, you are bound to third dimensional laws."

Ricky had a momentary flashback. "When I was Baniti, I remember teaching this. The people, like the pharaoh, the reptilians, and now the Order, bypass their fourth chakra somehow. They serve only themselves and not a spiritual concept. That's how they are able to gain power. I can recall seeing a reptilian in the outer dimensions. It had no heart chakra that was visible, but it still had power—or at least the ability to take other people's power."

I agreed, "That would make sense. I couldn't figure out how the Order still had so much energetic influence over the world. Now I understand. They jump over their heart, or their energy spirals up the spine and bypasses the heart nerves to reach the fifth chakra nerves on the spine. I get it now."

"Good," she acknowledged. "Ted, does that explain your question?"

"I think so. Let's move on. I'll ask more if I can't put it together."

"Here's where it gets interesting." She pointed to her paper to show us how far down she was. Then she read:

"In one day's time, I reached the Nile's throat.
There was much more to do. I knew not to gloat.

Speak truth and enter the Mediterranean Sea.
Speak false and sink to the rocks beneath thee.
Onward I went. I didn't know what would happen to me.
It'd all become such a grand mystery."

Ted spoke immediately, "This one is easy. It's your throat chakra. If you speak the truth, you must have a good energy flow, right?"

"Exactly," she nodded. "Good going, Ted. And here's number six:

"The only company was the voice in my head.
The voices wouldn't stop, not even if I was dead.

Maybe I should follow my thoughts all the way through.
Seek out the silence amidst all this blue.
Calm the mind and be with the One.
When you conquer this, your task will be done.

473

"This one is telling you to quiet not just your thoughts, but all senses. If you can do this, you can enter into Samadhi—union with the Divine."

I queried, "I thought that was the seventh chakra?"

"It can be, but it can be both. Let me explain after this part:

"I looked back at my life and saw nothing to hold.
It was barren and selfish and fully controlled.
It was time to turn my life to the One,
To let go of fear and become the humble son.

Into the water, I had left my boat.
I lay on my back and began to float.
I gave myself to the holy Creator.
It was time to learn from a new educator.

I rolled my head back with ears under water.
The sun was ablaze, it was getting much hotter.
It came to me what I must do.
Let go of it all, no longer accrue.

I offered my senses to be with the One.
When this was done, I knew I had won.
No sight, no sound, no thoughts to think.
My body let go, and I began to sink.

This was not death, it was the start of life.
I was held in a void, not the afterlife.
My lessons came quick with seas full of knowledge.
I had just begun in a new sort of college.

I thought the Mediterranean Sea was so grand,
But connected to it were oceans without sand.
Infinity had shown her graceful attire,
Songs were sung by the heavens' saintly choir."

"Do you get it?" We were all waiting for her to continue. "The sixth chakra

474

can be a doorway to infinity, to really touch the hand of your Godself."

"I'm still confused," declared Ted. "Where are the sixth and seventh chakras?"

"It all depends on whom you study with. Some say the sixth and seventh are the pituitary and then the pineal gland. Others teach it that it goes from your pineal gland to your pituitary gland."

I inquired, "What do you think it is?"

"That's where your other clue came in, Tumaini. It was the crook and flail that gave me the answer."

"It was?" I thought for a moment, and then I made the connection. "It was!" Ricky got it at the same time.

Ted was frustrated. "Would someone mind telling me what is going on with the heka and nekhakha?"

I held the crook up for him to see. "Look at the shaft. This must be the spine. And the curved part must be a representation of the energy pathway in the skull. So the energy goes up the spinal cord, through the medulla oblongata, past the pons, and then to the pineal and pituitary glands."

Ricky interjected, "But that's not all. See the round part? There's more to the pathway. Otherwise, it would be two dots at the top of the shaft."

"He's right," Laura concurred. "There's a lot more happening there."

"I've got an idea. Give me a second." I woke up my computer and typed in a search for the human brain. Once I had an image on the screen, I held the crook toward the picture. "This curved part goes through more than two parts of the brain. There's the pineal, the thalamus, the corpus callosum, the hypothalamus, and the pituitary. And the tip here, at the end, it seems to curve outward to the frontal lobe area."

Ted pointed to the computer screen. "And you got that all from a shepherd's staff?!"

"It was hiding in plain sight for all of these years. Who would have guessed?"

"But you never answered part of the riddle—the seventh chakra."

Laura pointed to the paper. "That's where this part comes in again, along with another clue that Michael mentioned on Thursday." She read again:

"No sight, no sound, no thoughts to think.
My body let go, and I began to sink.

This was not death, it was the start of life.
I was held in a void, not the afterlife.
My lessons came quick with seas full of knowledge.
I had just begun in a new sort of college.

"Once you get to this state of no thought, no emotion, no senses of any type, you've reached a great place in spiritual and energetic development. When you get here, you can do some awesome things, like what Baniti and Tumaini have done in the last few days."

Ted held both hands out in a question-like pose.

"Do you remember something that his friend from Egypt said, 'You have to go down to go up'? Well, that has to do with brain frequencies. When you meditate, you lower your brainwaves to an alpha or theta state."

Ted asserted, "I know this from my research. What's the up part?"

"I've got this one," I answered. "But I never put the two together until now. A lot of Buddhist Monks have meditated so long that their brainwaves actually increase to a gamma level. And if you've done this enough, you can eventually produce gamma bursts that create unlimited energy, levitations, telekinesis, and more."

Ricky included, "That's what we worked for in the priesthood—to reach this ability naturally, and without the use of drugs. If you use drugs, you can't control it. If you do it our way, with years of practice and service, you can control this great gift." His look changed. "But our intentions were to help. Others can use this method to cause real harm in a person, even kill them with their thought alone."

"When the Russians declassified a lot of their psychic programs, I saw a video of a woman doing telekinesis, and she made the heart of a frog stop," commented Ted. "I knew there was something to all of this that the governments didn't want us to know."

Ricky continued his thought out loud, "And when I was Baniti, I saw a reptilian torture another subordinate to death with his mental abilities. It was gruesome." That stunned me. I never knew they had that ability.

Laura pointed out, "That leaves the flail, and I'm still working on that one."

I had an instant flash of information. Two things came to mind that made sense, but I would have to prove it with practice. "I think I know what it is." I put down the crook and picked up the flail.

Ricky was nodding. "I sensed your thoughts, Tumaini. You're right. Tell them."

"To max out the energy, you have to focus on two more areas. The flail has three dangly things hanging from the tip." I shook it slightly to swing the three rods. "I know it means other things to many Egyptians, but to me, I sent this piece to remind me of the three major energy centers."

Ricky finished, "Your three dantians."

"Right." I continued, "You can have all of the chakra centers open, or even partially open, but you need an energy supply. If you aren't working on your energy supply, it's like having no batteries in a flashlight—no light, and no power."

Laura was excited. "Man you guys are good. I wish I'd been in your priesthood."

"You might have been at some point," I grinned. "And you have already shown a natural ability with your little lightning bolt."

Ted proclaimed, "This is great stuff. When do we get started?"

While he said that, I was having visions from when I'd read the poem. "Hold on a second, I'm...I'm trying to remember something. It's important—one of the missing pieces."

They remained quiet for a good while, but I couldn't get the full image in my mind. "Sorry guys, it will come to me. But I can't recall enough. It was something with skeletons and water." I raised my pointer finger. "But I will remember this. I know it's important. It's one of the missing clues to energy."

A few more seconds passed. "Nothing."

Laura smiled, "Relax, it'll come."

"I know. Hey, we've got a little bit before lunch. I'd like to meditate and focus on what we've learned today."

Ted asked, "Can we use some of that special incense?"

"Yup, got it right here."

Laura got excited when she saw a familiar object. "I know that incense box. Did you get it at my store?"

"I did, and it works perfectly. Couldn't have all those burning ashes around the papyrus. All of these clues could have gone up in smoke."

Ricky agreed, "That would have been a disaster."

Laura gave a gesture toward the street. "I almost forgot. I brought you something."

"Really, what is it?"

"I though you might like the books you were looking at the other day. I know we just came up with a lot of information, but they still might help. They're in the car."

"Thanks, Laura. That was thoughtful of you."

"Don't mention it."

"Well, how about we put all this knowledge into practice?" I lifted the lid, put in a fresh stick, and lit the incense. "Time to meet the Maker," I said comically.

Ricky chuckled, "See you on the other side, mon."

"See you there, my friend."

CHAPTER THIRTY-TWO

WEEKEND BOOT CAMP: SATURDAY P.M.

"Baniti, where are we going?" I asked.

"Tumaini, there is one more thing that I can teach you before we slumber amongst the stars. If I am correct, this can help your future timeline to succeed."

"What is it? What can I do to help?"

"We must travel to Deir el-Bahri in Thebes. To one of the tombs."

"Tomb? Who died? Why do we need to go to Thebes?"

"It's not about who died, Tumaini. It's about what is on one of the ceilings."

"The ceiling? What's so important about a ceiling? Can't we just project our minds there, like we do when we time travel or explore the ethers?"

"That is exactly why we are going to Thebes, Tumaini. You have mastered traveling by thought and projecting your consciousness at will through all of time and space. Now you must learn how to take your body with you when you travel."

I looked at him in wonder. "I didn't know that was possible."

"It is very possible, and the adepts have been doing it for countless millennia."

"But, Baniti, how are we getting to Thebes? Aren't all of the main camel paths and trade routes closely monitored by the pharaoh's guards? Won't we be caught?"

"If we go by the road most traveled, yes, we would most likely get caught. But we are not going by any man-made roads. We are taking the path of the adept."

"The path of the adept?"

"Tumaini, are you going to trust me, or do you want to ask a lot of questions all night long?"

"I do trust you, and you know that I'm going to ask a lot of questions. How else will I become an adept?"

Baniti knew he'd just trapped himself with his previous question. "You are right, my friend. You are *wise* to ask me many questions. It is the *fool* who does not gather information and follows another blindly." He nodded to me in respect. "Thank you for reminding me of an earlier, painful lesson in my life. Please accept my apology."

"No apology needed, *Master Baniti*." I gave him a humorous look and bow because I knew he didn't want to be called *Master* anymore. "I'm all ears, though. What can you show me in Thebes that will help our future?"

"It is best if we just do it." He looked at me and waited for my question.

"You are setting me up to ask another question—I know this. Well, my friend, you have always had my respect, and I trust your wisdom. Lead the way, and I will follow."

"Again, you honor me." He bowed one more time. "This may feel strange at first, but all you have to do is take my hand." He opened his palm toward me.

I laughed, "Where would you like me to take your hand to?" He laughed along. Then I nodded, "I am with you," and grabbed his hand.

Whoosh! I felt my body jerk and be pulled maliciously out of the very fabric of space and time by angles. My flesh stretched long until I felt that I could not hold myself together anymore. Then I felt a sudden stop. I was in a place where time did not move. *Whoosh!* My body was pulled from timelessness and stretched back toward another location on Earth with more angles. When I opened my eyes, we were in Senenmut's tomb at Deir el-Bahri. I turned away from Baniti, held my hand to my mouth, jerked violently, and then I threw up.

When I was through with my initial reaction, Baniti said comically,

"That happens a lot with new adepts. I wonder why?"

"For the life of me, I wouldn't know," I replied with a hint of sarcasm. Then I bent over for another convulsion.

When I was through with my bodily trauma, I looked over to Baniti. He was simply pointing to the ceiling with a big grin. "This is why we are here, Tumaini. Can you stand upright?"

"Yes. I'll be fine." I wiped my mouth, and then I glanced upward and just gawked in amazement at the artwork. "This is… I don't know how to describe it. The knowledge emanates from this masterful work, I can feel it."

"Yes, it was done with great care. And this, my friend, is what you just experienced. Do you see the circles and the soul making his journey to the Realm of Souls by moving ninety degrees from the Earth plane?" I nodded in confirmation. "You have just traveled from space and time, to time and space, and back again to a new location"—he paused, and then he continued while pointing to the soul in the picture—"without having to die. This is but one way to teleport yourself with your living body and your ka at the same time."

"So you weren't kidding when you said we could take our body anywhere?"

"Well, not so fast, my friend. You can take your living body with you, but if you teleport to a place where your body cannot survive—say, inside a lava pit—then you will have to give up being a vegetarian."

I laughed, "Then I would be the main course at a cookout."

"Only for the cannibals and meat eaters," he snickered.

"How do I do this?"

"I showed you the way. And because of your previous work and training, once you have experienced it in your lifetime, now you can do it on your own. And when you practice enough, you can take others with you."

"So I can take Bes and Talibah with me?"

"That's if you can get Bes out of the kitchen," he laughed.

"Are there any restrictions?"

"That depends"—he paused for just a second—"do you want to live afterwards?"

"That goes without saying."

"Then heed my words: Do not stop until you reach timelessness or your destination. If you do, your body and ka may be pulled apart by the force of space and time."

"Those are good words to heed." I took my time looking at the ceiling.

"What are these circles?"

"They reveal the Music of Creation, vibrations that make up all locations in space and time. If you know the coordinates of space, you could literally touch the edge of the Universe. Every place in God's creation has a coordinate. A place, if you will, with height, length, width, and time."

"I understand. What about time, though? Can I also time travel this way?"

"You can, but you must be cautious about time travel with your body. Without the proper energy, you could be stuck in a timeline with no return. It's best to start with locations."

"Do you die there?"

"Not always. Sometimes you are pulled back to your original place of origin." He looked at me with his old teacher look. "There are things that I am still learning, too. The Universe, and God's creation, is much more vast than my learnings as of yet."

"Well, I think you are doing a great job."

"You are a good student. More advanced than the others—and myself in many ways."

"I'm not greater than you, Baniti. Look at all you know."

"Knowledge isn't everything, Tumaini. There is more to a soul than facts and figures."

I nodded and thought about what he had said. Then I asked, "What other ways are there to travel with my body?"

"We will return to our encampment by another method. Instead of going by angles to timelessness and back, we are going to project our ka to the place we desire first." I looked at him with full attention. "Then, your physical body will dematerialize into another dimension and rematerialize with your ka. Mind you, this will all happen faster with practice. Eventually, you will be able to do it instantly." Before I grasped his comments, he disappeared.

"Baniti?!" I yelled out. I spun around to see if he was anywhere in the room, but he was gone. I looked up to the ceiling to find a possible clue, and when I looked back down, Baniti had reappeared against the far wall.

"As I was saying, you can do this faster with practice."

"Wow! This is truly amazing! Thank you for showing me this."

"It is my pleasure."

"OK, I have another question. Can anyone do this?"

"It does take a bit of preparation. Your body's energy systems must be clean, you must have the power, and your mind must be open. Any of these can prevent someone from performing this feat." He looked at me and gestured to the outer world. "Most have not done the work to accomplish such things. Remember, if you live for this world, then you are bound to its laws. Go beyond the trinkets, bobbles, and fame, and the Universe expands for you."

"Those are great words, Baniti."

"Well, I do what I can with what I have to work with," he chuckled.

"There's more to this work, though, I can feel it."

"Once again, you are on the path of adepthood. Your mind must not only be open and your body used to higher energies, but you must have opened the pathways."

"Yes, the pathways. We have worked on this long and hard in our studies."

"You have, Tumaini, you have. And you are ready to unlock more."

"I am?"

"I wouldn't have suggested it otherwise. Once you follow the path of the crook and flail and learn of your third energy pathway, you will become one of the greats."

"I'm not in this to become one of the greats, Baniti. You know this. I'm just here to help."

"I know. That is why it has been such an honor to share with you the knowledge of the Source, our Creator."

"What's the third energy pathway?"

"The lines that make up all living things. As humans, we have twelve primary energy pathways and eight extra special ones. When they are open, they look like the most beautiful constellations at night." He pointed to the ceiling. "Take another look. Grasp the image. Then we must return. I'll tell you more about the third pathway when we get back."

"This has been an incredible adventure."

"That it has, Tumaini." Then he said in a different sounding voice with his hand stretched out, "See you on the other side, mon."

"See you there, my friend." I grabbed his hand, and we returned to the remaining priests.

———————

Three hours had gone by. Laura, Ricky, Ted, Hara, and Constance had already eaten lunch. Laura had also gone to her car and retrieved the books that she wanted to give me and put them on my desk. Ricky stayed in the room to watch over me while the others were in the kitchen eating dessert. Then my hand started making jerking movements.

Ricky leaned over the railing and called to everyone below, "Hey guys, his hand is jerking around, but he's still in meditation. What should I do?"

After a moment, Laura answered back, "Hold on. I think I know what this is." They all came upstairs following Laura.

Ricky asked again, "What should I do?"

"Let me see his hand moving. If it's what I think it is, we'll need a tablet and a pen." She saw my thumb and finger making a pincer gesture.

Constance handed her a yellow tablet and a ballpoint pen. "Will this do?"

"Yes, that's perfect." She carefully placed the pen in my fingers and they closed automatically around the shaft.

Hara giggled, "What's Daddy doing? He looks funny."

"I think we are about to find out, honey."

With the pen in my fingers, my hand was making tiny circular motions. Laura put the tablet under the pen. "I think he might be trying to do automatic writing."

Ricky nodded, "She's right. He could do this when he was Tumaini. That's how he made the God Scrolls. He must be trying to tell himself something."

The pen was moving jerkily across the page. Somehow, when the pen got to the edge, my hand instinctively flew to the left and started writing again.

Ted commented, "He looks like a typewriter, only without the ding noise."

Hara chuckled, "*Ding!*"

"What's it say, Laura?" asked Constance.

"It's hard to read. The letters are really messy."

She laughed, "Penmanship was never his strong suit."

Ricky countered, "But he has so many more."

"Yes, he does"—Constance put her palm on his arm—"and I'm grateful for every one of them."

After I wrote a couple of lines, the pen stopped moving. Then, my hand slumped down like the life had been drained from it, and I opened my eyes.

"What?!" I asked. There were five people all gathered around and staring at me.

Constance answered, "You were in meditation for a long time, and you were writing in your sleep."

Hara laughed, "You were funny, Daddy."

"Was I, pumpkin?"

"You were automatic writing," explained Laura. "Ricky said you'd done this before with these God Scrolls that I haven't seen yet. *Hint, hint.*"

"Wow, was I?"

She held up the tablet. "You were."

I had a memory flashback. "I did this when I was in Cairo, too. I wrote in hieratic, and I had no idea what I had written until Omar deciphered it for me."

Ted held up two fingers. "Well, looks like you can do this on two continents."

I motioned for the tablet. "Here, let me see what I wrote." I only looked at it for a moment. "It's sloppy, but it's in English."

Constance asked, "What's it say?"

"There are five sentences. They say:

> *"The skeletons were floating on the water with their spines beneath the waves. A skeleton being sucked down in a whirlpool. I saw bodies on the water covered with hundreds of water beads. These beads kept sparkling like constellations in the sky. I swear that I could just about make out patterns and lines from the sparkles.*

"Whoa! I know what this is...and more."

Ricky urged, "Don't keep us waiting."

I looked down at the tablet, then back to Ricky. "I remember."

"Remember what?"

"What you taught me. You showed me how to teleport myself. That's why I was in meditation so long. I remember!" Then I pointed to the writing. "And these were the exact thoughts I had after I read Omar's translation about the chakra riddle. This is becoming so very clear."

Ted jested, "Glad it's clear to you. I can't read any of it." He looked at the tablet from multiple angles while tilting his head.

I saw the books on my desk that Laura had brought. "Those are—"

She finished, "Gifts that I told you about."

485

"Yes, yes, but those are pictures for what I wrote." I picked up the books for each sentence that I had written. "The skeleton with the whirlpool… that was symbolism for the chakras on the spine. The spine under the water was about connecting to Source energy." Then I looked at Ricky. "Do you remember? You taught me about the third energy system." I picked up the book with the Chinese meridian system and dantians. "It's the acupuncture lines on the body. When they are clear and lit up, they look like constellations in the sky. I remember all of it."

"Ya, mon, I remember it, too. When I was meditating, I kept seeing stars twinkling. We must have connected again."

"We did. You took me to Senenmut's tomb and showed me how to teleport my body." I turned to the computer. "Wait. I can show you the picture."

I scrambled with the keypad and mouse to get the illustration on the screen. "Do you see? This Egyptian guy is moving along at ninety degrees. That's one of the ways we did it, Baniti—I mean, Ricky. We transported through time and space!" I was so excited that I was practically yelling. "Then you told me about the third energy system that we needed to use in order to reach our full potential!"

He affirmed excitedly, but with a softer tone, "I do remember."

Constance grabbed my shoulders and shook. "This is so exciting!"

Laura added, "Yes, it is."

"This is great and all," questioned Ted, "but what does this have to do with the Order?"

"Everything!" I exclaimed. "And we have work to do. Ricky, you and I need to activate our abilities in this lifetime to teleport ourselves. Once we do it here, we can help others."

"I can do that. Once we get all three energy systems going, it should be no problem."

"I agree." I looked toward Ted. "And when we have this ability again, we can share it with you. Remember? When one person gets it, it makes it easier for the rest."

"Michael—sorry, Tumaini"—Ted put up both hands in an apology fashion—"are you talking about this hundredth monkey thing?"

"Yes, I am. And it's true. We've all seen this work with our kids. We can't do near what our children are doing on the computer these days."

Constance interrupted, "It's true. I feel like I'm being left in the dust."

"Right. They've picked up these new skills and made it easier for their friends. That's why everything is happening so fast with this technological boom. Instead of a hundred monkeys, it's a hundred kids."

Hara made a monkey noise, "*Ooh, ooh, ooh.* I like monkeys."

Constance kissed her head. "So do we, monkey," and she made a monkey noise, too.

Laura asked, "How can I help?"

Ted immediately followed, "Yeah, what's next?"

"Like I said, Ricky and I have work to do." I thought about school and pointed out a little dejectedly, "And believe it or not, I have papers to grade."

Ted reacted, "Seriously?! You're going to grade papers while the world is about to be taken over by the Order?"

"Those students are what we are doing this for. I can't stop teaching them now. Some of them are amazing!" I grabbed Hara and hugged her. "Including this one!" She giggled and squirmed.

Laura got a psychic hit when I mentioned my students. It didn't feel good to her, but she didn't say anything.

"Well, you're the boss," he agreed with some trepidation.

Constance reassured him, "He'll do the right thing, Ted. We still have to live in this primitive society and earn a paycheck to survive."

He smiled back to her, "Well, you do have a point." He looked at me. "Can you give me any guidance in the meantime?"

"Yes, while we remember how to integrate all three energy systems, I think it would help if you three"—I pointed individually to Ted, Laura, and Constance—"started meditating on your own and working to clear your blockages and open your energy systems."

Laura held up her fingers, and the lightning bolt was definitely brighter. "I've already been working on mine."

Hara burst, "That's so cool!"

Constance added, "It is, honey, isn't it?"

"Well, I guess I'm the slow horse out of the gate," reckoned Ted. "I've got my work cut out for me."

"So do I, Ted. You aren't alone," added Constance.

I glanced at all of them. "I have a favor to ask."

"What is it, Honey?"

"I'm famished, and it's been a long day. Do you think we could go out and just be friends for an early dinner? Then Ricky and I can come back and hit it hard."

Laura perked up. "That's a great idea. I would love to go out and just be friends."

"Ya, mon. What's the point of helping the world if we can't enjoy each other, too?"

Ted slapped his shoulder and mimicked in a terrible accent, "Ya, mon. What he said." Ricky smiled back at him.

"Excellent. Let me take care of the ashes, and we'll all go out."

Constance asked, "Where do you want to go?"

Hara yelled out, "Bongo Billy's Pizza House! Bongo Billy's Pizza House!"

"How about it, guys? Can we do pizza?" They all agreed heartily. "Pizza it is."

Hara jumped up and down. "Yea!"

———•———

Phillip showed up at the beginning of the frat party. Bruce excused himself from the two girls they'd met on Wednesday and came over to meet him. He put his arms around his shoulders and gave him a manly hug. "Dude, glad you could make it." He tilted his head in their direction. "The girls are anxious to see you again."

"They are?"

"Yeah, both of them wondered why you never called." He hit Phillip's chest with the back of his hand. "Smart move playing it cool and making them wait." He looked at the girls to make sure they were out of earshot. "They can't handle it sometimes when the guy doesn't chase them right away. It makes them try harder to get you to like them. Way to go, champ. I bet you'll score tonight."

"I didn't do it for that reason."

"Don't spoil the moment, dude. I was just beginning to have hope for you. We have a new pledge class coming up, and you'd make a great brother."

"Really? Thanks."

He tilted his head to motion for him to come along. "Let's go say hi!"

Phillip held him back for a moment and asked, "By the way, do you still have that ringing in your ears?"

"Yeah, I can't seem to make it stop. And something funny started happening since the other day."

"What's that?"

"I swear that I can hear the frequency change when I have certain thoughts. It's like everything I think or say is being monitored."

"I've had the same thing happen, too, including some really—"

"What?" Bruce leaned in for the answer.

"Nothing." The girls were giving them a suggestive *come here* motion with their fingers. "Let's go meet the girls."

"You're gonna get some, dude. Wait and see." Phillip just smiled toward him.

On the reptilian ship, the commanding lizard asked the two military men, "Hsssss. The programming, is it working?"

The older officer responded, "Just watch and see." He used the console and sent a coded message to the boys' Illuminati handlers. "I just gave the command to begin voice to skull communications. They will start hearing vocal instructions soon. If the programming has worked like we think it has, they will comply and take out your priest."

"Hsssss. Must work." The reptilian pointed its razor-sharp nail at the officer. "Hsssss. The priest must be removed."

"You realize we serve the Order, too. No need to get angry at me."

"Hsssss. Humans like you cannot be trusted."

He thought to himself, "Look who's talking."

The reptilian focused at the officer's heart. It sent images of his left and right ventricle exploding inside his chest. The officer reacted by falling to the ground beside the younger recruit. He was in immense pain and screaming, "Stop it! Stop it now! I beg you!" From the ground, he reached out in pain toward the reptilian.

The commander was taking great pleasure in hurting the officer. It inhaled the pain and anguish that he was emitting and gave a low sadistic growl. The younger recruit didn't dare look at the older guy on the floor.

One of the reptilians at the console reported, "Hsssss. The boy received the signal. He was told to touch the girl's lower flesh. The boy's thoughts were controlled and he could not resist. His fleshy hand is on her leg. We are receiving his thought patterns."

"Hsssss. It seems as if the program might work." It erased the image of the exploding heart from its mind. The officer on the floor gasped for air and

489

clutched his chest. The commander pointed at him and growled, "Hsssss. Do not question my authority again. I am in command." Still in pain, he nodded in submission.

The younger man stepped up. "Shall we proceed?"

"Hsssss. Yes. Send more commands. Make the boys comply with all suggestions."

"We can do that. When we mix messages with sexual thoughts, it weakens their ability to say *no*."

"Hsssss. Good. We feed on sex vibrations."

"Long live the Order," the young man declared. Then he walked up to the console and sent the Illuminati handlers a list of coded actions. "By the end of the night, he will have a weapon that he can use to kill the priest."

"Hsssss. You are now his superior. Do not fail me." The older officer stood up and stepped behind the younger man.

Ricky and I were in the study and we had just started meditating. I was going over the events that had transpired and smiled. As I was journeying toward my goal, I became distracted and thought about tomorrow. "These guys are coming back Sunday afternoon, and there's so much to do still. We have to call Egypt about the seers, I need to show Laura the scrolls..." My mind flew to another thought, "Scrolls! I haven't asked Ricky about the five songs. I wonder if he knows the tunes." The word *songs* distracted me yet again and a childhood song popped into my head and took me in another direction. It brought about a vision of my father helping me learn how to tie my shoes. After the memory faded, I caught myself drifting with my thoughts. It reminded me of the poem and drifting up the Nile. "No wonder people have trouble meditating. My thoughts are scrambled tonight. Focus, Michael, focus."

Ricky scolded me humorously, "Shhhh! You're thinking too loud."

I laughed, "Sorry."

He did it again, "Shhhh!" That made me snicker.

I asked in my head, "Are you listening to my thoughts, Baniti?"

He projected to me without words, "I was connected to you, Michael. My focus was on helping you. This allowed me to hear your thoughts." After a second of silence, "I didn't know I could do that in this lifetime."

"You are my friend, Ricky. I didn't shield myself from you."

"Nor I from you." Another moment of silence occurred between us. Then he commented telepathically, "We have two tasks to accomplish tonight. What shall we do first?"

"My goal was to focus on all of my meridians, including the eight special meridians."

"You memorized those acupuncture lines fast after dinner."

We were still speaking telepathically. "I can remember them from your teachings. Tumaini and Michael are beginning to blur some."

"I know what you mean; I keep getting feelings about being Baniti. His skills are flowing through me without any help from myself. I couldn't even imagine doing the things he's done in this lifetime—like that black ooze thing exploding off of your head."

"Thanks again for that. And I know what you mean; I've been holding back my past. Maybe I was trying to stop a destiny. Maybe I'm just scared."

"There's no fault in that. I'm also scared."

"What are you most afraid of, Ricky?"

"Not living up to being Baniti. And you?"

"The same…not living up to being Tumaini"—I paused—"and failing."

"I think, when the other priests are with us, that we can make a difference—with your guidance, of course. I mean, what you set up when you were Tumaini was nothing short of amazing. I'm still putting together the pieces that you left yourself."

"That makes two of us." He laughed at my comment.

"Hey, Ricky?"

"What?"

"Shhh!"

He laughed, "OK, Tumaini. Let's activate our super priest powers."

I had visions of superhero capes flowing in the wind. "Super priest powers, reactivate!" He laughed again.

We both focused once more and went into a deep meditation.

The reptilian commander asked the new military officer in charge, "Hsssss. Why is this taking so long? Take out the priest now!"

"There is a plan," he replied. "We have just dispatched one of our operatives. When he arrives, it will take a few days before we can do as you ask."

"Hsssss. You know our goal. Discredit him, make him suffer, then his disposal."

"It will be done in the name of the Order."

"Hsssss. It will be done effectively, or you will suffer the same fate as the others."

"The plan is in motion, commander. I will complete this mission."

"Hsssss. Rewards to you if you are successful." The officer smiled and thought of the riches he would receive. "Hsssss. Yes, many riches to you when he falls to the Order."

"Yes, falls to the Order."

———— • ————

Bruce and Phillip were downstairs with the girls. Each of them was showing exceedingly strong dominant traits. Phillip had his new girlfriend pinned against the wall with her hands held above her. He was biting her neck while she moaned and writhed beneath him. Bruce was passionately pulling on the other girl's hair while he was kissing her hard. His other hand held both of her hands behind her back.

In Bruce's mind, he heard a plain-sounding male voice, "You are needed at the front door. Move there now."

He tried to stop kissing the girl and comply, but he was lost in his heightened lust. "You will receive more of this. Pleasure is good. Walk to the front door for more pleasure." His brain couldn't stop what was being done to him. The ringing was sending him coded messages and bypassing his ethical upbringing, and the voices were now using psychological brainwashing methods. He pulled her hair a little harder, and she nibbled on his neck. "Pleasure is good. Sex is good. Go to the door for more pleasure."

He stopped immediately and stood up. His girl was a little surprised. "I have to go upstairs, babe. Wait right here. I'll be back to give you more."

She was still confused about the sudden stoppage and harrumphed. However, she still flirted with him and scraped his leg hard with her hand and nails. "Don't take too long, sugar."

The voice told him, "Pleasure is good. Do not deny your lust. More *rewards* come when you go upstairs. Take the other boy."

Phillip was grinding hard up against his girlfriend's body, and she was pressing right back onto his. Before he could lift up her skirt, he was grabbed by Bruce. "We have to go upstairs, now!"

In Phillip's head, he heard, "Go upstairs for more pleasure. Lust is good. Pleasure is good. More *rewards* when you go upstairs."

Phillip blurted, "I have to go upstairs. Pleasure is good."

She hummed back very seductively, "*Mmmmm, pleasure is* good. Don't keep me waiting too long." She pulled him in for another kiss and slid her tongue into his mouth.

In his mind, he heard, "Pleasure is good. Lust is good. Follow the other boy upstairs." He was so overcome with sexual urges that they completely overrode his critical thinking. He turned to Bruce. "What are we waiting for? Let's go upstairs so we can get back to the girls."

"Yes, upstairs." Both of them left.

Bruce was instructed to open the door and greet the officer. "Hello, Officer Dunse. Is everything alright?"

The officer looked inside the door. "You boys having a party tonight? Hmm. We were told to do our usual rounds on all of the fraternities. You don't have any underage drinking going on, do you?" He held his hands on his police belt.

Bruce replied, "No sir. We check all IDs at the door."

"I think you need to come down to the car."

In both Bruce's and Phillip's heads, they heard, "Go with the officer. Many pleasures and *rewards* for following your lust." They both received images of the girls in lewd positions in their minds.

The officer was well aware of their thoughts. He turned and went to the car. "I'll need to take your names, just to be sure. Stand at the back of the car while I get my notepad. There might be a *reward* for doing as you are told." Both of them complied with the command word he'd just spoken.

Bruce heard new thoughts being projected to him. "Pick up the box beneath the trunk and hold it behind your back until the officer leaves. Many *rewards* come to those who do as they are told." More suggestive images were flashed in his head. "Keep the box hidden from the camera in the squad car."

He had a hard time bending over from his excited state. Once he was kneeling, he faked tying his shoe and picked up the box. He held it behind his back when he stood up, just as he'd been instructed to do. Then the officer came to them. "You boys have been extremely cooperative. There's no need to take your names. I remember what it was like when I was in college. You will receive many *rewards* when you graduate."

"Thanks, Officer Dunse," answered Bruce, with his hand behind his back.

Phillip added, "Yes, thank you, Officer Dunse."

The man looked at both of them with a twisted grin. "All hail to the Order." He got in his car and drove off. Then Bruce and Phillip went inside.

Phillip heard, "*Rewards* are downstairs." He received another image of his new girlfriend in his mind.

Bruce received a different set of instructions. "Put the box in your room. Listen for us tomorrow." He received two more sets of ring tones in his ear, accompanied by the image of his girl completely naked.

He turned to Phillip. "I'll meet you downstairs. Tell the girls that I'll be right down."

He mimicked Bruce and lightly hit his arm with his fist. "You got it, dude."

———•————

The young military officer on the alien ship reported, "The package has been delivered, commander. All is in order."

"Hsssss. We are expecting your plan to work. Do not fail us."

"All hail the Order."

———•————

Ricky and I came out of meditation at the same time. He saw something new and shared, "I can see your body glowing. What you did must have worked."

"I can see your meridian lines, too. The only thing I can see that needs attention is your stomach meridian. It has some blockage to it."

"It's probably all of the meat I've been eating. Maybe it's time to lose the red flesh."

"You taught us it was best for our energy flow to be vegetarian back in the olden days."

He looked to the left for his past memories. "I did, didn't I?" He stretched a bit. "This isn't like the olden days, though."

I stretched, too. "No, no it's not. But it has its perks."

"You mean, Constance and Hara?"

"You're reading my mind again, aren't you?"

"It was still open." He looked to the tables. "So what's next on the clues list?"

"From what I got this afternoon, we need to energize everything and wake up our teleportation skills."

"Wasn't what you did in Laura's store enough?"

"I think we can do more when we merge all of our chakras, dantians, and meridians to the same goal. I just have this feeling."

"I can feel it, too." He looked at the light bulbs on the ceiling lamp. "What about those? Do you want to blow them out, too?" he laughed. "Constance might not be too happy if you have to rewire the entire house."

"That's a good point. How do we do this then? Do you remember?"

"I do, actually. This is strange. I just know Baniti's experiences, like they were my own thoughts and not his. We have to draw energy into our bodies, then compact it in our lower dantian. Then, we send it to the meridians to store for later use."

I was nodding, "You're right. I remember this teaching. You had me practice this technique after we left Senenmut's tomb."

"As I recall, you were pretty good at it."

I smiled, "Yeah, there were no light bulbs to blow out at our temple." I had a small image flash in my mind. "Except for the bulbs at Dendera, we blew those out pretty good, didn't we?"

He remembered and gave a hearty laugh, "Yeah, those exploded nicely. The workers in the crypts were pissed." We both laughed some more.

"Ricky, we both know how to do this. Let's just do it. Let's draw in as much energy as possible, store it, and then use it to attempt teleportation."

"Ya, mon. Let's do it."

I remembered that it was a visualization exercise that didn't require any special feat. All it took was focus, feeling the energy around the body, and bringing it into the lower dantian through the bottoms of the feet and crown of the head.

After a few minutes, Ricky exclaimed, "Holy cow, Michael. Can you tone it down some? You're so bright that you could pull a sleigh through a blizzard."

"Me? You should see yourself. I should find a way to plug a lamp into you and sell electricity." Then I looked down at my arms, torso, and legs. I could see all of my meridians, my lower chakras, and middle and lower dantian. They were ablaze with silver, gold, and white light. Sparkles were shining all throughout my energy bodies.

Ricky exclaimed, "This is amazing. I've never felt so much power before."

"Me, neither. And the lights are still standing. That's a good sign."

"Ya, mon."

I stretched an open palm out to him. "Where do you want to go?"

"Let's keep it simple. Somewhere close."

"I've got it. Let's drop in on Constance. She's in the kitchen making cookies. I can smell them."

"I like that idea. Simple, yet satisfying."

"Hope you like chocolate chip. She's got that one perfected."

"No stopping now." He grabbed my hand. Our bodies stretched like they had done in old Egypt. We slingshotted into timelessness with our focus held on the kitchen. Right after our bodies lengthened again—which only took less than a second—we materialized directly in front of Constance. She screamed, threw the pan upward, and cookies went flying everywhere.

She held her chest and gasped, "Don't you *ever* do that again without warning me!"

Ricky and I looked at each other with a guilty look. "I'm sorry, honey. We were trying to practice and focus. Your cookies were a great focal point."

She wasn't really mad, but she hit me with a hand towel. "You scared me half to death." Then she bent down to pick up the tray. "Just look at this mess."

Ricky stopped her. "I caused that. Let me help." He knelt down and started tossing cookies onto the sheet. He had melted chocolate all over his hands.

"Theeth are great, hon." I had a mouthful of one from the cooling rack. "Ricky, you'th gotta try one."

He looked up and smiled, "You sound like Bes right before prayer time."

That made me think back. "Bes…I wonder how the others are doing. I guess I'll find out tomorrow."

We finished cleaning up the kitchen and told Constance about our energy-gathering exercise.

"Well, you two'd better fill me in tomorrow and show me how all of this is done." She turned toward Ricky. "And Baniti, you're invited over anytime.

But can you please use the door? I don't want to keep tossing cookies every time I turn around."

"Sure, Constance. Anything for you."

"Ricky, I think we should call it a day. Do you want some to take with you?"

"No need to ask me twice. I love chocolate chips."

Constance packed him up a to-go bag and we walked him to the door. "Tomorrow at 1:00 p.m.?" he asked.

"Yep, everyone's coming at 1:00 p.m. See you then, old friend."

"See you then."

CHAPTER THIRTY-THREE

WEEKEND BOOT CAMP: SUNDAY

After a late brunch, I was in my study working on my students' papers. Constance walked in and mentioned, "It's almost 1:00 p.m. Is there anything I can do to help today?"

"You've been great. The best wife and partner a guy could ever ask for."

She blushed and said, "Thanks for spending time with Hara this morning before doing your work. You were right. It's not a bad idea to teach over the weekend. It makes our schedule very flexible—especially with all of this Tumaini stuff coming to the surface."

"Yeah, I never agreed with the go-to-school-Monday-through-Friday-for-eight-hours-a-day concept anyway. Forced schedules and forced education does not allow for open minds."

"Are you sure you are still my husband? I'm learning so many new things about how you think, and you still amaze me."

"That's makes two of us." She looked at me because she didn't know how to take my last statement. "I'm shocked about me, and you still amaze me." She grinned at my compliment. "You're just as open and willing to listen, and I respect you more than I respect most other people." I gestured with my hands, "Heck, you're smarter than most people I know, too."

"Aw, thanks hon." She came over and sat in my lap. "How about these students? Do you respect them?"

"Do you need to ask? These are great kids. You'd be surprised at some of their responses to the *I love you* assignment and the last one I gave."

"Serving others? I always liked that one."

I chuckled, "Some of the pairings even turned into boyfriend-girlfriend relationships."

"You're kidding. Anyone I know?"

"Robbie, and one other. I was completely surprised."

"Robbie? Now that is a surprise."

"He's had this girl chasing him all semester. This just gave them the opportunity to break the ice. He was so worried about getting in trouble for dating a student."

"Why? That doesn't make sense. He's not the teacher."

"I know, but he feels like he has to follow the same guidelines. I told him he'd make a great professor someday."

"I agree with you. He's a great kid, and a good soul."

In my head, I heard my name. "Tumaini. Ya, mon!" I laughed and laughed.

Constance asked, "What is it?" She gave me a funny look.

"It's Ricky." I pointed to my head. "Hold on a second."

I replied telepathically, "Hi, Ricky."

"Can I come in your house?"

"Are you outside?"

"No, mon. I want to *come in*. I need the practice."

"Oh, you mean *come in*. Let me tell Constance first."

I mentioned to her, "Honey, Ricky's coming in."

"Do you want me to get the door?"

I laughed again, "No, he's not using the door. Just wait a second." I told him that the coast was clear and where to enter. I pointed. "Look over there."

The papers on my desk blew a bit from the energy burst. Ricky had just appeared out of nowhere and was standing at the doorway to my study. Constance grabbed her chest and gasped, "My word! I don't know if I'll ever get used to that."

"Hello, Constance. Good to see you again." He gave her a small, respectful bow.

"Hello, Ricky," she breathed heavily. "How ever in the world do you do that?"

He said in a Baniti-like manner, "When you do the work, I will show you." He gave me a quick nod. "Unless you want to show her first, of course."

"We'll leave that one open for now." I gave him my teacher's wink.

She asked, "Do you two have any other new surprises that you want to tell me about?"

He looked at me, and then we both turned to her and replied together, "Nah."

"Honest, hon. I'm trying to show you everything I know as soon as I remember it."

"He ain't lyin'. He's not holding back."

"How do you know that?" she asked.

"I would see it in his aura. It would turn a dark color. Kind of hard to hide lies when you can see auras."

She shook her head in awe, "Well, you two—" The doorbell rang and interrupted her. She got off my lap and turned, "You two work. I'll get that," and she started heading down the stairs.

I gave Ricky a quirky look. "My turn to practice." I focused on our front door. With a quick trip to timelessness—including a lengthy body stretch—I was turning the knob to greet our guests.

Constance was at the last step when I pulled it open. "How did... How did you...?" She pointed upstairs, and then to me.

"Hi, Ted. Hi, Laura. Come on in." I teased Constance, "Beat ya."

Ted gave me a funny glance. "Do you want to tell me what just happened?"

Ricky was coming down the stairs at that moment. "Hi, folks."

Laura waved. "Hi, Ricky."

Ted continued, "In the short time that I've known you, Constance, I recognize that look—hands on hips with a not-so-nice smile at your husband."

She turned to me and said with a hint of huff, "You tell him. I wouldn't know where to begin."

Then I explained, "Ricky and I remembered how to dematerialize and rematerialize from timelessness to a new coordinate last night. It was cool. Cookies went flying everywhere."

She came over to hug Ted and Laura while scrunching her face at me. "A fancy way of saying *teleportation*."

Laura was all excited. "I thought only Indian fakirs could do that."

Ted inquired, "Cookies flying in the air? Indian fakirs? Do you want to tell me, or do I have to guess?"

Constance chimed, "Oh no, it's true. Ricky and Michael teleported into the kitchen last night, and cookies flew."

With great excitement, Ted asked, "You can teleport?!"

Ricky told Constance, "By the way, your cookies are awesome."

Laura got a glint in her eye. "Cookies? I could do some cookies."

"I'll go get you some." I motioned.

Constance mentioned, "They're in the yellow container."

This time, Ted yelled slowly, "Wait…a…minute! Are you telling me that you two can teleport?"

We all answered at once, "Yes!"

I remarked in an unfazed manner, "Where was I? Oh yes, cookies."

Ted threw his hands up in frustration. "What's next, levitating polar bears?"

"I don't know. Ricky," I laughed, "did you teach me that, too?"

He replied, "I think that was in Baniti and Tumaini go to the Arctic, the Sequel." All but Ted laughed.

Laura got our attention. "While you two were remembering an old skill, I did some research last night."

"Really? What did you come up with?" I asked.

"I was going over your riddle poem and piecing it together with the crook and flail. It turns out that your information was right on. I pulled out an old book that I had, *Book of the Master of the Hidden Place,* and on the cover was a picture of King Tut's coffinette. He was holding an exact duplicate of your heka and nekhakha." She held up the book to show us.

"There's a lot of symbolism in ancient Egypt." She giggled to herself for a moment. "Of course, you know this. You were there. Duh," she laughed again. "So the coffinette is a representation of your physical desires, just like you said in your riddle poem. When you stop being tempted by fruits of the flesh and coins for your pocket, those desires die away naturally, leaving you open to pursue your spiritual abilities—even your destiny."

"Sounds right to me," I replied. "Anything on the three dantians?"

"Yes. It turns out that your spine is only a pathway. A number of Eastern texts talk about moving energy from your lower dantian to the front of your belly button, to your sexual organs, down and around your perineum, and then to your spine."

Ricky was nodding, "You found one of our ancient teachings. Baniti would be proud."

She winked. "I'll settle for Ricky, if that's OK?"

"Good one, Laura," he bowed to her.

"And one more thing… The Eastern texts talk about returning energy back to the lower dantian—something about cooling down."

I concurred, "Yes, that was taught in a number of books that I researched a few years back. When you raise your energy, you can do damage by staying too hot. You're supposed to send it back through the meridians. What's that called? Oh, yes, the conception vessel and the governing vessel. Energy should move up and down again in an orbit."

Ricky was nodding in agreement, "That sounds right."

Ted and Constance had a look that said: *What are you talking about?*

I motioned to them. "Come upstairs. I can show you with the book Laura brought me yesterday. It's got some great illustrations."

Ted joked, "Does it have pop-ups, too?"

I laughed, "And pages for coloring."

"By the way"—he twisted around—"where is Hara?"

Constance answered, "She went to her friend's house for the rest of the day. She won't be back until late."

As we were going up the steps, she turned around and gibed, "Are you two going to walk, or are you going to meet us up there?"

"Walking's good for me. What do you say, Ricky?"

"Ya, mon. Gotta keep those legs a movin."

We all grabbed a chair in the study. Laura noted, "I found one more thing last night." She looked specifically at Ricky and me. "I remember watching Ricky pull in energy to his body when that black ooze monster attacked your head." We both nodded. "It seems that you can also generate energy another way, but it can be very dangerous."

Ted ribbed, "Wow, someone did her homework last night. What did you find?"

"In the Eastern system of energy, there is a hidden reference about *Being the Source.*"

I looked to Ricky. He admitted, "She's got me there." We both looked back to Laura.

"With enough focus on your center, you can tap directly into Source Energy."

It took me a moment. "Now I remember. It makes sense, too. In those same Eastern texts, I've read that the human body has the entire Universe built inside. If you want to go to the Source, you focus on the center of the Universe. And on our body, the center of the Universe would be the lower dantian."

Ricky asked, "So what's the bad news?"

"If your heart is not pure, the energy can burn you to bits. Only the pure of heart can handle that type of vibrational energy. That's why the Order has to steal energy from others to gain strength. They can't tap into Source energy and survive. They vibrate so low that it would short circuit their energetic bodies."

"Interesting…" I nodded. "And this energy, what can it do?"

"From what I've read, it's the highest energy source out there. It's touching the Creator—God." She got even more excited. "Infinite power! It would fry lesser beings."

I nudged Ricky. "Now that's one bright light bulb." He laughed.

"If used right, there would be no defense against it, which is why the Order hates the idea of anyone spiritually evolving beyond their control."

Ted gestured. "Now that makes sense to me. I understand that clearly."

Constance added, "So do I."

Getting Ricky's attention again, I asked, "Can you help fill them in on what we did last night? I need to call Hanif and Mudads."

Constance interrupted, "Oh, I want to listen in, too."

"Because we are on limited time today, do you mind if I call while Ricky fills you in on the techniques we've remembered? It might come in handy real soon."

Ted held up his fingers like Laura had done. "Do you mean that lightning bolt thingy?"

"That, and more. He can guide you in a short meditation to clear some of your blockages." I reassured Constance, "I won't be long. I just want to see if there are any more updates and to find out about the seers."

She was a little disappointed. "You're probably right. But tell Rehema I said hello."

"I will. And if you learn how to do telepathy, you can call her anytime that you'd like. Right, Ricky?"

"Right, mon."

Laura reminded me, "When you get back, would you show me the scrolls?"

I pointed in the air because I had forgotten already. "You betcha. I'll do that as soon as I get back."

On the reptilian ship, the commander received a report from a subordinate. It called for the military officer to come to the bridge. When he arrived, the reptilian motioned. "Hsssss. We cannot wait much longer. The priest is getting stronger. We received intelligence of intensified energy bursts from his location."

The naïve officer asked, "Can't you capture his ka thing again and put implants in him?"

"Hsssss. He is protected once again. We cannot penetrate his field at such a distance. Only when he is close can we hurt him."

He looked at its snarling face and announced, "We have news to report."

"Hsssss. Speak."

"The two boys will receive signals from their Illuminati handlers to take the gun and practice shooting today."

"Hsssss. More."

"We are ahead of schedule on our mainframe. It seems that we can push up one of the tests to this week. We've been spraying nanotechnology on the people for years via chemtrails. These nanobots are now ready to connect with each other and receive signals from our computers. We are set to run the first simulation through all of the cell phone towers."

"Hsssss. The population must fall to the Order."

"They will. We are going to activate all of the implants on the corporations' CEOs and financiers. Our plan is to have them institute a global economic crash in the next few days. If this works, we will know our programs are foolproof. Then we will initiate the entire mainframe program on the population." The reptilian commander growled in pleasure. "Then, the Order will make a killing by claiming more land, fallen stocks, and crumbled businesses, just like they did at the turn of the last two centuries. They'll be even richer than before."

The commander growled again, "Hsssss. Their suffering will feed us again."

The officer inquired, "Are the politicians and military heads still under reptilian control?"

"Hsssss. Controlled with our implants, yes. They remain subservient to us—even though they don't know it. Silly humans think their thoughts are all their own."

"Then this will be the final stage. Our mainframe, with your implants and soul-catcher, will conquer the planet. No one will escape or leave for millennia."

"Hsssss. Plan must come together. Priests must still fall."

"They will."

"Hsssss. Too many failures in the past. Send in the assassin to harm the group."

"As you wish. All hail the Order."

"Hsssss. Hail the Order." It growled and stomped away.

———————

Ring... "Hello," answered Phillip.

"Hey, dude. This is Bruce. What are you doing today?"

"What day is this?" His head was throbbing, and the ringing was intensified. All he could hear in his left ear was a tone that kept changing pitch every once in a while.

"It's Sunday, dude. How about that date last night? Was that awesome or what? Boy did we hit the jackpot and get *rewarded*." The handler's word was working perfectly. Bruce received another signal.

Phillip looked at his neck and saw the remnants of bite marks from his new girlfriend. "Yeah, *rewards* are good." He received a new signal as well, and then he smiled from his memory of hot sex.

"Hey, I've got an idea." The voice in Bruce's head was practically telling him what to say word for word. "Have you ever shot a gun before?"

Phillip had to think. It was hard for him to focus. "Never. Why do you ask?"

"Do you want to go do some target practice?"

"Yeah, sure. It sounds like fun. Will the girls be coming?"

"Not for this one. It's just you and me. It'll be fun. I'll pick you up in an hour."

"Cool. See you then." *Click.* Both boys received a new signal, and the pitch changed slightly in their ears.

———————

I had finished preparing two trays of cookies and drinks to take upstairs. I laughed because I felt like Rehema playing hostess. I could also smell the incense wafting through the house. I knew they had been meditating for a bit. "Time to call Mudads," I thought.

Hanif recited his familiar conversation phone jingle, "Hanif's Incense Shop, finest incense in all of Cairo. How may I help you?"

"Hi, Hanif. It's Michael—Tumaini."

"Oh my gosh, Michael. It's so good to hear from you, my friend."

"It's good to hear from you, too. How's Rehema?"

"She can't stop talking about how you helped her. She's been practicing with all of the priests over here."

"That's wonderful." A question came to my mind. "How come she hasn't used her telepathy with me since our first chat?"

Rehema's voice came over the phone next, "It's because I didn't want to interrupt what you were doing. Ramla sensed that you and Baniti were so close with completing your tasks that no one wanted to interfere."

"She is the perceptive one."

"That she is," she laughed.

"Hey, is Mudads there?"

"Hello, my friend."

"Mudads! Boy am I glad to hear your voice. Do you guys know how much I've missed you?"

"About as much as we've missed you."

Rehema asked, "When are you coming back to Egypt?"

That question threw me off for a moment. "To be honest, I hadn't given that much thought. I feel like I just got home."

Mudads chimed in next, "We need you here, Tumaini. Much has happened since you have gone."

"I know. I heard about more priests waking up. Who would have guessed that Omar, Karim, and Ehab were priests?"

Hanif expressed, "We were shocked, too."

"What about you and Mudads? Are you two of the remaining sixteen priests?"

Mudads responded, "No, my friend. Our roles were fulfilled as the believer and the provider. The others must be out amongst the sands of the Earth."

"Hmm. Ricky and I will have to do something about that."

Rehema asked, "Is Ricky really the reincarnation of Baniti?"

"Oh my gosh, yes! And he and I have so much to share with you."

"We are all very excited to meet with him again. The other priests have been training so hard since you left, but we need you and your guidance to help us."

"What about Ramla?"

"Her help has been invaluable, Michael, but she has told us that she is not one of the thirty-six priests. Her abilities came from her time as a kahuna. Your abilities are much like hers, but your magic is intermingled with the other Egyptian priests. It's our unity—the priesthood's unity—that creates our intensified power."

"That sounds logical to me. Let me tell you what has happened recently since I've met Baniti again."

For the next twenty minutes, I told them about teleporting, the implants, alien attacks, channeling with the God Scrolls, the Decans circle, the latest on the magic cross spread, and the red helicopter.

"What news do you have for me?"

Ramla's voice came over the phone, "Hello, Tumaini. It is good to hear you are doing well."

"Ramla!" I reacted excitedly. "The surprises keep coming."

"I made my way to Hanif's shop when I felt your desire to call today. I have been waiting to tell you about the seers."

"I'm all ears. Please share."

"Our seers believe they have located the mainframe, and it is close by—very close."

"Do you know the exact location?"

"They believe they have the exact location. Gahiji, Asim, and Jabari are working on a plan."

"Based on their names, I bet I know what that plan is."

"You are quite astute, Tumaini."

507

"I am also working on a plan, but I have been so involved with Ricky these past few days that I haven't had time to iron out any real details. All I have is a concept in the making."

"I am sure that you will devise an effective strategy, Tumaini. We are all very hopeful about your efforts. Did your magic cross reveal anything new?"

"Based on what's happened so far, whatever will happen next will be dictated by the mainframe. No other pieces have moved toward the remaining three spots."

"Do keep us informed, Tumaini. I am with you…always."

I thought in my mind, "I've heard that before."

Ramla replied telepathically, "Yes, you have, but it was not me."

Rehema said in both of our minds, "I heard that, too. This is so wonderful."

I smiled from both of their comments. Then I inquired out loud, "Is there anything else to share about the seers?"

"Only that they are working very hard to help all of us, Tumaini," replied Ramla. "We are close, very close."

"I'll tell Ricky—Baniti—about our call. He's remembering a lot and has been a great help these last few days."

Ramla stated, "I will communicate with him soon. Please tell him to expect my telepathic call so he is not wary of my voice."

"I will. Guys, it's been great talking with you again. I won't wait so long before our next chat."

Mudads said, "It's great to hear you again, too, my friend. I know that we will see you soon."

"I hope so." The others gave the same sentiment on the other end of the line.

"Oh, before I go, Constance told me to say, 'Hi, Rehema.'"

"She's so wonderful. I can't wait to meet her."

"You've helped her a lot. Thanks, Rehema."

"My pleasure. Bye, Michael."

"Bye, guys." *Click.*

Before going into the study, I made a detour to my bedroom and grabbed the box with the scrolls. "This ought to be fun," I thought.

When I walked in, surprisingly, everyone was still in meditation. I was about to close my eyes and join them when Ted and Constance slowly opened theirs. Both of them looked glazed over. Then Ricky and Laura opened their eyes, too.

I asked Constance, "Did you enjoy your meditation?" She came over and put her palms on my face. It felt like a steaming hot towel that the barber shops used. "Wow!" I exclaimed. "Those are hot!"

"Ricky used his abilities to open up some of my energy channels. I felt this immense heat emanating from my body. I've never felt this way before." She turned to him. "Thank you."

He bowed toward her. "I am here to serve."

"Ted, how was your meditation?" I asked. He didn't say anything, but he had the hugest smile that I had ever seen painted on his face. "OK…must have been good." He nodded slowly.

Laura got up and gave Ricky a hug. "I understand why you joined the priesthood with Baniti. I've already seen both of you in action, but now I know where you get your energy from."

Ricky asked, "What do you mean?"

"When you connected with me, I felt the power of the Source. It jolted me and made my body quake."

"That's your sixth chakra opening," he explained with his teacher's voice.

"It is? I thought my channels were already open. I must have been fooling myself for years."

Still in his teacher's voice, "One can open a valve slightly or fully. Yours was only stuck for a bit."

She bowed to him. "Thank you for helping me."

"Again, it was my pleasure to serve."

Laura put up her fingers, and an extremely powerful lighting bolt sparkled between them. "Oh my!"

Ted finally spoke, "Now that's power." She smiled from his comment and her progress.

Constance took a tray from my hand. "What's going on in Egypt?"

I passed around the other tray of cookies, and then I shared, "The seers might have found the location of the Order's mainframe. Gahiji, Asim, and Jabari are working on a plan."

"Who are they?" inquired Baniti.

"I told you before…Bes, Talibah, and… Actually, I don't know who Jabari is. It will be interesting to find out."

"Ah, yes, Bes and Talibah." He was acting more like Baniti than Ricky at the moment. "I miss them."

"Constance, you remember. I told you that they were our security guards and walked around all day with an Uzi to protect the tourists."

"I remember."

"They received some great training, and they are devising a plan. I imagine it is to take out the mainframe."

Laura took a cookie and passed the tray. "Do they know where it is?"

"Ramla mentioned it was close by. I can only imagine that she means somewhere in Egypt."

She got a psychic hit when I told her. "That feels right to me. Somewhere close, but I can't make out the location."

Ted remarked, "If the military is involved somehow, I bet they are shielding it with their psychic unit."

"That would explain why I can't see it clearly."

"Ted," I commended, "you've been a great resource during this whole endeavor. We'd still be in the dark about a lot of this stuff if it wasn't for you." Constance nodded in agreement.

"Thanks, Michael. It's probably the best way that I can help right now."

Then Constance added, "It's your friendship that counts most." He smiled back to her.

"I agree. You've become a good friend in a short time." I looked at the other two. "You, too. All of you have become great friends."

Ted motioned toward the tray. "Well, if you're done trying to make us cry, can you pass the cookie plate around again? These are awesome."

"Sure, help yourself."

Laura glanced in the box. "Are those what I think they are?"

"Those are the ones—the famous God Scrolls."

"Can I see them?"

"Let me wash my hands, and then I'll unroll them for you."

"Don't you trust me?" She saw her own hands covered in melted chocolate. "OK, point taken. I'll wait."

I was just across the hall in the bathroom while Laura was talking loudly to me. "I still have that weapon from the red helicopter in my safe. Do you want me to bring it to you?"

The towel was flapping in the air as I dried my hands in the doorway.

"No, I think it's best to keep it locked up. We can look into it later. It's better that we fine-tune our abilities instead of researching technology."

"I can do that." She got up and started walking toward the bathroom. "I think I'll wash my hands. I'd like to take a good look at these scrolls."

Constance told her, "There are extra towels by the sink."

"Thanks."

Ricky and Ted also got up. Ted added, "I'll need to wash up, too."

I laughed a bit, "I'll be here waiting."

As they cleaned up, I took the opportunity to separate the scrolls. I rolled out the God Scroll on the empty table and asked Constance to help me hold it down with the glass. Then I rolled out the scroll that already had writing on it and put it under the glass beside it. "There, those are the only two with markings. All of the rest are blank."

"Do you want to put them here?" She pointed to the glass.

"No, I remember something from a meditation a few days back. I think Ricky and I can solve the blank ones."

Ted walked in. "Are you going to serenade the scrolls?"

"Actually, yes."

Laura didn't understand. "Serenade?"

"It's a long story, but I used my magic to keep the scrolls from falling into the wrong hands. I sang a song with the Vowels of Creation, and these gold letters appeared on the God Scroll."

She pointed beside it. "And this one?"

"Those are the five songs I was given by Source."

"Do you mean God?"

"I think so."

She asked more seriously, "Do you mean the same god that preaches hellfire, brimstone, and damnation?"

"Not at all. This is not the same bi-polar Saturnian god of most alien-based religions—all loving one second and ruthless killer the next. This consciousness gave me instructions for building peaceful communities. That's what these are for. When I held this one, the instructions came right through me."

"Oh, good. I was just checking. Please continue."

I smiled from her comment and went on, "This voice that comes through me is special. It's the most loving, intelligent voice I've ever heard. What I've shared with the class so far is amazing."

Ted praised, "That was smart to hide them. If these communities catch on, that would terrify the Order. I can see why you hid them."

Ricky included, "They would have destroyed these for sure, Tumaini. I can remember visions of the pharaoh's guards burning all of our other scrolls."

Constance asked, "Do you think they were behind burning the Library of Alexandria?"

"Who knows? History has been tarnished by the Order so much that nobody really knows the truth anymore."

"Ain't that the truth!" exclaimed Ted.

Ricky hunched over the scrolls. "So, what were you hoping I could do?"

"Do you remember any of the songs?"

"Maybe when I was Baniti, but nothing's coming to mind."

"That's OK." I winked. "If I remember correctly from the other night, there are five songs in total. One song brought the God Scroll to life. The other four songs will revive these eight."

Ted held up three fingers. "And you have to sing it three times for it to stick."

"Right," I confirmed.

Constance added, "I saw this happen, Laura. These golden letters just appeared when he sang the song."

"I'd love to see that," she hinted. "Do you remember the other four songs?"

"I know the second one like the back of my hand. When I sang it in Hanif's shop, he dropped a tray full of coffee cups."

Ricky burst, "Really?!"

"Yes, really. That was one of the signals to prove to them I was Tumaini's reincarnation."

"Man, you really thought this through."

"When I was Tumaini, I did. It's all even written down right here." I gestured to the first parchment and the translation beside it. "Apparently, I passed all of the tests, including the songs."

Ted patted my shoulder. "Way to go, Tumaini."

"Well, don't pat me too soon. If this doesn't work, and we don't give the people a chance, none of this matters."

Constance encouraged me, "Stop being so hard on yourself. You've done great up till now."

"Thanks, hon." I checked with Ricky again, "Are you sure you don't remember? I hate singing alone."

"Sorry, mon. You're solo on this one."

"OK, here goes song number two."

Ted stopped me. "Aren't you forgetting something?"

"What?"

"You said that you need to be holding the scrolls."

"That's right! Good memory, Ted." I saw all of the other rolled up scrolls. "But which one? I'd have to sing the song while individually holding each one to find out."

Constance leaned over the table and instructed with her hands. "I have an idea. What if we stack the scrolls on the table like a fan, and then you place your hands on them? When you start singing, we should be able to see the letters appear. That will identify the scroll with the song."

"Great idea. And one song supposedly unlocks two scrolls from this point out."

"Right, hon. You are smart. Stop selling yourself short," she laughed.

"Hey, that's my line."

I explained to the others, "It's a personal joke. I usually tell her not to sell herself short and put on some high heels." They all laughed. "That's my special phrase for her." Then I smooched at Constance and smirked teasingly, "Line stealer."

"I know," she grinned. "Are you ready to sing?"

"Let's get the scrolls unrolled, and then I'll give it a try."

With a fan of papyrus all laid out, I recalled the second tune, breathed in with my hands on the parchments, and began singing.

Laura gasped, "Would you look at that?" Gold letters were appearing on two of the scrolls. "I've never seen anything like this, and that's strange to say considering what's happened lately."

Ted gibed, "I couldn't agree more."

When I finished, the letters remained visible. Once I pulled my hands off of the paper, they disappeared.

Ricky complimented me, "You sure knew what you were doing as Tumaini. Just look at this magic do its thing."

"Now we know which two scrolls they are. Help me pull them out, please." I motioned to Constance to pick up the other blank scrolls. "Thanks, hon. Let's see if this still works." I sang the song twice in a row with the vowel sounds. The letters reappeared and stayed on the papyrus.

Ted hit his head with his palm. "I should have been recording this. No one is ever going to believe me."

"Actually, I'm glad that we didn't. It makes it easier to protect everyone from the Order."

"Good point. I hadn't thought of that."

Laura repositioned the remaining scrolls. "So now what?"

"We do the same thing with the other six scrolls." I put my hands on the stack. "Three songs to go, and that should reveal the final gold writings."

"I sure wish I knew the songs. I love to sing. And to be a part of this is just…well, words can't even describe. I'm glad to be here."

"Glad to have you here with us," I smiled. "And you are part of the team."

Constance added, "Family."

"Yes, family." That made Laura blush.

"OK, here goes, the last three songs." With a perfected round of elimination, all eight scrolls were now filled with golden letters that I had recorded centuries ago. "That's it. My work is done," I laughed. "The rest is up to you guys. I'm toast."

"If only it were that easy," sighed Constance. "Our work"—she put her hands on my shoulders and looked at the others—"has just begun."

"Too right," added Ted.

"Too right," echoed Ricky.

"And, Michael?" implored Laura.

"We've discovered all of the clues. That's it. The rest is devising a workable plan to help bring hope to the world."

"What can we do until then?"

"Keep working on your meditation, and Laura, your new abilities. With Ricky's help, we should be able to start the schools again."

Laura asked, "You mean, like what you learned when you were priests?"

Ricky stepped closer. "Yes, we served the people—all people—no matter what their background, beliefs, or financial statuses were. We fed the hungry, healed the sick, and gave teachings to the people of the land. That was the school I remember so well."

"And that's a great plan for the future. Mixed with what I've taught with the God Scroll, it's a place I'd like to live in."

I put the last two scrolls back on the table. "I've got to teach tomorrow, and so do you, Ted. I'll see about translating these later. Shall we wrap this up and meet in a few days?"

"It's going to be hard going back to the fake world run by the Order after seeing this. I'm inspired," expressed Laura.

"So am I," chimed Constance. "One day at a time, and we'll make a difference."

"Ya, mon."

"What do you say, team? Sorry—I mean, Protectors of Souls. Let's meet in a few days. Besides the schools and new communities we could start, think of a way to bring hope to the people. We'll compare ideas and act on the best of them."

"Good plan, Michael," supported Ted.

"Sounds good to me." Laura put her hands on Constance's shoulders. "I'm so glad I met you."

"Me, too."

Out of nowhere, the number sixteen flashed in my head. I thought, "What's sixteen?"

Constance gave me a head tilt. "What is it? I know that look."

"The number sixteen just came to me. I was all ready to stop for today, but there must be something else to do."

Ricky spoke in Baniti's voice, "It's the other priests, Tumaini. We must call to them and help them out of their slumber."

"You're right. I even thought about that recently. By the way, do you realize that you spoke in Baniti's voice and not your own?"

He shook his head, and returned to his regular, soft Jamaican accent, "I what? I didn't..." Then he realized I was right. "Ya, mon, I did."

The others jested in a chorus, "Yes, you did."

"I think Baniti is coming back really strong."

Laura suggested, "I think it is because your powers are getting stronger, and those powers are generated from Baniti."

I added, "I wouldn't worry about that, Ricky. I'm having some of the same feelings when Tumaini's powers come through me. I'm still Michael in the end." He nodded in agreement.

Constance gave me a hug from the back. "What about the other priests? How are you going to wake them up?"

I chuckled, "The same way I've done the rest of this—wing it." They laughed. "Seriously, though, I think the easiest way is for Ricky and me to combine our intention with our energy and resurrect the others."

Laura offered, "We can help. You said it earlier: We can influence the future with more energy."

Ted concurred, "Sounds like a plan. Let's do it."

"I like this plan," included Constance. "It's about time I feel like I'm really helping."

"Honey"—I turned and hugged her—"you've been an awesome help."

"Thanks, but this is something different. I can put my energy with yours to bring about a great change."

"It's settled, then. We'll intensify our intention with all of our energy and revive the sixteen priests."

"Anything else?"

In Baniti's voice, Ricky urged, "They must return to our place of learning. They must go back to Egypt with haste."

Ted got Ricky's attention. "You're doing it again."

"I am?"

"Yes," I answered for Ted. "It's OK, Ricky. Just go with it. That's all I've been doing so far."

Laura chuckled, "The path of least resistance is sometimes the best."

Constance cheered, "Here, here! Can we send our intention now?"

"Yes"—I clapped once—"let's do it."

We closed our eyes and combined our energy into our intent. While in meditation, I felt that we had touched the souls of our past friends. Some were aware, and others were glad to have the remembering. When we opened our eyes, I affirmed, "It is done."

"Ya, mon. We reached them all. I felt them waking up."

"Me, too. I felt our friends. Their souls were so familiar, and the energy was definitely from our priesthood."

Ted pointed with his thumb to the East. "Do you think they will go to Egypt like you said?"

"Does a camel spit?" I laughed, and so did he.

"I'll send word to Ramla and the gang to look out for them. Some will come from great distances to be in Cairo."

Ricky exclaimed, "One was in Rio."

Constance added, "That's so cool."

"By the way, Ricky, Ramla said she would communicate with you telepathically. She asked me to tell you so you wouldn't be surprised or defensive."

"Thanks for the heads up."

Ted proposed, "Shall we call it a day?"

"I think we accomplished so much. I'm happy with our progress. Meeting is adjourned."

Constance winked and prodded, "What did you say?"

I got our little joke. "Like I said before, take a few days and think of ways to help bring hope to the people. Then we'll meet, say, Tuesday at seven o' clock?"

Laura giggled, "I was just about to say, *seven o' clock?*"

"Right," I laughed. "Come on. We'll walk you down."

Constance and I walked them to the door and bid them goodbye. I kissed her on her head and said, "It's coming together, honey. It's coming together."

"Yes, it is."

CHAPTER THIRTY-FOUR

THE ORDER STRIKES

I was almost to my classroom when I saw Robbie standing outside the door. It was strange because he was always the first one in the room to take attendance.

"Hi, Robbie. How are you today? Why are you standing out here?"

He had an odd look on his face and whispered, "Dean Shwermer is inside. He wants a word with you before you let any students in."

I shook my head and thought, "It's just like him to speak to me here—before class—instead of in either of our offices. He's so unprofessional."

I asked, "Is that why you are standing out here?"

"Yes." He whispered even softer, "And just between you and me, he gives me the creeps. I don't like him."

"I can understand why. Is he carrying his Bible today?"

He nodded *yes.* "He took another opportunity to read me one of his select scripture in the hopes that I would accept his faith."

I sighed, "This ought to be good. Let's do as he said and keep the students out until his majesty is ready." He snickered at my comment. "And I only confided in you this way because I look at you as a colleague, just without the actual job title to match your ability." He smiled.

I walked in with my best smile. "Hello, Dean Shwermer. What can I do for you today?"

He was reading his Bible and put it down. "I've had a number of complaints about your recent class, and I came to give you fair warning." I knew he was lying because I could see his dark aura.

"Really…a number of complaints? I can only think of one student, maybe two, who might have complained, and the entire room disagreed with both of them last class."

"It wasn't just two," he retorted smugly. "There have been multiple complaints about you." His aura was still a dark color.

I thought to myself, "He is setting me up for a threat, or he has another plan cooking in his brain. Either way, he's not to be trusted. He's lying, and I can see it."

Before he continued, he put his left pointer finger in his ear and wiggled it around. Then he wiped the wax off on the desk. "This blessed ringing won't go away." I immediately perked up because he had the same ringing that Bruce, Phillip, and I'd experienced from the Order. He looked back to me and continued, "Anyway, I've received numerous calls from parents with concerns about your class content."

"Numerous? Really? Can you tell me exactly who has a concern so I can address this myself in a *professional manner?*"

"Their names don't matter here. It's your style of teaching that I don't like. Your open discussions about religion and the negative insinuations about our wonderful working government are a threat to the *order* of this school." He put his finger in his ear again.

With my new heightened abilities, I scanned his energy bodies and saw a tracking tag. "I'm starting to get the picture here."

"Are you?!" he asked callously. "Since I was hired as dean a year ago, I have been watching you."

"That's good. Then you have noticed my class sizes have increased over the last five years, and more students have submitted requests to your office asking me to create additional classes so they can study with me beyond my 201 class. That's more revenue for the university."

He didn't like that I'd taken away his steam and scolded, "I'm still receiving complaints, and that tarnishes your record."

"I can't fix the situation unless you allow me to address it. Who is complaining?"

"As I said, it doesn't matter who."

"Of course it does, and it is very unprofessional to make accusations about my teaching without backing them up with proof. This I will take to the university president." He knew he was caught, and I saw his aura flare black and dark red.

He patted his Bible. "You know, if you would just accept *my views,* we would get along much better."

"Yes, I've seen videos online of you dancing with your Bible in the air at your church. You are very proud of your faith."

He gave me a very strange, ominous look. "Salvation is at hand, and everything would fall into *order.* I will be watching you."

"You're more than welcome to stay and actually see me teach. You haven't done that since you were hired."

"I might just do that."

I thought to myself, "Trying to get proof out of him is futile. He can't provide any because he is lying. Let's see where this goes. The Order is behind this, I can tell."

<hr>

The energy of the classroom was extremely high. Students were coming in smiling and laughing. Before Robbie gave me the all-in-attendance signal, some of the students were pointing at the stranger sitting in the back and whispering to each other.

"Hello, everyone," I greeted. "As you can see, we have a guest with us today. Dean Shwermer has decided to pay us a visit." Bruce smiled evilly, while the other students turned around quickly to get a glance.

One of the girls near the back chatted softly with her neighbor, "Is that who that is? I've never seen him before. He looks more like a ghost." The entire room heard her and laughed. The Dean just stared and wouldn't acknowledge her comment.

Rochelle gazed directly at him. "Hello, Dean. Did you get my request for more classes with Professor Whyse?" She added sarcastically, "I never get any replies from your office."

He spoke with a monotone voice to the room, "Hello. It's good to see all of you." Then he looked at Rochelle. "I will look into your request with due diligence, young lady." His aura was still dark black.

Todd muttered, "Sure he will. That's what they all say."

Rochelle whispered to Allen at the same time, "He sounds like another politician: all talk and no action." I gave them an open-palm sign to get them to go easy on the Dean.

Another girl called to him, "Hi, Dean. I hope that you do follow up with her. This is one of my favorite classes. I never miss it." A number of students smiled and nodded. This was making the Dean very uncomfortable. She added, "I'd love to take more classes with the Professor, and philosophy isn't even my major." More students nodded and gave verbal agreements.

Inside Phillip's head, he was hearing a very loud ringing tone mixed with whispering voices. "Do it now. Do it. *Rewards* come if you do it now." He was grimacing and holding both hands over his ears. He threatened back to the voices, "Get out of my head! I can't stand this anymore." He started to feel a slight pressure on his skull.

It was time to get started, so I addressed the class with my hand over my heart, "I appreciate all of your support. Really, I do. But we have a lot to cover today. Has anyone thought about your three O's assignment from last Friday?" A number of hands went up. "Great, let's begin."

Shwermer had a confused look on his face. "Sorry, the students already know what I am asking. I was referring to the concepts of omniscient, omnipotent, and omnipresent as they pertain to each person's religious teachings, upbringings, and non-religious ideologies. It was their assignment over the weekend."

I looked down for a moment to think. Then I engaged him and the entire class, "Do you mind if the Dean gets to ask questions like you do? It might help him to understand what we are doing in class." They all agreed.

Allen heckled just loud enough for the front few rows to hear, "Someone's about to get schooled." They laughed with him.

"Brandi, how about you go first?" Robbie sat up and looked at her.

"This was a good assignment. I was thinking about what you and Todd said last time. If you can't kill an immortal, then there are things that just can't be done without creating a paradox." The boy in the back laughed from the reminder of the paradox joke, and Todd nodded in agreement. "So, I thought of another one based on a childhood teaching." I motioned for her to continue. "If God is omnipresent and everywhere all at once, then you can't go anywhere that God isn't. And it brought up another point."

I remarked, "I like this one. Do you care to elaborate?" The Dean was scowling. I could tell that he didn't like me questioning this religious topic.

"Well, it's like you said about free will: You can't be free as a soul to go anywhere that God isn't—there's no place for you to go. So as a soul, you would be restricted to God's territory. And this made me think further." She shifted in her chair and recrossed her legs. Robbie was completely engrossed in what she was doing. She continued, "God's ability to be *nowhere* and *everywhere* at the same time wouldn't seem to work, either. It mirrors what you taught us: God can't know *everything* and *nothing* at the same time. It can't happen without creating a paradox to solve it."

"Excellent point! It fits right in with that concept. Good work, Brandi.

"Robbie, are you recording participation grades?" His head was buried in the gradebook and he gave me the hand gesture to say *yes*.

The shy boy in front volunteered meekly, "If what she said is true, and if God is everything and everywhere, then God couldn't leave God, either." That made a few students' heads jerk.

I chuckled from their reaction, "While some of you are processing his statement, he is correct. There would be nowhere to go if God is omnipresent. Good work." He smiled.

One of the girls near the back commented, "Here's a major contradiction involving free will and an all-knowing God."

"Being a philosophy teacher, I like contradictions. Please share."

"A lot of religions say that we have free will, and that's how they justify that their version of God has a right to punish each person—they say we choose to be bad, or something like that. But you've already pointed out that we aren't perfect, and then, according to some religions, we would still be punished anyway for our imperfections." I knew the point was coming and nodded in agreement. "Well, it seems that if there is an all-knowing God, if God is omniscient and all, then you couldn't have free will to do something that God doesn't already know. It could never happen."

"That's a great point," I applauded.

She continued, "It made me think last night. How could I ever have the freedom to do something that no one else would ever know about? If I was always monitored, then I would never be free to be the only one who knew. You wouldn't have free will to keep a secret."

"Another great point. Very well thought out," I smiled.

Rochelle laughed sarcastically, "And that's why the governments demand that people are on camera everywhere they go. We are being completely monitored. Nobody is free."

While fighting his assassin programming, Phillip snapped, "What's the point of it all then? If God knows everything, then what's the purpose? It would be like God watching a rerun of the same show over and over for eternity. That cancels out free will completely."

I was glad that he'd participated. "Thanks for sharing, Phillip. I like your observation."

Todd raised his hand, and I pointed toward him. "Todd?"

"This one took me a while, but I've got it. Do you remember how I said that God was supposed to be all powerful and stuff?" I showed him that I remembered. "Well, this one wipes out all three O's." Almost the entire class was focused on Todd. "If God was all powerful, then God could not know what it is like to be powerless at the exact same time, right? And if it's true what they say—that energy can't be destroyed, only changed—then God wouldn't have the knowledge or ability to do that, either. That wipes out being all-knowing and being omnipotent. And if God is everywhere, then God lacks the power to be anywhere that God isn't. That wipes out omnipotent and omnipresent even more. And since God can't know what it is like to be somewhere that God isn't, that wipes out being omnipresent, omniscient, and omnipotent." He gave a shrug with his shoulders and added, "Well, in theory of course."

"Very well done, Todd. And remember, this is philosophy class. We are philosophizing."

Daphnee partially raised her hand, and then quickly put it back down. "Do you have something to add, Daphnee?"

"I hate to admit this, but you have me questioning my own beliefs."

Rochelle interjected, "That's good."

"Daphnee, please continue."

"What I was taught sounded so good until we had to question it, like when you had me think about that New Age magnet example that I gave last week. I admit that I was rattled by that. But then I was thinking about limitations, or not being omnipotent—like I was taught by my mother—and I came up with a restriction."

"I'm all ears, Daphnee. Let's have it."

"I was also taught that God was everywhere. But then I thought, that creates a problem. If God is everywhere, meaning that God takes up all space—and I was taught that no two things can occupy the same space at the same time—then God can't know what it is like to duplicate itself in that exact same place. I mean, if that concept that I was taught was correct, then God could not know what it is like to be in the same place at the same time as anything else. God would lack the ability, and God couldn't overlap God. There can't be two *everythings,* so there couldn't be two or more Gods."

"I like how you said that: 'There can't be two *everythings.*' That makes complete logical sense. And to take it further, there can't be any multiple above one, based on your statements, which would include from *one* all the way up to *infinity.* There can't be an infinity of God all in the same place. Excellent thinking, Daphnee."

The Dean was furious. "I'm sorry to interrupt, but is your goal here to have the students leave their current faith?"

Bruce echoed snidely, "Yeah, Professor! What's up?!" That made the Dean happy.

Surprisingly, Beth spoke next. She turned and explained, "I kind of had the same feeling." The Dean smiled at her comment, too. "But what the Professor is doing is having us question so we can know who and what to trust." She looked at me and said, "I can't know true faith unless I also know doubt." This made the Dean frown.

"From what I have learned this year, I have strengthened my faith in some ways, and now I know that I can't believe everything that is taught by my priest, either, without looking at simple facts."

The Dean wanted to trick her and questioned condescendingly, "Can you honestly tell me that you don't hate losing your faith? Can you tell me one simple fact?" The class reacted negatively to the Dean's statement.

"I'm not losing my faith at all, just changing it. I guess you could say that I'm sharpening my faith and views." She looked to me, and then back to the Dean. "The Professor pointed out a simple contradiction to one of Jesus' teachings. And honestly, when I brought it up to my priest at our youth group, he couldn't deny it, either. And the rules do keep changing in most religions. I've seen it in my own lifetime." She turned to the front and continued, "I still believe, like you taught us to do, Professor, but now I have my reservations." The class cheered for her.

Rochelle yelled over the clapping, "Way to go, Beth!"

She swung back around. "And honestly, Dean Shwermer, the Professor made it very clear to us that he isn't trying to take us away from our faith. What did he say? Oh yes, something like: We are still us, and when we leave this class, we still have our faith. To be honest, I respect him for that. He's offered support and guidance. That's more than I've gotten from a lot of people I know, including at my church—especially when I ask questions. I was even threatened this past weekend by someone in our group for not accepting everything as truth."

Bruce and Phillip received another upload. The voices were now a consistent thought in their minds. The same program commanded, "Do it now! *Rewards* come to those who do it now!" Their handlers increased the pressure on the boys' brains.

Stacey raised her hand. I nodded. "Stacey?"

"I love this class. I hope you stay."

"Thanks, Stacey."

She wasn't done and held up a piece of paper. "I came up with a formula."

"You did? What is it?"

"Based on our assignment, I came up with a formula for the three O's."

"Now this I'd like to hear. Go on."

"I thought about this a lot, and…" She stopped and asked, "Can I just write this on the board? It will be a lot easier."

"Be my guest." I turned around and grabbed one of the markers to hand to her.

She walked up with her paper and a smile. "Thanks." She began furiously writing a mathematical equation on the board. Her hand was literally a blur. The majority of the formula was blocked by her body, but from what I could see, there were a lot of infinity signs and individual letters. I tried sneaking a peek at her paper, but she saw me and hid it from my view. A few seconds later, she chirped, "There, that does it." She was about to put down the marker, but added, "Oops, missed something." Then she walked to the end of her formula and placed a final bracket. With pride, she turned around and waited for approval. "What do you think?"

I was completely dumbfounded. I looked intensely at the equation. "It's a stroke of genius, Stacey. You're going to have to explain it to me, though, so I can see if I have it correct or not."

"My pleasure." She practically skipped a few steps back to the board to share her findings. Her long blonde hair flipped side-to-side with each step. "I wrote a short version"—as she pointed to the left equation—"and I wrote the long version next to it"—while pointing to the right.

"I'd like to hear what you've found. Please continue."

The Dean added, "So would I."

"The short version is this. When I looked back at some of my religious texts, I saw a phrase that said, 'God is infinite.' That made me think about limitations to infinity. Then I came up with this formula. It became more complicated"—a number of students chuckled because of the irony—"and I wrote it down. If God is the infinity sign, and God can't do certain things without creating a paradox, then you subtract X from the infinity sign. In short, God is: Infinity minus X, where X is greater than or equal to 1—the God Formula." She did a tiny curtsy.

Brandi asked with a confused look, "What is X again?"

"X stands for everything that the religious God can't do." She turned to me. "And when you think about it, that could reach infinity also, just like you said, Professor."

With my hand on my head in amazement, I expressed, "I'm thoroughly impressed."

"Wait, there's more."

I pointed to the class to look toward Stacey. "Stay with us, folks." Some of their eyes were glazed over, including the Dean's.

"Now"—she paused for effect—"the long version. It's pretty much the same idea, but with more concepts spelled out. This time, it's Infinity minus X plus Y, and it's multiplied by everything inside the brackets."

"Robbie, are you getting all of this down?" I asked. He was writing down her formula as she explained it.

"The bracket goes like this: It's Change times Infinity, times Form times Infinity, times Action times Infinity, times Reaction times Infinity, times Perception times Infinity, times Emotion times Infinity, minus XY, where XY is greater than one but less than Infinity. And that's all multiplied by the original Infinity minus X plus Y."

"Stacey, explain to us this part." I pointed to the board. "What's X and Y?"

She huffed because she thought it was simple to understand. "Let's start with the easy stuff. X is greater than one but less than Infinity—what God can't do. Y is God experiencing itself from an outside perspective—the paradox." She looked back to the Dean. "Are you getting all of this?" He had a not-so-happy-but-interested look.

Rochelle exclaimed, "I've got it! Inside the brackets, just take infinity times Change, Form, Action, Reaction, Perception, and Emotion minus XY. That what God can't do. It makes sense. I think?"

I inquired, "Is there more to this?"

Stacey perked right up because she wanted to go deeper. "I was hoping you would ask." With excitement, she used the marker to point at the board. "It's missing *time,* but *time* is a perception anyway. Time can speed up and slow down based upon many different factors. And, according to some, time is influenced by how dense something is or how close that object approaches the speed of light. That's why I left it as perception."

Allen interrupted, "Like Einstein's theory?"

She nodded multiple times to him very fast, "Precisely." She pointed to another section of the formula. "And this right here: Action includes concepts like distance, Change includes concepts like order and disorder, and, oh"—she paused to look at the class with a beaming smile—"I liked this one. Reaction is always controlled by Action—which is also infinite in its possibilities—and Action and Reaction control Perception and Emotion, minus one up to infinity." Her voice was raised at this point because she was extremely excited. "The possibilities are—"

I finished her sentence with her, "Infinite!" I was applauding because of how well she had done.

"And to conclude this, with your three O's assignment, there are now infinite possibilities of what the religious God *cannot* do without creating paradoxes." She bowed, and the class clapped for her.

"Outstanding, Stacey! Truly outstanding!" I applauded some more. She gave me a quick, small bow and returned to her seat.

The Dean was flabbergasted, and he went against his ringing programming from the Illuminati sector of the Order. "Is this what you are teaching your students to do? I've never seen this type of open thinking before."

I replied, "If that's a compliment, thank you." He didn't say anything.

Daphnee's hand went up. "I was taught that God experiences itself through us. And since we are limited, that provides God with all of the perceptions that God cannot have. Doesn't that still work?"

"That's a good point, Daphnee. Does anyone want to respond to that?"

Todd's arm shot up immediately. "I know what she's thinking. I thought about this a lot this weekend." His statement caught the Dean by surprise because he realized that my students were putting a lot of extra effort and thought into this class. "You can't ignore the paradox. Even if God were us, God could not know what it is like to experience being all powerful and powerless at the same time without"—he made a hand gesture to include everyone in the room—"*us!*"

I looked to Daphnee and asked, "Daphnee? Do you see his point?"

She was processing it all and tried to share her thoughts, "It makes sense the way he said it, but I still…"

Beth added, "I know exactly what you are thinking. Now you have to figure out if what you were taught is correct or not. And now you don't know who to trust anymore."

Allen turned to her. "I know all about that. The rug got pulled out from underneath me last week. Like when I learned about the bad stuff our American government does, and then I started learning the real truth. Who do you trust anymore? You can't trust the government—any of them—the media, the military, or the police." Rochelle grabbed his hand again and smiled. Then he continued, "My perception got thrown for another loop, too, when Rochelle pointed out that the U.S. military and government will fight to the death to preserve a democracy, but they'll all worship a sadistic, judgmental monarch as their god. Now that's just plain stupid!" He got a lot of laughs and applause.

Bruce, Phillip, and the Dean received another frequency change in their ears. The Dean interrupted, "Are you telling the students that they should not believe in an all-powerful God or our government?"

"On the contrary, I'm not telling the students what to believe or what not to believe. That has always been a rule of mine. It is up to them to decide." Almost the entire class was either nodding or verbally agreeing. "It's my job to get them to think for themselves without being brainwashed by power-hungry individuals. I just guide them with questions and thought. They still make the final ruling for themselves."

Stacey confirmed, "He's right, Dean Shwermer. He makes that very clear to us, and he says he supports us either way."

Rochelle turned to him. "He's also pointing out the repetitious flaws and greed-based motives that the authorities continue to shove down our throats, and he's giving us solutions to those problems."

The Dean looked angrily at Rochelle, and then he addressed his question to me, "Alright, I'll play student for the moment. Based on your findings, why don't you pray for help? Why don't you give homage, reverence, and respect to a higher power? Don't you *fear* the wrath of *God?*" He held up his Bible to show the class. Some of the students just sighed and groaned.

"Great question." I turned to Robbie. "Give the Dean credit for participating." The Dean wasn't amused and just twisted his Bible in the air to get my attention.

"Quite simply, it's because prayer doesn't work the way religions say it works. All of this prayer to the alien and man-made god doesn't seem to make a difference. Just look at all of the atrocities that have happened in our history—and continue to happen. If the religious god were as powerful as they all claim god is, then god would have stepped in and made changes during all of the world wars—all wars for that fact! Wars would never have happened in the first place if the religious god had deemed it so. And furthermore, the religious god would have stopped the Jews from burning in concentration camps, stopped the Indians from having their land taken from them by force, stopped the militaries and governments from using citizens as test subjects for their sadistic weapons and research, and god would have stopped the rich from enslaving the poor for all time. I could go on for days listing every atrocity all throughout history. But that hasn't happened, and you are well aware of this. There have been so many times when the religious man-made god should have stepped in, but nothing happened."

The Dean replied, "But that's because we have free will." Almost the entire class shook their heads in disbelief.

I countered with great emotion, "If the alien *god* isn't going to interfere in our affairs because we supposedly have free will…then why pray to the alien man-made *god* at all? It wouldn't matter." I paused so he could have time to comprehend what I'd said, and the class went wild. Then I added, "And if this man-made, reptilian version of god is going to do what it wants anyway because of some supposed plan, then why pray there, too?!" The Dean was stymied, and the students were pounding and clapping.

Allen hooted, "Score number twenty for Professor Whyse." Rochelle gave him a high five.

Stacey concluded, "That's a great point, Professor. I never thought of that before." She turned to the Dean and gloated, "He's right."

I sighed and addressed the entire room, "I'm sorry about that, class. That was not supposed to be about me again. Let's turn this back to you and pick up from the last day's discussion."

Todd supported me, "It's not your fault, Professor. He asked you a question, and you answered him." He said a little softer, "And boy did you answer him."

His Illuminati programmer was sending him more signals. The Dean wasn't satisfied and pursued further, "So you won't pray or live in fear of God?" He tapped his Bible.

"First off, if the religious god only responds to people who pray, then that is not an all-loving god, it's a god who shows favoritism. Not a very good role model in my book. And each religion has its own version of god, so each religion's version of god is showing favoritism only to that religion. I think history has completely proven that wrong. Nobody's religion is rising to the top because of prayer and favoritism.

"Secondly, there's a huge difference between supplicating to an amygdala-stimulating entity and asking someone for help."

I laughed because I saw that some of the students had not understood my use of adjectives. I pointed to my head comically and explained, "The amygdala…it's responsible for fear and anger responses. You can get quite addicted to those feelings, too. It's one of the worst drugs possible. And religions, the media, and the governments serve it up with multiple helpings."

The Dean was still looking at me to finish. "As I was saying, Dean, unlike most fear-based religions, you wouldn't have to pray to me to get help. I do my best to help my students all of the time, and not once have I asked any of them to pray to me, kneel to me, or send offerings. If they ask, I'll help—and not because of some hidden agenda or plan. And if the religious man-made god was all-knowing, then the religious man-made god would have already sent help where it was needed, or even fixed the situation before it ever happened. There would be no problems in all of Creation."

I looked to my class and asked, "Did I ever ask you to kneel to me?" All but two responded in my favor. "I teach my students to find ways to overcome any personal fears they might have and to live peacefully with one another. Fear is not the answer." That response received even more applause. "And sometimes, you have to stand up to those who continue to enslave you to their primitive, selfish, ego-driven thoughts and ideas."

Rochelle yelled, "You get 'em, Professor!"

"So, Dean Shwermer, I will not cower to a reptilian or man-made, amygdala-stimulating, created god, nor will I teach others to live in fear." I shook my finger to him and said rather loudly, "Children don't grow up being afraid of the Creator until someone teaches them to be afraid of the Creator." The class erupted into more cheers and applause. "And if you look at history, the only ones doing any punishing of people not cowering to god are other power-hungry people or aliens. It's the religious fanatics who are doing the preaching, punishing, torturing, and killing. It was the humans and aliens who wrote in the religious texts that man gets to punish man on god's behalf for not abiding by certain religious beliefs, commandments, or laws."

I engaged my class again, "Let's remove the human element, OK? No human in this room gets to say they are acting on the religious god's behalf, alright?" I looked directly at the Dean. "If the Creator wants me dead for misleading these students, then the Creator, and the Creator alone—no human hand involved—will strike me down immediately for teaching these students to disobey any commandment, or for saying that they should not live in fear of god." Nothing happened to me, and the students laughed when I put my arms up to show my point.

The voices in Phillip's and Bruce's heads were screaming, "Do it! Do it now! He deserves to die! Do it now and get *rewarded!*"

Phillip put his head down on his desk and covered it with his hands. Bruce's hand was twitching and his face was all scrunched. He was logically thinking about his instructions, and he was doing everything that he could to stop them from taking over completely. He received another loud ring in his ears. "Your time has come. Do it now and receive your *reward.*" His hand was twitching even more and moved toward his backpack. He pulled his twitching hand back with his other hand and slammed it down on his lap. His aura, and Phillip's aura, was a bright yellow and red color from all of their fear and hate.

"Dean Shwermer, at this point, as a new student, I would normally ask you to make an appointment to see me during my conference time so we could discuss this outside of class. If it's OK, I would like to move ahead with the goal for today." He didn't pursue his question and put up his hand to gesture that he would not ask any more on this topic. "And I support you in your pursuit of truth and your faith." He was taken aback by my last comment.

"Great. With the time remaining, we have some tidying up to do from last class and from your last two assignments. Anyone who would like his or her papers back can see Robbie at the end of class."

In my body, the voice grew from within my soul. It spoke to me directly this time, "Hold the *new* scroll while you speak. It will guide you on your mission. Your voice is what they should hear." I could only imagine that I would not be channeling this time but just receiving the knowledge needed to help my students. I picked up the second scroll and faced the class.

"Now, on Friday, we were discussing a community where everyone serves each other with his or her best abilities and gives them away freely, knowing that they would receive everything else in return for free. In this type of town, there would be no need for money, simply because money never created the basics for survival anyway. And that's what we will cover today."

Bruce challenged harshly, "Why don't you teach for free right now if you want to be in a no-money society so badly?" The Dean looked at him because his father was the only one who had called.

"I'm glad you brought that up, Bruce. I gave that a lot of thought while I was grading papers this weekend. I'll use a jury notice as an example.

"Let's say that I receive a jury notice. I'm mandated by a silly, made-up law to report and judge someone else for his or her imperfections—even though the judges, lawyers, politicians, and the police are also extremely imperfect and dishonest themselves. If I don't go to jury duty, nobody in my community cares; they won't even bat an eyelash. The only ones who would care are the marshals, who will then drag me—by brutal force—in front of a judge. Then, this imperfect judge will either fine me thousands of dollars or hold me in contempt of court and send me to prison for not judging someone else. So refusing to go won't mean a thing in the grand picture. Life goes on if I don't show up to jury duty.

"Furthermore, if I do go to jury duty and I make a vocal protest, I will be dragged off by some cop and beaten in some room because I didn't comply like a good little brainwashed citizen. Again, life goes on if I show up and don't want to participate in their childish games.

"The only way this would work is the Freedom Number." That got a lot of students to sit up.

Beth raised her hand. "What's the Freedom Number?"

"It's a term that I've used in the past to explain this concept. There is a certain number of souls—the Freedom Number—that the cabalistic Order is unwilling to kill or imprison before a change is made." I stopped to emphasize my point. "They can't kill all of us. They need slaves to do their bidding." That made a lot of the students nod their heads in agreement.

Then I turned and walked back to the board and wrote a huge question mark. "There's an unknown number that they fear. There're only a few of them, and a lot of us. You've heard the terms used in regard to financial inequality: the ninety-nine percenters and the one percenters. The cabalistic one percenters use the military and police to keep themselves in power. But somewhere down the road, the ninety-nine percenters *will* rise up against them. The masses will regain the freedom that was wrongly taken from them at birth—the Freedom Number."

Rochelle remarked, "That's what Gandhi did. He got the people to rise up against the enslaving British monarchy and freed India."

"She's right, Gandhi knew about this number. But, unfortunately, he never really freed the citizens of India. All he did was change the power structure a little. The people of India are still held as financial slaves to the world bankers, the corporations, and the Order."

After a short pause, I redirected the conversation. "Well, let's take this back to the enforced jury duty and money system. If the people rose up against the for-profit legal system, and all of them refused to comply with jury duty, there would be a change in the system toward freedom."

Todd pointed out, "The legal system is completely flawed anyway. Tons of innocent people get sent to jail. DNA testing has been proving this a lot lately. It is a for-profit business, so no one is really trying to fix the system. And all laws are based upon fear and are created by the rich to keep the rich in power. The lawyers love it; they get rich either way. I get it, Professor. It's about time that someone is saying all of this, and now I get it." The class applauded.

Bruce was furious. "So what does that have to do with money? Teach for free, then!" A number of students were very concerned by his anger, including the Dean. I saw his aura flash from the pain in his head.

"I'm getting to that, Bruce. If I don't use money, nobody cares. Life goes on. The government will just take everything I have because they'll say I owe taxes and can't pay them. We are forced and brainwashed to work in a money-dominated system by those who feed on power, or be sent to prison. Remember, taxation was a concept completely created by the reptilians and the Order."

The boy in the back interjected, "That's why they repossessed our house! Those dirty scumbags!" The Dean looked at him in shock. He was getting schooled in a new way.

"So…if I don't use money, so what? Nothing changes. If I don't pay taxes, so what? Nothing changes. If I make a stand on my own and refuse to use money, no one cares, and everyone goes on with his or her life in this brainwashed society. And, on top of all this, I still need the basics to survive, and so do you. I can't do it on my own, either, even though I want to. I still need food, water, shelter, and so on."

Stacey asserted, "I know where this is going. You need other people—well, other occupations—to do the things that you can't do on your own. And you are held in this system against your will by those who use fear and force to keep you there."

She turned to Bruce. "Even if he goes off grid and grows his own food, the government will still force him to pay property, land, and federal taxes, or they'll just take his land and possessions from him. He's in a no-win situation as long as the..." She spun around, "What did you call them, Professor, the reptilian cabalistic Order?" I nodded *yes*. Then she turned back to Bruce. "As long as the cabalistic Order is in control of the money, no one is free."

"Thanks, Stacey." I continued, "But if everyone stood up against this cabal, then the people could begin to live freely, without being forced, coerced, punished, beaten, or killed by the police and military."

Rochelle cautioned, "Be careful, Professor. You are starting to sound like an empowered individual."

Allen agreed, "I know. The military hates self-empowered people. You, Professor, are now an enemy of the state."

"Sadly, Allen, that's how things have turned out in our country."

Rochelle scowled, "And the world."

"I know that only partially answers your question, Bruce, but that's where I was headed with today's discussion. There are basic needs that a community must have in order to operate. I already mentioned three of them: we need food, water, and shelter. But there are four major groups beyond this. What are they?"

The football player contributed, "We need clothing. It's hard to play football without uniforms and pads."

"Right you are," I praised. "We need three more basics."

The Dean offered, "We need education." I gave him a point to acknowledge his answer.

Another girl added, "It's hard to fix your own broken leg, back, or do your own dental work, so we need dental, vision, and medical care."

"Man, you guys are sharp today. That leaves the last one."

Daphnee chimed in, "In the last class, when you were speaking in that strange voice, you said that we were given the ability to think and learn for entertainment. I guess that would be important. All work and no play makes for another slave. So entertainment would be useful."

I was glad that she remembered the God Scroll channeling. "Now it's time to get practical. The seven basic needs would guide the community's efforts. And each need is completed by experts in the field, people who really love doing what they are doing for enjoyment, and for the opportunity to serve others. And this philosophy would be taught to children from birth."

I grabbed the marker and wrote *food* on the open space. "Until we can get to a point of living off of Universal Energy Juice, we all need it." They laughed. "It's one of the basics. It brings people together and tightens a community. It teaches sharing, responsibility, and nurturing. It also helps provide entertainment in the way of creativity. So, if we need food, we need farmers and gatherers. No money is needed to do this. All food is provided in its rawest form for free."

"But doesn't some food need processed, grown, or cooked?" asked the shy boy in the front.

"Yes, and that would provide another opportunity to serve your neighbors. No money is needed in food processing. There are many native tribes all over the world that don't use money, and they care for each other in their clan willingly."

Daphnee beamed, "The same would go for water, too. Bringing water to a home, either through buckets or some natural distribution system, would also bring a community together. And nobody is creating water on this planet. It's all been provided for free."

"You've got it. And anything to do with water, such as drinking, cooking, personal hygiene, irrigation, and elimination would all fall under the water category. No money is needed for that. In a community like this, it would be about serving: How can I serve you today? Do you need any water?"

Brandi joshed, "Can we still have water parks?"

"I wouldn't see why not. That would be an awesome community project."

Allen stretched and yawned, "It seems a lot like going back to live like cavemen. Do you really think people would go for it?"

"It would depend on how much the people wanted to return to their roots or to give up modern-day comforts. I, for one, like having a refrigerator for food preservation and air-conditioning on those really hot days. And if we had the best inventors, we could distribute free, clean energy to everyone on the planet. With our best minds at work, instead of producing weapons that kill, we could produce machines that have no negative impact on the environment. Does that answer your question?"

He replied, "I could see it working, as long as I wouldn't have to live in a cave."

"Food for thought, Allen." I laughed at my own bad joke. "What if living in a cave was your only option for protection? Would you refuse to go inside because it wasn't shaped like a traditional house?"

He took a moment. "I guess not, as long as there weren't any bears inside," he chuckled.

"Of course there are many other factors for providing clean drinking water and food for a town, but we won't be able to solve everything in one class. So let's talk about the concept itself. In ancient Hawaii, the elders used to raise the children and pass along their knowledge and wisdom to the young ones while the parents took care of the seven basic needs. How would that be a benefit to a community like this?"

One of the girls in the back shared, "My sister recently had a baby, and she just turned eighteen. She's going to keep her baby girl, but she told me that she was too young to raise a child on her own. She's scared and is still trying to figure out life and what she wants to do. In this situation, the elders could help care for and teach her daughter while she learns and masters a skill."

"Great point. The elders would be passing down the best of their life experiences to help the child grow in love and service. That's exactly what they used to do in old Hawaii."

Rochelle gruffed, "You mean, until some greedy Americans took it away from them."

"Yes," I replied. "And the Hawaiians did have their share of wars between the islands. Even in paradise, there will be challenges if everyone doesn't live to serve others. That's why the concept needs to be taught from early childhood: peace, love, and service to others. Simple to say, but a challenge to accomplish."

The Dean wasn't convinced. "And with this concept, how does higher education fit in?"

Todd answered, "We covered that in the last class. Everyone would receive the best education for free. Having the smartest and most skilled people would benefit each town—and the entire world. Knowledge would be given freely, not held in secret to make money." He nodded with a smile.

I thought to myself, "I might not live to see this happen in my lifetime, but what if the seed just took root? Wouldn't that be awesome?"

He continued, "And as I thought about the list of seven things, the same would apply with medical care, entertainment, clothes making, and so on. Everyone, everywhere in the world, could have an opportunity to receive the best of everything for free—if people learned how to live for each other instead of for themselves. The Professor said something like this: When you share the best you have to offer with your neighbors and community, you also receive the best in return. I mean, who wouldn't want to live in a place like that?"

The Dean countered, "It is a lofty goal."

One of the girls in the front noted, "The Professor said it correctly in the last class, too. We have an opportunity to free ourselves from tyranny and oppression, or we can remain enslaved to the Order. Personally, I'd like to see us free ourselves and live for peace. It's better than what we have now." She got a number of verbal praises from the students.

The Dean received another tone in his ear. Then he questioned, "And you approve of such a place?"

"Don't you? It seems like a win-win to me." He didn't say anything in return.

Allen got my attention. "So how do you start? I mean, what's the next step? You know that the Order isn't going to just go quietly."

Rochelle put her hand on his arm. "It's the Freedom Number, remember?"

"Oh yeah, the Freedom Number. So we need to form an uprising?"

"It takes more than that, Allen," I corrected him. "Everyone would have to start deprogramming themselves from centuries of brainwashing. The first thing people would have to do is willingly, and I mean *willingly*, give up their control-based identities. If you force someone to give up an identity, like national pride, they might fight you to the death to keep it. That would go against a peaceful community."

Rochelle acclaimed, "It's not a hard choice. Peace over pride? I'd give up my identity for peace and freedom." A number of other students agreed with her, but a few shook their heads *no*.

Bruce and Phillip were receiving strong signals. The pressure on their brains was causing them immense pain, and the volume on the voices increased.

"I can see that we don't have a consensus on this, and that's fine. I'm not here to force anyone to change. But if you changed willingly, that's a start toward freedom."

"Kill him now! Do it and get *rewarded!* Kill him now!" The message kept repeating in both boys' heads. Bruce pulled his backpack into his lap and clutched it hard. His knuckles turned white from the pressure.

The football player spoke next, "I gave some thought to what you said last class. It would be hard for me to stop competing and to stop being proud of my team. I've been taught since I was a kid to win above all else. Team, team, team! That's what's ingrained in our heads: us over them. That's some tough reprogramming that would have to happen."

"I understand. It would be a challenge."

He continued, "I know that the coaches say it's character building—sportsmanship and all—but it is still us against them, isn't it? Instead of living for the betterment of everyone else, we are competing for ourselves. I have to admit, I struggled with this. And you are right—it's selfish."

"I honor your conclusions." I bowed to him.

The Dean challenged, "What about laws?"

Daphnee answered him, "We went over that in the last class, too. Love doesn't need laws, just guidance. And if everything is free, and given freely from one to another, then you can't steal what someone wants you to have anyway. This system eliminates the need for most laws." She paused for a moment. "It would seem, if love and peace were taught from childhood, that a loving, peaceful person would not deliberately harm another. Love, compassion, guidance, and serving others really do seem the way to go."

Todd added, "And it wipes out literally thousands of useless jobs that were only created because of money." Bruce looked angrily at him.

Allen asked, "So how would removing an identity help change things?"

I praised him, "Great question. In our current state of enslavement, countries make up laws that are enforced by the police and military, and these are all umbrellaed under the concept of a nation. The cabalistic leaders in the Order were very sneaky to create borders and nations. You see, if they could get you to accept a nationality, then you would be controlled by those in power of that nation. So, as soon as you are born, you are now mandated to live under all existing Order-made laws—even though you never got to vote on them in the first place."

I engaged the class, "Do you see how you've been enslaved to someone else's morals and ideals for power and greed before you were ever born?" They were nodding. "You never had the right to say if you wanted to be a part of that nation. The nations of the world claimed you by where you were born and bound you to those laws—by force. I'm telling you, you were all born into slavery—not freedom."

Allen was a little puzzled. "I still don't get how the Freedom Number works here. How do you start it?"

"I was getting to that, Allen. Thanks for your interest."

I addressed everyone in the room, "If enough people—the Freedom Number—no longer claimed to be of that nation, if they all willingly declared 'I will no longer identify myself as a U.S. slave, a British slave, a fill-in-your-own-blank slave, and I will no longer live under your laws', then the money-based U.S. government and other world governments could no longer control them or force them to live under the Order's laws. It's a numbers game. The majority can rule in favor of freedom again, instead of being enslaved by the few who run the Order-based governments."

Rochelle pumped her fist and shouted, "It's a revolution, then. Time to revolt!"

"Well," I calmly replied, "it would never be a revolution if people just didn't identify themselves as a citizen or a slave of any nation. There would be no war. It would be a simple act that changes everything *instantly*. There would be no violence offered by someone who says *I am not part of your greed-based group and laws.*"

Brandi was impressed. "You've really thought this through, haven't you?"

I was still holding the scroll. A message came through me. "You were all born free. You were meant to be free. And you will always remain free until someone tells you that you cannot do something. You were born unto a world without laws. It was the aliens and humans who created these laws to enslave you, and then they lied to you and told you that you have certain freedoms. This is still slavery and deception at its core.

"I tell you, My children, reclaim what was given to all as a birthright. You have the opportunity to reclaim your freedom and live in peace, love, and understanding. Serving others is a strength, not a weakness. It is the weak who must use deception and lies to control you. Your governments have lied to you from their inception, My children, and they will continue to lie to you. If they truly served the people, they would not ask for gold coin or compensation for their acts. Love and service do not ask for anything in return. You must see the deception if you are going to make a change and free yourselves."

The voice made a special emphasis for its final thought. "I tell you this, My children, hear Me and remember it well. This phrase will build a new world: *When we all serve each other, there are no masters! When we all serve each other, there are no masters! When we all serve each other, there are no masters!* This I say with love and guidance."

Rochelle expressed, "I love it when you speak in that voice. It sounds very…full of guidance. And you are right—we are born free until someone forces us to live by a law. And look how many laws there are in the U.S. that tell us what we can't do based upon someone else's morals and fears. I'm tired of it." A number of students were applauding.

Allen queried, "So, let me get this straight… If everyone stops calling themselves Americans and refuses to live by these enslaving laws, then the government could no longer control us?"

Robbie looked at me so he could answer him. I gave him an approval nod. "Only if you reach the Freedom Number. There have to be enough people who act. They have to unify and stand up to the oppression we've all been living under. If people keep being distracted by new technology, reality TV, sports, and the fear-based media, the cabalistic Order has won. People have to wake up and make a stand." He received numerous cheers and applause.

The signal in Bruce's head was overwhelming. His Illuminati handlers were screaming in his ear via the voice to brain technology. "Now! Do it now before he finishes! Do it now!" The handler increased his pain.

He couldn't take it anymore. The excruciating pressure on his brain was too intense. Bruce turned to the Dean and threatened, "This is what I am talking about." He pointed at me. "The Professor is putting evil thoughts in our heads. I'm telling you that greed is good! Money is good!" Students were adamantly disagreeing with him verbally.

He continued to point in anger. "He's insulting my financial major. This country was founded on greed, and look how great it's become. We were once the most powerful nation, but it's people like him who are destroying it. We need to rebuild our wealth and crush everyone else in the world." The class booed at him.

He stood up and turned to the Dean. "If you won't stop him, I will!" He reached into his backpack and pulled out the gun. Students around him started screaming and ducking for cover. Then he pointed the gun at me. "It's time for you to stop!" He pulled the trigger, and a single shot echoed in the room—*Bang!*

CHAPTER THIRTY-FIVE

EVERYTHING HITS THE FAN

I was on the floor, motionless, with my hands over my chest. Robbie and a few students from the front rows ran up and immediately knelt down. They encircled my body to see if I was alright.

Stacey started crying, "Please, Professor! Please, please don't die!"

Beth was also sobbing, "Noooo, this can't be happening. Somebody do something!"

Allen was shaking from his adrenaline. "Is he going to be alright?!"

Robbie took over. "Give him some room. Everyone back away! And someone call for help!"

The football player had already tackled Bruce and had him pinned on the ground. Bruce was easy to immobilize because he'd been frozen in his stance with the gun dangling loosely from his finger. The voices inside his head had ceased, and the pressure on his brain had stopped. He had no conscious idea about what had just happened. Before he was knocked down, he'd stood there like a lifeless mannequin.

Todd joined in to help and was holding Bruce's arms behind his back. He couldn't move, and he didn't put up a struggle. Then, the two guys from the back also came over to keep Bruce from escaping. The gun was on the floor by the windows.

Both the Dean and Phillip were receiving new instructions. "Pick up the gun and finish your assignment. *Rewards* come to those who follow instructions." That was the first time that the Dean had heard voices in his head. Meanwhile, Phillip was eyeing the gun.

Brandi was kneeling beside Robbie. "Is he going to live? Help him, Robbie."

The entire room was still in chaos. Some of the students had run out of the classroom in terror.

I gasped loudly—"Mduuuuhhhhh!"—sprang up into a seated position, and opened my eyes. That scared all of the students around me and made two of them jump backwards.

"Professor!" Robbie yelled. "Are you alright?" This was followed by a number of students asking the same thing.

I looked down to my shirt. There wasn't any blood, and I felt no wounds on my head or body. I had a strange feeling in my hand, though, like a small object was pinned inside of it. Then I opened it slowly. The bullet that had sped toward me at two thousand and five hundred feet per second was crushed into a little ball and lay there loosely in my palm. There was a trace of white powder around it.

Robbie was in shock. "How did you do that, Professor?"

Allen joked, "Is he some kind of ninja or something?" Rochelle slapped his chest with the back of her hand.

"It's magic!" exclaimed one of the other students.

"Pick up the gun and finish your assignment!" This message accompanied even more pain in Phillip's brain, and he knelt down hard because of the torture. "Finish it now, and the pain will stop. *Rewards* come to those who follow instructions." His Illuminati handler increased his pain one more level. He winced with tears streaming down his face.

Everyone else was still focused on Bruce and the Professor. When the pain receded slightly, he walked over to the wall and stood by the gun.

Meanwhile, I had a vision flash from my memory. When Bruce pointed the gun at my chest, I put my hand in front of me, and instinctively it had filled with an energy ball. The energy was stronger than anything I had ever felt before. It rose from my lower dantian and had made my arm buzz like I was holding a live electric wire.

I checked, "Is everyone OK? Is anyone hurt?"

Robbie answered, "No one else was shot at, and Bruce was tackled. He didn't move after the gun went off."

"Are you sure that no one else was hurt?" I stood up to look around.

Stacey confirmed, "We're all OK, and security has already been called."

"Are you sure?" I glanced around the room one more time. No one else seemed to be in any other danger.

Without conscious control, Phillip bent down, picked up the gun, and pointed it at me. "Professor, I'm sorry. But the voices just won't stop. They are hurting me!"

The remaining students went into another panic. All those around me ducked behind the podium and desk. Some of the students closest to him ran to the other side of the room, and three of them stepped toward Phillip.

He frantically pointed the gun at each of them and hollered, "Stop! I swear I'll shoot!" They immediately ceased moving toward him.

I yelled, "Nobody make a move! Phillip, put down the gun!" The Dean was the closest one to him. I looked to Shwermer to help, but he did nothing.

"The voices won't stop. Please make them stop!" He was shaking his arm and hand toward me. The gun was moving closer to my head.

"Phillip, those voices aren't yours. They are coming from the Order." He looked at me strangely. "They are using voice to skull technology to brainwash you. Don't listen to them!" With my hands and arms in an open, inviting position, I exclaimed, "I can help you!"

One of the other students blurted, "He's crazy, just like Bruce!"

"No!" I asserted. "He's being controlled by the Order, too. He has a handler giving him commands with voice to skull technology." I turned to Phillip. "Right? They are sending you messages."

"Please make them stop. They want me to kill you!"

"Don't give in, Phillip. You are a good person, and they are evil. Don't let them win!" I was taking small, cautious steps toward him.

"It hurts!"

"I know. Just don't give in! Hand me the gun."

His handler increased the pain, and he clutched his head with both hands. One student started to move toward him. Phillip regained himself and pointed the gun at him, and then at everyone else. More screams filled the room as the students ducked again from his wildly swinging arm. His hand finally steadied with its aim back at me.

I commanded, "Nobody else move toward him. Back away, now!" Everyone stood still. "I mean it. Back away, now!" They finally listened and backed away.

Bruce urged his friend, "Don't give in to the voices, Phillip!"

Todd put his hand on his head. "Shut up, murderer."

"Todd, don't hurt him, either. They've both been tagged and used by the Order."

Phillip screamed from another shot of pain, "Owwwww!" He re-aimed his gun at my head and focused to shoot.

"I know what they are doing to you, Phillip. These thoughts aren't your own. They are using you and sending you signals. I've experienced this myself."

That caught him off guard. "You, too?"

"Yes, I've gone through this same pain. It hurts, I know. But I can help you. Just put the gun down."

He received another piercing sting and shook his gun hand. "No, don't take another step. I have to stop the voices. They want me to kill you!" His finger started to squeeze.

"I can help you, Phillip."

"Aaaaahhhhhhh!" He was in agony. He stumbled from the pain for a moment, but then he regained his strength just enough to declare, "I'm not a murderer!" He withdrew his aim, but then his hand rushed to his neck with the gun barrel touching beneath his chin. "I have to make this stop!"

I thrust my hand out to him. "Noooo!" A burst of calming energy shot out of my body and wrapped around him before he could squeeze the trigger. I saw the white, sparkling mist envelop him. I refocused again while sending more energy his direction. "Don't do it. They aren't worth it."

He relaxed for a second because the energy had immensely eased his pain. "Think, Phillip. This is not who you are. Give me the gun."

He shoved the gun up under his chin one more time. "Help me!" He was crying and shaking.

"Stop! I can help you." I still had my palm facing to him, and I was sending everything I had to calm him down. A massive rush of warm energy flowed out from my body to meet his. I could see his aura start to change, and the dark red, yellow, and black colors turned to calmer shades.

He looked at me, winced hard, and then with a sigh put his hand down. He glanced at the gun one more time before throwing it out the open window. "I'm not a killer!" Then he collapsed to the ground in more tears.

I rushed over to him. "It's OK, Phillip. It's over." With my arms around him, I told the others to release Bruce. Reluctantly, they complied.

I looked at the remaining students. "This is what your government and military do to you if you don't live their way. They are the enemies, not Phillip and Bruce. Don't trust the CIA, FBI, NSA, CDC, FDA, the police, military, or any part of the government!"

The police had arrived on campus and swarmed the building. The officer who worked directly with the Order, Officer Dunse, saw the gun that he had given to the boys lying near one of the bushes. He let the other officers run inside while he looked around to see who was watching. Then he picked up the gun, put it inside his shirt, and went back to his squad car to hide it.

Inside the room, the Dean stood there with a dull look on his face. He didn't know if what had just happened was real or not. He'd heard the same voices, but he was in complete denial. He thought to himself, "This is the work of demons. Satan spoke to me."

I was kneeling over the boys. "I will get you help, I promise. You've been tagged by the Order."

Then the police came into the room in their standard scare-everyone-as-much-as-they-can formation, with guns and shields pointing toward each soul in the room. "Everyone, hands up in the air!" A number of students reacted and followed the ego-driven command.

They were still rushing in and surrounding everyone when I stood up with open arms. "Everything is under control…"

One of the officers lunged at me and used the butt end of his rifle to smash my face. The skin-ripping blow knocked me to the ground immediately. He shouted, "I said, hands up!"

Stacey screamed, "Stop it!"

Robbie yelled, "You idiot! He's the one they shot at!" He took a step toward me, but the officer pushed him back with his rifle barrel. He put his hands back in the air.

The officer who'd hit me aimed his rifle at my face with an empty-soul glare. I held my head and felt the warm blood pour from the deep gash.

Rochelle hollered at them, "You stupid, dumb-ass people! Is that all you know how to do? He's our teacher!" Another officer raised a gun to her.

The lead officer commanded, "Everyone keep your hands in the air. Who's in charge here?"

While I raised my bloody hand, Todd spat, "You hit the one in charge, bastard."

The Dean finally spoke up. "I'm the Dean here, and this is his classroom. No one is hurt here."

"Who's in charge?" the officer asked again.

My students pointed to me. "He is!" The policeman who'd hit me was still shoving his rifle in my face.

"I'm their teacher, and this is my room." Blood had completely covered the side of my head. "It was all done by the Order."

The officer in charge stated, "We had a report of shots being fired. Who was it?"

Bruce raised his hand, while other students pointed at him and Phillip. The police rushed them immediately and threw them to the ground with knees planted in their backs. "You are under arrest!"

"Wait!" I stopped them for a moment. "I am not pressing charges. They were under attack and had voice to skull technology used on them."

While the officers continued to manhandle the boys and read them their made-up rights, the leader looked at me in confusion. "Voice to what?"

"It's called voice to skull. The military, NSA, and CIA have used this for years. You're the police. Don't you know anything?" I exclaimed. Then I remembered that they work for the Order, too.

"These boys are under arrest for firing a weapon on school grounds."

I defended them, "And they were under an evil influence. These people who brainwashed them are the same people who blow up tall buildings with thousands of people in them just to start wars and make money." I looked at the boys. "I'm not pressing charges. They need help, not abuse."

Phillip and Bruce glanced at me with sorrow-filled eyes. I reiterated as I pointed to the boys, "They were used. Don't you know anything?" I continued in frustration. "I know you refuse to think that our government and military would do such a thing, but wake up! This is *them* using these boys for an evil purpose."

He scoffed, "You're a delusional conspiracy theory follower, aren't you?" He pointed to the boys. "They broke the law, and they will answer to a judge. That's how this goes." He motioned to the other officers. "Take them away!"

As they were being dragged out, I told the boys, "I will help you as much as I can. Just do as they say so they won't hurt you anymore." They were pulled out of the room and out of sight. I slumped down in one of the chairs from exhaustion.

Rochelle concluded, "What you've been saying all along is true. There is a cabalistic group called the Order."

"Yes," I replied. "And those boys need help."

Allen added, "We all do."

Some of the officers were already taking statements. I told my students to cooperate with them so they would not be physically harmed. I could see that some of them were giving the officers a hard time. What I had been teaching had taken root, and they were seeing the evil play out before their very eyes.

Brandi pulled a towel out of her gym bag. "Here, Professor"—she poured some water out of her bottle and wet it down—"let me help you with that." She was wiping away the blood.

"Thanks, Brandi."

Robbie asked, "Is there anything I can do for you?"

"This isn't over. When all of it unfolds and hits the fan, will you help me to look out for the other students?" I looked at Brandi, then back to him and winked. "And don't forget Brandi." She smiled, and so did he.

The Dean came up to me after giving his statement to the police. He was also receiving multiple uploads from his Illuminati handler. I mentioned to him, "I imagine that the campus is on lockdown. When this is done, would you please help the students in class get any counseling that they need?"

"I will. And I think it's best that you take an early sabbatical. I can't fire you, but I can't have you endanger the students any further. You are done here for the semester."

Robbie and Brandi both blurted, "What?!"

Stacey and the others echoed the same thing, "What?!"

Robbie continued, "Surely you can't be serious. He had nothing to do with it."

"I will take this to the president of the university. Besides, who will finish out the semester?"

He replied, "I will. Someone has to fix this mess."

The other students were in complete shock. Most of them were saying things like "I won't be back if you are the teacher" and "Flunk me if you want to."

He continued, "Take this up with the president if you'd like, but my mind is made up. Go home and wait for your hearing." Then he started to walk away.

Just before he got to the door, I said to him, "By the way, Dean Shwermer, you've been tagged by the Order. I know you are hearing a ringing sound and voices in your ear." He stopped and looked at me with a hint of fear. "I can help you, if you'll let me." He didn't say anything and left.

I looked at the others. "Unless he has his tag removed, don't trust him. He's under their influence, too."

Robbie reassured me, "I'll tell the other students."

Rochelle overheard and burst, "I'll tell the world."

After I gave my statement, the officers said they needed the room cleared to collect any evidence.

Todd mocked them, "You mean *plant* evidence." He was pushed behind the back by an officer to make him move. He turned around. "Hey, get off me! I'm not the bad guy here, you are!" He was still being pushed by the policeman's rifle.

I thought to myself, "This feels like only the beginning," and I walked the last few students out of the room.

On the reptilian ship, the young officer reported to the commander. "The programming worked well. The professor was sent home and injured by the police. We've also programmed the Dean to make sure that he fires him. The professor will lose his job." The commander hissed in approval.

"I have more to report. The boys are in prison, and the police won't believe their story about the voices in their heads. They've already been scheduled for a psychiatric evaluation. And we have the psychiatrists programmed, too," he laughed. "The mainstream psychiatrists won't even consider our voice to skull technology as valid. They still believe that their government works for them." He laughed harder.

The commander pointed a claw at him. "Hsssss. It is a good thing that you succeeded. The older one was tossed into space for failing me and being insolent." The young officer gulped. "Hsssss. Did you discredit the priest?"

"The police work for us, even though they don't know it." He laughed, "And we've got tons of loyal police who are already in the Order. Officer Dunse has planted evidence of drugs in the professor's classroom desk, and our computer guys at the NSA are falsifying his internet usage and linking it to some sort of wild porn. He'll be judged guilty by the entire world before he can ever clear his reputation, and the religious people will fry his honor and his name. It happens all of the time these days. And since we control the media, they'll make sure that he looks guilty. He's never going to get a job again."

"Hsssss. You have served the Order well."

"Should I initiate the first phase of the mainframe?"

"Hsssss. Yes, it is time to start. Activate the implants and watch their finances fall. Feast we will on their panic and suffering."

"It will be done as you've commanded. In a few days, the implants will control all of the CEOs and financial people on the planet. The mainframe program will instruct them to start selling stocks at a record pace and pull all of their gold and money out of the banks. There will be a complete global economic crash. Once we have successfully run our test, then we will initiate the full mainframe program. *Everyone* will be under our complete mind control soon." He gave his hand signal: a fist covering one eye to honor the Order's one-eyed god. "All hail the Order!"

"Hsssss. All hail the Order."

———————

In Cairo, ten new priests had shown up to Mudads' shop since Ricky and I sent out the prayer. He knew exactly what to do with them and sent each priest to see Ramla. She had already finished another day of teaching at their training grounds and told the new additions that they would start tomorrow. She walked up to Karim. "We are done for the day. Can you take me home now, please?"

He replied, "It is my honor to serve you." He grabbed her cane and handed it to her.

"You really are a sweet boy. Your pain will be healed in this lifetime."

He smiled to her. He knew she was right because he had been hurt badly throughout his lifetime.

Omar ran up to both of them. "Can I get a ride with you? My car won't start."

"Of course. I just have to take Ramla home."

He held up another envelope filled with translations. "I've finished two more of the parchments that Tumaini left behind. Can we stop at the post office so I can mail them?"

"Yes, my child," replied Ramla. "There is one only two blocks from my home."

"Great, thanks."

Karim asked, "Were they like the last ones?"

"Yes, some sort of riddle poem." He laughed, "He sure was good at hiding things."

Ramla agreed, "He was very thorough in his other lifetime."

"Has he developed his plan yet?" asked Omar.

"Not that I am aware of. I did, however, tell him about Gahiji's, Asim's, and Jabari's intentions."

Karim wondered, "Is that why they weren't here today?"

"They told me that they must make haste. Our seers have told them to move swiftly in their goal. Time is running out fast. They might be doing something at this very moment."

Omar remarked, "I don't think I want to know what they are doing. I saw all three of them yesterday carrying boxes of C4 explosives. They were being loaded into the back of a large truck."

Ramla suggested to Omar, "It would be best for you to keep your thoughts protected. The Order is always sweeping the ethers for information."

Karim was shocked. "They can do that?"

"Yes, I have felt them look right into my thoughts in the past. Since then, I've learned how to shield them so they cannot hear me anymore."

Omar requested, "You are so skilled at many things. Will you teach us?"

"Your skills are also improving, Omar. And if there is time, Tumaini, Baniti, and I will help you unlock all of your innate abilities." She looked at both of them. "And when Baniti and Tumaini return, they will be able to amplify your skills, as you were bonded in your goal. Tumaini is becoming very powerful as of late. His energy has surpassed mine."

"Even yours?" Karim was doubtful.

"Yes, even mine. Tumaini's heart is pure in serving others. He will show you how to combine all of your energy systems together to touch the Source of All Things. It is time for you to trust him, Karim. He is one of you, and you are a part of him."

"I have come to trust him more, Ramla. You know me, though; it is not easy for me to let people in."

"I know, my dear boy. I know."

Omar glanced at his watch. "The post office will close soon. Will we have time to make it?"

"I'll get you there in plenty of time," Karim laughed. "I'll take the hidden camel paths." He revved up his car and sped off.

———————

Gahiji nudged his older brother. "Jabari, did you double-check the coordinates for the mainframe? We need to go over our plan of attack for tonight."

"Yes, we will be heading southeast toward one of the pyramids." He pulled out his map to show them the location. He pointed below and to the right of the Giza Necropolis. "This is where we are going, about ten miles."

Asim leaned in to take a better look. "It's not Pyramid Neferirkare, is it?"

"Yes, and no," he replied. "From our intel, the target is under three of the pyramids at Abusir. Pyramid Neferirkare is just one of the pyramids. The entranceway to the mainframes is a secret tunnel located in Ptahshepses Mastaba, over here." He pointed to the building.

Gahiji questioned, "The non-royal tomb, right?"

"Yes. I guess the Order figured we would only look at sites linked to royalty, since they consider themselves to be above us and all. This place just happens to have been the most extensive of non-royal tombs near Cairo. It makes for a great hiding place."

Asim pointed to the first picture. "Where are the tunnels?"

Jabari pulled out the second photo. "Here is the secret tunnel entrance in the tomb. Once inside, the tunnel branches off underground and forks into two more tunnels. One tunnel goes north by northwest to the Pyramid of Sahure." He moved his finger in that direction. "This is the power plant for the mainframe and the mainframe backup. Gahiji, as we've discussed, this will be your target."

He looked up at Asim. "You and I are taking the underground tunnel that goes south by southwest to the pyramids of Nyuserre and Neferirkare. The first pyramid, Nyuserre, is the backup mainframe. I'll be taking that one. The furthest pyramid, Neferirkare, is the primary mainframe. Asim, you are in charge of blowing up that mainframe." He gestured to both of them. "Once the timers are set, we will leave the complex and watch for the explosions near the Sun Temple that's farther north."

Gahiji added, "We are going in light, too—backpacks filled with C4 and timers, including our gun belts and vests. We need to be able to run quickly through the tunnels to plant the explosives and then get out as fast as possible."

"Right," confirmed Jabari.

Asim signaled. "And don't forget to check your pack for wire cutters and detonators."

"I've already checked all three packs," remarked Gahiji, "but we should double-check them before taking the truck."

Asim checked his watch. "We have another hour before we need to go."

Gahiji's stomach growled. "Let's get something to eat first." His brother and Asim laughed. They'd heard all of the stories about Bes and his constant eating.

I was in my office packing up a few things that I wanted to take home. Ted walked up to the door and knocked. I motioned to him. "Come in. I'm almost done." Then I set two more books in my box and lifted my head into his view.

Ted exclaimed, "Holy cow! Are you alright?" He was looking at my deep cut. "Who did that?"

"I'll be fine. It was one of the officers who hit me with his rifle butt."

"Figures. That's all they know how to do in a crisis situation—maim first, ask questions later. Do you want to tell me what happened?"

"Sure…it started with the Dean in my room, and then an awesome discussion about a new type of society." After sharing that tidbit, I spent the next few minutes giving him the abridged version of the shooting. I also mentioned how both of the boys and the Dean had been tagged by the Order. "Yeah, Phillip and Bruce were in bad shape. They experienced the same intense pain that I went through with the implants. I was terrified that Phillip might take his own life because of the torture."

"I'm glad that he didn't."

"So am I. He's a good boy. They shouldn't have abused him like that. I'm going to check on them, if they'll let me."

Ted asked, "And what about the Dean? He's going to use this in his favor to get rid of you."

"I could tell that he was under the Order's influence, too. His actions were completely back and forth today. One minute he was asking a sincere question, and the next minute he was hating me and what I was teaching."

"That's a classic sign of someone who isn't strong enough to fight their programming. If he's hearing ringing in his ear, he's being monitored and being given instructions. You might as well consider him as a member of the dark side."

"I hate to admit it, Ted, but you are right."

"Have you called Constance yet?"

"No. I was just going to go home and process all of this. But maybe I should call her first."

"It's what I'd do. You don't want to walk in with a bloody shirt and a massive gash on your face without any warning." I nodded in agreement.

After picking up the box, I said, "I want to fight this, but there is another fight that is much more important. Since I'm not allowed back in the classroom until my hearing, it's time to focus completely on my plan that will affect the Order."

"It's not right what they are doing to you. The Dean never liked you, and he's using this against you. Can I help?"

"Sure. Can you come over tomorrow sometime? I could use a friend to collaborate with."

"I can do that. Maybe in the evening after classes?"

"Evening sounds great." I looked to the phone. "Thanks for coming to see me. I appreciate it. I should call Constance now."

"No problem. And you are right. Call her and let her know that you are OK. Er…well, as OK as you can be after being hit by the cops."

"I'll do that." Then he left and closed the door.

As soon as Karim got two blocks away from the parking lot, a black four-door sedan pulled out and started following him, but it remained at a distance. The black car tailed them for a good twenty minutes until they reached a narrow, unused road that followed along the Nile. Then the car sped up, and dust trails began spewing from the back tires.

Ramla was engrossed in conversation with Omar and Karim. She was telling them about a technique that would enhance their focus for meditations. She suggested, "Omar, if you consider doing this for your training, you would... What?!" She reacted because she sensed danger. "Karim, look behind you!"

Within seconds, the sedan rammed the back end of Karim's car and jolted everyone inside. Before he could react, the black car rammed him a second time. Then, his car started to hydroplane on the dirt road from the second impact. It was moving forward with the wheels turned hard, but the front end was aimed directly toward the water.

Omar looked behind him and saw the sedan coming for another hit. Karim finally got control as the car came out of the hydroplane. With a quick fishtail maneuver, he moved to the side to avoid another rear-end impact. The black car hit his back quarter panel instead.

Omar saw a man lean out of the passenger window. He yelled, "It's the assassin! He's holding a gun!"

The assassin took aim at Karim and shot. He missed him because Karim turned sharply toward the assassin's car at the exact same moment. Instead of killing him, the bullet blasted a hole in the engine. Unable to outrun the black sedan, Karim swerved his car into its side and smashed the doors. The assassin had pulled back inside just in time.

As soon as the cars separated, the assassin positioned himself outside of the window again and shot three times—*Bang! Bang! Bang!*

Everyone in Karim's car ducked down. When Karim returned upright again, steam started spewing out from his engine. He could barely see. In the mist, he heard another shot—*Bang!*

The black car hit its brakes as Karim's tire blew out. He completely lost control of the car and it turned ninety degrees toward the Nile. Then it began to flip over sideways multiple times, kicking up dirt and dust with each impact. After three complete flips, Karim's car finally bobbed a few times and landed upright. The windows were broken, and three bodies lay lifeless inside.

The sedan had now stopped. The assassin got out and looked inside. All three of them were covered in blood. He ran back to his car, and it sped off.

———————

Constance ran out to greet me at the car. "Oh my, I'm so sorry for what they did to you." She started crying because of the bloody shirt and lacerations. "What they are doing is so wrong."

I hugged her tightly. "I agree with you. The police never even listened to me. Those boys needed help, and all they cared about were their sadistic procedures. That's when my face got smashed in."

"I feel so helpless. We can't call the cops because the cops are part of the problem. What do we do?"

"I know how you feel. But don't go down the path of helplessness. We are the ones who are gaining power, not them."

She was sniffling, "How do you do that?"

"Do what?"

"When things get bad, you look for another route, another way that doesn't lead to fear."

"Maybe that's part of Tumaini coming through."

"I don't think so. Before you even went to Egypt, you were like this. It's one of the many things that I admire about you." She was still teary-eyed.

"Thanks, and I admire so many things about you, too." She smiled, but she still looked at me with concern. I tried to calm her by saying, "If they are attacking me in the open like this, that means that they are really scared. And frightened people are the ones who attack. It's a weakness, and they just showed how weak they are."

"How does that make them weak? They're the ones who hit you."

I replied in Tumaini's voice, "Someone who is confident and calm does not need to hit another to prove his point. They are being ruled by their lower emotions, and that is why they are not in control—we are! Our attack is not offensive; we act in defense so our planet will not be completely enslaved."

"You spoke in another voice."

I checked my short-term memory. "I did, didn't I? But what I said was completely logical, though."

"You are doing it again."

556

"What?"

"Finding a way to take the other road. And damn, you sure make a lot of sense, even if it's Tumaini's voice coming through."

I snickered, "I could be more confusing if you'd like."

"No, I like the common sense route. Thanks for being inspiring."

"Thanks for sticking with me. You're the brave one. You could have left me when all of this started. I'm the one who is in awe of you."

Before heading in, she mentioned, "Ricky and Laura called when they heard the news. They wanted to know how they can help."

"They can come over after dinner if they'd like. I also told Ted that he could come over tomorrow evening, but he can come over tonight, too."

"I'll call them and let them know. I bet they'd like to."

"It might be a good idea. We could practice."

"Or just enjoy their friendship."

"That, too."

⸻•◆•⸻

After dark fell, Jabari parked the truck two thousand yards away from their target. All three of them got out of the vehicle dressed completely in black, including black hoods to cover their faces.

Standing at the back, Asim passed out the packs and headsets. "When we get to the fork in the tunnel, keep in constant contact." He told Gahiji, "You'll be done setting charges before your brother, so you take point on the way out." He gave a fast nod. "I'll take the rear on both trips."

Jabari added, "Our intel said that the mainframe is not heavily guarded. Their feeling is that too many armed henchmen would draw way too much attention to the site."

His little brother included, "It makes sense. The Order is all about keeping *most* things hidden in plain sight."

"You're right, Gahiji. And let's not forget how important this mission is." He put a hand on each of their shoulders. "You, my fellow Protectors, can help stop this terrible reptilian and Anunnaki plot from unfolding."

"So can you, brother." He put his hand on his brother's shoulder, too.

"Alright, standard formation, just like we rehearsed this afternoon." He instructed Gahiji, "You're in charge of taking out any guards."

"Roger."

"And I'll call out any other targets," added Asim.

Jabari whispered, "Hand signals until we get to the tunnel." They both gave a thumbs up. "I've got point." Then he motioned for them to advance.

Like skilled hunters, they made their way to the tomb. The only person visible was a temple priest who was walking away from the mastaba and moving toward Nyuserre's pyramid.

They entered into the building with the slanted walls without being detected. Jabari gave the signal to move through the vestibule and chapel. From there, he led the other two through the pillared courtyard, and then to the burial chamber. He gave another hand signal for all three of them to lift the false bottom that was inside the huge granite sarcophagus. Once they placed it to the side, they could see electric lights descending downward with the stairs. Jabari went first, followed by Gahiji, and then Asim. At the fork, they turned on their headsets and split up.

Gahiji reported, "No one is here. There's nothing but a long black tunnel with lights. Coast is clear."

Jabari commented, "This is strange. We at least expected to see some resistance. Don't let your guard down."

Both Asim and Gahiji responded, "That's affirmative."

Jabari reached an empty cave under Nyuserre's pyramid first. He was confused. It wasn't a modern room at all, and it had no mainframe. "Gahiji, be on the lookout. We may have been led into a trap. There's no computer here. I'm heading to Neferirkare's pyramid." He told Asim, "Stay here and cover me." Asim nodded.

Gahiji reached Sahure's pyramid. "Guys, I think we got some bad intel. There's nothing here but a dugout cave."

His brother had just reached the final pyramid. "Nothing. It's an empty pit. Time to call off the mission. Regroup at the fork." The other two confirmed and backtracked to the entrance tunnel.

Gahiji got there first and called out, "I'm taking point. I'll sweep the tomb and cover you."

"Be careful, brother."

Being the professional that he was, Gahiji swept the burial area and waited for the other two. Once they came out of the sarcophagus, they replaced the false floor.

Jabari saw Gahiji by the courtyard entrance. He gave him the signal for both to move forward. When all three were together, he said, "No more hand signals. Something's not right. We need to get out of here."

Asim added, "I agree. I'll take point." Then he walked through the entrance to the pillars. As soon as he was around the corner, a single rifle shot rang out—*Bang!* Asim buckled down and grabbed his leg. Blood was pouring out onto the sandy floor.

Both brothers immediately pulled him back behind the wall. Asim looked down at his leg and grimaced, "Go! They must have hit an artery. It's gushing blood. I'll only slow you down."

Gahiji replied, "Not a chance. We all get out of here together."

"No, you need to go. I'll stay and cover you."

Jabari scolded, "We protect all souls. That includes yours. Now be quiet. I have some work to do." He turned to his brother. "Look for the sniper while I mend his wound."

"Got it!"

Asim motioned. "I have a tourniquet in my pack."

"You forget who you are talking to. You showed me what to do when you were Talibah, remember?" He cut the bleeding fabric on both sides of his leg. "It must have gone straight through. I can mend this."

"I trust you, my friend."

He turned to look for his brother, but he was not in sight. "Here, give me your hand. Your energy and healing skill will combine with mine to mend this faster." Asim gave him his hand, and a light ball grew around both of them. Then Jabari softly sang one of the prayer songs. White light blazed around Asim's leg and was even brighter at the gunshot wound. Within seconds, Asim's leg was no longer bleeding, and it had healed. The muscles that had been torn were repaired, and his flesh looked like a bullet had never pierced his skin.

Gahiji returned and reported, "The shooter must have moved. He's not in the courtyard." He looked where Asim's wound should have been. "Did you just heal him, brother?"

"Yes, but he might be a little weak. He's lost a lot of blood."

"I'll be fine, honest. I can make it. But we should get out of here."

Gahiji pointed behind him. "We shouldn't go back out the way we came in. On the other side of this wall, the stones at the perimeter are only two or three high. We can get over those easily and escape."

His brother agreed. "Lead the way. I'll take the rear."

With trained precision and guns drawn, all three men made it outside of the mastaba. Asim had a tiny limp, but he was able to keep up with the other two. They were about a thousand feet away from the truck when they heard a sound like a firecracker in the distance. The sniper had just pulled off another round.

———————

It was past dinner at the Whyse's residence. Constance met Laura and Ted at the door. Ted asked, "How's he doing?"

"He'll be fine. He's just a little rattled by everything that happened today at school."

Laura gave her a hug for comfort. "Who could blame him? That would rattle me, too."

"Come on up. Ricky's in the study with him. He was going to lift the glass and work on the magic cross."

Constance came in and saw both Ricky and I with a look of fear on our faces. "What's wrong? You look like you just saw a ghost."

I nodded toward the table. "One of the four cards just moved into this spot." Then I pointed to the number nine location.

"Really?!" exclaimed Laura.

"Which one was it?" inquired Ted.

They all gathered around and bent down to look. "It's the card with the number thirty-six and a dash beside it. I think it means thirty-six minus. I have a feeling that something bad just happened to one of our friends in the priesthood. One of our beloved souls has died."

CHAPTER THIRTY-SIX

DEATH IN EGYPT

Ricky spoke in Baniti's voice, "The beast is awake."

I tried to move the number nine card out to see if I was wrong, but it kept moving back into place. The other three cards were also repelled by the newly set timeline and flew out of the slot. This confirmed my speculation that a terrible event must have transpired. I said with some trepidation, "This means something involving the mainframe took place."

Ted shrugged. "What happened?"

"I'm not sure, but the cards have been perfect up till now. And I can't shake this feeling that one of our brethren has fallen. It's like a piece of our power is missing."

Ricky returned to his own voice. "We need to check in on Egypt. This isn't good."

"I agree." I glanced at the clock. "It's the middle of the night over there. I doubt we'll get any information until morning. Maybe—"

Constance interrupted and urged with a worried tone, "We have to try."

"I know, hon, we will. I was just about to say that I could contact Ramla and Rehema telepathically. If either of them are up, they could give us some answers." I looked at Laura and Constance. "Why don't you two go use the phone downstairs? Ricky and I will make our connections here."

Ted asked, "What should I do?"

"Send hope and love to our friends across the seas."

"I can do that. That's easy."

After the women left, I suggested to Ricky, "Ramla knows my voice, and you already had a telepathic connection with Rehema the other day. You try her, and I'll contact Ramla."

"Sounds good, mon."

Ricky closed his eyes and focused on Rehema. He called out to her multiple times, but didn't get a response.

I followed suit and made my attempt with Ramla. "Ramla, hear me. Ramla, hear me. Ramla, hear me. Are you there?" I waited for a few moments, but there was no voice on the other end. Then I opened my eyes and looked at Ricky. "I'm not getting any response. Are you?"

He shook his head *no*, "You are better at this than I am, though. I'm not sure I did it right."

"Let me try reaching Rehema." With my eyes closed, I made my call. After a few seconds, I reported, "Nothing. She must be asleep."

The girls were coming back up the stairs. Hara ran to her mother. "Mommy, what's going on?"

"We're trying to reach somebody, baby doll. We want to see if all of Daddy's and Ricky's friends are OK."

"Can I help?"

"That's so sweet," sang Laura.

Constance agreed, "Yes, honey, that was very nice of you. We'll let you know if you can do anything." She nodded to her mother. "Why don't you stay up here and play in the game room? If something happens that's fun, we'll call you in, OK?"

"OK," and she went to her own hieroglyph puzzle.

Constance stepped into the room. "Anything?"

Ricky nodded *no*, and I replied, "Nothing. But it's late. They could just be sleeping. We'll call them in the morning to give them our updates and find out if everyone is OK over there."

"It's all we can do for now."

Ted got up from his chair. "Hey, Laura, are you getting anything?"

"Only that Michael's and Ricky's intuition is correct. Something isn't right, and I think it has to do with the mainframe." She motioned to the card with her nod. "I think the Order has initiated some type of plan."

I looked at everyone in the room. "I don't feel any different. And I know what it's like to have implants in my body controlling me. I'm not experiencing anything like that."

Ted felt up and down his chest comically. "I'm not getting anything, either."

I chuckled at Ted and turned toward Ricky. "How about you?"

"I'm good." He turned to Constance. "You?"

"I'm fine. Nothing weird in my head."

"I just had a strange thought. What if it wasn't adults that they've targeted?" I made a whisper motion with one hand and pointed toward Hara with my other. "Let's check in on Hara, but don't go out there. We don't want to startle her by asking a lot of questions."

I poked my head out the door and looked toward the game room. Constance bent over me and her head was above mine. Laura was next, followed by Ted and Ricky. All five of our heads were stacked on top of each other.

Hara noticed and started laughing hysterically, "What?!"

I lost my balance, and we all fell forward with a big *Oof!* That made her laugh even harder.

"Sorry, mon." Ricky got off, and so did the others. "She seems alright to me."

Constance agreed, "She's just fine."

Hara came bouncing over. "You looked so funny." She giggled some more. "Can you do it again?"

I knelt and held both of her arms. "Honey, are you feeling any different?"

She looked to the right with a quizzical look, and then back to me. "No... but I could go for some ice cream."

"Not tonight," answered Constance. "Sorry to interrupt your puzzle." She pointed to the study with her head. "We adults need to go back inside and talk."

"OK... No ice cream?"

"No, no ice cream." She shrugged and went back to her puzzle.

"Well," I chuckled, "so much for keeping a low profile." They all laughed. We all went back inside and talked about the day and what might have happened to make a card move into the timeline.

Jabari was driving the truck as fast as he could to shake the two unmarked vehicles that were chasing them. When they passed the first main road a few miles up, he made an unsuspected move toward the west. When the tires hit the sand, he switched over to four-wheel drive and plowed over the first few dunes. "We'll lose them in the desert. They'll get stuck for sure." He quickly glanced at the other two. "Those cars aren't made for this type of terrain."

Asim looked behind in the rearview mirror. "You're right. They've stopped. I can see their headlights standing still on the main road."

Jabari kept driving over a few more hills toward the northwest. "I have a hunch that they are expecting us to loop back to the east and reconnect with the road. We're going to stay on this course instead until we reach the next main highway past Giza. They won't have a clue where we are."

Gahiji agreed, "That's a good plan." He lifted off his bandage, made a face, and reapplied it to his arm.

His brother asked, "How is it?"

"It's fine. The bullet just grazed me. It barely broke the skin."

Asim expressed his concern, "When we stop, your brother and I are going to take care of that for you."

"By the blood on your sleeve, that's more than just a scratch," scolded his older brother. "You shouldn't hold back vital information about your condition on a mission." Gahiji bounced his head sarcastically to mimic his comment.

Asim saw his reaction and laughed, "Can you feel the love?" He gave him a nudge. "He's only saying that because he cares about you." That made him stop and think, his eyes looked upward, and then he nodded because Asim was right.

Jabari stopped the truck when they reached the crest of another sand dune. "I'm sure that we've lost them. It's completely dark back there." He saw Gahiji's arm. "You're still losing blood. We should do this now."

Asim added, "It is bleeding more. Jabari, give me your hand." Asim took his palm and laid it on his brother's wound. "I'll sing this time."

From the outside of the truck, a jackal was on the prowl in the desert. As it trotted along looking for prey, it turned its head to the right and saw the cab of the truck light up. The positive energy emanated far enough that it reached the jackal and overwhelmed it with joy. The jackal sat down like a loving dog and pawed in the air toward the vehicle. It remained there calm, non-aggressive, and affectionate.

Gahiji pulled up his bloody sleeve. "It's healed." He put his hand on Asim's shoulder. "You were always so good at this as Talibah." He turned to Jabari. "And you too, brother. You've become quite adept at this."

Jabari motioned toward Asim. "I had a good teacher." Then he refocused on the road. "We should be going."

Asim nodded, "I agree."

He was in the act of repositioning himself when he saw something strange outside of the window. He looked across Jabari and pointed his flashlight. "Will you look at that?" Just beyond the driver's side, two jackals were sitting side by side, a cobra was raised with its hood open, and a scorpion sat next to it with open pincers. They were all peacefully facing the truck.

Jabari gawked for a moment. "Now that is a sight."

Gahiji added, "It must have been your healing energy. It calmed the hunters of the night. Now that was worth being shot for."

The other two looked at him and reacted, "What?!"

"OK, it wasn't worth getting shot for," he laughed, "but it seemed like the right thing to say at that moment." All three looked out the window and saw the night creatures disperse in peace.

Jabari said, "Let's get going," and the truck pulled forward. "We have a ways to drive until we reach the other side of the Necropolis."

———

On the deserted road, Karim picked his head up slowly from the steering wheel. His face was covered with blood from the deep cut above his eyebrow. He reached up to touch it. "Owww!" He groaned and struggled to sit upright.

There was enough light reflecting off the Nile from the half moon for him to see his bloodied hand. As Karim regained more consciousness, he turned toward Ramla. Her lifeless body rested against the door, and her cane was broken in two. Dried blood covered her arms, and cuts were etched on her face.

He shook her gently. "Ramla, Ramla, are you alright?" He struggled to get his bearings and remove his seatbelt. "Ramla, wake up." He started to cry. "Ramla, please be alive." Finally, his belt unclipped.

He turned to the back to see if Omar was injured and if he could give any aid. With the dim light, he saw Omar slumped over across the entire seat with his head crunched against the armrest. One arm hung down toward the floor, and his other arm partially covered his bloodied head. When Karim nudged him and called his name, Omar's hand fell from his head and revealed a bullet wound above his temple. Karim yelled, "Noooooo!" A number of birds flew off in terror, screeching from the scream.

———————

On the alien ship, the young officer came to the bridge. "You asked for me?"

The reptilian commander replied, "Hsssss. Yes, report."

"We have good news. The assassin struck a blow to the priest's group. The teacher was taken out, and possibly two more died in the car crash."

"Hsssss. Good. Other news. Report."

"An attack was attempted on the alternate mainframe site, and the ghosting techniques worked extremely well. Our psychic units have hidden the real location of the mainframe with a false image and led the assailants into a trap. When the attackers attempted to blow up the false site, one of our snipers hit two of them. There was a large pool of blood left at the mastaba. No one could have survived that much blood loss."

"Hsssss. Excellent. You are doing well and will receive many rewards. You are promoted to lead human commander for our final operation."

He smiled diabolically, "I won't let you down."

"Hsssss. See to it that you don't." The reptilian gave him a painful jab in the heart with his psychic power as a reminder.

The young officer grimaced from the pain, but did not change his stance. "What is your next order?"

"Hsssss. The mainframe is operating?"

"Yes."

"Hsssss. Time to initiate more nanotechnology in the skies. Send all planes to cover their world with more mind control nanobots. We must be ready for the final phase. See to it."

"I will do as you command. We will start immediately." He walked to the console and punched a few buttons. "I will take charge of this person-ally. Once I've relayed the message to our military outposts, the skies will be completely blanketed with our devilish mist. No one will escape the Order's mainframe or your soul-catcher ship."

"Hsssss. Good. We will feast on their pain. Report when their finances fall so we can initiate the final attack."

"It will be done." With his hand raised over his eye, he declared, "All hail the Order!"

"Hsssss. Hail the Order."

Ricky looked at the cut on my head. "I wish I could do something about that."

"You know, back at our temple you showed us how to do this type of healing. Talibah was a natural at it, too. Bes and I were always in awe of how well she helped the sick in the towns and surrounding farms." I touched my bandage lightly and flinched. "She used to sing something."

"Yeah, I remember something like a tune." He had his eyes closed, and his pointer finger was bobbing in the air while he tried to remember the past. After a dozen finger shakes, he blurted out, "I've got it! They were called healing songs, really close to what you sang to activate the God Scrolls."

"I remember, too." A flash of my past with Talibah brought back an entire song. "One of them went like this..." I took in a breath and began singing. Ricky joined me after a few notes.

While we both sang, he got up and walked over to me. Hara was curious about the melody she heard and came to the doorway. She stood there and watched intently. Then Ricky put both of his hands over my cut. While he sang, a white light filled the room, with the most intense part beam-ing from his hands. The other three were speechless as colored light rays danced in the air.

When the song reached its climax, the light burst gently and left little sparkles fading away throughout the room. Ricky removed his hands, and my cut was gone. The two mending strips were covering perfectly healthy skin.

Hara reacted first. "Whoa! This is the best house *ever!*"

Constance came over and touched my forehead. "It's a miracle."

In Baniti's voice, Ricky instructed, "No, it only seems like a miracle. Those who have studied the arts can do this easily."

Laura expressed, "I want to study those arts."

Ted tried to speak, but his throat was all dry. "I, ca…" After a quick cough, he said, "I want to study those, too."

"Ricky, I think we might *really* want to consider starting those schools again. It seems to me that we have some new recruits who are hungry for knowledge."

"Hungry?!" Laura gushed. "I'm famished for this type of knowledge."

Hara begged, "Can we have some ice cream?!"

I laughed, and then I pulled off the two medical strips. "I guess I won't be needing these anymore."

Constance put her hand on Hara's shoulder. "Not just yet, honey. Maybe in a bit."

Ted pointed to the table. "Guys, you might want to take a look." We all walked over.

Ricky observed, "There're more cards moving from the pile."

"I want to see!" Hara put her face close to the table.

Laura was counting, "There're one, two"—her finger pointed faster—"five, six, seven—seven new cards are moving toward the next spot."

Ricky added, "Seven, mon. That's a lot of potential futures."

Hara was jumping up and down excitedly. "Look! Another piece started moving!" A piece of papyrus came from under the pile and joined the other seven.

"Eight!" Constance exclaimed. "Eight new futures. What's going on, Michael?"

"It seems that the events from today have opened up a bunch of possible timelines."

Ted asked, "But which one? And what did the mainframe do?"

"I hate to use a cliché, but only time will tell." Ted gave me a little grunt of disapproval.

Constance proposed, "You know what we have to do next." She pointed to the cards.

Ricky answered, "We need to look for the picture behind the picture and then decode what it might mean."

Laura and I answered together, "Right."

Hara pulled on my sleeve. "Can I help?"

"Yes, honey, you can help," replied Constance.

"Yippee!"

Karim was leaning over Ramla's body and searching for a pulse. "Come on, Ramla. Please be alive." He held her wrist first, and then he put two flat fingers beneath her chin. There was no blood pumping through her veins that he could feel. "You can't die, Ramla. You are like a mother to me. You can't go." He was still crying.

Using all of his body weight on his door, he finally got out of the car to check on Omar. The door creaked loudly as it swung open. He had already thought the worst, but knew he needed to do all that he could. The back door on the driver's side was completely jammed from the collision, so he had to run around to the other side. When he opened the door, he caught Omar's head as it fell. He didn't move, and his body was completely limp. Karim checked for a heartbeat, but he knew he was dead.

"Omar, I'm so sorry," he sobbed quietly. "I should have done more to help you." When he repositioned Omar's body, he declared, "I will avenge you, my friend. I will avenge you."

Then he looked to the front seat. "Ramla, I must go get help. I will return. Please stay with us." He began running with a hint of a limp.

After a good fifteen minutes, Karim came running back to the car. He was completely winded when he opened the front passenger door. "Ramla..." He put his hand on his chest from the pain. "Ramla, help is on the way. Please be OK." He stopped talking again to catch his breath. "I barely have my powers, so I don't know how to heal you yet. Please be alive."

He rested his hand on her head and sent her all of his good intentions for health and wellness. His palm heated slightly, and then Ramla gasped softly with her eyes fluttering. "Aaaaahhhhh," she sighed with a raspy breath.

"Ramla, you're alive!"

She closed her eyes again and went motionless.

"No, no. What must I do? Think!" He thought back to what he had just done. He put his hand on her head again and wished her health and wellness.

"Ramla, please come back." He put his other hand on top of Ramla's head, too. A little more heat left his palms and entered into her body.

She breathed in harshly, "Aaaaahhhh." With a few blinks, her eyes remained open. Then she struggled to say, "Where…am I?"

"Help is on the way. Just stay with me, Ramla. Just stay with me."

She tried raising her hand toward him, as if she wanted to say something, but could only move it about twelve inches. Karim took both of her hands and held them. "What is it, Ramla? What can I do for you?"

In a soft, pain-filled voice, she whispered, "Tust, Umain…" She labored to fill her lungs again.

"Ramla, I couldn't understand. What did you say? What did you say?"

Her eyes rolled back into her head and her eyelids fluttered. When they came back down, she said in a raspy voice, "Trust…Tumaini."

"Trust Tumaini? I will. But what is it that you are trying to tell me?"

She coughed a little blood, breathed in slowly, and uttered in a decaying whisper, "Trust…Tumaini…" Her grip went soft as her head tilted to the right. Her eyes closed for the last time. Then Karim fell over her body crying.

The sounds of emergency vehicles were approaching. When he looked out of the broken window, he could see flashing lights from two ambulances. As his head lowered, he noticed Ramla's broken cane. He grabbed the top half and clenched it tightly. His white knuckles contrasted the dried blood on his hands. "My work is not done. I will finish this." He laid her down gently in the seat and met the paramedics.

I left the table where the others were all standing, and I sat down in one of the chairs. Constance asked, "What's wrong, hon?"

I had tears welling from inside. "I felt…I felt a dear friend. There was pain, then some more pain"—I wiped away a tear—"and then the pain instantly stopped." I looked back at Constance. "I think Ramla just died."

She reacted with a shocked tone, "No!" and the other three turned.

I searched inside and called out to her, but there was nothing but emptiness. I put my head in my hands and cried. Constance came over to give me some comfort, and nobody else spoke. Out of the corner of Ted's eye, he saw one of the cards move a little closer to the number eleven spot.

In the truck, Jabari had passed a number of smaller farm roads on his way toward the main highway near the Necropolis. He knew exactly where he wanted to go. He turned to his brother. "When we reach town, we're going to report at Hanif's shop." He also asked Asim, who was looking behind the truck, "Is anyone there?"

He replied, "Nothing. I haven't seen any lights coming from the desert. Only lights on the farm roads, and none of them were the two cars that followed us."

"Good. They won't be able to find us once we've entered the populated highways."

Gahiji suggested, "We should call Michael and tell him about the mission failure." His brother nodded in agreement. Then he continued, "But you know, it wasn't a complete failure. Now we know they are hiding the mainframe somewhere else. All we have to do is locate it. It also tells us how important it is to the Order."

Asim added, "That's the spirit. Good way to look at being shot at." They all laughed. "Seriously, though, you're right. This wasn't a complete failure. And next time, we'll be more prepared."

Jabari included, "Consider this our test run with the Order."

An hour later, they reached Hanif's shop. The front was locked, so they used the Protector's entrance through the basement. Gahiji whispered, "They must still be asleep. Let's not wake them." He smiled to his brother, "I'll take the couch," and he sprawled out before his brother could finish sitting down.

"Fine, brother." He straightened back up and went to the chair. Asim took the chair's twin and they all grabbed a little shut-eye.

"Michael, is there anything I can do to help?" Laura rubbed my shoulder.

It was almost ten o'clock, and I could see that the others were extremely tired. "No, you've all been a great help so far. Why don't we call it a night?"

Ted and Ricky looked over from the table. Ricky growled, "Rrrrr! We're so close to getting these last two cards."

Ted added, "Yeah, these were much harder to see than the last ones. We must have spent a good ten minutes on each piece. I still can't make out the ones that Laura and Ricky saw."

Constance tiptoed back in. "Hara's finally sleeping again. She keeps waking up because of the jets overhead. I swear that we've never heard that much air traffic before."

I glanced toward the ceiling because of the loud engine roar from another jet. "Now that you mention it, I've never heard that many planes before, either. Do you think the airlines diverted air traffic?"

Laura shook her head, "I don't think so. It's something else."

I pointed to my chest. "It wasn't from me meditating." That made Constance laugh.

I looked to Laura again. "Are you getting anything?"

"Just agitated feelings, nothing in particular." She walked back to the table. "These cards were rough. I'm usually pretty good at this type of puzzle, but I swear that I'm being blocked somehow."

I asked Ricky, "I shielded the house. Did you also shield it?"

"Ya, mon." He checked our energetic bodies. "I'm not picking anything up on any of you, unless it's some type of new Order technology that isn't visible to my inner sight."

"I wouldn't put it past them." I moved to the table. "But let's focus on what we do know. What did you guys come up with?"

Ted pulled out his paper. "We found a number twenty-two, something that resembles a large wave of water, three UFOs above a planet, a balanced scale..." He made a funny face. "And this is weird...we found another card with an exploding planet and another card with burning buildings, just like these two over here."

"Do you mean like the ones that were headed for the number nine spot?" He nodded *yes*. "That is odd. Maybe it's a stronger timeline than the others, and that's why they repeated for this location, too."

"Could be." He shrugged.

I stared at the last two cards for a moment. "Guys, I'm not in the frame of mind to work on this. Do you mind if I close my eyes for a bit?" They all gave their blessings.

Laura asked, "What about the last two cards?"

"You're more than welcome to stay and work if you'd like."

Constance added, "Uh huh. You can stay as long as you'd like. We both appreciate the help."

"What she said." I pointed to my wife. "I'm going to look in on Hara and then lie down on the bed. Don't be afraid to wake me if you find some Earth-saving information."

Ted replied, "We won't." Within an hour, Ricky, Laura, Ted, and Constance were also asleep in various chairs and positions.

<hr />

It was just past sunrise in Cairo when Karim showed up at Hanif's shop. The paramedics had treated him at the wreckage site and cleaned up his wounds, however, blood from Ramla and Omar still stained his clothes. The shop was closed, so he took the same entrance as the two brothers and Asim.

He staggered into the room and saw Gahiji asleep on the couch. The two chairs were also occupied, so he walked to the wall and sat down. He was still clenching the staff that Ramla used to carry, and he dejectedly put his head down and tried to rest.

Rehema and Hanif both heard the door close downstairs. Anxious to learn of any good news about the mission, they made their way to the first floor. When they saw three of the four bodies with blood on them, they panicked.

"Oh my word!" burst Rehema. She ran over to the sleeping trio.

"I'll call an ambulance," stated Hanif.

Karim got up off of the floor and sadly declined, "I don't need any help." That stopped Hanif abruptly from going to the next room.

At the same time, the brothers and Asim had also opened their eyes and sat up. Rehema was kneeling between Gahiji and Asim like a concerned mother. "There's blood all over your clothes. What can I do? Who's hurt?" She became very hands-on and touched each of them like a trained nurse.

Jabari replied first, "We are all fine. All of our wounds are healed, thanks to Asim, and Ramla's training."

Gahiji agreed, "We don't need an ambulance, Hanif. Come, come." He waved with his hand. "Honest, we are alright."

"Are you sure?"

"Yes." He was a little stiff from sleeping on the couch, so he stretched out his shoulders. "Talibah made a great return and helped heal me...and himself," he chuckled as he put his hand on Asim. His brother coughed at being excluded, so Gahiji motioned toward him. "With Jabari's help, of course." He nodded once for finally being included in the healing.

Asim humbly said, "It was nothing. All I did was help where I could."

Jabari reacted to Karim's clothes and walked toward him. "What happened to you? Where did all of that blood come from?"

Hanif pointed toward Asim. "He wasn't with you?"

"No, it was just the three of us."

The remaining four hurried over to Karim. Gahiji urged, "What's wrong, Karim?" Then he noticed Ramla's broken cane. "Where's Ramla?"

"Dead!" he lashed out. "And so is Omar!" Rehema put her hand to her mouth and gasped. He was shaking her cane as he spoke. "That blasted assassin killed our beloved Ramla, and he shot Omar. He killed both of them." His face turned completely red from anger. "He will die. I assure you."

All of them were in shock from Karim's news, and they offered as much comfort and aid to him as they could. Over the next thirty minutes, the four men shared their accounts of the night's terrible news.

———

Ring, ring…ring, ring…ring, ring…
Ring, ring…ring, ring…ring, ring…

"I'll get it," I said groggily. I noticed the clock. "It's the middle of the night. Who's calling?" I fumbled for the phone and slammed my hand down on the receiver to pick it up. Constance came in the room as I answered. "Hello?" The other three adults also staggered from the study as I fumbled for the light switch.

"Michael, this is Hanif."

With a scratchy voice, I replied, "Hanif, good to hear from you. What's up?"

"Michael, I have sad news for you." I knew what was coming next, and I didn't say anything right away. After a few seconds of silence, he asked, "Michael, are you still there?"

My head was hanging low in despair. "Yes, Hanif, I am. Give me a second. I'm going to put this on speakerphone." I called the others into the room. "We're on speaker. What's the problem?"

"I don't know how to put this gently, so I will just tell you." He sighed,

"Ramla and Omar have been killed by the assassin." The room instantly was filled with sadness. "And the mainframe still exists. Gahiji, Jabari, and Asim are OK right now, but two of them were shot. Asim lost a lot of blood, and Gahiji is mending well."

With a tear in my eye, I sniffled, "And how are you and Rehema faring?"

"We are overwhelmed by the loss."

Rehema was also on speakerphone. "Michael, we are so sorry."

"Thank you, Rehema." After a moment of silence, I inquired, "Is anyone else hurt?"

Hanif answered, "Karim was driving, and he barely got out alive. The same assassin who attacked you while you were here shot at them multiple times and hit Omar. The car overturned, and the impact killed Ramla."

"Where is Karim?"

"I am here, my brother."

"Karim, I'm so sorry. I know how much Ramla meant to you. Is there anything that I can do to help?"

He was slapping the cane into his other hand. "Not at this time, Tumaini. But Ramla did tell me something in her last dying words."

"What did she say?"

He hit his hand harder. "She said to trust you." He hit again. "Tell me that you have a plan to take down this hideous Order."

"She said to *trust* me?"

"Yes, and she made it a point. I know it was part of my learning in this lifetime. She was trying to teach me this. But, there is more." He hit his hand really hard this time. Rehema was also feeling his pain and winced. "Tell me that you have a plan."

"I am working on something as we speak, Karim, but it's not finished."

"Good!" He hit his hand a final time. "I look forward to exacting your plan. Do let me know when you have instructions for me."

"I'll do that, Karim. And please let me know what I can do in the meantime." He didn't reply, and I knew that he was extremely irate.

From the other end, I heard another voice. "Michael—Tumaini—this is Asim. It is good to hear from you, my friend, even in our time of loss."

"Asim! It's wonderful to hear you. Are you and the others alright?"

"We're fine. Jabari is turning out to be quite the healer." He smiled from the compliment. "But I'm afraid that we have other bad news to share."

I looked concernedly toward the others in the room. "What is it?"

"The mainframe was not where the seers said it would be. The intel led us to a trap in Abusir. When we went beneath the pyramids, there was nothing there but empty tunnels and caves. Then we were attacked by a sniper and chased."

Ted suggested, "The Order must have ghosted the main site."

Asim was confused by the new voice. "Ghosted? I've heard that term before from our seers. Who said that?"

I replied, "Oh, sorry. That's Ted." I smiled to him. "He's been our resident guru on the Order's hidden technology and strategies. He's been an invaluable help."

"Hello, Ted, this is Asim. It is an honor to be in your service."

He responded with some surprise and reservation, "Hello...?"

"What can you tell us about this ghosting?"

Ted explained, "The Order's psychic unit...well, the militaries around the world—they work for the Order—they have the ability to hide specific targets by making your seers think they are seeing one target, but they are really remote viewing the wrong one."

"They can do this?!" He called to Gahiji and Jabari, "Come closer. You need to hear what Ted has to say. Please continue, Ted."

I patted him on the shoulder. "See, you are our resident guru. Thanks, buddy."

Ted greeted the other two and continued, "Let's say that you are looking for the Cairo Museum. If the Order wanted to hide the museum from your seers, they would use their psychic abilities to put the image of, say, the Sphinx over it. So when the seers look for the museum, they would get an image of the Sphinx instead." He paused for a moment. "It wasn't bad intel; it was the Order using a tactical advantage. All you have to do is tell your seers how to look beyond any psychic ghosting techniques."

Gahiji inquired, "How do we do that?"

"I'll tell you." Ted spent the next five minutes describing how to overcome this energetic shielding used by the military and the Order.

Jabari complimented him, "Thank you, my friend. This is extremely valuable information, and we will pass this on to our seers. We won't be fooled again."

I said to him while shaking his shoulders, "You're the man, Ted."

"Stop that," he grumbled. I smiled because I knew it made him uncomfortable.

Gahiji asked, "What's our next move, Tumaini? What should we do?"

"I have a plan started, but I don't want to divulge it until I can tell all of the priests. What I want you to do is to find that mainframe for us."

"We've heard about your other phone calls," Jabari mentioned, "the ones describing some type of alien craft."

"Yes, and the plan will deal with both of them. If I'm right, the Order has stepped up its plans and has activated the mainframe."

"What does it do?"

"I'm not sure yet, and the magic cross hasn't revealed anything else. But I do know that they are using students and other people as assassins with their voice to skull technology and brainwashing implants."

"What?!"

Rehema interrupted, "Student assassins and voice to skull?"

Constance chimed in, "Hello, Rehema. Yes, Michael was shot at in his class by one of his students. The boy was being controlled by the Illuminati part of the Order. His handler sent commands directly to his brain."

"My word. They are hideous."

"Yes, they are," she agreed. "Luckily, he was not hurt by them, only the police." She made a sound of disappointment over the phone.

"Rehema," I asked, "have the other six priests shown up yet?"

"Not yet, Michael. But we are expecting them."

"Let me know what I can do to help.

"Hanif?"

"Yes, Michael?"

"Will you take care of Karim and the others?"

"It will be my honor to serve."

"And it has always been my honor to know all of you." I sniffed from the loss of my friends.

Gahiji commented, "I can feel your grief, Tumaini. We all miss Ramla and Omar, but more will fall if we don't continue to focus."

Jabari added, "My little brother said it wisely. We must keep ourselves on task. We should keep in touch daily until your return."

That took Constance by surprise, and she whispered to me, "Return? What's he talking about?"

I whispered back, "I'll tell you later." Ricky looked toward me and nodded. He already knew.

"Gahiji, Jabari, and Asim, will you please care for our friends, too? And please help Karim in his loss."

Asim replied, "We will, my brother from across the seas. We will."

Before they hung up, I could hear the roar of planes on the other end of the phone, and then I heard a jet fly close to our house. "That's odd," I thought. "Hey, are you guys getting a lot of air traffic over there?"

Hanif looked up for a moment. "Now that you mention it, I have noticed quite a lot of planes in the sky."

Laura, who had been quiet the entire time, broke her silence, "Michael, I think that's part of the plan."

"Hey guys"—I winked back at Laura—"one of our new friends, Laura, said she thinks that the planes might be part of the Order's plans. Please tell the other priests to continue to shield themselves and everyone else that they can."

Gahiji commented, "I remember all about shielding from when I was Bes. We've made a daily practice of it. Why?"

"Just a feeling that I've had. Please keep doing it, OK?"

"We will, Tumaini. We will."

"Thanks. If something new comes up today, I'll call. And please do the same thing. We should keep in touch a lot over the next few days."

Jabari fell back into character. "That's affirmative."

"Great, guys, thanks for calling me. You are in my thoughts."

Hanif replied, "And you are in ours, Tumaini." Then we both hung up.

We all walked to the study, and one of the two cards that hadn't been identified yet was closer to the magic cross spread. I noticed it and pointed it out to the others. "Do you see that? Another card has moved."

CHAPTER THIRTY-SEVEN

CHEMTRAILS, CHEMTRAILS, CHEMTRAILS

We were all gathered around the table. Ricky asked, "Which card moved?"

I replied, "It's this one, right here."

Ted remarked, "That's one of the two pieces we haven't been able to identify yet."

"Figures. We sure could use a break right now."

Ricky picked up the tweezers. "Do you mind if I give this another go? I bet I can figure it out."

"Not at all." I moved out of the way so he could pick it up. "I'm going to look at the other one that wasn't identified."

For the next few hours, we took turns looking at parchment pieces. While Ricky and I tried to solve it, Ted, Constance, and Laura practiced the techniques that we had shown them earlier. Unfortunately, no one was able to crack any more of the magic cross spread, but Laura's lightning bolt was gaining more power.

After I held up the tweezers for the next person to try again, Ted commented, "Michael, I'd love to stay, but I need to get home and change for class. We've been here all night."

I sighed a little because I couldn't go in to teach today. He heard me and empathized, "Sorry, I know you want to be back at school. If I have time, I'll check in with your TA."

"Thanks."

"I've got to get to my store today, too, Michael. Can you handle this without me?" asked Laura.

"Of course. You guys have been an incredible help so far. I can't ask any more of you."

"Oh, we're not done helping yet."

Ted echoed, "Same here."

Laura put her hand on my arm. "I can be back later today, if you'd like."

Constance chirped, "That would be wonderful. Your energy really helps to brighten the place." That made her smile.

"You guys are always welcome here." I motioned with my head to take them downstairs. "Come on, we'll see you to the door."

Light was just starting to break over the horizon. When we all walked onto the porch, we looked up into the skies.

I stated, "I've never seen that many chemtrails before in my life. There must be forty or fifty of them. It looks like they are playing an all-world tic-tac-toe tournament."

"And look, there're"—Ricky pointed in the sky to count—"seven more planes. They are lacing this place."

"This isn't good," worried Laura.

One of my neighbors was getting his paper. Ricky saw his energy body. He had hundreds of tiny dark speckles all over his skin. He nudged me. "Tumaini, take a look."

"What?"

"Use your sight. Take a look at him."

When I saw my neighbor, he was looking right back at me. I waved to try and cover up the troubling vision I'd just seen. "Guys, Ricky's right. He's got nanobots all over his body. I bet they are coming from those." I pointed to the sky. "It's up there. They're in the chemtrails. I can see them falling, and I don't like it."

Ted cursed, "It's in the chemtrails! It's in the chemtrails!"

"Don't worry," comforted Ricky. "We can clear you two if something gets on you. For now, you should be OK with our shielding." Both of them gave their thanks.

Ted started to walk away, and then he turned around. "I'm not gifted like Laura is, but I have a bad feeling about this."

"I know what you mean," I replied. "We'll do all we can to help." He looked up at the sky one more time, brushed his shoulders and arms, and then walked to his car.

I asked Ricky, "Do you need to go? You're more than welcome to stay if you'd like."

"No, mon. This is where I need to be. Right here with you guys."

Constance smiled from his dedication, "You are a special man, no matter what time period you are from."

"Thanks, Constance."

"I'm going to make some breakfast while you two work in the study. Will you get Hara up?"

"I can do that."

Hara was just coming out of her bedroom when she saw us. "Morning, pumpkin," I sang.

"Morning, Hara," greeted Ricky.

She was a little embarrassed because Ricky saw her in her pajamas. She covered her face and ducked into the bathroom.

"It's not you, Ricky, honest."

"I'm not taking it personally. I'd be a little jumpy, too, if I had on bunny slippers," he laughed, and I laughed from his quick wit.

When we walked into the study, he reminded me, "You know that we have to go back to Egypt. You haven't told Constance yet, have you?"

"No, but I will. I'm still working on the plan for the priests. Eventually, we will have to go back and meet with them. It's just happening so fast, and I haven't had much time to finalize anything."

"Ya, mon. It is picking up."

"Did you get any sleep last night?"

"I got a few winks after you went to bed, but not much, though."

"If you need to crash, there's always the couch, or you could use the spare bedroom."

"I might do that after breakfast. When I can't keep my eyes open anymore, I'll take you up on that."

"Sounds good. How about one more try on these cards?" He nodded, and we went to work.

———————

After breakfast, Constance told Hara to start on her next assignment and that she would be right up.

"Honey, I'll clean up so you can spend some extra time with Hara."

"OK," she smiled.

"And I need to mention Egypt again. I know you were surprised about me going back so soon, but—"

"Relax, savior boy. I figured out after the call last night that you would have to meet with the other priests. It just took me by surprise is all. I never even thought about you going back so soon, but it makes sense, with everything hitting the fan like it is."

Ricky professed, "You are one lucky guy."

"Yeah, he is," she snickered.

"I know I am." I pulled her in for a hug from behind. "Rehema even said it the other day—she is a gift from the gods."

Hara came back in the kitchen. "Mommy, why are all the planes flying overhead?"

"Sweety?"

"I looked out the window and saw all kinds of white lines in the sky." She walked to the back door to see out the window. "Look, there's a red one."

"A red one?" I asked.

"Hurry, Daddy. You'll miss it."

We all rushed out to the backyard. When we looked up in the sky, there was a red jet leaving another chemtrail. While it was flying, it was actually clearing a path ahead of it through all of the clouds and mist.

Constance declared, "Would you look at that? I've never seen a jet do that before."

Ricky added, "Me, neither."

"Is it a UFO again?" Hara asked. "I liked seeing the UFOs."

I put my hands on her shoulders. "I don't think so, baby. That's a jet, but it's doing something strange. And I have no idea why it's clearing a path."

Ricky used his inner sight again. "Look, Tumaini. It's leaving some kind of different spray."

I changed my view and saw it. "It's not the same black, speckled spray. That's a…that's a new type of spray." I nudged Ricky and told him to look again. "See. It's making the black specks bind together somehow. If those are nanobots, they are being connected by this new spray. It's like it's creating pathways for the nanobots to work in tandem when they are on a person's body."

Hara pointed to the west. "Look, Daddy, there's another red jet. It's doing the same thing. It's parting the clouds before it goes through."

Ricky suggested, "It's not creating a path for them to work together, I think it's parting the seas so the plane won't destroy the nanobots before they can connect and attack someone."

I touched his shoulder and pointed to Hara. I didn't want him to scare her. She reacted, "Attack someone?"

"Too late," I blurted in a concerned-but-joking manner.

"Sorry, mon."

Constance grabbed Hara's hand. "Come on inside, baby doll. Let's get your assignment started."

"I'll be in to help in a moment."

When Hara was walking away, she stopped and spun around. "Who are they attacking, Daddy?"

"Don't worry, pumpkin. We'll protect you. Daddy will protect you."

Constance reassured her, "We're going to help anyone who needs help. Let's get your problems solved."

"OK," she replied with a hint of worry.

"Sorry about that, Tumaini. I wasn't thinking."

"It's not your fault, it's the Order. Without them, there would be no chemtrails, and no threat." I put my hand on his shoulder. "Let's go inside. I'm going to help Hara and let Constance sleep."

"I think I'll grab a few winks myself."

———————

Hara finished her assignment, and I gave her a recess to go play. Just as I was hanging up the phone from giving Hanif and Rehema the morning's update, the receiver rang in my hand. It startled me, and it woke up both Ricky and Constance.

"Hello?"

"Hi, Michael."

"Hi, there. What's up?"

Constance whispered, "Who is it?"

I whispered back with my hand over the phone, "It's Tammy's mom."

"Hold on. I'll put you on speaker." I hit the button as Ricky walked to our bedroom door. "You sound panicked. What's wrong?"

"Do you guys need anything from the store? The place is going berserk over here."

"Why? What's going on?" asked Constance.

"Haven't you two been watching the news? The stock market nearly crashed today, and that sent everyone into a panic. People are coming to the stores like there won't be any tomorrow. They are saying things like *Black Tuesday from 1929* is happening all over again."

"I haven't heard a thing. Let me turn on the TV." I reached for the remote and hit the button. Then I put on the news channel.

"Constance, what do you need the most?"

She stammered, "Uh…I guess milk and eggs."

"They're out of those, and all of the bottled water is gone, too. The canned goods aisle is like a battle zone. I'll grab what's available and drop some off, OK?"

"That'd be great. Thanks for the heads up."

"I've got to go. They just made an announcement that a new delivery truck arrived." Before she disconnected, we heard her cart being rammed by another person in the store, and she yelled back, "Hey! Watch it, will ya'?!" Then the line went silent.

I jested, "That didn't sound good."

Ricky pointed to the TV, "The newscaster…she's outside interviewing people. And look in the background, there're tons of chemtrails behind her."

Constance asked, "Where's she reporting from?"

"The station logo says Boston."

"Let me turn to another channel." I flicked my thumb a few times until there was another news channel. "There. That guy's reporting outside, too. The skies are blanketed with chemtrails."

Constance was worried. "It's happening, Michael. The Order must have started their plan."

"I think she's right. I've never seen that many planes in the sky before."

I flipped to an international British channel. "It's happening everywhere.

It must be going on all over the world."

Constance suggested, "Try the Japanese news."

"Can't, I'm in the 70's...gotta go around the horn."

She laughed and took the remote from me, "Give me that." When she pushed in the right numbers, the same scene showed on the screen. "You're right. It is going on all over."

She put her head out the door. "Hara! We need to go to the store. Get your shoes on."

A reply came from downstairs, "OK!"

"Ricky," I requested, "why don't you come with us? Extra hands would be a huge help."

"I'm here to serve. I guess I'm camping out here for a while, too."

"We can stop and get you some extra clothes, since you're not heading back home."

"That'd be good. Stopping at the laundromat is getting old."

<hr>

After a couple of hours, a number of stops for food and clothes, and calls to Ted and Laura to see if they needed anything, we finally made it back home. Tammy's mother had already left the extra groceries for us on our back porch.

Constance started gathering bags. "I'm going to give her a call and thank her."

"Thank her for me, too."

"I will."

Ricky picked up half of her bags. "Here, Constance, let me get those for you." He walked behind her and Hara.

While I finished unloading the rest, Ted pulled up behind our car. "Hi, Ted. Good to see you so soon." I stopped for a moment to wonder. "Why are you here so soon?"

"They cancelled all classes for the rest of the day because of the craziness. Turns out that I showed up for nothing."

"Sorry to hear that."

"I'm not. This is much more important at the moment."

"We picked up some extra food for you and Laura. Your stuff is in the back."

"Thanks. I hate going to the store when people are in a panic."

"I know what you mean. I almost got my arm chewed off when I picked up a case of organic fruit that someone else wanted."

After he grabbed some bags, I asked, "Hey, do you think this stock market thing is the Order's M.O.?"

"Their modus operandi? Is the pope Catholic?" he quipped.

"I know it was a silly question, but I wanted your input."

"This is as fishy as the cat's tuna. Of course this is their M.O. They did this in '29, the early 70's, in 2008, and now they are doing it again."

"And if memory serves me right, they'll clean up when they buy all of the foreclosed businesses, land, and homes."

"That's the setup. These are greedy bastards at the helm."

"Let's get this inside. By the way, I need to tell you about the red jet."

"Red jet? That's a new one."

"We saw it do this…" I told him all of the details as we walked the rest of the groceries inside.

As the cupboards were being stocked, I had the urge to go look at the table in the study. When I got there, the two unknown cards were even closer to the number eleven slot.

Ricky came in and looked with me. "I think those two are pulling away from the pack. We might have a winner."

"Yeah, but what are they?" I gazed beyond the geometric figures on the papyrus. "I'm starting to get something."

"Really, what is it?"

"It has my name on it, and two funny lines."

"Michael?"

"No, it's Tumaini. Here, take a look."

"I see it now. There's a main line, and another line branching off of it. Whoa! It doesn't just say *Tumaini*, it says *Tumaini Timeline*."

"You're pulling my leg."

"See for yourself." He moved aside so I could look again.

"Wow, you're right. It does say that." I took the paper that listed the other six cards. "And the lines do this." I drew them under the words I'd just written. "If this is a set timeline, then maybe this is a possible offshoot. Maybe

586

it's a timeline that I can influence. See how it branches off of the main line? And it does say *Tumaini Timeline*."

"It's possible. But from what we've remembered, it would take a lot of energy to make that much of a change."

"Maybe there's more to it. Maybe it's a way to beat the Order."

"Or maybe it's just another timeline that only works for you, but not for the rest of the world."

"Hmm. I hadn't thought of it that way. Good call, old friend."

"There're still too many possible meanings for one card." He pointed to its running mate. "Did you make out that one?"

"I just started to look. Can you see anything?"

"Give me a moment." We both stared, but the parchment didn't reveal its secret yet.

"It'll come. It just needs more events to make it visible."

"Let's hope it's not a bunch of bad events."

We heard the doorbell downstairs. Then we heard Constance greeting Laura. We both went to the stairs to say *hi*. When she saw us, she blurted, "It's crazy out there. People are driving like madmen. I saw two accidents on the way over here."

Constance closed the door. "Well, I'm glad that you made it here safely. We picked you up a bunch of groceries and supplies. We have them back here." She walked her into the kitchen.

I yelled downstairs, "When you two are done, we need to show you something."

Ted reacted, "I don't need to wait; you can show me now." He took three stairs at a time to reach us.

On the reptilian spaceship, the young officer reported to the reptilian commander, "The sell-offs have started. By tomorrow, we should see more economic collapse. We expect the entire banking system to fall by the third day."

"Hsssss. Yes, we have begun to feed on their fear and misery."

"Should I have our planes continue to deliver the nanobots?"

"Hsssss. Continue with the mist. All humans must be covered before we can use the final program. Cover the globe you should."

"I'll contact our ranking officers and give them the orders to continue. Is there anything else?"

"Hsssss. The Queen of Reptilious is coming to initiate the final mainframe program and to start the enhanced soul-catcher device."

"I didn't know there was a queen."

"Hsssss. Queen is royalty and does not appear unless it is a monumental occasion. The complete enslavement of the humans will make it happy. Feast well, the queen will."

"Then we will double our efforts to ensure our success."

"Hsssss. The queen will reward your loyalty." It pointed its sharp nail at him. "Do not wait. Execute your orders now."

"As you command. All hail the Order."

"Hsssss. Hail the Order."

Constance and Laura followed right behind Ted and joined Ricky and me in the study. When they saw the *Tumaini Timeline* card, each of them came up with a completely different interpretation of its meaning. I smirked, "Well, so much for any consensus. That piece can do a lot, or it will do nothing."

Laura slightly tilted her head and raised an eyebrow at me. "You know something about this card, but you don't remember it yet. I can feel it."

"Whatever you feel," I chuckled, "can you feel the answer, please?"

Ricky nodded, "I agree with her. There's something to this card, and I think it involves me, too."

"All of this means nothing, though, if it doesn't go here," Constance emphasized while she pointed to the cross. "It's just as close as this one." She gestured to the card next to it.

Ted added, "And we can't rule out the other six cards, either. They could easily leapfrog these two and still make the open spot based upon our actions."

"He's right," I agreed. "There's still too much that can influence the future."

"So what do we do now?" Laura yawned really big and stretched.

"I think…" Her yawn reminded me that I hadn't gotten much sleep last night, either, and I yawned next. "I think we should make it a point to get some rest tonight. We all put in a long day yesterday." All of them nodded.

"I'm sure that we have things to do besides look at these cards."

Laura asked Ricky if he could help her increase her energy, and Constance mentioned that she needed to start Hara's next lesson.

I got Ted's attention. "Do you want to go to the station with me? I'd like to check in on Bruce and Phillip and see if I can do anything to help."

"I'm not doing anything else today, and you could use a witness if you are visiting the police. They can't be trusted."

"I'm with you there."

I glanced at Constance. She indicated, "It's OK. I'll be fine here. Do you all want to come over for dinner? We have plenty of food now."

Ricky nodded *yes*, while Laura answered, "I'd love to come back over. Maybe we could meditate again tonight."

"Ted?"

"I'm not one to turn down free food. Are any of those cookies still around?"

"No, but Hara and I can make some more while you are gone. I'll work that into her math assignment. We'll use the measurements to teach her fractions."

"Smart girl."

"Great!" I exclaimed. "Let's meet for a casual dinner and a short meditation. Then we'll call it a day so we can all sleep."

"Sounds good," replied Ricky. "Come on, Laura. We can practice at your shop."

———

At the police station, Ted and I met a lot of resistance trying to see the boys. No one would even let us talk to them. When we were about to leave, Officer Dunse came up to me with a yellow envelope and spoke in a non-friendly voice, "Mr. Whyse, I have some important evidence regarding you and the shooting. I need you to come with me."

Ted looked at me, then at Officer Dunse and mocked, "Important evidence?"

"I will explain this back at my desk. It would be good for you to comply, or do I need to get more officers to escort you there?"

I saw his aura. It was black, red, and yellow. I gave Ted a look to trust me. "His energy is not of this world. We have a few minutes." Ted immediately figured out what I was trying to say. He nodded, but wasn't happy about sticking around any longer than he had to.

At his desk, he had another officer from the Order join him. He stared at me, dumped out the envelope, and accused smugly, "It turns out that we found these drugs in your classroom at school. Do you have anything you would like to say? Are you a user or a pusher?"

Ted was extremely offended and started to stand. He was motioning for me to leave. "Don't answer anything without representation."

I put my hand on his arm and instinctively calmed him with my energy. "Ted, it's OK, honest."

At that moment, I felt as if I was being given the right words to say by some loving part of myself that would alleviate the tense situation. I addressed Officer Dunse, "First off, that classroom is used by more than ten different teachers throughout the week, so it's not only my desk." Ted instantly smiled with confidence and turned to me to see what I would say next. "Second, the room isn't locked throughout the day because of all of the student traffic. It's also used for student meetings and study groups in the evening, so it could easily have come from hundreds of different people." Both officers' faces began to scowl. "And third, do you have any proof that I had anything to do with that bag? Are there any prints on it besides your own? What do you have that links that bag to me?" Officer Dunce put his head down and slapped it with his hand because he knew that he'd just screwed up royally.

Ted cheered, "Way to go, Tumaini."

"Do you have an answer for me Officer Dunse, or do I need to report this as an attempt to plant evidence?"

The other officer whispered in his ear, but we both heard him say, "You'd better drop this. There's nothing to link him."

His aura spiked red. "I'm not done with you."

"If you have any evidence that points that bag to me, you'd better show it to me right now. If not, we are through here. And I already know that you are not an honest cop; I can see it. So anything that you say from this point is not to be honored as truth." His face was completely red.

I looked at the officer sitting at the next desk and touched his arm. A warm energy flowed from me to him. "Would you please be a witness to this? The officer here just tried to pin this bag on me, but he has no proof. Since he can't be trusted, and he might tamper with evidence just to win, would you ask him for the proof right now, too?"

Surprisingly, the other officer asked, "Well, Dunse?"

He fired back, "Fine. You are free to go, but don't consider this a closed case."

I turned to the officer who had helped. "Thanks for asking." He nodded and went back to his work, not knowing why he'd been so cooperative with me. We also took down his name to keep for our records.

While we were walking away, Ted asked, "How did you know?"

"I saw his aura, and I saw that he was tagged—along with the other cop. It just seemed too predictable. The Order isn't as smart as they make themselves out to be."

"I can see why the governments don't want people developing their psychic skills. We would all know who is lying and who is tagged."

"Too right, Ted. Too right. Let's get out of here as fast as we can, though. It's not safe in this place."

"I agree."

———•◆•———

During dinner, we decided to turn on the news. The reporter had just stated that the stock market had been forced to close early today but would reopen tomorrow to try and salvage a complete market meltdown.

Ted gruffed, "This is all being manipulated." Laura nodded in agreement.

Ricky motioned with his hands. "I wasn't aware of a lot of this stuff two weeks ago, but even I can see that there is foul play going on."

"This is the Order, I know it is"—I shook my finger to emphasize—"but I don't know how the mainframe fits into all of this. People are panicked, but they aren't walking around like zombies."

Ted laughed, "So mindless, brainwashed sheeple that believe their government cares about them are OK, and zombies aren't?"

I snickered back, "That's a good point."

Constance motioned to the TV. "Do you think it's just the heads of the money industry that are being manipulated to do this?"

"It could be." I thought for a moment. "Actually, that would make a lot of sense. If the brokers and corporate CEOs were controlled, then those above them—the Anunnaki bloodlines—they would make even more money. Greed squashes everyone below the top of the pyramid." I congratulated

Constance. "That was really smart, hon. Way to go."

She smiled, "Do you think that's what the mainframe did?"

"It's quite possible, and it's the most logical connection so far."

Ricky brought up something, "Speaking of pyramids, have you called Egypt since this morning?"

"No, and it's after midnight there. I'll call them first thing tomorrow."

"I wonder how the other priests are doing without Ramla."

"I'm sure they are fine. Plenty of people have remembered how to do things. Just look at all you and I have remembered on our own. I bet we'll be surprised when we get there."

"I keep forgetting that stuff. This going back and forth between the old me and the Baniti me is still a trip."

"I know what you mean. I had that spontaneously happen at the police station."

Constance's head jerked. "The police?"

"Yes…" I told the others about the drugs being planted and the officers who were tagged. I also shared how part of Tumaini came in and calmed down the situation.

Laura cautioned, "They're gunning for you. Just be careful."

"I will."

We watched TV for a few more minutes while we finished eating. I remembered my dear friends who were no longer with us.

Ricky asked, "What's wrong? I can see your energy change."

"I was just thinking about Ramla and Omar. They helped me so much. I only knew them for a short time, but I miss them."

Constance put her hand on my leg for comfort. "And now you will pick up where she left off. You and Ricky can start teaching the real arts."

"Ya, mon. I've been thinking about the schools again. The priesthood could start up, with your help."

I was nodding, "I know that's what needs to happen, but—"

Ted added, "We need to focus on the mainframe and soul-catcher."

"Right." I pointed to him. "That has to come first, or I'm afraid we'll be fighting a losing battle."

"You're right, Michael," affirmed Ricky. "That's why you are the leader right now and not me."

For the remainder of the night, we all did a short meditation, worked on increasing our energy flow, and parted ways so we could get a lot of rest.

We agreed to start early the next day.

———◆———

At eight o'clock, they all showed up at the door. The news reports in the morning were horrifying. Massive selloffs had occurred overseas, and all of the European and offshore banks had been cleared out by the largest money holders in the world. As a result, the banks in the western countries closed before 10:00 a.m., and an announcement was made that all credit card balances, loans, and mortgages were to be repaid immediately or they would be in default. This created immense panic worldwide.

Throughout the day, we continued seeing reports of large-scale riots breaking out, and thousands of innocents souls were killed as a result. Each news report added more to the death toll.

The entire financial structure had crumbled by 5:00 p.m. Most of the countries had suspended all ground and air transportation. Reports were also coming in that certain nations were closing their borders. The world was going into complete lockdown.

"Guys, I need to have some time alone with Ricky upstairs. I think you should stay here for the night. It's not safe out there."

Ted expressed, "Thanks for the offer, and I don't mind a bit." He gave a soft chuckle, "I don't relish being shot at just so I can sleep in my own bed. The couch looks just fine."

Laura also thanked us. "I'm grateful just to be here with friends. I wouldn't want to be anywhere else."

Another news report flashed a gruesome scene. People were shooting and stabbing each other to get food supplies from a truck. I was intensely irate because of the senseless killing and tremendous loss of life. "This is terrible! I can't stand it anymore." The scene on the TV turned even more violent. The reporter announced that they had just killed the driver, and the crowds were rocking the truck trying to turn it over. "It's getting out of hand. It's time to make a change."

Constance asked, "What change?"

At that moment, off in the distance, a couple of gunshots rang loudly in our own neighborhood. "A change that will make a difference." Ricky was already looking to me. I motioned upstairs with a small head bob. Then I said to the others, "I don't know how long we will be, but unless you hear

screams for help, stay down here." I turned to Ricky. "Come on, Baniti, we
have work to do."

CHAPTER THIRTY-EIGHT

TUMAINI TIMELINES

Hara, Constance, Ted, and Laura were downstairs. They were alternating between watching the news and looking upstairs to see the waves of light flashing from under the door of the study. Rays of pinks, blues, and wild flashes of white light filled the game room and upper stairway.

Hara asked, "What's Daddy doing?"

"He and Ricky are trying to help all of us," she answered.

"Ooo, did you see that one?" Hara was bouncing up and down on her chair and pointed upwards.

Laura exclaimed, "That was a flash of a rainbow. They bent the light somehow." She covered her mouth in awe. "How did they splinter light? Now that was awesome."

"I have to admit, I'm impressed," chimed Ted.

It happened two more times. A ray of white light split outward into seven visible colors and painted the upper ceiling. All heads below were tilted at ninety degrees, and their eyes were glued to the spectacle above.

A fog-like smoke began to filter from under the door. As it flowed even stronger, it looked like dry ice creeping down the stairs. Then the door burst open, and Ricky and I walked out. We both had little sparkles floating around our bodies.

Constance called out with concern, "Are you OK? Is everything alright?" She walked up the first few steps.

"It's alright. Ricky and I were just adding energy to a future timeline."

"Well, you should have seen the light spectacle out here. It was incredible!"

I pointed to the room. "We saw it in there."

She laughed, "I guess you did. What exactly did you do?"

"We tried to help bring hope back to humanity." Ricky nodded along. "The only way to know if it worked is from the future."

Laura inquired, "Couldn't you just time travel forward to see it?"

Ricky answered, "Believe it or not, we tried that and—"

I interrupted, "It's a work in progress. I could see some of this as Tumaini from ancient Egypt, but as Michael, something is different."

On the TV, the emergency signal began screeching above all of our talk. *Beep! Beep! Beep!* It repeated again. *Beep! Beep! Beep!*

This is the Emergency Broadcast System. This is not a test. This is the Emergency Broadcast System. This is not a test.

Martial law has been instituted in all United States towns, cities, districts, and municipalities. All citizens are now under curfew and instructed to stay inside. Curfew will be lifted between the hours of 7:00 a.m. and 7:00 p.m. Any citizen breaking curfew will be arrested on sight and treated as a prisoner of the Department of Homeland Security. The use of deadly force has been authorized as a means to keep *order*. Do not venture outside unless it is an emergency situation.

This new law will stay in effect until further notice. All citizens are now under control of the Department of Homeland Security. Any dissidents will be detained without due process and held at the surrounding FEMA camps.

This has been a message of the Emergency Broadcast System.

The entire message repeated again.

"Uh oh!" Ted groaned. "You know what this means?"

"What?" asked Laura.

"If the Department of Useless Homeland Security is involved, then you know the Order has initiated its plan. As soon as President Smush created the DHS back in the early 2000's—you know, as a means to cover up for the CIA's and NSA's false terrorist attacks on behalf of the Order—all citizens' rights went out the window. Now you know why it was created back then. They just finally got to the point of being able to enact it permanently."

"This is horrible news. How can they do this?"

I responded, "They can do this because the sheeple aren't standing up to the politicians and government. The sheeple are allowing a few rich, old farts to control the many."

Laura touched my arm. "You like that word, don't you?"

"Sheeple?"

"Yes, that's the one."

"It does paint a pretty good picture of how things are going right now, don't you think? Ted likes that word, too." He nodded vigorously.

"I hate to admit it, but you are right. The masses have been duped into this false life by the Order. The majority of people still believe that their national governments and politicians will solve the problems."

Constance jumped in excitedly, "That's what I said last week when I learned about all of this from Ted and Michael. And the governments—"

Ted interjected, "But the governments aren't trying to solve anything. It's the same problems over and over again. Unless we initiate Michael's money-free society, nothing will change."

I perked up. "How did you know about that?"

"I saw Robbie on campus yesterday and we talked for a while. He told me how excited he was about your idea. He also said that other students were anxious to talk with you more about it."

"It wasn't just my idea. It came to me from the God Scrolls."

"Well, wherever it came from, it's a great fix to a terrible, ongoing problem."

I smiled, "That's the best news I've heard so far today."

"Robbie also mentioned that the students were signing petitions to get you reinstated. Then we found out that all classes were cancelled."

Laura urged, "Can you tell us about this idea? I'd love to hear about it."

"Sure, I'd be happy to. And since we're under house arrest by the DHS, let me tell you how well this money-free world would work."

For the next two hours, we shared our thoughts on how great this idea was. We also made a complete set of plans for starting one money-free community when this nightmare finally ends. Just as we were about to finish our discussion, we heard the same Emergency Broadcast System message coming from loudspeakers outside. Then we saw flashing lights. A police vehicle was making its way through the neighborhood to frighten the people.

———————

An hour later, I glanced at the clock, and then I looked at Ricky. He confirmed, "It's time."

"Time for what?" Constance asked.

"Oh, it's late enough that we can call the gang in Cairo. I'll bet they are up by now."

Ted yawned. "Late here and early there. Why can't everyone be on the same time zone?" We laughed with him.

I counted down the seconds until it was exactly past eleven o'clock. "Now I can call." That made Constance and Laura look at each other with funny faces.

"Is there something going on that you would like to tell us about, hon?" Constance gave me her don't-keep-secrets-from-me look.

"You're going to have to trust me on this. It's best that you don't know just yet. I heard that the Order has psychics who sweep the ethers and track our conversations. Right, Ted?"

"Well, from what I've heard, that's correct. Besides listening in through our phone calls, TVs, computers, and hacking our emails, it's just another way of keeping tabs on us."

"Trust me, hon. Let me keep this one, OK?"

"Alright, but you will let me know when it's safe, won't you?"

"I will." I pointed up to the bedroom. "I'm going to call upstairs."

———————

"Hello," said a familiar voice.

"Ehab? Is that you?"

"Yes, this is Ehab. Is this you, Tumaini?"

"It is. It's great to hear from you again."

"It is good to hear from you, too. We all miss you here."

"Ehab, I'm confused. Did I call the right place?"

"Yes, this is still Hanif's shop. He and Rehema are helping the others who came in last night. I told them that I would man the phones for them."

"The others?"

"The priests. They got inside the borders before they closed at midnight. Two of them had to pay to be smuggled inside."

"You're kidding? Did all six arrive then?"

"From all over the globe, they came. Hanif's store has always been a hub for the Protectors, so they just keep showing up here. And with the final six, that completes all of the priests from the times of old."

I sighed because I remembered the loss of Omar and Ramla. "Did you say that they closed Egypt's borders?"

"Yes, and martial law has been imposed in Cairo. No one is allowed out after dusk. The soldiers have been given permission to shoot anyone on sight after dark."

"The same orders have been given here, too, Ehab. It's crazy."

"That's a good word to choose. It is mad over here. People went into a panic when the banks closed."

More gunshots rang out in our neighborhood. "People are still frightened here as well. The loss of life is too much. We need to act—and now!"

"What should I do, Tumaini?"

"I need to speak with Gahiji, Jabari, and Asim."

"Asim is here. The two brothers are helping Karim with the funeral arrangements."

"Can you put him on?"

"Sure, give me a moment."

"Tumaini, this is Asim. I am ready to help."

"Excellent. Is Rehema there?"

"She's right here."

"Good."

In Rehema's mind, I asked, "Hello, Rehema, can you hear me?"

The reply came in my head, "Hello, Tumaini, I can hear you just fine."

I asked inside of Asim's mind, "Hello, Asim, can you hear me?"

"Tumaini, it has been a long time since I have heard your voice this way. Talibah would be proud."

I clapped my hands together in excitement. "Now we're cooking. And I'm proud of all of you, no matter what time period we're in."

Rehema giggled, "What are you cooking?"

I laughed, "Nothing as good as your pastries. And Asim, thank Ehab for me and hang up the phone."

Ehab spoke in my mind, "You can thank me yourself. I can hear you clearly, my friend. I've already hung up."

"More of the priests are remembering the old ways, Tumaini," added Rehema telepathically, "just like the first group did when they awakened a week ago."

"Wonderful. This will make things easier, too. Hold on for a second. I need to get Ricky in here." I called Ricky telepathically. He excused himself from the group and joined me upstairs.

"Everyone, this is Baniti. This is the first time you've gotten to hear his voice in this timeline."

Asim reacted first, "Baniti—Ricky—this is Talibah. I've missed you so."

"I've missed all of you as well. As Ricky, I don't recognize your voices as much, but I do know the feel of your souls. I am very glad to be with you once again."

"We are glad you are with us, Baniti," chimed Rehema.

Ehab asked, "What do you want us to do, Baniti?"

"This is still Tumaini's show. He's in charge, and I listen to him."

"So do we," agreed Rehema.

"Guys, I'm glad that you got to hear Baniti's current voice. What I need to know now is about the intel. Have the seers been able to crack the ghosting techniques and find the mainframe?"

Asim answered, "Yes, they have. Do you want us to tell you?"

"Not until Ricky and I get there. When we arrive, have Jabari and Gahiji ready. Five of us have a mission to do."

Rehema inquired, "How are you going to get here? All of the airlines are shut down, and the borders are closed."

"Leave that to Ricky and me. Expect us in an hour."

Rehema still didn't know what I was talking about, but Ehab and Asim were smiling. Ehab asked, "Where will you meet us?"

I thought for a moment. "Until Ricky and I are at full strength with our energy and skills, we need a place that has a portal."

"A portal?" questioned Asim.

"Yes. Rehema, can you still get inside the pyramids?"

"I think so. They haven't closed all of the ruins to the tourists who are stuck here. I heard that tour groups are still taking the risk to visit. They're bringing at least triple the security guards with them." After a second, Rehema figured out what Ricky and I were going to do. "Oh my! You can do this in this lifetime?! No one else can do it yet over here."

Ricky confirmed, "We can do it. But Michael is right, we need the extra energy source."

"Baniti, this is Rehema. I will meet you there in one hour."

I added, "Good, and have the brothers ready with the intel and their supplies. Oh, and have them join you as security at the portal. That will make it easier for us to look like tourists."

"Very well. Safe travel." The other two gave similar well wishes.

"Bye, friends." Our telepathic communication ceased.

Ricky opened his eyes and turned to me. "That was…that was cool. Our old friends are with us."

"That they are."

"You know, I think I could travel there without the use of the portal for energy."

"I think I can, too, but this is too risky. I want to do all we can to ensure our success."

"You've got a point. What are you going to tell Constance?"

"I'll tell her that you and I have to leave for the night, and we should both be back by dawn. I don't want to say more because she could get hurt if they find out."

"I trust you."

"Thanks, Ricky." I got up to walk downstairs. "Let me explain things, and then you and I can get ready to go."

"I'll be here waiting."

"Thanks."

It took about twenty minutes to convince Constance and the others that Ricky and I had to leave and that we would not get caught by the local police. Once I made it back to the room, I changed into tourist clothes and grabbed my backpack. When I met Ricky in the study, he asked, "Are they OK down there?"

"Constance didn't like that I was holding back information, but she understood it when I said it was best for her, Hara, and the other two."

"She's a good person. If this works, she'll be glad." He grabbed the extra backpack and laughed, "So, what are we doing?"

"We're going to teleport to a portal in the Great Pyramid. Rehema, Jabari, and I saw it when I was there recently."

"I didn't know they had one there."

"I didn't either, but it seemed to be a fixed location. And since it takes energy to keep a portal like that working, we can piggyback off of it."

"That's a great idea."

"It'll be a great idea if it works." I checked the clock. "I asked them to give us about ten minutes, and then the others could get some sleep."

"Do you think they'll sleep with all of this going on?"

"They'll need to. I mentioned that we could take shifts sleeping until this is over."

"You've thought a lot of this through, haven't you?"

I shrugged. "Some of it, but most of it I'm making up as we go. And speaking of going, let's focus on the Well of the pyramid."

"Can you show me a picture of that place so I know where I am going?"

"Sure." I pulled up the image on the computer. "Are you good?"

"Yes. I'm ready." He extended his hand and I grabbed it. We both were stretched into timelessness and back again. When the mist cleared, we were standing in the middle of the Well deep inside the Great Pyramid. We turned around to see if anyone was with us. No one was there, but the portal made a zapping noise.

"It worked!" Ricky exclaimed. "And that must have been the portal you talked about."

I was rubbing my neck. "It did work, but that snapping in and out of time space sure does take its toll on the body sometimes."

"Can you go on?"

"Sure, but we need to wait for Rehema to show up. That was part of the plan."

———•·•———

Rehema, Jabari, Gahiji, Asim, and Ehab met us not much later in the Well. As soon as Gahiji made it through the tunnel, he nodded to us. Then he scouted the area and stood guard while the others came through. As soon as Rehema emerged from the tiny tunnel, she ran up to me and gave me a really tight hug. "It's so good to see you again, Michael."

"You, too."

Before I could say any more, she turned to Ricky. "And you must be my old teacher, Baniti." She gave him a similar hug, which caught him by surprise. The others came up and also gave us warm greetings. They were especially interested in meeting Ricky.

"Master Baniti, it is so good to see you again," expressed Gahiji.

"Likewise," added Asim. He and the others bowed to their old teacher.

This made him even more uncomfortable. He replied humbly, "It's so good to feel your souls again. And if it's OK with you, *Ricky* will do just fine."

Asim came forward. "Please don't be offended if I let a *Baniti* slip out every once in a while. I keep sliding back and forth between my old self and this one."

"I won't, Talibah, my old friend. And I know what you mean. Sometimes I don't know if Baniti is speaking or if I am."

Gahiji picked up his pack. "I've had that happen more than once since I met Tumaini. How are you handling it?"

"I just remembered less than a week ago. If I figure out what to do, I'll tell you," he chuckled.

Jabari asked, "We are ready to rally the other priests. Do you want us to send out the call?"

"No." I laughed, "You can let the pigeons rest."

Ricky had a puzzled look on his face. "I'll tell you later." I winked. Then he raised one eyebrow at me, which made me laugh even harder.

I turned back to the other four. "This assignment will be just us, excluding Rehema and Ehab." They both looked surprised. "I need you two to stay ready to escort us out of here if it doesn't work."

"If what doesn't work?" asked Rehema.

"Here is the plan..." I gestured to the brothers and Asim. "Did you bring the location and the supplies?"

The brothers turned to show me their packs, while Asim slung his off of his shoulder and opened it. "We have the detonators, C4, timers, and the communicators if we need them."

"Good," I nodded. "But we can all talk telepathically on this one. No need for those just yet."

The three replied, "Roger."

"While Rehema and Ehab wait in the pyramid, you three, Ricky, and I are going to use the portal again to reach the location."

Gahiji contended, "But we don't know how to do that yet."

"It's OK. Ricky and I can take you there and back. If we meet any resistance and Ricky and I don't make it, you can still return the same way. All it takes is one time for you to know how to do it."

"That simple, huh?" questioned Jabari with a hint of sarcasm.

Ricky stepped forward. "It's true. I showed Tumaini how to do this back in the olden times, and he could do it from that point on. You can do the same thing, too. I remember this."

"I'm in," chimed Asim. The brothers nodded as well.

"So once we are at the location, we drop the C4, hit the timer button, and return back here. It will happen so fast that they won't have any time to react."

Jabari patted his side. "And if we do meet resistance, we brought along these." He pulled open his security jacket to show us his Uzi and silencer. The other two did the same thing.

Gahiji chuckled, "You did ask for triple security, didn't you?"

I laughed with him, "Yes, I did."

Asim knelt down and started drawing in the sand. "The intel we received this time shows the mainframe in this room here, the backup is beside it, and the generator is in a shielded room next to it."

Jabari knelt down and crossed out the generator. "We figured that we don't need to spend any time on the generator since the two mainframes are in adjoining rooms. All we need to do is set charges here"—he marked the spot on the crude drawing—"and here"—he marked the other spot.

Gahiji pulled out one of the timers. "If we are going to teleport in, that will shave off all of the travel time we had already planned. This makes it even better." He turned to his brother and Asim. "That means we can set the charges and be out of there in less than thirty seconds."

He spoke to Ricky and me next, "We have all of the timers linked to this main timer here. It's set for ten seconds. As soon as we hit the button, they'll go off simultaneously at *zero*."

"The entire mission will take less than a minute. Excellent!" Asim enthused. "We'll be back in the Well, and no one will be the wiser on either end." He focused on Rehema and Ehab. "From here, you'll take us out as if our tour is over."

I inquired, "Are Ricky and I setting charges?"

"No," replied Gahiji. "I'll have the backup supplies in case something goes wrong, and I'm taking point on this mission. All Asim and Jabari have to do is place the C4 and turn on the power to the timer. You two will now be responsible for getting us in and out."

"That's great work," I praised. "No need to make any revisions, either. Did the seers mention resistance?"

Jabari answered, "They only get hints of technicians coming in and out of the rooms. All of the security is above ground and in the tunnels."

Ricky added, "That's good news, as long as they're right."

"And two more things..." Jabari got more serious. "The seers mentioned that the cell towers and communication grids are hooked into these mainframes. If we don't take them out, the entire world will start receiving signals through their electronic devices. Even the radio waves will be affected."

"What's the other thing?" I prodded.

"There were hints of someone important coming onto the soul-catcher ship in the near future. Nothing concrete, but a new presence was felt."

I had a worried look. "That means that they are either ready to start the soul-catcher over the entire Earth, or they've already started it."

Gahiji asked, "Do they know any more about this soul-catcher?"

I looked to Ricky, and he just nodded to me. "No, but I have a plan in action for this ship. That will be Ricky's and my responsibility."

Rehema put her hand on my shoulder. "What about the other priests? What are we to do?"

"If my plan works, there won't be anything for you to do. You'll be able to help society get back on its feet and start the schools again."

"You can't do this all on your own, Tumaini," she said with a concerned tone.

"I won't be. I have you guys and Baniti to help. If we need the others, I'll call for you, OK?" She wasn't convinced, but she agreed.

I requested of Ehab, "Take care of Rehema while we are gone."

"I'll make sure she is nice and safe."

The brothers and Asim were double-checking their backpacks and timers. Asim announced, "I'm all set."

Jabari zipped up his bag. "I'm all set, too. What about you, brother?"

"Mine is set as well. All backups are ready."

"Tumaini, Baniti, are you ready to take us there?"

I nodded, "Yes, just give us the coordinates now and show us the picture. You three grab hands, and then Ricky and I will grab yours. We'll slingshot to no-time and back again."

Ricky started to laugh a little. I shrugged. "What?"

"Guys, just be ready for some nausea the first time. When Tumaini did this, he was yacking all over Senenmut's tomb."

I laughed because he was right. Then I looked at the group. "Good. If there aren't any other questions, we need to go."

Rehema and Ehab backed up to the far wall and away from the portal. Asim laughed, "Smart move. You don't want to get sucked in with us." Rehema had a worried look on her face.

"All right, you three grab hands. Ricky, are you ready?"

"Ya, mon." He held his hand out to mine.

"On three, we'll grab your hands. One, two, three..."

In a flash, all five of us were standing in the doorway between the two mainframes. Gahiji held up his Uzi and started to look around, but he was hit by a small wave of nausea and spit out a mouthful of vomit.

Asim hit his shoulder on the way to his target. He joked telepathically, "You never could keep your cookies down as Bes."

He replied in our minds, "I'm fine, Talibah. Eight seconds."

The other two replied by thought, "Roger."

Jabari and Asim ran to two different places on each mainframe and stuck on the C4 devices. Gahiji stood in watch and counted out, "Fifteen seconds."

Ricky and I were sweating while we waited. Time stood still as we watched each of the three trained priests exercise his precise maneuvers to complete the goal.

"Twenty seconds," came from Gahiji's telepathic voice.

Asim commented, "No one is around. It's hot in here from these computers."

Jabari spat back, "Stop the chatter. My timer is set. Detonator *on*."

"Twenty-five seconds."

"My timer is set, too. Detonator *on*."

Gahiji commanded, "Main timer power is *on*. Thirty seconds."

Asim and Jabari rejoined us in the middle of the doorway. A siren began to bellow loudly. I warned telepathically, "They're on to us. We have to go now."

Jabari looked at the switch for the main timer. "Set. Countdown starting...now!"

10...

9...

8...

7...

"Hold out your hands," I urged.

5...

"They're at the door!" stressed Ricky. Asim, Gahiji, and Jabari held hands and reached out to us.

"Now Ricky! Now!" I yelled.

2...

1...

Booooooooooooooooommmmmmmmmmmmmm!!!

———•◆•———

After the dust had cleared, Rehema was shaking my body, and Ehab was bent over the others. "Michael! Michael! Are you alright?"

"Gahiji, wake up! Asim, Jabari, come on. Wake up!"

Rehema was now shaking Ricky's body. "Please be alright. Please!"

Ricky started to cough. "Where am I?" He coughed some more. The two brothers and Asim were also slowly getting up off of the ground.

Rehema was bent over me. "Michael, come back to us."

After five more seconds, a nasty sound filled the Well. "Owww!" I grabbed in the middle of my back. I had landed on a medium-sized rock. "Owww! That hurts."

"Are you OK?" asked Ricky and Rehema.

I rolled over slowly. "I don't *ever* remember the return trip being that painful."

Ehab came over and helped me up. The other three walked over, too. Jabari stated, "Mission accomplished. The shockwave from the blast must have traveled with us and knocked us off our feet when we landed."

"Mission accomplished," added Gahiji. "I felt the explosion just as we left. With the amount of C4 that we put there, the rooms must have been destroyed."

"And the mainframes with them," included Asim confidently.

Ricky put his hand on Jabari's shoulder and shook his hand. "You guys were impressive. Great work!" He did the same for the other two.

Gahiji came over. "That was awesome how we teleported like that. I don't remember being taught that as Bes."

"You were not taught that, my friend," replied Ricky in Baniti's voice. "But now you have been shown the way. Use this gift wisely." He shook his head and said as Ricky, "Did I...? Yes, I did. Baniti strikes again." We all laughed with him.

I grabbed my back and winced. Rehema pulled me over. "Here, let me take a look at that." She lifted up my shirt and saw that my back was cut. She put her hand on my laceration and took in a deep breath. My lower back became very warm, like a hot water bottle was being pressed against it. "There, that should do it."

I wiggled around while the others looked. "That's feels great."

She smiled and sang, "You're welcome."

"Thanks."

Ricky laughed, "Boy, this being a priest stuff is really cool."

"I couldn't agree more." I looked to the others. "Are you all OK?"

They nodded, and Asim confirmed, "We're doing just fine. Thanks for helping us bring *hope* to the world."

"We did it as a team." I gestured to Ehab. "And thanks for looking out for Rehema."

"Are you kidding? I had the easy job."

"Everything we do in service to another is a blessing. You are all wonderful priests...and people. And guys"—I looked to our three-man security team—"your training was top notch in that room. Bravo!" I applauded and was joined by Ricky, Ehab, and Rehema. They stood there, humble and appreciative.

Gahiji asked, "What's next?"

"Ricky and I have to go back."

"Back?!" exclaimed Rehema. "But you just got here."

"I know, but Ricky and I need to do something back home."

"Can we come along?" requested Asim.

I shook my head *no*, "What I need you to do is to confirm our mission with the seers. If all goes well, I'll be able to call you in a day or two with good news."

"Michael, you aren't telling us everything. I can see it in your aura," hinted Ehab.

I smiled to him, "You're right." I laughed toward Ricky, "Man, this can bite you in the butt on either side of the battle." I turned back to Ehab. "I can't tell you just yet, but I promise that I will include you in the rest of the plan after Ricky and I complete this next part."

"If that's what you wish. You are in charge, Tumaini." He put his hand on my shoulder. The others joined him.

"Our thoughts and well-wishes are with you, my friend," added Asim.

"Tell all of the other priests, Protectors, Hanif, and Mudads that we are here for you," I said.

"We will," replied Jabari.

"Ricky, are you ready?" I held out my hand.

"We should go solo back to your study. I need the practice by myself."

"You're right. And so we don't land in the same spot, I'm going to aim for my backyard."

"See you there, my friend."

"See you there, Baniti." I glanced at my other friends in the small cave and gave them a goodbye look. Then I vanished.

Whoosh! We were back home in less time than it takes Hara to get excited about going to Bongo Billy's Pizza House. When I opened the back door, Constance was sitting at the kitchen table. I could tell that she was a nervous wreck.

"It's so good to be home. Why are you still up?" I walked up to give her a quick kiss.

She glared at me. "Do you really think that I would have gone to sleep with you out there?" She took a sniff. "And why do you smell like burnt toast?" Then she looked at my clothes and asked even louder, "And why is there a bloodstain on the back of your shirt?"

Ricky came down the stairs. In an effort to bring some levity to the situation, I pointed to Ricky and greeted him cheerfully, "Hello. I see that you made it back safely."

"Don't you change the subject, mister! What happened?" She turned me around to get a better look at my back.

As I lifted my shirt to show her that I had no cut, I explained, "Ricky and

I went to Egypt to take out the mainframe. Isn't that right?" He nodded. "We were in and out in less than a minute. And if Jabari, Gahiji, and Asim planted enough C4, the Order will be back to using abacuses again." Ricky smirked from the joke.

"And this bloodstain?"

"That happened on the landing. I fell on a rock, and then Rehema patched me up. I'm as good as new." I moved my body like I was spinning a hula hoop. "See…?"

She looked to Ricky for confirmation. He told her, "That's pretty much the whole story. It happened so fast that I'm still trying to process everything."

"We're OK, hon, honest."

"Did you really take out the mainframe?"

"I didn't take out the mainframe; that was the other three. Ricky and I were just the bus drivers. I can barely get the grill going, remember?"

"Constance," he beamed, "the plan was foolproof. If those were the real mainframes, then a major blow was struck to the Order's plans."

"I don't know what to say." She put her arms around my neck for a hug. She motioned to Ricky. "Come over here." When he stepped closer, she grabbed him in for a group hug. "Thank you." She kissed both of our cheeks, and he blushed.

I whispered, "We did this all for you…and the rest of the world." She squeezed one more time and let go.

"What do we do now?" she asked.

"Sleep. I could use some. How about you, Ricky?"

"I could use about forty winks."

"Did Laura and Ted stay here?"

"They're both camped out on the couches."

"Good, then let's not wake them." We called it a night and went to sleep.

————————

Over breakfast, we told Ted and Laura about our mission. Both of them had their mouths open in awe. Laura pleaded, "You have to teach me how to do this stuff. I know that I can be a help."

"What she said," added Ted.

"We'll get to that, but there is something else that has to be done today."

"What?" shrugged Laura.

"Do you still have that raygun in your safe?"

"Yes. Ricky and I were looking at it the other day. I think we can put it back together. I didn't do it yet, but it looks like it just fell apart."

"I think she's right," he nodded.

"Ted, will you go with Laura and me to her shop?"

"Of course. The streets aren't completely safe yet."

"Honey, do you have any plans for yourself and Hara?"

"We were going over to Tammy's house to drop off some of the cookies we made. Hara wanted to play since she's been cooped up here."

"OK, change of plans then. Ted, I'd like you to go with Constance. Ricky, you stay here. And I'll go with Laura."

Constance blurted out, "I don't need a chaperone." She had her hands on her hips.

"Honey, this isn't up for discussion. Ted's right, we don't go anywhere without extra help." He nodded in agreement. "And while you are on your way back, maybe you can see if any stores are open and get extra supplies and fuel."

Ted snorted, "Now I know you'll need extra company. If the stores are open, it'll be a madhouse."

"OK, but I do this under protest," she fumed.

I snickered, "Protest away, but thanks for seeing it my way." I kissed her head, which helped soften the tension.

Ricky asked, "What am I supposed to do?"

"Work on the cross and see if you can figure out that unknown card." I gave him a wink. "Maybe add some energy to the future."

"Roger." His reply reminded me of our Protector friends.

Hara came in with a glint in her eye. "Did you say we can go to Tammy's house?"

"Yes, pumpkin, and Mr. Ted is coming, too. Can you help him when Mommy goes shopping afterwards?" She nodded and smiled. "He might need you to hold his hand." He got a little frightened from what I'd said. "See, he needs help, too." She giggled.

"Fantastic. Let's get going, then."

On the way to Laura's shop, we saw a number of burning cars, a few houses on fire, and some of the food and convenient stores had been ransacked. There were other people on the roads, but not many.

Luckily, her shop had not been damaged or looted. We went to the safe, picked up the pieces, and started to leave. Laura stopped me before I got to the door. "I want to pick up some fun stuff for Hara. Can you spare a moment?"

"Of course. Do you need a bag?"

"That's a great idea." She took two of the largest ones from behind the counter and started filling them to the brim with books, knickknacks, games, and toys. I used a third bag and put the gun parts in it.

I saw her packing the bags with stuff and laughed, "She just had her birthday. She's going to think that she's getting two in one month."

"Really? A birthday? Then we'll just call this a belated present, shall we?"

"She'll love it."

———————

Back at the house, Ricky was upstairs working on the papyrus piece. He started to get an image, but he was interrupted by a loud pounding on the front door. He went downstairs and looked out the side window cautiously. He saw a police car and a military jeep parked out front. The pounding rattled the door again.

He partially opened it. "Can I help you?"

The officer was accompanied by two military police and another officer. He demanded, "Is this the home of Professor Whyse?"

Ricky didn't answer right away. Then the officer started to walk in, but Ricky blocked his entrance with his energy. The officer didn't know why he couldn't move beyond him, and he stepped back. His expression showed how startled he was, and in an effort not to lose face in front of the others, he placed his hand on his gun and telescoping baton. "Who are you, and where is Professor Whyse?!"

Ricky saw the name on the badge. It was Officer Dunse. "I'm house-sitting. What do you need?"

"When will he be back?"

"I'm not sure." Ricky knew something evil was up, and he was being very guarded with his answers. He peered around the door and saw another set of officers and military vehicles a block away. Down the street, one of the neighbors was being taken away in handcuffs. The man's wife came out screaming, "You have the wrong man! He didn't do anything!"

Ricky stepped back. "What's going on?"

"We are taking dissidents to the holding camps for questioning." The officer made another move to step inside, and the others began to join him. Ricky instantly put up his strongest energy shield and actually pushed all three of them back into their stance.

To cover his actions, Ricky began closing the door. "I'll tell him that you were here. Have a good day." As he latched the door, he sent a wave of energy to repel any offensive actions from the police. He stayed there with his hand on the door and his eyes scrunched for a good fifteen seconds. The officers tried to move forward, but none of them could reach the door knob or advance. In frustration, Officer Dunse spat, "Tell him we will be back for his family if he doesn't comply." Ricky stood there unfazed and kept pouring out energy to block their evil intentions. Finally, they retreated, confused and dazed about their inability to enter.

When the vehicles left, Ricky called out telepathically, "Tumaini, hear me. Tumaini, hear me. Tumaini, hear me."

"Ricky, what is it?"

"Tumaini, the police and military were just here. They are taking people away to camps for questioning."

"Are you OK?"

"Yes. I was able to repel them, but they said they'd be back for your family if you don't comply. It was Officer Dunse."

I shook my head in disgust, "We knew this was going to happen. Thanks for the heads-up. Do me a favor and call Constance and Ted. Her number is on the tablet by the refrigerator. Tell them what happened and not to come home yet. This is part of the Order's plan. Will you do this for me?"

"Of course. Should I do the other thing?"

"Not yet. You were awesome. I wish I could have seen you stop them."

He laughed, "I wished I could have seen it, too. I had my eyes closed."

I laughed, then added, "Laura and I are on our way. It may take us a few extra minutes because of the police and military vehicles. See you soon."

"Ya, mon." The telepathic conversation ended.

"Laura, we have to go now. They've started gathering dissidents to take to the FEMA camps."

"Oh no!" she exclaimed in horror. "Was Ricky hurt?"

"No, they weren't after him. I don't even think they knew who he was."

"We should take the bypass to the freeway to get home."

"Agreed."

In the car, we made our way down a number of side streets and alleys to reach the bypass. When we got to the entrance, it was blocked off by barbed wire and two military vehicles with mounted machine guns on top. Overhead, we saw a number of military helicopters flying by in formation.

"We can't go this way, Laura. Hurry up, turn around. We have to get out of here."

She peeled down one of the feeder roads. As we looked at the highway, we saw tanks taking formation in both directions with their turrets aimed at car level. The next entrance was also blocked. "I bet they cordoned off the entire highway. The town is being blockaded."

"I bet you're right. Look up there." We saw up to the next entrance. A pickup truck was trying to run the blockade and break through the wire. The two military jeeps opened fire on it with machine guns. Then a soldier used a rocket launcher and blew it up in a cloud of red, yellow, and black flames.

Laura screamed, and I pointed across her face. "Turn down here. We've got to get away from the main roads."

In a panic, she struggled to say, "We have to cross Main Street at some point. It's the only way across town." She pushed her foot down to the floor, and we sped off.

"Turn right. Let's go over here." We drove down three more blocks and turned left to cross Main Street. When we got there, a tank was rolling down the middle of the road and blocked our path. From behind, a military police car came bouncing down the alley with its sirens blaring. "Laura, I'll explain later." I picked up the three bags from the store. "Take my hand." She put the car in park and grabbed hold.

Whoosh! We were now standing side by side in our backyard. She teetered for a moment, and after her fear subsided, she exclaimed, "That... was...awesome!"

"I'm glad you didn't get sick. Hurry, we've got to get inside."

Ricky was upstairs when I came in the door. "Michael? Laura?"

"It's us. We had to make a fast getaway."

"I'm glad you're back. I watched from the upstairs window. They arrested another person on your block and took an entire family away."

"This is getting out of hand."

Ricky gave us the *come here* sign. "I think I got the last piece for the slot."

We ran up the steps and I got into the study first. "What did you find?"

"Look for yourselves, and tell me what you see."

Laura and I gazed at the papyrus. I saw it and said in disbelief, "It can't be!"

"I haven't seen it yet. What is it?"

I could hear the sound of military helicopters off in the distance, and the metallic clanking of a tank made its way onto our long street. Above the house, the loud roar of a fighter jet flew overhead.

I pointed outside. "It's those."

"You mean...! Holy cow! It's the image from Seti's Temple in Abydos. It's the plane, the helicopter, and the tank. How did you...?"

"It must have been part of the timeline that I'd seen." Another fighter jet flew overhead. Then I gave Ricky the bag with the raygun parts. "You'll have to put this together with Laura. I've got to do something that I'm not looking forward to."

"You don't have to do it this way, Tumaini."

Laura was confused. "What's he talking about?" She turned to me. "What are you going to do?"

"Ricky, you know the arrangement. Put this together and meet me at the planned coordinates."

I went into my desk and put on my amulet. "I am a Protector of Souls, and this is my vow to help those in their direst of needs."

Ricky walked over to me and put his hand on my shoulder. "I am a Protector of Souls, and I help those in their direst of needs."

"Michael, what are you going to do?" Laura was pleading with me.

A loud pounding sound came from the front door. "Open up! This is the police!"

I glanced at both of them. "It'll be OK. I have to do this. Tell Constance that I love her and that I will meet her again." I leaned in toward Ricky. "You know how to find me."

"I will find you, my friend. Stay strong."

I started to walk away, but Laura grabbed my arm. "You can't go!"

"Ricky, keep them safe."

I walked downstairs, while Ricky kept Laura in the study. I opened the door to a not-so-friendly face. "Officer Dunse, I'm ready to go with you." I added softly, "And I have something that might interest you."

He flipped me around and put cuffs on my wrists and played along. "You don't have anything of interest to me."

I whispered only loud enough so he could hear, "That's what I want to talk to you about."

He motioned to the others to walk down to the car. "He's not giving us any resistance. Let's go." As they walked away, he held me back. "Alright, talk."

"I know that you're probably in hot water for messing up the planted drugs. I'm betting that won't get you any speedy advancement in the Order. But if you brought in the lead ancient Egyptian priest to the reptilian commander, that would look mighty good on your résumé."

An evil smile grew on his face. "Move, priest."

As I walked to the car, I turned around and looked up to the study. Ricky and Laura were watching, and I could see Laura crying. Officer Dunse pushed my shoulder to get me looking straight ahead. I walked to the car and got in.

Dunse told the other officer, "We have the main priest. We're taking him directly to military head command. They'll know what to do with him."

We drove past a number of checkpoints and entered the Air Force base one town over. I was escorted by armed soldiers to the general in charge. Dunse also came along.

I was pushed toward the four-star general. "This is the priest that the reptilian commander was trying to kill. I think he would make a great offering on board their soul-catcher." He laughed sadistically, "Maybe he can be the first to be put in the black box to suffer."

"You brought him in?" questioned the general.

"Yes. He fell right into my trap." I could see that he was lying. There was no trap.

"Very well, then. We can use the Order's teleporter in the lower hangar. Take him there and wait. I will make contact and see what the reptilian wants to do with him."

I was driven over to Hangar Eighteen and dragged inside. We passed numerous alien spaceships, some of which were in pieces. They looked like they were being taken apart for reverse engineering. I was pushed from behind by a soldier. "Eyes straight ahead!"

At the back of the hangar was a device that resembled a tall, open shoe box sitting on its side. It was made of a dark black metal and stood at least twelve feet tall, sixteen feet wide, and ten feet deep. There was a control panel on a console to the left of the opening.

"The general just called in. We are to wait here for him," instructed the soldier. "Then he will take the prisoner to the reptilian."

Officer Dunse whispered in my ear, "Now who's in charge? You won't like it up there." He sneered and chuckled to himself.

When the general arrived, his escort and four soldiers walked in a parade to the teleporter. "Put him inside," he commanded.

I was surrounded by the four officers and roughly pushed to the middle. Officer Dunse came in next, followed by the general. He looked to the attendant outside the teleporter. "You have the coordinates. Seven to teleport up to the reptilian ship. Commence transport."

A few extra buttons were pushed, and then a strange whirring noise filled the hangar. Everyone stopped doing their work to watch. A translucent bluish and white energy screen covered the front of the black box. The six vertical energy bars that ran the height of the box began to glow a reddish-yellow color. As they got brighter, the buzzing sound got louder. When they radiated white, a single loud crack sounded in the box and flashed a blinding light into the hangar. In an instant, we were on the reptilian ship.

"Ricky?" I called telepathically. "I'm inside the ship. Do you have it working?"

"Tumaini... Yes, Laura and I were able to reassemble it. The parts slid together just like we thought they would. We tested it once, and it works."

"Can you home in on my amulet?"

"I can feel it, yes. And I contacted the priests. The small attack force is ready to come on the ship and rescue you."

"Good. The plan is working. Have Jabari bring the extra backup pack from the mission. We can set off the C4 on the main bridge."

The reptilian queen and the commander came into the teleport room. As soon as the commander saw me, it thrust its hand out toward me. I hit the ground in agony. "Hsssss. Silly priest. Your powers are weak in such close contact. You should have been prepared. Hsssss." The queen hissed along in pleasure from my pain. "Stronger shield you need when near us. Hsssss."

Ricky could hear my pain. "Tumaini, are you alright? What can I do?"

The commander dropped his hand and I had a moment of relief. I groaned, "That hurt."

The commander did it again. I screamed in agony. The general and Dunse were pleased at my torture.

"Tumaini, I'm coming up now. I'll stun them with this gun."

I was still writhing on the floor. The reptilian put up both hands, and I curled up into a ball. "Arghhhh!"

"Hsssss. You should have died with the rest of the priests millennia ago." It put its claws down.

I struggled to tell Ricky, "No, don't come yet."

"Hsssss. We feed on pain. The queen commands your pain." Its claws were directed at me again.

It was the most intense agony that I'd ever imagined. I screamed, "Help meeee!"

"I'm coming, Tumaini. I'm coming."

I started to say, "No, Ricky. Wait for the others." But it was too late. Ricky teleported onto the ship and was standing right next to me. Before he could raise the raygun, the reptilian commander was already in the process of striking me for a fourth time. Ricky got hit with me and crashed to the ground. The gun fell from his hands, and the soldiers rushed over and grabbed it. We both screamed in pain.

The reptilian growled in anger, "Hsssss. Other priest. You must die." It hit us one more time with an excruciating blow.

The queen signaled to the commander. "Hsssss. Execute them now. Do not delay. No chance to escape for them. Dump them in space."

The commander motioned to the general, and he nodded to two of the soldiers. They grabbed our shoulders and had us kneel. The reptilian kept us in pain so we couldn't focus enough to teleport ourselves off of the ship. I felt the cold metal from the gun barrel on the back of my neck. I was still wincing in pain. Then I felt a sharp jab as two shots blasted in the teleport room. *Bang! Bang!*

After checking the bodies and bullet holes, the general told his soldiers to put them in the teleport machine and send them into deep space. With a few pushes of the buttons, and a flash of light, no priest remained on the ship.

CHAPTER THIRTY-NINE

TIME AFTER TIME

Hara, Constance, Ted, and Laura were downstairs. They were alternating between watching the news and looking upstairs to see the waves of light flashing from under the door of the study. Rays of pinks, blues, and wild flashes of white light filled the game room and upper stairway.

Hara asked, "What's Daddy doing?"

"He and Ricky are trying to help all of us," she answered.

"Ooo, did you see that one?" Hara was bouncing up and down on her chair and pointed upwards.

Laura exclaimed, "That was a flash of a rainbow. They bent the light somehow." She covered her mouth in awe. "How did they splinter light? Now that was awesome."

"I have to admit, I'm impressed," chimed Ted.

It happened two more times. A ray of white light split out into seven visible colors and painted the upper ceiling. All heads below were tilted at ninety degrees, and their eyes were glued to the spectacle above.

Without warning, two violent thuds rocked the house. It sounded like two heavy sandbags hitting the upper floor. Hara jumped and yelped from the noise. Then a fog-like smoke began to filter from under the door. As it flowed even stronger, it looked like dry ice creeping down the stairs. Then the door burst open, and I started to walk out. I had little sparkles floating around my body.

Constance called out with concern, "Are you OK? Is everything alright?" She walked up the first few steps.

"It's alright." I was grabbing the back of my neck from being shot on the soul-catcher. "I'll be down in a moment."

I looked over to Ricky. "You're alive! I'm so glad." I walked over to help him up. "I can't tell you how happy I am that you made it back."

"What happened, mon?" He also grabbed the back of his neck.

"The timeline didn't stick. We both died, and then we were slingshot-ted back to the point where we tried to manipulate the magic cross. The *Tumaini Timeline* failed!"

"No! We tried so hard to make it work. What happened?"

Constance was standing at the top of the steps and staring. "Will you please tell me what is going on?"

I saw the others coming up as well. "Well, it's over now, so there's no harm in telling you."

Ted asked, "Tell us what?" He pointed to the ceiling. "That was a pretty intense light show, by the way."

Ricky had a funny look on his face. "I'm confused. Shouldn't *time* still have gone forward like all other time travel? We should be two days in the future."

"I had the same thought, but we didn't time travel in this timeline, we splintered off, remember? If we time traveled in this timeline, we would be two days in the future, but we're right back where we started because of the split."

Constance stomped her foot. "Will someone please tell me what's going on?" Hara was standing beside her and mimicked her mother and stomped.

"I will, hon, just give me a moment, please." I grabbed the back of my neck again. "Come in to the study, and I'll explain everything."

Everyone walked in before I did, with Ricky bringing up the rear. I scanned him with my inner sight, and I could see that his energy field had a hole in it from the gunshot. "Ricky, come here." I placed my hand on the back of his neck. It got really warm under my palm as I softly sang a healing song. The light glowed brightly around his shoulders. Then he spun his neck like he was doing neck stretches.

"That feels much better. I'm whole again." He turned me around. "Your turn." With expert healing, he fixed the tear in my energy body and patched me up.

"I hope I don't have to go through that again." Constance and the others were looking at us in the doorway. "Coming, dear."

I walked over to the table. "You see, guys, I was angry—I mean, really angry. People were dying all over the world because of what the Order did with the financial meltdown. I wanted to see if Ricky and I could alter the timeline somehow and fix everything." I pointed to the magic cross. "Wow, would you look at that?"

Laura gasped, "Oh my!"

"What is it, Tumaini?" asked Ricky.

"Look at the card. It's all burnt up and out of the slot." I picked it up, and it fell apart into ash. Little grayish-black pieces floated out of my hand like fried tissue paper.

Constance stuttered, "Did...did...did you...?"

"This was the *Tumaini Timeline* card. Ricky and I used our white magic on the number eleven spot to attract this papyrus piece to it." I chuckled, "Well, what's left of it anyway." I rubbed my fingers together to make some smoke and dust. "We also put our magic on the *Tumaini Timeline* card to be stronger than all of the other timelines. Our goal was to stop all of the senseless death just so some old farts could get richer. And the way Baniti explained it to me back in ancient Egypt was, if we died, the odds were pretty good we would slingshot back to the original timeline. We gave that intention a lot of energy, too, so we took the chance and went."

Laura picked up some of the dust. "But why this card?"

I laughed because of the serendipity, "You asked me in the other timeline if I time traveled to see something, *and I did*. I traveled as far as my sight would let me in the *Tumaini Timeline*. We blew up the mainframe there and got onto the soul-catcher ship. Then the vision stopped. I thought it was the most successful answer to this terrible problem."

Ricky chimed in, "Yeah, and he distracted you in the other timeline, too. He switched subjects to cover it up."

"So you are a cover-up artist," gibed Ted.

I nodded, "Yes, but this was for the betterment of everyone, not my bank account."

"Good point."

Constance stared at me. "So you tried to do this on your own, huh?"

I laughed again, "Rehema said something similar to me in the Well. No, hon, I had Ricky with me. And all of you helped me in the other timeline, too. Ted was watching over you and Hara, Laura went with me to get the raygun and put it back together, and Ricky came to rescue me on the soul-catcher. That's when we were shot and our bodies were dumped into deep space."

She flipped, "You were shot?! Dumped?!"

"Ya, mon!"

I gave Ricky the not-now look and gesture with my hands. "Yes, we were both shot trying to bring hope to the world. But we're not dead here; we were only dead over there."

She walked up to me with a few tears in her eyes, and then she laid her head on my shoulder. Hara came over and grabbed around my waist. "I can't believe that you were shot. You were actually dead." She put her arms around me and cried a little. "I love you so much. I don't know what I'd do without you." Hara squeezed a little more.

"I know, hon, I love you, too"—I grabbed Hara tighter—"both of you. We did this for everyone."

"It's just hard. I know you are doing this to help. Hara and I are extremely lucky, but"—she wiped away her tears—"you're doing too much on your own. You have to include us."

"I did"—I paused—"and I didn't. I included you in the *Tumaini Timeline*, but not in this one for the last few hours. But now we are back here, and you're included again. Is that OK?"

"Some..."

Laura asked, "What would happen if you returned over there?"

"Our role in that fixer-upper debacle would have been over, and it would be entirely up to you guys to make a difference—that is, if that timeline had stuck in the magic cross."

Ted pointed to the table. "Speaking of magic crosses, have you noticed something?" The last of the eight cards had moved into place. "I'd say that a new event has just taken over your valiant attempt." Hara still held on, but she looked over with interest.

Ricky hinted, "I bet I know what it is."

"This may sound strange," Laura grinned, "but I think I know what it is, too." She picked it up with the tweezers and looked at it.

She and Ricky said at the same time, "It's planes, tanks, and helicopters—" and he finished, "—from Seti's Temple in Abydos. We saw this in the other timeline, too."

"Exactly." She lowered her hand but didn't let go of the tweezers. "Whoa! That was déjà vu happening."

"No," I corrected her. "This happened in the other timeline. It just happened later, is all. Both of you—"

Ted interrupted, "It's true, then. There are multiple timelines all sitting on top of each other, like parallel dimensions. And"—he picked up Laura's hand to hold the card higher—"there are possible crossovers." Laura nodded with him.

"From what we've just experienced, I'd have to agree. And it appears that some things can happen in multiple timelines." Constance looked worried because Ricky and I were previously executed. "But I know about getting shot, and that won't happen again."

Laura put the card on the table, but next to the cross. It slid back into the spot. "Just checking." Hara smiled because she'd seen it move on its own.

Ted scratched his head some. "I'm curious, though. I don't get it. Why didn't it work? I mean, the *Tumaini Timeline*. Why didn't it work? And don't get me wrong, I'm glad you're both back here and alive."

"I think that this timeline"—I pointed toward my feet to emphasize the here and now—"has the strongest chance for success. Ricky and I couldn't do it on our own in the *Tumaini Timeline*, so something else must have to happen in this particular future to beat the Order."

The TV downstairs began blaring above all of our talk. It was the Emergency Broadcast signal. "I think we need to hear this message. Hurry!" I motioned for us to go down quickly. After our human stampede, we were gathered around the TV. It was on its second round of emergency tones.

Beep! Beep! Beep!
This is the Emergency Broadcast System. This is not a test. This is the Emergency Broadcast System. This is not a test.

Martial law has been instituted in all United States towns, cities, districts, and municipalities. All citizens are now under curfew and instructed to stay inside. Curfew will be lifted between the hours of 7:00 a.m. and 7:00 p.m. Any citizen breaking curfew will be arrested on sight and treated as a prisoner of the Department of Homeland Security. The use of deadly force has been authorized as a means to keep *order*. Do not venture outside unless it is an emergency situation.

This new law will stay in effect until further notice. All citizens are now under control of the Department of Homeland Security. Any dissidents will be detained without due process and held at the surrounding FEMA camps.

This has been a message of the Emergency Broadcast System.

The entire message repeated again.

"Uh oh!" Ted groaned. "You know what this means?"

"What?" asked Laura. "Whoa! It's happening again. Go on, Ted. I think I know what you are going to say."

He gave here a funny look. "OK...? If the Department of Useless Homeland Security is involved, then you know the Order has initiated its plan. As soon as President Smush created the DHS back in the early 2000's—you know, as a means to cover up for the CIA's and NSA's false terrorist attacks on behalf of the Order—all citizens' rights went out the window. Now you know why it was created back then. They just finally got to the point of being able to enact it permanently."

Laura, Ricky, and I were laughing. "What?" He shrugged.

"You said the exact same thing in the other timeline—word for word. It was one of those strong crossovers."

Constance jumped in, "Does that mean we are still living out the other timeline where you both get shot?"

"No, it's already changed, honest. We've already seen the plane, helicopter, and tank card go into the number eleven spot, and that didn't happen until later tomorrow in the *Tumaini Timeline*. The events are mostly different, I can tell."

"Are you sure?"

"I'm positive."

I checked with Ted, "Didn't you meet with Robbie yesterday?" Before he could respond, I glanced back to Constance. "OK, some things might be the same. But I won't get shot." I made an X sign over my heart to promise.

He answered in surprise, "I did meet with him. He told me that the students were trying to get you back and signed a bunch of petitions. But with the schools closed, it's a moot point."

"See, he didn't say the same thing this time. The timeline is different."

"OK," she conceded, "I'll trust you."

"He also was... How do I put this? He was very proud of you—something to do with money-free societies. He wouldn't stop talking about it. He wants to know more. You've really made an impression on him."

"He's a great TA."

"He also said that students want to meet with you, even if it's not at school. They want to put this money-free community into motion somewhere."

"That's awesome news. You didn't say that in the last timeline, either."

"Well, I'll try to get my act straight between parallel dimensions." We all laughed.

Hara spoke up, "What's parallel dimensions?"

Constance replied, "It's like getting to eat a banana split at home at 12:00 p.m., and you get to eat a hot fudge sundae at 12:00 p.m. at Tammy's house, but they both happen at the same time."

Hara gave a confused look. "What?"

"It's OK, Hara. I'll explain it better later."

Laura laughed, "I know I've probably heard this before, but can you tell us about this money-free community in this timeline?"

"Sure, I'd be happy to. And since we're under house arrest by the DHS, let me tell you how well this money-free world would work." I put my finger up because I remembered something else. "I got the information from the God Scrolls. Let me get them and share all I know. It's really important that this gets passed along to others."

Ricky asked, "Have you used the other scrolls yet?"

"Not all of them. I've only used three of the ten: one for the songs, and the other two for channeling. There's got to be so much more that these scrolls can tell us."

"I bet there is. I might have to give a go at channeling these scrolls."

"You're more than welcome. You were there when I wrote some of them."

He was nodding his head *yes,* "You're right. I do remember. I can see the gold paint and the brush in your hand in the back of my mind. And I bet that I can channel them in this timeline."

"Why don't we give it a shot?"

I came back with the rolled-up papyrus. For the first hour and a half, while holding the God Scroll, I covered all of the information on why the community is needed and how to start one. They were stunned at the messages that I was bringing forth. Constance, Ted, and Laura were furiously taking notes.

Laura reacted excitedly, "This is incredible! I've never heard so many inspiring words in my life. It makes me want to start one of these communities right now."

"I know what you mean," I added. "When I said these words at school, I was filled with this voice that sounded so loving and full of guidance."

Constance enthused, "You sounded that way right here. I was moved to tears sometimes."

"Ya, mon."

"Hey, Ricky"—I grabbed one of the new scrolls—"your turn."

Ted held up his finger. "Hold on a second, I'm still writing. This information is *gold*." Then he snickered, "OK, it's priceless. If I say gold too loud, the Order will come a runnin' to claim it." We all laughed with him.

"OK, Ted," agreed Ricky, "this is too important to rush through." He looked at me. "And in the next few days, maybe we can go over the other scrolls."

"After the mainframe and soul-catcher are gone, we'll focus on all of them." I expressed with more emphasis, "We have to get the word out."

"Tumaini, the God Scrolls are a godsend. Thank you."

"Baniti"—I bowed to him—"it was because of you and our other friends that I was able to do this. Thank you." He nodded in appreciation.

"Ted, are you caught up?"

"I'm good. Time for God Scrolls part two."

"Let's hear it, Ricky." He picked up the scroll and channeled more inspiring messages of peace, service, and love.

When he was done channeling, and Ted was finishing up his work, we heard the same Emergency Broadcast System message coming from loudspeakers outside. Then we saw flashing lights. A police vehicle was making its way through the neighborhood to frighten the people.

"It's OK"—I motioned toward the car—"this is still part of their plan." I remembered back to the other timeline, and they were all looking at me. "It will be an hour until I can call Egypt. I think it would be smart for us to make an emergency backpack for everyone—you know, extra clothes and provisions, in case we have to leave right away."

Constance squinted at me. "What aren't you telling us?"

Hara wasn't looking directly at me, so I gave a head nod toward her with the don't-scare-Hara look. Constance got the idea and motioned. "Come on, Hara, let's do what Daddy said and get some stuff prepared in your pack. And then it's bedtime."

"Awwww, do I have to?"

I walked over and gave her a quick kiss on her head. "Yes, pumpkin, you've stayed up really late tonight. You need to get some rest."

Ted was yawning and stretched, "I could use some rest, too."

Constance giggled, "Ted, we can tuck you in later, but you need to get some supplies ready first."

He gave her a one-eyed look, but then he smiled, "Do I get a bedtime story?"

"Only if you are a good boy," she smiled back.

I picked up the scrolls and glanced toward the study. "I have some packing to do as well." I requested to Laura and Ricky, "Can you guys go in the kitchen and start organizing some food and water for each person? I'll be down as soon as I put the scrolls away."

Laura answered, "I can do that. I'm pretty handy in the kitchen."

Constance pointed from the doorway. "Water is over here, and all of the long-term food is in these cupboards. There're extra storage containers in the cabinets by the refrigerator."

"We'll find our way around," asserted Ricky. "And most of my clothes are still in the shopping bag. It won't take me long to get my stuff ready."

"Thanks, guys." I waved as I went upstairs.

Ted motioned to the kitchen. "I didn't bring any extra clothes, so I'll help you two."

On her way up, Constance told him, "I'm sure we can find some of Michael's clothes that might fit you. And Laura, I'll put some clothes together for you." Laura and Ted smiled before going into the kitchen.

An hour later, Hara was in bed, and everyone had a travel bag filled with clothes and goodies. I grabbed the phone. "I need to make a call to Egypt. In the last timeline, I had to keep it a secret, but I'd like it if you all joined me for this one."

"Ya, mon. You were pretty stealthy in that timeline." He came over and put his arm around me. "And it almost worked. But this one will do even better, I can feel it."

Constance sighed, "I sure hope so." Then she turned to me. "You don't have any more secret timelines up your sleeve, do you?"

I pulled up my make-believe sleeves like a magician. "No tricks in here"—I thought for a moment about the remaining papyrus pieces—"but there must be some more cards heading to the new slot by now."

With excitement, Ted blurted, "You're right. We should go look."

"We will, but I need to call Egypt first. Then we can see if any new cards moved."

Laura made a *tsk*, noise. "Hara won't be happy if she misses any new cards." That made us laugh.

"We'll show her in the morning." I started dialing. "Shhhh. There's a lot of crackling on the line."

"Hello, Hanif's…scrrrrr…incen…scrrrr. How may I scrrrrr?"

"Hanif? Is that you…scrrrr? We have a…scrrrr…interference."

"Scrrrr. No. This is Ehab…scrrrr."

"Hold on. Let me call…scrrrr…let me…scrrrrr…let me call you right back." *Click.* "Man, there's a lot of phone interference."

While I redialed, Ted suggested, "Maybe there is something going on in the atmosphere from all of the chemtrails."

"Or a new mainframe signal," added Ricky.

"It's possible." The phone was on speaker this time and ringing.

"Hello, Tumaini?"

"Yes, that's much better. I can hear you. Is this Ehab?"

"Yes, it's me, old friend. And I can hear you just fine now."

"Boy is it good to hear your voice again. Did I call Hanif's shop?"

"You did. He and Rehema are helping the group of priests who came in last night before they closed the borders."

I smiled at Ricky, "Our prayer to reunite the last priests must have worked." He nodded back.

"Did you say that they closed the borders?"

"Yes. Two of the priests had to pay a smuggling ring just to get inside safely."

"You're kidding."

"Not at all. But the remaining priests are all finally here. The original Protectors of Souls are back, and we are ready to serve." He paused for a moment. "Tumaini, they also instituted martial law in Cairo, Luxor, Alexandria, and most other cities. No one is allowed out after dusk. The soldiers have been given permission to shoot anyone on sight after dark.

They were even shooting at shadows and stone walls last night."

Ted snickered, "Even the walls aren't safe anymore." We laughed, and Constance gave him a *shoosh* sign.

"The same orders have been given here, too, Ehab. It's crazy."

"That's a good word to choose. It is mad over here. People went into a panic when the banks closed."

More shooting broke out in our neighborhood. "Were those gunshots I just heard, Tumaini? Are you alright?"

"Yes, and we're all fine. It was off in the distance. Ehab, people are frightened here as well. The loss of life is too much. We need to act—and now!"

"We are the Protectors, and we are ready to serve. What would you have me do?"

"I need to speak with Gahiji, Jabari, and Asim. Are they around?"

"The two brothers are helping Karim with the funeral arrangements. Asim is here, though."

"Ehab, we are all sorry for your loss over here."

"Thanks, my friend. We are sorry for your loss as well. Should I get Asim?"

"Yes, and is Rehema close by?"

"She is. I'll get her, too."

"Great. We'll be here waiting."

I turned to the others. "I may need to do some telepathic communication with them. It's part of the plan I've been putting together."

Constance begged, "Just promise to fill us in later."

"I will."

"Tumaini, this is Asim. I'm glad you are OK, especially with all of this madness going on in the world."

"I'm glad you're OK, too," I sighed in relief. "You have no idea how good it is to hear your voices again. Is Rehema there?"

Their phone was put on speaker. "I'm here, Tumaini."

From over my shoulder, Constance piped in, "Hello, Rehema."

"Oh, hi, Constance. Nice to hear your voice. You sound lovely today."

I could tell that they were about to go into a girls' talk. "Ladies, there'll be plenty of time for that later. Focus, please."

They both apologized, "Sorry."

Asim spoke next, "Tumaini, we need you back here. Is your plan ready?"

"I have most of it worked out. I also have a way of getting in."

"Getting in?!" exclaimed Rehema. "How will you do that with all of the borders closed? They're killing anyone who tries to leave or enter the country."

I laughed, "Let's just say that I already did a test run for rejoining with you guys, and it worked perfectly. And if I'm right, it will work again." Ricky laughed as well.

"What are you talking about?" she asked.

"Rehema, hear me. Rehema, hear me. Rehema, hear me," I called telepathically.

"Hello, Tumaini," she voiced in my head.

"Asim, hear me. Asim, hear—"

He interrupted, "It has been a long time since I've heard your voice this way. Talibah would be proud." Then he murmured, "That was some major déjà vu."

I replied in his mind, "Excellent!" I clapped my hands together. "Now we're cooking. And that déjà vu might be happening a lot in the next day or two."

"Tumaini, hear me. Tumaini, hear me. Tumaini, hear me."

"Ehab?"

"It is I!" He was very excited. "It worked. I can hear you in my mind."

"Good, and I have a surprise for all three of you. Can you hang up the phone on your end? We need to speak beyond the ears of the Order."

I spoke to Ricky telepathically, "Time to join in the conversation." Constance saw my hand signal and hung up our phone after we heard the *click*. They just looked at us for the rest of the conversation.

"Everyone," I said, "Baniti is with us. He can hear our thoughts."

He greeted telepathically in Baniti's voice, "Hello, my old friends. I can feel your souls. I am glad to be with you once again."

Rehema just about burst, "Baniti! Oh my word. It's been so long. I have missed you." The others also gave similar greetings.

After the pleasantries, Ehab asked, "What do you want us to do, Baniti?"

Ricky stammered for a moment. "Uh…to be honest, I just remembered who I was last week. Tumaini is in charge. I'm doing what he says."

Rehema added, "So are we."

"Yes, you are the one in charge," affirmed Asim. "What's the plan?"

"Did the seers get any new intel on the real location of the mainframe?"

"They did. Ted's advice on cracking the ghosting technique worked. The energy signature has been verified, too. We're sure that they have a generator and a backup."

"Wonderful news. Please pass along my gratitude to the seers."

"We will."

Ricky spoke next, "Rehema, we have a way back into Cairo that will bypass the borders. Are they still letting tourists visit the Great Pyramid?"

"Why, yes. How did you know?"

"It was a lucky guess." I laughed with him.

"What do you two know that we don't?"

"Rehema"—I paused for a moment—"it would take too long for this conversation, but I will tell you about our little advantage later."

"OK, please continue."

"I can't tell you exactly when, but Ricky and I will be meeting you in the Well in the Great Pyramid. We are going to use the portal's energy to help transport us there."

Ehab gasped, "The portal! I remember Jabari telling me about the portal after you and Rehema were in there."

"Yes, it seems to be a fixed dimensional window. Rehema?"

"I have a feeling I already know what you are going to ask."

"Chalk it up to déjà vu again." She laughed from my comment. "How soon do you think you could get there?"

"Since there's very little traffic, I could be there in less than twenty minutes."

"Good. I'll call you telepathically when we'll need you. And have the security team meet us there as well. It will make us look like tourists who were stranded when the borders were closed."

"Security team? Stranded tourists? You know more than I do. Would you care to fill me in, please?"

"I know. This all sounds confusing, but you'll have to trust me."

"I do."

"When you go to the Well, bring Ehab, Asim, Jabari, and Gahiji with you."

Ricky nudged me. "Should they bring the special backpacks?"

"No, no backpacks. Just be there to help when I call. Can you do that?"

Rehema, Asim, and Ehab all answered, "Yes."

"Tumaini, is this part of the plan?" questioned Asim.

"It's part of the plan, but not all of it. There's still a missing piece or two."

"I know that Karim is anxious to hear the details."

"I've been thinking about him. He's included. Tell him that I have him in my thoughts."

"I'll do that for you."

As I was thinking through part of my plan, I added, "And guys, can you have alternate transportation ready? I have a feeling that we may need it."

Rehema told me, "I can read your thoughts. It will be done."

"Excellent. Please tell the priests that Baniti and Tumaini are coming. We have work to do as soon as we arrive."

"We'll do that for you. Is there anything else?"

"Just accept my thanks. You've been awesome friends—in all places."

"Bye, Tumaini. Bye, Baniti."

We both bade, "Goodbye, my friends." That ended our telepathic communication.

"Well?" asked Ted. My eyes were still adjusting to the light.

Ricky burst, "That was so cool. I felt them, Tumaini. I felt their essence. The Protectors of Souls are with us again."

I smiled and put my hand on his shoulder, "Yes, they are."

Ted asked with a little more insistence, "Well?!"

Constance followed, "What's going on, Michael?"

I shared with them, "I've been putting together a plan that might take down the mainframe and the soul-catcher ship. It's going to involve all of you, the priests, and the rest of the Protectors of Souls."

Laura chimed in, "I'm ready. What do you want me to do?"

"I'm more than willing to help, too," added Constance.

Ricky was still glowing from his experience. I smiled to him, "I know you are happy, I can feel it."

"I am. I can't wait to see all of our old friends and what they look like today."

I laughed, "I hadn't thought about that. They are all going to be in different bodies. It will be hard to know who is who."

"I'll know. I could already feel Talibah's soul. It was like being back home again."

Ted asked a third time, "Well?! What's this plan?! What did you say in your conversation?!"

I pointed. "Got it. Here's part of the plan that I have in mind."

I used a blank piece of paper and drew a crude computer and spaceship. "Ricky and I are going to teleport to Egypt to be with the priests. We are going to take out the mainframe and ship." I crossed those two out. Then I wrote the word *intel* on the sheet. "Ted, you are going to feed us any new information that we might need at the last second—you know, info that you know about the Order."

"I can do that."

"Good. Your information has been invaluable so far. If there's anything you can tell us about this nanotechnology, it might help us find a way to cure everyone who has been infected with it."

Constance urged, "What am I supposed to do?"

"I need you to help Ted on the computer. You know your way around the internet like no other. With two of you looking up information, we can get it much faster."

"I guess that I'm going to help somehow, too?" included Laura.

"I'd like you to help Constance look out for Hara." I paused for a moment. "And one more thing… Do you think you could get the parts for the raygun out of your safe tomorrow? I have a feeling that we might need it."

"I can do that. Ricky and I believe we found a way to put it back together last night. I think it just fell apart when it hit the ground."

I mentioned to Ricky, "Oh, and take a look at a picture of the Well. That way you'll already know where we are headed when it's time to teleport."

"You've got it, Master Tumaini."

I laughed, "I'm no master. You are."

"Maybe in another time, but you're doing pretty good here."

I leaned over. "Shhh, I'm making this up as I go. Don't tell the others." They all laughed, too.

Constance asked with a little worry, "How are the two of you going to take out the ship and mainframe?"

"Let's just say that I have one of the best security teams in the world over in Cairo. These guys really know their stuff."

Ricky expressed, "They're good, too. I've seen them in action. I've never witnessed such precision executed on a mission. They really are top notch." His comment made Constance feel a little better.

I continued, "And with the rest of the Protectors and priests, I'll bet that we can use our powers to wipe out these horrible machines."

Ted inquired, "When's all of this going to take place?"

"Tomorrow. We start everything tomorrow."

"And the new cards for the next slot?"

"Oh yeah, I almost forgot. We can see if anything has moved, and then we can get a good night's sleep." Another few gunshots rang out in the neighborhood, followed by a woman's scream off in the distance. I could see the fear on the girls' faces. "We'll be OK. We'll protect you."

Ricky chuckled, "We are the Protectors of Souls."

"Let's go look at the table and see if the planes, tanks, and helicopters card has started the next event on the magic cross."

On the way, Laura pointed out, "You know, it's odd that we haven't seen anything that deals with those yet."

"I have a feeling that we will see all three by morning."

She got a psychic hit. "You're right, and the cross has been true to form ever since you showed it to me."

As we walked to the table, sure enough, we all saw that three more cards were on their way to the next spot. "If these cards moved"—I motioned—"then that means that eleven is locked in for sure, even though we haven't seen it happen yet."

"That means no more *Tumaini Timeline,* right?" begged Constance.

"Right."

Then she asked, "Can you make them out?"

"Only one way to find out. Let's take a look."

We took turns at each of them. The only card that we could make out was an exploding planet. Ted joked, "That one has come up more than once on this cross. It's a persistent little bugger, isn't it?"

Ricky answered, "Let's hope that it's not going to end that way."

"Yeah, they already tried to do that back in the 60's. Thank goodness they failed back then."

"It's like you said when you read us the God Scroll," added Constance, "no one should have that much power over the planet."

I pulled her in sideways. "I agree with you." Then I pointed to the table. "What do you see here?"

She peered down at one of the two cards. "I'm not getting anything. There must be too many things that have to happen yet before it appears, just like before."

"You're probably right."

Ricky leaned back to get Laura's attention. "Can you sense anything?"

She put her hand over one of the two cards. She closed her eyes and felt with her intuition. "One is...one is good for us." She pulled her hand away and put it back in the same place. "Yes, this one is definitely good. This one gives...gives...gives us a chance."

"And?" asked Ted.

As soon as she placed her hand over the other card, she pulled it away faster than a frightened girl who'd just touched a spider. "Oh my gosh! This one is terrible." She covered her mouth in horror. "Let's hope that this one doesn't go into the twelfth spot." She shuddered from the bad energy. "I don't want to feel that one again."

"Well, I guess that gives us a clue to these two cards: one good, one bad," chuckled Ted. "Anyone care to take a guess?"

From overhead, we could hear more jets. "It's probably something to do with those, but we won't know until it becomes visible." I was pointing to the ceiling. Then I walked over and opened the window. "The chemtrails are still falling. The Order isn't stopping."

"Neither are we," asserted Ricky in a very confident voice. "Neither are we."

Ted yawned again, "I'm tired."

"Good point," I said. "We should get as much sleep as we can. We've got plenty of places to rest. Find a pullout couch or bed and call it a night. Tomorrow, we put the plan into action."

CHAPTER FORTY

GATHERING OF PRIESTS

"Michael, Constance, wake up!" Laura was shaking both of us.

"Wha…wha…what time is it?" stammered Constance.

"It's three in the morning. You've got to get up." She peered out the window. "Hurry!"

"Can't we have five more years?" I mumbled in a deep, slumbered voice.

"No, you have to get up now. This is important." She shook me some more.

Ted and Ricky had just finished walking like zombies toward our bedroom door. Ted scowled and pointed at Laura. "It's…too…early!"

She scolded him, "No! You have to listen!"

She spun back around. "I usually get up a couple hours before sunrise to meditate, check messages, and stuff. I must have turned my phone off last night and didn't hear any calls. But my employee—the one who has a crush on you, Ricky—well, she said that they've started gathering people to take to the FEMA camps."

I woke up a little more. "FEMA camps?" Constance sat up with me.

"Yes. She said that they have a list for anyone who poses a threat to the Order. She has a friend who showed her one. I'm on it because of my metaphysical shop"—she pointed to me—"you're on it"—then she turned to Ted—"and so are you." He reacted with a surprised head jerk. "We've got to be prepared."

Ricky caught my attention. "This has all happened before."

"And it will happen again," I replied, "if the crossover is strong enough."

"Aren't you concerned?" she pleaded with a trembling voice.

Constance put her arm on mine. "What are we going to do?"

I nodded once toward Laura and Ted. "They don't know you are here, so don't go home. And don't go to your shop—at least not by yourself. They won't know to look for either of you at this house, so you should be safe."

"And what if they come here?" asked Constance.

"We'll be safe. I promise."

"How can you say that?"

"Because I have a plan." She looked at me with doubt in her eyes. "I know you don't believe me, hon, but I'm savior boy, remember?" That didn't put a smile on her face, but I could tell that she understood some.

I yawned again, "Well, we're up. How about some breakfast? We've got three full baths, too, so we can all get cleaned up."

Constance mentioned, "I'll get Hara. You guys can use our bathroom first."

"Thanks." Ted motioned at the door. "I'll take dibs on this one—too much coffee last night."

Laura said, "I'll use the one downstairs."

"I guess I'll wait for Hara to get done first," chuckled Ricky.

———•◦•◦•◦•———

In the kitchen, I asked Constance to turn on the TV while I prepared something to eat. Off in the distance, I could hear a low whirring noise. I checked out the little window over the counter as the sound was getting louder. I could just barely make out a squad of six attack helicopters flying in formation. Their lights were on, and they were coming our way. We both went to the backyard to take a look.

"They're the helicopters from the card." She pointed to the heavily armed choppers.

On the opposite horizon, two F-35s flew behind us and made their familiar jet roar as they blazed through the sky. "I've never seen them fly so low before," I remarked. "It's like a scene out of a war movie. We'd better get inside and eat while we can."

In the kitchen, Ted was helping himself to some juice. "What was out there? It sounded like an airshow." The F-35s made another pass, and he rushed to the back door to catch a glimpse. "Man, those are fast." Then the helicopters finally flew over the house.

"Mommy, Mommy, did you hear that?" Hara came running in.

"We heard it. Did you get all cleaned up?"

"Uh huh. Those were loud. Were they UFOs?"

"Sorry, hon," I answered, "not this time." I gave her a plate of food. "You need to eat up quick, OK?" She shook her head *yes*. "Those were military planes and helicopters."

"Like the ones in the card I saw?"

"Yep."

Constance told her, "Ms. Laura and Mr. Ted will be here to play with you today if you want. Maybe you can get them to help you decipher your puzzle."

She replied excitedly, "I'm almost done with one of them. It's a funny story about an Egyptian boy, with love and kissing and stuff."

"Really?" I asked. "You still aren't interested in those things yet, are you?"

She giggled, "No. Boys spit, remember?"

I laughed, which made me choke a little on my juice. "Good memory. You just keep that in mind if a boy asks you out on a date."

Constance playfully slapped me on the arm. "Stop that."

Laura came in with a handful of towels. "Would you like me to help with some laundry?" Then she caught a glimpse of the newscast. They were showing pictures of all the local on-ramps being blocked off with barricades and barbed wire. Behind the newscaster, another squad of helicopters flew over the highway. "Look!" She motioned.

We all turned to the TV. I hit the volume button, and then we heard:

The town is now on lockdown. The military has issued a statement that all traffic in or out of the city limits must go through the checkpoint at exit 29a. Only emergency vehicles and law enforcement personnel are permitted to use the highways at this time.

The cameraman zoomed to the exit. Below the chemtrails, you could see two military jeeps with machine guns mounted on top. A blue pickup truck attempted to run the blockade behind them to escape being imprisoned in the city. As it approached, the soldiers opened fire, followed by another soldier using a rocket launcher on the truck. It blew up before it could ram the barriers.

The newscaster reported excitedly, "Oh my gosh, folks! We just witnessed a protective measure being enforced by our loyal troops." The driver was completely engulfed in flames as he fell out the open door. "Please… This is horrible. This may not be suitable for our younger viewers."

Hara's eyes were already covered by her mother's hands. Luckily, she didn't see the gruesome scene. Then the cameraman panned to the highway. Three tanks, with turrets aimed at car level, were coming into view from the south. He moved his camera to the north, and three more heavy tanks filled the viewscreen.

The reporter implored, "These troops mean business. Do not, please, do not panic. I'm sure this is being done for the betterment of everyone in each town." More tanks were coming down the feeder roads as well. "This is one patriotic display, folks."

Ricky was standing in the doorway to the kitchen. "Did I just see what I thought I saw?"

I was in shock. "I'm not sure what to say. They just incinerated that driver."

Ted looked at Hara and curbed his rage, "Those…those…those dirty…!" He breathed in heavily with anger. "And that reporter was so…errrrr. This is infuriating!"

Constance was speechless. She just held onto Hara tightly.

I informed Laura, "You're not going to your shop today. It's too dangerous."

"Don't you need the raygun? I can still go across Main Street."

"No. They are looking for you, and it's just not safe. Stay here with us." I grabbed the handful of towels from her. "I insist!"

"Constance, honey," I requested, "would you mind turning that off? I think we've seen enough."

"With pleasure." *Click.*

She looked at all of us and said shakily, "Alright, eat. We need to keep our strength up."

"Agreed," I nodded. "Take all that you want. And after breakfast, we should double-check our bags and see if we can pack any extra provisions."

Ricky asked, "Did you see this coming?"

I replied softly so only he could hear, "Some of this happened in the other timeline. I didn't expect so much to be the same."

"Me, neither," he whispered.

"Make sure you get to eat. We may need to move faster than I thought." He gave me a thumbs up.

———————

An hour later, we all had our packs stuffed as much as possible. Ted expressed, "Thanks for lending me so many clothes. This duffle bag is jam-packed." He set it down heavily. "I don't think we can even get an extra strand of spaghetti in there, it's so full."

"It's the least we could do, Ted," responded Constance.

Laura came over with her pack. "That goes double for me. You are a blessing, both of you."

Hara bounced over. "What about me?"

"You're a special little blessing." Laura touched her nose, and that made her wiggle her shoulders and smile. Then she ran up the stairs to play.

From inside the top of Laura's pack, her phone started ringing. "Who can that be?" She grabbed it and answered, "Hello...

"Oh my! You're not serious...?

"They took your brother's family...

"They're going street by street...

"What can I do...?

"Just stay there. Don't go outside..."

From the phone, Laura could hear banging on her shop helper's door. We could all hear a tiny voice in the background. "Open up! This is the police!" It sounded like a door was broken down, a scream followed, and then the phone went dead.

Constance was worried and yelled upstairs, "Hara, is your pack ready?!" She told me, "I'm going to check on her."

I mentioned to the others, "When Ricky and I come back from Egypt, we need to find a safe place to stay."

"We could always go by foot and stay at my house," suggested Ricky.

"That might not be a bad idea."

From down the street, we could hear the sound of tanks and other military vehicles. "Stay here!" I ran outside to take a quick look. They all ignored me and followed right behind. Two blocks away, we saw a group of soldiers and policemen going house by house. They were arresting two people and also marched an entire family out to a police van. "Hurry! Everyone back inside!"

Ted pushed the door shut and locked it behind us. "This isn't right what they are doing."

"No need trying to convince me," added Ricky.

"OK, this is what I need you to do. All of you go up to the study, and don't come down for any reason, no matter what you hear or see. You have to promise me that. Will you promise?" They all agreed. "Good. I need to get some things ready. Let's go."

I ran up first to get the black trunk that I'd used in Egypt. "Ricky, help me to put everything inside."

Constance came out of Hara's room. "What's going on?"

"I don't have much time to explain. Just promise me that you'll keep Hara upstairs."

"You have that look in your eye. What aren't you telling me?"

"Just promise me. I know what I am doing. Now promise."

Her face was covered with anxiety and she struggled to say, "I promise."

"And don't come downstairs. You have to keep Hara safe."

"I will."

"Ricky, get all of the scrolls, parchments, and magic cross pieces. Put them in the bags and load them in the trunk. And keep the pieces that we've already found for the magic cross separate. Put them in this one." I handed him an extra clear plastic bag.

Ted asked, "Do you need me to help?"

"Yes, help Ricky. This all needs to be packed up. Go! Do this now!"

Laura came over to assist. "Please help Constance and Hara. Keep them up here."

"I will. What are you going to do?"

"I'm helping bring hope to the world. Trust me."

While the two men were organizing everything in the trunk, I was grabbing all of the backpacks and running them into the study.

I went over to Hara and Constance. "I love you both so much. Stay here, OK?" I kissed and hugged both of them.

"Whatever you are going to do, don't do it." Constance pleaded with me, "Please?"

"I have to do this. It's the only way to keep all of you safe."

"Please! I can't lose you!" She was holding back her tears.

I kissed Hara again on the head and Constance on the lips. Then I looked to Ted and Ricky. "Don't open the door for any reason."

"Tumaini, what are you going to do?" asked Ricky.

"Trust me, old friend." I gave him a wink. "Trust me."

I motioned to Ted. "Follow behind me and lock the door."

"No!" yelled Constance.

The sound of the tanks and police sirens were at the end of our street. I looked out the side window and saw Officer Dunse walking down the middle of the road with his billy club clenched in one hand.

"I love you guys!" I turned, ran down the stairs, opened the door, and went out to the street.

"Officer, I'm here. I give myself up to you freely."

Constance and Hara were in the window. I could see them crying. Officer Dunse swung me around callously. Then he called into the microphone pinned to his shoulder, "We have Whyse. Bring around the car."

While he was putting the zip tie handcuffs on me, I tried my best to keep him distracted from going into the house. "Do you know who you really have?"

"Don't talk! You don't have anything to say to me."

"I'm the priest."

He used his billy club and hit me in the back of the legs. I dropped to the ground hard on my knees. Then he grabbed my hair and pulled my head back. "What did you say?"

"I'm the priest that they are looking for."

"Priest, what priest?" He told the other officer from the station, "I've got this. Get the car ready. This house is finished." He glared back at me. "Now, talk."

"I'm the reincarnated Egyptian priest that the Order has been looking for. I'm the one that the reptilians want."

In a cold voice, he hissed, "You are, are you?"

"Yes. And think how good this would look for you if you brought me in to your superiors."

He called into his microphone, "Hurry up with my car. This one is going in with me."

In an evil voice, he whispered, "You're going to regret where I'm taking you." Then he hit me in the back with his club. I arched and winced as the car pulled up. He threw me in the back seat and closed the door. As we drove off, I saw that the tanks and the police vans were past my house.

Dunse told his partner, "We have the Egyptian priest. Take him to the next town. We're going to see the general at the Air Force base." He gave him a testosterone-filled nod.

The officer drove for another thirty minutes and took us through a number of checkpoints. When we arrived at the entrance of the base, I asked, "Where are you taking me?"

He laughed sinisterly, "You should never have come out to the street."

"I did what I had to do."

"Well, you're going to do as I say now. And when I turn you over, I'm going to get a *huge* reward."

"Good. You'll get what's coming to you." I looked at the floor of the car, and then back to him. "Tell me…what do they do when you fail more than once in the Order?"

"What?"

I closed my eyes and focused my thoughts.

"What's he doing?!" the driver called out.

"Hurry up! Pull over!" yelled Dunse. "I can't reach him because of the glass."

As the car crunched down on a number of stones, I finally relaxed my thoughts. And in a flash of light and smoke, I vanished from the back of the car and reappeared in my bedroom.

Hara saw me first. "Daddy!" The others rushed toward me. Constance threw her arms around my shoulders and was still crying. I almost fell over because I was off balance.

"Ricky, get these things off of me." He grabbed a pair of metal scissors off of my desk and worked to cut the plastic. Ted also came to help.

I rubbed my wrists. "That hurt."

Ted grinned, "You had that planned all along, didn't you?"

"Let me take a look at those." Constance held my wrists.

"I had to do something to keep them from coming into the house. They would have arrested all of you."

"You sly dog, you." He slapped my shoulder.

Laura went downstairs to help Constance get some ice.

Ricky cheered, "Tumaini, you're the man!"

"No, I'm like you taught me to be, Baniti. I'm a Protector of Souls."

"No, you were inspiring."

"It's what any Protector would have done," I said humbly.

"Here, put this on your wrists." Constance had the towel wrapped around my hands. "I don't know what to say. Thank you for keeping us safe." She kissed the side of my face.

"I love you."

"I love you, too." She hugged me tightly.

Laura warned, "They're going to come back for you."

"I know. It's time for Plan B."

"Plan B?"

"Yes. Ricky and I can't leave you behind; it's not safe. We are all going to Egypt. Grab your bags in the study and hold on."

"Daddy, are we going for a ride?" asked Hara.

"We're going for a big ride. Don't forget your favorite stuffed toy." She ran into her room and grabbed it.

Laura grunted as she picked up her pack. "Are you serious?"

"No joking. Ricky and I are going to get you there safe and sound."

We could hear sirens coming around the corner. "Hurry, everyone gather around the trunk." We all encircled the black case. I laughed for a moment, "I've never seen such huge eyes from all four of you before. Relax, we'll be alright."

Constance was rigidly shaking. "The sirens are right outside, Michael. Hurry!"

"All four of you, hold hands. Ricky, are you ready?"

The front door was knocked down. "Police! You're all under arrest!"

Hara was shaking and pleading for me to hurry, "Daddy?!"

"Come on, Michael," urged Ted with his teeth closed.

"On three. One…"

We could hear multiple footsteps heavily stomping up the stairs.

"Two…"

"Don't move!" The yell came from the game room.

Calmly, I counted, "Three." We grabbed their hands and vanished with the trunk before the policemen's eyes. We reappeared instantly inside the Well.

———◆———

After a minute of waiting in the stone cave structure, Constance, Ted, and Laura were all still bent over and heaving on the floor. Hara was tugging on my hand and yelled excitedly, "Whoa! That was cool. We *have* to do that again!"

Ricky came over to her while I tended to Constance. "I'm proud of you, Hara. You didn't get scared once while we flew."

"Master Ricky," she begged, "can you take me on another trip?"

He blushed, looked at me, and then answered her in Baniti's voice, "I appreciate the honor you have bestowed upon me, precious one. In time, you will be showing me how to do many wondrous things." That caught me by surprise. I wondered if he had an insight that I wasn't aware of.

Constance was getting better and gave me the *I'm fine* look. At that point, I was standing between her and Ted's kneeling body. I placed my hands on his shoulders during his last spasm. He gruffed and moved my hand away, "Enough already. I'll be fine." He wiped off his mouth with the back of his hand. "Go tend to the others. I'm OK, thanks." Then he got up slowly, and I smiled because it was classic Ted.

Ricky had pulled out some water from his pack and handed it to both him and Constance. Then he walked over to check on Laura. She was still dazed from our trip to timelessness and was lying on her back next to a rock and her pack. I laughed because I remembered that rock.

I moved to the place where the portal was. Hara was busy exploring the shelf part of the Well. Then she ran up to me, hid behind my legs, and held my hand. "Daddy?!" she expressed in a concerned voice.

A man had just poked through the small entranceway. He stood up and pulled out his gun and looked around the room. He aimed everywhere and at everyone. He stared directly into my eyes, and then looked around one more time.

Before I could greet him, Rehema came through the entranceway. She ran up to me and gave me a hug. "You're alive! Oh, I'm so happy that you escaped from those dreadful men."

I hugged her back. "Thanks for meeting us here on such short notice."

She gave me one more squeeze, then she walked up to Constance. "And you must be..." Before she could finish, she and Constance were already embraced in each other arms like they were reunited college friends. Hara walked over, and she pulled her in like a loving Aunt who'd just seen her niece at the family reunion. Hara smiled and hugged her back.

Ted was a little alarmed by the four armed men who were standing at the mouth of the tunnel entrance. I motioned to him. "It's OK, Ted, they're with me." Then they came up in a line to greet us. Laura was also getting her bearings at that moment and stood up.

"Everyone," I announced, "this is Gahiji, his brother Jabari, Ehab, and Asim. And some of you have already met Rehema." The three girls were smiling. "These are some of the Protectors of Souls—the original priests."

In a wave-like fashion, they bowed to Ricky. Ehab greeted him, "Baniti"— he looked up with a grin—"Ricky, it's wonderful to be in your presence again." Ricky nodded back quickly and humbly.

They straightened up and bowed to me next. "We are very happy to see you again, Tumaini," added Jabari. Gahiji gave me a nod and turned to keep an eye on the entrance. "We are humble priests and are ready to serve."

I practically ran up to all four of them. "You have no idea how glad I am to see all of you." I held my hand out toward Hara and Constance. "Guys, this is my wife, Constance, and my daughter, Hara"—I pointed to the other side of the Well—"this is Ted"—he nodded in their direction—"and this is Laura." After I gave each of the men a proper *hello* greeting, they walked over to introduce themselves to the rest of our travel party. Rehema was busy giving everyone motherly hugs. Laura welcomed it graciously, but it made Ted uncomfortable.

Asim asked, "What's with the trunk?"

"I had to bring all of the parchments and scrolls. I didn't want to leave them to fall into the hands of the Order."

"Smart move, Tumaini."

Constance came up to me. "I don't understand. How did they come here so fast?"

Rehema jumped in, "Oh, I can tell you that. While he was in the police car, he contacted me telepathically and told me the alternate plan. We left right away to meet you." She nudged her. "He's one smart guy."

She turned to me next. "And my gift is getting stronger, Michael. I could hear your thoughts without you speaking to me."

Ted questioned, "So you're a mind reader?"

"Well, I'm a priest, and I have a special gift." She gestured to all of the others. "We all have special talents. Some heal, some travel, and others...well, others can do many things." She winked at Ricky and me to acknowledge our many powers.

Laura came up to her with a purpose. "We need to talk." Rehema just smiled modestly.

Gahiji motioned toward the door. "We should get out of here soon."

"He's right." I picked up my pack and added, "We need to go out and look like tourists."

Ehab patted the trunk. "We've already made plans for this."

"I thought you might have," I said. "Did Rehema tell you about it?"

"From your thoughts, yes."

Jabari looked toward his brother. "They should be here by now. Would you check on them?" He nodded and closed his eyes.

Laura asked, "Is someone else coming?"

Rehema laughed, "In a matter of speaking."

Constance sighed, "I know, trust you."

"We've got this covered, hon."

I turned to Ehab. "Did you come in the tourist bus?"

"We did, but we aren't going back that way. The roads have gotten even more dangerous for Americans. We're taking alternate transportation." He gave me a secretive wink.

"I thought so. Are there still armed guards inside the Necropolis?"

Jabari replied, "Yes. And we have a number of Protectors on the grounds to help, just in case."

"Wonderful. That should keep everyone safe." I turned to the security team. "Would you escort them out of here and take them to the rendezvous location?"

Constance pulled my arm. "Aren't you coming with us?"

I got Laura's, Ted's, Ricky's, Hara's, and Constance's attention. "You're going to go with these friendly people." I pointed toward Rehema, Gahiji, Ehab, and Asim. "I'm going to stay here with Jabari to get the trunk out."

"How are you going to do that?"

Laura nudged her. "He's got this covered. I can feel it in his energy. Trust him."

"I do," she confirmed.

Rehema bent down to Hara. "Are you ready to do some exploring? We have to crawl through this little cave. It'll be fun."

"Yeah!" She was holding on tightly to her stuffed toy.

I handed Ehab a small roll of Egyptian pounds that I had left over from my previous trips. "Here, this is for the pyramid priests and guards. This might keep them happy, and hopefully they won't ask any questions about our group leaving the pyramid."

"You haven't lost your touch, Tumaini. You know this land well."

Rehema held Hara's hand. "Are you ready?" She was completely comfortable with her and giggled, even though Rehema had been a total stranger less than five minutes ago. Both Constance and I smiled because she could feel Rehema's warmth and love.

"Laura, Ted, are you going to be OK?"

"We'll be fine," he replied.

"Just another day at the office," joked Laura.

"Ricky?"

"Ya, mon." That made the Egyptian party laugh. It was the first time that they'd heard someone from the beautiful island of Jamaica say that.

Gahiji informed us, "It's all arranged. We'll meet you there in about fifteen minutes."

"You guys are impressive. My hats off to all of you." I bowed to them. "I can't thank you enough."

Jabari smiled, "We are like you: Protectors of Souls. We are ready to serve."

"That you are. And I'm honored to know all of you, no matter what timeline." Jabari looked at me funny because he didn't know what I was referring to. "I'll fill you in back at Hanif's shop."

"As you wish, Tumaini."

I walked over to Constance, "I'll see you in just a bit. You're in the best hands possible. I trust these guys with my life." I gave each of them a look of confidence.

"I remember you telling me about them." She pulled my arm again. "We'll be OK, though, right?"

"Better than OK. You have the Protector team on your side."

Ted added, "Something that the Order is completely clueless about. Friends like you are the best gift ever."

"Thanks, Ted. I feel the same way about you." I leaned over and whispered to him, "Can you help take care of Constance and Hara?" He felt needed again and smiled.

Gahiji gave the order, "I've got point. Ehab, you take up the middle, and Asim, you take up the rear—three people between each of us."

They both replied, "Roger."

Gahiji looked to the group. "Alright team, time to move out. The rest of you grab your backpacks and stay close to your Protector." He knelt down to Hara. "And I'll help you up the long stairs and with your pack, OK, sweety?" She nodded back to him, and he lovingly placed his hand on her head. "Let's move." He picked up her bag and went through the tunnel.

Once Asim left the tiny square opening and was able to stand upright, he and some of the others looked back. From the dark tunnel, they saw a white light flash from the Well and a little mist came out of the entrance. He affirmed, "They're good. Let's go."

After a long climb to the place where the corridor branches off to the King's and Queen's chambers, Gahiji motioned to Ehab. "You and Rehema should stay right behind me and talk to the pyramid guards while we exit. You can distract them and keep them from looking at our new friends as they leave."

"Good plan," complimented Ehab. He pulled out the roll of cash and picked out a few bills.

Ted took a moment and spun around in place. "Man, I wish we had more time to visit. I've never been here before."

Rehema walked over. "Maybe when this is all over, I can take you on a special tour. I used to do a lot of archeological work here." Then she whispered, "But you should pretend that you are excited and just got done seeing it so you don't tip off the pyramid guards, OK?"

"Right." He winked.

Constance was holding Hara's hand. "How are you doing, pumpkin?"

"This is an awesome place, Mommy. We have to come back."

Rehema bent down. "I could take you on a special tour, too. Would you like that?"

"Oh, yes, very much, Ms. Rehema." She was jumping up and down.

Laura leaned in. "Can I come, too, Ms. Rehema?"

"Of course you can, dear."

Asim announced, "OK, if everyone has caught his breath, we should be going. We still have to meet at the rendezvous point."

Gahiji instructed, "The rest of you wait a minute at the entrance so Rehema and Ehab can distract the guards. Then follow us tightly down the stone steps. Got it?" They all acknowledged the plan. "When we get through the door, don't look back at the guards." He picked up Hara's pack again and led them up the last set of stairs.

Everything went smoothly outside of the pyramid. There were a handful of other tourists, but not many. Gahiji took point again. "This way, folks, down to the Sphinx." He turned to Rehema. "I think you and Ehab should act like tour guides and talk to the others on the way."

"Oh, I can do that. I'm a woman, remember?"

The newly arrived guests were gawking at all of the pyramids and the Sphinx. Rehema pointed to the temple next door. "Come on, we're going over here."

Constance asked, "Where're Michael and Jabari?"

"We should be meeting them soon." She got the others' attention. "We have to go to the back of this wall."

Ted touched one of the old columns. "There's not much to look at in this one."

"I know," agreed Rehema. "Khafre's Temple isn't near the attention getter as the others"—she pushed on the large stone at the back wall and made it move inwards—"but it does have its hidden secrets."

Jabari was pulling out a few floodlights from his pack and passed them to the security team, while Laura gasped, "Wow, a hidden tunnel."

Asim hushed her, "Shhh. We don't want to alert anyone else. Hurry!" He waved Laura, Hara, and Constance inside. Rehema ducked down and followed.

Ted was looking around like a jackrabbit scouting its hole before going inside. Then he crouched down into the black tunnel, followed closely by Asim. Before letting the door close, Asim made a hand signal to one of the Protectors who was watching over them. Then he gave a thumbs up for the Protectors to leave the Necropolis and meet at the second rendezvous point. Once inside, the stone door swung shut behind him.

"Careful down these stairs, pumpkin," warned Constance.

Ted professed, "This is incredible. I never knew this was here."

"Most people don't," remarked Rehema.

The security team used their lights to help them all the way down. I was waiting for them at the bottom of the stairs. When Constance and Hara reached the last step, they jumped into my arms. "You...are...amazing!" she exclaimed.

I kissed her back. "I still think that you are the amazing one. Thanks for trusting me."

Ricky let go of the railing after getting his footing. "Even as Baniti, I didn't know they'd built this."

Asim came up to him. "The Protectors have used this tunnel for centuries. We have an offshoot to take us to our main meeting place."

Gahiji gestured down the dark tunnel. "We made transportation arrangements and should leave quickly. Let's stick to Tumaini's plan, and we can all visit at Hanif's shop."

Laura heard a deep-sounding snort. "What's down there? What part of the plan is this?"

"That would be our ride." I pointed to the darkness.

"That ride isn't going to eat us, is it?" worried Ted. That made our Egyptian friends laugh.

Rehema giggled, "Come, meet our American-eating friends." Gahiji led the way, followed by a laughing Rehema and Ricky.

Ehab motioned for the rest to follow. He took three funny steps down to the floor. "This way," he chuckled. "It's safe, honest."

We walked about thirty feet or so and met up with Hanif, Mudads, Karim, and two other priests: Zuberi and Umi. They were standing in a group in front of five donkeys who were all hitched to carts. Rehema introduced the newly-arrived team to our drivers and hosts.

"Everyone"—she put her arm around his back and one hand on his chest—"this is my husband, Hanif. This is Mudads, his brother"—they both bowed—"next to him is Karim, a dear friend"—he nodded—"and these two handsome brothers are Zuberi and Umi"—they also bowed.

Zuberi stood six foot three and had the figure of a body builder. His shirt sleeves were straining to keep in his biceps. Umi was two inches shorter and had a similar problem. Both of them had short black haircuts and well-chiseled faces.

Laura whispered to Constance, "I'm riding with them."

The five men came up and gave everyone a proper hello. The two brothers spent a few more minutes talking with Ricky, who spoke to them in Baniti's voice.

One of the donkeys snorted again. I grabbed Hara's hand. "Do you want to pet them?"

"Yeah!"

Hanif and Rehema took Hara's hand from mine and walked her up to the first one. "This is Daisy," introduced Hanif. "Your father named her."

"Hello, Daisy." She touched the coarse mane cautiously. Then she petted her with a number of strokes down her neck.

"This big fellow is Duke." She petted him next. "And these three are Molly, Angel, and Little Mikey—we left Ginger and Pepper at home."

Mudads came over to say hello to Hara. After his gentle greeting, I asked him, "I thought you didn't name your animals."

"We did it in your honor. It seemed strange to name one and not the others."

"Good thing I didn't name your car." He smirked from my short joke.

Zuberi and Umi picked up the black trunk and loaded it on the first cart. "Who's riding with us?"

Laura just about ran Ted and Ricky over. "That'd be me!"

Both guys turned to each other and flexed their smaller biceps. Ricky jested, "I can't compete with that."

Ted grunted, "Yeah, right. You're in better shape than I am, and you're also Baniti. I've got nothing." They both laughed.

Constance came up behind them and put her hands on each of their shoulders. "Well, you guys are super to me. Don't change a thing."

I came up behind her and added, "That goes double for me."

"Thanks, Constance," replied Ted.

"We wouldn't be here if it wasn't for your help." I patted their shoulders one more time.

Ricky joked, "I thought we were here because of your plan."

"OK"—I acknowledged with my hands that he was right—"I had something to do with the location."

Jabari came over to us. "Time to load up—if that's OK with you, Tumaini?"

"Lead the way, Jabari. Let's get back to Hanif's."

———————

Once we got beyond the part of the tunnel that the government and smugglers used, we were finally trotting down the Protector's secret branch. Asim gave us the signal that it was safe to talk openly again. Each cart was buzzing with questions directed to the five drivers. I just sat back and listened to the excitement.

When we reached Hanif's basement, he, his brother, and Karim took the carts up the ramp to unhitch the donkeys; Rehema played hostess and took us up to the shop; and Ehab and Asim carried the trunk up with them.

She announced to the group, "Consider yourselves family, and please make yourselves at home." She waved her arms to the familiar red velvet couch and chairs. "We do a lot of talking down here, but Hanif and I have our home upstairs."

Then she tapped Zuberi and Umi on the shoulders. "Would you be dears and grab the extra chairs from the cellar and workroom? We have a lot of new guests today."

Zuberi nodded, "It would be my pleasure to serve."

"Me, too," added Umi.

I gestured to Ted and Ricky. "Come on guys, we can help."

When we returned and gave everyone a seat, Laura complimented her, "You have a lovely store."

"Oh, thank you. And please tell Hanif. He takes great pride in pleasing his customers."

Ted was sniffing in the air. Constance asked, "What is it?"

"I can smell it." He took a very long, slow breath through his nose. "I smell it." I was already laughing. "It's over here." He pointed and walked with a purpose to the back wall.

Laura was following him. "What do you smell?"

He went right to the box full of special incense. "Don't you recognize this? It's—"

We all answered with him in a chorus, "*Incense from the Temple Gods.*" The group laughed together. I chuckled, "See, just like home."

Mudads and the others came back from tending to the donkeys. Karim had Ramla's broken staff in his hand and came over to talk with me. Meanwhile, Hara was walking around the store and looking at all of the pretty perfume bottles and diffusers. When she saw a bottle on the shelf that looked like the one she'd received as a gift, she grabbed it and ran over to her mother. Constance and Laura were already telling Hanif how wonderful everything looked and smelled.

"Mommy, Mommy, this is just like the one Daddy brought me."

I overheard and jumped in, "That was a gift from Mr. Hanif. What do you say?"

"Oh, thank you, Mr. Hanif. I use this every day at home."

He bowed. "You honor me, Ms. Hara. Did you like the oil, too?"

"It smells cool." Then she laughed, "Sometimes, when I put too much water in the bulb, it gets too hot and water explodes out of the steam hole." She giggled some more.

"Well, I think you should have a different one with some prettier smelling oil, don't you?" He winked to me and Constance.

"Can I?"

"Come, let's go pick them out together."

Karim motioned for me to return so we could finish talking, and except for Hanif, the other men followed. Rehema saw us gathering and took the two ladies upstairs to give them a tour of a modern-day Egyptian home.

"I'm glad you are here, my friend," thanked Karim. "I gave my oath to Ramla and Omar that they would not have died in vain. What can I do to help?" While staring at me, he resumed sanding down the tip of the cane to a fine point.

"I have a plan, but I don't want to divulge much without including the women. They are part of everything."

Karim was sanding harder. "Can you tell us anything?"

"Yes. I know that it's possible to take out the mainframe, but what I need is the latest report from the seers." I inquired from Jabari and Gahiji, "Have they found the location for the mainframe?"

Gahiji answered first, "It's one of the energy spots in Egypt. The seers had to use their knowledge of Sacred Geometry to find it."

"How'd they do that?"

Jabari stepped forward. "They used the Fibonacci spiral to pinpoint the center on a map. Believe it or not, the location isn't that far away."

I gave them a look that begged for more explanation. "I'm a little rusty on my spirals. Can you show me?" Ted and Ricky were nodding along.

Jabari took three bottles off of the shelf and positioned them on the floor in a tiny arc. "You see, these three bottles are like the three stars in Orion's Belt. They form a slight curve."

Ted remarked, "The pyramids at Giza were built to mirror them, right?"

"Exactly." He pointed to him. "The seers followed the Fibonacci spiral along these pyramids and located a vortex of energy. When they peered deeper to go beyond the ghosting techniques—the ones you told us about—they found two mainframes and a generator."

Ricky picked up one of the bottles, then set it back. "But, why there?"

Mudads answered, "It's an unnatural, vile, negative vortex in the Earth that was created by the Order. Which also means that the power of the mainframe's programming will be intensified by it."

Ricky gestured with his hands. "I'm still not following."

Mudads bent down to the bottles. "It makes perfect sense, based on what the Order wants to do with the mind control nanobots. Michael and Ted said that their initial plan is to use the cell towers, radio waves, satellite signals, and electronic devices to control the masses. But if the power goes out anywhere on the planet, the vortex energy will still send out the signal. The people will still be controlled to do the bidding of the Order."

I knelt down and traced the spiral to the center. "Have you double-checked this intel?"

Asim responded, "We've found three electronic energy signatures at that exact location. One is the generator, and the other two are the mainframe and backup."

"That's good work," I praised.

Hanif came over, and the three women were down the steps. Hara joined Constance by her side with a new bottle of oil and a diffuser. "Great timing. We were just going over some of the intel that the seers provided."

"I know." Rehema tugged on her earlobe. "I could hear your thoughts so loud that I said we had to go down and listen. This is more important than our pillow cases."

"Wow, you weren't kidding when you told me that your gift had gotten stronger." She blushed.

Laura tapped her shoulder. "Are you going to teach that to me?" Rehema nodded back.

Ted was a little worried. "Can you hear all of our thoughts?"

"I'm not an eavesdropper," she giggled. "Tumaini and I have a unique connection. His thoughts stand out particularly strong. Once my gift opened a few days ago, I actually had to start tuning him out most of the time."

Hanif laughed, "Sometimes she thought I was talking to her out loud, but it was your thinking, my friend."

"That might come in handy in the future," I thought out loud. "Does anyone else have this ability?"

"No, she's the only one."

"Speaking of abilities, I could use a refresher on the powers of each priest.

I'll need to know that when I give out assignments." I looked to the trunk. "This will help even better." I pulled out the page that had the Decans circle on it with all of the priests' names. Then I pulled out a pen and handed it to Constance. "Your penmanship is better than mine. Can you record their gifts by each name? Oh, and take down their current names, too."

"My pleasure."

For the next ten minutes, everyone in the room listed his and her abilities, and they gave the abilities of the other priests. Constance wrote down all that she could, including a couple of other Protectors' abilities.

"That's some list," declared Ricky. "I can't wait to see what they've remembered."

"If it's anything like the last timeline, we're going to have to act fast. Not much time to rehearse or practice."

Jabari inquired, "You mentioned something about another timeline in the Well. What's that all about?"

"I was really mad about the massive loss of life happening just to satiate the greed of the Order. So, Ricky"—I put my hand on his shoulder—"Baniti and I used our powers to try and fix everything without any of you getting hurt or killed."

Ricky pointed to the security team and burst, "You guys were amazing! You blew up the mainframe in less than a minute. We teleported in and jumped back out before anyone from the Order had a chance to react." The three men were shocked by what he'd said, and their eyes were as big as saucers.

"We did?" Gahiji scratched his head.

"Yes, Bes, you three were the definition of precision—truly awesome! The only bad part was that the *Tumaini Timeline* failed and we both died on the soul-catcher."

Mudads was horrified. "You died?!"

"Yes, but it was for a very good cause," I assured. "Then Ricky and I were pulled back to this timeline. And here we are."

"Back here?" Mudads pointed to the ground.

"This one seems to have the most chance for success. That's why the other one didn't stick, even though we wanted it to." I gazed around the group. "But the good thing about our incomplete mission is that we retrieved vital information."

Ehab raised a finger to get our attention. "What's the soul-catcher that you mentioned?"

"I'm getting to that. Some of you in the room already know that there's a reptilian spaceship orbiting the planet that has the capability of capturing the energy of the soul when a person dies."

Karim spat, "Yes, we already know this."

"I know, sorry, Karim." I could tell he was still hurting from his loss. "Well, in the *Tumaini Timeline*, I turned myself in to a policeman who works for the Order. I told him that I was the ancient Egyptian priest that they were looking for, so he took me to an Air Force base with a lot of UFO stuff. From there, I was teleported onto that very reptilian spaceship."

I paused for a moment. Before I could continue, Ted cracked snidely, "Well? We're waiting."

I smiled and went on, "The crossover of some events has been incredibly strong from that timeline to this one. And I'm betting that the soul-catcher ship is a strong crossover. If that's the case, then Ricky and I know how to get on that alien craft." I re-emphasized even louder, "Ricky and I know how to get on that alien craft!"

Constance reacted before the others could say anything, "You turned yourself over to the police in that timeline, too?"

"Yes, it's what any Protector would have done."

A number of them agreed, "Here, here!"

"See?" I kissed her on the cheek. "I was just doing the Protector thingy."

I addressed the group again, "And there's more… If the events are similar enough, then they haven't turned on the soul-catcher machine over the entire planet yet."

Zuberi sighed in relief, "That's good news."

"But," Ricky interjected, "we don't know for sure. The timelines could be changed enough by the people's actions."

"Right." I pointed to him. "We also have two more important pieces of information that need to be passed along. If we ever get into a tangle with a reptilian close up, we need to increase our shielding. Ricky and I both got hammered hard by them. That's how they were able to kill us. Their mental abilities can overpower a human's mind if they get a chance to focus before we do."

"That's good to know," acknowledged Asim. "What's the other part?"

"Again, this is based on strong crossovers between parallel timelines. The reptilian queen was on that ship. It's possible that it might already be there in this timeline to turn on the soul-catcher and start the mainframe program."

Umi boasted, "We'll be ready."

"That's the spirit," chimed Hanif.

I glanced at the two new brothers. "I might have something special for you guys." They both looked back at me inquisitively. "Your names don't have anything to do with strength, do they?"

Zuberi laughed, "Actually, yes. How did you know?"

"It was a hunch." My other Egyptian friends laughed with me.

Umi stated first, "My name means life, servant, and energy."

"Mine is *strong*," added Zuberi. His muscles were flexing uncontrollably.

"That doesn't surprise me one bit. I have something special in mind for you and Karim—if you're up to it?" Karim's head perked up.

He pointed at me with the tip of the cane. "What is it?"

"I'll tell you later. Best not to share this one just yet."

I quickly turned to Rehema. "And no reading my mind on this one, OK?"

"As you wish, Tumaini."

Mudads asked, "What's this *Tumaini Timeline* that you've talked about?"

"Do you remember all of those papyrus pieces?" I stopped myself from going on. "Of course you and Hanif remember all of the papyrus pieces." I motioned to the trunk. "It was one of the cards on the magic cross."

Gahiji piped in, "Magic cross? I've heard it mentioned from your phone calls, but I've never seen it."

"I think you should all see it now, don't you?" I walked over to the trunk and pulled out the two bags filled with papyrus pieces. Then I turned to Hanif and Mudads. "Have I ever thanked you for being so loyal to your mission?" They were both looking back humbly. "Without you two, none of this would have worked out this way. Thank you so very much."

"We are here to serve," bowed Mudads. He was smiling bigger than I'd ever seen him smile.

Rehema was squeezing Hanif from behind. "Like my brother shared, it was a pleasure to be of service, Tumaini."

After we all expressed our gratitude, I pulled open the bag with all of the unused pieces first. "You guys are going to be amazed at what happens with these magical pieces of wood." Some of the others put on gloves and helped me to arrange them on the counter nearest to the back of the store.

Hara came up beside me. "Can I help?"

"Of course, honey. Can you get me the paper from the trunk that has my notes on it for the cross?"

She whispered, "Are you going to let all of the pieces go into place?"

"Yes." She jumped up and down happily.

I turned to Ricky and Laura. "Would you lay the cross pieces down?"

Mudads was smiling, "Would you like some help with that?"

They both looked at me. "He's the expert at this. Let him put it together."

He lifted up the pieces that he knew and placed them precisely in each spot. When he got to the remaining cards, he commented, "I don't remember these. What do I do with them?"

"Do you want to see something cool?" I asked. Hara was ready to explode with excitement.

"Why are you looking at me that way?"

"Daddy, can I tell him?"

"Yes, child, please tell me." The entire room was watching Hara.

She walked behind the counter to stand beside him. "Daddy found this out about the cross. If you put the pieces in the wrong spots, they'll magically move to the right location."

"You mean, like this?" Hanif picked up one of the cards and put it in the open nine slot.

Hara was confused. "How come it didn't work?"

I stepped beside them. "Don't you remember, pumpkin? The cross has to be put together up to the point where the timelines are set. We need to fill the other holes and leave the last two blank."

"Oh yeah, duh!" She got a lot of laughs from the crowd.

"Mr. Mudads, can I put them down for you?"

"Yes, child, please do." He backed up so she could put them in.

"Any old spot, right, Daddy?"

"Any old spot—except for the last two. And let's mix them up, shall we?"

"Goody!" She used the tweezers and filled in two more spots. "Only one left."

Mudads, Rehema, and Hanif were especially curious, as they'd already seen the partial cross put together in the shop. I snickered, "Are you guys ready?"

Rehema was a little perplexed, "I don't understand. What's so special?"

"Show them, Hara. Put down the last card in the wrong spot."

With care, she let the last piece fall gently into the eleventh spot. Her eyes got big in anticipation. Then the glass began to vibrate and hummed like a wine glass being stroked. It started shaking on the hinges and bounced a little. The cards were jiggling and vibrating like an earthquake was erupting under each piece. Then the four cards flipped in the air—two of them crashing together—and they finally landed in the correct spots.

"Did you see, Mr. Mudads?! Did you see that?!" trumpeted Hara.

The main party in the room was stunned. Mudads exclaimed, "I've never seen them do that before! They came to life and moved all on their own."

I put my hand on his shoulder. "That's because you've probably never put them out of order, have you?"

"Well, no. I've always done what my father taught me. I've never made a mistake with them."

"Watch this… Ricky, Hara, come help me mix them all up." We rearranged all of the pieces and heard the glass vibrate and hum again. With more energy than before, the pieces jolted into the correct pattern and formed an eleven-piece cross.

Asim gave me a tiny head bow. "Tumaini, your magic is incredible!"

Ricky chirped, "I know. I remember him showing this idea to me in the sand when I was Baniti. It was ingenious."

Gahiji added, "It's still ingenious." He scratched his head. "I have vague memories of this, too. And there were scrolls, right?"

"Yes." I motioned to Ted and Constance. "Can you get those and bring them over, please?" I turned back to my Egyptian friends. "Like I said on the phone a few days ago, the scrolls came alive when I sang the magical songs. All of the—"

Jabari interrupted, "All of the golden letters appeared. I can see this just like you were writing them when you were Tumaini. Well, one of them at least. I wasn't there for the first five scrolls that you wrote, but I remember you singing a magical prayer song that hid the lettering."

"I remember now," Asim recalled. "You taught us these prayer songs, and we passed those down to the local farmers."

Hanif included, "And those were passed down through our families until Tumaini was reunited with them again."

"This is so exciting," expressed Rehema.

Ted pointed to the table. "Look!" The same three pieces of papyrus started moving toward the number twelve spot.

Umi stared at the magic cross. "What do all of these pieces mean?"

"This is awesome." Ricky went on to explain, "Tumaini time traveled into the future to learn how to hide a picture in a picture. Each of these cards has a picture of the current timeline behind it." He pointed to the large group of loose papyrus. "And these are potential futures, or events that won't happen in this timeline because another event took its place. We told all of you this when you took the vow as priests to come back to this timeline. You just haven't remembered all of the details yet. Heck, I'm still remembering!" They laughed with him.

Constance and Ted returned with the scrolls and set them on the counter. "Ah, good. These are most important." I opened the God Scroll and laid it flat. I used some of the bottles to hold down the edges, just like I'd done weeks ago. "When I held these after the words had reappeared, I started channeling these godly instructions to help solve the world's problems."

"My word!" gasped Rehema.

I laughed, "I don't think it was my words. But they were incredibly inspiring messages."

Laura added, "Isn't that the truth."

"No matter what," I emphasized, "these scrolls have to be kept safe. They are the answer to a lot of the world's problems."

Karim stopped sanding Ramla's cane. "But what happens if something happens to you? Won't they be useless?"

"Great question. It turns out that Ricky can also channel this information. He just held the scroll and let the words come out." I looked at the other priests. "And if I'm right, I'll bet that any of you can do it, too."

I pointed to the cross a few times to get everyone's attention. "We have to refocus on this for the moment. This is an important key to the scrolls' success. If we fail here, nothing else matters." I picked up my notes and read out each event to match the corresponding card. "This timeline's events have perfectly matched up with these eleven cards. There have been no errors up to this point." I motioned to the three new pieces of papyrus. "We've also seen that this card is another picture of a planet exploding, which I'm assuming is Earth, but we had to leave town before we could make out the last two options for the twelfth slot. Whatever these are will be our next possible future."

Zuberi nodded once to Ricky. "You weren't kidding when you said it was awesome."

"What I'd like for you to do is to use the gloves and tweezers to learn how to see beyond the geometric figures. Once you've done it the first time, you can do it again. Then we can all look at these last two cards and see if the images can be seen or not."

"Why can't they be seen now?" asked Asim. "I don't remember this as much as I'd like from old Egypt."

Constance answered him, "It's because there have to be enough events happening in the present that will unlock the possible futures."

"Great job, honey. Expertly said."

"That makes sense," he replied. "Thanks, Constance."

"Alright, practice with the pieces on the cross, and let's help the future."

It didn't take long for everyone to begin seeing images. Most of them were shouting out things like "I can see it!" and "I got it!"

Ehab was the first to get one of the two pieces. "It's a picture of these two." He pointed to the number nine and eleven cards. "There's a mainframe on the right, a soul-catcher on the left, and a number of human stick figures underneath in handcuffs."

Ted gulped, and Ricky proposed, "I'm guessing that this one is the bad news card that Laura felt."

She put her hand near it and jerked it back. "Yup, that's the one."

Laura motioned to the card. "If this is the bad one, let me see if I can figure out the good one."

"Are you sure it's a good one?" questioned Karim.

"It feels good to me." She spent less than a minute on it. "I've figured it out. It's the exact same picture as the one Ehab described. But this is cool…"

"What?" begged Constance. We all gathered around her. "Isn't that a bad news card again?"

Laura answered, "I can see the soul-catcher crossed out and the mainframe crossed out. This must be the victory card."

"Or," I added, "at least a potential future for victory."

Constance glanced toward me. "Can't you use your magic on this one and make it stick?"

I laughed, "I wish we could, but our group's actions and thoughts will be the magic that decides if it will be triumphant or not."

Ricky spoke in Baniti's voice, "It is wise of Tumaini to speak the words of truth. We, alone, can no longer force the future for all. But together, we, the Protectors of Souls, can bring hope to the people of the land once again."

The group loved hearing Baniti's voice. Umi beamed, "Master Baniti, you've returned."

He shook his head briskly, "Whoa! That's a trip. I don't know if I'll ever get used to that."

Ted slapped him on the back. "Welcome back, Ricky." He moved his shoulder to wash off the sting. "You'll always be Ricky to me."

I was recording the papyrus information on my notes when Mudads and Hanif approached me. "Michael, we've made arrangements for an early dinner and for all of you to be amongst the other priests and Protectors."

"Great. I can't wait to see them all again. Where are we meeting?"

Hanif explained, "Because of the curfew, we are meeting outside of town, deep in the desert."

"We'll be staying there overnight until curfew is lifted again"—Mudads looked at me for approval—"if that's OK with your plans?"

"Are all of the remaining priests going to be there?"

"Yes," he replied. "The deserts aren't being patrolled. It will give us the freedom to reacquaint ourselves with everyone and for you to divulge your plan well after dark."

"It sounds like a great idea. I was wondering how we were going to do this under the current circumstances."

Hanif checked his watch. "It will be nightfall in a few hours. We need to leave in less than thirty minutes so we can get there by dinner."

"Everyone, get your backpacks and gear ready." I looked back to Hanif and Mudads. "Hey, guys"—I motioned to the papyrus and scrolls—"will this be safe here?"

"Of course," Hanif laughed. "No one is looting perfume stores. I have some silk cloth upstairs. We'll put it over the pieces, and then I'll cover it with a piece of plywood. It will be safe."

Mudads called Gahiji, Jabari, Asim, and Ehab in closer. "Our security team—" He turned to me. "That's what you called them, right?" I nodded. "—well, they made the arrangements for us, so let's have them tell everyone what's going on."

Jabari called everyone over, "Hello, folks. We are going to dinner in the desert shortly. We will be meeting the other priests and Protectors at their tents." Hara, Constance, and Laura got excited. "To keep us safe, we will be taking two security trucks to the camel roads. That will hide the fact that we are transporting Americans." Ted gave him a thumbs up. "Once we get to the path, we will leave the trucks about a mile into the desert. Our contacts will meet us there with our second form of transportation."

Ricky raised his hand. "What form of transportation?"

He continued with a half smile, "If one is going to the camel roads, it would seem that we might be riding"—he paused for a moment—"camels." He looked for Hara's reaction.

She gasped with her hand over her mouth. Then she burst, "Camels?!"

Gahiji grinned, "Yes, Hara. Would you like to ride a camel?"

"Would I?!"

"Wonderful, then. We'll leave in…" He looked to Hanif, Mudads, and me.

Mudads said, "We'll leave in thirty minutes. That will give everyone plenty of time to freshen up, use the facilities, and take care of any last-minute arrangements."

Laura turned to Constance, Ted, and Hara. "This is going to be exciting." They all were smiling. "I've never been on a camel before."

Hara joked, "Be careful. They spit like boys."

I smiled at her, "Good girl."

Hanif called to Rehema,"Would you help me get the silk covers from upstairs?"

"Of course." They both walked away.

"Hey, Asim," I asked, "what about the Protectors who were at the Necropolis? Will they be joining us?"

"Absolutely. Just before going down in the tunnel, I gave them the hand signal to meet us at the second rendezvous point."

"Second rendezvous point?"

"Yes!" He was nodding with a big smile. "You'll like this. As you've heard, we are going to the tent city." He paused because I had a questioning look on my face. "I'm sorry, let me explain better. We are going to the ancient temple site where we all learned our skills so many years ago under Baniti's and the other masters' guidance. It's not there anymore—the columns and buildings—but we've been gathering there recently to practice everything that we have remembered. We are going back home." He knew I would get it in a second. "It's not just any tent city, Tumaini. It's the tent city of the Protectors of Souls. Our temple grounds—our home!"

"Awesome!"

Gahiji came up and put his hands on both of our shoulders and said in Bes' voice, "Come on, guys. I'm hungry."

"Home!" I reminisced. "Home!"

CHAPTER FORTY-ONE

THE PLAN

Gahiji and Jabari drove their trucks deep into the desert as planned. The extraordinarily tall sand dune was a marker to let them know they were close. Once they made their way safely down the steep slope, both jeeps pulled behind a smaller sand dune and parked. After looking around to secure the location, the brothers went to the rear and opened the back doors. Ehab, Asim, Zuberi, and Umi accompanied them and formed a protective perimeter.

"We're here, everybody." Jabari held out his hand to help everyone. "It's safe to come out."

Ted and Ricky were the first to crawl through. Ted groaned, "Boy am I glad to stand up again." He arched his back to straighten his spine.

Ricky did the same thing. "A little cramped back there."

Ehab laughed, "Next time, we'll take the bus with all of the windows that show your faces really well. But for this trip, we thought it was best not to get shot at."

"Good point," smirked Ted.

Mudads and Hanif were the last ones to exit. As their feet touched the sand, we saw a small caravan of camels approaching over the next mound.

Laura asked, "How did they know to meet us here?"

Without missing a beat, Rehema tapped her temple and chimed, "I called them."

"I should have known." She put her hand on her arm. "Would you teach me how to do that, even though I'm not a priest?"

Rehema pulled her in for a hug. "It would be my pleasure."

"Look, Hara"—I got her to glance up the hill—"here's our next ride."

"They're cool, Daddy."

Rehema asked Constance, "Can Hara ride with me? I have a story that I would like to share with her."

"Of course. I'd like to hear the story, too."

Karim walked up to our party. "These are our camels—well, part of the herd, at least." He got us to start moving toward them. "One of the Protectors who does tours around the pyramids owns them. He brought a few out here to shuttle us to the tent city."

"That was awfully nice of him," commented Constance. "Please pass along our gratitude."

He nodded with a smile. Then he asked Hara, "Do you have a favorite?"

"I like that one, Mr. Karim, the one with the red blanket."

"Then that's the one you should ride. It's the nicest female we have."

"Can I call her Fluffy?"

"Of course you can."

"Hello, Fluffy!"

I walked up and gave him my gratitude, "That was very nice of you, Karim, thanks."

"It is my honor to serve." After his bow, he asked, "Have you finished devising your plan?"

"All but one part. When we get to the tent city, there's something that I want Rehema to do for me. Then I'll be able to give out assignments."

"I know that Ramla said to trust you, but do you know what you are doing?"

I laughed a little, "Thanks for the vote of confidence, Karim. I'll tell you this: I know the objectives, and I have an idea for how to neutralize the soul-catcher and the mainframe. Our priests, with all of their abilities, can do the job. I just hope that no one gets hurt."

"But we have been hurt." He slapped Ramla's cane in his hand.

I put my hand on his shoulder. "I know your pain, and it will heal in this lifetime. I'm sure of it."

"How did you…how did you know to say that?"

"What?"

"Ramla said the same thing to me the day she died."

"I have this feeling, is all. I know you have been sad for a while. I even remember this when you were a priest. But you will fulfill your vow, and you will be able to rest."

He sighed, "I've remembered bits and pieces from my past. You were always kind to me in the priesthood, and I haven't always been the nicest to you in return." He put his hand on the back of his head and rubbed it in a circular motion. "I don't know why, either. Maybe it's part of my personality. But I will change, I promise you."

"Thanks, Karim. I'm just glad you're here."

Hara's camel made a loud growl as it began to stand. "Daddy, did you hear that?" She was giggling hard. Rehema was holding on to her tightly as the camel's front legs straightened up.

"Hara, your voice has changed," I snickered. "You be nice to that camel, pumpkin."

"I didn't do anything," she laughed. Her camel lifted its head and growled one more time. "Easy, Fluffy." She petted the side of its neck.

Before I got up on my camel, the security team came up to me carrying two black wooden boxes with rope handles. Asim informed us, "It's the C4. We're going to take this to the camp."

Ricky put his hand on Asim's backpack. "I remember this from—"

"The other timeline," I finished for him. The four men were staring at us. "I'll tell you more of the details on the way, and we'll be needing that for sure. Do you have the detonators?"

Gahiji turned around to show us his backpack. "They're in here. How did you know to ask?"

"Let's just say that we had a successful dry run in the *Tumaini Timeline*."

Ricky grimaced, "Well, your part was successful."

"The fact that you are here means that you were successful, too. You could still be dead," added Gahiji.

Rehema projected in our heads, "Good way to think about the positive." We all turned to her quickly and smiled. She just sat there behind Hara with a huge grin.

I responded telepathically, "I'll need your special skill when we get to the camp."

"As you wish, my friend."

With the women all on their camels, the men followed suit and were lifted high into the air. More camel growls blasted in the desert.

Gahiji got his brother's attention and pointed to the far right. Jabari grinned at me, "He always likes to keep watch from a distance."

"I know what you mean. He did the same thing when we first met in Luxor." I looked in his direction and nodded. "You'll miss your success story from the other timeline."

As he was riding off, he yelled, "I'll write a new one in this timeline!"

During our long, wobbly camel trip, Rehema kept Constance, Laura, and Hara deeply engrossed with her tale about the magic priests of old. Ricky and I had most of the other men's ears with details from the previous timeline's mission, including the relearning of our current abilities. Hanif and Mudads also shared accounts of the priests' skills and how they had spontaneously remembered parts of their past.

Gahiji was on top of a dune ahead of our group. He made some hand motions and began galloping our way. In less than a minute, he pulled up beside us. "I saw the tents. They are just around this hill."

Ted grumbled, "It's about time. My butt hurts."

Our camels rounded the turn at a steady pace. From a distance, we saw a dozen tents pitched in a circle. Some were extremely ornate, with golden, yellow, and black felt tapestries which formed large box-styled tents. Jutting out from the fronts were longer tapestries that created covered porch settings. The box-shaped tents were a good twenty-five by twenty-five feet in dimension. Three of the other tents were the traditional circular, brownish-grey Bedouin tents. And the last remaining tent was an open-styled tent with four wooden posts at the borders and one taller post in the middle. The edges of the purple fabric had golden tassels all the way around, and the sandy floor was covered with carpets, pillows, and a fireplace near the center.

As we came forward, a number of the priests ran up to meet us. Many of them were dressed in comfortable, touristy clothes. "Baniti," I said exuberantly, "it's our old friends."

"That, they are."

I laughed, "And you wouldn't know it by the looks of them."

"Or us," he laughed back.

Our reunion was overflowing with tears of joy. We hugged, embraced, admired how each of us looked in this lifetime, and hugged some more.

Hanif and Mudads were already halfway between the camels and the tents. Mudads waved to us to follow. "Dinner is waiting. We should go eat." Gahiji perked up.

Ehab caught my attention and held on to two of the camels' leads. "Go ahead. We'll gather the camels and join you in a minute." Zuberi, Umi, and Asim helped and led them to the holding area beside the tents.

"Oh my," remarked Laura while sniffing in the air. "Do you smell that? It smells wonderful!"

"That's not college cafeteria food," smirked Ted.

Constance added, "And it's not the camels, either." Hara laughed at her joke. "Dinner smells divine."

We had just reached the circle of tents. I stood between Mudads and Hanif. "I thought we were meeting all of the Protectors, too. Where are they?"

Rehema was smiling really big. Mudads replied comically, "What?" He motioned to the tents with both arms outstretched. "Don't you think they could all be in there? You guys have some pretty powerful magic, you know."

Ricky and I looked at each other. He scoffed a little, "You're pulling my leg. We don't know how to—"

Hanif and Mudads interrupted him and started laughing. Hanif gave his familiar *come here* motion and walked through the tent circle and exited the other side. We all followed like little lost goats chasing their herder to get to the watering hole.

Hanif's feet stopped abruptly at the edge of a cliff, and he turned to us. We ended up in a straight line facing directly at him. "Look down here." He pointed below to the valley. Our bodies bent forward to peer down. What we saw was hundreds upon hundreds of colorful tents covering the desert floor as far as the eye could see, with fires glowing in strategic spots. It was reminiscent of a scene from an ancient battle, and our army of soul protectors was down below. We were witness to thousands of loving people deeply engaged in helping their brothers and sisters inside the valley.

"These are our Protectors," he acclaimed. We stood there speechless, with our mouths gaping wide open. Mudads and Hanif knew we were all stunned by the vast number of people.

Rehema broke the silence, "Do you remember me telling you a good while back that droves of people were joining the Protectors? Once word got out about the Order's plans to enslave the Earth and what you were doing to help, they all started taking the vow to protect those who can't protect themselves. It just kept growing and growing. It's wonderful, isn't it?"

I struggled to speak, "That's…that's incredible. I don't know what to say."

Mudads put his hand on my shoulder. "After dinner, we are going down to address the group. They'll want to hear from you."

"No pressure, huh?" I said meekly.

Ricky bent over farther and looked across the line. "You've got this, Tumaini."

"Come on, folks," directed Mudads, "time to go eat."

I pulled Rehema aside. "Do you mind if I ask you something? We can let them eat first."

"Not one bit. I've been waiting for you to ask for my help." She walked toward the open-walled tent. "Will this do?"

"Perfect." We sat down near the roaring fire.

"You've gotten nervous all of the sudden, Tumaini. What's wrong?" She grabbed my hand. "Your mind is all scrambled. I can hear it. Relax."

After a few seconds, I shared, "I still have this one fear dangling at the back of my brain. I'm actually surprised that it resurfaced so fast."

"It's the same fear that Ricky was thinking about during our camel ride."

"You know about his same fear?"

"His thoughts were dwelling on it, and now yours are, too." She leaned over and put her hand on my knee. "You're afraid that you won't live up to your previous self's name."

"It's more than that. They're all counting on me for this plan, and I know we can do it, but—"

Rehema interrupted me, "Michael—Tumaini—do you remember what I told you a few weeks back in your hotel room?"

"Can I ask for a refresher course on that?"

"We were all sitting together, and you were wearing your worry on your shirtsleeve. When you and I had a chance to speak back then, I told you—"

"I'm starting to remember."

"Good… I told you that you only have one mission for this lifetime. And so far, from what I've seen, you've been doing an amazingly good job at it." I was nodding along while she talked. "Tumaini, whether we succeed or fail, whether we live or die from this mission, is not up to you—not one bit." She shook my knee. "Not one bit! We all have our own part in this endeavor. And you, my dear old friend, only have one job.

"Do you remember what I said?" My head was down at that point, and I partially raised it to look at her. "I said to you, 'Michael, if you are Tumaini, do you know what that means?'"

I was smiling more because I remembered this conversation better. I played the past with her and asked, "What does it mean, Rehema?"

She smiled back, "Tumaini just means—"

We both answered together, "Hope!"

"Well done, savior boy." I laughed hard with her.

"Is this all you wanted of me?"

"You already know that isn't it." I stood up and took a few steps. "I hate asking this because it could put you in danger."

"We're in danger if I don't do anything." She stood up with me and showed her stern motherly side. "Let me decide if it's too much." Then she had me sit back down again. "Out with it, then. I want to know if I'm picking up the right thoughts from you."

"OK. What I want you to do is to listen in on the reptilian commander's mind. I need to know what is happening on that ship. They are controlling everything from behind the scenes. If it's giving special commands, we need to know so we can act."

"How does that put me in danger?"

"From my short experience with them, it seems that their mental capabilities are pretty strong. I don't want the reptilian to discover who you are from your telepathic link."

"That risk is not for you to decide, Tumaini. And if it helps our cause, the risk is well worth it."

"You are a brave one, Rehema."

She patted my knee one more time. "So are you. Let me see if I can zero in on this spaceship and scan for any thought patterns." She closed her eyes and went into a meditative state. A good minute went by, and then she gasped in horror, "Mdaaaaaaah!"

"What is it?!"

Her eyes looked like she'd just seen a ghost. "This beast is evil. I could feel its anger and hatred when I read its thoughts. It was ghastly."

I was just about to ask if she was alright, when she continued, "I'm fine. It just caught me by surprise. These reptilians really hate us."

671

"Did you hear anything important?"

"Give me a moment. I need to go back and listen again. I think I can pick up thoughts from its past. There was something about the assassin."

"I'll be right here for you."

She closed her eyes again. I could tell immediately when she connected with the reptilian because her body shuddered. "I can feel it. It's horrible in that mind—so much cruelty and carnage. But its thoughts…it's saying, 'Hsssss. Priest is in Egypt. Can feel its energy some. Send the assassin to kill him once and for all. Hsssss.'"

She opened her eyes. "There's a human with him. Some type of military officer. That's who it was speaking to."

"Can you read his mind?"

"Let me try." Her eyes scrunched this time. "He's easier to read. He's… he's…he's acknowledging the command. It was given less than an hour ago. He's thinking about his rewards."

"Anything else?"

"He doesn't know where to send the assassin. Your signal isn't strong enough to pinpoint."

"Excellent. This will work out perfectly."

"How?"

"I'm going to lure him away from this area. We can't let him learn about this place by searching for me."

"What are you going to do?"

I put my hand on my head and scratched my scalp. "My timetable's just been moved up drastically. I was hoping to start everything in a day or two, but I think what you've just told me has given us the edge."

"Michael?"

"Trust me." I stood up, and so did she. "Do you think that you can keep me informed about any new instructions from either of them?"

"I'll do my best."

"And your best has always been good enough. Shall we go eat?"

"Let's." She put her arm in mine and we walked over together. Hanif and Mudads were at the end of the food line, and I escorted her to her husband.

"Did you get him all straightened out?" laughed Hanif.

Before she could speak, I grinned, "She's an awesome therapist. And we didn't even use the full hour."

"Would you like some food, Michael?" asked Mudads.

"I'd love some. Can you fix me a plate? I need to go talk with those guys." I pointed to the security team.

"I'll bring it right over."

I sat on one of the pillows with the enhanced security team. "Guys, my plans have been moved up. I just found out that the assassin is looking for me again, and we can't risk him finding me here. That would lead the entire Order to destroy this place. We've got to act in the next hour or two."

Karim put his fork on his plate and placed his hand on Ramla's cane. "What do you want me to do?"

"You're going to be one of my team leaders." That made him smile.

"Hold on, let me get Ricky over here." I got his attention, and he walked to our meeting with his dinner plate.

"What's up?"

"The assassin is looking for me. I have a plan."

"Well, don't keep it to yourself."

"We have to get as far away from here as we can, but still stay in Egypt."

Asim stated, "That would be Alexandria or Abu Simbel."

"Hmmm. Alexandria would be too crowded, and the curfew is going to take effect in about three hours."

Ehab pointed out, "Abu Simbel would work perfectly because there won't be anyone there. I heard on the way over that all of the tourist sites are now closed and the soldiers are no longer protecting the sites."

"They aren't?" asked Ricky.

"No," affirmed Jabari. "All of the soldiers are now being used to block off the major cities after tonight's curfew. The temple priests are abandoning the ruins as we speak."

"Abu Simbel it is, then." I gestured. "How soon can you guys be ready to leave?"

Gahiji inquired, "What do you need us to bring?"

"How many of those special backpacks can you guys make up with the C4 that you brought?"

"Six at least, maybe seven. We can be ready in two hours."

"Good." I looked to Karim, Zuberi, and Umi. "Are you guys up for a special assignment?" All three of them nodded. "To make this work, we are going to teleport the original security team, plus you three, to Abu Simbel."

I glanced over at Ehab. "You, my friend, have to stay here."

"What am I going to do here, Tumaini?"

"You know the priests' abilities pretty well, don't you?"

"Yes, rather well, actually. Call it *a gift*." I laughed because that's what his name meant.

"Then I want you to be the team leader at this location. You'll put ten of the best priests on a special assignment." I leaned over and whispered to him, "I'll tell you about that one after I'm done here." I readdressed the group again. "The others will be working with the Protectors down below. It will be up to you to decide who is best for each job."

"I can do that."

"What about the mainframe and soul-catcher?" asked Jabari.

"I was getting to that. After we show you how to teleport once, you'll be able to do it again on your own. Jabari, you can do it already because we both teleported from the Well to the tunnel." He gave an understanding nod.

"This feels like déjà vu," commented Gahiji.

Ricky said to him, "We've done this before"—he tilted his head to the left twice—"other timeline."

"Got it." He winked.

I continued, "After we teleport to the temples down south, we'll stay there until the assassin shows. I'm going to lift my protective shield so I can be located. I'll do something to create an energy spike. Then the security team will go directly to the mainframe and take it out."

"We just got the latest intel on the location," informed Asim. "It's just like the seers told us before."

Ricky made a circular motion with his finger. "Something to do with that Fibonacci spiral, right?"

"That's affirmative."

"Good," I concluded. "Then this won't be much of a surprise. You guys are going to be awesome." They gave looks of confidence to each other. "When you're done at the mainframe, you'll teleport back here and wait for Ricky and me to call you."

"Roger," all three nodded once.

Ehab raised his hand. "What about your family and friends?"

"I'm sending Rehema, Hanif, Mudads, my friends, and my family back to the shop. They'll be working on the magic cross and sending me updates." I turned to the brothers. "Can Hanif and Mudads take your jeeps?"

"Of course." Jabari started digging for his keys. "But you don't want to wait too long. They have to get in before they barricade the city."

"Rehema can help them avoid any danger by reading the soldiers' thoughts."

Karim was patting Ramla's cane in his hand. "Good plan so far. What else?"

Ricky caught my attention by tapping between his eyebrows. "We need to do this."

"I know. Before we set off, Ricky and I are going to give each of you an energy boost."

He was laughing, "When Tumaini did this for me in Laura's shop, he blew out all of the light bulbs. We'd better make sure we strengthen the shield in this area so the Order won't pick up any energy spikes."

"Yeah, or the black helicopters and drones will arrive to spy on us," added Asim.

"I'm telling you guys, after Tumaini's—" He turned to me. "What did you call it? Shaktipat?" I nodded my head *yes*. "—my powers were intensified a thousandfold. I felt like I was hooked up to a turbine generator. I could fire lightning bolts."

"We saw Ramla do this for Tumaini when he was here," mentioned Karim. "It is powerful. She said that you would do this for us when you returned."

Zuberi and Umi were quiet during the entire conversation. I checked on them, "Do you guys have any questions?"

Umi replied, "We just remembered who we were three days ago and got into Cairo the other night. I'm barely catching up on everything."

Zuberi chimed in next, "Yeah, but we'll help any way that we can."

"You guys will be just fine. Your job will be to help me and Karim keep the assassin away from the main group." Both brothers gave me an affirmative nod. "When you are done there, I'd like you to teleport to Hanif's shop."

Mudads was standing off to the side patiently. He approached with a plate of food. "I hope I'm not interrupting."

"Not one bit. I was just telling the guys about part of the plan. Once everyone is done eating, I'm going to share it with all of the priests."

"I'm sure they are all anxious to help."

I carried my plate over to my backpack and pulled out an envelope. Then I called for Ehab and Rehema. When he stepped up, I informed him, "I have something special for your group of ten priests." I sat down with him to talk, and Rehema showed up. "Hold on for a second. I need to ask

Rehema something first."

"What is it?" she asked.

"I know you can hear others' thoughts. Can you also send a message and mask it so it won't appear like it's coming from you?"

"I think I can."

"Good. I want you to send a thought to the military commander on the spaceship that I'm in Abu Simbel. We need the assassin to travel there as quickly as possible."

"I could have him think of a military jet or helicopter for transport. They are the only ones flying right now."

Ehab pointed out, "A helicopter would get him there the fastest from the Simbel airport."

"Great suggestion. Send that. Put him on a military jet and get him to the airport, quick. Then have him chopper in." Rehema walked away to focus on her assignment.

"OK, Ehab, here's what I want you to do..."

On the soul-catcher, the reptilian queen's transport had just landed inside the docking platform. A squadron of reptilians and a small detachment of human military personnel were there to greet it. As the queen's feet stomped down the shuttle's ramp, all in attendance snapped to attention.

The queen stood four feet taller than the reptilian commander and resembled an ominous black dragon. Its long, leathery wings were tucked behind it, and its spiked tail dragged on the ground. When it opened its elongated snout to speak, rows of dagger-like teeth were set apart by four pairs of tiered fangs on the top and bottom jaws. They glistened from the spotlights in the bay.

"Hssssss. Report," is all it said.

The commander stepped forward. "Hssssss. Mainframe will be fully ready for the entire planet in less than twenty-four hours. The new soul-catcher is awaiting your command."

"Hssssss. I must feast first. Bring me one of them." It lifted its claw and pointed toward the humans. The commander gave the order to bring the offering.

Two reptilians were dragging a tall man out onto the platform. He was screaming at the top of his lungs, "It's not my fault! I didn't know he could do that!" When Officer Dunse saw the reptilian queen, he froze in horror. The queen, commander, and rows of reptilians were all breathing in his fear and snarling. The queen made a low-guttural noise to drink up more of his terror. It stomped forward as he screamed, "Nooooo!"

With one snap of its jaws, the queen bit off his head. It held his quivering body in its claws and tipped him upside down to drain all of Dunse's blood into its mouth. When his life force stopped flowing, the queen flung his body aside like a ragdoll.

"Hsssss. Bridge now." The entire detachment turned and followed the beastly dragon onto the command center.

"Hsssss. Explain the machine," the queen demanded of the young officer in charge.

He stepped forward and explained, "It's an ingenious device, and it's a major upgrade from the etheric strands that you used in the past to capture a soul. As soon as it's turned on, the soul-catcher will send out a cascading particle beam toward the Earth. When the beam hits the planet's atmosphere, it will spread and create an energetic net around the entire surface. It's more like a funnel, really, and any departing energy source will be sent directly to this ship and collected."

Next, he picked up a small black cube. "Souls are pure energy, so the human souls will be separated and stored in these tiny black boxes made of *soulandrum*. No human soul can escape this metallic box unless it's opened by the master switch on this ship."

"Hsssss. Explain more."

"When the soul is ready to be reinstituted into the reptilians' new matrix on Earth, the soul will be released and attached to a human clone or a newly born baby. The bodies on Earth will already be implanted with the Order's nanobots to create a perfectly engineered slave race."

"Hsssss. Suffer they must."

"Their suffering will increase beyond measure. If the people think it's bad now, they'll think they are in a living hell when the Order's entire plan is instituted."

"Hsssss. Souls must not escape this particle beam. Some have powers."

"We've thought of that. Our mainframe has a program that will read each person's thoughts and history. When a person dies, his soul will immediately be met by images of relatives and friends. These fake images will guide the unsuspecting soul toward a false white light tunnel on the other side of the firmament. This false white light is the energy funnel that will take them directly to this ship."

"Hsssss. Memories they will have. Plan will fail. They will fight us in the new body. Hsssss."

"Forgive me, your highness, but that has also been taken care of. When the soul passes through the Earth's firmament, each soul's memories will be wiped clean by the negative energy field that's created by the funnel. It will be like placing a powerful magnet on a computer. The soul won't remember where it came from or where it is going." He stated this part with great pride, "And we can maintain this process until the soul has no more energy to survive. We figure that we can get at least four hundred to five hundred incarnations out of each soul. That's four to five hundred lifetimes of complete misery."

The reptilian commander gave a sadistic laugh, "Hsssss. We will feast and breed a new race of reptilians to rule from the skies. They will never know what has happened to them or why they suffer so much."

"Hsssss. Much fear and pain they will feel. Make sure of this."

"It's programmed into each person's mind control program. They will be docile, afraid, and compliant. Reinforcement signals will be sent through all new technologies on the planet."

"Hsssss. When can this begin?"

"The mainframe is running its final glitch-removal program right now and will be ready tomorrow. The soul-catcher is awaiting your command."

The reptilian queen gave a sadistic growl, "Hsssss. Command is given. Turn on the machine."

Two of the reptilians at the console looked to the commander. It nodded, and they turned to press a sequence of lights on the panel. On the viewscreen, the ship turned slightly to realign with the Earth in order to create a straight shot. As the soul-catcher was fed more energy from the fuel cells, the ship began to vibrate slightly. A high-pitched sound grew for eight seconds, and then a blasting pulse sound filled the bridge as a solid particle beam shot toward Earth.

———•◦•———

Mudads asked me, "Is it time to talk with the others in the valley?"

"First, I want to share the plan with all of the priests. Then we'll go down to the Protectors."

Vhhhwwwoooooooooooommm!!! The deafening sound filled the skies in all directions and was louder than any thunder blast we'd ever heard. Everyone's head looked up at once. A number of people in the tents were also startled by the sudden noise and dropped their plates.

Rehema came running over to me. "Michael! Michael! I just heard." Then she said a little softer so only the people around could hear, "They started the soul-catcher!"

"What?!"

Mudads and I ran outside, followed by a number of priests. We were all looking to the sky. Rehema pointed up and repeated again, "They've started the soul-catcher."

Constance and the others ran up to me and looked with us. Hara grabbed my hand. "What is it, Daddy?"

"It came from the UFO, pumpkin. It's not good."

Laura was scared. "What do we do?"

Ted chirped, "Don't die." He got a number of unpleasant looks. "OK, at least not until Tumaini and the others take it out."

"Alright," I stressed, "the first thing to do is *not* to panic. This was inevitable, and we knew it would happen."

The rest of the priests were now outside and looking with us. Ricky motioned upward. "Use your vision. I can see it."

Constance asked, "What do you see?"

"I can see it, too," I affirmed. A number of others could also pick it up with their inner sight.

He continued, "It looks like an energy field. It's pulsing everywhere and is covering the entire sky." He pointed to the north. "And it has a huge funnel over Egypt—like we are inside a massive teardrop looking out."

"I can see these beautiful spheres of light flowing in that direction," commented Asim. "They are flowing out into space. What are those?"

Rehema gasped, "Those…those…those are souls. " She buried her head into Hanif's chest. "How could they be so despicable?"

The viewscreen showed glowing orbs being drawn into the

energy-capturing appendage on the outside of the soul-catcher. The young officer reported, "It's working. We've just gathered the first round of souls."

The queen demanded, "Hsssss. What is capacity?"

"On average, around five to eight thousand people die every hour. With the current conditions, we expect that to be around ten thousand. A soul doesn't take much room, and this ship can easily hold up to five hundred thousand in these tiny boxes. When we initiate the mainframe tomorrow, we can start reinstituting the captured souls back onto Earth to feed your blood lust. From that point, we'll just keep the cycle going until we've exhausted every soul on Earth. Then we'll move on."

"Hsssss. Good! You will receive many rewards."

He broke face and smiled a little. Then he gave the hand signal. "All hail the Order!"

"Hsssss!"

I looked at the security team and pointed to outer space. "That's our last target."

Mudads informed me, "The Protectors down below are scared. We need to help them."

"I agree. You and Hanif go down to help. I'm going to give the plan to the priests and boost their energy. It won't take more than twenty minutes. Then we'll follow you down."

I called to Rehema, "Are you getting anything?"

"Give me a moment." She was still holding a hand on Hanif's chest. "Yes, the assassin has been sent down south. He's on the way, maybe two hours until he gets there." Then she held up her finger. "Wait!" Her hand was motionless. "There's a powerful presence on the ship—stronger than the reptilian commander. Its evil is beyond compare."

Ricky grimaced, "That's probably the queen. I can sense it, too."

"Mudads, Hanif, you guys go down below. Laura, Ted, Constance, after we are done talking with the Protectors, I'll need you to go with Rehema and those two back to Hanif's shop. We need you to keep working on the cross and send us information."

Both brothers walked toward the camels. Ted asked, "Are you sure you don't want me to help here?"

I leaned in closer. "I'd like you to help protect my family, please. Keep them safe."

"I'll do what I can. Consider me a Protector of Souls."

I put my hand on his shoulder. "You were already one of those before I met you."

"Thanks, Michael."

"You bet."

Laura came up and offered, "I can be of assistance."

"Actually, I need to ask you something." We walked away from the others, talked for a moment, and I wrote something down on a piece of paper.

"Is that all you need?"

"That'll be perfect. And can you help watch over the others back at the shop?"

"It's like Ted said, 'Consider me a Protector of Souls.'" I gave her a humble smile and a hug.

"Ricky, we need to get everyone gathered around."

Most of the priests were still in shock over the recent event. Some were pointing to the sky, while others were huddled in smaller groups talking.

Ricky motioned and yelled for them all to come closer, "Everyone, gather 'round!" The first few who came up sat down in front of us, while the others stood behind them. "You're on," and he moved to the side.

I stepped forward to address them. "My friends, my dear friends, I share your concern for the people of the world. I, too, have loved ones that I care for deeply and who are in the grasp of the Order's deadly jaws." I glanced over to Constance and Hara and then back to my friends. "And now is the time for you to fulfill your vow to help those in their direst of needs. Now is the time to revive your duty and your service. Now is the time to show that you truly are…the Protectors of Souls!" A number of them nodded with enthusiasm.

"When we fell to the pharaoh's guards so long ago, we suspended our souls in space for the purpose of reincarnating at the right time—the right time to come back as a group and help the world. Well, as you can see by their wicked actions, *now* is that time to help."

I pointed to the energy funnel. "There is an alien ship up there that is collecting souls for some evil purpose, and the Order has initiated the first phase of the mainframe which sent the world into a global financial disaster. Ricky and I have also seen these mind control nanobots that they've been spraying on everyone through the chemtrails. When they start the final phase of the mainframe, the people of the world will be completely helpless to their will. They will become mindless zombies to the Order and feed the insatiable hunger of the reptilians and other evil aliens.

"I tell you, we have the ability to stop them. We have the powers to turn the tides. And we can use all of our effort and strength to take back that which was wrongfully taken from all of the people so many millennia ago. We, the Protectors of Souls, will give freedom back to the people of the land. We will give their souls a chance again. We will free all of the people of Earth!" A number of them clapped and cheered.

"I know that you've been wondering about my plan. I've already spoken with a few of you and assigned team leaders to complete specific tasks." I held my hand out toward Karim. "Your team, Ricky, and I are going to Abu Simbel to lead the assassin away from this location. Jabari and his team are in charge of taking out the mainframe. Another designated group will take out the soul-catcher device." I looked to Ehab. "And Ehab has two special assignments. Based upon your abilities, he will split the rest of you into two groups."

Asim raised his hand. "What about the Protectors down in the valley?"

"That's what one of Ehab's groups will focus on. We will have that group lead all of the Protectors in the valley in the healing songs. They'll focus their intent on different spots all over the world. The entire globe will be covered by our magical, healing energy. Maybe, just maybe, this will give the people enough of a fighting chance—and a way to find their own strength—to stand up to the Order's military and police forces."

"What about—?" asked Karim.

I interrupted before he could finish, "I'm sorry, Karim. Ehab already knows his other assignment and will tell that group what to do." I read-dressed the priests. "What we have to do next is to boost each one of your energy systems. When we do this, you will be able to fully embrace and utilize your personal powers. Ricky and I will touch each one of you on the forehead and give you shaktipat." A number of them turned to their neighbors and expressed excitement.

"Your team leaders will fill you in on the rest of the details. Are there any other questions?" No one raised his hand. "Excellent. My brothers, my sisters, thank you for your vow and for your efforts to continue the tradition of the Protectors of Souls. If you'll come forward, Ricky and I have a treat for you."

I leaned over to Ricky. "Before we start, we need to strengthen the shielding over this valley."

"Agreed." We both held hands, closed our eyes, and placed more energy over our beloved group.

One by one, the priests came forward. With each person that I touched, the power and energy increased through me a hundredfold. By the time I touched my seventh person, I could barely keep the energy from tearing my body apart, and that person fell backwards. He blurted, "Wow! What a rush!" When he stood up, his upward motion lifted him off of the ground. He levitated for a few seconds and landed safely.

Ricky was completely astonished. "What's going on, Tumaini?!" The other priests gathered around to hear.

I looked down at both of my palms in amazement and with a little worry. "Ricky, I was getting visions and feelings of the initial Creative Force. I was feeling what I can only describe as Source Energy flowing through me. I was actually losing myself to it. The power was incredible. It felt like there wasn't anything that I couldn't do."

Laura was watching and spoke up, "I know what's going on. I mentioned this to you a few days ago. You have opened your energy system up so much that you are touching into the All That Is. You've found the way to touch the Fabric of all Energy, the very Source of Creation."

Ricky stepped in front of me and bowed a little. "Do it. Do it again."

I placed my entire hand over his brow. The brightest and warmest light flowed through me and filled Ricky's entire body. He actually looked like a human light bulb.

"Holy cow! I've never felt such power before." He looked at the others. "Everyone that I've touched, you need to have him do this to you." They nodded and lined up.

"Can you handle it?" he asked.

Even though my feet were planted firmly on the ground, my body was spiraling in the air uncontrollably from the powerful force. "I think so. When I did it to you, I lost consciousness for a moment. It's pure energy."

For the next few minutes, I finished transferring power to all but one of the priests. The last one standing in front of me was Rehema. As I placed my hand on her, Aurora lights glowed from her body and remained there even after I removed my hand. Then I fell to the ground in exhaustion.

When I regained consciousness, I mumbled, "Where am I?"

Rehema touched my shoulder. "Are you OK?"

Karim added, "You're with us. Thank you for this gift." A number of others were expressing their gratitude.

"Tumaini, are you OK?" she asked again. "Can you stand?"

I got up and looked at my hands once more. "I…I…almost merged with this power, this energy. I don't know if I can describe it."

Asim stepped forward. "You were glowing, just like Ricky and Rehema."

Laura still had both hands in front of her mouth. "I've never seen anything like this. You really touched Source."

I laughed just a little, "Yeah, and if I'd held on any longer, I don't think I would be here."

"What do you mean?"

"I think I would have lost all individuality. I think I would have merged with the Infinite Power and become One."

She gasped, "Oh my!" A number of others did the same thing. "Would you do it for me, please? Can you give me an energy boost?"

Rehema got her attention. "He needs his rest. Let me help you." She looked to me for confirmation. I nodded, and she pronounced, "Receive that which was always and rightfully yours."

She placed her finger between Laura's eyebrows. Her body shuddered uncontrollably for a few seconds as the energy flowed in and filled her soul. Then Laura fell to the ground in supplication. "Do not kneel to me, my dear friend. This is your gift returning back to yourself. Please stand and be amongst your friends."

Laura stood back up and breathed deeply. "I can feel things that I've never felt before." She raised her hand and touched the air out in front of her face. "This is amazing. I can actually see the energy waves in the air." Then she held up her hands with her palms facing together. She focused, and we could all see bright lightning bolts sparking between them."

Ricky spoke in Baniti's voice, "You have done the work, and now you have graduated with honors. Use this gift wisely."

I added in Tumaini's voice, "It is our blessing to have witnessed a rebirth of your spirit. Please pass along your knowledge to those who might ask."

She bowed to both of us. "It is my honor to serve."

I looked over toward Ted and Constance. Ted joked, "Don't look at me. I haven't done the work yet."

Constance whispered in my ear, "When my time comes, I'll know. But it's not today."

Baniti's voice came next, "You are wise to know where your growth level is. When you are ready to receive, it will come to you in many blessed ways." Then he shook his head and said as Ricky, "And I will help you both," he laughed, "whether I'm Ricky or Baniti."

I ribbed in my own voice, "Does this mean we have multiple personalities?" We all laughed together.

Gahiji pointed toward the valley. "They're waiting down below."

"Yes, we need to see all of the Protectors and tell them our mission. It's time to act."

Ehab came over and informed me, "I have already chosen my two groups and given them their tasks."

"Excellent. I'd like for you to talk to the Protectors and take charge here. As soon as we are ready, I need to send Mudads and the gang back to the shop and the other teams to their locations."

"It will be done." Then we all made our way down the steep hill.

———◆———

By the time we arrived, Mudads and Hanif had already gathered all of the Protectors into a central location. As we walked toward the front of the group, we heard some of them say, "The priests are here. The priests are here."

Mudads called to them, "Please, everyone, please have a seat!" After the commotion had settled down, we all humbly bowed to the group.

Ehab stepped forward and addressed the crowd, "My friends, as you have heard from the sky, we do not have much time. The Order has started their hideous device and has already begun taking innocent souls from the Earth. Tumaini"—he pointed to me, I nodded, and then he returned his focus to the large group and continued—"Tumaini has asked me to unite all of the Protectors in the valley to help the people of the world. With our combined intentions, we can send an energy field around the planet that will help heal and protect the rest of humanity. While we do this, a number of other priests will take out that dastardly machine and their menacing mainframe. I ask you, my friends, fellow Protectors, will you help me?!" A loud roar of applause and confirmation filled the valley.

He pointed to the priests who would be staying with them. "My friends here will guide you in our healing songs. They are very easy to learn and sing. I would like for each of you to pick a unique spot on the globe to send your song. Just follow your intuition and send it with confidence that you have chosen the best location. Will you do this, please?" Another round of applause and affirmations echoed back.

"To show you the power of intention, I would like for our priests to sing the first healing song." He turned to us and began singing. When we joined in, a visible energy field began growing from inside our group. As it strengthened, light began to circle all of the priests as if we were standing in a white dome. Then the light changed from white to many shades of greens, blues, purples, and pinks. As the light expanded over our heads, the emanations looked like the Aurora borealis lights that dance and fill the northern skies.

The Protectors were in complete admiration of the sight that was taking place before their eyes. Ehab announced, "When you know the simple melody, please join in." One by one, the Protectors started singing. With each new voice, the dome of energy expanded even higher and wider. By the time a quarter of the group was singing, the dancing lights had spread beyond the entire valley. And once the entire group was engaged, the energy field encircled the Earth.

He yelled as loud as he could, "My friends, fellow Protectors, please keep singing to help the world. We, all of us, applaud your efforts. Please continue to help those who cannot help themselves, and continue singing until the people have the strength and courage to unite against the dastardly Order and stand on their own."

The priests who were to remain continued leading the crowd. The rest of us stopped and began to walk away. I expressed to Ehab, "Very nicely done. Go ahead and send the other ten priests with the envelope to the tents to complete the next assignment. And don't forget to tell the group to sing in shifts. You'll see that the energy field will be sustained, even with a few people reciting the healing songs."

"Good luck, my friend."

"Good luck to you, as well." The others were already a few steps ahead, and I ran to catch up.

"Hsssss," reported one of the reptilians on the ship's bridge. "A new energy field has grown inside our net. Stopping the flow of souls."

"Hsssss. Where is the source?" demanded the commander

"Hsssss. It is growing all over the planet. There's no one location."

"Hsssss. Remote viewers. Use the remote viewers and backtrack the energy signal to the source. Then annihilate it."

———————

We rejoined Constance and the others at the tents. Hara raised her hand to the sky. "I saw it grow, Daddy. I saw it. That's power!"

Ted pointed his thumb to Hara. "I'm with her."

Hanif, Mudads, and Rehema were waiting by the camels. I motioned in their direction. "Guys, I need you to go back to the shop, fast. It'll take you less than an hour, and you'll be there before they close the city's borders. Stay at the shop until we come back for you, OK?"

Constance clasped my hands. "And what are we to do again?"

"We need updates on the magic cross. If any of the pieces move or change, we need to know about it right away."

Laura was still checking out her new abilities. "I feel like I can move mountains."

Ricky supported her, "You'll be able to do more than that with practice."

I asked her, "Can you help them?"

"Or course. And don't forget that paper."

"I won't." I patted my chest pocket.

Constance started to speak, and then stopped. I knew what she was going to say and helped, "I know. I love you, too. And I'll see you soon…promise." I kissed her, and then I hugged her. Then I bent down and hugged Hara. "Keep Mommy safe, OK?" She nodded back to me. "I love you." I kissed her cheek and walked them to the camels.

I was about to say something to Rehema, but she spoke first, "I'll let you know when we arrive. I'll be your contact from here on out."

"What would I have done without you?" I turned to both brothers. "Thank you."

Mudads reassured me, "We have this under control. Now go kick the Order's ass!" He shook my hand vigorously.

Hanif was surprised by his brother's uncharacteristic outburst and gave him a quick glance. Then he smiled and shared, "My thoughts go with you. And no matter what happens here today, you have brought me hope." He shook my hand, too.

"Alright everyone," yelled Mudads, "time to move out."

I helped Hara and Constance onto their camels, blew them both a kiss, and watched them walk away.

Ricky came to my side. "Ehab's second group went into the large tent to work, and the others are getting their things together."

"The C4?"

"Yes."

Karim, Zuberi, and Umi came over. Karim urged, "It's time to put the rest of your plan into action."

"Agreed."

CHAPTER FORTY-TWO

BATTLE SCENES

Jabari called to his little brother, "Hand me the wire cutters when you are done."

"Don't forget to set your timers for thirty seconds." Gahiji shook his head, "More of that déjà vu stuff just happened. I wonder if that will ever stop when we finish this assignment and the magic cross is completed."

Asim laughed, "Maybe those feelings are supposed to happen this way, no matter what." He zipped up his backpack. "My two are finished." He handed Jabari another five-pound brick of C4. "That should be the last for your pack." He placed the remaining brick of explosives by Gahiji's feet.

"Thanks. Here're the cutters." Gahiji tossed them to his brother. "Where are Tumaini and Ricky? We're almost done."

Asim answered, "Both of them went down with Karim's team to sing along with the Protectors." He opened his outside pocket. "Good, my detonators and timers are ready."

"We should call them."

Jabari zipped up all of the pockets on his pack. "I'm through. Let's check all of our gun clips first."

"Got it," replied his brother.

I took a break from singing to check the sky. The Aurora lights were glowing even stronger than before and were successfully blocking off the funnel. I got the other men's attention. "It's time to go. They're ready up there, and Ehab and the Protectors are doing just fine down here." All five of us dusted off the sand and waved goodbye to the hundreds of Protectors who were singing. Ehab waved back, and we hurried to climb the hill.

As we passed the tent where Ehab's second team of priests was working, I motioned for the others to go on ahead. "I want to stop in for a moment."

Karim tapped Ricky's chest with the back of his hand. "What's he up to in there?"

"I'm not quite sure, but I know it's part of the plan."

The three-man security team came up to them wearing their gun belts and backpacks. "Where's Tumaini?" asked Asim.

Zuberi pointed to the tent. Just as he was about to speak, I came out and walked over. "How many packs were you able to make?"

Jabari put up five fingers plus one thumb. "We left the other three in our tent. We'll resupply for the next target after we blow up the mainframe."

Karim inquired, "What's going on in there?"

"I'll tell you when we get to Abu. We'll have some downtime until the assassin shows."

Umi was a little apprehensive and raised his hand. "What's going to happen next—this teleportation thing?"

Ricky laughed, "Relax. It's just a quick stop over into timelessness, and then we slingshot to our desired location."

I pulled out a picture from my top pocket. "This is Abu Simbel. Take a look. Once you see where you are going, or if you know the space time coordinates, you can teleport anywhere you'd like." I shrugged my shoulders with my hands open. "Well, in theory, of course. Ricky and I haven't gone everywhere yet to prove it."

Zuberi slapped Umi on the shoulder. "Come on, brother, buck it up. You know these guys have skills."

"Oh, one other thing," mentioned Ricky. "Your thoughts have to be centered. It's not like in the movies where you can teleport in the middle of a fistfight or something."

"Good to know," replied Umi.

After they all looked at the picture, I motioned to the tent. "I'll be right back."

Karim stuffed Ramla's cane into his back pocket. Gahiji cautioned, "Careful with that tip. You could put an eye out."

"I'll be careful with it. It's the other guy who should keep an eye out."

I came back to the group and informed them, "Hold on to your cookies, it's time to travel."

"Cookies?" asked Gahiji with his eyes really wide.

Ricky and I laughed. Then Ricky added, "Just know that you could experience some nausea. You did that in the other timeline." Gahiji nodded.

I told the others, "If you are ready, hold out your hands and grab hold." They all clasped hands, and the two on the ends held theirs out to Ricky and me. "OK, Ricky, on three. One…two…three…" The dust settled from our departure, and we landed safely between the Great Temple and the Small Temple at Abu Simbel.

All four brothers, Karim, and Asim were a little shaken by the trip. Jabari stumbled for a moment. "That's my second go at this. It will still take some getting used to."

Gahiji quickly fell into character. "Focus. We need to scout the area." The three men pulled out their guns and made a security sweep while the rest of us watched.

"All clear. There's no one here. It's abandoned," reported Asim.

"All clear," echoed Jabari.

"It's like a ghost town," added Gahiji.

"Thanks, guys. Well done!" I praised. "It's just like Jabari said it would be, too. They've abandoned the ruins." I pointed to the tree near the left corner of Nefertari's Temple. "Why don't you guys meet under there? I have to do something."

Ricky asked, "Your shield?"

"Right. I have to take it down and create an energy surge."

Zuberi laughed, "After what you did with the shaktipat, it shouldn't be too hard. Do you need some help?"

"No, I need them to pick up on me. They shouldn't know that you guys are here. Stay shielded."

"Got it."

Once they were under the tree, I focused my thoughts, dropped my shield, and then I raised my hands to the sky. The Aurora lights were still glowing. I motioned for the others to look as well. As their eyes were gazed upwards, I pulled my arms down in the same formation as the Protector's amulet. Then I closed my eyes, drew in as much Universal Energy as I could, and sent it out in a single blast. Aurora lights sped out from my body in the same fashion as when the priests sang the healing songs—only this time it happened in a split second. It grew and merged with the protective dome in the sky.

Ricky yelled over, "That should do it!" I just smiled back to him.

———•─•———

"Hsssss. Commander, we've detected the priest's signal. It's confirmed in Abu Simbel. Major energy spike."

The human officer approached the reptilian. "I've already sent the assassin there. He should be landing at the airport any minute. Our remote viewers have confirmed this as well. They can see him standing in the main temple."

"Hsssss. Good. Make sure that he does not fail."

"It will be taken care of, I assure you. He'll get the job done."

"Hsssss. Priest's powers have grown beyond that of a normal mortal. Make sure the assassin does not fail!" It sent a mental projection to stab the officer's heart.

He stumbled for a moment and held his chest. "Arrrgh!" After a hard breath, he stood back up. "Understood. I'll handle this matter personally. I will check in on the viewers."

"Hsssss."

———•─•———

I heard Rehema's message in my head, "Tumaini, this is Rehema."

"Yes? I can hear you just fine," I replied telepathically.

"I just picked up some information from the reptilian. They know you are there because of an energy surge. Was that you?"

"Yes, it was."

"The lights are glowing in the sky here in Cairo, just like they were at the tent city."

"Did everyone arrive at the shop safely?"

"We are all fine." There was a moment of silence. "The assassin's on his way."

"Can you hear anything else?"

"Hold on." Rehema shut her eyes and refocused on the reptilian commander.

———•••———

"Hsssss. Report on the soul-catcher. Where is the secondary shield coming from?" It shook its head furiously like it was trying to get something off of it. Then it did it again, but longer this time. It followed by putting its claw over its earhole.

The commander stomped toward the console in anger. "Hsssss. Something is listening in. Find it!" It pounded the console with its fist. "Hsssss. Find its location. Nasty human tried to read my thoughts."

"Hsssss. We're tracking it. Somewhere in Cairo."

"Hsssss. Find it, and kill it. Dirty human. Hsssss. Where is it coming from? Exact location."

"Hsssss. The signal location is shielded. We cannot pinpoint the correct spot."

The commander pounded the console again and cracked off part of the edge. It pointed a clawed finger at the reptilian closest to it. "Hsssss. Find this human and send two of our best troops to snap it in two. Then I want to see the body parts."

"Hsssss. Command accepted. Retracing signal now." It looked at the panel and touched a number of buttons and screens.

The reptilian focused its anger and tried to hurt the human who had listened in. "Hsssss. I will find you. Hsssss." Then it growled and stomped away.

———•••———

"Ow," cried Rehema, as she grabbed her head. Hanif ran up to her, but she held her hand up in a stop motion.

"Are you OK?" I asked telepathically.

"Yes, the reptilian tried to hit me with a painful shot. I think my shield weakened the blow."

Hanif couldn't help himself. "Rehema, are you alright?"

"Yes, yes, thanks, Hanif. Let me finish talking with Michael, please." He understood and waited by her side. "I'll be OK." She patted his arm to reassure him.

"Rehema, you don't have to keep doing this," I implored.

"Don't be silly. You're putting your life on the line to help, and neither of us is going to stop. Let me help the best way that I know how."

"I know better than to argue with you."

I was about to tell her that we had teleported safely, but she interrupted. "I can sense where you are. I'm glad you made it. Give me a second, I need to check something."

———◆———

At the airport, the assassin left the fighter jet and walked across the tarmac. He wore black military tactical pants with stuffed side pockets and a tight black shirt. He was met by the pilot of the helicopter about twenty feet from the chopper. They both gave the hand signal for the Order.

The pilot spoke first, "The remote viewers have confirmed. The priest is still there. They say he's somewhere in the Great Temple's Hypostyle Hall."

"Good. Let's not let him get away. Keep getting updates from the viewers until we land." Before getting inside, he asked, "That's the one with the two rows of eight statues inside it, isn't it?"

"Yes. The other one has six columns. Don't get them mixed up."

"I won't." They both boarded through the open side door. Once seated, the pilot began punching in the lengthy startup sequence, and the assassin put on his headgear. With the final switch flipped over, the high-pitched whine of the motor grew in intensity, followed by the rotors slicing through the air with increased speed. Then it took off.

———◆———

The officer reported, "The assassin is almost to the site. Our viewers still confirm that the priest is in the Hypostyle Hall."

"Hsssss. Keep me informed."

"As you command."

———◆———

"Michael, can you hear me?"

"I can hear you, Rehema."

"The assassin has just taken off from the airport."

"We'll be ready. Has the magic cross changed?"

"The exploding planet card hasn't moved, but the other two papyrus pieces have moved closer to the number twelve spot."

"Is one closer than the other?"

"They are both the same, Michael."

"So we have a fifty-fifty chance for success."

"It would seem so."

"Rehema, I need to go tell our team what to do. Please pass along my love, and stay in touch."

"I will." Our telepathic communication ended for the moment.

"Guys, it's time to move." I looked at Jabari. "Are you ready for phase one?"

"Roger."

"Karim, are you and your team ready to keep the assassin busy?"

He pulled out his sharpened cane. "More than busy."

Ricky and I are going out of sight while you complete your missions. This will hopefully keep the assassin from finding me or the Protectors. We have to keep him distracted."

Zuberi and Umi both were looking at Karim. He instructed, "Follow my lead. We're going into Nefertari's Temple—the Small Temple. And don't forget to turn on the microphones and earpieces that Jabari gave us."

The chopper pilot indicated to the assassin through his headphones, "We're ten minutes out. I'll drop you off and head back to the airport as instructed." He handed him a mic set. "We'll stay in contact this way. When you do away with the priest, I'll come back for you."

"Any change on his location?"

"Last report had him in the Great Temple. The viewers said he was look-ing at a map."

"A map? Of what?"

"That's all they could tell me. Just do your job so we can get our reward." He looked at the clock. "Nine minutes out. Do you have what you need?"

"I brought everything with me." He patted one of his thigh pockets. "Drop me off between the two structures."

"Roger that."

———————

"OK, guys," I joked, "time to play hide the priest."

Ricky laughed, "I assume that you are talking about yourself."

"Yes. If you hide the target, it's hard for the marksman to hit it. We have to keep him away from the main group and Hanif's shop as long as possible."

Jabari pulled out the photo and coordinates for the mainframe. "Take a look again. I don't want anyone teleporting to the wrong spot."

"Roger," nodded Asim and Gahiji.

"We're ready to go."

"Keep in touch through Rehema. And when your team is done at the mainframe, go back to the tent city and wait for my call."

Karim pointed to the tree by the Small Temple. "Umi, do you think you can get up there and hide? It's the best spot to see the entire complex."

"I can get up there. I'll call out any movement he makes."

"If you guys are set here, then Ricky and I need to move."

Zuberi nodded to Jabari's team. "Good hunting."

"You too," replied Gahiji.

"Ricky, take my hand." He grabbed it, and we vanished.

Asim held out his hand. Gahiji clasped it and held his free hand to his brother. "Game on," he said with confidence. When Jabari grabbed his brother's hand, all three vanished.

Karim directed, "Everyone, to their spots."

———————

The young officer came back onto the bridge and stood in front of the reptilian commander and queen. "Our ground forces have narrowed down the source that's creating the energy field. It's also in Egypt."

"Hsssss. Those priests are becoming a menace," growled the commander. "Hsssss. Have your air units ready to destroy them."

"Hsssss," added the queen. "Put them in special black soul boxes. They return in the first rebirth to suffer the most."

"It will be done." He laughed hard to himself and gave a wicked grin to the reptilians. "Once they go back, we can put them in our most recent genetically enhanced clones. These newer clones have a much longer life span than the old models that we used with the politicians and military leaders. Our drug companies will keep these clone bodies alive well past their expected life span. These pathetic priests will have to suffer in their aging bodies and work for pennies just to keep buying their drugs."

"Hsssss. Good plan," snarled the queen. "Hsssss. Your mind is evil. Will go far in our Order, you will."

"All hail the Order."

"Hsssss. Find the energy source." The commander motioned for the officer to leave.

Umi had climbed to the densest part of the tree and pulled in a few leafy branches. As he finished moving the last branch to cover his face, the sound of a helicopter became audible. It grew louder from behind the temple mound.

"He's here. The chopper's here!" Umi yelled into his microphone.

Asim, Gahiji, and Jabari landed exactly as planned in between the two mainframes. They quickly looked around to get their bearings and saw a number of technicians turning toward them. "Who are you?! How did you get in here?!" questioned one of them.

A security guard was standing behind them in the backup mainframe room. He pointed his machine gun at the trio and threatened, "Hold it right there!"

The two brothers and Asim looked at each other. Jabari instructed telepathically, "Don't react just yet. Stay calm."

"Put your hands up!" the guard ordered.

Gahiji asked in their heads, "What do we do? You're in charge."

"Follow my lead." His brother put his hands up first and announced out loud, "We give up." Gahiji and Asim did the same and reluctantly raised their arms.

The military helicopter came in low, hugging the temple mound as it flew up and over the rocky surface. When it reached Lake Nassir a few hundred feet away, the back end of the chopper reared down like a horse coming to a quick stop. The chopper hovered for a moment, creating a circular wake on the water, then it turned slowly and moved toward the tourist viewing area.

The assassin hollered above the noise, "Just get me close to the ground. I can jump from here."

The pilot received a message. "The report's the same." He pointed to the larger temple mound. "He's in there."

"Good. Get a little closer." The chopper hovered a few feet from the ground. A wave of dust and sand masked his exit. "I'm down!" he yelled. Without hesitation, the craft made a vertical climb and tilted forward to head back to the airport.

—————————

Telepathically, Asim asked each of them, "What are we going to do?"

The security guard was walking closer. The technicians had all stopped working. "Go back to your business. I've got this covered." He turned to the trio. "Who are you? Keep your hands up!"

Jabari replied in their minds, "Gahiji, I've seen you shooting energy balls at targets. Can you shoot one at him?" He gave a slight nod. "Good. When I tell you to, drop straight back to the ground. The packs will break our fall. He won't expect all three of us to go down together, and we can surprise him."

"And?" asked Asim.

"When we do, Gahiji, you blast him, and then we'll both charge."

The guard was less than ten feet away and walking slowly, never taking his eyes off of the three men.

Jabari commanded telepathically, "Drop now...now...now!" All three of them fell backwards. Gahiji landed in a sitting position. The guard reacted instinctively and pulled off a fast burst from his gun. The bullets sprayed and hit the technicians, killing them instantly. Gahiji pulled back his right arm and hit him with a lightning bolt. The guard flew backwards from the force of the jolt, which continued to assail his body until he smashed into the backup computer. Then his body fell to the ground, and it remained still.

Asim got up first and ran over, followed by Jabari. "Good work, Gahiji," Asim congratulated.

"I guess that energy boost from Tumaini really helped."

"I'll say," as he took the guard's gun and supplies away from him.

A deafening siren went off unexpectedly in the rooms. *Aaaaanh! Aaaaanh! Aaaaanh! Aaaaanh!*

———————

The assassin was slowing down from his sprint into the Great Hall. He thought to himself, "Where is he? No one is here." He turned around and looked behind all of the towering Osiris statues. "There's no one here!"

He grabbed the microphone on his front right shoulder and called in the information, "I'm in the Hypostyle. The priest is missing."

The chopper pilot answered, "Hold on. I'll check."

"I'm moving into the vestibule and sanctuary in the back."

As he ran to the two rear rooms of the temple, the pilot informed him, "He's supposed to be there. They're still getting his image."

The assassin was mad. "I'm telling you, no one is here!"

"Backtrack to the side storage chambers. Maybe he's hiding." After a moment of silence, he reiterated, "They're telling me he's there and that there are eight separate storage rooms off of the Hypostyle. Check them all."

He kicked at the ground in frustration, turned, and ran back to the room with the twenty-foot statues.

———————

"Toss me another clip. I'm almost out!" yelled Gahiji. He and Asim were trading Uzi bursts down the hallway at the Order's troops.

When Asim pulled back for cover, he asked Jabari, "How are the timers coming?"

"They're both busted. We must have broken them when we fell backwards on our packs. I don't think I can fix them." He put the timers back into the packs.

The guards made a small advancement. Gahiji shouted, "Here they come!" Jabari sprinted to the door and fired his gun to stop them from being overrun.

———•••———

The young officer ran up to the reptilian commander. "We've located the main power source that's blocking our soul-catcher. It's coming from the desert south of Cairo. Here're the coordinates." He handed him the computer pad.

"Hsssss." It looked at the pad and gave it back to him. "Send attack squad now. Kill everyone on sight." He came to a quick snap and turned to exit the bridge. The Commander growled, which made him pause before leaving. "Hsssss. Kill them all! And get the soul-catcher working."

"I'll have an attack squad of helicopters there in thirty minutes." He walked away at a fast pace.

———•••———

The assassin finished looking in the five chambers that were on the right side of the hall. He pressed his microphone button. "I'm going to the storage rooms on the left. Nobody was in the right side. Ask for further instructions."

"Roger," is all the pilot said.

———•••———

Jabari laid down his gun and extra clips. "Do you think you can keep them busy for the next few minutes? I'm going to place the charges."

"What do you have in mind?" asked Asim. He poked his head through the open door and sprayed the hall with more bullets.

"Gahiji, your timer is still working. I've checked it out."

"But we need at least two sets of timers for this plan to work," he stated.

"I know, and we shouldn't use the backups at the camp. We need those for the next assignment."

"They won't do us much good if we don't complete this one," contended Asim.

"Just keep them busy." Gahiji took a turn and blazed more bullets through the door. His brother turned, stayed in a crouched position, and grabbed both packs with the explosives.

While the two of them kept the Order's troop from advancing any farther, Jabari jumped over the dead bodies and placed one backpack in the central part of the main computer. He opened the zippers to expose the bricks of C4.

Asim motioned toward Jabari with a nod. "What's he doing?"

"Setting charges," quipped Gahiji.

"Ha-ha, I can see that. What's his plan?"

Jabari ducked just in time to miss being shot, and sparks flew from the terminals. He stayed low and used the rest of the computer towers as protection.

"I don't know what he has planned yet," said his brother. "Just keep him covered."

Asim shot down the hall again, while Jabari made it safely into the backup mainframe room. In the same manner, he placed the pack in the middle of the computer towers and opened it. After Gahiji gave him cover fire, Jabari sprinted back toward them.

Asim leaned back and panted, "There're too many. We need to do something fast, or we'll be swarmed."

"You're right, we can't take them out with our guns, even if we teleport behind them," added Jabari. "They're too spread out."

Gahiji said excitedly, "I've got an idea." He pulled out two bricks of C4 and the only working timer. "I'll do it."

"Do you think you can get in and out without being shot?" urged his brother.

"Only one way to find out. Cover me, and I'll get this ready." He took the detonator and timer and started hooking them up to the explosives. His brother picked up his gun and took his turn shooting down the hall.

At the military base near Cairo, twelve heavily armed attack helicopters started taking off from the airstrip. Once in the air, they moved into a V formation and flew south toward the tent city.

———————

"I'm done checking all of the rooms," reported the assassin. "Unless this guy is inside one of these statues, he's not here."

"I've got the intel from the viewers. They keep giving me the same information. He's looking at a map inside that room."

"I don't care what they are seeing. I'm right here, and I'm telling you that I'm the only one in this temple. I'm going on my own."

"That's not what your orders are."

"Screw my orders. I'm taking care of this guy once and for all." The assassin ripped off his communicator and ran out of the Great Hall.

The chopper pilot tried to communicate further with him, but all he got was static.

Umi whispered, "He's back out in the open. What do you want me to do?"

"Stay hidden," replied Karim. "He'll be coming in here shortly."

———————

Gahiji held a brick in each hand. The detonator and timer were on the right brick, and a connecting wire ran from the right explosive to the left one. "I'm thinking ten seconds ought to do it."

"Are you sure?" asked his brother. "That's cutting it awfully close."

"We don't want to give them any reaction time. I'm going to start the timer here, teleport behind them, and zip right back out before they get off a shot." He put down the brick with the timer and set the counter to ten.

"It's too risky," cautioned Asim.

"Too late now." He picked the bricks back up and placed his thumb over the start button. Then he closed his eyes to focus. "If I'm not back in ten seconds, set off the other two bags."

Jabari stopped shooting long enough to say, "I love you, brother."

"Don't get mushy on me now. Save it for later." He breathed in to calm his nerves. When he was settled, he pressed the timer button and vanished.

Asim bent forward to shoot at the Order's soldiers. Just as he pulled off his round, Gahiji appeared behind the enemy lines. One of Asim's bullets hit the wall right beside his head. Then Asim's face filled with terror.

To cover quickly for his brother, Jabari fell through the door, hit flat on the floor, and sprayed his Uzi to the wall opposite from where Gahiji was kneeling. Seconds later, Asim regained his composure and pulled Jabari back inside by his boots. As soon as Asim and Jabari got back inside, bullets came blazing in their direction.

From down the hall, they heard a soldier yell, "Hey!" A number of gunshots echoed from that direction. Gahiji had just slid the two bricks into the middle of the soldier's position, closed his eyes, and disappeared.

Jabari put his gun hand around the corner. "Cover fire!" He sprayed left, then right, and left again.

Gahiji reappeared beside Asim while counting calmly, "Three...two... one..."

Boooooooom! The doors, walls, and frames shook, as the remaining glass above them shattered from the blast's shockwave.

When the smoke cleared, Jabari looked down the corridor and saw dead bodies lacing the floor. "Clear!" He turned to see that Gahiji was safely back with the group. "Now I'll say it. I love you, brother."

"Love you, too." He brushed off some of the dust and glass from his arms and legs.

Asim commended him, "Nice going, and sorry about that back there." He held out his hand to help him stand.

"No worries. You were just doing it to protect my soul." Asim patted his arm in appreciation.

Jabari looked down the hall one more time. None of the soldiers were moving. "Let's check the timers. If we can't get them fixed in two minutes, I have another idea."

Asim replied, "Got it." They both went to the backup mainframe, while Jabari checked on the main one.

The officer informed the reptilian commander, "The attack squad is on its way, and the assassin is looking for the priest."

The commander growled in anger, "Hsssss. Almost had that filthy human. Grrrrr. Had its thoughts for a moment." It turned to the officer. "Hsssss. Continue with the plan. Get the soul-catcher working."

He snapped to attention and left the bridge.

Before entering the Small Hall, the assassin reached into his right leg pants pocket. He pulled out a fleur de lis club that was similar to the one he'd used during the attack at the restaurant. This one was blood red and gold in color, and it was slightly longer and larger than the original. He looked at it, flicked one of the side petals, and a six inch double-edged blade sprang out.

Inside the smaller Hypostyle Hall stood six columns with floor-length carvings of the goddess Hathor. The sanctuary at the rear was separated by two ornate walls. The two walls were divided, which created an open door in the middle, and it had two additional openings at each of the outermost sides.

"He just went in," whispered Umi into his microphone.

"Follow him," replied Karim. Umi began to climb down quickly so he could catch up.

The assassin skidded to a halt beside the first two columns and looked around. He paused for a moment, peered cautiously toward the sanctuary, and flipped the knife over in his hand. He sneered while scanning the room, "Where are you?"

Karim and Zuberi were out of sight and waiting for him on the other side of the wall. Karim was standing by the middle doorway and motioned to Zuberi, who stood at the far side. He indicated that he would go straight toward the assassin to distract him and that Zuberi should run behind the columns and tackle him from the side.

Zuberi nodded, but as he turned, he unknowingly kicked a small rock. The noise alerted the assassin, which gave him enough time to pull his right arm into a throwing position.

When Karim finally moved through the doorway, the assassin changed his aim from the left column. He cursed when he saw Karim's familiar face, "You!" With one deliberate step and a forceful throw, the assassin let the dagger fly through the air.

When Umi entered the hall, he saw Karim falling to his knees and clenching the assassin's wooden club that was sticking out from his chest. "Noooo!" Umi screamed.

The assassin turned clockwise toward Umi. While in mid-turn, Zuberi lept through the air and tackled him at the waist. Umi rushed in to help his brother, and a fierce hand-to-hand fight ensued.

———————————

Asim threw the box to the ground. "This timer is toast. There's no way it'll work."

"I can't salvage this one, either," added Jabari.

Gahiji asked, "What was your idea?"

All three walked to the doorway between the two rooms. Jabari turned toward his brother. "Do you think that you can blast both bags at the same time?"

"I've never done that before." He gazed at both of his palms, which were glowing white from his intention. Then he turned to the side wall and shot both arms outward. Lightning bolts streamed from his shoulders down to his fingertips and zapped the wall fifteen feet away. When he pulled his arms down, two flaming circles lit up that area as debris fell to the floor.

Asim laughed, "I guess you can."

"Wait a minute," reacted Gahiji. "If I blast both bags at the same time, won't that be a *bad* thing?"

"Only if we stick around for the boom," jabbed his brother.

"No kidding," included Asim.

"And?" inquired Gahiji.

"Here's my plan. At the same time that you blast the two bags, Asim and I will put our hands on your body and teleport all of us safely back to the tent city."

"At the same time?" he asked anxiously. "Now that's cutting it close, don't you think?"

"Do you have a better idea, brother?"

"Not at the moment. Can you call me in a week or two?"

Jabari chuckled, "Come on, we can do this."

Asim nodded his head and added, "We can do this, Bes."

"How about you two go on, and I'll stay behind and blast the bags on my own. That will ensure our success."

"Not a chance," negated his brother. "We're with you on this. Trust me. We can all get back alive and still blow these things to kingdom come."

"OK. We can do this." He took a breath. "On the third *now*?"

"Yes. Let's get into position before we start, though," suggested Jabari.

All three men sat on the ground. Gahiji was in the middle with his arms aimed at the two bags. Jabari sat on his right with his palm inches away from Gahiji's knee. Asim did the same thing on the left.

Asim shared, "Before we go, I just want you to know how proud I am of both of you."

They both looked to the left, and Gahiji grinned, "See you on the other side, Talibah."

"You mean, at the tent city, *right?*"

Jabari took over. "OK, here we go. Now...now..."—Gahiji's arms shot two streams of lightning at each of the waiting piles of exposed C4. As they ignited, and the molecular explosions grew exponentially, Jabari yelled the third word—"now!" The powerful blasts decimated the computer panels and surrounding mainframe pillars, leaving nothing but a massive pile of shredded metal and burnt silicon.

As Umi's punch was blocked by the assassin, and Zuberi got up off the floor for another bout, Karim painfully and slowly slid the dagger out from his chest. He looked down at his hands and saw everything covered in blood. In a state of shock, he let the dagger fall slowly from his loosened grip. It hit the floor blade first and clanged in the hall.

The assassin heard the noise and looked toward Karim's punctured body. The distraction gave Zuberi just enough of an edge as he connected his fist to the assassin's jaw. His body and head jerked wildly from Zuberi's powerful punch, and two teeth came flying out of his mouth.

The assassin spit a mouthful of blood to the side and countered quickly with a flying roundhouse kick to Zuberi's chest. The force knocked him backwards through the air and into one of the middle columns. As Umi attacked from his rear, the assassin spun around, flung both of his legs into the air—grabbing Umi's head between his feet—and finished with a Teeth of Tiger throw. Umi's body spun uncontrollably to the ground and rolled three times before coming to a stop.

Karim staggered to stand with his right arm held behind his back. The assassin turned to him and threatened, "Time for you to die!"

Before the assassin could charge the injured Karim, Zuberi jumped up and taunted, "Hey, over here!" The assassin tried to hit Zuberi with a side kick to the head, but Zuberi deliberately dropped to the ground and dodged his forceful blow. Then he immediately spun around with his leg sweeping underneath the assassin's legs to perform a Dragon's Tail Sweep. The assassin's legs went flying into the air as he hit the ground hard on his upper back.

Umi saw the stunned, prostrate body and flew down with a locked elbow to smash the assassin's face, but the assassin put his hands behind his head and kicked back up before Umi could connect. As Umi hit the floor hard, and as the assassin tried to regain his balance, Zuberi ran up from behind him, leaped over Umi, and did a perfect flying drop kick.

While Zuberi's body landed beside his brother, the assassin was uncontrollably flying through the air toward the staggering Karim. As the assassin's body tackled him, Karim flung his right arm forward from behind his back. They both fell hard to the ground, with the assassin lying on top of him.

Zuberi and Umi got up and sprinted over to Karim. When they looked down, neither he nor the assassin was moving. "Hurry! Help me!" urged Umi.

One brother pushed, while the other pulled the assassin off. As the body rolled away from Karim, Ramla's staff was sticking out of the assassin's chest. His head tilted toward Karim, and then his eyes closed in death.

Karim sighed, "Omar...Ramla...I have avenged you."

———————◆◆◆◆———————

Jabari, Asim, and Gahiji were finally regaining consciousness inside their personal tent. The sound of the Protectors singing in the valley calmed the newly arrived trio. Jabari checked himself first, then looked to the other two. "Is everyone alright?" He slowly got up from the ground.

"Ow! That blast left a mark," remarked Asim, as he held the side of his blackened face.

"Are you hurt?"

"No, just residue from the blast."

Jabari shook his brother. "Gahiji, are you still with us?"

"I'm here." He put his finger in his ear and shook it because of the blast's deafening effect. "No doubt about that explosion."

"No doubt indeed." He patted his brother on the shoulder. "That was a great job."

Asim added, "But we're not done. We need to report in to Rehema and pass along our intel."

Rehema spoke telepathically to all three, "I can hear your thoughts just fine. I'm so very proud of all of you."

"Thanks," replied Gahiji.

"Please tell Tumaini that the mainframe is burning to cinders," added Jabari.

"I will. He'll be thrilled, as we all are."

Asim asked, "Is there anything else to report?"

"Let me try and connect…"

————————

"Hsssss. It's the human!" yelled the reptilian commander. "Hsssss. Have you now." It pounded out the coordinates on the console. "Hsssss. Send the two attackers."

————————

"Oh my!" she exclaimed.

"What is it?" asked Gahiji.

"I was so busy working on the magic cross that I didn't listen in on the Order. They've sent helicopters to your site. They are going to attack the tent city!"

"Rehema?"

"And…and something is coming here. I've got to go warn the others!" Her telepathic communication ended.

"Let's get down below and tell Ehab and the Protectors."

The two brothers and Asim sprang right up. But before the three men could get out of the tent, the squadron of helicopters came over the hill in stealth mode. Flames from multiple rocket launches immediately lit up the sky, followed by all of the machine gun cannons letting loose. The miniguns sprayed the valley with six-thousand rounds per second and killed hundreds of Protectors instantly. The explosions from the rockets also ripped the crowds apart and sent huge bloody sandblasts and body parts into the air.

The entire valley was in a panic. The singing stopped, and the Aurora lights began to fade. The three men stood at the edge of the valley and shot their Uzis toward the choppers, but they were too fast and out of range.

Once the choppers were done with their first attack run, they swung around and reformed for another killing spree.

———•+•———

Karim was lying on his back with his head propped up. "Karim, what can we do to help?" asked Zuberi.

"I'm afraid that my wounds are fatal." He coughed hard, and then he spat some blood. "I don't think you can heal me."

Umi uttered with remorse, "I wish we knew how to mend your wounds, but we never got that training. We just got in—"

"It's OK, I'm finally...I'm finally at peace." Karim labored to cough again. "I have found forgiveness and can rest once more." He put his hand on Umi's.

Zuberi offered, "We can sing the healing songs. Maybe that will help." The two brothers placed their hands over his wound and sang to him.

———•+•———

"The shield is down. We can start the soul-catcher again," declared the officer.

"Hsssss. Many lives lost. Send the squadron through once more. The new deaths will make up for the missing souls."

"Consider it done."

As he left the bridge, the reptilian commander pushed one of the soldiers away from the console. "Hsssss. Why haven't the two attackers left?"

"Hsssss. The transport could not get through their shield. We can send them now that it's down."

"Hsssss. Send them. Kill this human."

———•+•———

Ehab's second team of priests came running out of the tent and joined the security trio. They were horrified by the carnage that had been left from the Order's attack helicopters.

Asim ran up to them. "Where's Ehab?"

One of the priests pointed to the valley. "He's down there somewhere."

Jabari knelt down in a shooting position. "Here they come again!" He and Asim opened fired at the choppers.

Ehab gathered the remaining priests around him in the valley. "We can use our skills against them. Use the elements. Use the wind and fire!" Four priests, including Ehab, stood in a circle facing each other. They held hands and closed their eyes. "Send the elements of wind and fire to protect our brethren."

The helicopters opened fire with a round of rockets and miniguns. The remaining Protectors in the valley had begun screaming and running for their lives. Tents were blowing apart, and bodies were being torn to shreds from the heavy streams of bullets and rockets.

Ehab guided the other four. "Now, wind!" The desert floor came to life with more than two dozen mini vortexes of sand and stone. The powerful circular motion picked up the earthen floor and created towering tornados that reached far into the sky. The chopper pilots were not prepared for any immediate resistance and two of them were torn apart by the mighty forces of nature. Choppers began weaving in and out of the twisting obstructions, and the squadron had finally been forced to break formation.

"Now, fire!" commanded Ehab. All of the camp fires grew in intensity, just as the tornados had done. Streams of fire lept into the sky and touched the clouds. One helicopter dove immediately to the right to miss the blazing inferno, but the chopper that followed close behind did not react in time. The last thing that the chopper pilot saw was his craft engulfed in a red and yellow fireball, and then it exploded.

One of the helicopters that had veered off from the group focused on the Protectors who were climbing the hill. As it was making its attack run, Gahiji bent his left knee and stepped back with his right leg. He squeezed his eyes closed as he drew in all of the surrounding energy that he could. His body was encased in a vibrant ball of light. He quickly opened his eyes, focused on the chopper, and shot his hands toward it. The brightest lightning bolts imaginable streamed from his shoulders, down his arms, and blasted the chopper, just as the pilot was pressing the trigger for the minigun.

Outside of Hanif's shop, two eight-foot-tall reptilians materialized in the street. "Hsssss. In there," growled the first one.

The larger of the two snapped gruffly, "Hsssss. Move!" and pushed the first one out of the way. Then the larger reptilian smashed right through the glass door. At the back of the store, Hara gave a high-pitched scream and ran into her mother's arms. This caught the first reptilian off guard, and it froze. Laura was standing behind them, completely petrified by the hideous creature.

The smaller reptilian was stepping through the glass, when Hanif yelled, "Not in my store!" He swung a wooden bat at the reptilian's midsection, and it splintered in two. The reptilian, unfazed by Hanif's action, picked him up and threw him to the back of the room. He landed hard on the couch, and it slid across the floor until it tipped over. Rehema ran over to help him.

At the same time, Mudads and Ted both looked toward Hanif and the terrified women. Then they gave their best battle cry and charged at the reptilians, "Aaaaaaahhhhhhhh!"

Ted was struck first by the larger one. The reptilian raised its muscular arm and batted him away with one stroke. Ted's body went flying sideways and smashed into the wall with all of the perfume bottles and oil burners. Glass shelves, mirrors, and bottles shattered and covered Ted's limp body. His right arm was visibly broken in two places.

In the meantime, Mudads jumped through the air to tackle the smaller of the two reptilians. The beast pushed a second too late to completely throw Mudads off, and Mudads ended up with his arms around the reptilian's neck. With his forward momentum, and the reptilian's ducking motion, Mudads swung onto the reptilian's back. He was holding on for dear life, trying to strangle the reptilian to the ground.

The larger reptilian was making its way to the four women. Hara was screaming as the heavy foot stomps rocked the remaining shelves. In midstride, the reptilian grabbed a three-foot intricate blade from its back. "Hsssss. The smaller one dies first."

Laura stepped in front of Hara and Constance. "These are my friends! Go to hell!" She pushed her hands together in front of her chest, and lightning bolts filled her palms and fingers.

The reptilian looked surprised for a moment, and then continued its attack. Laura threw her hands toward it and directed the intense flickering lights at the beast's chest. The bolts hit the reptilian and pushed it backwards, almost to the same place where Mudads was still riding the other reptilian. Its feet were digging into the floor to stop from being pushed any farther.

A fierce standoff ensued. With each step the reptilian made, Laura grunted and was pushed backward. She refocused as best she could and added more voltage to the energy bolts.

The other reptilian couldn't reach behind well enough to grab Mudads. In frustration, it ran backwards and smashed Mudads between itself and a wall. The reptilian did this two more times until Mudads fell unconsciously to the floor.

Ten feet away, Laura and the larger reptilian were still pushing back and forth, each determined to defeat the other's death throes.

Rehema stood up from helping Hanif. "You will not hurt my friends anymore." She held out her right hand and lowered her head slightly. Her face scowled with concentration, and an energy force left her hand and picked up the smaller beast. It struggled helplessly with its feet dangling in the air as she kept it levitated two feet off of the floor. Then Rehema rapidly lifted her other hand, and the reptilian sped upwards and smashed hard into the ceiling. Satisfied, she released it by suddenly dropping her hands, and it fell to the floor with a huge *thud*. Bricks, wood, and other debris partially covered the stunned leathery demon.

"I'm losing it." The larger reptilian's strength was pushing Laura backwards even farther.

The smaller reptilian got up, bared its sharp fangs, and growled at Rehema. Hara screamed from the terrifying sight, and Constance protected her with her body.

Rehema used both hands and levitated the beast again. She thrust her hands above and behind her head, which pulled the reptilian almost to her face. "The exit is behind you!" she commanded. Then she flung her arms in front of her toward the street. The reptilian—completely helpless against her powers—flew through the air, smashed through the main window, and careened into the brick wall across the street. It left an indentation of its body in the wall as it peeled off slowly and crashed to the ground.

Laura was pushed back one more step. Sweat was running down her face. The larger reptilian growled and stepped again. Then she yelled,

"Nooooooo!" She pushed forward with her shoulders and then flung her arms in the same direction. The lightning bolts that flowed out from her glowing hands had instantly turned into pure streams of energy.

The reptilian froze like a statue from the intense surge. It was barely able to say, "Hsssss. You don't have the power!"

"I said"—she pushed again with her hands and strengthened the beam— "go to hell!" The reptilian immediately caught fire and burned to ashes in seconds. When nothing remained but a pile of dust, Laura collapsed to the floor in exhaustion.

———————

The priests above the valley copied what had been done by the team below and sent additional sand tornadoes and fire streams at the remaining choppers. With their protective efforts, they were able to knock out three more. Jabari and Asim joined in, while Gahiji continued to send lightning blasts into the sky.

Despite the Order's losses, the remaining two helicopters stayed in the battle and added to the carnage and onslaught. Both teams of priests saw them firing again at the Protectors, and they converged all of their tornadoes at the flying ships.

The two choppers lined up one behind the other and flew toward Ehab's group. With skilled banking and turns, they both dodged the flaming cyclones and sand twisters. Unexpectedly, from behind, a blast of fire hit the rear rotor of the second chopper. The blades stopped moving, and it began spinning uncontrollably. The pilot struggled with the stick to regain control and glanced down. When he looked back through his window, Gahiji's blast, combined with two other vortexes of fire, hit the pilot and destroyed the chopper. The wreckage continued spinning as it crashed to the desert floor.

The first chopper continued its attack run and dodged three tornadoes on the right by banking down to the left. Then it made an immediate bank to the opposite side to miss being hit by flaming twisters and climbed straight up into the sky. It performed a rollover maneuver directly over Ehab's group. As it made its downward turn, the pilot coldly said, "Target in sight. Fox Two, away." As he flicked the rocket switch and released his final weapon, three tornadoes were directed from the priests above the valley and smashed the chopper with sand and flame. Before the debris hit the Earth, an explosion occurred directly below.

Zuberi and Umi had finished singing the healing songs. Karim's breath was thin, and his life force was fading. He raised his hands to them. "Brothers, friends, I will always be with you. Thank you for all that you have done. I...I...love...you." His hand fell limp, and both brothers hung their heads.

"Hsssss. Report," demanded the reptilian commander. "Hsssss. The queen expects death."

The officer replied, "The soul-catcher has regained full power and has captured all the souls of the newly dead. And the priests in the desert were obliterated by our squad. But..."

"Hsssss. But what?"

"The squadron was also lost."

"Hsssss. Acceptable losses. Bring the queen the new soul count."

"As you wish. Hail the Order."

"Hsssss."

Rehema's hands were over Ted's forearm. Her final transfer of healing energy had fused his bones perfectly. "There now, see how that feels."

Ted moved his arm like he was a chicken flapping its wing. "That feels wonderful. How can I ever repay you?"

"Shhhh, rest now. You already paid in full when you risked your life to save ours." Constance and Laura also gave their thanks.

Hara came over and stood beside Rehema and Ted. "You were brave, Mr. Ted. I was really scared."

"Thanks, Hara." She sat beside him, and he pulled her in close.

Constance exclaimed to Rehema and Laura, "You two were amazing!"

Hanif added, "I agree. You've been holding out on me, Rehema." She smiled. "I had no idea that you had such powers. Thanks!"

Mudads was still limping a bit. Rehema stood up and went to help. "I can fix this." She put her hand up and sang him a healing song.

Constance leaned a bit toward Laura. "We've got to get these schools started up when this is all over."

"I'll be the first to join."

In the back room, Zuberi and Umi had just teleported with Karim's body. They stepped out quietly into the main shop.

"Zuberi! Umi!" shouted Hanif in a welcoming voice. They looked at him meekly. "How did everything go?" Both brothers turned their heads and stared at each other. Neither one wanted to speak first.

Rehema gasped with her hand to her mouth. Then she urged, "Where is he?" They both walked silently to the back room, and everyone followed.

Rehema knelt down beside his body. Mudads and Hanif joined her, and Mudads took Karim's hand in his. "My dear friend, I will miss you."

"He was very noble in his cause," praised Zuberi. "After he killed the assassin, he said that he had found forgiveness, and then he left this world in peace."

Umi asked Hanif, "What happened here?"

———————

All of the priests were making their way to the valley floor. Every time they encountered an injured person, they would use their skills to heal his wounds. Along the way, Gahiji asked one of the priests from Ehab's group, "What were all of you doing in the tent?"

A younger woman in her late teens pulled out two old pictures. One was a picture of me holding a tourist map of Abu Simbel, and the other was a photo of the Great Hall. "Ehab told us that we were to focus Michael's image inside the Great Hall near these eight statues. He said that it would give the illusion to anyone looking for him that he was there instead of being on his next assignment. It was some kind of military ghosting technique." She put the first picture on top of the second one. "We had to stack them this way: Michael's image over this one."

"That sly dog," grinned Jabari. "He used the military's own techniques against the Order."

Asim added, "That was a great diversion tactic." He looked up at the sky for a moment; the energy funnel was visible again. "We aren't done yet, by a long shot. I wonder how the team did with the assassin."

Before anyone could check in telepathically, they arrived at the spot where the five priests had been standing. A huge rocket crater now dotted the location, and a few remaining fires were still smoldering from the chopper's wreckage.

Three of the Protectors came over and guided them to their burnt bodies. "We're so sorry," one of them lamented. "We saw them get hit by the bomb. No one survived." They all stood there, silent. The Protector continued humbly, "We could use your help. There are still many more wounded." The soft moans of pain were not far off.

Asim motioned. "Come on, everyone. Let's help where we can."

Gahiji asked, "What about Tumaini?"

Jabari answered, "He'll contact us as soon as he needs us. Let's put our backpacks over by this tent."

The remaining priests scattered to help the wounded and dying.

——————————

I shook the repaired raygun. "We did it, Ricky. I think it's finally working."

"Ya, mon. It only took twenty tries. We had to get it right some time."

"I'm going to contact the others." I focused on Karim first to see if the assassin was still at the site. "I can't hear his thoughts. I don't know what's wrong."

"I'll try him," he added with a chipper voice, "then you can contact Rehema and the security team." He closed his eyes and called out for Karim. Again, there was no reply.

"Let me see if I can reach Asim." I closed my eyes again and began my hail, "Asim, hear me. Asim, hear—"

"I can hear you, Tumaini," he replied telepathically.

"Ah, good. I was beginning to wonder if I'd lost my touch."

"What?"

"I tried reaching Karim for a report and couldn't get anything."

"He must be busy. Are you safe?"

"Yes. Ricky and I are inside Laura's shop. We've been working on the raygun."

"Ah, I get it. That must have been why you spoke with her alone before leaving."

"I needed to get the combination for her safe."

"And that explains the piece of paper."

"How are you doing?"

"We've had one great success and a majorly terrible setback. Have you looked outside lately?"

"No. We've been hiding from the Order's police and military. They've completely shut down the city and are dragging people away by the thousands to the camps. Why? What happened?" I tapped Ricky. "Listen to this."

"Hello?" he asked telepathically.

"Ricky, this is Asim. We've had a huge success with the mainframe. It's been blown to pieces."

"Awesome!" he cheered.

"Congratulations!" I added.

"But..."

"What's wrong?" asked Ricky.

"The entire tent city has been destroyed. The Order's attack copters..." He got choked up and stopped to regain his composure. "The Order has killed hundreds of our Protectors, and they also killed Ehab and four other priests. It's...it's too gruesome to even describe."

"I...I don't know what to say."

"I'm so sorry," sighed Ricky.

"When you get a chance to look, the protective shield has come down. And the Order's soul-catcher must be working again. I can see the energy funnel with souls going into it."

I was in shock and still trying to emotionally process everything he'd just said. "Then we have work to do, don't we?"

"Ya, mon."

"Ricky and I have a plan for that ship. Do you still have the packs ready?"

"Three of them. They're with us."

"I need to talk with Rehema before we leave. She'll give us the best locations for success."

"When do you want our group to come?"

"The fewer of us in the beginning, the better. The last time we went, we got shot at right away. But this time, with Rehema's help, we'll have an edge."

Ricky nodded, "I agree. I think it's best if we start the mission and then call for you guys to blow up the ship."

"But how are we going to find you? What about the captured souls?"

"That's why I need to talk with Rehema. I'm going to have her guide us."

Ricky remembered something and shared, "Hey, Asim, this worked well in the last timeline. I'm already wearing Tumaini's amulet—it's on. When we get to the ship, lock onto its energy signal. You'll be able to come right to us."

"We can do that. How many of us do you want to come?"

"Keep it simple. I imagine the other priests are tending to the Protectors."

"Yes, they are."

"Have them continue with their healing work, and then you three will come to the ship. You're the most skilled with explosives."

"I agree with you," he concurred. "We'll pass along our best to the others for you."

"Thanks. Just wait for our call."

"We will. Our thoughts go with both of you."

"And our thoughts are with you," replied Ricky. Then the communication ended.

———————

The queen asked, "Hsssss. How many souls now?"

The officer tallied before responding. "Even with the temporary stoppage, we are up to"—he tapped his pad—"fifteen thousand."

"Hsssss. Continue processing the souls."

He stood there with a fearful look. The commander grunted, "Hsssss. Report!"

He answered shakily, "We've also received word. Both mainframes have been destroyed."

In a rage, the commander stomped toward the officer and picked him up with one claw. "Hsssss. We should never have trusted humans." It dropped him roughly, and he fell to the floor. "Hsssss. That is why we copied all programs to our ship's computer." It pointed for him to leave. "Hsssss. Go to the soul-catcher and stay out of sight. I will see to a new mainframe on that retched planet."

"As you wish." He got up and left in a hurry.

On Earth, the reptilian outside of Hanif's store regained consciousness. It tried to push up off the ground, but its wounds were too severe and it fell back down. Then it struggled with its arm to get its communicator and called the ship.

"Hsssss," bellowed a reptilian at the console. "The two attackers have failed, and the first one is fatally injured. The human still lives."

"Hsssss. Aaaaaarrrrrrrgggggghhhhhh!" screamed the commander.

The queen immediately ordered, "Hsssss. Send five more attackers. Give *me* her body this time."

"Hsssss. Pick them myself," growled the commander. It walked over to the reptilian at the console and snapped its neck. "Hsssss. No excuses anymore."

After it flung the body aside, it pointed to a waiting reptilian by the door. "Hsssss. Take it away, and then resume its post." Before leaving, it finished with, "Hsssss. And tell the first attacker to join in the new group—or die!" The commander left the bridge as the other reptilian dragged the dead body away.

"Tumaini, Baniti, this is Rehema," she called telepathically.

Ricky looked to me because he'd heard her voice at the same time I did. He shut his eyes, and I replied, "We both hear you fine, and we've finally got the raygun working."

"That's good news."

"Rehema, I tried reaching Karim. Do you know anything on his whereabouts?"

She put her hand to her mouth and got a little choked up. "He...he died, Michael, while stopping the assassin." Ricky's head dropped in disbelief.

"I'm sorry, Rehema," I sighed. "He was a good man."

She sniffled, "He was a very good man, but"—she sniffled again—"his suffering has not ended."

I could hear her thoughts now. She was thinking about him being captured by the soul-catcher. "You're right. We need to stop that ship."

"Rehema, is my family safe?"

"They are all fine." She told us about the reptilian attack. "Zuberi and Umi came back to the shop like you told them to do. They'll help protect them."

Ricky piped in, "Have you heard about the others?"

"No," she replied. After a few minutes of telling her about the Protectors and priests at the tent city, she was completely distraught.

"I know this is hard, Rehema. I'm very sorry."

Sniffling, she said, "I know. I'll tell Hanif and the rest. They should learn about the tent city, too."

"I agree. Can you also tell everyone how much we love them?"

"I will." After a short pause, she asked, "Now, what do you want me to do?" Before I could reply, she added, "Give me a moment. I'll listen in to the human officer." Ricky and I glanced at each other while we waited. "They've…they've learned about the mainframe being destroyed. There's a copy of the program on board."

Ricky deduced, "That means we need to blow up the ship, or they'll just create another mainframe."

"He's right," I affirmed. "Is there any vulnerability to the soul-catcher?"

"He's standing in the room with all of these black boxes. Oh my! That's where they are keeping all of the souls."

"Keep going. This is good information."

"To get in that room, he passed the ship's fuel cells. Not many reptilians on board, it's mostly self-sustaining. The ship can almost run itself."

"Not much resistance then," Ricky stated with a more positive voice. "That's good to know."

"If the fuel cells are ignited, it might destroy the entire spaceship. Wait… he's looking at a panel by the machine. A counter is in progress to keep track of every soul that's been collected. And there's another panel. It's the…I think it's the release command center. There seems to be a way to send the souls back out."

"How can we get in that room, Rehema? I can get us on the ship from my previous experience, but we need to be in the soul-catcher room first."

"He has something on his belt. It's a policemen's baton." Ricky and I looked to each other. "It has some residual energy left on it, and it's not the military officer's."

"I have a feeling that I know whose it is."

"I'm picking up a name—Dunse." We both smiled.

"Is there anyone else with him?"

"One reptilian is at the door. His post is to guard the fuel cell room and this one."

"Hsssss. The queen demands the human's body. Don't come back without it." The commander finished addressing the squad and turned to the one at the controls. "Hsssss. Send them now." The teleporter hummed and glowed. Then the five reptilians vanished.

"Rehema, can you keep the telepathic line open? We'll need your help until we're done."

"I'll do what I can."

"Ricky, are you ready?"

"As I'll ever be."

"When we get onto the ship, you take out the guard"—I shook the raygun—"and I'll handle the officer."

"Michael, I need to go—*now!*"

"Rehema?"

"Go, Michael, go! I'll be in touch."

Ricky grimaced, "That didn't sound good."

"Let's not disappoint the lady. We have business to do. Get your stuff ready."

"Right."

"Hsssss. Get up, or die," threatened the leader of the five reptilians. They were all huddled around the wounded reptilian. "Hsssss. You know the law: only the strong survive."

The injured reptilian couldn't stand all the way up and stumbled down hard to its knees. "Hsssss. Decision made." The leader took its sword from its back and stabbed the kneeling beast. It fell off the blade and hit the ground sideways. Then it snarled to the other four, "Hsssss. The female priest is mine."

The sound of broken glass crunching under shoes alerted the five reptilians that they were not alone. Facing directly toward them in a straight line were Zuberi, Hanif, Laura, Rehema, Ted, Mudads, and Umi. They stood there, motionless and silent, glaring into the reptilians' eyes. It was an alien-human Mexican standoff.

Rehema spoke, "You have a chance to leave here peacefully. We don't want any more bloodshed."

All five reptilians rolled their heads, hunched down, and growled at the row of Protectors.

Ted quipped, "I think that means *no*."

Laura put her hands in front of her and started her powers. Light balls filled her palms, with electrical currents flowing around them. The lightning was accentuated by the darkness of night.

The lead reptilian pointed the bloodied blade at Rehema. "Hsssss. Your compassion is your weakness—human. You will die first!"

"Very well, then…but not today!" She looked back to Hara, who was standing just inside the broken door beside her mother. "Now, child!"

Hara started screaming at the top of her lungs. Her high, shrill voice echoed between the stone buildings and distracted the five attackers.

"Move!" yelled Mudads.

Laura and the three priests took two steps forward, while Hanif, Ted, and Mudads stepped backwards and picked up clubs to protect Constance and Hara. As the reptilians began their charge, Rehema grabbed ahold of the leader with her levitation power, looked down the street, and sent it flying until it smashed through the front window of a delivery truck.

A reptilian had cut across its group and came at Laura. She hit it on its forehead with a quick jolt, and it fell over hard onto the rocky pavement.

Zuberi and Umi looked across to each other with their fists clenched and ready to deliver their powerful blows. As two reptilians came at them, they channeled all of their energy into the front of their knuckles and connected with each of the leathery chests. *Bdwooosssshhhhzzzz!* Shockwaves spread out from each of their punches and sent the two reptilians flying backwards into the brick wall. Piles of stones and dust fell on top of them and covered their bodies.

The fifth reptilian had dodged one of Laura's bolts and tackled Zuberi. The one that she'd hit a few seconds earlier also got up and re-entered the battle. Umi tackled the beast before it could swing its blade at Laura's neck.

The reptilian crawled out of the truck and roared at Rehema. It was leaning forward while running full speed at her. She picked it up again with one hand before it could take another step. This time, she threw it in the other direction, even higher and farther than before. It landed head first into a store front a block away.

Zuberi and Umi were doing their best to dodge the flesh-tearing blades. With every swing of the reptilians' swords, they countered with bone-crushing blows to the beasts' bodies. When Zuberi missed with one of his punches, the reptilian's blade slashed across his chest. "Aaaahhhhh!" he screamed.

Rehema saw it and levitated the attacker into the air. She called to Laura, "Hit it!" She turned to help and shot the suspended target head-on with two bolts of lightning. It sent the reptilian flying on a collision course with a parked car.

———⊷+⊶———

"We weren't prepared last time and got hit hard," I remembered. "Don't forget to keep your shielding up and your focus strong. It's the only way to protect against their mental attack."

"Got it." He held out his hand. "Time to go."

In a flash, we were on the soul-catcher ship. Ricky immediately knelt as soon as he saw the reptilian; his arms were already blazing with electricity. When he let loose, his shot fried a hole in the reptilian's chest. It fell back like a stone statue, with smoke lifting from its leathery hide.

The young officer had his hands up as I pointed the raygun at him. "No need to shoot," he squealed in a shaky voice. "Maybe we could make a deal."

I looked at the black boxes behind him. The counter on the panel was adding new souls to the tally. I scolded with disgust, "How could you do this to your own kind?"

Without missing a beat, he replied, "Money and power, of course—lots and lots of money and power. What? Do you think I want to live on your kind of salary?" He laughed arrogantly.

I pulled the trigger and hit him with a beam from the gun. He went down in agony, begging me to stop. We both watched him as he curled up in a ball from the intense pain. I released my finger and waited for him to get back up.

"He means business," said Ricky. "I'd cooperate with him if I were you."

I pointed the gun toward the machine, and then back to his head. "How do you stop this?"

"I...I don't know." He held his hands out to defend himself.

I pulled the trigger and took a step forward. When the beam stopped, I taunted, "I can do this all day...your choice. How do you stop this terrible machine?"

"OK, OK, I'll tell you. Just don't shoot me with that raygun again."

He walked to the panel beside the counter and started pushing in a sequence of buttons. "You know, you'll never stop us. The Order is everywhere. I don't even know who's in charge."

I pulled the trigger for two seconds and released it. The officer arched his back in pain. "We'll take our chances. For now, just stop that device!"

He looked at me with his finger over a red button. "This is the final switch. If I turn it now, it will override the commands from the bridge and shut off the machine. The entire ship will be notified that something is wrong."

I shook the gun at him. "What are you waiting for? Do it!" His finger pressed the last button in the sequence, and the cascading particle beam stopped shooting toward the Earth. *Byrrrruuuzzzuuuggghhhh!* The buzzing noise ceased, and the soul counter remained the same.

Ricky and I looked at the machine, then we looked at each other and smiled. The officer moved his hand slowly from the button to his belt. While we spied around the room to find the release panel, the officer pulled out his baton and smashed the raygun. It fell to the floor in several pieces. Then he swung it and hit my head, and I fell to the ground.

He took a step to stand over me, and I looked to Ricky. "You got this?"

"Ya, mon." He pulled back his right arm and paused, "Time to meet your maker." He forcefully shot it forward, and a pure stream of energy flowed down his arm. The officer had a hole burned right through his midsection. He fell straight to his knees, and then the remainder of his dead body slumped forward and hit the floor.

"Thanks."

"No problem. But now we don't know how to release all of these souls."

"Let me call Rehema."

———————

Hanif and Ted were hanging on to a reptilian who had broken through the priests' lines. Mudads was on the ground grasping onto its leg. Ted yelled over, "Rehema, we could use your help right now!"

"I'm a little busy myself." She had the lead reptilian levitated three hundred feet directly above them. Ted and Hanif were knocked off when the reptilian spun around inside the shattered doorway. The frame stripped their bodies away, and they both fell on top of Mudads.

Hara and Constance were at the back of the shop. Constance stood in front of Hara in a defensive stance with a club in her hands. "You leave my child alone!" she demanded. In an instant, the reptilian was ripped from where it stood and was pulled out to the other side of the street. Hara and Constance heard the *whoosh!* sound as it left. Rehema was standing just outside the door as the others looked toward her. From their viewpoint, they saw the first reptilian smash into the wall and fall down hard to the stones below. Two seconds later, the lead reptilian came crashing from way up in the sky onto a pile of bricks beside it. We all heard a loud *thud,* mixed with the sound of bricks and wood flying everywhere.

Laura yelled, "That's enough!" She remembered how Ricky had pulled energy into his body when he fought the black ooze. Her hands were whirling around her as streams of light and energy filled her body. From her head down to her waist, her body lit up like a three-foot candle flame. With both arms pointed at the fallen reptilians, she shot white streams of light directly at them. She took three steps and intensified the burning lightning bolts. With one final step, both bodies incinerated before everyone's eyes.

A bloodied Zuberi and Umi took advantage of the distraction and jumped feet first toward the two reptilians in front of them. They grabbed hold of their necks, just like the assassin had done to Umi, and they twisted them to the ground with the Teeth of Tiger throw.

The fifth reptilian, which had been thrown into the car earlier, got out and ran toward the others.

Rehema came forward with both hands stretched out at shoulder height. "Time for you to leave the planet!" She dropped her palms to her side,

725

and then she lifted them quickly above her shoulders. All three reptilians blasted off of the ground like speeding rockets and sped into the night sky. Laura stepped beside her and gathered another round of energy. While Rehema kept her hands in the air, Laura clasped her hands over her head and directed a three-foot diameter light beam into the heavens. It struck the floating beasts and fried them beside the partially lit moon. Cinder and ash fell slowly to the ground and ended the bloody battle.

After a few moments of silence, Rehema asked, "Are you sure that you weren't a priest? You sure have the skills of one."

She was touching a cut on her head that she'd received during the fight. "It was you, Ricky, and Michael that helped me get this far. I couldn't have done it without you."

"Well, you'll always be a priest in my book." They both smiled and gave each other a hug.

When the others joined them, all of the people from the surrounding homes and businesses opened their windows and doors and began to clap and cheer for them. Slowly, people broke the curfew and started coming out into the street.

Rehema pointed to the sky. "I can see it. The soul-catcher's energy web is gone."

———————

"Try her again," Ricky said.

"Let's both try her again. She must have been busy."

"Rehema, hear me. Reh—"

"Tumaini, Ricky, I can hear you. You did it. That evil funnel is gone."

"Good," I replied. "And before the rest of the ship comes down on us, how do we release all of the captured souls?"

She focused on the residual thoughts that were left in the room. "The panel on the right; do this sequence."

Ricky was standing guard at the door, while I looked at the strange configuration in front of me. "I'm here. Walk me through it."

"The three buttons on the left…move them up simultaneously."

I shoved them upward and they made a funny mechanical noise. "Done."

"Next, swipe your hand from left to right on the screen at the top of the panel."

"OK, next step."

Ricky fired a blast toward two human soldiers. "They're coming!" He fired again, striking both of them, and their bodies fell to the floor. "Never mind."

"Rehema, what do I do next?"

"Sorry, it took me a moment. This one is a thought command. You *think* how many souls that you want released and where you want them to go, and then you swipe that same screen in the opposite direction."

"OK...that's weird. Where do I send them?"

"Send them home, Tumaini. Send them home."

"Do it, Tumaini!" Ricky yelled. "There're more coming! Do it now!"

I thought, "All souls go home to the Creator. Go to the Realm of Souls." Then I swiped the panel from right to left.

The machine came to life and began to bellow. *Errrr! Errrr! Errrr! Errrr!* Rows upon rows of the soulandrum boxes immediately opened at the sides. The tubes that connected to them filled with brilliant, vibrant, glowing souls. When the final door opened at the front of the ship's soul-catching appendage, the vacuum of space opened up a pathway toward freedom.

We watched on the monitor as the souls sped off to go home, and the counter finally read *zero* again. Thousands upon thousands of multi-colored souls were outside of the spaceship and disappearing safely back to the Realm of Souls.

On the bridge, the queen was furious at the failure of the mission. "Hsssss. Fix the machine. Find the perpetrators. Kill them. Kill them all!"

"Hsssss. It will be done." The reptilian at the console started pushing buttons furiously.

"Ricky, help me give this a blast. We have to destroy this."

"Good idea. But where do we go when it ignites?"

"We know where the teleporter is. That's our destination."

"We've only got one shot at this."

"I know. Hit it on three. One...two...three!" Waves of pure energy streamed from both of our bodies, down our arms, and connected with the two panels. Small explosions decimated the device and left it burning in flames.

"Go now!" The explosion grew quickly, and we teleported out of the soul-catcher room.

As soon as our bodies rematerialized in the teleporter room, the reptilian commander was standing behind us and picked us up by our necks. "Hsssss. You will suffer for what you have done. The queen will feast on your flesh." We struggled in the air with our feet dangling below. Our hands grasped helplessly at the strong, clenching claws.

The reptilian was choking off our air supply. "Ricky," I managed to say telepathically, "put your hand on its head." He struggled to raise his palm.

"Hsssss. Can hear your thoughts this close. You can't harm me." We both put our hands on either side of its head. "Hsssss. Can barely even raise your filthy arms. Finished you are."

"Now!" Both of us sent a shock to the reptilian. It wasn't a full blast, but it was enough for him to drop us both. On the floor, we held our necks and gasped.

As the reptilian came to, Ricky asserted, "My turn." He grabbed onto its leg, and electrical currents ran up its body. I followed suit and grabbed its other leg. Strands of lightning were coming out of its ears, eyes, and mouth, while electrical streamers covered the rest of its body. It was spasming uncontrollably from the energy surges.

Ricky and I let go at the same time. He moved behind the reptilian and gave it another shot. The blast knocked it off balance and it fell into the teleporter. Before it could regain full consciousness, I scrambled to the panel and hit the button to close the energy screen. It snarled fiercely and pounded at the newly-formed energy shield.

Ricky hurried over to me. "Where do we send it?"

"Deep space." I punched in some wild coordinates and turned to Ricky. "Time for *it* to meet *its* maker."

"Ya, mon." He pushed the button that I pointed to, and the reptilian screamed, "Hsssss. Nooooo!" It dematerialized into nothingness.

"Ricky, Michael, are you OK?" asked Rehema.

Ricky coughed and cleared his throat, while I rubbed the back of my neck. He punned, "We're living."

"Rehema, we need a diversion so we can get to the bridge."

"Yes, I hear you."

"While Ricky and I fend off any new attacks, have the security trio meet us with their packs. Have them zero in on Ricky's amulet."

"I'll do that right away."

"And please keep everyone there informed."

We were about to head to the bridge, but three reptilians came down the passageway with blasters and started firing at us. We retreated back inside the teleporter room and traded shots with them.

"They're getting closer!" yelled Ricky.

"We're not done yet. The ship's computer has to be destroyed."

He took off his amulet and set it beside the control panel. "Good move," I remarked. "Don't want them landing on your head." A shot from a blaster zinged by my ear and hit the corner of the doorway.

Flash! Asim, Gahiji, and Jabari were standing in the teleporter. They saw the mini-explosions from the blaster and rushed over right away.

"Having some problems up here?" joked Jabari.

"You know, trouble with the neighbors and stuff," laughed Ricky. "Do you want to give us a hand?" He turned down the hall and let another energy blast go.

Gahiji pulled out a stun grenade. "Let the professionals handle this." I bowed with an arm gesture to let them by.

He knelt down by the door and looked back to see if Asim and Jabari were ready. After the signal, he pulled the pin and threw the grenade down the hall. After the loud bang and flash of light, Jabari fell flat to the floor outside of the door. He sprayed his Uzi multiple times until we heard three thuds. Then Asim pulled him back in by his boots.

Gahiji ducked around the corner quickly for a look. "Clear!"

"Man, you guys really are the professionals." I clapped. "Nice maneuver."

Asim laughed, "You like that? We did the same thing back at the mainframe. Worked like a charm."

Ricky added, "I'll say. Great job!"

Jabari got up and inquired, "So, what's next?"

Ricky and I filled them in about the soul-catcher being destroyed and the commander being teleported into deep space. I continued, "Rehema told us that they've copied all of the mainframe's programs onto this ship's computers. It's not enough to just destroy the soul-catcher; we need to take out the entire ship."

"How are we going to do that?" asked Asim.

Ricky picked up the amulet and put it back on. "Good thinking." I put my hand on his shoulder. "We might be able to use it again."

Then I turned to the security trio. "There're a bunch of fuel cells back by the soul-catcher device. I'm thinking that one bag goes there, one bag should go near a wall in the middle of the ship, and the last bag should go off on the bridge."

"I like that plan. Sounds like a simple solution for a big problem," agreed Asim.

"Makes sense, given the resources that you brought along," I replied.

"Who goes where?" asked Ricky.

"I'll take the fuel cell room," volunteered Jabari.

Asim pulled his pack down to ready his detonator. "I'll stay in this location and get as close to an outer wall as I can."

"Great." I motioned to Gahiji. "Looks like you're with Ricky and me."

"Couldn't think of a better pair to be with."

His brother snorted, "Figures, after all we've been through."

"OK, best secondary pair." We laughed for a second.

I looked at the security team. "When we are done here, we all go back to Hanif's shop."

"Roger that," they replied.

"Let me contact Rehema."

"I'm here," she responded telepathically to all of us.

"Any last information?"

"There's a lot of confusion. The queen is angry, and there aren't many left on board—a handful of reptilians, and three human military men."

"Where are they?" asked Jabari.

"They seem to all be scattered throughout the ship: three on the bridge, one in the middle, and two near the fuel cells."

Asim praised, "Best intel we've had so far. Thanks, Rehema."

I checked with Gahiji, "What do you want us to do?"

"I'll take the rear and cover you. Just be careful when you round any corners." Ricky and I nodded in acknowledgement.

Gahiji got the other two's attention. "Asim, Jabari, are you ready?"

"Affirmative," they replied.

"Telepathic communication all the way," I suggested. "Rehema, please help out where you can."

She was surrounded by everyone in the shop. We heard her thoughts, "They all wish you love and luck."

"Tell them that we love them, too."

The five of us were in a circle. Jabari broke the silence, "Let's get this done. The people on Earth need us." We all nodded.

Gahiji looked down the corridor and saw that it was still clear. He motioned for Ricky and me to move first. Then he waived his brother and Asim out the door. He checked his gun and followed behind.

In our heads, Rehema was giving specific directions to each party, "Jabari, go down this long hall and turn left at the junction. Asim, stay to the right and follow the open door. If you go to the left, you'll run into a reptilian. Gahiji, you guys go up the ramp to the long hall. That will lead you to the bridge."

"Hsssss. Report," demanded the queen.

"Hsssss. The soul-catcher is completely destroyed, the human officers on board are mostly dead, and the commander is not to be found."

"Hsssss. Reptilians left?"

"Hsssss. There are less than a half-dozen on the ship."

"Hsssss. Prepare to leave orbit within the hour. We will come back with an armada and destroy this putrid planet."

"Hsssss." The two reptilians began departure procedures.

Rehema communicated in my head, "After the second reptilian attack, Laura and Ted went back to the magic cross. Luckily, it wasn't damaged in the melee. The card with the soul-catcher and mainframe crossed out has moved closer."

"Thanks for the update. Wait a minute—second attack?"

"We're all fine, just a few cuts and bruises that are being tended to. You would have been proud of Hara."

731

Gahiji reminded us, "Focus. Keep your mind on the mission."

"Got it," I replied. "You'll fill me in later, won't you?"

"Of course I will."

Jabari called out, "Taking fire near the fuel cell. Two reptilians."

"Can you handle them?" asked his brother.

"I've got this. Keep moving."

When we got closer to the top of the ramp, one of the human soldiers stepped out from behind a closed hatch. He saw Gahiji and fired a round. It missed and ricocheted off of the wall. He directed sternly, "Keep moving."

As Gahiji swung around to return fire, the soldier hit him in the shoulder. Gahiji fell as he pulled the trigger. His shots sprayed wildly into the air, and then his body lost control and began sliding down the ramp.

The soldier fired two more shots. One missed his head, but the other hit him in the leg. Gahiji fought to sit upright as he slid down. With a reactive squeeze of the trigger, he hit the soldier with multiple shots and killed him.

We had already reached the top of the ramp and called back to him, "Gahiji, we're coming down to help."

"No, stay where you are. The bullet just grazed my leg."

His brother chided telepathically, "Don't hide vital information on a mission."

"I'll be up there in a minute. Go to the bridge and secure the location."

Ricky turned to go back, but I held his arm. "I need you on this. I can't do it alone."

Rehema chimed in, "He's right. He needs your help, Ricky. Go with him."

Gahiji added, "I'll get the detonator ready while I'm down here, and I'll be up as soon as I get it connected."

———◦———

"Hsssss." The queen pointed its clawed finger at one of the two reptilians. "Shooting outside. Go kill it."

———◦———

Rehema warned us, "Ricky, Michael, the queen just sent a reptilian your way."

"Thanks, for the heads-up. Ricky and I will be ready."

Asim gave us a tip, "Lay on the ground, they won't expect an attack from down there."

As soon as we both got on the floor, the reptilian stomped rapidly out of the bridge. With four arms pointed at its chest, Ricky and I let loose a blast from each hand and stopped it dead in its tracks.

Asim reported in, "I'm finished. Just need to know what to set the timer for."

Jabari gave an answer, "Make it short, ten seconds."

"Agreed," Gahiji added.

Ricky and I cautiously made our way to the bridge. Rehema told us that the queen and another reptilian were the only thoughts she could pick up. "I'll take the queen; you zap the reptilian at the console." He nodded.

"Michael, you're close enough. The queen can hear your thoughts."

We turned the corner, and I immediately fired at the queen. It was ready for my attack and had a protective shield around its huge body. Ricky fired at the unsuspecting reptilian at the console and sent it flying through the air. Its heavy body crashed to the floor, with smoke smoldering from the blast.

The queen countered and hit Ricky. His body smashed against the inner wall of the bridge and lay there stunned.

I screamed, "Noooo!" I glared back at the queen and shot a light blast at its shield. Sparks flew off in all directions from its protective bubble. The queen hissed at me and sent a powerful black energy bolt in return. With both hands up, a white wall formed in front of me and absorbed all of the dark energy until it dissipated. The queen did it again, and the energy from the strengthened black bolt pushed me up against the wall.

Rehema tried to call me, but I kept my focus on the battle. Ricky was still knocked out on the floor. While the queen was re-energizing, I started a new line of attack and formed flaming energy balls in both hands. In a pitcher-like fashion, I threw energy ball after energy ball at the queen's body. After ten direct hits, I could see visible cracks in its shield.

"Hsssss. Your powers are no match for mine." The queen's hands sent out streams of black smoke. "Hsssss. Black magic will destroy you." The lines of smoke sped toward my body and went right through my shield. They wrapped around my body and squeezed me like a python squeezes its prey.

"Hssss. You will die now!" The queen clenched its hands, and the smoke mimicked its actions. I was lifted off of the ground and was being squeezed to death.

Ricky shook his head and struggled to lift himself off of the floor. In a fit of rage, the queen snarled and dug its claws into the air. The smoke formed dagger-like tips and ripped down the front of my body. "Aaaaaaahhhhhhhhhh!"

Alarmed at the sight of my torture, Ricky stood up and drew in the surrounding energy to his body. He was glowing brighter than I'd ever seen. Before the queen could redirect its attack, Ricky hit it with both arms. The power behind his energy cut through the cracks in its shield and seared the queen's skin.

"Skreeeeee!" it screamed, and danced around in pain from his powerful blast. He gathered more energy and hit the queen again. "Skreeeeee!" It spun around and spat something at Ricky. The acid spray hit his arm and burned his flesh. With the queen in pain, the black magic smoke dissipated, and I fell to the floor.

"Tumaini," Rehema called.

"Not now, Rehema." I threw another round of flaming balls at the queen and hit it in the face. The queen screamed and fell to the floor hard. "Skreeeeee!"

"Come on, Ricky!" I picked him up while he nursed his arm. "It's too strong to go head to head." I dragged him out of the bridge. "Go check on Gahiji. I think I can do something to stop it out here."

"I won't leave you."

"You have to. Besides, Gahiji should have been here by now."

Gahiji moaned to us telepathically, "Uuuhhh. I've lost a lot of blood and can barely walk. I need help."

His brother called out in concern, "Gahiji!"

"Go!" I pointed for Ricky to head down the ramp. Heavy foot stomps were coming our way. "Go! Trust me!"

"Alright." I could see fear in his eyes before he hurried away.

I told myself, "It's now or never." I thought back to the shaktipat energy and how powerful it was. The memory brought back the feeling instantly. "I can do this."

I sat on the floor in a meditative position. I closed down my thoughts as best I could to allow the Source of All Energy to flow through me. Before my last thought dissipated, I heard Rehema's voice in the distance. "Don't do this, Tumaini."

I thought back one word to her, "Hope." My mind went blank.

The reptilian queen came stomping to the doorway. Its claws grabbed hold of each side as its head peered into the corridor. It looked right, and then its head swung fiercely to the left. When it saw me, it bent down and roared like a dragon, with its head twisting violently in the air. Its large wings spread open as it walked out and blocked the light from the bridge.

"Hsssss. You are dead now."

As it stepped forward, I focused solely on Source, the Creator, the Energy behind all Living Things. With my thoughts stilled and unwavering, the Energy of Creation welled up from inside of me and generated a blazing white field around my body. Then, Aurora lights grew instantly and hardened the energy field. Within seconds, the ball of dancing light was more than ten feet in diameter.

Enraged, the queen sent black energy bolt after energy bolt at me, but they had no effect. They bounced off my growing light and careened toward the surrounding walls. The walls began to blast apart from the intense impact and started a cascade of explosions throughout the ship's electrical system.

Ricky had reached Gahiji and helped him partway up the ramp. When they looked in my direction, they could no longer see my body. The light emanating from the Creative Energy was so bright that they had to shield their eyes.

Asim and Jabari called in, "What's happening?!" But neither of the two responded.

The ship began to shake from the redirected black energy bolts. The queen shot everything it could at the powerful shield created by Source. As the energy sphere kept growing, it made its way to the queen's clawed feet. When it touched it, its skin burned. "Skreeeeee!" Sparks and smoke flamed from the impact.

Retreating to the doorway, the queen roared like a dragon. Then it said, "Hsssss. Black magic will destroy you once and for all!" The queen chanted and made growling guttural noises. It did it again and again as it spun around multiple times. During the spinning process, the queen's body transformed into a fifteen-foot cloud of black smoke. Then the smoke took on the shape of the queen's body.

In a calm voice, I called to Ricky; the others could hear me as well, "Ricky, I'm losing myself. I'm losing consciousness. All there is is energy. It's too intense. I'm losing myself to Source."

"Hold on, I'm coming!"

Calmly and slowly, I replied, "No, stay away. You could get hurt."

He let Gahiji rest on the floor and tried to come near, but the emanations were too strong for him to approach. He was shielding his eyes with his arm and sliding backwards.

"Ricky, get out of here. I'm going to lose control of this energy. It's taking over my body. I'm...I'm...I'm going!"

The black smoke dragon flew through the air and made a final diving attack at the blazing shield. "Hsssss. Diiiieeeee!" At the same moment, Source Energy filled my body one last time and expanded outward in a three hundred and sixty degree fashion. *Bzzzzzwwwaaaaahhhhhhh!* As the powerful Energy of the Creator hit the black demon, it began to incinerate the queen. Its smoke-like body disintegrated painfully and slowly from its toothy snout all the way down to its spiked tail. Within seconds, the queen's agonizing screams died away, and nothing remained of the reptilian beast. Then the walls to the bridge blew out and knocked Ricky over, followed by explosions and flames flying over Gahiji's and Ricky's bodies.

Another explosion shook the entire ship. "We've got to go!" exclaimed Jabari.

Ricky ran up to Michael's motionless body. "Tumaini, Tumaini, wake up." He put his ear to his chest. "I'm not getting a pulse." He put his hand on Michael's ribs and sent a healing blast. His body cavity lit up, but there was no response.

Gahiji finally made it beside Ricky. "Please tell me he's alive."

"He's not breathing, and there's no pulse." His palm lit up on Michael's chest. "He had too much energy running through him. It may have killed him." He put his ear to his nose and lips. "No breath."

An explosion occurred farther down the corridor. Asim yelled out, "This place is going to blow! Set the charges just to make sure, and let's teleport out of here."

Ricky bent over and gave Michael's body another jolt of healing energy. "I'm not going without him."

"We can teleport Tumaini back home, but we have to go—now!"

Gahiji was limping to the bridge. "I'm setting my timer for twenty seconds. You guys turn on your timers and leave."

"That's affirmative," replied Jabari. "Timer set. It will go off before yours. See you at home, brother."

"Timer on," echoed Asim. "Get out now, guys. Best of luck."

Gahiji touched the button. "Timer is running." He ran with a limp to Ricky. "Can you take us all back? I'm too weak to go on my own."

He held out his hand. "As long as all three of us go together."

Gahiji bent down and took Michael's lifeless hand in his. Then he held out his other hand to Ricky. The bomb near the fuel cells exploded, and the back end of the ship started ripping apart in pieces. Then the middle of the ship shook violently from the second bomb.

Ricky's hand grabbed Michael's as the fireballs swept forward through the rest of the ship. "I love you, Tumaini." He grabbed Gahiji's hand, just as the wall of fire reached the bridge. The timer clicked, and the last bag of C4 went off and obliterated the entire area. In one cataclysmic blast, the soul-catcher ship imploded for a second. Then it blew up with the force of a super nova. Four exploding energy rings expanded outward, as pieces of debris scattered into deep space.

CHAPTER FORTY-THREE

HOPE'S MYSTERY

One minute earlier, Ted and Laura were standing at the glass counter with the magic cross. Laura blurted out excitedly, "Guys, guys, the good card moved into the spot!" All but Rehema made their way over. She remained upstairs with her hands over her face and sobbed quietly. She'd heard all of the thoughts from the spaceship and knew about the terrible news.

Hara skipped for the last few steps. "Which one was it?"

"The one with the mainframe and the soul-catcher crossed out. That means they must have won!" She held Hara's hands, and they jumped up and down. The others congratulated each other on the defeat of the reptilian ship.

In the back room, Jabari teleported safely inside Hanif's shop. A few seconds later, Asim appeared beside him. Zuberi and Umi saw them and motioned with their heads to the new arrivals. The rest of the group looked their way.

From outside, a huge flash of light filled the sky. It lasted for a moment, and then it faded to black.

Constance felt that something was wrong. "Where's Michael? Where is he?" She looked around the room for him. "Where is he?"

Behind Asim and Jabari, Ricky, Gahiji, and Michael's bodies instantly materialized...then time stood still.

Moments later, Ricky looked across the room at Constance; her face was filled with horror. Laura gasped and pulled Hara into her side.

Constance screamed, "Noooo!" She ran up to him, fell to the ground, and clutched his body tightly. "You can't be..." Tears started streaming down her face. "You can't be... I don't know what I'd do without you." She cried more and pleaded, "I love you, Michael. Don't you dare die. I love you!" Her body went limp onto his.

Hara left Laura's grip and ran to her mother's side. Then she knelt down beside her father's body and sobbed uncontrollably. Ricky put his hands on both to console them.

Gahiji fell over from the immense loss of blood. His brother and Asim immediately came to his aid, and Asim encouraged him, "We can heal you, Bes. Just lie quietly. Try not to move." They both put their hands over his wounds and started singing. Warm light radiated into his body and began the healing process.

Hanif, Mudads, and Ted were all teary-eyed and stood close by. Ricky moved backwards to let Laura kneel between Constance and Hara. Constance's tear-soaked face was on Michael's lifeless chest.

Rehema walked up completely distraught. "We must try to help him. We must."

Hara was still crying, "Daddy, please don't die." She squeezed his hand, hoping for a reaction from him. "Please don't die."

Ted put his fingers to the bridge of his nose. He tried to hold back, but his emotions took over and he broke down. Mudads put a hand on his shoulder to help.

Rehema bent over Michael and tried to sing a healing song. She stuttered the first few notes and cried softly. Hanif knelt with her and held her close. She tried to sing again but couldn't make a sound.

Zuberi and Umi came and knelt down on Michael's other side. They put their hands on his body and began to sing. Light filled their fingers as they focused their healing intent on his soul. Ricky joined in, and the radiance grew in intensity. While he sang, he took off Tumaini's amulet, placed it on his chest, and held his hands over it.

Gahiji was regaining consciousness and fluttered his eyes. He looked over to Tumaini and saw him lying still. "No, it can't be!"

Jabari looked at his brother and struggled to whisper, "I'm...I'm glad you are OK, Gahiji."

Asim held his composure and moved to Tumaini's body. He joined with the others and sang the healing song. The glow around Tumaini's body grew even more and wrapped around him like a cocoon.

The rest of the group knelt all around Tumaini. One by one, each person added his healing voice. No one wanted *hope* to die.

Hara lifted her head; she was still holding her father's hand. "Daddy, please come back. I promise that I'll be good. I'll do anything you say. Just please come back." Her daughter's plea sent Constance and Laura into another wave of tears.

Rehema patted Hanif's hand. Then she rested both of her hands on Tumaini's chest. "Come back to us, you dear soul. Come back." Her singing was louder than the others', and the healing cocoon became brighter.

For the next ten minutes, all who could sang healing songs into Tumaini's body. The light filled him from their touch, but as soon as someone would remove his hand, the light faded.

Rehema was emotionally exhausted. "I can't..." She regained her composure after a moment and said, "He had so much of the Creator's energy running through his body to destroy that evil reptilian queen, I don't know if we can bring him back."

Constance was holding her husband's hand with Hara. She was rocking back and forth, waiting for a sign of life.

"Wait a minute, I'm getting a familiar sensation," Rehema exclaimed. "His soul is still around us. I can feel him. He's not crossed over yet." She looked at Constance. "If there is a way, we'll bring him back to you."

The group kept vigil and began singing in shifts through the night. Rehema, Constance, and Hara never left his side.

———————

After his shift, Ricky walked over to Ted, Hanif, and Mudads. They were standing by the magic cross spread with the security team. "He was...he was amazing. He never thought of himself the entire time. He gave his all to help bring *hope* to the world."

"What happened up there?" asked Hanif.

Each of them traded off giving his account of the final battle. After Ricky told them about the queen using black magic to transform itself into smoke so it could kill Tumaini, Mudads' head jerked back in disbelief.

"That's exactly like the dream I had just before Michael arrived a few weeks ago. A black dragon that looked like an ominous black mist tried to destroy the white dragon. It was attacking without mercy. Tumaini, the white dragon, was calm inside a goldish-white light. Nothing could hurt him while he was in that sphere." He shook his head, "I never saw the ending because I woke up in horror."

Ricky continued, "And now you know that the white dragon prevailed. The queen, with all its dark magic, was destroyed by the godly power that flowed through Tumaini. The Creative Energy of Source was too much for the reptilian queen, and it disintegrated."

"And it took a powerful soul to defeat such evil," remarked Mudads. "If only we could have helped more."

Jabari spoke next, "I don't know what else we could have done. Each of us put our souls on the line to help humanity."

Ricky agreed, "He's right. We all gave a part of ourselves. And many did lose their lives in this battle."

"There's more work to be done," added Asim. "The priests down south are still helping the injured. We lost many Protectors and priests today."

Gahiji asked, "Do they need our help down there?"

"I spoke with them after my shift. They'll be fine, and they said to do what we could up here to start recruiting again."

"And those FEMA prison camps back home… There're a lot of people who were taken away," included Ted.

Ricky nodded and pointed to Tumaini's body. He praised in Baniti's voice, "He did what he was supposed to do. He gave the people of the world a chance." He stopped speaking, and then motioned to the group. "All of you gave the people of the world a chance." They nodded in respect. "With the mainframe destroyed, and the soul-catcher blown to kingdom come, it's now up to the people to stand against the Order. They have to free themselves from tyranny. No one person, savior, or alien race can do it for them." All of the men were agreeing with what was said.

"If I've learned anything from the past few days, it's that the people have to wake up and stop being led by the rich, greedy, power-hungry cabal. The Order still needs to be stopped." He received a lot of verbal support from the group. "We'll help, but the people of the world must make a stand."

Ted pointed to the cross. "I hate to bring this up, but look." Two cards had moved toward the last spot.

Laura came over and requested, "Can someone take my place for a moment, please?"

The security team looked at her. Asim offered, "We'll give everyone a break." They knelt down by Tumaini's body and began singing.

Rehema left Tumaini's side for a moment. "I can still feel his soul. Tumaini—*hope*—is still with us. It's like he is waiting for something."

"What's he waiting for?" asked Hanif.

Laura was looking at one of the cards. "I can see something. It's the word *Hope*. It's crossed out, with people standing below in handcuffs."

Ted chimed, "I can see it, too. That's a dismal card." He pointed to the final slot on the magic cross. "I sure don't want to wake up tomorrow if it goes there." He looked at the other papyrus piece. "What's the other card? Can anyone make it out?"

Mudads got a huge grin. "I see it. I see it. It's the word *HOPE*. It's as big as the paper, and the people of the world are holding hands around it."

"That's a much better sign," sighed Rehema. "Maybe that's what Tumaini is waiting for."

Constance came over with Hara. "I want to thank all of you for what you've done. Michael—Tumaini—he couldn't have asked to be with a better group of people. We're blessed to have known you—all of you. I just want to say *thanks*."

Hanif gestured to the cross. "It's not over yet. There's a chance he may come back to us. Rehema can still feel his soul. He's not leaving yet."

"You can still feel him after all this time?" she asked with a bit of excitement.

Rehema answered with her hand on Constance's arm, "Yes, dear."

"Why won't Daddy come back now?" sniffed Hara. Then she wiped her nose with a tissue. "I want him back."

She knelt down to talk with her. "Your father showed so much love for others that he helped way beyond what anyone has ever asked of him. What he did was...well, it was very brave, kind, and giving. He served others without asking for anything in return. He was a true Protector of Souls." Hara nodded her head with a little smile. "And if people will do the same for their friends and family—and strangers, too—then your daddy might come back. If they love their family so much that they won't allow mean men and women to control them for money, power, or greed, then your daddy just might wake up again and hold you, hug you, and kiss you all over your pretty little face."

After she giggled, Hara inquired, "So it's up to someone else if my daddy lives?"

"It seems that Tumaini—*Hope*—will live or die based on what the people do next."

Hara stomped once and responded emphatically, "Then I want them do what it takes so my daddy can live!"

"So do we, dear. So do we." Rehema received a lot of verbal support.

Laura pointed to the scrolls and parchments. "And with these tools—the God Scrolls—we can show the people how they can live in harmony again."

"Here, here!" came from those standing around.

"What can I do to help?" asked Hara.

CHAPTER FORTY-FOUR

HOPE'S FATE

A strong wind blew through the room. It rattled the glass top where the cards were placed, but none of them were scattered by the force. It flowed through each person in Hanif's shop.

Constance gasped with excitement, "I felt him! I felt him! That was my husband! That was Michael!"

Hara was jumping up and down. "I felt him, too! That was Daddy. He's not gone yet!"

Rehema had a small tear in her eye. "His soul is still here. He wants to live. *Hope* wants to live." Everyone felt Tumaini's presence and was beaming with joy.

Hara begged, "Oh please, people! Please, people! Do what it takes so my Daddy can live!"

Ted shook his head and quipped, "They won't do it." Everyone turned and looked at him.

Laura slapped his arm. "Shoosh! Give the people a chance."

The countertop started to rattle with force. The papyrus pieces were all shaking in their spots. Hanif called the others over, "Hurry! Come, come! I think the people have decided." The rest of the priests and Protectors quickly gathered around.

"Look!" exclaimed Ricky. "One of the two pieces moved into the last spot!"

Constance gasped, "Which one?!"

The End...

Of Book One

EPILOGUE

You decide. Does Hope live? Will you stand up against the oppressive governments, police, military, and the Order? Or does Hope die, and we remain enslaved to the greedy, power-hungry, evil controllers of the Matrix?

It's up to us—all of us! We can make a difference if we all do it together—the Freedom Number. We can be the real-life *Protectors of Souls*.

CHARACTERS IN ORDER OF APPEARANCE

Michael Whyse (Tumaini)
Mudads
Hara Whyse
Constance Whyse
Hanif
Rehema
Shannon
Omar
Karim
The Assassin
Onuris
Ramla
Gahiji (Bes)
Asim (Talibah)
Talibah
Bes
Tumaini
Baniti
Ehab
Jabari
Ted
Robbie

Rochelle
Brandi
Todd
Stacey
Beth
Phillip
Principal Snoot
Bruce
Daphnee
Allen
Ricky (Maverick Priestly/
    Master Baniti)
Laura
Older Military Officer
Reptilian Commander
Younger Military Officer
Officer Dunse
Dean Shwermer
Zuberi
Umi
Reptilian Queen

ABOUT THE AUTHOR

MICHAEL J. RHODES is an award-winning author, an award-winning musician, and a published composer. His earlier background includes performing with numerous orchestras and teaching music at the university, high school, and middle school levels. He is also a motivational speaker, an advanced certified clinical hypnotist, and he has created and taught classes on metaphysical, spiritual, and extraterrestrial topics.

His journey for truth eventually led him to the evil alien and New World Order agenda, and the horrible actions, tactics, and mindsets of the greed-driven politicians, judges, lawyers, corporate owners, military, police forces, and bankers—the cabal.

Michael is available for speaking engagements and presentations. Please contact him at info@AncientEldersPress.com.